The Ghastly Gothic Tomes

Vol. 10

The Ghastly Gothic Tomes

Vol. 10

Published by NRM Books.

ISBN: 978-1-965179-13-0

CREDITS
Cover Art by: Nathan Reese Maher

COPYRIGHT

The Ghastly Gothic Tomes are protected under the copyright laws of the United States of America. Any reproductions or unauthorized use of the contents herein including, but not limited to, artwork and text is prohibited without written permission from the author. Novels, poems, plays and short stories published herein are part of the public domain.

Copyright 1st Edition October 14th, 2024, all rights reserved.

Table of Contents

"The Woman in White"
by Wilkie Collins
Published 1860, p. 2-616

"The Marble Faun"
by Nathaniel Hawthorne
Published 1851, p. 616-768

The Woman in White

By Wilkie Collins

THE STORY BEGUN BY WALTER HARTRIGHT

(of Clement's Inn, Teacher of Drawing)

This is the story of what a Woman's patience can endure, and what a Man's resolution can achieve.

If the machinery of the Law could be depended on to fathom every case of suspicion, and to conduct every process of inquiry, with moderate assistance only from the lubricating influences of oil of gold, the events which fill these pages might have claimed their share of the public attention in a Court of Justice.

But the Law is still, in certain inevitable cases, the pre-engaged servant of the long purse; and the story is left to be told, for the first time, in this place. As the Judge might once have heard it, so the Reader shall hear it now. No circumstance of importance, from the beginning to the end of the disclosure, shall be related on hearsay evidence. When the writer of these introductory lines (Walter Hartright by name) happens to be more closely connected than others with the incidents to be recorded, he will describe them in his own person. When his experience fails, he will retire from the position of narrator; and his task will be continued, from the point at which he has left it off, by other persons who can speak to the circumstances under notice from their own knowledge, just as clearly and positively as he has spoken before them.

Thus, the story here presented will be told by more than one pen, as the story of an offence against the laws is told in Court by more than one witness — with the same object, in both cases, to present the truth always in its most direct and most intelligible aspect; and to trace the course of one complete series of events, by making the persons who have been most closely connected with them, at each successive stage, relate their own experience, word for word.

Let Walter Hartright, teacher of drawing, aged twenty-eight years, be heard first.

II

It was the last day of July. The long hot summer was drawing to a close; and we, the weary pilgrims of the London pavement, were beginning to think of the cloud-shadows on the corn-fields, and the autumn breezes on the sea-shore.

For my own poor part, the fading summer left me out of health, out of spirits, and, if the truth must be told, out of money as well. During the past year I had not managed my professional resources as carefully as usual; and my extravagance now limited me to the prospect of spending the autumn economically between my mother's cottage at Hampstead and my own chambers in town.

The evening, I remember, was still and cloudy; the London air was at its heaviest; the distant hum of the street-traffic was at its faintest; the small pulse of the life within me, and the great heart of the city around me, seemed to be sinking in unison, languidly and more languidly, with the sinking sun. I roused myself from the book which I was dreaming over rather than reading, and left my chambers to meet the cool night air in the suburbs. It was one of the two evenings in every week which I was accustomed to spend with my mother and my sister. So I turned my steps northward in the direction of Hampstead.

Events which I have yet to relate make it necessary to mention in this place that my father had been dead some years at the period of which I am now writing; and that my sister Sarah and I were the sole survivors of a family of five children. My father was a drawing-master before me. His exertions had made him highly successful in his profession; and his affectionate anxiety to provide for the future of those who were dependent on his labours had impelled him, from the time of his marriage, to devote to the insuring of his life a much larger portion of his income than most men consider it necessary to set aside for that purpose. Thanks to his admirable prudence and self-denial my mother and sister were left, after his death, as independent of the world as they had been during his lifetime. I succeeded to his connection, and had every reason to feel grateful for the prospect that awaited me at my starting in life.

The quiet twilight was still trembling on the topmost ridges of the heath; and the view of London below me had sunk into a black gulf in the shadow of the cloudy night, when I stood before the gate of my mother's cottage. I had hardly rung the bell before the house door was opened violently; my worthy Italian friend, Professor Pesca, appeared in the servant's place;

and darted out joyously to receive me, with a shrill foreign parody on an English cheer.

On his own account, and, I must be allowed to add, on mine also, the Professor merits the honour of a formal introduction. Accident has made him the starting-point of the strange family story which it is the purpose of these pages to unfold.

I had first become acquainted with my Italian friend by meeting him at certain great houses where he taught his own language and I taught drawing. All I then knew of the history of his life was, that he had once held a situation in the University of Padua; that he had left Italy for political reasons (the nature of which he uniformly declined to mention to any one); and that he had been for many years respectably established in London as a teacher of languages.

Without being actually a dwarf—for he was perfectly well proportioned from head to foot—Pesca was, I think, the smallest human being I ever saw out of a show-room. Remarkable anywhere, by his personal appearance, he was still further distinguished among the rank and file of mankind by the harmless eccentricity of his character. The ruling idea of his life appeared to be, that he was bound to show his gratitude to the country which had afforded him an asylum and a means of subsistence by doing his utmost to turn himself into an Englishman. Not content with paying the nation in general the compliment of invariably carrying an umbrella, and invariably wearing gaiters and a white hat, the Professor further aspired to become an Englishman in his habits and amusements, as well as in his personal appearance. Finding us distinguished, as a nation, by our love of athletic exercises, the little man, in the innocence of his heart, devoted himself impromptu to all our English sports and pastimes whenever he had the opportunity of joining them; firmly persuaded that he could adopt our national amusements of the field by an effort of will precisely as he had adopted our national gaiters and our national white hat.

I had seen him risk his limbs blindly at a fox-hunt and in a cricket-field; and soon afterwards I saw him risk his life, just as blindly, in the sea at Brighton.

We had met there accidentally, and were bathing together. If we had been engaged in any exercise peculiar to my own nation I should, of course, have looked after Pesca carefully; but as foreigners are generally quite as well able to take care of themselves in the water as Englishmen, it never occurred to me that the art of swimming might merely add one more to the list of manly exercises which the Professor believed that he could learn impromptu. Soon after we had both struck out from shore, I stopped, finding my friend did not gain on me, and turned round to look for him. To my horror and amazement, I saw nothing between me and the beach but two little white arms which struggled for an instant above the surface of the water, and then disappeared from view. When I dived for him, the poor little man was lying quietly coiled up at the bottom, in a hollow of shingle, looking by many degrees smaller than I had ever seen him look before. During the few minutes that elapsed while I was taking him in, the air revived him, and he ascended the steps of the machine with my assistance. With the partial recovery of his animation came the return of his wonderful delusion on the subject of swimming. As soon as his chattering teeth would let him speak, he smiled vacantly, and said he thought it must have been the Cramp.

When he had thoroughly recovered himself, and had joined me on the beach, his warm Southern nature broke through all artificial English restraints in a moment. He overwhelmed me with the wildest expressions of affection—exclaimed passionately, in his exaggerated Italian way, that he would hold his life henceforth at my disposal—and declared that he should never be happy again until he had found an opportunity of proving his gratitude by rendering me some service which I might remember, on my side, to the end of my days.

I did my best to stop the torrent of his tears and protestations by persisting in treating the whole adventure as a good subject for a joke; and succeeded at last, as I imagined, in lessening Pesca's overwhelming sense of obligation to me. Little did I think then—little did I think afterwards when our pleasant holiday had drawn to an end—that the opportunity of serving me for which my grateful companion so ardently longed was soon to come; that he was eagerly to seize it on the instant; and that by so doing he was to turn the whole current of my existence into a new channel, and to alter me to myself almost past recognition.

Yet so it was. If I had not dived for Professor Pesca when he lay under water on his shingle bed, I should in all human probability never have been connected with the story which these pages will relate—I should never, perhaps, have heard even the name of the woman who has lived in all my thoughts, who has possessed herself of all my energies, who has become the one guiding influence that now directs the purpose of my life.

III

Pesca's face and manner, on the evening when we confronted each other at my mother's gate, were more than sufficient to inform me that something extraordinary had happened. It was quite useless, however, to ask him for an immediate explanation. I could only conjecture, while he was dragging me in by both hands, that (knowing my habits) he had come to the cottage to make sure of meeting me that night, and that he had some news to tell of an unusually agreeable kind.

We both bounced into the parlour in a highly abrupt and undignified manner. My mother sat by the open window laughing and fanning herself. Pesca was one of her especial favourites and his wildest eccentricities were always pardonable in her eyes. Poor dear soul! from the first moment when she found out that the little Professor was deeply and gratefully attached to her son, she opened her heart to him unreservedly, and took all his puzzling foreign peculiarities for granted, without so much as attempting to understand any one of them.

My sister Sarah, with all the advantages of youth, was, strangely enough, less pliable. She did full justice to Pesca's excellent qualities of heart; but she could not accept him implicitly, as my mother accepted him, for my sake. Her insular notions of propriety rose in perpetual revolt against Pesca's constitutional contempt for appearances; and she was always more or less undisguisedly astonished at her mother's familiarity with the eccentric little foreigner. I have observed, not only in my sister's case, but in the instances of others, that we of the young generation are nothing like so hearty and so impulsive as some of our elders. I constantly see old people flushed and excited by the prospect of some anticipated pleasure which altogether fails to ruffle the tranquillity of their serene grandchildren. Are we, I wonder, quite such genuine boys and girls now as our seniors were in their time? Has the great advance in education taken rather too long a stride; and are we in these modern days, just the least trifle in the world too well brought up?

Without attempting to answer those questions decisively, I may at least record that I never saw my mother and my sister together in Pesca's society, without finding my mother much the younger woman of the two. On this occasion, for example, while the old lady was laughing heartily over the boyish manner in which we tumbled into the parlour, Sarah was perturbedly picking up the broken pieces of a teacup, which the

Professor had knocked off the table in his precipitate advance to meet me at the door.

"I don't know what would have happened, Walter," said my mother, "if you had delayed much longer. Pesca has been half mad with impatience, and I have been half mad with curiosity. The Professor has brought some wonderful news with him, in which he says you are concerned; and he has cruelly refused to give us the smallest hint of it till his friend Walter appeared."

"Very provoking: it spoils the Set," murmured Sarah to herself, mournfully absorbed over the ruins of the broken cup.

While these words were being spoken, Pesca, happily and fussily unconscious of the irreparable wrong which the crockery had suffered at his hands, was dragging a large arm-chair to the opposite end of the room, so as to command us all three, in the character of a public speaker addressing an audience. Having turned the chair with its back towards us, he jumped into it on his knees, and excitedly addressed his small congregation of three from an impromptu pulpit.

"Now, my good dears," began Pesca (who always said "good dears" when he meant "worthy friends"), "listen to me. The time has come—I recite my good news—I speak at last."

"Hear, hear!" said my mother, humouring the joke.

"The next thing he will break, mamma," whispered Sarah, "will be the back of the best arm-chair."

"I go back into my life, and I address myself to the noblest of created beings," continued Pesca, vehemently apostrophising my unworthy self over the top rail of the chair. "Who found me dead at the bottom of the sea (through Cramp); and who pulled me up to the top; and what did I say when I got into my own life and my own clothes again?"

"Much more than was at all necessary," I answered as doggedly as possible; for the least encouragement in connection with this subject invariably let loose the Professor's emotions in a flood of tears.

"I said," persisted Pesca, "that my life belonged to my dear friend, Walter, for the rest of my days—and so it does. I said that I should never be happy again till I had found the opportunity of doing a good Something for Walter—and I have never been contented with myself till this most blessed day.

Now," cried the enthusiastic little man at the top of his voice, "the overflowing happiness bursts out of me at every pore of my skin, like a perspiration; for on my faith, and soul, and honour, the something is done at last, and the only word to say now is—Right-all-right!"

It may be necessary to explain here that Pesca prided himself on being a perfect Englishman in his language, as well as in his dress, manners, and amusements. Having picked up a few of our most familiar colloquial expressions, he scattered them about over his conversation whenever they happened to occur to him, turning them, in his high relish for their sound and his general ignorance of their sense, into compound words and repetitions of his own, and always running them into each other, as if they consisted of one long syllable.

"Among the fine London Houses where I teach the language of my native country," said the Professor, rushing into his long-deferred explanation without another word of preface, "there is one, mighty fine, in the big place called Portland. You all know where that is? Yes, yes—course-of-course. The fine house, my good dears, has got inside it a fine family. A Mamma, fair and fat; three young Misses, fair and fat; two young Misters, fair and fat; and a Papa, the fairest and the fattest of all, who is a mighty merchant, up to his eyes in gold—a fine man once, but seeing that he has got a naked head and two chins, fine no longer at the present time. Now mind! I teach the sublime Dante to the young Misses, and ah!—my-soul-bless-my-soul!—it is not in human language to say how the sublime Dante puzzles the pretty heads of all three! No matter—all in good time—and the more lessons the better for me. Now mind! Imagine to yourselves that I am teaching the young Misses to-day, as usual. We are all four of us down together in the Hell of Dante. At the Seventh Circle—but no matter for that: all the Circles are alike to the three young Misses, fair and fat,—at the Seventh Circle, nevertheless, my pupils are sticking fast; and I, to set them going again, recite, explain, and blow myself up red-hot with useless enthusiasm, when—a creak of boots in the passage outside, and in comes the golden Papa, the mighty merchant with the naked head and the two chins.—Ha! my good dears, I am closer than you think for to the business, now. Have you been patient so far? or have you said to yourselves, 'Deuce-what-the-deuce! Pesca is long-winded to-night?'"

We declared that we were deeply interested. The Professor went on:

"In his hand, the golden Papa has a letter; and after he has

The Woman in White

made his excuse for disturbing us in our Infernal Region with the common mortal Business of the house, he addresses himself to the three young Misses, and begins, as you English begin everything in this blessed world that you have to say, with a great O. 'O, my dears,' says the mighty merchant, 'I have got here a letter from my friend, Mr. — —' (the name has slipped out of my mind; but no matter; we shall come back to that; yes, yes—right-all-right). So the Papa says, 'I have got a letter from my friend, the Mister; and he wants a recommend from me, of a drawing-master, to go down to his house in the country.' My-soul-bless-my-soul! when I heard the golden Papa say those words, if I had been big enough to reach up to him, I should have put my arms round his neck, and pressed him to my bosom in a long and grateful hug! As it was, I only bounced upon my chair. My seat was on thorns, and my soul was on fire to speak but I held my tongue, and let Papa go on. 'Perhaps you know,' says this good man of money, twiddling his friend's letter this way and that, in his golden fingers and thumbs, 'perhaps you know, my dears, of a drawing-master that I can recommend?' The three young Misses all look at each other, and then say (with the indispensable great O to begin) "O, dear no, Papa! But here is Mr. Pesca— —' At the mention of myself I can hold no longer—the thought of you, my good dears, mounts like blood to my head—I start from my seat, as if a spike had grown up from the ground through the bottom of my chair—I address myself to the mighty merchant, and I say (English phrase) 'Dear sir, I have the man! The first and foremost drawing-master of the world! Recommend him by the post to-night, and send him off, bag and baggage (English phrase again—ha!), send him off, bag and baggage, by the train to-morrow!' 'Stop, stop,' says Papa; 'is he a foreigner, or an Englishman?' 'English to the bone of his back,' I answer. 'Respectable?' says Papa. 'Sir,' I say (for this last question of his outrages me, and I have done being familiar with him—) 'Sir! the immortal fire of genius burns in this Englishman's bosom, and, what is more, his father had it before him!' 'Never mind,' says the golden barbarian of a Papa, 'never mind about his genius, Mr. Pesca. We don't want genius in this country, unless it is accompanied by respectability—and then we are very glad to have it, very glad indeed. Can your friend produce testimonials—letters that speak to his character?' I wave my hand negligently. 'Letters?' I say. 'Ha! my-soul-bless-my-soul! I should think so, indeed! Volumes of letters and portfolios of testimonials, if you like!' 'One or two will do,' says this man of phlegm and money. 'Let him send them to me, with his name and address. And—stop, stop, Mr. Pesca—before you go to your friend, you had better take a note.' 'Bank-note!' I say, indignantly. 'No bank-note, if you please, till my brave

Englishman has earned it first.' 'Bank-note!' says Papa, in a great surprise, 'who talked of bank-note? I mean a note of the terms—a memorandum of what he is expected to do. Go on with your lesson, Mr. Pesca, and I will give you the necessary extract from my friend's letter.' Down sits the man of merchandise and money to his pen, ink, and paper; and down I go once again into the Hell of Dante, with my three young Misses after me. In ten minutes' time the note is written, and the boots of Papa are creaking themselves away in the passage outside. From that moment, on my faith, and soul, and honour, I know nothing more! The glorious thought that I have caught my opportunity at last, and that my grateful service for my dearest friend in the world is as good as done already, flies up into my head and makes me drunk. How I pull my young Misses and myself out of our Infernal Region again, how my other business is done afterwards, how my little bit of dinner slides itself down my throat, I know no more than a man in the moon. Enough for me, that here I am, with the mighty merchant's note in my hand, as large as life, as hot as fire, and as happy as a king! Ha! ha! ha! right-right-right-all-right!" Here the Professor waved the memorandum of terms over his head, and ended his long and voluble narrative with his shrill Italian parody on an English cheer.

My mother rose the moment he had done, with flushed cheeks and brightened eyes. She caught the little man warmly by both hands.

"My dear, good Pesca," she said, "I never doubted your true affection for Walter—but I am more than ever persuaded of it now!"

"I am sure we are very much obliged to Professor Pesca, for Walter's sake," added Sarah. She half rose, while she spoke, as if to approach the arm-chair, in her turn; but, observing that Pesca was rapturously kissing my mother's hands, looked serious, and resumed her seat. "If the familiar little man treats my mother in that way, how will he treat me?" Faces sometimes tell truth; and that was unquestionably the thought in Sarah's mind, as she sat down again.

Although I myself was gratefully sensible of the kindness of Pesca's motives, my spirits were hardly so much elevated as they ought to have been by the prospect of future employment now placed before me. When the Professor had quite done with my mother's hand, and when I had warmly thanked him for his interference on my behalf, I asked to be allowed to look at the note of terms which his respectable patron had drawn up for my inspection.

Pesca handed me the paper, with a triumphant flourish of the hand.

"Read!" said the little man majestically. "I promise you my friend, the writing of the golden Papa speaks with a tongue of trumpets for itself."

The note of terms was plain, straightforward, and comprehensive, at any rate. It informed me,

First, That Frederick Fairlie, Esquire, of Limmeridge House, Cumberland, wanted to engage the services of a thoroughly competent drawing-master, for a period of four months certain.

Secondly, That the duties which the master was expected to perform would be of a twofold kind. He was to superintend the instruction of two young ladies in the art of painting in water-colours; and he was to devote his leisure time, afterwards, to the business of repairing and mounting a valuable collection of drawings, which had been suffered to fall into a condition of total neglect.

Thirdly, That the terms offered to the person who should undertake and properly perform these duties were four guineas a week; that he was to reside at Limmeridge House; and that he was to be treated there on the footing of a gentleman.

Fourthly, and lastly, That no person need think of applying for this situation unless he could furnish the most unexceptionable references to character and abilities. The references were to be sent to Mr. Fairlie's friend in London, who was empowered to conclude all necessary arrangements. These instructions were followed by the name and address of Pesca's employer in Portland Place—and there the note, or memorandum, ended.

The prospect which this offer of an engagement held out was certainly an attractive one. The employment was likely to be both easy and agreeable; it was proposed to me at the autumn time of the year when I was least occupied; and the terms, judging by my personal experience in my profession, were surprisingly liberal. I knew this; I knew that I ought to consider myself very fortunate if I succeeded in securing the offered employment—and yet, no sooner had I read the memorandum than I felt an inexplicable unwillingness within me to stir in the matter. I had never in the whole of my previous experience found my duty and my inclination so painfully and so unaccountably at variance as I found them now.

"Oh, Walter, your father never had such a chance as this!" said my mother, when she had read the note of terms and had handed it back to me.

"Such distinguished people to know," remarked Sarah, straightening herself in the chair; "and on such gratifying terms of equality too!"

"Yes, yes; the terms, in every sense, are tempting enough," I replied impatiently. "But before I send in my testimonials, I should like a little time to consider — —"

"Consider!" exclaimed my mother. "Why, Walter, what is the matter with you?"

"Consider!" echoed my sister. "What a very extraordinary thing to say, under the circumstances!"

"Consider!" chimed in the Professor. "What is there to consider about? Answer me this! Have you not been complaining of your health, and have you not been longing for what you call a smack of the country breeze? Well! there in your hand is the paper that offers you perpetual choking mouthfuls of country breeze for four months' time. Is it not so? Ha! Again — you want money. Well! Is four golden guineas a week nothing? My-soul-bless-my-soul! only give it to me — and my boots shall creak like the golden Papa's, with a sense of the overpowering richness of the man who walks in them! Four guineas a week, and, more than that, the charming society of two young misses! and, more than that, your bed, your breakfast, your dinner, your gorging English teas and lunches and drinks of foaming beer, all for nothing — why, Walter, my dear good friend — deuce-what-the-deuce! — for the first time in my life I have not eyes enough in my head to look, and wonder at you!"

Neither my mother's evident astonishment at my behaviour, nor Pesca's fervid enumeration of the advantages offered to me by the new employment, had any effect in shaking my unreasonable disinclination to go to Limmeridge House. After starting all the petty objections that I could think of to going to Cumberland, and after hearing them answered, one after another, to my own complete discomfiture, I tried to set up a last obstacle by asking what was to become of my pupils in London while I was teaching Mr. Fairlie's young ladies to

The Woman in White

sketch from nature. The obvious answer to this was, that the greater part of them would be away on their autumn travels, and that the few who remained at home might be confided to the care of one of my brother drawing-masters, whose pupils I had once taken off his hands under similar circumstances. My sister reminded me that this gentleman had expressly placed his services at my disposal, during the present season, in case I wished to leave town; my mother seriously appealed to me not to let an idle caprice stand in the way of my own interests and my own health; and Pesca piteously entreated that I would not wound him to the heart by rejecting the first grateful offer of service that he had been able to make to the friend who had saved his life.

The evident sincerity and affection which inspired these remonstrances would have influenced any man with an atom of good feeling in his composition. Though I could not conquer my own unaccountable perversity, I had at least virtue enough to be heartily ashamed of it, and to end the discussion pleasantly by giving way, and promising to do all that was wanted of me.

The rest of the evening passed merrily enough in humorous anticipations of my coming life with the two young ladies in Cumberland. Pesca, inspired by our national grog, which appeared to get into his head, in the most marvellous manner, five minutes after it had gone down his throat, asserted his claims to be considered a complete Englishman by making a series of speeches in rapid succession, proposing my mother's health, my sister's health, my health, and the healths, in mass, of Mr. Fairlie and the two young Misses, pathetically returning thanks himself, immediately afterwards, for the whole party. "A secret, Walter," said my little friend confidentially, as we walked home together. "I am flushed by the recollection of my own eloquence. My soul bursts itself with ambition. One of these days I go into your noble Parliament. It is the dream of my whole life to be Honourable Pesca, M.P.!"

The next morning I sent my testimonials to the Professor's employer in Portland Place. Three days passed, and I concluded, with secret satisfaction, that my papers had not been found sufficiently explicit. On the fourth day, however, an answer came. It announced that Mr. Fairlie accepted my services, and requested me to start for Cumberland immediately. All the necessary instructions for my journey were carefully and clearly added in a postscript.

I made my arrangements, unwillingly enough, for leaving London early the next day. Towards evening Pesca looked in, on his way to a dinner-party, to bid me good-bye.

"I shall dry my tears in your absence," said the Professor gaily, "with this glorious thought. It is my auspicious hand that has given the first push to your fortune in the world. Go, my friend! When your sun shines in Cumberland (English proverb), in the name of heaven make your hay. Marry one of the two young Misses; become Honourable Hartright, M.P.; and when you are on the top of the ladder remember that Pesca, at the bottom, has done it all!"

I tried to laugh with my little friend over his parting jest, but my spirits were not to be commanded. Something jarred in me almost painfully while he was speaking his light farewell words.

When I was left alone again nothing remained to be done but to walk to the Hampstead cottage and bid my mother and Sarah good-bye.

IV

The heat had been painfully oppressive all day, and it was now a close and sultry night.

My mother and sister had spoken so many last words, and had begged me to wait another five minutes so many times, that it was nearly midnight when the servant locked the garden-gate behind me. I walked forward a few paces on the shortest way back to London, then stopped and hesitated.

The moon was full and broad in the dark blue starless sky, and the broken ground of the heath looked wild enough in the mysterious light to be hundreds of miles away from the great city that lay beneath it. The idea of descending any sooner than I could help into the heat and gloom of London repelled me. The prospect of going to bed in my airless chambers, and the prospect of gradual suffocation, seemed, in my present restless frame of mind and body, to be one and the same thing. I determined to stroll home in the purer air by the most roundabout way I could take; to follow the white winding paths across the lonely heath; and to approach London through its most open suburb by striking into the Finchley Road, and so getting back, in the cool of the new morning, by the western side of the Regent's Park.

I wound my way down slowly over the heath, enjoying the divine stillness of the scene, and admiring the soft alternations of light and shade as they followed each other over the broken ground on every side of me. So long as I was proceeding through this first and prettiest part of my night walk my mind remained passively open to the impressions produced by the view; and I thought but little on any subject — indeed, so far as my own sensations were concerned, I can hardly say that I thought at all.

But when I had left the heath and had turned into the by-road, where there was less to see, the ideas naturally engendered by the approaching change in my habits and occupations gradually drew more and more of my attention exclusively to themselves. By the time I had arrived at the end of the road I had become completely absorbed in my own fanciful visions of Limmeridge House, of Mr. Fairlie, and of the two ladies whose practice in the art of water-colour painting I was so soon to superintend.

I had now arrived at that particular point of my walk where four roads met — the road to Hampstead, along which I had returned, the road to Finchley, the road to West End, and the road back to London. I had mechanically turned in this latter direction, and was strolling along the lonely high-road—idly wondering, I remember, what the Cumberland young ladies would look like—when, in one moment, every drop of blood in my body was brought to a stop by the touch of a hand laid lightly and suddenly on my shoulder from behind me.

I turned on the instant, with my fingers tightening round the handle of my stick.

There, in the middle of the broad bright high-road—there, as if it had that moment sprung out of the earth or dropped from the heaven—stood the figure of a solitary Woman, dressed from head to foot in white garments, her face bent in grave inquiry on mine, her hand pointing to the dark cloud over London, as I faced her.

I was far too seriously startled by the suddenness with which this extraordinary apparition stood before me, in the dead of night and in that lonely place, to ask what she wanted. The strange woman spoke first.

"Is that the road to London?" she said.

I looked attentively at her, as she put that singular question to me. It was then nearly one o'clock. All I could discern distinctly by the moonlight was a colourless, youthful face, meagre and sharp to look at about the cheeks and chin; large, grave, wistfully attentive eyes; nervous, uncertain lips; and light hair of a pale, brownish-yellow hue. There was nothing wild, nothing immodest in her manner: it was quiet and self-controlled, a little melancholy and a little touched by suspicion; not exactly the manner of a lady, and, at the same time, not the manner of a woman in the humblest rank of life. The voice, little as I had yet heard of it, had something curiously still and mechanical in its tones, and the utterance was remarkably rapid. She held a small bag in her hand: and her dress—bonnet, shawl, and gown all of white—was, so far as I could guess, certainly not composed of very delicate or very expensive materials. Her figure was slight, and rather above the average height—her gait and actions free from the slightest approach to extravagance. This was all that I could observe of her in the dim light and under the perplexingly strange circumstances of our meeting. What sort of a woman she was, and how she came to be out alone in the high-road, an hour after midnight, I altogether failed to guess. The one thing of which I felt certain was, that the grossest of mankind could not have misconstrued her motive in speaking, even at that suspiciously late hour and in that suspiciously lonely place.

"Did you hear me?" she said, still quietly and rapidly, and without the least fretfulness or impatience. "I asked if that was the way to London."

"Yes," I replied, "that is the way: it leads to St. John's Wood and the Regent's Park. You must excuse my not answering you before. I was rather startled by your sudden appearance in the road; and I am, even now, quite unable to account for it."

"You don't suspect me of doing anything wrong, do you? I have done nothing wrong. I have met with an accident—I am very unfortunate in being here alone so late. Why do you suspect me of doing wrong?"

She spoke with unnecessary earnestness and agitation, and shrank back from me several paces. I did my best to reassure her.

"Pray don't suppose that I have any idea of suspecting you," I said, "or any other wish than to be of assistance to you, if I can. I only wondered at your appearance in the road, because it seemed to me to be empty the instant before I saw you."

She turned, and pointed back to a place at the junction of the road to London and the road to Hampstead, where there was a gap in the hedge.

"I heard you coming," she said, "and hid there to see what sort of man you were, before I risked speaking. I doubted and feared about it till you passed; and then I was obliged to steal after you, and touch you."

Steal after me and touch me? Why not call to me? Strange, to say the least of it.

"May I trust you?" she asked. "You don't think the worse of me because I have met with an accident?" She stopped in confusion; shifted her bag from one hand to the other; and sighed bitterly.

The loneliness and helplessness of the woman touched me. The natural impulse to assist her and to spare her got the better of the judgment, the caution, the worldly tact, which an older, wiser, and colder man might have summoned to help him in this strange emergency.

"You may trust me for any harmless purpose," I said. "If it troubles you to explain your strange situation to me, don't think of returning to the subject again. I have no right to ask you for any explanations. Tell me how I can help you; and if I can, I will."

"You are very kind, and I am very, very thankful to have met you." The first touch of womanly tenderness that I had heard from her trembled in her voice as she said the words; but no tears glistened in those large, wistfully attentive eyes of hers, which were still fixed on me. "I have only been in London once before," she went on, more and more rapidly, "and I know nothing about that side of it, yonder. Can I get a fly, or a carriage of any kind? Is it too late? I don't know. If you could show me where to get a fly — and if you will only promise not to interfere with me, and to let me leave you, when and how I please — I have a friend in London who will be glad to receive me — I want nothing else — will you promise?"

She looked anxiously up and down the road; shifted her bag again from one hand to the other; repeated the words, "Will you promise?" and looked hard in my face, with a pleading fear and confusion that it troubled me to see.

What could I do? Here was a stranger utterly and helplessly at my mercy — and that stranger a forlorn woman. No house was near; no one was passing whom I could consult; and no earthly right existed on my part to give me a power of control over her, even if I had known how to exercise it. I trace these lines, self-distrustfully, with the shadows of after-events darkening the very paper I write on; and still I say, what could I do?

What I did do, was to try and gain time by questioning her. "Are you sure that your friend in London will receive you at such a late hour as this?" I said.

"Quite sure. Only say you will let me leave you when and how I please — only say you won't interfere with me. Will you promise?"

As she repeated the words for the third time, she came close to me and laid her hand, with a sudden gentle stealthiness, on my bosom — a thin hand; a cold hand (when I removed it with mine) even on that sultry night. Remember that I was young; remember that the hand which touched me was a woman's.

"Will you promise?"

"Yes."

One word! The little familiar word that is on everybody's lips, every hour in the day. Oh me! and I tremble, now, when I write it.

We set our faces towards London, and walked on together in the first still hour of the new day—I, and this woman, whose name, whose character, whose story, whose objects in life, whose very presence by my side, at that moment, were fathomless mysteries to me. It was like a dream. Was I Walter Hartright? Was this the well-known, uneventful road, where holiday people strolled on Sundays? Had I really left, little more than an hour since, the quiet, decent, conventionally domestic atmosphere of my mother's cottage? I was too bewildered—too conscious also of a vague sense of something like self-reproach—to speak to my strange companion for some minutes. It was her voice again that first broke the silence between us.

"I want to ask you something," she said suddenly. "Do you know many people in London?"

"Yes, a great many."

"Many men of rank and title?" There was an unmistakable tone of suspicion in the strange question. I hesitated about answering it.

"Some," I said, after a moment's silence.

"Many"—she came to a full stop, and looked me searchingly in the face—"many men of the rank of Baronet?"

Too much astonished to reply, I questioned her in my turn.

"Why do you ask?"

"Because I hope, for my own sake, there is one Baronet that you don't know."

"Will you tell me his name?"

"I can't—I daren't—I forget myself when I mention it." She spoke loudly and almost fiercely, raised her clenched hand in the air, and shook it passionately; then, on a sudden, controlled herself again, and added, in tones lowered to a whisper "Tell me which of them you know."

I could hardly refuse to humour her in such a trifle, and I mentioned three names. Two, the names of fathers of families whose daughters I taught; one, the name of a bachelor who had once taken me a cruise in his yacht, to make sketches for him.

"Ah! you don't know him," she said, with a sigh of relief. "Are you a man of rank and title yourself?"

"Far from it. I am only a drawing-master."

As the reply passed my lips—a little bitterly, perhaps—she took my arm with the abruptness which characterised all her actions.

"Not a man of rank and title," she repeated to herself. "Thank God! I may trust him."

I had hitherto contrived to master my curiosity out of consideration for my companion; but it got the better of me now.

"I am afraid you have serious reason to complain of some man of rank and title?" I said. "I am afraid the baronet, whose name you are unwilling to mention to me, has done you some grievous wrong? Is he the cause of your being out here at this strange time of night?"

"Don't ask me: don't make me talk of it," she answered. "I'm not fit now. I have been cruelly used and cruelly wronged. You will be kinder than ever, if you will walk on fast, and not speak to me. I sadly want to quiet myself, if I can."

We moved forward again at a quick pace; and for half an hour, at least, not a word passed on either side. From time to time, being forbidden to make any more inquiries, I stole a look at her face. It was always the same; the lips close shut, the brow frowning, the eyes looking straight forward, eagerly and yet absently. We had reached the first houses, and were close on the new Wesleyan college, before her set features relaxed and she spoke once more.

"Do you live in London?" she said.

"Yes." As I answered, it struck me that she might have formed some intention of appealing to me for assistance or advice, and that I ought to spare her a possible disappointment by warning her of my approaching absence from home. So I added, "But to-morrow I shall be away from London for some time. I am going into the country."

"Where?" she asked. "North or south?"

"North—to Cumberland."

"Cumberland!" she repeated the word tenderly. "Ah! I wish I was going there too. I was once happy in Cumberland."

I tried again to lift the veil that hung between this woman and me.

"Perhaps you were born," I said, "in the beautiful Lake country."

"No," she answered. "I was born in Hampshire; but I once went to school for a little while in Cumberland. Lakes? I don't remember any lakes. It's Limmeridge village, and Limmeridge House, I should like to see again."

It was my turn now to stop suddenly. In the excited state of my curiosity, at that moment, the chance reference to Mr. Fairlie's place of residence, on the lips of my strange companion, staggered me with astonishment.

"Did you hear anybody calling after us?" she asked, looking up and down the road affrightedly, the instant I stopped.

"No, no. I was only struck by the name of Limmeridge House. I heard it mentioned by some Cumberland people a few days since."

"Ah! not my people. Mrs. Fairlie is dead; and her husband is dead; and their little girl may be married and gone away by this time. I can't say who lives at Limmeridge now. If any more are left there of that name, I only know I love them for Mrs. Fairlie's sake."

She seemed about to say more; but while she was speaking, we came within view of the turnpike, at the top of the Avenue Road. Her hand tightened round my arm, and she looked anxiously at the gate before us.

"Is the turnpike man looking out?" she asked.

He was not looking out; no one else was near the place when we passed through the gate. The sight of the gas-lamps and houses seemed to agitate her, and to make her impatient.

"This is London," she said. "Do you see any carriage I can get? I am tired and frightened. I want to shut myself in and be driven away."

I explained to her that we must walk a little further to get to a cab-stand, unless we were fortunate enough to meet with an empty vehicle; and then tried to resume the subject of Cumberland. It was useless. That idea of shutting herself in, and being driven away, had now got full possession of her mind. She could think and talk of nothing else.

We had hardly proceeded a third of the way down the Avenue Road when I saw a cab draw up at a house a few doors below us, on the opposite side of the way. A gentleman got out and let himself in at the garden door. I hailed the cab, as the driver mounted the box again. When we crossed the road, my companion's impatience increased to such an extent that she almost forced me to run.

"It's so late," she said. "I am only in a hurry because it's so late."

"I can't take you, sir, if you're not going towards Tottenham Court Road," said the driver civilly, when I opened the cab door. "My horse is dead beat, and I can't get him no further than the stable."

"Yes, yes. That will do for me. I'm going that way — I'm going that way." She spoke with breathless eagerness, and pressed by me into the cab.

I had assured myself that the man was sober as well as civil before I let her enter the vehicle. And now, when she was seated inside, I entreated her to let me see her set down safely at her destination.

"No, no, no," she said vehemently. "I'm quite safe, and quite happy now. If you are a gentleman, remember your promise. Let him drive on till I stop him. Thank you — oh! thank you, thank you!"

My hand was on the cab door. She caught it in hers, kissed it, and pushed it away. The cab drove off at the same moment — I started into the road, with some vague idea of stopping it again, I hardly knew why — hesitated from dread of frightening and distressing her — called, at last, but not loudly enough to attract the driver's attention. The sound of the wheels grew fainter in the distance — the cab melted into the black shadows

The Woman in White

on the road—the woman in white was gone.

Ten minutes or more had passed. I was still on the same side of the way; now mechanically walking forward a few paces; now stopping again absently. At one moment I found myself doubting the reality of my own adventure; at another I was perplexed and distressed by an uneasy sense of having done wrong, which yet left me confusedly ignorant of how I could have done right. I hardly knew where I was going, or what I meant to do next; I was conscious of nothing but the confusion of my own thoughts, when I was abruptly recalled to myself—awakened, I might almost say—by the sound of rapidly approaching wheels close behind me.

I was on the dark side of the road, in the thick shadow of some garden trees, when I stopped to look round. On the opposite and lighter side of the way, a short distance below me, a policeman was strolling along in the direction of the Regent's Park.

The carriage passed me—an open chaise driven by two men.

"Stop!" cried one. "There's a policeman. Let's ask him."

The horse was instantly pulled up, a few yards beyond the dark place where I stood.

"Policeman!" cried the first speaker. "Have you seen a woman pass this way?"

"What sort of woman, sir?"

"A woman in a lavender-coloured gown——"

"No, no," interposed the second man. "The clothes we gave her were found on her bed. She must have gone away in the clothes she wore when she came to us. In white, policeman. A woman in white."

"I haven't seen her, sir."

"If you or any of your men meet with the woman, stop her, and send her in careful keeping to that address. I'll pay all expenses, and a fair reward into the bargain."

The policeman looked at the card that was handed down to

him.

"Why are we to stop her, sir? What has she done?"

"Done! She has escaped from my Asylum. Don't forget; a woman in white. Drive on."

V

"She has escaped from my Asylum!"

I cannot say with truth that the terrible inference which those words suggested flashed upon me like a new revelation. Some of the strange questions put to me by the woman in white, after my ill-considered promise to leave her free to act as she pleased, had suggested the conclusion either that she was naturally flighty and unsettled, or that some recent shock of terror had disturbed the balance of her faculties. But the idea of absolute insanity which we all associate with the very name of an Asylum, had, I can honestly declare, never occurred to me, in connection with her. I had seen nothing, in her language or her actions, to justify it at the time; and even with the new light thrown on her by the words which the stranger had addressed to the policeman, I could see nothing to justify it now.

What had I done? Assisted the victim of the most horrible of all false imprisonments to escape; or cast loose on the wide world of London an unfortunate creature, whose actions it was my duty, and every man's duty, mercifully to control? I turned sick at heart when the question occurred to me, and when I felt self-reproachfully that it was asked too late.

In the disturbed state of my mind, it was useless to think of going to bed, when I at last got back to my chambers in Clement's Inn. Before many hours elapsed it would be necessary to start on my journey to Cumberland. I sat down and tried, first to sketch, then to read—but the woman in white got between me and my pencil, between me and my book. Had the forlorn creature come to any harm? That was my first thought, though I shrank selfishly from confronting it. Other thoughts followed, on which it was less harrowing to dwell. Where had she stopped the cab? What had become of her now? Had she been traced and captured by the men in the chaise? Or was she still capable of controlling her own actions; and were we two following our widely parted roads towards one point in the mysterious future, at which we were to meet once more?

It was a relief when the hour came to lock my door, to bid farewell to London pursuits, London pupils, and London friends, and to be in movement again towards new interests and a new life. Even the bustle and confusion at the railway terminus, so wearisome and bewildering at other times, roused me and did me good.

My travelling instructions directed me to go to Carlisle, and then to diverge by a branch railway which ran in the direction of the coast. As a misfortune to begin with, our engine broke down between Lancaster and Carlisle. The delay occasioned by this accident caused me to be too late for the branch train, by which I was to have gone on immediately. I had to wait some hours; and when a later train finally deposited me at the nearest station to Limmeridge House, it was past ten, and the night was so dark that I could hardly see my way to the pony-chaise which Mr. Fairlie had ordered to be in waiting for me.

The driver was evidently discomposed by the lateness of my arrival. He was in that state of highly respectful sulkiness which is peculiar to English servants. We drove away slowly through the darkness in perfect silence. The roads were bad, and the dense obscurity of the night increased the difficulty of getting over the ground quickly. It was, by my watch, nearly an hour and a half from the time of our leaving the station before I heard the sound of the sea in the distance, and the crunch of our wheels on a smooth gravel drive. We had passed one gate before entering the drive, and we passed another before we drew up at the house. I was received by a solemn man-servant out of livery, was informed that the family had retired for the night, and was then led into a large and lofty room where my supper was awaiting me, in a forlorn manner, at one extremity of a lonesome mahogany wilderness of dining-table.

I was too tired and out of spirits to eat or drink much, especially with the solemn servant waiting on me as elaborately as if a small dinner party had arrived at the house instead of a solitary man. In a quarter of an hour I was ready to be taken up to my bedchamber. The solemn servant conducted me into a prettily furnished room—said, "Breakfast at nine o'clock, sir"—looked all round him to see that everything was in its proper place, and noiselessly withdrew.

"What shall I see in my dreams to-night?" I thought to myself, as I put out the candle; "the woman in white? or the unknown inhabitants of this Cumberland mansion?" It was a strange sensation to be sleeping in the house, like a friend of the family, and yet not to know one of the inmates, even by sight!

VI

When I rose the next morning and drew up my blind, the sea opened before me joyously under the broad August sunlight, and the distant coast of Scotland fringed the horizon with its lines of melting blue.

The view was such a surprise, and such a change to me, after my weary London experience of brick and mortar landscape, that I seemed to burst into a new life and a new set of thoughts the moment I looked at it. A confused sensation of having suddenly lost my familiarity with the past, without acquiring any additional clearness of idea in reference to the present or the future, took possession of my mind. Circumstances that were but a few days old faded back in my memory, as if they had happened months and months since. Pesca's quaint announcement of the means by which he had procured me my present employment; the farewell evening I had passed with my mother and sister; even my mysterious adventure on the way home from Hampstead—had all become like events which might have occurred at some former epoch of my existence. Although the woman in white was still in my mind, the image of her seemed to have grown dull and faint already.

A little before nine o'clock, I descended to the ground-floor of the house. The solemn man-servant of the night before met me wandering among the passages, and compassionately showed me the way to the breakfast-room.

My first glance round me, as the man opened the door, disclosed a well-furnished breakfast-table, standing in the middle of a long room, with many windows in it. I looked from the table to the window farthest from me, and saw a lady standing at it, with her back turned towards me. The instant my eyes rested on her, I was struck by the rare beauty of her form, and by the unaffected grace of her attitude. Her figure was tall, yet not too tall; comely and well-developed, yet not fat; her head set on her shoulders with an easy, pliant firmness; her waist, perfection in the eyes of a man, for it occupied its natural place, it filled out its natural circle, it was visibly and delightfully undeformed by stays. She had not heard my entrance into the room; and I allowed myself the luxury of admiring her for a few moments, before I moved one of the chairs near me, as the least embarrassing means of attracting her attention. She turned towards me immediately. The easy elegance of every movement of her limbs and body as soon as she began to advance from the far end of the room, set me in a flutter of expectation to see her face clearly. She left the window—and I said to myself, The lady is dark. She moved forward a few steps—and I said to myself, The lady is young. She approached nearer—and I said to myself (with a sense of surprise which words fail me to express), The lady is ugly!

Never was the old conventional maxim, that Nature cannot err, more flatly contradicted—never was the fair promise of a lovely figure more strangely and startlingly belied by the face and head that crowned it. The lady's complexion was almost swarthy, and the dark down on her upper lip was almost a moustache. She had a large, firm, masculine mouth and jaw; prominent, piercing, resolute brown eyes; and thick, coal-black hair, growing unusually low down on her forehead. Her expression—bright, frank, and intelligent—appeared, while she was silent, to be altogether wanting in those feminine attractions of gentleness and pliability, without which the beauty of the handsomest woman alive is beauty incomplete. To see such a face as this set on shoulders that a sculptor would have longed to model—to be charmed by the modest graces of action through which the symmetrical limbs betrayed their beauty when they moved, and then to be almost repelled by the masculine form and masculine look of the features in which the perfectly shaped figure ended—was to feel a sensation oddly akin to the helpless discomfort familiar to us all in sleep, when we recognise yet cannot reconcile the anomalies and contradictions of a dream.

"Mr. Hartright?" said the lady interrogatively, her dark face lighting up with a smile, and softening and growing womanly the moment she began to speak. "We resigned all hope of you last night, and went to bed as usual. Accept my apologies for our apparent want of attention; and allow me to introduce myself as one of your pupils. Shall we shake hands? I suppose we must come to it sooner or later—and why not sooner?"

These odd words of welcome were spoken in a clear, ringing, pleasant voice. The offered hand—rather large, but beautifully formed—was given to me with the easy, unaffected self-reliance of a highly-bred woman. We sat down together at the breakfast-table in as cordial and customary a manner as if we had known each other for years, and had met at Limmeridge House to talk over old times by previous appointment.

"I hope you come here good-humouredly determined to make the best of your position," continued the lady. "You will have to begin this morning by putting up with no other company at breakfast than mine. My sister is in her own room, nursing that essentially feminine malady, a slight headache; and her old governess, Mrs. Vesey, is charitably attending on her with restorative tea. My uncle, Mr. Fairlie, never joins us at any of our meals: he is an invalid, and keeps bachelor state in his own apartments. There is nobody else in the house but me. Two young ladies have been staying here, but they went away yesterday, in despair; and no wonder. All through their visit (in consequence of Mr. Fairlie's invalid condition) we produced no such convenience in the house as a flirtable, danceable, small-talkable creature of the male sex; and the consequence was, we did nothing but quarrel, especially at dinner-time. How can you expect four women to dine together alone every day, and not quarrel? We are such fools, we can't entertain each other at table. You see I don't think much of my own sex, Mr. Hartright—which will you have, tea or coffee?—no woman does think much of her own sex, although few of them confess it as freely as I do. Dear me, you look puzzled. Why? Are you wondering what you will have for breakfast? or are you surprised at my careless way of talking? In the first case, I advise you, as a friend, to have nothing to do with that cold ham at your elbow, and to wait till the omelette comes in. In the second case, I will give you some tea to compose your spirits, and do all a woman can (which is very little, by-the-bye) to hold my tongue."

She handed me my cup of tea, laughing gaily. Her light flow of talk, and her lively familiarity of manner with a total stranger, were accompanied by an unaffected naturalness and an easy inborn confidence in herself and her position, which would have secured her the respect of the most audacious man breathing. While it was impossible to be formal and reserved in her company, it was more than impossible to take the faintest vestige of a liberty with her, even in thought. I felt this instinctively, even while I caught the infection of her own bright gaiety of spirits—even while I did my best to answer her in her own frank, lively way.

"Yes, yes," she said, when I had suggested the only explanation I could offer, to account for my perplexed looks, "I understand. You are such a perfect stranger in the house, that you are puzzled by my familiar references to the worthy inhabitants. Natural enough: I ought to have thought of it before. At any rate, I can set it right now. Suppose I begin with myself, so as to get done with that part of the subject as soon as possible? My name is Marian Halcombe; and I am as inaccurate as women usually are, in calling Mr. Fairlie my uncle, and Miss Fairlie my sister. My mother was twice married: the first time to Mr. Halcombe, my father; the second time to Mr. Fairlie, my half-sister's father. Except that we are both orphans, we are in every respect as unlike each other as possible. My father was a poor man, and Miss Fairlie's father was a rich man. I have got nothing, and she has a fortune. I am dark and ugly, and she is fair and pretty. Everybody thinks me crabbed and odd (with perfect justice); and everybody thinks her sweet-tempered and charming (with more justice still). In short, she is an angel; and I am — — Try some of that marmalade, Mr. Hartright, and finish the sentence, in the name of female propriety, for yourself. What am I to tell you about Mr. Fairlie? Upon my honour, I hardly know. He is sure to send for you after breakfast, and you can study him for yourself. In the meantime, I may inform you, first, that he is the late Mr. Fairlie's younger brother; secondly, that he is a single man; and thirdly, that he is Miss Fairlie's guardian. I won't live without her, and she can't live without me; and that is how I come to be at Limmeridge House. My sister and I are honestly fond of each other; which, you will say, is perfectly unaccountable, under the circumstances, and I quite agree with you — but so it is. You must please both of us, Mr. Hartright, or please neither of us: and, what is still more trying, you will be thrown entirely upon our society. Mrs. Vesey is an excellent person, who possesses all the cardinal virtues, and counts for nothing; and Mr. Fairlie is too great an invalid to be a companion for anybody. I don't know what is the matter with him, and the doctors don't know what is the matter with him, and he doesn't know himself what is the matter with him. We all say it's on the nerves, and we none of us know what we mean when we say it. However, I advise you to humour his little peculiarities, when you see him to-day. Admire his collection of coins, prints, and water-colour drawings, and you will win his heart. Upon my word, if you can be contented with a quiet country life, I don't see why you should not get on very well here. From breakfast to lunch, Mr. Fairlie's drawings will occupy you. After lunch, Miss Fairlie and I shoulder our sketch-books, and go out to misrepresent Nature, under your directions. Drawing is her favourite whim, mind, not mine. Women can't draw — their minds are too flighty, and their eyes are too inattentive. No matter — my sister likes it; so I waste paint and spoil paper, for her sake, as composedly as any woman in England. As for the evenings, I think we can help you through them. Miss Fairlie plays delightfully. For my own poor part, I don't know one note of music from the other; but I can match you at chess, backgammon, ecarte, and (with the inevitable female drawbacks) even at billiards as well. What do you think of the programme? Can you reconcile yourself to our quiet, regular life? or do you mean to be restless, and secretly thirst for change and adventure, in the humdrum atmosphere of Limmeridge House?"

She had run on thus far, in her gracefully bantering way, with no other interruptions on my part than the unimportant replies which politeness required of me. The turn of the expression, however, in her last question, or rather the one chance word, "adventure," lightly as it fell from her lips, recalled my thoughts to my meeting with the woman in white, and urged me to discover the connection which the stranger's own reference to Mrs. Fairlie informed me must once have existed between the nameless fugitive from the Asylum, and the former mistress of Limmeridge House.

"Even if I were the most restless of mankind," I said, "I should be in no danger of thirsting after adventures for some time to come. The very night before I arrived at this house, I met with an adventure; and the wonder and excitement of it, I can assure you, Miss Halcombe, will last me for the whole term of my stay in Cumberland, if not for a much longer period."

"You don't say so, Mr. Hartright! May I hear it?"

"You have a claim to hear it. The chief person in the adventure was a total stranger to me, and may perhaps be a total stranger to you; but she certainly mentioned the name of the late Mrs. Fairlie in terms of the sincerest gratitude and regard."

"Mentioned my mother's name! You interest me indescribably. Pray go on."

I at once related the circumstances under which I had met the woman in white, exactly as they had occurred; and I repeated what she had said to me about Mrs. Fairlie and Limmeridge House, word for word.

Miss Halcombe's bright resolute eyes looked eagerly into mine, from the beginning of the narrative to the end. Her face expressed vivid interest and astonishment, but nothing more. She was evidently as far from knowing of any clue to the mystery as I was myself.

"Are you quite sure of those words referring to my mother?" she asked.

"Quite sure," I replied. "Whoever she may be, the woman was once at school in the village of Limmeridge, was treated with especial kindness by Mrs. Fairlie, and, in grateful remembrance of that kindness, feels an affectionate interest in all surviving members of the family. She knew that Mrs. Fairlie and her husband were both dead; and she spoke of Miss Fairlie as if they had known each other when they were children."

"You said, I think, that she denied belonging to this place?"

"Yes, she told me she came from Hampshire."

"And you entirely failed to find out her name?"

"Entirely."

"Very strange. I think you were quite justified, Mr. Hartright, in giving the poor creature her liberty, for she seems to have done nothing in your presence to show herself unfit to enjoy it. But I wish you had been a little more resolute about finding out her name. We must really clear up this mystery, in some way. You had better not speak of it yet to Mr. Fairlie, or to my sister. They are both of them, I am certain, quite as ignorant of who the woman is, and of what her past history in connection with us can be, as I am myself. But they are also, in widely different ways, rather nervous and sensitive; and you would only fidget one and alarm the other to no purpose. As for myself, I am all aflame with curiosity, and I devote my whole energies to the business of discovery from this moment. When my mother came here, after her second marriage, she certainly established the village school just as it exists at the present time. But the old teachers are all dead, or gone elsewhere; and no enlightenment is to be hoped for from that quarter. The only other alternative I can think of— —"

At this point we were interrupted by the entrance of the servant, with a message from Mr. Fairlie, intimating that he would be glad to see me, as soon as I had done breakfast.

"Wait in the hall," said Miss Halcombe, answering the servant for me, in her quick, ready way. "Mr. Hartright will come out directly. I was about to say," she went on, addressing me again, "that my sister and I have a large collection of my mother's letters, addressed to my father and to hers. In the absence of any other means of getting information, I will pass the morning in looking over my mother's correspondence with Mr. Fairlie. He was fond of London, and was constantly away from his country home; and she was accustomed, at such times, to write and report to him how things went on at Limmeridge. Her letters are full of references to the school in which she took so strong an interest; and I think it more than likely that I may have discovered something when we meet again. The luncheon hour is two, Mr. Hartright. I shall have the pleasure of introducing you to my sister by that time, and we will occupy the afternoon in driving round the neighbourhood and showing you all our pet points of view. Till two o'clock, then, farewell."

She nodded to me with the lively grace, the delightful refinement of familiarity, which characterised all that she did and all that she said; and disappeared by a door at the lower end of the room. As soon as she had left me, I turned my steps towards the hall, and followed the servant, on my way, for the first time, to the presence of Mr. Fairlie.

VII

My conductor led me upstairs into a passage which took us back to the bedchamber in which I had slept during the past night; and opening the door next to it, begged me to look in.

"I have my master's orders to show you your own sitting-room, sir," said the man, "and to inquire if you approve of the situation and the light."

I must have been hard to please, indeed, if I had not approved of the room, and of everything about it. The bow-window looked out on the same lovely view which I had admired, in the morning, from my bedroom. The furniture was the perfection of luxury and beauty; the table in the centre was bright with gaily bound books, elegant conveniences for writing, and beautiful flowers; the second table, near the window, was covered with all the necessary materials for mounting water-colour drawings, and had a little easel attached to it, which I could expand or fold up at will; the walls were hung with gaily tinted chintz; and the floor was spread with Indian matting in maize-colour and red. It was the prettiest and most luxurious little sitting-room I had ever seen; and I admired it with the warmest enthusiasm.

The solemn servant was far too highly trained to betray the slightest satisfaction. He bowed with icy deference when my terms of eulogy were all exhausted, and silently opened the door for me to go out into the passage again.

We turned a corner, and entered a long second passage, ascended a short flight of stairs at the end, crossed a small circular upper hall, and stopped in front of a door covered with dark baize. The servant opened this door, and led me on a few yards to a second; opened that also, and disclosed two curtains of pale sea-green silk hanging before us; raised one of them noiselessly; softly uttered the words, "Mr. Hartright," and left me.

I found myself in a large, lofty room, with a magnificent carved ceiling, and with a carpet over the floor, so thick and soft that it felt like piles of velvet under my feet. One side of the room was occupied by a long book-case of some rare inlaid wood that was quite new to me. It was not more than six feet high, and the top was adorned with statuettes in marble, ranged at regular distances one from the other. On the opposite side stood two antique cabinets; and between them, and above them, hung a picture of the Virgin and Child, protected by glass, and bearing Raphael's name on the gilt tablet at the bottom of the frame. On my right hand and on my left, as I stood inside the door, were chiffoniers and little stands in buhl and marquetterie, loaded with figures in Dresden china, with rare vases, ivory ornaments, and toys and curiosities that sparkled at all points with gold, silver, and precious stones. At the lower end of the room, opposite to me, the windows were concealed and the sunlight was tempered by large blinds of the same pale sea-green colour as the curtains over the door. The light thus produced was deliciously soft, mysterious, and subdued; it fell equally upon all the objects in the room; it helped to intensify the deep silence, and the air of profound seclusion that possessed the place; and it surrounded, with an appropriate halo of repose, the solitary figure of the master of the house, leaning back, listlessly composed, in a large easy-chair, with a reading-easel fastened on one of its arms, and a little table on the other.

If a man's personal appearance, when he is out of his dressing-room, and when he has passed forty, can be accepted as a safe guide to his time of life—which is more than doubtful—Mr. Fairlie's age, when I saw him, might have been reasonably computed at over fifty and under sixty years. His beardless face was thin, worn, and transparently pale, but not wrinkled; his nose was high and hooked; his eyes were of a dim greyish blue, large, prominent, and rather red round the rims of the eyelids; his hair was scanty, soft to look at, and of that light sandy colour which is the last to disclose its own changes towards grey. He was dressed in a dark frock-coat, of some substance much thinner than cloth, and in waistcoat and trousers of spotless white. His feet were effeminately small, and were clad in buff-coloured silk stockings, and little womanish bronze-leather slippers. Two rings adorned his white delicate hands, the value of which even my inexperienced observation detected to be all but priceless. Upon the whole, he had a frail, languidly-fretful, over-refined look—something singularly and unpleasantly delicate in its association with a man, and, at the same time, something which could by no possibility have looked natural and appropriate if it had been transferred to the personal appearance of a woman. My morning's experience of Miss Halcombe had predisposed me to be pleased with everybody in the house; but my sympathies shut themselves up resolutely at the first sight of Mr. Fairlie.

On approaching nearer to him, I discovered that he was not so entirely without occupation as I had at first supposed. Placed amid the other rare and beautiful objects on a large round table near him, was a dwarf cabinet in ebony and silver, containing coins of all shapes and sizes, set out in little drawers lined with dark purple velvet. One of these drawers lay on the small table attached to his chair; and near it were some tiny jeweller's brushes, a wash-leather "stump," and a little bottle of liquid, all waiting to be used in various ways for the removal of any accidental impurities which might be discovered on the coins. His frail white fingers were listlessly toying with something which looked, to my uninstructed eyes, like a dirty pewter medal with ragged edges, when I advanced within a respectful distance of his chair, and stopped to make my bow.

"So glad to possess you at Limmeridge, Mr. Hartright," he said in a querulous, croaking voice, which combined, in anything but an agreeable manner, a discordantly high tone with a drowsily languid utterance. "Pray sit down. And don't trouble yourself to move the chair, please. In the wretched state of my nerves, movement of any kind is exquisitely painful to me. Have you seen your studio? Will it do?"

"I have just come from seeing the room, Mr. Fairlie; and I assure you— —"

He stopped me in the middle of the sentence, by closing his eyes, and holding up one of his white hands imploringly. I paused in astonishment; and the croaking voice honoured me with this explanation—

"Pray excuse me. But could you contrive to speak in a lower key? In the wretched state of my nerves, loud sound of any kind is indescribable torture to me. You will pardon an invalid? I only say to you what the lamentable state of my health obliges me to say to everybody. Yes. And you really like the room?"

"I could wish for nothing prettier and nothing more comfortable," I answered, dropping my voice, and beginning to discover already that Mr. Fairlie's selfish affectation and Mr. Fairlie's wretched nerves meant one and the same thing.

"So glad. You will find your position here, Mr. Hartright, properly recognised. There is none of the horrid English barbarity of feeling about the social position of an artist in this house. So much of my early life has been passed abroad, that I have quite cast my insular skin in that respect. I wish I could say the same of the gentry—detestable word, but I suppose I must use it—of the gentry in the neighbourhood. They are sad Goths in Art, Mr. Hartright. People, I do assure you, who would have opened their eyes in astonishment, if they had seen Charles the Fifth pick up Titian's brush for him. Do you mind putting this tray of coins back in the cabinet, and giving me the next one to it? In the wretched state of my nerves, exertion of any kind is unspeakably disagreeable to me. Yes. Thank you."

As a practical commentary on the liberal social theory which he had just favoured me by illustrating, Mr. Fairlie's cool request rather amused me. I put back one drawer and gave him the other, with all possible politeness. He began trifling with the new set of coins and the little brushes immediately; languidly looking at them and admiring them all the time he was speaking to me.

"A thousand thanks and a thousand excuses. Do you like coins? Yes. So glad we have another taste in common besides our taste for Art. Now, about the pecuniary arrangements between us — do tell me — are they satisfactory?"

"Most satisfactory, Mr. Fairlie."

"So glad. And — what next? Ah! I remember. Yes. In reference to the consideration which you are good enough to accept for giving me the benefit of your accomplishments in art, my steward will wait on you at the end of the first week, to ascertain your wishes. And — what next? Curious, is it not? I had a great deal more to say: and I appear to have quite forgotten it. Do you mind touching the bell? In that corner. Yes. Thank you."

I rang; and a new servant noiselessly made his appearance — a foreigner, with a set smile and perfectly brushed hair — a valet every inch of him.

"Louis," said Mr. Fairlie, dreamily dusting the tips of his fingers with one of the tiny brushes for the coins, "I made some entries in my tablettes this morning. Find my tablettes. A thousand pardons, Mr. Hartright, I'm afraid I bore you."

As he wearily closed his eyes again, before I could answer, and as he did most assuredly bore me, I sat silent, and looked up at the Madonna and Child by Raphael. In the meantime, the valet left the room, and returned shortly with a little ivory book. Mr. Fairlie, after first relieving himself by a gentle sigh, let the book drop open with one hand, and held up the tiny brush with the other, as a sign to the servant to wait for further orders.

"Yes. Just so!" said Mr. Fairlie, consulting the tablettes. "Louis, take down that portfolio." He pointed, as he spoke, to several portfolios placed near the window, on mahogany stands. "No. Not the one with the green back — that contains my

Rembrandt etchings, Mr. Hartright. Do you like etchings? Yes? So glad we have another taste in common. The portfolio with the red back, Louis. Don't drop it! You have no idea of the tortures I should suffer, Mr. Hartright, if Louis dropped that portfolio. Is it safe on the chair? Do you think it safe, Mr. Hartright? Yes? So glad. Will you oblige me by looking at the drawings, if you really think they are quite safe. Louis, go away. What an ass you are. Don't you see me holding the tablettes? Do you suppose I want to hold them? Then why not relieve me of the tablettes without being told? A thousand pardons, Mr. Hartright; servants are such asses, are they not? Do tell me — what do you think of the drawings? They have come from a sale in a shocking state — I thought they smelt of horrid dealers' and brokers' fingers when I looked at them last. Can you undertake them?"

Although my nerves were not delicate enough to detect the odour of plebeian fingers which had offended Mr. Fairlie's nostrils, my taste was sufficiently educated to enable me to appreciate the value of the drawings, while I turned them over. They were, for the most part, really fine specimens of English water-colour art; and they had deserved much better treatment at the hands of their former possessor than they appeared to have received.

"The drawings," I answered, "require careful straining and mounting; and, in my opinion, they are well worth— —"

"I beg your pardon," interposed Mr. Fairlie. "Do you mind my closing my eyes while you speak? Even this light is too much for them. Yes?"

"I was about to say that the drawings are well worth all the time and trouble— —"

Mr. Fairlie suddenly opened his eyes again, and rolled them with an expression of helpless alarm in the direction of the window.

"I entreat you to excuse me, Mr. Hartright," he said in a feeble flutter. "But surely I hear some horrid children in the garden — my private garden — below?"

"I can't say, Mr. Fairlie. I heard nothing myself."

"Oblige me — you have been so very good in humouring my poor nerves — oblige me by lifting up a corner of the blind. Don't let the sun in on me, Mr. Hartright! Have you got the

The Woman in White

blind up? Yes? Then will you be so very kind as to look into the garden and make quite sure?"

I complied with this new request. The garden was carefully walled in, all round. Not a human creature, large or small, appeared in any part of the sacred seclusion. I reported that gratifying fact to Mr. Fairlie.

"A thousand thanks. My fancy, I suppose. There are no children, thank Heaven, in the house; but the servants (persons born without nerves) will encourage the children from the village. Such brats—oh, dear me, such brats! Shall I confess it, Mr. Hartright?—I sadly want a reform in the construction of children. Nature's only idea seems to be to make them machines for the production of incessant noise. Surely our delightful Raffaello's conception is infinitely preferable?"

He pointed to the picture of the Madonna, the upper part of which represented the conventional cherubs of Italian Art, celestially provided with sitting accommodation for their chins, on balloons of buff-coloured cloud.

"Quite a model family!" said Mr. Fairlie, leering at the cherubs. "Such nice round faces, and such nice soft wings, and—nothing else. No dirty little legs to run about on, and no noisy little lungs to scream with. How immeasurably superior to the existing construction! I will close my eyes again, if you will allow me. And you really can manage the drawings? So glad. Is there anything else to settle? if there is, I think I have forgotten it. Shall we ring for Louis again?"

Being, by this time, quite as anxious, on my side, as Mr. Fairlie evidently was on his, to bring the interview to a speedy conclusion, I thought I would try to render the summoning of the servant unnecessary, by offering the requisite suggestion on my own responsibility.

"The only point, Mr. Fairlie, that remains to be discussed," I said, "refers, I think, to the instruction in sketching which I am engaged to communicate to the two young ladies."

"Ah! just so," said Mr. Fairlie. "I wish I felt strong enough to go into that part of the arrangement—but I don't. The ladies who profit by your kind services, Mr. Hartright, must settle, and decide, and so on, for themselves. My niece is fond of your charming art. She knows just enough about it to be conscious of her own sad defects. Please take pains with her. Yes. Is there anything else? No. We quite understand each other—don't we?

I have no right to detain you any longer from your delightful pursuit—have I? So pleasant to have settled everything—such a sensible relief to have done business. Do you mind ringing for Louis to carry the portfolio to your own room?"

"I will carry it there myself, Mr. Fairlie, if you will allow me."

"Will you really? Are you strong enough? How nice to be so strong! Are you sure you won't drop it? So glad to possess you at Limmeridge, Mr. Hartright. I am such a sufferer that I hardly dare hope to enjoy much of your society. Would you mind taking great pains not to let the doors bang, and not to drop the portfolio? Thank you. Gently with the curtains, please—the slightest noise from them goes through me like a knife. Yes. Good morning!"

When the sea-green curtains were closed, and when the two baize doors were shut behind me, I stopped for a moment in the little circular hall beyond, and drew a long, luxurious breath of relief. It was like coming to the surface of the water after deep diving, to find myself once more on the outside of Mr. Fairlie's room.

As soon as I was comfortably established for the morning in my pretty little studio, the first resolution at which I arrived was to turn my steps no more in the direction of the apartments occupied by the master of the house, except in the very improbable event of his honouring me with a special invitation to pay him another visit. Having settled this satisfactory plan of future conduct in reference to Mr. Fairlie, I soon recovered the serenity of temper of which my employer's haughty familiarity and impudent politeness had, for the moment, deprived me. The remaining hours of the morning passed away pleasantly enough, in looking over the drawings, arranging them in sets, trimming their ragged edges, and accomplishing the other necessary preparations in anticipation of the business of mounting them. I ought, perhaps, to have made more progress than this; but, as the luncheon-time drew near, I grew restless and unsettled, and felt unable to fix my attention on work, even though that work was only of the humble manual kind.

At two o'clock I descended again to the breakfast-room, a little anxiously. Expectations of some interest were connected with my approaching reappearance in that part of the house. My introduction to Miss Fairlie was now close at hand; and, if Miss Halcombe's search through her mother's letters had produced the result which she anticipated, the time had come for clearing up the mystery of the woman in white.

VIII

When I entered the room, I found Miss Halcombe and an elderly lady seated at the luncheon-table.

The elderly lady, when I was presented to her, proved to be Miss Fairlie's former governess, Mrs. Vesey, who had been briefly described to me by my lively companion at the breakfast-table, as possessed of "all the cardinal virtues, and counting for nothing." I can do little more than offer my humble testimony to the truthfulness of Miss Halcombe's sketch of the old lady's character. Mrs. Vesey looked the personification of human composure and female amiability. A calm enjoyment of a calm existence beamed in drowsy smiles on her plump, placid face. Some of us rush through life, and some of us saunter through life. Mrs. Vesey sat through life. Sat in the house, early and late; sat in the garden; sat in unexpected window-seats in passages; sat (on a camp-stool) when her friends tried to take her out walking; sat before she looked at anything, before she talked of anything, before she answered Yes, or No, to the commonest question—always with the same serene smile on her lips, the same vacantly-attentive turn of the head, the same snugly-comfortable position of her hands and arms, under every possible change of domestic circumstances. A mild, a compliant, an unutterably tranquil and harmless old lady, who never by any chance suggested the idea that she had been actually alive since the hour of her birth. Nature has so much to do in this world, and is engaged in generating such a vast variety of co-existent productions, that she must surely be now and then too flurried and confused to distinguish between the different processes that she is carrying on at the same time. Starting from this point of view, it will always remain my private persuasion that Nature was absorbed in making cabbages when Mrs. Vesey was born, and that the good lady suffered the consequences of a vegetable preoccupation in the mind of the Mother of us all.

"Now, Mrs. Vesey," said Miss Halcombe, looking brighter, sharper, and readier than ever, by contrast with the undemonstrative old lady at her side, "what will you have? A cutlet?"

Mrs. Vesey crossed her dimpled hands on the edge of the table, smiled placidly, and said, "Yes, dear."

"What is that opposite Mr. Hartright? Boiled chicken, is it not? I thought you liked boiled chicken better than cutlet, Mrs. Vesey?"

Mrs. Vesey took her dimpled hands off the edge of the table and crossed them on her lap instead; nodded contemplatively at the boiled chicken, and said, "Yes, dear."

"Well, but which will you have, to-day? Shall Mr. Hartright give you some chicken? or shall I give you some cutlet?"

Mrs. Vesey put one of her dimpled hands back again on the edge of the table; hesitated drowsily, and said, "Which you please, dear."

"Mercy on me! it's a question for your taste, my good lady, not for mine. Suppose you have a little of both? and suppose you begin with the chicken, because Mr. Hartright looks devoured by anxiety to carve for you."

Mrs. Vesey put the other dimpled hand back on the edge of the table; brightened dimly one moment; went out again the next; bowed obediently, and said, "If you please, sir."

Surely a mild, a compliant, an unutterably tranquil and harmless old lady! But enough, perhaps, for the present, of Mrs. Vesey.

All this time, there were no signs of Miss Fairlie. We finished our luncheon; and still she never appeared. Miss Halcombe, whose quick eye nothing escaped, noticed the looks that I cast, from time to time, in the direction of the door.

"I understand you, Mr. Hartright," she said; "you are wondering what has become of your other pupil. She has been downstairs, and has got over her headache; but has not sufficiently recovered her appetite to join us at lunch. If you will put yourself under my charge, I think I can undertake to find her somewhere in the garden."

She took up a parasol lying on a chair near her, and led the way out, by a long window at the bottom of the room, which opened on to the lawn. It is almost unnecessary to say that we left Mrs. Vesey still seated at the table, with her dimpled hands still crossed on the edge of it; apparently settled in that position for the rest of the afternoon.

As we crossed the lawn, Miss Halcombe looked at me significantly, and shook her head.

The Woman in White

"That mysterious adventure of yours," she said, "still remains involved in its own appropriate midnight darkness. I have been all the morning looking over my mother's letters, and I have made no discoveries yet. However, don't despair, Mr. Hartright. This is a matter of curiosity; and you have got a woman for your ally. Under such conditions success is certain, sooner or later. The letters are not exhausted. I have three packets still left, and you may confidently rely on my spending the whole evening over them."

Here, then, was one of my anticipations of the morning still unfulfilled. I began to wonder, next, whether my introduction to Miss Fairlie would disappoint the expectations that I had been forming of her since breakfast-time.

"And how did you get on with Mr. Fairlie?" inquired Miss Halcombe, as we left the lawn and turned into a shrubbery. "Was he particularly nervous this morning? Never mind considering about your answer, Mr. Hartright. The mere fact of your being obliged to consider is enough for me. I see in your face that he was particularly nervous; and, as I am amiably unwilling to throw you into the same condition, I ask no more."

We turned off into a winding path while she was speaking, and approached a pretty summer-house, built of wood, in the form of a miniature Swiss chalet. The one room of the summer-house, as we ascended the steps of the door, was occupied by a young lady. She was standing near a rustic table, looking out at the inland view of moor and hill presented by a gap in the trees, and absently turning over the leaves of a little sketch-book that lay at her side. This was Miss Fairlie.

How can I describe her? How can I separate her from my own sensations, and from all that has happened in the later time? How can I see her again as she looked when my eyes first rested on her — as she should look, now, to the eyes that are about to see her in these pages?

The water-colour drawing that I made of Laura Fairlie, at an after period, in the place and attitude in which I first saw her, lies on my desk while I write. I look at it, and there dawns upon me brightly, from the dark greenish-brown background of the summer-house, a light, youthful figure, clothed in a simple muslin dress, the pattern of it formed by broad alternate stripes of delicate blue and white. A scarf of the same material sits crisply and closely round her shoulders, and a little straw hat of the natural colour, plainly and sparingly trimmed with ribbon to match the gown, covers her head, and throws its soft pearly shadow over the upper part of her face. Her hair is of so faint and pale a brown—not flaxen, and yet almost as light; not golden, and yet almost as glossy—that it nearly melts, here and there, into the shadow of the hat. It is plainly parted and drawn back over her ears, and the line of it ripples naturally as it crosses her forehead. The eyebrows are rather darker than the hair; and the eyes are of that soft, limpid, turquoise blue, so often sung by the poets, so seldom seen in real life. Lovely eyes in colour, lovely eyes in form—large and tender and quietly thoughtful—but beautiful above all things in the clear truthfulness of look that dwells in their inmost depths, and shines through all their changes of expression with the light of a purer and a better world. The charm—most gently and yet most distinctly expressed—which they shed over the whole face, so covers and transforms its little natural human blemishes elsewhere, that it is difficult to estimate the relative merits and defects of the other features. It is hard to see that the lower part of the face is too delicately refined away towards the chin to be in full and fair proportion with the upper part; that the nose, in escaping the aquiline bend (always hard and cruel in a woman, no matter how abstractedly perfect it may be), has erred a little in the other extreme, and has missed the ideal straightness of line; and that the sweet, sensitive lips are subject to a slight nervous contraction, when she smiles, which draws them upward a little at one corner, towards the cheek. It might be possible to note these blemishes in another woman's face but it is not easy to dwell on them in hers, so subtly are they connected with all that is individual and characteristic in her expression, and so closely does the expression depend for its full play and life, in every other feature, on the moving impulse of the eyes.

Does my poor portrait of her, my fond, patient labour of long and happy days, show me these things? Ah, how few of them are in the dim mechanical drawing, and how many in the mind with which I regard it! A fair, delicate girl, in a pretty light dress, trifling with the leaves of a sketch-book, while she looks up from it with truthful, innocent blue eyes—that is all the drawing can say; all, perhaps, that even the deeper reach of thought and pen can say in their language, either. The woman who first gives life, light, and form to our shadowy conceptions of beauty, fills a void in our spiritual nature that has remained unknown to us till she appeared. Sympathies that lie too deep for words, too deep almost for thoughts, are touched, at such times, by other charms than those which the senses feel and which the resources of expression can realise. The mystery which underlies the beauty of women is never raised above the reach of all expression until it has claimed kindred with the deeper mystery in our own souls. Then, and then only, has it passed beyond the narrow region on which light falls, in this world, from the pencil and the pen.

Think of her as you thought of the first woman who quickened the pulses within you that the rest of her sex had no art to stir. Let the kind, candid blue eyes meet yours, as they met mine, with the one matchless look which we both remember so well. Let her voice speak the music that you once loved best, attuned as sweetly to your ear as to mine. Let her footstep, as she comes and goes, in these pages, be like that other footstep to whose airy fall your own heart once beat time. Take her as the visionary nursling of your own fancy; and she will grow upon you, all the more clearly, as the living woman who dwells in mine.

Among the sensations that crowded on me, when my eyes first looked upon her—familiar sensations which we all know, which spring to life in most of our hearts, die again in so many, and renew their bright existence in so few—there was one that troubled and perplexed me: one that seemed strangely inconsistent and unaccountably out of place in Miss Fairlie's presence.

Mingling with the vivid impression produced by the charm of her fair face and head, her sweet expression, and her winning simplicity of manner, was another impression, which, in a shadowy way, suggested to me the idea of something wanting. At one time it seemed like something wanting in her: at another, like something wanting in myself, which hindered me from understanding her as I ought. The impression was always strongest in the most contradictory manner, when she looked at me; or, in other words, when I was most conscious of the harmony and charm of her face, and yet, at the same time, most troubled by the sense of an incompleteness which it was impossible to discover. Something wanting, something wanting—and where it was, and what it was, I could not say.

The effect of this curious caprice of fancy (as I thought it then) was not of a nature to set me at my ease, during a first interview with Miss Fairlie. The few kind words of welcome which she spoke found me hardly self-possessed enough to thank her in the customary phrases of reply. Observing my hesitation, and no doubt attributing it, naturally enough, to some momentary shyness on my part, Miss Halcombe took the business of talking, as easily and readily as usual, into her own hands.

"Look there, Mr. Hartright," she said, pointing to the sketch-book on the table, and to the little delicate wandering hand that was still trifling with it. "Surely you will acknowledge that your model pupil is found at last? The moment she hears that you are in the house, she seizes her inestimable sketch-book, looks universal Nature straight in the face, and longs to begin!"

Miss Fairlie laughed with a ready good-humour, which broke out as brightly as if it had been part of the sunshine above us, over her lovely face.

"I must not take credit to myself where no credit is due," she said, her clear, truthful blue eyes looking alternately at Miss Halcombe and at me. "Fond as I am of drawing, I am so conscious of my own ignorance that I am more afraid than anxious to begin. Now I know you are here, Mr. Hartright, I find myself looking over my sketches, as I used to look over my lessons when I was a little girl, and when I was sadly afraid that I should turn out not fit to be heard."

She made the confession very prettily and simply, and, with quaint, childish earnestness, drew the sketch-book away close to her own side of the table. Miss Halcombe cut the knot of the little embarrassment forthwith, in her resolute, downright way.

"Good, bad, or indifferent," she said, "the pupil's sketches must pass through the fiery ordeal of the master's judgment—and there's an end of it. Suppose we take them with us in the carriage, Laura, and let Mr. Hartright see them, for the first time, under circumstances of perpetual jolting and interruption? If we can only confuse him all through the drive, between Nature as it is, when he looks up at the view, and Nature as it is not when he looks down again at our sketch-books, we shall drive him into the last desperate refuge of paying us compliments, and shall slip through his professional fingers with our pet feathers of vanity all unruffled."

"I hope Mr. Hartright will pay me no compliments," said Miss Fairlie, as we all left the summer-house.

"May I venture to inquire why you express that hope?" I asked.

"Because I shall believe all that you say to me," she answered simply.

In those few words she unconsciously gave me the key to her whole character: to that generous trust in others which, in her nature, grew innocently out of the sense of her own truth. I only knew it intuitively then. I know it by experience now.

We merely waited to rouse good Mrs. Vesey from the place which she still occupied at the deserted luncheon-table, before we entered the open carriage for our promised drive. The old lady and Miss Halcombe occupied the back seat, and Miss Fairlie and I sat together in front, with the sketch-book open between us, fairly exhibited at last to my professional eyes. All serious criticism on the drawings, even if I had been disposed to volunteer it, was rendered impossible by Miss Halcombe's lively resolution to see nothing but the ridiculous side of the Fine Arts, as practised by herself, her sister, and ladies in general. I can remember the conversation that passed far more easily than the sketches that I mechanically looked over. That part of the talk, especially, in which Miss Fairlie took any share, is still as vividly impressed on my memory as if I had heard it only a few hours ago.

Yes! let me acknowledge that on this first day I let the charm of her presence lure me from the recollection of myself and my position. The most trifling of the questions that she put to me, on the subject of using her pencil and mixing her colours; the slightest alterations of expression in the lovely eyes that looked into mine with such an earnest desire to learn all that I could teach, and to discover all that I could show, attracted more of my attention than the finest view we passed through, or the grandest changes of light and shade, as they flowed into each other over the waving moorland and the level beach. At any time, and under any circumstances of human interest, is it not strange to see how little real hold the objects of the natural world amid which we live can gain on our hearts and minds? We go to Nature for comfort in trouble, and sympathy in joy, only in books. Admiration of those beauties of the inanimate world, which modern poetry so largely and so eloquently describes, is not, even in the best of us, one of the original instincts of our nature. As children, we none of us possess it. No uninstructed man or woman possesses it. Those whose lives are most exclusively passed amid the ever-changing wonders of sea and land are also those who are most universally insensible to every aspect of Nature not directly associated with the human interest of their calling. Our capacity of appreciating the beauties of the earth we live on is, in truth, one of the civilised accomplishments which we all learn as an Art; and, more, that very capacity is rarely practised by any of us except when our minds are most indolent and most unoccupied. How much share have the attractions of Nature ever had in the pleasurable or painful interests and emotions of ourselves or our friends?

What space do they ever occupy in the thousand little narratives of personal experience which pass every day by word of mouth from one of us to the other? All that our minds can compass, all that our hearts can learn, can be accomplished with equal certainty, equal profit, and equal satisfaction to ourselves, in the poorest as in the richest prospect that the face of the earth can show. There is surely a reason for this want of inborn sympathy between the creature and the creation around it, a reason which may perhaps be found in the widely-differing destinies of man and his earthly sphere. The grandest mountain prospect that the eye can range over is appointed to annihilation. The smallest human interest that the pure heart can feel is appointed to immortality.

We had been out nearly three hours, when the carriage again passed through the gates of Limmeridge House.

On our way back I had let the ladies settle for themselves the first point of view which they were to sketch, under my instructions, on the afternoon of the next day. When they withdrew to dress for dinner, and when I was alone again in my little sitting-room, my spirits seemed to leave me on a sudden. I felt ill at ease and dissatisfied with myself, I hardly knew why. Perhaps I was now conscious for the first time of having enjoyed our drive too much in the character of a guest, and too little in the character of a drawing-master. Perhaps that strange sense of something wanting, either in Miss Fairlie or in myself, which had perplexed me when I was first introduced to her, haunted me still. Anyhow, it was a relief to my spirits when the dinner-hour called me out of my solitude, and took me back to the society of the ladies of the house.

I was struck, on entering the drawing-room, by the curious contrast, rather in material than in colour, of the dresses which they now wore. While Mrs. Vesey and Miss Halcombe were richly clad (each in the manner most becoming to her age), the first in silver-grey, and the second in that delicate primrose-yellow colour which matches so well with a dark complexion and black hair, Miss Fairlie was unpretendingly and almost poorly dressed in plain white muslin. It was spotlessly pure: it was beautifully put on; but still it was the sort of dress which the wife or daughter of a poor man might have worn, and it made her, so far as externals went, look less affluent in circumstances than her own governess. At a later period, when I learnt to know more of Miss Fairlie's character, I discovered that this curious contrast, on the wrong side, was due to her natural delicacy of feeling and natural intensity of aversion to the slightest personal display of her own wealth. Neither Mrs.

Vesey nor Miss Halcombe could ever induce her to let the advantage in dress desert the two ladies who were poor, to lean to the side of the one lady who was rich.

When the dinner was over we returned together to the drawing-room. Although Mr. Fairlie (emulating the magnificent condescension of the monarch who had picked up Titian's brush for him) had instructed his butler to consult my wishes in relation to the wine that I might prefer after dinner, I was resolute enough to resist the temptation of sitting in solitary grandeur among bottles of my own choosing, and sensible enough to ask the ladies' permission to leave the table with them habitually, on the civilised foreign plan, during the period of my residence at Limmeridge House.

The drawing-room, to which we had now withdrawn for the rest of the evening, was on the ground-floor, and was of the same shape and size as the breakfast-room. Large glass doors at the lower end opened on to a terrace, beautifully ornamented along its whole length with a profusion of flowers. The soft, hazy twilight was just shading leaf and blossom alike into harmony with its own sober hues as we entered the room, and the sweet evening scent of the flowers met us with its fragrant welcome through the open glass doors. Good Mrs. Vesey (always the first of the party to sit down) took possession of an arm-chair in a corner, and dozed off comfortably to sleep. At my request Miss Fairlie placed herself at the piano. As I followed her to a seat near the instrument, I saw Miss Halcombe retire into a recess of one of the side windows, to proceed with the search through her mother's letters by the last quiet rays of the evening light.

How vividly that peaceful home-picture of the drawing-room comes back to me while I write! From the place where I sat I could see Miss Halcombe's graceful figure, half of it in soft light, half in mysterious shadow, bending intently over the letters in her lap; while, nearer to me, the fair profile of the player at the piano was just delicately defined against the faintly-deepening background of the inner wall of the room. Outside, on the terrace, the clustering flowers and long grasses and creepers waved so gently in the light evening air, that the sound of their rustling never reached us. The sky was without a cloud, and the dawning mystery of moonlight began to tremble already in the region of the eastern heaven. The sense of peace and seclusion soothed all thought and feeling into a rapt, unearthly repose; and the balmy quiet, that deepened ever with the deepening light, seemed to hover over us with a gentler influence still, when there stole upon it from the piano the heavenly tenderness of the music of Mozart. It was an evening of sights and sounds never to forget.

We all sat silent in the places we had chosen—Mrs. Vesey still sleeping, Miss Fairlie still playing, Miss Halcombe still reading—till the light failed us. By this time the moon had stolen round to the terrace, and soft, mysterious rays of light were slanting already across the lower end of the room. The change from the twilight obscurity was so beautiful that we banished the lamps, by common consent, when the servant brought them in, and kept the large room unlighted, except by the glimmer of the two candles at the piano.

For half an hour more the music still went on. After that the beauty of the moonlight view on the terrace tempted Miss Fairlie out to look at it, and I followed her. When the candles at the piano had been lighted Miss Halcombe had changed her place, so as to continue her examination of the letters by their assistance. We left her, on a low chair, at one side of the instrument, so absorbed over her reading that she did not seem to notice when we moved.

We had been out on the terrace together, just in front of the glass doors, hardly so long as five minutes, I should think; and Miss Fairlie was, by my advice, just tying her white handkerchief over her head as a precaution against the night air—when I heard Miss Halcombe's voice—low, eager, and altered from its natural lively tone—pronounce my name.

"Mr. Hartright," she said, "will you come here for a minute? I want to speak to you."

I entered the room again immediately. The piano stood about half-way down along the inner wall. On the side of the instrument farthest from the terrace Miss Halcombe was sitting with the letters scattered on her lap, and with one in her hand selected from them, and held close to the candle. On the side nearest to the terrace there stood a low ottoman, on which I took my place. In this position I was not far from the glass doors, and I could see Miss Fairlie plainly, as she passed and repassed the opening on to the terrace, walking slowly from end to end of it in the full radiance of the moon.

"I want you to listen while I read the concluding passages in this letter," said Miss Halcombe. "Tell me if you think they throw any light upon your strange adventure on the road to London. The letter is addressed by my mother to her second husband, Mr. Fairlie, and the date refers to a period of between eleven and twelve years since. At that time Mr. and Mrs. Fairlie, and my half-sister Laura, had been living for years in this house; and I was away from them completing my education at a school in Paris."

She looked and spoke earnestly, and, as I thought, a little uneasily as well. At the moment when she raised the letter to the candle before beginning to read it, Miss Fairlie passed us on the terrace, looked in for a moment, and seeing that we were engaged, slowly walked on.

Miss Halcombe began to read as follows:—

"'You will be tired, my dear Philip, of hearing perpetually about my schools and my scholars. Lay the blame, pray, on the dull uniformity of life at Limmeridge, and not on me. Besides, this time I have something really interesting to tell you about a new scholar.

"'You know old Mrs. Kempe at the village shop. Well, after years of ailing, the doctor has at last given her up, and she is dying slowly day by day. Her only living relation, a sister, arrived last week to take care of her. This sister comes all the way from Hampshire—her name is Mrs. Catherick. Four days ago Mrs. Catherick came here to see me, and brought her only child with her, a sweet little girl about a year older than our darling Laura——'"

As the last sentence fell from the reader's lips, Miss Fairlie passed us on the terrace once more. She was softly singing to herself one of the melodies which she had been playing earlier in the evening. Miss Halcombe waited till she had passed out of sight again, and then went on with the letter—

"'Mrs. Catherick is a decent, well-behaved, respectable woman; middle-aged, and with the remains of having been moderately, only moderately, nice-looking. There is something in her manner and in her appearance, however, which I can't make out. She is reserved about herself to the point of downright secrecy, and there is a look in her face—I can't describe it—which suggests to me that she has something on her mind. She is altogether what you would call a walking mystery. Her errand at Limmeridge House, however, was simple enough. When she left Hampshire to nurse her sister, Mrs. Kempe, through her last illness, she had been obliged to bring her daughter with her, through having no one at home to take care of the little girl. Mrs. Kempe may die in a week's time, or may linger on for months; and Mrs. Catherick's object was to ask me to let her daughter, Anne, have the benefit of attending my school, subject to the condition of her being removed from it to go home again with her mother, after Mrs. Kempe's death. I consented at once, and when Laura and I went out for our walk, we took the little girl (who is just eleven years old) to the school that very day.'"

Once more Miss Fairlie's figure, bright and soft in its snowy muslin dress—her face prettily framed by the white folds of the handkerchief which she had tied under her chin—passed by us in the moonlight. Once more Miss Halcombe waited till she was out of sight, and then went on—

"'I have taken a violent fancy, Philip, to my new scholar, for a reason which I mean to keep till the last for the sake of surprising you. Her mother having told me as little about the child as she told me of herself, I was left to discover (which I did on the first day when we tried her at lessons) that the poor little thing's intellect is not developed as it ought to be at her age. Seeing this I had her up to the house the next day, and privately arranged with the doctor to come and watch her and question her, and tell me what he thought. His opinion is that she will grow out of it. But he says her careful bringing-up at school is a matter of great importance just now, because her unusual slowness in acquiring ideas implies an unusual tenacity in keeping them, when they are once received into her mind. Now, my love, you must not imagine, in your off-hand way, that I have been attaching myself to an idiot. This poor little Anne Catherick is a sweet, affectionate, grateful girl, and says the quaintest, prettiest things (as you shall judge by an instance), in the most oddly sudden, surprised, half-frightened way. Although she is dressed very neatly, her clothes show a sad want of taste in colour and pattern. So I arranged, yesterday, that some of our darling Laura's old white frocks and white hats should be altered for Anne Catherick, explaining to her that little girls of her complexion looked neater and better all in white than in anything else. She hesitated and seemed puzzled for a minute, then flushed up, and appeared to understand. Her little hand clasped mine suddenly. She kissed it, Philip, and said (oh, so earnestly!), "I will always wear white as long as I live. It will help me to remember you, ma'am, and to think that I am pleasing you still, when I go away and see you no more." This is only one specimen of the quaint things she says so prettily. Poor little soul! She shall have a stock of white frocks, made with good deep tucks, to let out for her as she grows— —'"

Miss Halcombe paused, and looked at me across the piano.

"Did the forlorn woman whom you met in the high-road seem young?" she asked. "Young enough to be two- or three-and-twenty?"

"Yes, Miss Halcombe, as young as that."

"And she was strangely dressed, from head to foot, all in white?"

"All in white."

While the answer was passing my lips Miss Fairlie glided into view on the terrace for the third time. Instead of proceeding on her walk, she stopped, with her back turned towards us, and, leaning on the balustrade of the terrace, looked down into the garden beyond. My eyes fixed upon the white gleam of her muslin gown and head-dress in the moonlight, and a sensation, for which I can find no name—a sensation that quickened my pulse, and raised a fluttering at my heart—began to steal over me.

"All in white?" Miss Halcombe repeated. "The most important sentences in the letter, Mr. Hartright, are those at the end, which I will read to you immediately. But I can't help dwelling a little upon the coincidence of the white costume of the woman you met, and the white frocks which produced that strange answer from my mother's little scholar. The doctor may have been wrong when he discovered the child's defects of intellect, and predicted that she would 'grow out of them.' She may never have grown out of them, and the old grateful fancy about dressing in white, which was a serious feeling to the girl, may be a serious feeling to the woman still."

I said a few words in answer—I hardly know what. All my attention was concentrated on the white gleam of Miss Fairlie's muslin dress.

"Listen to the last sentences of the letter," said Miss Halcombe. "I think they will surprise you."

As she raised the letter to the light of the candle, Miss Fairlie turned from the balustrade, looked doubtfully up and down the terrace, advanced a step towards the glass doors, and then stopped, facing us.

Meanwhile Miss Halcombe read me the last sentences to which she had referred—

"'And now, my love, seeing that I am at the end of my paper, now for the real reason, the surprising reason, for my fondness for little Anne Catherick. My dear Philip, although she is not half so pretty, she is, nevertheless, by one of those extraordinary caprices of accidental resemblance which one sometimes sees, the living likeness, in her hair, her complexion, the colour of her eyes, and the shape of her face——'"

I started up from the ottoman before Miss Halcombe could pronounce the next words. A thrill of the same feeling which ran through me when the touch was laid upon my shoulder on the lonely high-road chilled me again.

There stood Miss Fairlie, a white figure, alone in the moonlight; in her attitude, in the turn of her head, in her complexion, in the shape of her face, the living image, at that distance and under those circumstances, of the woman in white! The doubt which had troubled my mind for hours and hours past flashed into conviction in an instant. That "something wanting" was my own recognition of the ominous likeness between the fugitive from the asylum and my pupil at Limmeridge House.

"You see it!" said Miss Halcombe. She dropped the useless letter, and her eyes flashed as they met mine. "You see it now, as my mother saw it eleven years since!"

"I see it—more unwillingly than I can say. To associate that forlorn, friendless, lost woman, even by an accidental likeness only, with Miss Fairlie, seems like casting a shadow on the future of the bright creature who stands looking at us now. Let me lose the impression again as soon as possible. Call her in, out of the dreary moonlight—pray call her in!"

"Mr. Hartright, you surprise me. Whatever women may be, I thought that men, in the nineteenth century, were above superstition."

"Pray call her in!"

"Hush, hush! She is coming of her own accord. Say nothing in her presence. Let this discovery of the likeness be kept a secret between you and me. Come in, Laura, come in, and wake Mrs. Vesey with the piano. Mr. Hartright is petitioning for some more music, and he wants it, this time, of the lightest and liveliest kind."

IX

So ended my eventful first day at Limmeridge House.

Miss Halcombe and I kept our secret. After the discovery of the likeness no fresh light seemed destined to break over the mystery of the woman in white. At the first safe opportunity Miss Halcombe cautiously led her half-sister to speak of their mother, of old times, and of Anne Catherick. Miss Fairlie's recollections of the little scholar at Limmeridge were, however, only of the most vague and general kind. She remembered the likeness between herself and her mother's favourite pupil, as something which had been supposed to exist in past times; but she did not refer to the gift of the white dresses, or to the singular form of words in which the child had artlessly expressed her gratitude for them. She remembered that Anne had remained at Limmeridge for a few months only, and had then left it to go back to her home in Hampshire; but she could not say whether the mother and daughter had ever returned, or had ever been heard of afterwards. No further search, on Miss Halcombe's part, through the few letters of Mrs. Fairlie's writing which she had left unread, assisted in clearing up the uncertainties still left to perplex us. We had identified the unhappy woman whom I had met in the night-time with Anne Catherick—we had made some advance, at least, towards connecting the probably defective condition of the poor creature's intellect with the peculiarity of her being dressed all in white, and with the continuance, in her maturer years, of her childish gratitude towards Mrs. Fairlie—and there, so far as we knew at that time, our discoveries had ended.

The days passed on, the weeks passed on, and the track of the golden autumn wound its bright way visibly through the green summer of the trees. Peaceful, fast-flowing, happy time! my story glides by you now as swiftly as you once glided by me. Of all the treasures of enjoyment that you poured so freely into my heart, how much is left me that has purpose and value enough to be written on this page? Nothing but the saddest of all confessions that a man can make—the confession of his own folly.

The secret which that confession discloses should be told with little effort, for it has indirectly escaped me already. The poor weak words, which have failed to describe Miss Fairlie, have succeeded in betraying the sensations she awakened in me. It is so with us all. Our words are giants when they do us an injury, and dwarfs when they do us a service.

I loved her.

Ah! how well I know all the sadness and all the mockery that is contained in those three words. I can sigh over my mournful confession with the tenderest woman who reads it and pities me. I can laugh at it as bitterly as the hardest man who tosses it from him in contempt. I loved her! Feel for me, or despise me, I confess it with the same immovable resolution to own the truth.

Was there no excuse for me? There was some excuse to be found, surely, in the conditions under which my term of hired service was passed at Limmeridge House.

My morning hours succeeded each other calmly in the quiet and seclusion of my own room. I had just work enough to do, in mounting my employer's drawings, to keep my hands and eyes pleasurably employed, while my mind was left free to enjoy the dangerous luxury of its own unbridled thoughts. A perilous solitude, for it lasted long enough to enervate, not long enough to fortify me. A perilous solitude, for it was followed by afternoons and evenings spent, day after day and week after week alone in the society of two women, one of whom possessed all the accomplishments of grace, wit, and high-breeding, the other all the charms of beauty, gentleness, and simple truth, that can purify and subdue the heart of man. Not a day passed, in that dangerous intimacy of teacher and pupil, in which my hand was not close to Miss Fairlie's; my cheek, as we bent together over her sketch-book, almost touching hers. The more attentively she watched every movement of my brush, the more closely I was breathing the perfume of her hair, and the warm fragrance of her breath. It was part of my service to live in the very light of her eyes—at one time to be bending over her, so close to her bosom as to tremble at the thought of touching it; at another, to feel her bending over me, bending so close to see what I was about, that her voice sank low when she spoke to me, and her ribbons brushed my cheek in the wind before she could draw them back.

The evenings which followed the sketching excursions of the afternoon varied, rather than checked, these innocent, these inevitable familiarities. My natural fondness for the music which she played with such tender feeling, such delicate womanly taste, and her natural enjoyment of giving me back, by the practice of her art, the pleasure which I had offered to her by the practice of mine, only wove another tie which drew us closer and closer to one another. The accidents of conversation; the simple habits which regulated even such a little thing as the position of our places at table; the play of Miss Halcombe's ever-ready raillery, always directed against my anxiety as teacher, while it sparkled over her enthusiasm as pupil; the harmless expression of poor Mrs. Vesey's drowsy approval, which connected Miss Fairlie and me as two model young people who never disturbed her—every one of these trifles, and many more, combined to fold us together in the same domestic atmosphere, and to lead us both insensibly to the same hopeless end.

I should have remembered my position, and have put myself secretly on my guard. I did so, but not till it was too late. All the discretion, all the experience, which had availed me with other women, and secured me against other temptations, failed me with her. It had been my profession, for years past, to be in this close contact with young girls of all ages, and of all orders of beauty. I had accepted the position as part of my calling in life; I had trained myself to leave all the sympathies natural to my age in my employer's outer hall, as coolly as I left my umbrella there before I went upstairs. I had long since learnt to understand, composedly and as a matter of course, that my situation in life was considered a guarantee against any of my female pupils feeling more than the most ordinary interest in me, and that I was admitted among beautiful and captivating women much as a harmless domestic animal is admitted among them. This guardian experience I had gained early; this guardian experience had sternly and strictly guided me straight along my own poor narrow path, without once letting me stray aside, to the right hand or to the left. And now I and my trusty talisman were parted for the first time. Yes, my hardly-earned self-control was as completely lost to me as if I had never possessed it; lost to me, as it is lost every day to other men, in other critical situations, where women are concerned. I know, now, that I should have questioned myself from the first. I should have asked why any room in the house was better than home to me when she entered it, and barren as a desert when she went out again—why I always noticed and remembered the little changes in her dress that I had noticed and remembered in no other woman's before—why I saw her, heard her, and touched her (when we shook hands at night and morning) as I had never seen, heard, and touched any other woman in my life? I should have looked into my own heart, and found this new growth springing up there, and plucked it out while it was young. Why was this easiest, simplest work of self-culture always too much for me? The explanation has been written already in the three words that were many enough, and plain enough, for my confession. I loved her.

The days passed, the weeks passed; it was approaching the third month of my stay in Cumberland. The delicious monotony of life in our calm seclusion flowed on with me, like a smooth stream with a swimmer who glides down the current. All memory of the past, all thought of the future, all sense of the falseness and hopelessness of my own position, lay hushed within me into deceitful rest. Lulled by the Syren-song that my own heart sung to me, with eyes shut to all sight, and ears closed to all sound of danger, I drifted nearer and nearer to the fatal rocks. The warning that aroused me at last, and startled me into sudden, self-accusing consciousness of my own weakness, was the plainest, the truest, the kindest of all warnings, for it came silently from her.

We had parted one night as usual. No word had fallen from my lips, at that time or at any time before it, that could betray me, or startle her into sudden knowledge of the truth. But when we met again in the morning, a change had come over her — a change that told me all.

I shrank then — I shrink still — from invading the innermost sanctuary of her heart, and laying it open to others, as I have laid open my own. Let it be enough to say that the time when she first surprised my secret was, I firmly believe, the time when she first surprised her own, and the time, also, when she changed towards me in the interval of one night. Her nature, too truthful to deceive others, was too noble to deceive itself. When the doubt that I had hushed asleep first laid its weary weight on her heart, the true face owned all, and said, in its own frank, simple language — I am sorry for him; I am sorry for myself.

It said this, and more, which I could not then interpret. I understood but too well the change in her manner, to greater kindness and quicker readiness in interpreting all my wishes, before others — to constraint and sadness, and nervous anxiety to absorb herself in the first occupation she could seize on, whenever we happened to be left together alone. I understood why the sweet sensitive lips smiled so rarely and so restrainedly now, and why the clear blue eyes looked at me, sometimes with the pity of an angel, sometimes with the innocent perplexity of a child. But the change meant more than this. There was a coldness in her hand, there was an unnatural immobility in her face, there was in all her movements the mute expression of constant fear and clinging self-reproach. The sensations that I could trace to herself and to me, the unacknowledged sensations that we were feeling in common, were not these. There were certain elements of the change in her that were still secretly drawing us together, and others that were, as secretly, beginning to drive us apart.

In my doubt and perplexity, in my vague suspicion of something hidden which I was left to find by my own unaided efforts, I examined Miss Halcombe's looks and manner for enlightenment. Living in such intimacy as ours, no serious alteration could take place in any one of us which did not sympathetically affect the others. The change in Miss Fairlie was reflected in her half-sister. Although not a word escaped Miss Halcombe which hinted at an altered state of feeling towards myself, her penetrating eyes had contracted a new habit of always watching me. Sometimes the look was like suppressed anger, sometimes like suppressed dread, sometimes like neither—like nothing, in short, which I could understand. A week elapsed, leaving us all three still in this position of secret constraint towards one another. My situation, aggravated by the sense of my own miserable weakness and forgetfulness of myself, now too late awakened in me, was becoming intolerable. I felt that I must cast off the oppression under which I was living, at once and for ever—yet how to act for the best, or what to say first, was more than I could tell.

From this position of helplessness and humiliation I was rescued by Miss Halcombe. Her lips told me the bitter, the necessary, the unexpected truth; her hearty kindness sustained me under the shock of hearing it; her sense and courage turned to its right use an event which threatened the worst that could happen, to me and to others, in Limmeridge House.

The Woman in White

X

It was on a Thursday in the week, and nearly at the end of the third month of my sojourn in Cumberland.

In the morning, when I went down into the breakfast-room at the usual hour, Miss Halcombe, for the first time since I had known her, was absent from her customary place at the table.

Miss Fairlie was out on the lawn. She bowed to me, but did not come in. Not a word had dropped from my lips, or from hers, that could unsettle either of us—and yet the same unacknowledged sense of embarrassment made us shrink alike from meeting one another alone. She waited on the lawn, and I waited in the breakfast-room, till Mrs. Vesey or Miss Halcombe came in. How quickly I should have joined her: how readily we should have shaken hands, and glided into our customary talk, only a fortnight ago.

In a few minutes Miss Halcombe entered. She had a preoccupied look, and she made her apologies for being late rather absently.

"I have been detained," she said, "by a consultation with Mr. Fairlie on a domestic matter which he wished to speak to me about."

Miss Fairlie came in from the garden, and the usual morning greeting passed between us. Her hand struck colder to mine than ever. She did not look at me, and she was very pale. Even Mrs. Vesey noticed it when she entered the room a moment after.

"I suppose it is the change in the wind," said the old lady. "The winter is coming—ah, my love, the winter is coming soon!"

In her heart and in mine it had come already!

Our morning meal—once so full of pleasant good-humoured discussion of the plans for the day—was short and silent. Miss Fairlie seemed to feel the oppression of the long pauses in the conversation, and looked appealingly to her sister to fill them up. Miss Halcombe, after once or twice hesitating and checking herself, in a most uncharacteristic manner, spoke at last.

"I have seen your uncle this morning, Laura," she said. "He thinks the purple room is the one that ought to be got ready, and he confirms what I told you. Monday is the day—not Tuesday."

While these words were being spoken Miss Fairlie looked down at the table beneath her. Her fingers moved nervously among the crumbs that were scattered on the cloth. The paleness on her cheeks spread to her lips, and the lips themselves trembled visibly. I was not the only person present who noticed this. Miss Halcombe saw it, too, and at once set us the example of rising from table.

Mrs. Vesey and Miss Fairlie left the room together. The kind sorrowful blue eyes looked at me, for a moment, with the prescient sadness of a coming and a long farewell. I felt the answering pang in my own heart—the pang that told me I must lose her soon, and love her the more unchangeably for the loss.

I turned towards the garden when the door had closed on her. Miss Halcombe was standing with her hat in her hand, and her shawl over her arm, by the large window that led out to the lawn, and was looking at me attentively.

"Have you any leisure time to spare," she asked, "before you begin to work in your own room?"

"Certainly, Miss Halcombe. I have always time at your service."

"I want to say a word to you in private, Mr. Hartright. Get your hat and come out into the garden. We are not likely to be disturbed there at this hour in the morning."

As we stepped out on to the lawn, one of the under-gardeners—a mere lad—passed us on his way to the house, with a letter in his hand. Miss Halcombe stopped him.

"Is that letter for me?" she asked.

"Nay, miss; it's just said to be for Miss Fairlie," answered the lad, holding out the letter as he spoke.

Miss Halcombe took it from him and looked at the address.

"A strange handwriting," she said to herself. "Who can Laura's correspondent be? Where did you get this?" she continued, addressing the gardener.

"Well, miss," said the lad, "I just got it from a woman."

"What woman?"

"A woman well stricken in age."

"Oh, an old woman. Any one you knew?"

"I canna' tak' it on mysel' to say that she was other than a stranger to me."

"Which way did she go?"

"That gate," said the under-gardener, turning with great deliberation towards the south, and embracing the whole of that part of England with one comprehensive sweep of his arm.

"Curious," said Miss Halcombe; "I suppose it must be a begging-letter. There," she added, handing the letter back to the lad, "take it to the house, and give it to one of the servants. And now, Mr. Hartright, if you have no objection, let us walk this way."

She led me across the lawn, along the same path by which I had followed her on the day after my arrival at Limmeridge.

At the little summer-house, in which Laura Fairlie and I had first seen each other, she stopped, and broke the silence which she had steadily maintained while we were walking together.

"What I have to say to you I can say here."

With those words she entered the summer-house, took one of the chairs at the little round table inside, and signed to me to take the other. I suspected what was coming when she spoke to me in the breakfast-room; I felt certain of it now.

"Mr. Hartright," she said, "I am going to begin by making a frank avowal to you. I am going to say—without phrase-making, which I detest, or paying compliments, which I heartily despise—that I have come, in the course of your residence with us, to feel a strong friendly regard for you. I was predisposed in your favour when you first told me of your conduct towards that unhappy woman whom you met under such remarkable circumstances. Your management of the affair might not have been prudent, but it showed the self-control, the delicacy, and the compassion of a man who was naturally a gentleman. It made me expect good things from you, and you have not disappointed my expectations."

She paused—but held up her hand at the same time, as a sign that she awaited no answer from me before she proceeded. When I entered the summer-house, no thought was in me of the woman in white. But now, Miss Halcombe's own words had put the memory of my adventure back in my mind. It remained there throughout the interview—remained, and not without a result.

"As your friend," she proceeded, "I am going to tell you, at once, in my own plain, blunt, downright language, that I have discovered your secret—without help or hint, mind, from any one else. Mr. Hartright, you have thoughtlessly allowed yourself to form an attachment—a serious and devoted attachment I am afraid—to my sister Laura. I don't put you to the pain of confessing it in so many words, because I see and know that you are too honest to deny it. I don't even blame you—I pity you for opening your heart to a hopeless affection. You have not attempted to take any underhand advantage— you have not spoken to my sister in secret. You are guilty of weakness and want of attention to your own best interests, but of nothing worse. If you had acted, in any single respect, less delicately and less modestly, I should have told you to leave the house without an instant's notice, or an instant's consultation of anybody. As it is, I blame the misfortune of your years and your position—I don't blame you. Shake hands—I have given you pain; I am going to give you more, but there is no help for it— shake hands with your friend, Marian Halcombe, first."

The sudden kindness—the warm, high-minded, fearless sympathy which met me on such mercifully equal terms, which appealed with such delicate and generous abruptness straight to my heart, my honour, and my courage, overcame me in an instant. I tried to look at her when she took my hand, but my eyes were dim. I tried to thank her, but my voice failed me.

"Listen to me," she said, considerately avoiding all notice of my loss of self-control. "Listen to me, and let us get it over at once. It is a real true relief to me that I am not obliged, in what I have now to say, to enter into the question—the hard and cruel question as I think it—of social inequalities. Circumstances which will try you to the quick, spare me the ungracious necessity of paining a man who has lived in friendly intimacy under the same roof with myself by any humiliating reference to matters of rank and station. You must leave Limmeridge House, Mr. Hartright, before more harm is done. It is my duty to say that to you; and it would be equally my duty to say it, under precisely the same serious necessity, if you were the representative of the oldest and wealthiest family in England.

You must leave us, not because you are a teacher of drawing—"

She waited a moment, turned her face full on me, and reaching across the table, laid her hand firmly on my arm.

"Not because you are a teacher of drawing," she repeated, "but because Laura Fairlie is engaged to be married."

The last word went like a bullet to my heart. My arm lost all sensation of the hand that grasped it. I never moved and never spoke. The sharp autumn breeze that scattered the dead leaves at our feet came as cold to me, on a sudden, as if my own mad hopes were dead leaves too, whirled away by the wind like the rest. Hopes! Betrothed, or not betrothed, she was equally far from me. Would other men have remembered that in my place? Not if they had loved her as I did.

The pang passed, and nothing but the dull numbing pain of it remained. I felt Miss Halcombe's hand again, tightening its hold on my arm—I raised my head and looked at her. Her large black eyes were rooted on me, watching the white change on my face, which I felt, and which she saw.

"Crush it!" she said. "Here, where you first saw her, crush it! Don't shrink under it like a woman. Tear it out; trample it under foot like a man!"

The suppressed vehemence with which she spoke, the strength which her will—concentrated in the look she fixed on me, and in the hold on my arm that she had not yet relinquished—communicated to mine, steadied me. We both waited for a minute in silence. At the end of that time I had justified her generous faith in my manhood—I had, outwardly at least, recovered my self-control.

"Are you yourself again?"

"Enough myself, Miss Halcombe, to ask your pardon and hers. Enough myself to be guided by your advice, and to prove my gratitude in that way, if I can prove it in no other."

"You have proved it already," she answered, "by those words. Mr. Hartright, concealment is at an end between us. I cannot affect to hide from you what my sister has unconsciously shown to me. You must leave us for her sake, as well as for your own. Your presence here, your necessary intimacy with us, harmless as it has been, God knows, in all other respects, has unsteadied her and made her wretched. I, who love her better than my own life—I, who have learnt to believe in that pure, noble, innocent nature as I believe in my religion—know but too well the secret misery of self-reproach that she has been suffering since the first shadow of a feeling disloyal to her marriage engagement entered her heart in spite of her. I don't say—it would be useless to attempt to say it after what has happened—that her engagement has ever had a strong hold on her affections. It is an engagement of honour, not of love; her father sanctioned it on his deathbed, two years since; she herself neither welcomed it nor shrank from it—she was content to make it. Till you came here she was in the position of hundreds of other women, who marry men without being greatly attracted to them or greatly repelled by them, and who learn to love them (when they don't learn to hate!) after marriage, instead of before. I hope more earnestly than words can say— and you should have the self-sacrificing courage to hope too— that the new thoughts and feelings which have disturbed the old calmness and the old content have not taken root too deeply to be ever removed. Your absence (if I had less belief in your honour, and your courage, and your sense, I should not trust to them as I am trusting now) your absence will help my efforts, and time will help us all three. It is something to know that my first confidence in you was not all misplaced. It is something to know that you will not be less honest, less manly, less considerate towards the pupil whose relation to yourself you have had the misfortune to forget, than towards the stranger and the outcast whose appeal to you was not made in vain."

Again the chance reference to the woman in white! Was there no possibility of speaking of Miss Fairlie and of me without raising the memory of Anne Catherick, and setting her between us like a fatality that it was hopeless to avoid?

"Tell me what apology I can make to Mr. Fairlie for breaking my engagement," I said. "Tell me when to go after that apology is accepted. I promise implicit obedience to you and to your advice."

"Time is every way of importance," she answered. "You heard me refer this morning to Monday next, and to the necessity of setting the purple room in order. The visitor whom we expect on Monday— —"

I could not wait for her to be more explicit. Knowing what I knew now, the memory of Miss Fairlie's look and manner at the breakfast-table told me that the expected visitor at Limmeridge House was her future husband. I tried to force it back; but

The Woman in White

something rose within me at that moment stronger than my own will, and I interrupted Miss Halcombe.

"Let me go to-day," I said bitterly. "The sooner the better."

"No, not to-day," she replied. "The only reason you can assign to Mr. Fairlie for your departure, before the end of your engagement, must be that an unforeseen necessity compels you to ask his permission to return at once to London. You must wait till to-morrow to tell him that, at the time when the post comes in, because he will then understand the sudden change in your plans, by associating it with the arrival of a letter from London. It is miserable and sickening to descend to deceit, even of the most harmless kind — but I know Mr. Fairlie, and if you once excite his suspicions that you are trifling with him, he will refuse to release you. Speak to him on Friday morning: occupy yourself afterwards (for the sake of your own interests with your employer) in leaving your unfinished work in as little confusion as possible, and quit this place on Saturday. It will be time enough then, Mr. Hartright, for you, and for all of us."

Before I could assure her that she might depend on my acting in the strictest accordance with her wishes, we were both startled by advancing footsteps in the shrubbery. Some one was coming from the house to seek for us! I felt the blood rush into my cheeks and then leave them again. Could the third person who was fast approaching us, at such a time and under such circumstances, be Miss Fairlie?

It was a relief — so sadly, so hopelessly was my position towards her changed already — it was absolutely a relief to me, when the person who had disturbed us appeared at the entrance of the summer-house, and proved to be only Miss Fairlie's maid.

"Could I speak to you for a moment, miss?" said the girl, in rather a flurried, unsettled manner.

Miss Halcombe descended the steps into the shrubbery, and walked aside a few paces with the maid.

Left by myself, my mind reverted, with a sense of forlorn wretchedness which it is not in any words that I can find to describe, to my approaching return to the solitude and the despair of my lonely London home. Thoughts of my kind old mother, and of my sister, who had rejoiced with her so innocently over my prospects in Cumberland — thoughts whose long banishment from my heart it was now my shame and my reproach to realise for the first time—came back to me with the loving mournfulness of old, neglected friends. My mother and my sister, what would they feel when I returned to them from my broken engagement, with the confession of my miserable secret—they who had parted from me so hopefully on that last happy night in the Hampstead cottage!

Anne Catherick again! Even the memory of the farewell evening with my mother and my sister could not return to me now unconnected with that other memory of the moonlight walk back to London. What did it mean? Were that woman and I to meet once more? It was possible, at the least. Did she know that I lived in London? Yes; I had told her so, either before or after that strange question of hers, when she had asked me so distrustfully if I knew many men of the rank of Baronet. Either before or after—my mind was not calm enough, then, to remember which.

A few minutes elapsed before Miss Halcombe dismissed the maid and came back to me. She, too, looked flurried and unsettled now.

"We have arranged all that is necessary, Mr. Hartright," she said. "We have understood each other, as friends should, and we may go back at once to the house. To tell you the truth, I am uneasy about Laura. She has sent to say she wants to see me directly, and the maid reports that her mistress is apparently very much agitated by a letter that she has received this morning—the same letter, no doubt, which I sent on to the house before we came here."

We retraced our steps together hastily along the shrubbery path. Although Miss Halcombe had ended all that she thought it necessary to say on her side, I had not ended all that I wanted to say on mine. From the moment when I had discovered that the expected visitor at Limmeridge was Miss Fairlie's future husband, I had felt a bitter curiosity, a burning envious eagerness, to know who he was. It was possible that a future opportunity of putting the question might not easily offer, so I risked asking it on our way back to the house.

"Now that you are kind enough to tell me we have understood each other, Miss Halcombe," I said, "now that you are sure of my gratitude for your forbearance and my obedience to your wishes, may I venture to ask who"—(I hesitated—I had forced myself to think of him, but it was harder still to speak of him, as her promised husband)—"who the gentleman engaged to Miss Fairlie is?"

Her mind was evidently occupied with the message she had received from her sister. She answered in a hasty, absent way—

"A gentleman of large property in Hampshire."

Hampshire! Anne Catherick's native place. Again, and yet again, the woman in white. There was a fatality in it.

"And his name?" I said, as quietly and indifferently as I could.

"Sir Percival Glyde."

Sir—Sir Percival! Anne Catherick's question—that suspicious question about the men of the rank of Baronet whom I might happen to know—had hardly been dismissed from my mind by Miss Halcombe's return to me in the summer-house, before it was recalled again by her own answer. I stopped suddenly, and looked at her.

"Sir Percival Glyde," she repeated, imagining that I had not heard her former reply.

"Knight, or Baronet?" I asked, with an agitation that I could hide no longer.

She paused for a moment, and then answered, rather coldly—

"Baronet, of course."

XI

Not a word more was said, on either side, as we walked back to the house. Miss Halcombe hastened immediately to her sister's room, and I withdrew to my studio to set in order all of Mr. Fairlie's drawings that I had not yet mounted and restored before I resigned them to the care of other hands. Thoughts that I had hitherto restrained, thoughts that made my position harder than ever to endure, crowded on me now that I was alone.

She was engaged to be married, and her future husband was Sir Percival Glyde. A man of the rank of Baronet, and the owner of property in Hampshire.

There were hundreds of baronets in England, and dozens of landowners in Hampshire. Judging by the ordinary rules of evidence, I had not the shadow of a reason, thus far, for connecting Sir Percival Glyde with the suspicious words of inquiry that had been spoken to me by the woman in white. And yet, I did connect him with them. Was it because he had now become associated in my mind with Miss Fairlie, Miss Fairlie being, in her turn, associated with Anne Catherick, since the night when I had discovered the ominous likeness between them? Had the events of the morning so unnerved me already that I was at the mercy of any delusion which common chances and common coincidences might suggest to my imagination? Impossible to say. I could only feel that what had passed between Miss Halcombe and myself, on our way from the summer-house, had affected me very strangely. The foreboding of some undiscoverable danger lying hid from us all in the darkness of the future was strong on me. The doubt whether I was not linked already to a chain of events which even my approaching departure from Cumberland would be powerless to snap asunder—the doubt whether we any of us saw the end as the end would really be—gathered more and more darkly over my mind. Poignant as it was, the sense of suffering caused by the miserable end of my brief, presumptuous love seemed to be blunted and deadened by the still stronger sense of something obscurely impending, something invisibly threatening, that Time was holding over our heads.

I had been engaged with the drawings little more than half an hour, when there was a knock at the door. It opened, on my answering; and, to my surprise, Miss Halcombe entered the room.

Her manner was angry and agitated. She caught up a chair

The Woman in White

for herself before I could give her one, and sat down in it, close at my side.

"Mr. Hartright," she said, "I had hoped that all painful subjects of conversation were exhausted between us, for to-day at least. But it is not to be so. There is some underhand villainy at work to frighten my sister about her approaching marriage. You saw me send the gardener on to the house, with a letter addressed, in a strange handwriting, to Miss Fairlie?"

"Certainly."

"The letter is an anonymous letter—a vile attempt to injure Sir Percival Glyde in my sister's estimation. It has so agitated and alarmed her that I have had the greatest possible difficulty in composing her spirits sufficiently to allow me to leave her room and come here. I know this is a family matter on which I ought not to consult you, and in which you can feel no concern or interest——"

"I beg your pardon, Miss Halcombe. I feel the strongest possible concern and interest in anything that affects Miss Fairlie's happiness or yours."

"I am glad to hear you say so. You are the only person in the house, or out of it, who can advise me. Mr. Fairlie, in his state of health and with his horror of difficulties and mysteries of all kinds, is not to be thought of. The clergyman is a good, weak man, who knows nothing out of the routine of his duties; and our neighbours are just the sort of comfortable, jog-trot acquaintances whom one cannot disturb in times of trouble and danger. What I want to know is this: ought I at once to take such steps as I can to discover the writer of the letter? or ought I to wait, and apply to Mr. Fairlie's legal adviser to-morrow? It is a question—perhaps a very important one—of gaining or losing a day. Tell me what you think, Mr. Hartright. If necessity had not already obliged me to take you into my confidence under very delicate circumstances, even my helpless situation would, perhaps, be no excuse for me. But as things are I cannot surely be wrong, after all that has passed between us, in forgetting that you are a friend of only three months' standing."

She gave me the letter. It began abruptly, without any preliminary form of address, as follows—

"Do you believe in dreams? I hope, for your own sake, that

you do. See what Scripture says about dreams and their fulfilment (Genesis xl. 8, xli. 25; Daniel iv. 18-25), and take the warning I send you before it is too late.

"Last night I dreamed about you, Miss Fairlie. I dreamed that I was standing inside the communion rails of a church—I on one side of the altar-table, and the clergyman, with his surplice and his prayer-book, on the other.

"After a time there walked towards us, down the aisle of the church, a man and a woman, coming to be married. You were the woman. You looked so pretty and innocent in your beautiful white silk dress, and your long white lace veil, that my heart felt for you, and the tears came into my eyes.

"They were tears of pity, young lady, that heaven blesses and instead of falling from my eyes like the everyday tears that we all of us shed, they turned into two rays of light which slanted nearer and nearer to the man standing at the altar with you, till they touched his breast. The two rays sprang in arches like two rainbows between me and him. I looked along them, and I saw down into his inmost heart.

"The outside of the man you were marrying was fair enough to see. He was neither tall nor short—he was a little below the middle size. A light, active, high-spirited man—about five-and-forty years old, to look at. He had a pale face, and was bald over the forehead, but had dark hair on the rest of his head. His beard was shaven on his chin, but was let to grow, of a fine rich brown, on his cheeks and his upper lip. His eyes were brown too, and very bright; his nose straight and handsome and delicate enough to have done for a woman's. His hands the same. He was troubled from time to time with a dry hacking cough, and when he put up his white right hand to his mouth, he showed the red scar of an old wound across the back of it. Have I dreamt of the right man? You know best, Miss Fairlie; and you can say if I was deceived or not. Read next, what I saw beneath the outside—I entreat you, read, and profit.

"I looked along the two rays of light, and I saw down into his inmost heart. It was black as night, and on it were written, in the red flaming letters which are the handwriting of the fallen angel, 'Without pity and without remorse. He has strewn with misery the paths of others, and he will live to strew with misery the path of this woman by his side.' I read that, and then the rays of light shifted and pointed over his shoulder; and there, behind him, stood a fiend laughing. And the rays of light shifted once more, and pointed over your shoulder; and there behind you, stood an angel weeping. And the rays of light shifted for the third time, and pointed straight between you and that man. They widened and widened, thrusting you both asunder, one from the other. And the clergyman looked for the marriage-service in vain: it was gone out of the book, and he shut up the leaves, and put it from him in despair. And I woke with my eyes full of tears and my heart beating—for I believe in dreams.

"Believe too, Miss Fairlie—I beg of you, for your own sake, believe as I do. Joseph and Daniel, and others in Scripture, believed in dreams. Inquire into the past life of that man with the scar on his hand, before you say the words that make you his miserable wife. I don't give you this warning on my account, but on yours. I have an interest in your well-being that will live as long as I draw breath. Your mother's daughter has a tender place in my heart—for your mother was my first, my best, my only friend."

There the extraordinary letter ended, without signature of any sort.

The handwriting afforded no prospect of a clue. It was traced on ruled lines, in the cramped, conventional, copy-book character technically termed "small hand." It was feeble and faint, and defaced by blots, but had otherwise nothing to distinguish it.

"That is not an illiterate letter," said Miss Halcombe, "and at the same time, it is surely too incoherent to be the letter of an educated person in the higher ranks of life. The reference to the bridal dress and veil, and other little expressions, seem to point to it as the production of some woman. What do you think, Mr. Hartright?"

"I think so too. It seems to me to be not only the letter of a woman, but of a woman whose mind must be——"

"Deranged?" suggested Miss Halcombe. "It struck me in that light too."

I did not answer. While I was speaking, my eyes rested on the last sentence of the letter: "Your mother's daughter has a tender place in my heart—for your mother was my first, my best, my only friend." Those words and the doubt which had just escaped me as to the sanity of the writer of the letter, acting together on my mind, suggested an idea, which I was literally afraid to express openly, or even to encourage secretly. I began to doubt whether my own faculties were not in danger of losing their balance. It seemed almost like a monomania to be tracing back everything strange that happened, everything unexpected that was said, always to the same hidden source and the same sinister influence. I resolved, this time, in defence of my own courage and my own sense, to come to no decision that plain fact did not warrant, and to turn my back resolutely on everything that tempted me in the shape of surmise.

"If we have any chance of tracing the person who has written this," I said, returning the letter to Miss Halcombe, "there can be no harm in seizing our opportunity the moment it offers. I think we ought to speak to the gardener again about the elderly woman who gave him the letter, and then to continue our inquiries in the village. But first let me ask a question. You mentioned just now the alternative of consulting Mr. Fairlie's legal adviser to-morrow. Is there no possibility of communicating with him earlier? Why not to-day?"

"I can only explain," replied Miss Halcombe, "by entering into certain particulars, connected with my sister's marriage-engagement, which I did not think it necessary or desirable to mention to you this morning. One of Sir Percival Glyde's objects in coming here on Monday, is to fix the period of his marriage, which has hitherto been left quite unsettled. He is anxious that the event should take place before the end of the year."

"Does Miss Fairlie know of that wish?" I asked eagerly.

"She has no suspicion of it, and after what has happened, I shall not take the responsibility upon myself of enlightening her. Sir Percival has only mentioned his views to Mr. Fairlie, who has told me himself that he is ready and anxious, as Laura's guardian, to forward them. He has written to London, to the family solicitor, Mr. Gilmore. Mr. Gilmore happens to be away in Glasgow on business, and he has replied by proposing to stop at Limmeridge House on his way back to town. He will arrive to-morrow, and will stay with us a few days, so as to allow Sir Percival time to plead his own cause. If he succeeds, Mr. Gilmore will then return to London, taking with him his instructions for my sister's marriage-settlement. You understand now, Mr. Hartright, why I speak of waiting to take legal advice until to-morrow? Mr. Gilmore is the old and tried friend of two generations of Fairlies, and we can trust him, as we could trust no one else."

The marriage-settlement! The mere hearing of those two

words stung me with a jealous despair that was poison to my higher and better instincts. I began to think—it is hard to confess this, but I must suppress nothing from beginning to end of the terrible story that I now stand committed to reveal—I began to think, with a hateful eagerness of hope, of the vague charges against Sir Percival Glyde which the anonymous letter contained. What if those wild accusations rested on a foundation of truth? What if their truth could be proved before the fatal words of consent were spoken, and the marriage-settlement was drawn? I have tried to think since, that the feeling which then animated me began and ended in pure devotion to Miss Fairlie's interests, but I have never succeeded in deceiving myself into believing it, and I must not now attempt to deceive others. The feeling began and ended in reckless, vindictive, hopeless hatred of the man who was to marry her.

"If we are to find out anything," I said, speaking under the new influence which was now directing me, "we had better not let another minute slip by us unemployed. I can only suggest, once more, the propriety of questioning the gardener a second time, and of inquiring in the village immediately afterwards."

"I think I may be of help to you in both cases," said Miss Halcombe, rising. "Let us go, Mr. Hartright, at once, and do the best we can together."

I had the door in my hand to open it for her—but I stopped, on a sudden, to ask an important question before we set forth.

"One of the paragraphs of the anonymous letter," I said, "contains some sentences of minute personal description. Sir Percival Glyde's name is not mentioned, I know—but does that description at all resemble him?"

"Accurately—even in stating his age to be forty-five——"

Forty-five; and she was not yet twenty-one! Men of his age married wives of her age every day—and experience had shown those marriages to be often the happiest ones. I knew that—and yet even the mention of his age, when I contrasted it with hers, added to my blind hatred and distrust of him.

"Accurately," Miss Halcombe continued, "even to the scar on his right hand, which is the scar of a wound that he received years since when he was travelling in Italy. There can be no doubt that every peculiarity of his personal appearance is thoroughly well known to the writer of the letter."

"Even a cough that he is troubled with is mentioned, if I remember right?"

"Yes, and mentioned correctly. He treats it lightly himself, though it sometimes makes his friends anxious about him."

"I suppose no whispers have ever been heard against his character?"

"Mr. Hartright! I hope you are not unjust enough to let that infamous letter influence you?"

I felt the blood rush into my cheeks, for I knew that it had influenced me.

"I hope not," I answered confusedly. "Perhaps I had no right to ask the question."

"I am not sorry you asked it," she said, "for it enables me to do justice to Sir Percival's reputation. Not a whisper, Mr. Hartright, has ever reached me, or my family, against him. He has fought successfully two contested elections, and has come out of the ordeal unscathed. A man who can do that, in England, is a man whose character is established."

I opened the door for her in silence, and followed her out. She had not convinced me. If the recording angel had come down from heaven to confirm her, and had opened his book to my mortal eyes, the recording angel would not have convinced me.

We found the gardener at work as usual. No amount of questioning could extract a single answer of any importance from the lad's impenetrable stupidity. The woman who had given him the letter was an elderly woman; she had not spoken a word to him, and she had gone away towards the south in a great hurry. That was all the gardener could tell us.

The village lay southward of the house. So to the village we went next.

XII

Our inquiries at Limmeridge were patiently pursued in all directions, and among all sorts and conditions of people. But nothing came of them. Three of the villagers did certainly assure us that they had seen the woman, but as they were quite unable to describe her, and quite incapable of agreeing about the exact direction in which she was proceeding when they last saw her, these three bright exceptions to the general rule of total ignorance afforded no more real assistance to us than the mass of their unhelpful and unobservant neighbours.

The course of our useless investigations brought us, in time, to the end of the village at which the schools established by Mrs. Fairlie were situated. As we passed the side of the building appropriated to the use of the boys, I suggested the propriety of making a last inquiry of the schoolmaster, whom we might presume to be, in virtue of his office, the most intelligent man in the place.

"I am afraid the schoolmaster must have been occupied with his scholars," said Miss Halcombe, "just at the time when the woman passed through the village and returned again. However, we can but try."

We entered the playground enclosure, and walked by the schoolroom window to get round to the door, which was situated at the back of the building. I stopped for a moment at the window and looked in.

The schoolmaster was sitting at his high desk, with his back to me, apparently haranguing the pupils, who were all gathered together in front of him, with one exception. The one exception was a sturdy white-headed boy, standing apart from all the rest on a stool in a corner—a forlorn little Crusoe, isolated in his own desert island of solitary penal disgrace.

The door, when we got round to it, was ajar, and the schoolmaster's voice reached us plainly, as we both stopped for a minute under the porch.

"Now, boys," said the voice, "mind what I tell you. If I hear another word spoken about ghosts in this school, it will be the worse for all of you. There are no such things as ghosts, and therefore any boy who believes in ghosts believes in what can't possibly be; and a boy who belongs to Limmeridge School, and believes in what can't possibly be, sets up his back against reason and discipline, and must be punished accordingly. You all see Jacob Postlethwaite standing up on the stool there in disgrace. He has been punished, not because he said he saw a ghost last night, but because he is too impudent and too obstinate to listen to reason, and because he persists in saying he saw the ghost after I have told him that no such thing can possibly be. If nothing else will do, I mean to cane the ghost out of Jacob Postlethwaite, and if the thing spreads among any of the rest of you, I mean to go a step farther, and cane the ghost out of the whole school."

"We seem to have chosen an awkward moment for our visit," said Miss Halcombe, pushing open the door at the end of the schoolmaster's address, and leading the way in.

Our appearance produced a strong sensation among the boys. They appeared to think that we had arrived for the express purpose of seeing Jacob Postlethwaite caned.

"Go home all of you to dinner," said the schoolmaster, "except Jacob. Jacob must stop where he is; and the ghost may bring him his dinner, if the ghost pleases."

Jacob's fortitude deserted him at the double disappearance of his schoolfellows and his prospect of dinner. He took his hands out of his pockets, looked hard at his knuckles, raised them with great deliberation to his eyes, and when they got there, ground them round and round slowly, accompanying the action by short spasms of sniffing, which followed each other at regular intervals—the nasal minute guns of juvenile distress.

"We came here to ask you a question, Mr. Dempster," said Miss Halcombe, addressing the schoolmaster; "and we little expected to find you occupied in exorcising a ghost. What does it all mean? What has really happened?"

"That wicked boy has been frightening the whole school, Miss Halcombe, by declaring that he saw a ghost yesterday evening," answered the master; "and he still persists in his absurd story, in spite of all that I can say to him."

"Most extraordinary," said Miss Halcombe, "I should not have thought it possible that any of the boys had imagination enough to see a ghost. This is a new accession indeed to the hard labour of forming the youthful mind at Limmeridge, and I heartily wish you well through it, Mr. Dempster. In the meantime, let me explain why you see me here, and what it is I want."

She then put the same question to the schoolmaster which we had asked already of almost every one else in the village. It was met by the same discouraging answer. Mr. Dempster had not set eyes on the stranger of whom we were in search.

"We may as well return to the house, Mr. Hartright," said Miss Halcombe; "the information we want is evidently not to be found."

She had bowed to Mr. Dempster, and was about to leave the schoolroom, when the forlorn position of Jacob Postlethwaite, piteously sniffing on the stool of penitence, attracted her attention as she passed him, and made her stop good-humouredly to speak a word to the little prisoner before she opened the door.

"You foolish boy," she said, "why don't you beg Mr. Dempster's pardon, and hold your tongue about the ghost?"

"Eh! — but I saw t' ghaist," persisted Jacob Postlethwaite, with a stare of terror and a burst of tears.

"Stuff and nonsense! You saw nothing of the kind. Ghost indeed! What ghost — —"

"I beg your pardon, Miss Halcombe," interposed the schoolmaster a little uneasily — "but I think you had better not question the boy. The obstinate folly of his story is beyond all belief; and you might lead him into ignorantly — —"

"Ignorantly what?" inquired Miss Halcombe sharply.

"Ignorantly shocking your feelings," said Mr. Dempster, looking very much discomposed.

"Upon my word, Mr. Dempster, you pay my feelings a great compliment in thinking them weak enough to be shocked by such an urchin as that!" She turned with an air of satirical defiance to little Jacob, and began to question him directly. "Come!" she said, "I mean to know all about this. You naughty boy, when did you see the ghost?"

"Yestere'en, at the gloaming," replied Jacob.

"Oh! you saw it yesterday evening, in the twilight? And what was it like?"

"Arl in white — as a ghaist should be," answered the ghostseer, with a confidence beyond his years.

"And where was it?"

"Away yander, in t' kirkyard—where a ghaist ought to be."

"As a 'ghaist' should be—where a 'ghaist' ought to be—why, you little fool, you talk as if the manners and customs of ghosts had been familiar to you from your infancy! You have got your story at your fingers' ends, at any rate. I suppose I shall hear next that you can actually tell me whose ghost it was?"

"Eh! but I just can," replied Jacob, nodding his head with an air of gloomy triumph.

Mr. Dempster had already tried several times to speak while Miss Halcombe was examining his pupil, and he now interposed resolutely enough to make himself heard.

"Excuse me, Miss Halcombe," he said, "if I venture to say that you are only encouraging the boy by asking him these questions."

"I will merely ask one more, Mr. Dempster, and then I shall be quite satisfied. Well," she continued, turning to the boy, "and whose ghost was it?"

"T' ghaist of Mistress Fairlie," answered Jacob in a whisper.

The effect which this extraordinary reply produced on Miss Halcombe fully justified the anxiety which the schoolmaster had shown to prevent her from hearing it. Her face crimsoned with indignation—she turned upon little Jacob with an angry suddenness which terrified him into a fresh burst of tears—opened her lips to speak to him—then controlled herself, and addressed the master instead of the boy.

"It is useless," she said, "to hold such a child as that responsible for what he says. I have little doubt that the idea has been put into his head by others. If there are people in this village, Mr. Dempster, who have forgotten the respect and gratitude due from every soul in it to my mother's memory, I will find them out, and if I have any influence with Mr. Fairlie, they shall suffer for it."

"I hope—indeed, I am sure, Miss Halcombe—that you are mistaken," said the schoolmaster. "The matter begins and ends with the boy's own perversity and folly. He saw, or thought he

The Woman in White

saw, a woman in white, yesterday evening, as he was passing the churchyard; and the figure, real or fancied, was standing by the marble cross, which he and every one else in Limmeridge knows to be the monument over Mrs. Fairlie's grave. These two circumstances are surely sufficient to have suggested to the boy himself the answer which has so naturally shocked you?"

Although Miss Halcombe did not seem to be convinced, she evidently felt that the schoolmaster's statement of the case was too sensible to be openly combated. She merely replied by thanking him for his attention, and by promising to see him again when her doubts were satisfied. This said, she bowed, and led the way out of the schoolroom.

Throughout the whole of this strange scene I had stood apart, listening attentively, and drawing my own conclusions. As soon as we were alone again, Miss Halcombe asked me if I had formed any opinion on what I had heard.

"A very strong opinion," I answered; "the boy's story, as I believe, has a foundation in fact. I confess I am anxious to see the monument over Mrs. Fairlie's grave, and to examine the ground about it."

"You shall see the grave."

She paused after making that reply, and reflected a little as we walked on. "What has happened in the schoolroom," she resumed, "has so completely distracted my attention from the subject of the letter, that I feel a little bewildered when I try to return to it. Must we give up all idea of making any further inquiries, and wait to place the thing in Mr. Gilmore's hands tomorrow?"

"By no means, Miss Halcombe. What has happened in the schoolroom encourages me to persevere in the investigation."

"Why does it encourage you?"

"Because it strengthens a suspicion I felt when you gave me the letter to read."

"I suppose you had your reasons, Mr. Hartright, for concealing that suspicion from me till this moment?"

"I was afraid to encourage it in myself. I thought it was utterly preposterous—I distrusted it as the result of some perversity in my own imagination. But I can do so no longer.

Not only the boy's own answers to your questions, but even a chance expression that dropped from the schoolmaster's lips in explaining his story, have forced the idea back into my mind. Events may yet prove that idea to be a delusion, Miss Halcombe; but the belief is strong in me, at this moment, that the fancied ghost in the churchyard, and the writer of the anonymous letter, are one and the same person."

She stopped, turned pale, and looked me eagerly in the face.

"What person?"

"The schoolmaster unconsciously told you. When he spoke of the figure that the boy saw in the churchyard he called it 'a woman in white.'"

"Not Anne Catherick?"

"Yes, Anne Catherick."

She put her hand through my arm and leaned on it heavily.

"I don't know why," she said in low tones, "but there is something in this suspicion of yours that seems to startle and unnerve me. I feel — — " She stopped, and tried to laugh it off. "Mr. Hartright," she went on, "I will show you the grave, and then go back at once to the house. I had better not leave Laura too long alone. I had better go back and sit with her."

We were close to the churchyard when she spoke. The church, a dreary building of grey stone, was situated in a little valley, so as to be sheltered from the bleak winds blowing over the moorland all round it. The burial-ground advanced, from the side of the church, a little way up the slope of the hill. It was surrounded by a rough, low stone wall, and was bare and open to the sky, except at one extremity, where a brook trickled down the stony hill-side, and a clump of dwarf trees threw their narrow shadows over the short, meagre grass. Just beyond the brook and the trees, and not far from one of the three stone stiles which afforded entrance, at various points, to the churchyard, rose the white marble cross that distinguished Mrs. Fairlie's grave from the humbler monuments scattered about it.

"I need go no farther with you," said Miss Halcombe, pointing to the grave. "You will let me know if you find anything to confirm the idea you have just mentioned to me. Let us meet again at the house."

The Woman in White

She left me. I descended at once to the churchyard, and crossed the stile which led directly to Mrs. Fairlie's grave.

The grass about it was too short, and the ground too hard, to show any marks of footsteps. Disappointed thus far, I next looked attentively at the cross, and at the square block of marble below it, on which the inscription was cut.

The natural whiteness of the cross was a little clouded, here and there, by weather stains, and rather more than one half of the square block beneath it, on the side which bore the inscription, was in the same condition. The other half, however, attracted my attention at once by its singular freedom from stain or impurity of any kind. I looked closer, and saw that it had been cleaned — recently cleaned, in a downward direction from top to bottom. The boundary line between the part that had been cleaned and the part that had not was traceable wherever the inscription left a blank space of marble — sharply traceable as a line that had been produced by artificial means. Who had begun the cleansing of the marble, and who had left it unfinished?

I looked about me, wondering how the question was to be solved. No sign of a habitation could be discerned from the point at which I was standing — the burial-ground was left in the lonely possession of the dead. I returned to the church, and walked round it till I came to the back of the building; then crossed the boundary wall beyond, by another of the stone stiles, and found myself at the head of a path leading down into a deserted stone quarry. Against one side of the quarry a little two-room cottage was built, and just outside the door an old woman was engaged in washing.

I walked up to her, and entered into conversation about the church and burial-ground. She was ready enough to talk, and almost the first words she said informed me that her husband filled the two offices of clerk and sexton. I said a few words next in praise of Mrs. Fairlie's monument. The old woman shook her head, and told me I had not seen it at its best. It was her husband's business to look after it, but he had been so ailing and weak for months and months past, that he had hardly been able to crawl into church on Sundays to do his duty, and the monument had been neglected in consequence. He was getting a little better now, and in a week or ten days' time he hoped to be strong enough to set to work and clean it.

This information — extracted from a long rambling answer in the broadest Cumberland dialect — told me all that I most wanted to know. I gave the poor woman a trifle, and returned at once to Limmeridge House.

The partial cleansing of the monument had evidently been accomplished by a strange hand. Connecting what I had discovered, thus far, with what I had suspected after hearing the story of the ghost seen at twilight, I wanted nothing more to confirm my resolution to watch Mrs. Fairlie's grave, in secret, that evening, returning to it at sunset, and waiting within sight of it till the night fell. The work of cleansing the monument had been left unfinished, and the person by whom it had been begun might return to complete it.

On getting back to the house I informed Miss Halcombe of what I intended to do. She looked surprised and uneasy while I was explaining my purpose, but she made no positive objection to the execution of it. She only said, "I hope it may end well."

Just as she was leaving me again, I stopped her to inquire, as calmly as I could, after Miss Fairlie's health. She was in better spirits, and Miss Halcombe hoped she might be induced to take a little walking exercise while the afternoon sun lasted.

I returned to my own room to resume setting the drawings in order. It was necessary to do this, and doubly necessary to keep my mind employed on anything that would help to distract my attention from myself, and from the hopeless future that lay before me. From time to time I paused in my work to look out of window and watch the sky as the sun sank nearer and nearer to the horizon. On one of those occasions I saw a figure on the broad gravel walk under my window. It was Miss Fairlie.

I had not seen her since the morning, and I had hardly spoken to her then. Another day at Limmeridge was all that remained to me, and after that day my eyes might never look on her again. This thought was enough to hold me at the window. I had sufficient consideration for her to arrange the blind so that she might not see me if she looked up, but I had no strength to resist the temptation of letting my eyes, at least, follow her as far as they could on her walk.

She was dressed in a brown cloak, with a plain black silk gown under it. On her head was the same simple straw hat which she had worn on the morning when we first met. A veil was attached to it now which hid her face from me. By her side trotted a little Italian greyhound, the pet companion of all her walks, smartly dressed in a scarlet cloth wrapper, to keep the

84

sharp air from his delicate skin. She did not seem to notice the dog. She walked straight forward, with her head drooping a little, and her arms folded in her cloak. The dead leaves, which had whirled in the wind before me when I had heard of her marriage engagement in the morning, whirled in the wind before her, and rose and fell and scattered themselves at her feet as she walked on in the pale waning sunlight. The dog shivered and trembled, and pressed against her dress impatiently for notice and encouragement. But she never heeded him. She walked on, farther and farther away from me, with the dead leaves whirling about her on the path—walked on, till my aching eyes could see her no more, and I was left alone again with my own heavy heart.

In another hour's time I had done my work, and the sunset was at hand. I got my hat and coat in the hall, and slipped out of the house without meeting any one.

The clouds were wild in the western heaven, and the wind blew chill from the sea. Far as the shore was, the sound of the surf swept over the intervening moorland, and beat drearily in my ears when I entered the churchyard. Not a living creature was in sight. The place looked lonelier than ever as I chose my position, and waited and watched, with my eyes on the white cross that rose over Mrs. Fairlie's grave.

XIII

The exposed situation of the churchyard had obliged me to be cautious in choosing the position that I was to occupy.

The main entrance to the church was on the side next to the burial-ground, and the door was screened by a porch walled in on either side. After some little hesitation, caused by natural reluctance to conceal myself, indispensable as that concealment was to the object in view, I had resolved on entering the porch. A loophole window was pierced in each of its side walls. Through one of these windows I could see Mrs. Fairlie's grave. The other looked towards the stone quarry in which the sexton's cottage was built. Before me, fronting the porch entrance, was a patch of bare burial-ground, a line of low stone wall, and a strip of lonely brown hill, with the sunset clouds sailing heavily over it before the strong, steady wind. No living creature was visible or audible—no bird flew by me, no dog barked from the sexton's cottage. The pauses in the dull beating of the surf were filled up by the dreary rustling of the dwarf trees near the grave, and the cold faint bubble of the brook over its stony bed. A dreary scene and a dreary hour. My spirits sank fast as I counted out the minutes of the evening in my hiding-place under the church porch.

It was not twilight yet—the light of the setting sun still lingered in the heavens, and little more than the first half-hour of my solitary watch had elapsed—when I heard footsteps and a voice. The footsteps were approaching from the other side of the church, and the voice was a woman's.

"Don't you fret, my dear, about the letter," said the voice. "I gave it to the lad quite safe, and the lad he took it from me without a word. He went his way and I went mine, and not a living soul followed me afterwards—that I'll warrant."

These words strung up my attention to a pitch of expectation that was almost painful. There was a pause of silence, but the footsteps still advanced. In another moment two persons, both women, passed within my range of view from the porch window. They were walking straight towards the grave; and therefore they had their backs turned towards me.

One of the women was dressed in a bonnet and shawl. The other wore a long travelling-cloak of a dark-blue colour, with the hood drawn over her head. A few inches of her gown were visible below the cloak. My heart beat fast as I noted the colour—it was white.

The Woman in White

After advancing about half-way between the church and the grave they stopped, and the woman in the cloak turned her head towards her companion. But her side face, which a bonnet might now have allowed me to see, was hidden by the heavy, projecting edge of the hood.

"Mind you keep that comfortable warm cloak on," said the same voice which I had already heard — the voice of the woman in the shawl. "Mrs. Todd is right about your looking too particular, yesterday, all in white. I'll walk about a little while you're here, churchyards being not at all in my way, whatever they may be in yours. Finish what you want to do before I come back, and let us be sure and get home again before night."

With those words she turned about, and retracing her steps, advanced with her face towards me. It was the face of an elderly woman, brown, rugged, and healthy, with nothing dishonest or suspicious in the look of it. Close to the church she stopped to pull her shawl closer round her.

"Queer," she said to herself, "always queer, with her whims and her ways, ever since I can remember her. Harmless, though — as harmless, poor soul, as a little child."

She sighed — looked about the burial-ground nervously — shook her head, as if the dreary prospect by no means pleased her, and disappeared round the corner of the church.

I doubted for a moment whether I ought to follow and speak to her or not. My intense anxiety to find myself face to face with her companion helped me to decide in the negative. I could ensure seeing the woman in the shawl by waiting near the churchyard until she came back — although it seemed more than doubtful whether she could give me the information of which I was in search. The person who had delivered the letter was of little consequence. The person who had written it was the one centre of interest, and the one source of information, and that person I now felt convinced was before me in the churchyard.

While these ideas were passing through my mind I saw the woman in the cloak approach close to the grave, and stand looking at it for a little while. She then glanced all round her, and taking a white linen cloth or handkerchief from under her cloak, turned aside towards the brook. The little stream ran into the churchyard under a tiny archway in the bottom of the wall, and ran out again, after a winding course of a few dozen yards, under a similar opening. She dipped the cloth in the water, and returned to the grave. I saw her kiss the white cross, then kneel down before the inscription, and apply her wet cloth to the cleansing of it.

After considering how I could show myself with the least possible chance of frightening her, I resolved to cross the wall before me, to skirt round it outside, and to enter the churchyard again by the stile near the grave, in order that she might see me as I approached. She was so absorbed over her employment that she did not hear me coming until I had stepped over the stile. Then she looked up, started to her feet with a faint cry, and stood facing me in speechless and motionless terror.

"Don't be frightened," I said. "Surely you remember me?"

I stopped while I spoke—then advanced a few steps gently—then stopped again—and so approached by little and little till I was close to her. If there had been any doubt still left in my mind, it must have been now set at rest. There, speaking affrightedly for itself—there was the same face confronting me over Mrs. Fairlie's grave which had first looked into mine on the high-road by night.

"You remember me?" I said. "We met very late, and I helped you to find the way to London. Surely you have not forgotten that?"

Her features relaxed, and she drew a heavy breath of relief. I saw the new life of recognition stirring slowly under the death-like stillness which fear had set on her face.

"Don't attempt to speak to me just yet," I went on. "Take time to recover yourself—take time to feel quite certain that I am a friend."

"You are very kind to me," she murmured. "As kind now as you were then."

She stopped, and I kept silence on my side. I was not granting time for composure to her only, I was gaining time also for myself. Under the wan wild evening light, that woman and I were met together again, a grave between us, the dead about us, the lonesome hills closing us round on every side. The time, the place, the circumstances under which we now stood face to face in the evening stillness of that dreary valley—the lifelong interests which might hang suspended on the next chance words that passed between us—the sense that, for aught I knew to the contrary, the whole future of Laura Fairlie's life might be determined, for good or for evil, by my winning or losing the

The Woman in White

confidence of the forlorn creature who stood trembling by her mother's grave—all threatened to shake the steadiness and the self-control on which every inch of the progress I might yet make now depended. I tried hard, as I felt this, to possess myself of all my resources; I did my utmost to turn the few moments for reflection to the best account.

"Are you calmer now?" I said, as soon as I thought it time to speak again. "Can you talk to me without feeling frightened, and without forgetting that I am a friend?"

"How did you come here?" she asked, without noticing what I had just said to her.

"Don't you remember my telling you, when we last met, that I was going to Cumberland? I have been in Cumberland ever since—I have been staying all the time at Limmeridge House."

"At Limmeridge House!" Her pale face brightened as she repeated the words, her wandering eyes fixed on me with a sudden interest. "Ah, how happy you must have been!" she said, looking at me eagerly, without a shadow of its former distrust left in her expression.

I took advantage of her newly-aroused confidence in me to observe her face, with an attention and a curiosity which I had hitherto restrained myself from showing, for caution's sake. I looked at her, with my mind full of that other lovely face which had so ominously recalled her to my memory on the terrace by moonlight. I had seen Anne Catherick's likeness in Miss Fairlie. I now saw Miss Fairlie's likeness in Anne Catherick—saw it all the more clearly because the points of dissimilarity between the two were presented to me as well as the points of resemblance. In the general outline of the countenance and general proportion of the features—in the colour of the hair and in the little nervous uncertainty about the lips—in the height and size of the figure, and the carriage of the head and body, the likeness appeared even more startling than I had ever felt it to be yet. But there the resemblance ended, and the dissimilarity, in details, began. The delicate beauty of Miss Fairlie's complexion, the transparent clearness of her eyes, the smooth purity of her skin, the tender bloom of colour on her lips, were all missing from the worn weary face that was now turned towards mine. Although I hated myself even for thinking such a thing, still, while I looked at the woman before me, the idea would force itself into my mind that one sad change, in the future, was all that was wanting to make the likeness complete, which I now saw to be so imperfect in detail. If ever sorrow and suffering set their profaning marks on the youth and beauty of Miss Fairlie's face, then, and then only, Anne Catherick and she would be the twin-sisters of chance resemblance, the living reflections of one another.

I shuddered at the thought. There was something horrible in the blind unreasoning distrust of the future which the mere passage of it through my mind seemed to imply. It was a welcome interruption to be roused by feeling Anne Catherick's hand laid on my shoulder. The touch was as stealthy and as sudden as that other touch which had petrified me from head to foot on the night when we first met.

"You are looking at me, and you are thinking of something," she said, with her strange breathless rapidity of utterance. "What is it?"

"Nothing extraordinary," I answered. "I was only wondering how you came here."

"I came with a friend who is very good to me. I have only been here two days."

"And you found your way to this place yesterday?"

"How do you know that?"

"I only guessed it."

She turned from me, and knelt down before the inscription once more.

"Where should I go if not here?" she said. "The friend who was better than a mother to me is the only friend I have to visit at Limmeridge. Oh, it makes my heart ache to see a stain on her tomb! It ought to be kept white as snow, for her sake. I was tempted to begin cleaning it yesterday, and I can't help coming back to go on with it to-day. Is there anything wrong in that? I hope not. Surely nothing can be wrong that I do for Mrs. Fairlie's sake?"

The old grateful sense of her benefactress's kindness was evidently the ruling idea still in the poor creature's mind — the narrow mind which had but too plainly opened to no other lasting impression since that first impression of her younger and happier days. I saw that my best chance of winning her confidence lay in encouraging her to proceed with the artless employment which she had come into the burial-ground to

The Woman in White

pursue. She resumed it at once, on my telling her she might do so, touching the hard marble as tenderly as if it had been a sentient thing, and whispering the words of the inscription to herself, over and over again, as if the lost days of her girlhood had returned and she was patiently learning her lesson once more at Mrs. Fairlie's knees.

"Should you wonder very much," I said, preparing the way as cautiously as I could for the questions that were to come, "if I owned that it is a satisfaction to me, as well as a surprise, to see you here? I felt very uneasy about you after you left me in the cab."

She looked up quickly and suspiciously.

"Uneasy," she repeated. "Why?"

"A strange thing happened after we parted that night. Two men overtook me in a chaise. They did not see where I was standing, but they stopped near me, and spoke to a policeman on the other side of the way."

She instantly suspended her employment. The hand holding the damp cloth with which she had been cleaning the inscription dropped to her side. The other hand grasped the marble cross at the head of the grave. Her face turned towards me slowly, with the blank look of terror set rigidly on it once more. I went on at all hazards—it was too late now to draw back.

"The two men spoke to the policeman," I said, "and asked him if he had seen you. He had not seen you; and then one of the men spoke again, and said you had escaped from his Asylum."

She sprang to her feet as if my last words had set the pursuers on her track.

"Stop! and hear the end," I cried. "Stop! and you shall know how I befriended you. A word from me would have told the men which way you had gone—and I never spoke that word. I helped your escape—I made it safe and certain. Think, try to think. Try to understand what I tell you."

My manner seemed to influence her more than my words. She made an effort to grasp the new idea. Her hands shifted the damp cloth hesitatingly from one to the other, exactly as they had shifted the little travelling-bag on the night when I first saw her. Slowly the purpose of my words seemed to force its way through the confusion and agitation of her mind. Slowly her features relaxed, and her eyes looked at me with their expression gaining in curiosity what it was fast losing in fear.

"You don't think I ought to be back in the Asylum, do you?" she said.

"Certainly not. I am glad you escaped from it—I am glad I helped you."

"Yes, yes, you did help me indeed; you helped me at the hard part," she went on a little vacantly. "It was easy to escape, or I should not have got away. They never suspected me as they suspected the others. I was so quiet, and so obedient, and so easily frightened. The finding London was the hard part, and there you helped me. Did I thank you at the time? I thank you now very kindly."

"Was the Asylum far from where you met me? Come! show that you believe me to be your friend, and tell me where it was."

She mentioned the place—a private Asylum, as its situation informed me; a private Asylum not very far from the spot where I had seen her—and then, with evident suspicion of the use to which I might put her answer, anxiously repeated her former inquiry, "You don't think I ought to be taken back, do you?"

"Once again, I am glad you escaped—I am glad you prospered well after you left me," I answered. "You said you had a friend in London to go to. Did you find the friend?"

"Yes. It was very late, but there was a girl up at needle-work in the house, and she helped me to rouse Mrs. Clements. Mrs. Clements is my friend. A good, kind woman, but not like Mrs. Fairlie. Ah no, nobody is like Mrs. Fairlie!"

"Is Mrs. Clements an old friend of yours? Have you known her a long time?"

"Yes, she was a neighbour of ours once, at home, in Hampshire, and liked me, and took care of me when I was a little girl. Years ago, when she went away from us, she wrote down in my Prayer-book for me where she was going to live in London, and she said, 'If you are ever in trouble, Anne, come to me. I have no husband alive to say me nay, and no children to look after, and I will take care of you.' Kind words, were they

92

The Woman in White

not? I suppose I remember them because they were kind. It's little enough I remember besides—little enough, little enough!"

"Had you no father or mother to take care of you?"

"Father?—I never saw him—I never heard mother speak of him. Father? Ah, dear! he is dead, I suppose."

"And your mother?"

"I don't get on well with her. We are a trouble and a fear to each other."

A trouble and a fear to each other! At those words the suspicion crossed my mind, for the first time, that her mother might be the person who had placed her under restraint.

"Don't ask me about mother," she went on. "I'd rather talk of Mrs. Clements. Mrs. Clements is like you, she doesn't think that I ought to be back in the Asylum, and she is as glad as you are that I escaped from it. She cried over my misfortune, and said it must be kept secret from everybody."

Her "misfortune." In what sense was she using that word? In a sense which might explain her motive in writing the anonymous letter? In a sense which might show it to be the too common and too customary motive that has led many a woman to interpose anonymous hindrances to the marriage of the man who has ruined her? I resolved to attempt the clearing up of this doubt before more words passed between us on either side.

"What misfortune?" I asked.

"The misfortune of my being shut up," she answered, with every appearance of feeling surprised at my question. "What other misfortune could there be?"

I determined to persist, as delicately and forbearingly as possible. It was of very great importance that I should be absolutely sure of every step in the investigation which I now gained in advance.

"There is another misfortune," I said, "to which a woman may be liable, and by which she may suffer lifelong sorrow and shame."

"What is it?" she asked eagerly.

"The misfortune of believing too innocently in her own virtue, and in the faith and honour of the man she loves," I answered.

She looked up at me with the artless bewilderment of a child. Not the slightest confusion or change of colour—not the faintest trace of any secret consciousness of shame struggling to the surface appeared in her face—that face which betrayed every other emotion with such transparent clearness. No words that ever were spoken could have assured me, as her look and manner now assured me, that the motive which I had assigned for her writing the letter and sending it to Miss Fairlie was plainly and distinctly the wrong one. That doubt, at any rate, was now set at rest; but the very removal of it opened a new prospect of uncertainty. The letter, as I knew from positive testimony, pointed at Sir Percival Glyde, though it did not name him. She must have had some strong motive, originating in some deep sense of injury, for secretly denouncing him to Miss Fairlie in such terms as she had employed, and that motive was unquestionably not to be traced to the loss of her innocence and her character. Whatever wrong he might have inflicted on her was not of that nature. Of what nature could it be?

"I don't understand you," she said, after evidently trying hard, and trying in vain, to discover the meaning of the words I had last said to her.

"Never mind," I answered. "Let us go on with what we were talking about. Tell me how long you stayed with Mrs. Clements in London, and how you came here."

"How long?" she repeated. "I stayed with Mrs. Clements till we both came to this place, two days ago."

"You are living in the village, then?" I said. "It is strange I should not have heard of you, though you have only been here two days."

"No, no, not in the village. Three miles away at a farm. Do you know the farm? They call it Todd's Corner."

I remembered the place perfectly—we had often passed by it in our drives. It was one of the oldest farms in the neighbourhood, situated in a solitary, sheltered spot, inland at the junction of two hills.

"They are relations of Mrs. Clements at Todd's Corner," she went on, "and they had often asked her to go and see them. She said she would go, and take me with her, for the quiet and the fresh air. It was very kind, was it not? I would have gone anywhere to be quiet, and safe, and out of the way. But when I heard that Todd's Corner was near Limmeridge—oh! I was so happy I would have walked all the way barefoot to get there, and see the schools and the village and Limmeridge House again. They are very good people at Todd's Corner. I hope I shall stay there a long time. There is only one thing I don't like about them, and don't like about Mrs. Clements——"

"What is it?"

"They will tease me about dressing all in white—they say it looks so particular. How do they know? Mrs. Fairlie knew best. Mrs. Fairlie would never have made me wear this ugly blue cloak! Ah! she was fond of white in her lifetime, and here is white stone about her grave—and I am making it whiter for her sake. She often wore white herself, and she always dressed her little daughter in white. Is Miss Fairlie well and happy? Does she wear white now, as she used when she was a girl?"

Her voice sank when she put the questions about Miss Fairlie, and she turned her head farther and farther away from me. I thought I detected, in the alteration of her manner, an uneasy consciousness of the risk she had run in sending the anonymous letter, and I instantly determined so to frame my answer as to surprise her into owning it.

"Miss Fairlie was not very well or very happy this morning," I said.

She murmured a few words, but they were spoken so confusedly, and in such a low tone, that I could not even guess at what they meant.

"Did you ask me why Miss Fairlie was neither well nor happy this morning?" I continued.

"No," she said quickly and eagerly—"oh no, I never asked that."

"I will tell you without your asking," I went on. "Miss Fairlie has received your letter."

She had been down on her knees for some little time past, carefully removing the last weather-stains left about the inscription while we were speaking together. The first sentence of the words I had just addressed to her made her pause in her occupation, and turn slowly without rising from her knees, so as to face me. The second sentence literally petrified her. The cloth she had been holding dropped from her hands—her lips fell apart—all the little colour that there was naturally in her face left it in an instant.

"How do you know?" she said faintly. "Who showed it to you?" The blood rushed back into her face—rushed overwhelmingly, as the sense rushed upon her mind that her own words had betrayed her. She struck her hands together in despair. "I never wrote it," she gasped affrightedly; "I know nothing about it!"

"Yes," I said, "you wrote it, and you know about it. It was wrong to send such a letter, it was wrong to frighten Miss Fairlie. If you had anything to say that it was right and necessary for her to hear, you should have gone yourself to Limmeridge House—you should have spoken to the young lady with your own lips."

She crouched down over the flat stone of the grave, till her face was hidden on it, and made no reply.

"Miss Fairlie will be as good and kind to you as her mother was, if you mean well," I went on. "Miss Fairlie will keep your secret, and not let you come to any harm. Will you see her to-morrow at the farm? Will you meet her in the garden at Limmeridge House?"

"Oh, if I could die, and be hidden and at rest with you!" Her lips murmured the words close on the grave-stone, murmured them in tones of passionate endearment, to the dead remains beneath. "You know how I love your child, for your sake! Oh, Mrs. Fairlie! Mrs. Fairlie! tell me how to save her. Be my darling and my mother once more, and tell me what to do for the best."

I heard her lips kissing the stone—I saw her hands beating on it passionately. The sound and the sight deeply affected me. I stooped down, and took the poor helpless hands tenderly in mine, and tried to soothe her.

It was useless. She snatched her hands from me, and never moved her face from the stone. Seeing the urgent necessity of quieting her at any hazard and by any means, I appealed to the only anxiety that she appeared to feel, in connection with me and with my opinion of her—the anxiety to convince me of her fitness to be mistress of her own actions.

"Come, come," I said gently. "Try to compose yourself, or you will make me alter my opinion of you. Don't let me think that the person who put you in the Asylum might have had some excuse — —"

The next words died away on my lips. The instant I risked that chance reference to the person who had put her in the Asylum she sprang up on her knees. A most extraordinary and startling change passed over her. Her face, at all ordinary times so touching to look at, in its nervous sensitiveness, weakness, and uncertainty, became suddenly darkened by an expression of maniacally intense hatred and fear, which communicated a wild, unnatural force to every feature. Her eyes dilated in the dim evening light, like the eyes of a wild animal. She caught up the cloth that had fallen at her side, as if it had been a living creature that she could kill, and crushed it in both her hands with such convulsive strength, that the few drops of moisture left in it trickled down on the stone beneath her.

"Talk of something else," she said, whispering through her teeth. "I shall lose myself if you talk of that."

Every vestige of the gentler thoughts which had filled her mind hardly a minute since seemed to be swept from it now. It was evident that the impression left by Mrs. Fairlie's kindness was not, as I had supposed, the only strong impression on her memory. With the grateful remembrance of her school-days at Limmeridge, there existed the vindictive remembrance of the wrong inflicted on her by her confinement in the Asylum. Who had done that wrong? Could it really be her mother?

It was hard to give up pursuing the inquiry to that final point, but I forced myself to abandon all idea of continuing it. Seeing her as I saw her now, it would have been cruel to think of anything but the necessity and the humanity of restoring her composure.

"I will talk of nothing to distress you," I said soothingly.

"You want something," she answered sharply and suspiciously. "Don't look at me like that. Speak to me — tell me what you want."

"I only want you to quiet yourself, and when you are calmer, to think over what I have said."

"Said?" She paused — twisted the cloth in her hands, backwards and forwards, and whispered to herself, "What is it he said?" She turned again towards me, and shook her head impatiently. "Why don't you help me?" she asked, with angry suddenness.

"Yes, yes," I said, "I will help you, and you will soon remember. I ask you to see Miss Fairlie to-morrow and to tell her the truth about the letter."

"Ah! Miss Fairlie—Fairlie—Fairlie——"

The mere utterance of the loved familiar name seemed to quiet her. Her face softened and grew like itself again.

"You need have no fear of Miss Fairlie," I continued, "and no fear of getting into trouble through the letter. She knows so much about it already, that you will have no difficulty in telling her all. There can be little necessity for concealment where there is hardly anything left to conceal. You mention no names in the letter; but Miss Fairlie knows that the person you write of is Sir Percival Glyde——"

The instant I pronounced that name she started to her feet, and a scream burst from her that rang through the churchyard, and made my heart leap in me with the terror of it. The dark deformity of the expression which had just left her face lowered on it once more, with doubled and trebled intensity. The shriek at the name, the reiterated look of hatred and fear that instantly followed, told all. Not even a last doubt now remained. Her mother was guiltless of imprisoning her in the Asylum. A man had shut her up—and that man was Sir Percival Glyde.

The scream had reached other ears than mine. On one side I heard the door of the sexton's cottage open; on the other I heard the voice of her companion, the woman in the shawl, the woman whom she had spoken of as Mrs. Clements.

"I'm coming! I'm coming!" cried the voice from behind the clump of dwarf trees.

In a moment more Mrs. Clements hurried into view.

"Who are you?" she cried, facing me resolutely as she set her foot on the stile. "How dare you frighten a poor helpless woman like that?"

She was at Anne Catherick's side, and had put one arm around her, before I could answer. "What is it, my dear?" she said. "What has he done to you?"

"Nothing," the poor creature answered. "Nothing. I'm only frightened."

Mrs. Clements turned on me with a fearless indignation, for which I respected her.

"I should be heartily ashamed of myself if I deserved that angry look," I said. "But I do not deserve it. I have unfortunately startled her without intending it. This is not the first time she has seen me. Ask her yourself, and she will tell you that I am incapable of willingly harming her or any woman."

I spoke distinctly, so that Anne Catherick might hear and understand me, and I saw that the words and their meaning had reached her.

"Yes, yes," she said — "he was good to me once — he helped me — —" She whispered the rest into her friend's ear.

"Strange, indeed!" said Mrs. Clements, with a look of perplexity. "It makes all the difference, though. I'm sorry I spoke so rough to you, sir; but you must own that appearances looked suspicious to a stranger. It's more my fault than yours, for humouring her whims, and letting her be alone in such a place as this. Come, my dear — come home now."

I thought the good woman looked a little uneasy at the prospect of the walk back, and I offered to go with them until they were both within sight of home. Mrs. Clements thanked me civilly, and declined. She said they were sure to meet some of the farm-labourers as soon as they got to the moor.

"Try to forgive me," I said, when Anne Catherick took her friend's arm to go away. Innocent as I had been of any intention to terrify and agitate her, my heart smote me as I looked at the poor, pale, frightened face.

"I will try," she answered. "But you know too much — I'm afraid you'll always frighten me now."

Mrs. Clements glanced at me, and shook her head pityingly.

"Good-night, sir," she said. "You couldn't help it, I know; but I wish it was me you had frightened, and not her."

They moved away a few steps. I thought they had left me, but Anne suddenly stopped, and separated herself from her friend.

"Wait a little," she said. "I must say good-bye."

She returned to the grave, rested both hands tenderly on the marble cross, and kissed it.

"I'm better now," she sighed, looking up at me quietly. "I forgive you."

She joined her companion again, and they left the burial-ground. I saw them stop near the church and speak to the sexton's wife, who had come from the cottage, and had waited, watching us from a distance. Then they went on again up the path that led to the moor. I looked after Anne Catherick as she disappeared, till all trace of her had faded in the twilight—looked as anxiously and sorrowfully as if that was the last I was to see in this weary world of the woman in white.

XIV

Half an hour later I was back at the house, and was informing Miss Halcombe of all that had happened.

She listened to me from beginning to end with a steady, silent attention, which, in a woman of her temperament and disposition, was the strongest proof that could be offered of the serious manner in which my narrative affected her.

"My mind misgives me," was all she said when I had done. "My mind misgives me sadly about the future."

"The future may depend," I suggested, "on the use we make of the present. It is not improbable that Anne Catherick may speak more readily and unreservedly to a woman than she has spoken to me. If Miss Fairlie— —"

"Not to be thought of for a moment," interposed Miss Halcombe, in her most decided manner.

"Let me suggest, then," I continued, "that you should see Anne Catherick yourself, and do all you can to win her confidence. For my own part, I shrink from the idea of alarming the poor creature a second time, as I have most unhappily alarmed her already. Do you see any objection to accompanying me to the farmhouse to-morrow?"

"None whatever. I will go anywhere and do anything to serve Laura's interests. What did you say the place was called?"

"You must know it well. It is called Todd's Corner."

"Certainly. Todd's Corner is one of Mr. Fairlie's farms. Our dairymaid here is the farmer's second daughter. She goes backwards and forwards constantly between this house and her father's farm, and she may have heard or seen something which it may be useful to us to know. Shall I ascertain, at once, if the girl is downstairs?"

She rang the bell, and sent the servant with his message. He returned, and announced that the dairymaid was then at the farm. She had not been there for the last three days, and the housekeeper had given her leave to go home for an hour or two that evening.

"I can speak to her to-morrow," said Miss Halcombe, when the servant had left the room again. "In the meantime, let me thoroughly understand the object to be gained by my interview with Anne Catherick. Is there no doubt in your mind that the person who confined her in the Asylum was Sir Percival Glyde?"

"There is not the shadow of a doubt. The only mystery that remains is the mystery of his motive. Looking to the great difference between his station in life and hers, which seems to preclude all idea of the most distant relationship between them, it is of the last importance—even assuming that she really required to be placed under restraint—to know why he should have been the person to assume the serious responsibility of shutting her up——"

"In a private Asylum, I think you said?"

"Yes, in a private Asylum, where a sum of money, which no poor person could afford to give, must have been paid for her maintenance as a patient."

"I see where the doubt lies, Mr. Hartright, and I promise you that it shall be set at rest, whether Anne Catherick assists us to-morrow or not. Sir Percival Glyde shall not be long in this house without satisfying Mr. Gilmore, and satisfying me. My sister's future is my dearest care in life, and I have influence enough over her to give me some power, where her marriage is concerned, in the disposal of it."

We parted for the night.

After breakfast the next morning, an obstacle, which the events of the evening before had put out of my memory, interposed to prevent our proceeding immediately to the farm. This was my last day at Limmeridge House, and it was necessary, as soon as the post came in, to follow Miss Halcombe's advice, and to ask Mr. Fairlie's permission to shorten my engagement by a month, in consideration of an unforeseen necessity for my return to London.

Fortunately for the probability of this excuse, so far as appearances were concerned, the post brought me two letters from London friends that morning. I took them away at once to my own room, and sent the servant with a message to Mr. Fairlie, requesting to know when I could see him on a matter of business.

I awaited the man's return, free from the slightest feeling of anxiety about the manner in which his master might receive my application. With Mr. Fairlie's leave or without it, I must go. The consciousness of having now taken the first step on the dreary journey which was henceforth to separate my life from Miss Fairlie's seemed to have blunted my sensibility to every consideration connected with myself. I had done with my poor man's touchy pride—I had done with all my little artist vanities. No insolence of Mr. Fairlie's, if he chose to be insolent, could wound me now.

The servant returned with a message for which I was not unprepared. Mr. Fairlie regretted that the state of his health, on that particular morning, was such as to preclude all hope of his having the pleasure of receiving me. He begged, therefore, that I would accept his apologies, and kindly communicate what I had to say in the form of a letter. Similar messages to this had reached me, at various intervals, during my three months' residence in the house. Throughout the whole of that period Mr. Fairlie had been rejoiced to "possess" me, but had never been well enough to see me for a second time. The servant took every fresh batch of drawings that I mounted and restored back to his master with my "respects," and returned empty-handed with Mr. Fairlie's "kind compliments," "best thanks," and "sincere regrets" that the state of his health still obliged him to remain a solitary prisoner in his own room. A more satisfactory arrangement to both sides could not possibly have been adopted. It would be hard to say which of us, under the circumstances, felt the most grateful sense of obligation to Mr. Fairlie's accommodating nerves.

I sat down at once to write the letter, expressing myself in it as civilly, as clearly, and as briefly as possible. Mr. Fairlie did not hurry his reply. Nearly an hour elapsed before the answer was placed in my hands. It was written with beautiful regularity and neatness of character, in violet-coloured ink, on note-paper as smooth as ivory and almost as thick as cardboard, and it addressed me in these terms—

"Mr. Fairlie's compliments to Mr. Hartright. Mr. Fairlie is more surprised and disappointed than he can say (in the present state of his health) by Mr. Hartright's application. Mr. Fairlie is not a man of business, but he has consulted his steward, who is, and that person confirms Mr. Fairlie's opinion that Mr. Hartright's request to be allowed to break his engagement cannot be justified by any necessity whatever, excepting perhaps a case of life and death. If the highly-appreciative feeling towards Art and its professors, which it is the consolation and happiness of Mr. Fairlie's suffering existence to cultivate, could be easily shaken, Mr. Hartright's present proceeding would have shaken it. It has not done so—except in the instance of Mr. Hartright himself.

"Having stated his opinion—so far, that is to say, as acute nervous suffering will allow him to state anything—Mr. Fairlie has nothing to add but the expression of his decision, in reference to the highly irregular application that has been made to him. Perfect repose of body and mind being to the last degree important in his case, Mr. Fairlie will not suffer Mr. Hartright to disturb that repose by remaining in the house under circumstances of an essentially irritating nature to both sides. Accordingly, Mr. Fairlie waives his right of refusal, purely with a view to the preservation of his own tranquillity—and informs Mr. Hartright that he may go."

I folded the letter up, and put it away with my other papers. The time had been when I should have resented it as an insult—I accepted it now as a written release from my engagement. It was off my mind, it was almost out of my memory, when I went downstairs to the breakfast-room, and informed Miss Halcombe that I was ready to walk with her to the farm.

"Has Mr. Fairlie given you a satisfactory answer?" she asked as we left the house.

"He has allowed me to go, Miss Halcombe."

She looked up at me quickly, and then, for the first time since I had known her, took my arm of her own accord. No words could have expressed so delicately that she understood how the permission to leave my employment had been granted, and that she gave me her sympathy, not as my superior, but as my friend. I had not felt the man's insolent letter, but I felt deeply the woman's atoning kindness.

On our way to the farm we arranged that Miss Halcombe was to enter the house alone, and that I was to wait outside, within call. We adopted this mode of proceeding from an apprehension that my presence, after what had happened in the churchyard the evening before, might have the effect of renewing Anne Catherick's nervous dread, and of rendering her additionally distrustful of the advances of a lady who was a stranger to her. Miss Halcombe left me, with the intention of speaking, in the first instance, to the farmer's wife (of whose friendly readiness to help her in any way she was well assured), while I waited for her in the near neighbourhood of the house.

I had fully expected to be left alone for some time. To my surprise, however, little more than five minutes had elapsed before Miss Halcombe returned.

"Does Anne Catherick refuse to see you?" I asked in astonishment.

"Anne Catherick is gone," replied Miss Halcombe.

"Gone?"

"Gone with Mrs. Clements. They both left the farm at eight o'clock this morning."

I could say nothing—I could only feel that our last chance of discovery had gone with them.

"All that Mrs. Todd knows about her guests, I know," Miss Halcombe went on, "and it leaves me, as it leaves her, in the dark. They both came back safe last night, after they left you, and they passed the first part of the evening with Mr. Todd's family as usual. Just before supper-time, however, Anne Catherick startled them all by being suddenly seized with faintness. She had had a similar attack, of a less alarming kind, on the day she arrived at the farm; and Mrs. Todd had connected it, on that occasion, with something she was reading at the time in our local newspaper, which lay on the farm table, and which she had taken up only a minute or two before."

"Does Mrs. Todd know what particular passage in the newspaper affected her in that way?" I inquired.

"No," replied Miss Halcombe. "She had looked it over, and had seen nothing in it to agitate any one. I asked leave, however, to look it over in my turn, and at the very first page I opened I found that the editor had enriched his small stock of news by drawing upon our family affairs, and had published my sister's marriage engagement, among his other announcements, copied from the London papers, of Marriages in High Life. I concluded at once that this was the paragraph which had so strangely affected Anne Catherick, and I thought I saw in it, also, the origin of the letter which she sent to our house the next day."

"There can be no doubt in either case. But what did you hear about her second attack of faintness yesterday evening?"

"Nothing. The cause of it is a complete mystery. There was

no stranger in the room. The only visitor was our dairymaid, who, as I told you, is one of Mr. Todd's daughters, and the only conversation was the usual gossip about local affairs. They heard her cry out, and saw her turn deadly pale, without the slightest apparent reason. Mrs. Todd and Mrs. Clements took her upstairs, and Mrs. Clements remained with her. They were heard talking together until long after the usual bedtime, and early this morning Mrs. Clements took Mrs. Todd aside, and amazed her beyond all power of expression by saying that they must go. The only explanation Mrs. Todd could extract from her guest was, that something had happened, which was not the fault of any one at the farmhouse, but which was serious enough to make Anne Catherick resolve to leave Limmeridge immediately. It was quite useless to press Mrs. Clements to be more explicit. She only shook her head, and said that, for Anne's sake, she must beg and pray that no one would question her. All she could repeat, with every appearance of being seriously agitated herself, was that Anne must go, that she must go with her, and that the destination to which they might both betake themselves must be kept a secret from everybody. I spare you the recital of Mrs. Todd's hospitable remonstrances and refusals. It ended in her driving them both to the nearest station, more than three hours since. She tried hard on the way to get them to speak more plainly, but without success; and she set them down outside the station-door, so hurt and offended by the unceremonious abruptness of their departure and their unfriendly reluctance to place the least confidence in her, that she drove away in anger, without so much as stopping to bid them good-bye. That is exactly what has taken place. Search your own memory, Mr. Hartright, and tell me if anything happened in the burial-ground yesterday evening which can at all account for the extraordinary departure of those two women this morning."

"I should like to account first, Miss Halcombe, for the sudden change in Anne Catherick which alarmed them at the farmhouse, hours after she and I had parted, and when time enough had elapsed to quiet any violent agitation that I might have been unfortunate enough to cause. Did you inquire particularly about the gossip which was going on in the room when she turned faint?"

"Yes. But Mrs. Todd's household affairs seem to have divided her attention that evening with the talk in the farmhouse parlour. She could only tell me that it was 'just the news,'—meaning, I suppose, that they all talked as usual about each other."

The Woman in White

"The dairymaid's memory may be better than her mother's," I said. "It may be as well for you to speak to the girl, Miss Halcombe, as soon as we get back."

My suggestion was acted on the moment we returned to the house. Miss Halcombe led me round to the servants' offices, and we found the girl in the dairy, with her sleeves tucked up to her shoulders, cleaning a large milk-pan and singing blithely over her work.

"I have brought this gentleman to see your dairy, Hannah," said Miss Halcombe. "It is one of the sights of the house, and it always does you credit."

The girl blushed and curtseyed, and said shyly that she hoped she always did her best to keep things neat and clean.

"We have just come from your father's," Miss Halcombe continued. "You were there yesterday evening, I hear, and you found visitors at the house?"

"Yes, miss."

"One of them was taken faint and ill, I am told. I suppose nothing was said or done to frighten her? You were not talking of anything very terrible, were you?"

"Oh no, miss!" said the girl, laughing. "We were only talking of the news."

"Your sisters told you the news at Todd's Corner, I suppose?"

"Yes, miss."

"And you told them the news at Limmeridge House?"

"Yes, miss. And I'm quite sure nothing was said to frighten the poor thing, for I was talking when she was taken ill. It gave me quite a turn, miss, to see it, never having been taken faint myself."

Before any more questions could be put to her, she was called away to receive a basket of eggs at the dairy door. As she left us I whispered to Miss Halcombe—

"Ask her if she happened to mention, last night, that visitors were expected at Limmeridge House."

Miss Halcombe showed me, by a look, that she understood, and put the question as soon as the dairymaid returned to us.

"Oh yes, miss, I mentioned that," said the girl simply. "The company coming, and the accident to the brindled cow, was all the news I had to take to the farm."

"Did you mention names? Did you tell them that Sir Percival Glyde was expected on Monday?"

"Yes, miss—I told them Sir Percival Glyde was coming. I hope there was no harm in it—I hope I didn't do wrong."

"Oh no, no harm. Come, Mr. Hartright, Hannah will begin to think us in the way, if we interrupt her any longer over her work."

We stopped and looked at one another the moment we were alone again.

"Is there any doubt in your mind, now, Miss Halcombe?"

"Sir Percival Glyde shall remove that doubt, Mr. Hartright—or Laura Fairlie shall never be his wife."

XV

As we walked round to the front of the house a fly from the railway approached us along the drive. Miss Halcombe waited on the door-steps until the fly drew up, and then advanced to shake hands with an old gentleman, who got out briskly the moment the steps were let down. Mr. Gilmore had arrived.

I looked at him, when we were introduced to each other, with an interest and a curiosity which I could hardly conceal. This old man was to remain at Limmeridge House after I had left it, he was to hear Sir Percival Glyde's explanation, and was to give Miss Halcombe the assistance of his experience in forming her judgment; he was to wait until the question of the marriage was set at rest; and his hand, if that question were decided in the affirmative, was to draw the settlement which bound Miss Fairlie irrevocably to her engagement. Even then, when I knew nothing by comparison with what I know now, I looked at the family lawyer with an interest which I had never felt before in the presence of any man breathing who was a total stranger to me.

In external appearance Mr. Gilmore was the exact opposite of the conventional idea of an old lawyer. His complexion was florid — his white hair was worn rather long and kept carefully brushed — his black coat, waistcoat, and trousers fitted him with perfect neatness — his white cravat was carefully tied, and his lavender-coloured kid gloves might have adorned the hands of a fashionable clergyman, without fear and without reproach. His manners were pleasantly marked by the formal grace and refinement of the old school of politeness, quickened by the invigorating sharpness and readiness of a man whose business in life obliges him always to keep his faculties in good working order. A sanguine constitution and fair prospects to begin with — a long subsequent career of creditable and comfortable prosperity — a cheerful, diligent, widely-respected old age — such were the general impressions I derived from my introduction to Mr. Gilmore, and it is but fair to him to add, that the knowledge I gained by later and better experience only tended to confirm them.

I left the old gentleman and Miss Halcombe to enter the house together, and to talk of family matters undisturbed by the restraint of a stranger's presence. They crossed the hall on their way to the drawing-room, and I descended the steps again to wander about the garden alone.

My hours were numbered at Limmeridge House — my

departure the next morning was irrevocably settled — my share in the investigation which the anonymous letter had rendered necessary was at an end. No harm could be done to any one but myself if I let my heart loose again, for the little time that was left me, from the cold cruelty of restraint which necessity had forced me to inflict upon it, and took my farewell of the scenes which were associated with the brief dream-time of my happiness and my love.

I turned instinctively to the walk beneath my study-window, where I had seen her the evening before with her little dog, and followed the path which her dear feet had trodden so often, till I came to the wicket gate that led into her rose garden. The winter bareness spread drearily over it now. The flowers that she had taught me to distinguish by their names, the flowers that I had taught her to paint from, were gone, and the tiny white paths that led between the beds were damp and green already. I went on to the avenue of trees, where we had breathed together the warm fragrance of August evenings, where we had admired together the myriad combinations of shade and sunlight that dappled the ground at our feet. The leaves fell about me from the groaning branches, and the earthy decay in the atmosphere chilled me to the bones. A little farther on, and I was out of the grounds, and following the lane that wound gently upward to the nearest hills. The old felled tree by the wayside, on which we had sat to rest, was sodden with rain, and the tuft of ferns and grasses which I had drawn for her, nestling under the rough stone wall in front of us, had turned to a pool of water, stagnating round an island of draggled weeds. I gained the summit of the hill, and looked at the view which we had so often admired in the happier time. It was cold and barren — it was no longer the view that I remembered. The sunshine of her presence was far from me — the charm of her voice no longer murmured in my ear. She had talked to me, on the spot from which I now looked down, of her father, who was her last surviving parent — had told me how fond of each other they had been, and how sadly she missed him still when she entered certain rooms in the house, and when she took up forgotten occupations and amusements with which he had been associated. Was the view that I had seen, while listening to those words, the view that I saw now, standing on the hill-top by myself? I turned and left it — I wound my way back again, over the moor, and round the sandhills, down to the beach. There was the white rage of the surf, and the multitudinous glory of the leaping waves — but where was the place on which she had once drawn idle figures with her parasol in the sand — the place where we had sat together, while she talked to me about myself and my home, while she asked me a woman's

The Woman in White

minutely observant questions about my mother and my sister, and innocently wondered whether I should ever leave my lonely chambers and have a wife and a house of my own? Wind and wave had long since smoothed out the trace of her which she had left in those marks on the sand. I looked over the wide monotony of the sea-side prospect, and the place in which we two had idled away the sunny hours was as lost to me as if I had never known it, as strange to me as if I stood already on a foreign shore.

The empty silence of the beach struck cold to my heart. I returned to the house and the garden, where traces were left to speak of her at every turn.

On the west terrace walk I met Mr. Gilmore. He was evidently in search of me, for he quickened his pace when we caught sight of each other. The state of my spirits little fitted me for the society of a stranger; but the meeting was inevitable, and I resigned myself to make the best of it.

"You are the very person I wanted to see," said the old gentleman. "I had two words to say to you, my dear sir; and if you have no objection I will avail myself of the present opportunity. To put it plainly, Miss Halcombe and I have been talking over family affairs—affairs which are the cause of my being here—and in the course of our conversation she was naturally led to tell me of this unpleasant matter connected with the anonymous letter, and of the share which you have most creditably and properly taken in the proceedings so far. That share, I quite understand, gives you an interest which you might not otherwise have felt, in knowing that the future management of the investigation which you have begun will be placed in safe hands. My dear sir, make yourself quite easy on that point—it will be placed in my hands."

"You are, in every way, Mr. Gilmore, much fitter to advise and to act in the matter than I am. Is it an indiscretion on my part to ask if you have decided yet on a course of proceeding?"

"So far as it is possible to decide, Mr. Hartright, I have decided. I mean to send a copy of the letter, accompanied by a statement of the circumstances, to Sir Percival Glyde's solicitor in London, with whom I have some acquaintance. The letter itself I shall keep here to show to Sir Percival as soon as he arrives. The tracing of the two women I have already provided for, by sending one of Mr. Fairlie's servants—a confidential person—to the station to make inquiries. The man has his money and his directions, and he will follow the women in the event of his finding any clue. This is all that can be done until Sir Percival comes on Monday. I have no doubt myself that every explanation which can be expected from a gentleman and a man of honour, he will readily give. Sir Percival stands very high, sir—an eminent position, a reputation above suspicion—I feel quite easy about results—quite easy, I am rejoiced to assure you. Things of this sort happen constantly in my experience. Anonymous letters—unfortunate woman—sad state of society. I don't deny that there are peculiar complications in this case; but the case itself is, most unhappily, common—common."

"I am afraid, Mr. Gilmore, I have the misfortune to differ from you in the view I take of the case."

"Just so, my dear sir—just so. I am an old man, and I take the practical view. You are a young man, and you take the romantic view. Let us not dispute about our views. I live professionally in an atmosphere of disputation, Mr. Hartright, and I am only too glad to escape from it, as I am escaping here. We will wait for events—yes, yes, yes—we will wait for events. Charming place this. Good shooting? Probably not, none of Mr. Fairlie's land is preserved, I think. Charming place, though, and delightful people. You draw and paint, I hear, Mr. Hartright? Enviable accomplishment. What style?"

We dropped into general conversation, or rather, Mr. Gilmore talked and I listened. My attention was far from him, and from the topics on which he discoursed so fluently. The solitary walk of the last two hours had wrought its effect on me—it had set the idea in my mind of hastening my departure from Limmeridge House. Why should I prolong the hard trial of saying farewell by one unnecessary minute? What further service was required of me by any one? There was no useful purpose to be served by my stay in Cumberland—there was no restriction of time in the permission to leave which my employer had granted to me. Why not end it there and then?

I determined to end it. There were some hours of daylight still left—there was no reason why my journey back to London should not begin on that afternoon. I made the first civil excuse that occurred to me for leaving Mr. Gilmore, and returned at once to the house.

On my way up to my own room I met Miss Halcombe on the stairs. She saw, by the hurry of my movements and the change in my manner, that I had some new purpose in view, and asked what had happened.

The Woman in White

I told her the reasons which induced me to think of hastening my departure, exactly as I have told them here.

"No, no," she said, earnestly and kindly, "leave us like a friend—break bread with us once more. Stay here and dine, stay here and help us to spend our last evening with you as happily, as like our first evenings, as we can. It is my invitation—Mrs. Vesey's invitation——" she hesitated a little, and then added, "Laura's invitation as well."

I promised to remain. God knows I had no wish to leave even the shadow of a sorrowful impression with any one of them.

My own room was the best place for me till the dinner bell rang. I waited there till it was time to go downstairs.

I had not spoken to Miss Fairlie—I had not even seen her—all that day. The first meeting with her, when I entered the drawing-room, was a hard trial to her self-control and to mine. She, too, had done her best to make our last evening renew the golden bygone time—the time that could never come again. She had put on the dress which I used to admire more than any other that she possessed—a dark blue silk, trimmed quaintly and prettily with old-fashioned lace; she came forward to meet me with her former readiness—she gave me her hand with the frank, innocent good-will of happier days. The cold fingers that trembled round mine—the pale cheeks with a bright red spot burning in the midst of them—the faint smile that struggled to live on her lips and died away from them while I looked at it, told me at what sacrifice of herself her outward composure was maintained. My heart could take her no closer to me, or I should have loved her then as I had never loved her yet.

Mr. Gilmore was a great assistance to us. He was in high good-humour, and he led the conversation with unflagging spirit. Miss Halcombe seconded him resolutely, and I did all I could to follow her example. The kind blue eyes, whose slightest changes of expression I had learnt to interpret so well, looked at me appealingly when we first sat down to table. Help my sister—the sweet anxious face seemed to say—help my sister, and you will help me.

We got through the dinner, to all outward appearance at least, happily enough. When the ladies had risen from table, and Mr. Gilmore and I were left alone in the dining-room, a new interest presented itself to occupy our attention, and to give me an opportunity of quieting myself by a few minutes of needful and welcome silence. The servant who had been despatched to trace Anne Catherick and Mrs. Clements returned with his report, and was shown into the dining-room immediately.

"Well," said Mr. Gilmore, "what have you found out?"

"I have found out, sir," answered the man, "that both the women took tickets at our station here for Carlisle."

"You went to Carlisle, of course, when you heard that?"

"I did, sir, but I am sorry to say I could find no further trace of them."

"You inquired at the railway?"

"Yes, sir."

"And at the different inns?"

"Yes, sir."

"And you left the statement I wrote for you at the police station?"

"I did, sir."

"Well, my friend, you have done all you could, and I have done all I could, and there the matter must rest till further notice. We have played our trump cards, Mr. Hartright," continued the old gentleman when the servant had withdrawn. "For the present, at least, the women have outmanoeuvred us, and our only resource now is to wait till Sir Percival Glyde comes here on Monday next. Won't you fill your glass again? Good bottle of port, that—sound, substantial, old wine. I have got better in my own cellar, though."

We returned to the drawing-room—the room in which the happiest evenings of my life had been passed—the room which, after this last night, I was never to see again. Its aspect was altered since the days had shortened and the weather had grown cold. The glass doors on the terrace side were closed, and hidden by thick curtains. Instead of the soft twilight obscurity, in which we used to sit, the bright radiant glow of lamplight now dazzled my eyes. All was changed—indoors and out all was changed.

Miss Halcombe and Mr. Gilmore sat down together at the

The Woman in White

card-table — Mrs. Vesey took her customary chair. There was no restraint on the disposal of their evening, and I felt the restraint on the disposal of mine all the more painfully from observing it. I saw Miss Fairlie lingering near the music-stand. The time had been when I might have joined her there. I waited irresolutely — I knew neither where to go nor what to do next. She cast one quick glance at me, took a piece of music suddenly from the stand, and came towards me of her own accord.

"Shall I play some of those little melodies of Mozart's which you used to like so much?" she asked, opening the music nervously, and looking down at it while she spoke.

Before I could thank her she hastened to the piano. The chair near it, which I had always been accustomed to occupy, stood empty. She struck a few chords — then glanced round at me — then looked back again at her music.

"Won't you take your old place?" she said, speaking very abruptly and in very low tones.

"I may take it on the last night," I answered.

She did not reply — she kept her attention riveted on the music — music which she knew by memory, which she had played over and over again, in former times, without the book. I only knew that she had heard me, I only knew that she was aware of my being close to her, by seeing the red spot on the cheek that was nearest to me fade out, and the face grow pale all over.

"I am very sorry you are going," she said, her voice almost sinking to a whisper, her eyes looking more and more intently at the music, her fingers flying over the keys of the piano with a strange feverish energy which I had never noticed in her before.

"I shall remember those kind words, Miss Fairlie, long after to-morrow has come and gone."

The paleness grew whiter on her face, and she turned it farther away from me.

"Don't speak of to-morrow," she said. "Let the music speak to us of to-night, in a happier language than ours."

Her lips trembled — a faint sigh fluttered from them, which she tried vainly to suppress. Her fingers wavered on the piano — she struck a false note, confused herself in trying to set it right, and dropped her hands angrily on her lap. Miss Halcombe and Mr. Gilmore looked up in astonishment from the card-table at which they were playing. Even Mrs. Vesey, dozing in her chair, woke at the sudden cessation of the music, and inquired what had happened.

"You play at whist, Mr. Hartright?" asked Miss Halcombe, with her eyes directed significantly at the place I occupied.

I knew what she meant—I knew she was right, and I rose at once to go to the card-table. As I left the piano Miss Fairlie turned a page of the music, and touched the keys again with a surer hand.

"I will play it," she said, striking the notes almost passionately. "I will play it on the last night."

"Come, Mrs. Vesey," said Miss Halcombe, "Mr. Gilmore and I are tired of ecarte—come and be Mr. Hartright's partner at whist."

The old lawyer smiled satirically. His had been the winning hand, and he had just turned up a king. He evidently attributed Miss Halcombe's abrupt change in the card-table arrangements to a lady's inability to play the losing game.

The rest of the evening passed without a word or a look from her. She kept her place at the piano, and I kept mine at the card-table. She played unintermittingly—played as if the music was her only refuge from herself. Sometimes her fingers touched the notes with a lingering fondness—a soft, plaintive, dying tenderness, unutterably beautiful and mournful to hear; sometimes they faltered and failed her, or hurried over the instrument mechanically, as if their task was a burden to them. But still, change and waver as they might in the expression they imparted to the music, their resolution to play never faltered. She only rose from the piano when we all rose to say good night.

Mrs. Vesey was the nearest to the door, and the first to shake hands with me.

"I shall not see you again, Mr. Hartright," said the old lady. "I am truly sorry you are going away. You have been very kind and attentive, and an old woman like me feels kindness and attention. I wish you happy, sir—I wish you a kind good-bye."

Mr. Gilmore came next.

"I hope we shall have a future opportunity of bettering our acquaintance, Mr. Hartright. You quite understand about that little matter of business being safe in my hands? Yes, yes, of course. Bless me, how cold it is! Don't let me keep you at the door. Bon voyage, my dear sir—bon voyage, as the French say."

Miss Halcombe followed.

"Half-past seven to-morrow morning," she said—then added in a whisper, "I have heard and seen more than you think. Your conduct to-night has made me your friend for life."

Miss Fairlie came last. I could not trust myself to look at her when I took her hand, and when I thought of the next morning.

"My departure must be a very early one," I said. "I shall be gone, Miss Fairlie, before you— —"

"No, no," she interposed hastily, "not before I am out of my room. I shall be down to breakfast with Marian. I am not so ungrateful, not so forgetful of the past three months— —"

Her voice failed her, her hand closed gently round mine—then dropped it suddenly. Before I could say "Good-night" she was gone.

The end comes fast to meet me—comes inevitably, as the light of the last morning came at Limmeridge House.

It was barely half-past seven when I went downstairs, but I found them both at the breakfast-table waiting for me. In the chill air, in the dim light, in the gloomy morning silence of the house, we three sat down together, and tried to eat, tried to talk. The struggle to preserve appearances was hopeless and useless, and I rose to end it.

As I held out my hand, as Miss Halcombe, who was nearest to me, took it, Miss Fairlie turned away suddenly and hurried from the room.

"Better so," said Miss Halcombe, when the door had closed—"better so, for you and for her."

I waited a moment before I could speak—it was hard to lose her, without a parting word or a parting look. I controlled myself—I tried to take leave of Miss Halcombe in fitting terms;

but all the farewell words I would fain have spoken dwindled to one sentence.

"Have I deserved that you should write to me?" was all I could say.

"You have nobly deserved everything that I can do for you, as long as we both live. Whatever the end is you shall know it."

"And if I can ever be of help again, at any future time, long after the memory of my presumption and my folly is forgotten . . ."

I could add no more. My voice faltered, my eyes moistened in spite of me.

She caught me by both hands — she pressed them with the strong, steady grasp of a man — her dark eyes glittered — her brown complexion flushed deep — the force and energy of her face glowed and grew beautiful with the pure inner light of her generosity and her pity.

"I will trust you — if ever the time comes I will trust you as my friend and her friend, as my brother and her brother." She stopped, drew me nearer to her — the fearless, noble creature — touched my forehead, sister-like, with her lips, and called me by my Christian name. "God bless you, Walter!" she said. "Wait here alone and compose yourself — I had better not stay for both our sakes — I had better see you go from the balcony upstairs."

She left the room. I turned away towards the window, where nothing faced me but the lonely autumn landscape — I turned away to master myself, before I too left the room in my turn, and left it for ever.

A minute passed — it could hardly have been more — when I heard the door open again softly, and the rustling of a woman's dress on the carpet moved towards me. My heart beat violently as I turned round. Miss Fairlie was approaching me from the farther end of the room.

She stopped and hesitated when our eyes met, and when she saw that we were alone. Then, with that courage which women lose so often in the small emergency, and so seldom in the great, she came on nearer to me, strangely pale and strangely quiet, drawing one hand after her along the table by which she walked, and holding something at her side in the other, which was hidden by the folds of her dress.

The Woman in White

"I only went into the drawing-room," she said, "to look for this. It may remind you of your visit here, and of the friends you leave behind you. You told me I had improved very much when I did it, and I thought you might like— —"

She turned her head away, and offered me a little sketch, drawn throughout by her own pencil, of the summer-house in which we had first met. The paper trembled in her hand as she held it out to me—trembled in mine as I took it from her.

I was afraid to say what I felt—I only answered, "It shall never leave me—all my life long it shall be the treasure that I prize most. I am very grateful for it—very grateful to you, for not letting me go away without bidding you good-bye."

"Oh!" she said innocently, "how could I let you go, after we have passed so many happy days together!"

"Those days may never return, Miss Fairlie—my way of life and yours are very far apart. But if a time should come, when the devotion of my whole heart and soul and strength will give you a moment's happiness, or spare you a moment's sorrow, will you try to remember the poor drawing-master who has taught you? Miss Halcombe has promised to trust me—will you promise too?"

The farewell sadness in the kind blue eyes shone dimly through her gathering tears.

"I promise it," she said in broken tones. "Oh, don't look at me like that! I promise it with all my heart."

I ventured a little nearer to her, and held out my hand.

"You have many friends who love you, Miss Fairlie. Your happy future is the dear object of many hopes. May I say, at parting, that it is the dear object of my hopes too?"

The tears flowed fast down her cheeks. She rested one trembling hand on the table to steady herself while she gave me the other. I took it in mine—I held it fast. My head drooped over it, my tears fell on it, my lips pressed it—not in love; oh, not in love, at that last moment, but in the agony and the self-abandonment of despair.

"For God's sake, leave me!" she said faintly.

The confession of her heart's secret burst from her in those pleading words. I had no right to hear them, no right to answer them—they were the words that banished me, in the name of her sacred weakness, from the room. It was all over. I dropped her hand, I said no more. The blinding tears shut her out from my eyes, and I dashed them away to look at her for the last time. One look as she sank into a chair, as her arms fell on the table, as her fair head dropped on them wearily. One farewell look, and the door had closed upon her—the great gulf of separation had opened between us—the image of Laura Fairlie was a memory of the past already.

The End of Hartright's Narrative.

THE STORY CONTINUED BY VINCENT GILMORE

(of Chancery Lane, Solicitor)

I

I write these lines at the request of my friend, Mr. Walter Hartright. They are intended to convey a description of certain events which seriously affected Miss Fairlie's interests, and which took place after the period of Mr. Hartright's departure from Limmeridge House.

There is no need for me to say whether my own opinion does or does not sanction the disclosure of the remarkable family story, of which my narrative forms an important component part. Mr. Hartright has taken that responsibility on himself, and circumstances yet to be related will show that he has amply earned the right to do so, if he chooses to exercise it. The plan he has adopted for presenting the story to others, in the most truthful and most vivid manner, requires that it should be told, at each successive stage in the march of events, by the persons who were directly concerned in those events at the time of their occurrence. My appearance here, as narrator, is the necessary consequence of this arrangement. I was present during the sojourn of Sir Percival Glyde in Cumberland, and was personally concerned in one important result of his short residence under Mr. Fairlie's roof. It is my duty, therefore, to add these new links to the chain of events, and to take up the chain itself at the point where, for the present only, Mr. Hartright has dropped it.

I arrived at Limmeridge House on Friday the second of November.

My object was to remain at Mr. Fairlie's until the arrival of Sir Percival Glyde. If that event led to the appointment of any given day for Sir Percival's union with Miss Fairlie, I was to take the necessary instructions back with me to London, and to occupy myself in drawing the lady's marriage-settlement.

On the Friday I was not favoured by Mr. Fairlie with an interview. He had been, or had fancied himself to be, an invalid for years past, and he was not well enough to receive me. Miss Halcombe was the first member of the family whom I saw. She met me at the house door, and introduced me to Mr. Hartright, who had been staying at Limmeridge for some time past.

I did not see Miss Fairlie until later in the day, at dinner-time. She was not looking well, and I was sorry to observe it. She is a sweet lovable girl, as amiable and attentive to every one about her as her excellent mother used to be—though, personally speaking, she takes after her father. Mrs. Fairlie had dark eyes and hair, and her elder daughter, Miss Halcombe, strongly reminds me of her. Miss Fairlie played to us in the evening—not so well as usual, I thought. We had a rubber at whist, a mere profanation, so far as play was concerned, of that noble game. I had been favourably impressed by Mr. Hartright on our first introduction to one another, but I soon discovered that he was not free from the social failings incidental to his age. There are three things that none of the young men of the present generation can do. They can't sit over their wine, they can't play at whist, and they can't pay a lady a compliment. Mr. Hartright was no exception to the general rule. Otherwise, even in those early days and on that short acquaintance, he struck me as being a modest and gentlemanlike young man.

So the Friday passed. I say nothing about the more serious matters which engaged my attention on that day—the anonymous letter to Miss Fairlie, the measures I thought it right to adopt when the matter was mentioned to me, and the conviction I entertained that every possible explanation of the circumstances would be readily afforded by Sir Percival Glyde, having all been fully noticed, as I understand, in the narrative which precedes this.

On the Saturday Mr. Hartright had left before I got down to breakfast. Miss Fairlie kept her room all day, and Miss Halcombe appeared to me to be out of spirits. The house was not what it used to be in the time of Mr. and Mrs. Philip Fairlie. I took a walk by myself in the forenoon, and looked about at some of the places which I first saw when I was staying at Limmeridge to transact family business, more than thirty years since. They were not what they used to be either.

At two o'clock Mr. Fairlie sent to say he was well enough to see me. He had not altered, at any rate, since I first knew him. His talk was to the same purpose as usual—all about himself and his ailments, his wonderful coins, and his matchless Rembrandt etchings. The moment I tried to speak of the business that had brought me to his house, he shut his eyes and said I "upset" him. I persisted in upsetting him by returning again and again to the subject. All I could ascertain was that he looked on his niece's marriage as a settled thing, that her father had sanctioned it, that he sanctioned it himself, that it was a desirable marriage, and that he should be personally rejoiced when the worry of it was over. As to the settlements, if I would consult his niece, and afterwards dive as deeply as I pleased into my own knowledge of the family affairs, and get everything ready, and limit his share in the business, as guardian, to saying Yes, at the right moment—why, of course he would meet my views, and everybody else's views, with infinite pleasure. In the meantime, there I saw him, a helpless sufferer, confined to his room. Did I think he looked as if he wanted teasing? No. Then why tease him?

I might, perhaps, have been a little astonished at this extraordinary absence of all self-assertion on Mr. Fairlie's part, in the character of guardian, if my knowledge of the family affairs had not been sufficient to remind me that he was a single man, and that he had nothing more than a life-interest in the Limmeridge property. As matters stood, therefore, I was neither surprised nor disappointed at the result of the interview. Mr. Fairlie had simply justified my expectations—and there was an end of it.

Sunday was a dull day, out of doors and in. A letter arrived for me from Sir Percival Glyde's solicitor, acknowledging the receipt of my copy of the anonymous letter and my accompanying statement of the case. Miss Fairlie joined us in the afternoon, looking pale and depressed, and altogether unlike herself. I had some talk with her, and ventured on a delicate allusion to Sir Percival. She listened and said nothing. All other subjects she pursued willingly, but this subject she allowed to drop. I began to doubt whether she might not be repenting of her engagement—just as young ladies often do, when repentance comes too late.

On Monday Sir Percival Glyde arrived.

I found him to be a most prepossessing man, so far as manners and appearance were concerned. He looked rather older than I had expected, his head being bald over the forehead, and his face somewhat marked and worn, but his movements were as active and his spirits as high as a young man's. His meeting with Miss Halcombe was delightfully hearty and unaffected, and his reception of me, upon my being presented to him, was so easy and pleasant that we got on together like old friends. Miss Fairlie was not with us when he arrived, but she entered the room about ten minutes afterwards. Sir Percival rose and paid his compliments with perfect grace. His evident concern on seeing the change for the worse in the young lady's looks was expressed with a mixture of tenderness and respect, with an unassuming delicacy of tone, voice, and manner, which did equal credit to his good breeding and his good sense. I was rather surprised, under these circumstances, to see that Miss Fairlie continued to be constrained and uneasy in his presence, and that she took the first opportunity of leaving the room again. Sir Percival neither noticed the restraint in her reception of him, nor her sudden withdrawal from our society. He had not obtruded his attentions on her while she was present, and he did not embarrass Miss Halcombe by any allusion to her departure when she was gone. His tact and taste were never at fault on this or on any other occasion while I was in his company at Limmeridge House.

As soon as Miss Fairlie had left the room he spared us all embarrassment on the subject of the anonymous letter, by adverting to it of his own accord. He had stopped in London on his way from Hampshire, had seen his solicitor, had read the documents forwarded by me, and had travelled on to Cumberland, anxious to satisfy our minds by the speediest and the fullest explanation that words could convey. On hearing him express himself to this effect, I offered him the original letter, which I had kept for his inspection. He thanked me, and declined to look at it, saying that he had seen the copy, and that he was quite willing to leave the original in our hands.

The statement itself, on which he immediately entered, was as simple and satisfactory as I had all along anticipated it would be.

Mrs. Catherick, he informed us, had in past years laid him under some obligations for faithful services rendered to his family connections and to himself. She had been doubly unfortunate in being married to a husband who had deserted her, and in having an only child whose mental faculties had been in a disturbed condition from a very early age. Although her marriage had removed her to a part of Hampshire far distant from the neighbourhood in which Sir Percival's property was situated, he had taken care not to lose sight of her — his friendly feeling towards the poor woman, in consideration of her past services, having been greatly strengthened by his admiration of the patience and courage with which she supported her calamities. In course of time the symptoms of mental affliction in her unhappy daughter increased to such a serious extent, as to make it a matter of necessity to place her under proper medical care. Mrs. Catherick herself recognised this necessity, but she also felt the prejudice common to persons occupying her respectable station, against allowing her child to be admitted, as a pauper, into a public Asylum. Sir Percival had respected this prejudice, as he respected honest independence of feeling in any rank of life, and had resolved to mark his grateful sense of Mrs. Catherick's early attachment to the interests of himself and his family, by defraying the expense of her daughter's maintenance in a trustworthy private Asylum. To her mother's regret, and to his own regret, the unfortunate creature had discovered the share which circumstances had induced him to take in placing her under restraint, and had conceived the most intense hatred and distrust of him in consequence. To that hatred and distrust—which had expressed itself in various ways in the Asylum—the anonymous letter, written after her escape, was plainly attributable. If Miss Halcombe's or Mr. Gilmore's recollection of the document did not confirm that view, or if they wished for any additional particulars about the Asylum (the address of which he mentioned, as well as the names and addresses of the two doctors on whose certificates the patient was admitted), he was ready to answer any question and to clear up any uncertainty. He had done his duty to the unhappy young woman, by instructing his solicitor to spare no expense in tracing her, and in restoring her once more to medical care, and he was now only anxious to do his duty towards Miss Fairlie and towards her family, in the same plain, straightforward way.

I was the first to speak in answer to this appeal. My own course was plain to me. It is the great beauty of the Law that it can dispute any human statement, made under any circumstances, and reduced to any form. If I had felt professionally called upon to set up a case against Sir Percival Glyde, on the strength of his own explanation, I could have done so beyond all doubt. But my duty did not lie in this direction—my function was of the purely judicial kind. I was to weigh the explanation we had just heard, to allow all due force to the high reputation of the gentleman who offered it, and to decide honestly whether the probabilities, on Sir Percival's own showing, were plainly with him, or plainly against him. My own conviction was that they were plainly with him, and I accordingly declared that his explanation was, to my mind, unquestionably a satisfactory one.

Miss Halcombe, after looking at me very earnestly, said a few words, on her side, to the same effect—with a certain hesitation of manner, however, which the circumstances did not seem to me to warrant. I am unable to say, positively, whether

Sir Percival noticed this or not. My opinion is that he did, seeing that he pointedly resumed the subject, although he might now, with all propriety, have allowed it to drop.

"If my plain statement of facts had only been addressed to Mr. Gilmore," he said, "I should consider any further reference to this unhappy matter as unnecessary. I may fairly expect Mr. Gilmore, as a gentleman, to believe me on my word, and when he has done me that justice, all discussion of the subject between us has come to an end. But my position with a lady is not the same. I owe to her—what I would concede to no man alive—a proof of the truth of my assertion. You cannot ask for that proof, Miss Halcombe, and it is therefore my duty to you, and still more to Miss Fairlie, to offer it. May I beg that you will write at once to the mother of this unfortunate woman—to Mrs. Catherick—to ask for her testimony in support of the explanation which I have just offered to you."

I saw Miss Halcombe change colour, and look a little uneasy. Sir Percival's suggestion, politely as it was expressed, appeared to her, as it appeared to me, to point very delicately at the hesitation which her manner had betrayed a moment or two since.

"I hope, Sir Percival, you don't do me the injustice to suppose that I distrust you," she said quickly.

"Certainly not, Miss Halcombe. I make my proposal purely as an act of attention to you. Will you excuse my obstinacy if I still venture to press it?"

He walked to the writing-table as he spoke, drew a chair to it, and opened the paper case.

"Let me beg you to write the note," he said, "as a favour to me. It need not occupy you more than a few minutes. You have only to ask Mrs. Catherick two questions. First, if her daughter was placed in the Asylum with her knowledge and approval. Secondly, if the share I took in the matter was such as to merit the expression of her gratitude towards myself? Mr. Gilmore's mind is at ease on this unpleasant subject, and your mind is at ease—pray set my mind at ease also by writing the note."

"You oblige me to grant your request, Sir Percival, when I would much rather refuse it."

With those words Miss Halcombe rose from her place and went to the writing-table. Sir Percival thanked her, handed her a pen, and then walked away towards the fireplace. Miss Fairlie's little Italian greyhound was lying on the rug. He held out his hand, and called to the dog good-humouredly.

"Come, Nina," he said, "we remember each other, don't we?"

The little beast, cowardly and cross-grained, as pet-dogs usually are, looked up at him sharply, shrank away from his outstretched hand, whined, shivered, and hid itself under a sofa. It was scarcely possible that he could have been put out by such a trifle as a dog's reception of him, but I observed, nevertheless, that he walked away towards the window very suddenly. Perhaps his temper is irritable at times. If so, I can sympathise with him. My temper is irritable at times too.

Miss Halcombe was not long in writing the note. When it was done she rose from the writing-table, and handed the open sheet of paper to Sir Percival. He bowed, took it from her, folded it up immediately without looking at the contents, sealed it, wrote the address, and handed it back to her in silence. I never saw anything more gracefully and more becomingly done in my life.

"You insist on my posting this letter, Sir Percival?" said Miss Halcombe.

"I beg you will post it," he answered. "And now that it is written and sealed up, allow me to ask one or two last questions about the unhappy woman to whom it refers. I have read the communication which Mr. Gilmore kindly addressed to my solicitor, describing the circumstances under which the writer of the anonymous letter was identified. But there are certain points to which that statement does not refer. Did Anne Catherick see Miss Fairlie?"

"Certainly not," replied Miss Halcombe.

"Did she see you?"

"No."

"She saw nobody from the house then, except a certain Mr. Hartright, who accidentally met with her in the churchyard here?"

"Nobody else."

"Mr. Hartright was employed at Limmeridge as a drawing-master, I believe? Is he a member of one of the Water-Colour Societies?"

"I believe he is," answered Miss Halcombe.

He paused for a moment, as if he was thinking over the last answer, and then added —

"Did you find out where Anne Catherick was living, when she was in this neighbourhood?"

"Yes. At a farm on the moor, called Todd's Corner."

"It is a duty we all owe to the poor creature herself to trace her," continued Sir Percival. "She may have said something at Todd's Corner which may help us to find her. I will go there and make inquiries on the chance. In the meantime, as I cannot prevail on myself to discuss this painful subject with Miss Fairlie, may I beg, Miss Halcombe, that you will kindly undertake to give her the necessary explanation, deferring it of course until you have received the reply to that note."

Miss Halcombe promised to comply with his request. He thanked her, nodded pleasantly, and left us, to go and establish himself in his own room. As he opened the door the cross-grained greyhound poked out her sharp muzzle from under the sofa, and barked and snapped at him.

"A good morning's work, Miss Halcombe," I said, as soon as we were alone. "Here is an anxious day well ended already."

"Yes," she answered; "no doubt. I am very glad your mind is satisfied."

"My mind! Surely, with that note in your hand, your mind is at ease too?"

"Oh yes — how can it be otherwise? I know the thing could not be," she went on, speaking more to herself than to me; "but I almost wish Walter Hartright had stayed here long enough to be present at the explanation, and to hear the proposal to me to write this note."

I was a little surprised — perhaps a little piqued also — by these last words.

"Events, it is true, connected Mr. Hartright very remarkably with the affair of the letter," I said; "and I readily admit that he conducted himself, all things considered, with great delicacy and discretion. But I am quite at a loss to understand what useful influence his presence could have exercised in relation to the effect of Sir Percival's statement on your mind or mine."

"It was only a fancy," she said absently. "There is no need to discuss it, Mr. Gilmore. Your experience ought to be, and is, the best guide I can desire."

I did not altogether like her thrusting the whole responsibility, in this marked manner, on my shoulders. If Mr. Fairlie had done it, I should not have been surprised. But resolute, clear-minded Miss Halcombe was the very last person in the world whom I should have expected to find shrinking from the expression of an opinion of her own.

"If any doubts still trouble you," I said, "why not mention them to me at once? Tell me plainly, have you any reason to distrust Sir Percival Glyde?"

"None whatever."

"Do you see anything improbable, or contradictory, in his explanation?"

"How can I say I do, after the proof he has offered me of the truth of it? Can there be better testimony in his favour, Mr. Gilmore, than the testimony of the woman's mother?"

"None better. If the answer to your note of inquiry proves to be satisfactory, I for one cannot see what more any friend of Sir Percival's can possibly expect from him."

"Then we will post the note," she said, rising to leave the room, "and dismiss all further reference to the subject until the answer arrives. Don't attach any weight to my hesitation. I can give no better reason for it than that I have been over-anxious about Laura lately—and anxiety, Mr. Gilmore, unsettles the strongest of us."

She left me abruptly, her naturally firm voice faltering as she spoke those last words. A sensitive, vehement, passionate nature—a woman of ten thousand in these trivial, superficial times. I had known her from her earliest years—I had seen her tested, as she grew up, in more than one trying family crisis, and my long experience made me attach an importance to her hesitation under the circumstances here detailed, which I should certainly not have felt in the case of another woman. I could see no cause for any uneasiness or any doubt, but she had made me a little uneasy, and a little doubtful, nevertheless. In my youth, I should have chafed and fretted under the irritation of my own unreasonable state of mind. In my age, I knew better, and went out philosophically to walk it off.

II

We all met again at dinner-time.

Sir Percival was in such boisterous high spirits that I hardly recognised him as the same man whose quiet tact, refinement, and good sense had impressed me so strongly at the interview of the morning. The only trace of his former self that I could detect reappeared, every now and then, in his manner towards Miss Fairlie. A look or a word from her suspended his loudest laugh, checked his gayest flow of talk, and rendered him all attention to her, and to no one else at table, in an instant. Although he never openly tried to draw her into the conversation, he never lost the slightest chance she gave him of letting her drift into it by accident, and of saying the words to her, under those favourable circumstances, which a man with less tact and delicacy would have pointedly addressed to her the moment they occurred to him. Rather to my surprise, Miss Fairlie appeared to be sensible of his attentions without being moved by them. She was a little confused from time to time when he looked at her, or spoke to her; but she never warmed towards him. Rank, fortune, good breeding, good looks, the respect of a gentleman, and the devotion of a lover were all humbly placed at her feet, and, so far as appearances went, were all offered in vain.

On the next day, the Tuesday, Sir Percival went in the morning (taking one of the servants with him as a guide) to Todd's Corner. His inquiries, as I afterwards heard, led to no results. On his return he had an interview with Mr. Fairlie, and in the afternoon he and Miss Halcombe rode out together. Nothing else happened worthy of record. The evening passed as usual. There was no change in Sir Percival, and no change in Miss Fairlie.

The Wednesday's post brought with it an event—the reply from Mrs. Catherick. I took a copy of the document, which I have preserved, and which I may as well present in this place. It ran as follows—

"MADAM,—I beg to acknowledge the receipt of your letter, inquiring whether my daughter, Anne, was placed under medical superintendence with my knowledge and approval, and whether the share taken in the matter by Sir Percival Glyde was such as to merit the expression of my gratitude towards that gentleman. Be pleased to accept my answer in the affirmative to both those questions, and believe me to remain, your obedient servant,

"JANE ANNE CATHERICK."

Short, sharp, and to the point; in form rather a business-like letter for a woman to write—in substance as plain a confirmation as could be desired of Sir Percival Glyde's statement. This was my opinion, and with certain minor reservations, Miss Halcombe's opinion also. Sir Percival, when the letter was shown to him, did not appear to be struck by the sharp, short tone of it. He told us that Mrs. Catherick was a woman of few words, a clear-headed, straightforward, unimaginative person, who wrote briefly and plainly, just as she spoke.

The next duty to be accomplished, now that the answer had been received, was to acquaint Miss Fairlie with Sir Percival's explanation. Miss Halcombe had undertaken to do this, and had left the room to go to her sister, when she suddenly returned again, and sat down by the easy-chair in which I was reading the newspaper. Sir Percival had gone out a minute before to look at the stables, and no one was in the room but ourselves.

"I suppose we have really and truly done all we can?" she said, turning and twisting Mrs. Catherick's letter in her hand.

"If we are friends of Sir Percival's, who know him and trust him, we have done all, and more than all, that is necessary," I answered, a little annoyed by this return of her hesitation. "But if we are enemies who suspect him——"

"That alternative is not even to be thought of," she interposed. "We are Sir Percival's friends, and if generosity and forbearance can add to our regard for him, we ought to be Sir Percival's admirers as well. You know that he saw Mr. Fairlie yesterday, and that he afterwards went out with me."

"Yes. I saw you riding away together."

"We began the ride by talking about Anne Catherick, and about the singular manner in which Mr. Hartright met with her. But we soon dropped that subject, and Sir Percival spoke next, in the most unselfish terms, of his engagement with Laura. He said he had observed that she was out of spirits, and he was willing, if not informed to the contrary, to attribute to that cause the alteration in her manner towards him during his present visit. If, however, there was any more serious reason for the change, he would entreat that no constraint might be placed on her inclinations either by Mr. Fairlie or by me. All he asked, in that case, was that she would recall to mind, for the last time, what the circumstances were under which the engagement between them was made, and what his conduct had been from the beginning of the courtship to the present time. If, after due reflection on those two subjects, she seriously desired that he should withdraw his pretensions to the honour of becoming her husband—and if she would tell him so plainly with her own lips—he would sacrifice himself by leaving her perfectly free to withdraw from the engagement."

"No man could say more than that, Miss Halcombe. As to my experience, few men in his situation would have said as much."

She paused after I had spoken those words, and looked at me with a singular expression of perplexity and distress.

"I accuse nobody, and I suspect nothing," she broke out abruptly. "But I cannot and will not accept the responsibility of persuading Laura to this marriage."

"That is exactly the course which Sir Percival Glyde has himself requested you to take," I replied in astonishment. "He has begged you not to force her inclinations."

"And he indirectly obliges me to force them, if I give her his message."

"How can that possibly be?"

"Consult your own knowledge of Laura, Mr. Gilmore. If I tell her to reflect on the circumstances of her engagement, I at once appeal to two of the strongest feelings in her nature—to her love for her father's memory, and to her strict regard for truth. You know that she never broke a promise in her life—you know that she entered on this engagement at the beginning of her father's fatal illness, and that he spoke hopefully and happily of her marriage to Sir Percival Glyde on his deathbed."

I own that I was a little shocked at this view of the case.

"Surely," I said, "you don't mean to infer that when Sir Percival spoke to you yesterday he speculated on such a result as you have just mentioned?"

Her frank, fearless face answered for her before she spoke.

"Do you think I would remain an instant in the company of any man whom I suspected of such baseness as that?" she asked angrily.

I liked to feel her hearty indignation flash out on me in that way. We see so much malice and so little indignation in my profession.

"In that case," I said, "excuse me if I tell you, in our legal phrase, that you are travelling out of the record. Whatever the consequences may be, Sir Percival has a right to expect that your sister should carefully consider her engagement from every reasonable point of view before she claims her release from it. If that unlucky letter has prejudiced her against him, go at once, and tell her that he has cleared himself in your eyes and in mine. What objection can she urge against him after that? What excuse can she possibly have for changing her mind about a man whom she had virtually accepted for her husband more than two years ago?"

"In the eyes of law and reason, Mr. Gilmore, no excuse, I daresay. If she still hesitates, and if I still hesitate, you must attribute our strange conduct, if you like, to caprice in both cases, and we must bear the imputation as well as we can."

With those words she suddenly rose and left me. When a sensible woman has a serious question put to her, and evades it by a flippant answer, it is a sure sign, in ninety-nine cases out of a hundred, that she has something to conceal. I returned to the perusal of the newspaper, strongly suspecting that Miss Halcombe and Miss Fairlie had a secret between them which they were keeping from Sir Percival, and keeping from me. I thought this hard on both of us, especially on Sir Percival.

My doubts—or to speak more correctly, my convictions—were confirmed by Miss Halcombe's language and manner when I saw her again later in the day. She was suspiciously brief and reserved in telling me the result of her interview with her sister. Miss Fairlie, it appeared, had listened quietly while the affair of the letter was placed before her in the right point of view, but when Miss Halcombe next proceeded to say that the object of Sir Percival's visit at Limmeridge was to prevail on her to let a day be fixed for the marriage she checked all further reference to the subject by begging for time. If Sir Percival would consent to spare her for the present, she would undertake to give him his final answer before the end of the year. She pleaded for this delay with such anxiety and agitation, that Miss Halcombe had promised to use her influence, if necessary, to obtain it, and there, at Miss Fairlie's earnest entreaty, all further discussion of the marriage question had ended.

The purely temporary arrangement thus proposed might have been convenient enough to the young lady, but it proved somewhat embarrassing to the writer of these lines. That morning's post had brought a letter from my partner, which obliged me to return to town the next day by the afternoon train. It was extremely probable that I should find no second opportunity of presenting myself at Limmeridge House during the remainder of the year. In that case, supposing Miss Fairlie ultimately decided on holding to her engagement, my necessary personal communication with her, before I drew her settlement, would become something like a downright impossibility, and we should be obliged to commit to writing questions which ought always to be discussed on both sides by word of mouth. I said nothing about this difficulty until Sir Percival had been consulted on the subject of the desired delay. He was too gallant a gentleman not to grant the request immediately. When Miss Halcombe informed me of this I told her that I must absolutely speak to her sister before I left Limmeridge, and it was, therefore, arranged that I should see Miss Fairlie in her own sitting-room the next morning. She did not come down to dinner, or join us in the evening. Indisposition was the excuse, and I thought Sir Percival looked, as well he might, a little annoyed when he heard of it.

The next morning, as soon as breakfast was over, I went up to Miss Fairlie's sitting-room. The poor girl looked so pale and sad, and came forward to welcome me so readily and prettily, that the resolution to lecture her on her caprice and indecision, which I had been forming all the way upstairs, failed me on the spot. I led her back to the chair from which she had risen, and placed myself opposite to her. Her cross-grained pet greyhound was in the room, and I fully expected a barking and snapping reception. Strange to say, the whimsical little brute falsified my expectations by jumping into my lap and poking its sharp muzzle familiarly into my hand the moment I sat down.

"You used often to sit on my knee when you were a child, my dear," I said, "and now your little dog seems determined to succeed you in the vacant throne. Is that pretty drawing your doing?"

I pointed to a little album which lay on the table by her side and which she had evidently been looking over when I came in. The page that lay open had a small water-colour landscape very neatly mounted on it. This was the drawing which had suggested my question — an idle question enough — but how could I begin to talk of business to her the moment I opened my lips?

"No," she said, looking away from the drawing rather confusedly, "it is not my doing."

Her fingers had a restless habit, which I remembered in her as a child, of always playing with the first thing that came to hand whenever any one was talking to her. On this occasion they wandered to the album, and toyed absently about the margin of the little water-colour drawing. The expression of melancholy deepened on her face. She did not look at the drawing, or look at me. Her eyes moved uneasily from object to object in the room, betraying plainly that she suspected what my purpose was in coming to speak to her. Seeing that, I thought it best to get to the purpose with as little delay as possible.

"One of the errands, my dear, which brings me here is to bid you good-bye," I began. "I must get back to London to-day: and, before I leave, I want to have a word with you on the subject of your own affairs."

"I am very sorry you are going, Mr. Gilmore," she said, looking at me kindly. "It is like the happy old times to have you here."

"I hope I may be able to come back and recall those pleasant memories once more," I continued; "but as there is some uncertainty about the future, I must take my opportunity when I can get it, and speak to you now. I am your old lawyer and your old friend, and I may remind you, I am sure, without offence, of the possibility of your marrying Sir Percival Glyde."

She took her hand off the little album as suddenly as if it had turned hot and burnt her. Her fingers twined together nervously in her lap, her eyes looked down again at the floor, and an expression of constraint settled on her face which looked almost like an expression of pain.

"Is it absolutely necessary to speak of my marriage engagement?" she asked in low tones.

"It is necessary to refer to it," I answered, "but not to dwell on it. Let us merely say that you may marry, or that you may not marry. In the first case, I must be prepared, beforehand, to

The Woman in White

draw your settlement, and I ought not to do that without, as a matter of politeness, first consulting you. This may be my only chance of hearing what your wishes are. Let us, therefore, suppose the case of your marrying, and let me inform you, in as few words as possible, what your position is now, and what you may make it, if you please, in the future."

I explained to her the object of a marriage-settlement, and then told her exactly what her prospects were—in the first place, on her coming of age, and in the second place, on the decease of her uncle—marking the distinction between the property in which she had a life-interest only, and the property which was left at her own control. She listened attentively, with the constrained expression still on her face, and her hands still nervously clasped together in her lap.

"And now," I said in conclusion, "tell me if you can think of any condition which, in the case we have supposed, you would wish me to make for you—subject, of course, to your guardian's approval, as you are not yet of age."

She moved uneasily in her chair, then looked in my face on a sudden very earnestly.

"If it does happen," she began faintly, "if I am——"

"If you are married," I added, helping her out.

"Don't let him part me from Marian," she cried, with a sudden outbreak of energy. "Oh, Mr. Gilmore, pray make it law that Marian is to live with me!"

Under other circumstances I might, perhaps, have been amused at this essentially feminine interpretation of my question, and of the long explanation which had preceded it. But her looks and tones, when she spoke, were of a kind to make me more than serious—they distressed me. Her words, few as they were, betrayed a desperate clinging to the past which boded ill for the future.

"Your having Marian Halcombe to live with you can easily be settled by private arrangement," I said. "You hardly understood my question, I think. It referred to your own property—to the disposal of your money. Supposing you were to make a will when you come of age, who would you like the money to go to?"

"Marian has been mother and sister both to me," said the

good, affectionate girl, her pretty blue eyes glistening while she spoke. "May I leave it to Marian, Mr. Gilmore?"

"Certainly, my love," I answered. "But remember what a large sum it is. Would you like it all to go to Miss Halcombe?"

She hesitated; her colour came and went, and her hand stole back again to the little album.

"Not all of it," she said. "There is some one else besides Marian — —"

She stopped; her colour heightened, and the fingers of the hand that rested upon the album beat gently on the margin of the drawing, as if her memory had set them going mechanically with the remembrance of a favourite tune.

"You mean some other member of the family besides Miss Halcombe?" I suggested, seeing her at a loss to proceed.

The heightening colour spread to her forehead and her neck, and the nervous fingers suddenly clasped themselves fast round the edge of the book.

"There is some one else," she said, not noticing my last words, though she had evidently heard them; "there is some one else who might like a little keepsake if — if I might leave it. There would be no harm if I should die first — —"

She paused again. The colour that had spread over her cheeks suddenly, as suddenly left them. The hand on the album resigned its hold, trembled a little, and moved the book away from her. She looked at me for an instant — then turned her head aside in the chair. Her handkerchief fell to the floor as she changed her position, and she hurriedly hid her face from me in her hands.

Sad! To remember her, as I did, the liveliest, happiest child that ever laughed the day through, and to see her now, in the flower of her age and her beauty, so broken and so brought down as this!

In the distress that she caused me I forgot the years that had passed, and the change they had made in our position towards one another. I moved my chair close to her, and picked up her handkerchief from the carpet, and drew her hands from her face gently. "Don't cry, my love," I said, and dried the tears that were gathering in her eyes with my own hand, as if she had been the little Laura Fairlie of ten long years ago.

It was the best way I could have taken to compose her. She laid her head on my shoulder, and smiled faintly through her tears.

"I am very sorry for forgetting myself," she said artlessly. "I have not been well—I have felt sadly weak and nervous lately, and I often cry without reason when I am alone. I am better now—I can answer you as I ought, Mr. Gilmore, I can indeed."

"No, no, my dear," I replied, "we will consider the subject as done with for the present. You have said enough to sanction my taking the best possible care of your interests, and we can settle details at another opportunity. Let us have done with business now, and talk of something else."

I led her at once into speaking on other topics. In ten minutes' time she was in better spirits, and I rose to take my leave.

"Come here again," she said earnestly. "I will try to be worthier of your kind feeling for me and for my interests if you will only come again."

Still clinging to the past—that past which I represented to her, in my way, as Miss Halcombe did in hers! It troubled me sorely to see her looking back, at the beginning of her career, just as I look back at the end of mine.

"If I do come again, I hope I shall find you better," I said; "better and happier. God bless you, my dear!"

She only answered by putting up her cheek to me to be kissed. Even lawyers have hearts, and mine ached a little as I took leave of her.

The whole interview between us had hardly lasted more than half an hour—she had not breathed a word, in my presence, to explain the mystery of her evident distress and dismay at the prospect of her marriage, and yet she had contrived to win me over to her side of the question, I neither knew how nor why. I had entered the room, feeling that Sir Percival Glyde had fair reason to complain of the manner in which she was treating him. I left it, secretly hoping that matters might end in her taking him at his word and claiming her release. A man of my age and experience ought to have known better than to vacillate in this unreasonable manner. I can make no excuse for myself; I can only tell the truth, and say—so it was.

The hour for my departure was now drawing near. I sent to Mr. Fairlie to say that I would wait on him to take leave if he liked, but that he must excuse my being rather in a hurry. He sent a message back, written in pencil on a slip of paper: "Kind love and best wishes, dear Gilmore. Hurry of any kind is inexpressibly injurious to me. Pray take care of yourself. Good-bye."

Just before I left I saw Miss Halcombe for a moment alone.

"Have you said all you wanted to Laura?" she asked.

"Yes," I replied. "She is very weak and nervous—I am glad she has you to take care of her."

Miss Halcombe's sharp eyes studied my face attentively.

"You are altering your opinion about Laura," she said. "You are readier to make allowances for her than you were yesterday."

No sensible man ever engages, unprepared, in a fencing match of words with a woman. I only answered—

"Let me know what happens. I will do nothing till I hear from you."

She still looked hard in my face. "I wish it was all over, and well over, Mr. Gilmore—and so do you." With those words she left me.

Sir Percival most politely insisted on seeing me to the carriage door.

"If you are ever in my neighbourhood," he said, "pray don't forget that I am sincerely anxious to improve our acquaintance. The tried and trusted old friend of this family will be always a welcome visitor in any house of mine."

A really irresistible man—courteous, considerate, delightfully free from pride—a gentleman, every inch of him. As I drove away to the station I felt as if I could cheerfully do anything to promote the interests of Sir Percival Glyde—anything in the world, except drawing the marriage settlement of his wife.

III

A week passed, after my return to London, without the receipt of any communication from Miss Halcombe.

On the eighth day a letter in her handwriting was placed among the other letters on my table.

It announced that Sir Percival Glyde had been definitely accepted, and that the marriage was to take place, as he had originally desired, before the end of the year. In all probability the ceremony would be performed during the last fortnight in December. Miss Fairlie's twenty-first birthday was late in March. She would, therefore, by this arrangement, become Sir Percival's wife about three months before she was of age.

I ought not to have been surprised, I ought not to have been sorry, but I was surprised and sorry, nevertheless. Some little disappointment, caused by the unsatisfactory shortness of Miss Halcombe's letter, mingled itself with these feelings, and contributed its share towards upsetting my serenity for the day. In six lines my correspondent announced the proposed marriage — in three more, she told me that Sir Percival had left Cumberland to return to his house in Hampshire, and in two concluding sentences she informed me, first, that Laura was sadly in want of change and cheerful society; secondly, that she had resolved to try the effect of some such change forthwith, by taking her sister away with her on a visit to certain old friends in Yorkshire. There the letter ended, without a word to explain what the circumstances were which had decided Miss Fairlie to accept Sir Percival Glyde in one short week from the time when I had last seen her.

At a later period the cause of this sudden determination was fully explained to me. It is not my business to relate it imperfectly, on hearsay evidence. The circumstances came within the personal experience of Miss Halcombe, and when her narrative succeeds mine, she will describe them in every particular exactly as they happened. In the meantime, the plain duty for me to perform — before I, in my turn, lay down my pen and withdraw from the story — is to relate the one remaining event connected with Miss Fairlie's proposed marriage in which I was concerned, namely, the drawing of the settlement.

It is impossible to refer intelligibly to this document without first entering into certain particulars in relation to the bride's pecuniary affairs. I will try to make my explanation briefly and plainly, and to keep it free from professional obscurities and technicalities. The matter is of the utmost importance. I warn all readers of these lines that Miss Fairlie's inheritance is a very serious part of Miss Fairlie's story, and that Mr. Gilmore's experience, in this particular, must be their experience also, if they wish to understand the narratives which are yet to come.

Miss Fairlie's expectations, then, were of a twofold kind, comprising her possible inheritance of real property, or land, when her uncle died, and her absolute inheritance of personal property, or money, when she came of age.

Let us take the land first.

In the time of Miss Fairlie's paternal grandfather (whom we will call Mr. Fairlie, the elder) the entailed succession to the Limmeridge estate stood thus—

Mr. Fairlie, the elder, died and left three sons, Philip, Frederick, and Arthur. As eldest son, Philip succeeded to the estate. If he died without leaving a son, the property went to the second brother, Frederick; and if Frederick died also without leaving a son, the property went to the third brother, Arthur.

As events turned out, Mr. Philip Fairlie died leaving an only daughter, the Laura of this story, and the estate, in consequence, went, in course of law, to the second brother, Frederick, a single man. The third brother, Arthur, had died many years before the decease of Philip, leaving a son and a daughter. The son, at the age of eighteen, was drowned at Oxford. His death left Laura, the daughter of Mr. Philip Fairlie, presumptive heiress to the estate, with every chance of succeeding to it, in the ordinary course of nature, on her uncle Frederick's death, if the said Frederick died without leaving male issue.

Except in the event, then, of Mr. Frederick Fairlie's marrying and leaving an heir (the two very last things in the world that he was likely to do), his niece, Laura, would have the property on his death, possessing, it must be remembered, nothing more than a life-interest in it. If she died single, or died childless, the estate would revert to her cousin, Magdalen, the daughter of Mr. Arthur Fairlie. If she married, with a proper settlement—or, in other words, with the settlement I meant to make for her— the income from the estate (a good three thousand a year) would, during her lifetime, be at her own disposal. If she died before her husband, he would naturally expect to be left in the enjoyment of the income, for his lifetime. If she had a son, that son would be the heir, to the exclusion of her cousin Magdalen. Thus, Sir Percival's prospects in marrying Miss Fairlie (so far as his wife's expectations from real property were concerned) promised him these two advantages, on Mr. Frederick Fairlie's death: First, the use of three thousand a year (by his wife's permission, while she lived, and in his own right, on her death, if he survived her); and, secondly, the inheritance of Limmeridge for his son, if he had one.

So much for the landed property, and for the disposal of the income from it, on the occasion of Miss Fairlie's marriage. Thus far, no difficulty or difference of opinion on the lady's settlement was at all likely to arise between Sir Percival's lawyer and myself.

The personal estate, or, in other words, the money to which Miss Fairlie would become entitled on reaching the age of twenty-one years, is the next point to consider.

This part of her inheritance was, in itself, a comfortable little fortune. It was derived under her father's will, and it amounted to the sum of twenty thousand pounds. Besides this, she had a life-interest in ten thousand pounds more, which latter amount was to go, on her decease, to her aunt Eleanor, her father's only sister. It will greatly assist in setting the family affairs before the reader in the clearest possible light, if I stop here for a moment, to explain why the aunt had been kept waiting for her legacy until the death of the niece.

Mr. Philip Fairlie had lived on excellent terms with his sister Eleanor, as long as she remained a single woman. But when her marriage took place, somewhat late in life, and when that marriage united her to an Italian gentleman named Fosco, or, rather, to an Italian nobleman—seeing that he rejoiced in the title of Count—Mr. Fairlie disapproved of her conduct so strongly that he ceased to hold any communication with her, and even went the length of striking her name out of his will. The other members of the family all thought this serious manifestation of resentment at his sister's marriage more or less unreasonable. Count Fosco, though not a rich man, was not a penniless adventurer either. He had a small but sufficient income of his own. He had lived many years in England, and he held an excellent position in society. These recommendations, however, availed nothing with Mr. Fairlie. In many of his opinions he was an Englishman of the old school, and he hated a foreigner simply and solely because he was a foreigner. The utmost that he could be prevailed on to do, in after years— mainly at Miss Fairlie's intercession—was to restore his sister's name to its former place in his will, but to keep her waiting for her legacy by giving the income of the money to his daughter for life, and the money itself, if her aunt died before her, to her cousin Magdalen. Considering the relative ages of the two ladies, the aunt's chance, in the ordinary course of nature, of receiving the ten thousand pounds, was thus rendered doubtful in the extreme; and Madame Fosco resented her brother's treatment of her as unjustly as usual in such cases, by refusing to see her niece, and declining to believe that Miss Fairlie's intercession had ever been exerted to restore her name to Mr. Fairlie's will.

Such was the history of the ten thousand pounds. Here again no difficulty could arise with Sir Percival's legal adviser. The income would be at the wife's disposal, and the principal would go to her aunt or her cousin on her death.

All preliminary explanations being now cleared out of the way, I come at last to the real knot of the case—to the twenty thousand pounds.

This sum was absolutely Miss Fairlie's own on her completing her twenty-first year, and the whole future disposition of it depended, in the first instance, on the conditions I could obtain for her in her marriage-settlement. The other clauses contained in that document were of a formal kind, and need not be recited here. But the clause relating to the money is too important to be passed over. A few lines will be sufficient to give the necessary abstract of it.

My stipulation in regard to the twenty thousand pounds was simply this: The whole amount was to be settled so as to give the income to the lady for her life—afterwards to Sir Percival for his life—and the principal to the children of the marriage. In default of issue, the principal was to be disposed of as the lady might by her will direct, for which purpose I reserved to her the right of making a will. The effect of these conditions may be thus summed up. If Lady Glyde died without leaving children, her half-sister Miss Halcombe, and any other relatives or friends whom she might be anxious to benefit, would, on her husband's death, divide among them such shares of her money as she desired them to have. If, on the other hand, she died leaving children, then their interest, naturally and necessarily, superseded all other interests whatsoever. This was the clause—and no one who reads it can fail, I think, to agree with me that it meted out equal justice to all parties.

We shall see how my proposals were met on the husband's side.

The Woman in White

At the time when Miss Halcombe's letter reached me I was even more busily occupied than usual. But I contrived to make leisure for the settlement. I had drawn it, and had sent it for approval to Sir Percival's solicitor, in less than a week from the time when Miss Halcombe had informed me of the proposed marriage.

After a lapse of two days the document was returned to me, with notes and remarks of the baronet's lawyer. His objections, in general, proved to be of the most trifling and technical kind, until he came to the clause relating to the twenty thousand pounds. Against this there were double lines drawn in red ink, and the following note was appended to them—

"Not admissible. The principal to go to Sir Percival Glyde, in the event of his surviving Lady Glyde, and there being no issue."

That is to say, not one farthing of the twenty thousand pounds was to go to Miss Halcombe, or to any other relative or friend of Lady Glyde's. The whole sum, if she left no children, was to slip into the pockets of her husband.

The answer I wrote to this audacious proposal was as short and sharp as I could make it. "My dear sir. Miss Fairlie's settlement. I maintain the clause to which you object, exactly as it stands. Yours truly." The rejoinder came back in a quarter of an hour. "My dear sir. Miss Fairlie's settlement. I maintain the red ink to which you object, exactly as it stands. Yours truly." In the detestable slang of the day, we were now both "at a deadlock," and nothing was left for it but to refer to our clients on either side.

As matters stood, my client—Miss Fairlie not having yet completed her twenty-first year—Mr. Frederick Fairlie, was her guardian. I wrote by that day's post, and put the case before him exactly as it stood, not only urging every argument I could think of to induce him to maintain the clause as I had drawn it, but stating to him plainly the mercenary motive which was at the bottom of the opposition to my settlement of the twenty thousand pounds. The knowledge of Sir Percival's affairs which I had necessarily gained when the provisions of the deed on his side were submitted in due course to my examination, had but too plainly informed me that the debts on his estate were enormous, and that his income, though nominally a large one, was virtually, for a man in his position, next to nothing. The want of ready money was the practical necessity of Sir Percival's existence, and his lawyer's note on the clause in the settlement was nothing but the frankly selfish expression of it.

Mr. Fairlie's answer reached me by return of post, and proved to be wandering and irrelevant in the extreme. Turned into plain English, it practically expressed itself to this effect: "Would dear Gilmore be so very obliging as not to worry his friend and client about such a trifle as a remote contingency? Was it likely that a young woman of twenty-one would die before a man of forty five, and die without children? On the other hand, in such a miserable world as this, was it possible to over-estimate the value of peace and quietness? If those two heavenly blessings were offered in exchange for such an earthly trifle as a remote chance of twenty thousand pounds, was it not a fair bargain? Surely, yes. Then why not make it?"

I threw the letter away in disgust. Just as it had fluttered to the ground, there was a knock at my door, and Sir Percival's solicitor, Mr. Merriman, was shown in. There are many varieties of sharp practitioners in this world, but I think the hardest of all to deal with are the men who overreach you under the disguise of inveterate good-humour. A fat, well fed, smiling, friendly man of business is of all parties to a bargain the most hopeless to deal with. Mr. Merriman was one of this class.

"And how is good Mr. Gilmore?" he began, all in a glow with the warmth of his own amiability. "Glad to see you, sir, in such excellent health. I was passing your door, and I thought I would look in in case you might have something to say to me. Do — now pray do let us settle this little difference of ours by word of mouth, if we can! Have you heard from your client yet?"

"Yes. Have you heard from yours?"

"My dear, good sir! I wish I had heard from him to any purpose — I wish, with all my heart, the responsibility was off my shoulders; but he is obstinate — or let me rather say, resolute — and he won't take it off. 'Merriman, I leave details to you. Do what you think right for my interests, and consider me as having personally withdrawn from the business until it is all over.' Those were Sir Percival's words a fortnight ago, and all I can get him to do now is to repeat them. I am not a hard man, Mr. Gilmore, as you know. Personally and privately, I do assure you, I should like to sponge out that note of mine at this very moment. But if Sir Percival won't go into the matter, if Sir Percival will blindly leave all his interests in my sole care, what course can I possibly take except the course of asserting them? My hands are bound — don't you see, my dear sir? — my hands are bound."

"You maintain your note on the clause, then, to the letter?" I said.

"Yes—deuce take it! I have no other alternative." He walked to the fireplace and warmed himself, humming the fag end of a tune in a rich convivial bass voice. "What does your side say?" he went on; "now pray tell me—what does your side say?"

I was ashamed to tell him. I attempted to gain time—nay, I did worse. My legal instincts got the better of me, and I even tried to bargain.

"Twenty thousand pounds is rather a large sum to be given up by the lady's friends at two days' notice," I said.

"Very true," replied Mr. Merriman, looking down thoughtfully at his boots. "Properly put, sir—most properly put!"

"A compromise, recognising the interests of the lady's family as well as the interests of the husband, might not perhaps have frightened my client quite so much," I went on. "Come, come! this contingency resolves itself into a matter of bargaining after all. What is the least you will take?"

"The least we will take," said Mr. Merriman, "is nineteen-thousand-nine-hundred-and-ninety-nine-pounds-nineteen-shillings-and-elevenpence-three-farthings. Ha! ha! ha! Excuse me, Mr. Gilmore. I must have my little joke."

"Little enough," I remarked. "The joke is just worth the odd farthing it was made for."

Mr. Merriman was delighted. He laughed over my retort till the room rang again. I was not half so good-humoured on my side; I came back to business, and closed the interview.

"This is Friday," I said. "Give us till Tuesday next for our final answer."

"By all means," replied Mr. Merriman. "Longer, my dear sir, if you like." He took up his hat to go, and then addressed me again. "By the way," he said, "your clients in Cumberland have not heard anything more of the woman who wrote the anonymous letter, have they?"

"Nothing more," I answered. "Have you found no trace of her?"

"Not yet," said my legal friend. "But we don't despair. Sir Percival has his suspicions that Somebody is keeping her in hiding, and we are having that Somebody watched."

"You mean the old woman who was with her in Cumberland," I said.

"Quite another party, sir," answered Mr. Merriman. "We don't happen to have laid hands on the old woman yet. Our Somebody is a man. We have got him close under our eye here in London, and we strongly suspect he had something to do with helping her in the first instance to escape from the Asylum. Sir Percival wanted to question him at once, but I said, 'No. Questioning him will only put him on his guard—watch him, and wait.' We shall see what happens. A dangerous woman to be at large, Mr. Gilmore; nobody knows what she may do next. I wish you good-morning, sir. On Tuesday next I shall hope for the pleasure of hearing from you." He smiled amiably and went out.

My mind had been rather absent during the latter part of the conversation with my legal friend. I was so anxious about the matter of the settlement that I had little attention to give to any other subject, and the moment I was left alone again I began to think over what my next proceeding ought to be.

In the case of any other client I should have acted on my instructions, however personally distasteful to me, and have given up the point about the twenty thousand pounds on the spot. But I could not act with this business-like indifference towards Miss Fairlie. I had an honest feeling of affection and admiration for her—I remembered gratefully that her father had been the kindest patron and friend to me that ever man had—I had felt towards her while I was drawing the settlement as I might have felt, if I had not been an old bachelor, towards a daughter of my own, and I was determined to spare no personal sacrifice in her service and where her interests were concerned. Writing a second time to Mr. Fairlie was not to be thought of—it would only be giving him a second opportunity of slipping through my fingers. Seeing him and personally remonstrating with him might possibly be of more use. The next day was Saturday. I determined to take a return ticket and jolt my old bones down to Cumberland, on the chance of persuading him to adopt the just, the independent, and the honourable course. It was a poor chance enough, no doubt, but when I had tried it my conscience would be at ease. I should then have done all that a man in my position could do to serve the interests of my old friend's only child.

The weather on Saturday was beautiful, a west wind and a bright sun. Having felt latterly a return of that fulness and oppression of the head, against which my doctor warned me so seriously more than two years since, I resolved to take the opportunity of getting a little extra exercise by sending my bag on before me and walking to the terminus in Euston Square. As I came out into Holborn a gentleman walking by rapidly stopped and spoke to me. It was Mr. Walter Hartright.

If he had not been the first to greet me I should certainly have passed him. He was so changed that I hardly knew him again. His face looked pale and haggard — his manner was hurried and uncertain — and his dress, which I remembered as neat and gentlemanlike when I saw him at Limmeridge, was so slovenly now that I should really have been ashamed of the appearance of it on one of my own clerks.

"Have you been long back from Cumberland?" he asked. "I heard from Miss Halcombe lately. I am aware that Sir Percival Glyde's explanation has been considered satisfactory. Will the marriage take place soon? Do you happen to know, Mr. Gilmore?"

He spoke so fast, and crowded his questions together so strangely and confusedly, that I could hardly follow him. However accidentally intimate he might have been with the family at Limmeridge, I could not see that he had any right to expect information on their private affairs, and I determined to drop him, as easily as might be, on the subject of Miss Fairlie's marriage.

"Time will show, Mr. Hartright," I said — "time will show. I dare say if we look out for the marriage in the papers we shall not be far wrong. Excuse my noticing it, but I am sorry to see you not looking so well as you were when we last met."

A momentary nervous contraction quivered about his lips and eyes, and made me half reproach myself for having answered him in such a significantly guarded manner.

"I had no right to ask about her marriage," he said bitterly. "I must wait to see it in the newspapers like other people. Yes," — he went on before I could make any apologies — "I have not been well lately. I am going to another country to try a change of scene and occupation. Miss Halcombe has kindly assisted me with her influence, and my testimonials have been found satisfactory. It is a long distance off, but I don't care where I go, what the climate is, or how long I am away." He looked about him while he said this at the throng of strangers passing us by on either side, in a strange, suspicious manner, as if he thought that some of them might be watching us.

"I wish you well through it, and safe back again," I said, and then added, so as not to keep him altogether at arm's length on the subject of the Fairlies, "I am going down to Limmeridge to-day on business. Miss Halcombe and Miss Fairlie are away just now on a visit to some friends in Yorkshire."

His eyes brightened, and he seemed about to say something in answer, but the same momentary nervous spasm crossed his face again. He took my hand, pressed it hard, and disappeared among the crowd without saying another word. Though he was little more than a stranger to me, I waited for a moment, looking after him almost with a feeling of regret. I had gained in my profession sufficient experience of young men to know what the outward signs and tokens were of their beginning to go wrong, and when I resumed my walk to the railway I am sorry to say I felt more than doubtful about Mr. Hartright's future.

IV

Leaving by an early train, I got to Limmeridge in time for dinner. The house was oppressively empty and dull. I had expected that good Mrs. Vesey would have been company for me in the absence of the young ladies, but she was confined to her room by a cold. The servants were so surprised at seeing me that they hurried and bustled absurdly, and made all sorts of annoying mistakes. Even the butler, who was old enough to have known better, brought me a bottle of port that was chilled. The reports of Mr. Fairlie's health were just as usual, and when I sent up a message to announce my arrival, I was told that he would be delighted to see me the next morning but that the sudden news of my appearance had prostrated him with palpitations for the rest of the evening. The wind howled dismally all night, and strange cracking and groaning noises sounded here, there, and everywhere in the empty house. I slept as wretchedly as possible, and got up in a mighty bad humour to breakfast by myself the next morning.

At ten o'clock I was conducted to Mr. Fairlie's apartments. He was in his usual room, his usual chair, and his usual aggravating state of mind and body. When I went in, his valet was standing before him, holding up for inspection a heavy volume of etchings, as long and as broad as my office writing-desk. The miserable foreigner grinned in the most abject manner, and looked ready to drop with fatigue, while his master composedly turned over the etchings, and brought their hidden beauties to light with the help of a magnifying glass.

"You very best of good old friends," said Mr. Fairlie, leaning back lazily before he could look at me, "are you quite well? How nice of you to come here and see me in my solitude. Dear Gilmore!"

I had expected that the valet would be dismissed when I appeared, but nothing of the sort happened. There he stood, in front of his master's chair, trembling under the weight of the etchings, and there Mr. Fairlie sat, serenely twirling the magnifying glass between his white fingers and thumbs.

"I have come to speak to you on a very important matter," I said, "and you will therefore excuse me, if I suggest that we had better be alone."

The unfortunate valet looked at me gratefully. Mr. Fairlie faintly repeated my last three words, "better be alone," with every appearance of the utmost possible astonishment.

I was in no humour for trifling, and I resolved to make him understand what I meant.

"Oblige me by giving that man permission to withdraw," I said, pointing to the valet.

Mr. Fairlie arched his eyebrows and pursed up his lips in sarcastic surprise.

"Man?" he repeated. "You provoking old Gilmore, what can you possibly mean by calling him a man? He's nothing of the sort. He might have been a man half an hour ago, before I wanted my etchings, and he may be a man half an hour hence, when I don't want them any longer. At present he is simply a portfolio stand. Why object, Gilmore, to a portfolio stand?"

"I do object. For the third time, Mr. Fairlie, I beg that we may be alone."

My tone and manner left him no alternative but to comply with my request. He looked at the servant, and pointed peevishly to a chair at his side.

"Put down the etchings and go away," he said. "Don't upset me by losing my place. Have you, or have you not, lost my place? Are you sure you have not? And have you put my hand-bell quite within my reach? Yes? Then why the devil don't you go?"

The valet went out. Mr. Fairlie twisted himself round in his chair, polished the magnifying glass with his delicate cambric handkerchief, and indulged himself with a sidelong inspection of the open volume of etchings. It was not easy to keep my temper under these circumstances, but I did keep it.

"I have come here at great personal inconvenience," I said, "to serve the interests of your niece and your family, and I think I have established some slight claim to be favoured with your attention in return."

"Don't bully me!" exclaimed Mr. Fairlie, falling back helplessly in the chair, and closing his eyes. "Please don't bully me. I'm not strong enough."

I was determined not to let him provoke me, for Laura Fairlie's sake.

"My object," I went on, "is to entreat you to reconsider your letter, and not to force me to abandon the just rights of your niece, and of all who belong to her. Let me state the case to you once more, and for the last time."

Mr. Fairlie shook his head and sighed piteously.

"This is heartless of you, Gilmore—very heartless," he said. "Never mind, go on."

I put all the points to him carefully—I set the matter before him in every conceivable light. He lay back in the chair the whole time I was speaking with his eyes closed. When I had done he opened them indolently, took his silver smelling-bottle from the table, and sniffed at it with an air of gentle relish.

"Good Gilmore!" he said between the sniffs, "how very nice this is of you! How you reconcile one to human nature!"

"Give me a plain answer to a plain question, Mr. Fairlie. I tell you again, Sir Percival Glyde has no shadow of a claim to expect more than the income of the money. The money itself if your niece has no children, ought to be under her control, and to return to her family. If you stand firm, Sir Percival must give way—he must give way, I tell you, or he exposes himself to the base imputation of marrying Miss Fairlie entirely from mercenary motives."

Mr. Fairlie shook the silver smelling-bottle at me playfully.

"You dear old Gilmore, how you do hate rank and family, don't you? How you detest Glyde because he happens to be a baronet. What a Radical you are—oh, dear me, what a Radical you are!"

A Radical!!! I could put up with a good deal of provocation, but, after holding the soundest Conservative principles all my life, I could not put up with being called a Radical. My blood boiled at it—I started out of my chair—I was speechless with Indignation.

"Don't shake the room!" cried Mr. Fairlie—"for Heaven's sake don't shake the room! Worthiest of all possible Gilmores, I meant no offence. My own views are so extremely liberal that I think I am a Radical myself. Yes. We are a pair of Radicals. Please don't be angry. I can't quarrel—I haven't stamina enough. Shall we drop the subject? Yes. Come and look at these sweet etchings. Do let me teach you to understand the heavenly pearliness of these lines. Do now, there's a good Gilmore!"

While he was maundering on in this way I was, fortunately for my own self-respect, returning to my senses. When I spoke again I was composed enough to treat his impertinence with the silent contempt that it deserved.

"You are entirely wrong, sir," I said, "in supposing that I speak from any prejudice against Sir Percival Glyde. I may regret that he has so unreservedly resigned himself in this matter to his lawyer's direction as to make any appeal to himself impossible, but I am not prejudiced against him. What I have said would equally apply to any other man in his situation, high or low. The principle I maintain is a recognised principle. If you were to apply at the nearest town here, to the first respectable solicitor you could find, he would tell you as a stranger what I tell you as a friend. He would inform you that it is against all rule to abandon the lady's money entirely to the man she marries. He would decline, on grounds of common legal caution, to give the husband, under any circumstances whatever, an interest of twenty thousand pounds in his wife's death."

"Would he really, Gilmore?" said Mr. Fairlie. "If he said anything half so horrid, I do assure you I should tinkle my bell for Louis, and have him sent out of the house immediately."

"You shall not irritate me, Mr. Fairlie—for your niece's sake and for her father's sake, you shall not irritate me. You shall take the whole responsibility of this discreditable settlement on your own shoulders before I leave the room."

"Don't!—now please don't!" said Mr. Fairlie. "Think how precious your time is, Gilmore, and don't throw it away. I would dispute with you if I could, but I can't—I haven't stamina enough. You want to upset me, to upset yourself, to upset Glyde, and to upset Laura; and—oh, dear me!—all for the sake of the very last thing in the world that is likely to happen. No, dear friend—in the interests of peace and quietness, positively No!"

"I am to understand, then, that you hold by the determination expressed in your letter?"

"Yes, please. So glad we understand each other at last. Sit down again—do!"

I walked at once to the door, and Mr. Fairlie resignedly "tinkled" his hand-bell. Before I left the room I turned round and addressed him for the last time.

"Whatever happens in the future, sir," I said, "remember that my plain duty of warning you has been performed. As the faithful friend and servant of your family, I tell you, at parting, that no daughter of mine should be married to any man alive under such a settlement as you are forcing me to make for Miss Fairlie."

The door opened behind me, and the valet stood waiting on the threshold.

"Louis," said Mr. Fairlie, "show Mr. Gilmore out, and then come back and hold up my etchings for me again. Make them give you a good lunch downstairs. Do, Gilmore, make my idle beasts of servants give you a good lunch!"

I was too much disgusted to reply—I turned on my heel, and left him in silence. There was an up train at two o'clock in the afternoon, and by that train I returned to London.

On the Tuesday I sent in the altered settlement, which practically disinherited the very persons whom Miss Fairlie's own lips had informed me she was most anxious to benefit. I had no choice. Another lawyer would have drawn up the deed if I had refused to undertake it.

My task is done. My personal share in the events of the family story extends no farther than the point which I have just reached. Other pens than mine will describe the strange circumstances which are now shortly to follow. Seriously and sorrowfully I close this brief record. Seriously and sorrowfully I repeat here the parting words that I spoke at Limmeridge House:—No daughter of mine should have been married to any man alive under such a settlement as I was compelled to make for Laura Fairlie.

The End of Mr. Gilmore's Narrative.

THE STORY CONTINUED BY MARIAN HALCOMBE

(in Extracts from her Diary)

LIMMERIDGE HOUSE, Nov. 8.[1]

[1] The passages omitted, here and elsewhere, in Miss Halcombe's Diary are only those which bear no reference to Miss Fairlie or to any of the persons with whom she is associated in these pages.

This morning Mr. Gilmore left us.

His interview with Laura had evidently grieved and surprised him more than he liked to confess. I felt afraid, from his look and manner when we parted, that she might have inadvertently betrayed to him the real secret of her depression and my anxiety. This doubt grew on me so, after he had gone, that I declined riding out with Sir Percival, and went up to Laura's room instead.

I have been sadly distrustful of myself, in this difficult and lamentable matter, ever since I found out my own ignorance of the strength of Laura's unhappy attachment. I ought to have known that the delicacy and forbearance and sense of honour which drew me to poor Hartright, and made me so sincerely admire and respect him, were just the qualities to appeal most irresistibly to Laura's natural sensitiveness and natural generosity of nature. And yet, until she opened her heart to me of her own accord, I had no suspicion that this new feeling had taken root so deeply. I once thought time and care might remove it. I now fear that it will remain with her and alter her for life. The discovery that I have committed such an error in judgment as this makes me hesitate about everything else. I hesitate about Sir Percival, in the face of the plainest proofs. I hesitate even in speaking to Laura. On this very morning I doubted, with my hand on the door, whether I should ask her the questions I had come to put, or not.

When I went into her room I found her walking up and down in great impatience. She looked flushed and excited, and she came forward at once, and spoke to me before I could open

The Woman in White

my lips.

"I wanted you," she said. "Come and sit down on the sofa with me. Marian! I can bear this no longer—I must and will end it."

There was too much colour in her cheeks, too much energy in her manner, too much firmness in her voice. The little book of Hartright's drawings—the fatal book that she will dream over whenever she is alone—was in one of her hands. I began by gently and firmly taking it from her, and putting it out of sight on a side-table.

"Tell me quietly, my darling, what you wish to do," I said. "Has Mr. Gilmore been advising you?"

She shook her head. "No, not in what I am thinking of now. He was very kind and good to me, Marian, and I am ashamed to say I distressed him by crying. I am miserably helpless—I can't control myself. For my own sake, and for all our sakes, I must have courage enough to end it."

"Do you mean courage enough to claim your release?" I asked.

"No," she said simply. "Courage, dear, to tell the truth."

She put her arms round my neck, and rested her head quietly on my bosom. On the opposite wall hung the miniature portrait of her father. I bent over her, and saw that she was looking at it while her head lay on my breast.

"I can never claim my release from my engagement," she went on. "Whatever way it ends it must end wretchedly for me. All I can do, Marian, is not to add the remembrance that I have broken my promise and forgotten my father's dying words, to make that wretchedness worse."

"What is it you propose, then?" I asked.

"To tell Sir Percival Glyde the truth with my own lips," she answered, "and to let him release me, if he will, not because I ask him, but because he knows all."

"What do you mean, Laura, by 'all'? Sir Percival will know enough (he has told me so himself) if he knows that the engagement is opposed to your own wishes."

"Can I tell him that, when the engagement was made for me by my father, with my own consent? I should have kept my promise, not happily, I am afraid, but still contentedly—" she stopped, turned her face to me, and laid her cheek close against mine—"I should have kept my engagement, Marian, if another love had not grown up in my heart, which was not there when I first promised to be Sir Percival's wife."

"Laura! you will never lower yourself by making a confession to him?"

"I shall lower myself, indeed, if I gain my release by hiding from him what he has a right to know."

"He has not the shadow of a right to know it!"

"Wrong, Marian, wrong! I ought to deceive no one—least of all the man to whom my father gave me, and to whom I gave myself." She put her lips to mine, and kissed me. "My own love," she said softly, "you are so much too fond of me, and so much too proud of me, that you forget, in my case, what you would remember in your own. Better that Sir Percival should doubt my motives, and misjudge my conduct if he will, than that I should be first false to him in thought, and then mean enough to serve my own interests by hiding the falsehood."

I held her away from me in astonishment. For the first time in our lives we had changed places—the resolution was all on her side, the hesitation all on mine. I looked into the pale, quiet, resigned young face—I saw the pure, innocent heart, in the loving eyes that looked back at me—and the poor worldly cautions and objections that rose to my lips dwindled and died away in their own emptiness. I hung my head in silence. In her place the despicably small pride which makes so many women deceitful would have been my pride, and would have made me deceitful too.

"Don't be angry with me, Marian," she said, mistaking my silence.

I only answered by drawing her close to me again. I was afraid of crying if I spoke. My tears do not flow so easily as they ought—they come almost like men's tears, with sobs that seem to tear me in pieces, and that frighten every one about me.

"I have thought of this, love, for many days," she went on, twining and twisting my hair with that childish restlessness in her fingers, which poor Mrs. Vesey still tries so patiently and so vainly to cure her of—"I have thought of it very seriously, and I can be sure of my courage when my own conscience tells me I am right. Let me speak to him to-morrow—in your presence, Marian. I will say nothing that is wrong, nothing that you or I need be ashamed of—but, oh, it will ease my heart so to end this miserable concealment! Only let me know and feel that I have no deception to answer for on my side, and then, when he has heard what I have to say, let him act towards me as he will."

She sighed, and put her head back in its old position on my bosom. Sad misgivings about what the end would be weighed upon my mind, but still distrusting myself, I told her that I would do as she wished. She thanked me, and we passed gradually into talking of other things.

At dinner she joined us again, and was more easy and more herself with Sir Percival than I have seen her yet. In the evening she went to the piano, choosing new music of the dexterous, tuneless, florid kind. The lovely old melodies of Mozart, which poor Hartright was so fond of, she has never played since he left. The book is no longer in the music-stand. She took the volume away herself, so that nobody might find it out and ask her to play from it.

I had no opportunity of discovering whether her purpose of the morning had changed or not, until she wished Sir Percival good-night—and then her own words informed me that it was unaltered. She said, very quietly, that she wished to speak to him after breakfast, and that he would find her in her sitting-room with me. He changed colour at those words, and I felt his hand trembling a little when it came to my turn to take it. The event of the next morning would decide his future life, and he evidently knew it.

I went in, as usual, through the door between our two bedrooms, to bid Laura good-night before she went to sleep. In stooping over her to kiss her I saw the little book of Hartright's drawings half hidden under her pillow, just in the place where she used to hide her favourite toys when she was a child. I could not find it in my heart to say anything, but I pointed to the book and shook my head. She reached both hands up to my cheeks, and drew my face down to hers till our lips met.

"Leave it there to-night," she whispered; "to-morrow may be cruel, and may make me say good-bye to it for ever."

9th. — The first event of the morning was not of a kind to raise my spirits — a letter arrived for me from poor Walter Hartright. It is the answer to mine describing the manner in which Sir Percival cleared himself of the suspicions raised by Anne Catherick's letter. He writes shortly and bitterly about Sir Percival's explanations, only saying that he has no right to offer an opinion on the conduct of those who are above him. This is sad, but his occasional references to himself grieve me still more. He says that the effort to return to his old habits and pursuits grows harder instead of easier to him every day and he implores me, if I have any interest, to exert it to get him employment that will necessitate his absence from England, and take him among new scenes and new people. I have been made all the readier to comply with this request by a passage at the end of his letter, which has almost alarmed me.

After mentioning that he has neither seen nor heard anything of Anne Catherick, he suddenly breaks off, and hints in the most abrupt, mysterious manner, that he has been perpetually watched and followed by strange men ever since he returned to London. He acknowledges that he cannot prove this extraordinary suspicion by fixing on any particular persons, but he declares that the suspicion itself is present to him night and day. This has frightened me, because it looks as if his one fixed idea about Laura was becoming too much for his mind. I will write immediately to some of my mother's influential old friends in London, and press his claims on their notice. Change of scene and change of occupation may really be the salvation of him at this crisis in his life.

Greatly to my relief, Sir Percival sent an apology for not joining us at breakfast. He had taken an early cup of coffee in his own room, and he was still engaged there in writing letters. At eleven o'clock, if that hour was convenient, he would do himself the honour of waiting on Miss Fairlie and Miss Halcombe.

My eyes were on Laura's face while the message was being delivered. I had found her unaccountably quiet and composed on going into her room in the morning, and so she remained all through breakfast. Even when we were sitting together on the sofa in her room, waiting for Sir Percival, she still preserved her self-control.

"Don't be afraid of me, Marian," was all she said; "I may forget myself with an old friend like Mr. Gilmore, or with a dear sister like you, but I will not forget myself with Sir Percival Glyde."

The Woman in White

I looked at her, and listened to her in silent surprise. Through all the years of our close intimacy this passive force in her character had been hidden from me—hidden even from herself, till love found it, and suffering called it forth.

As the clock on the mantelpiece struck eleven Sir Percival knocked at the door and came in. There was suppressed anxiety and agitation in every line of his face. The dry, sharp cough, which teases him at most times, seemed to be troubling him more incessantly than ever. He sat down opposite to us at the table, and Laura remained by me. I looked attentively at them both, and he was the palest of the two.

He said a few unimportant words, with a visible effort to preserve his customary ease of manner. But his voice was not to be steadied, and the restless uneasiness in his eyes was not to be concealed. He must have felt this himself, for he stopped in the middle of a sentence, and gave up even the attempt to hide his embarrassment any longer.

There was just one moment of dead silence before Laura addressed him.

"I wish to speak to you, Sir Percival," she said, "on a subject that is very important to us both. My sister is here, because her presence helps me and gives me confidence. She has not suggested one word of what I am going to say—I speak from my own thoughts, not from hers. I am sure you will be kind enough to understand that before I go any farther?"

Sir Percival bowed. She had proceeded thus far, with perfect outward tranquillity and perfect propriety of manner. She looked at him, and he looked at her. They seemed, at the outset, at least, resolved to understand one another plainly.

"I have heard from Marian," she went on, "that I have only to claim my release from our engagement to obtain that release from you. It was forbearing and generous on your part, Sir Percival, to send me such a message. It is only doing you justice to say that I am grateful for the offer, and I hope and believe that it is only doing myself justice to tell you that I decline to accept it."

His attentive face relaxed a little. But I saw one of his feet, softly, quietly, incessantly beating on the carpet under the table, and I felt that he was secretly as anxious as ever.

"I have not forgotten," she said, "that you asked my father's permission before you honoured me with a proposal of marriage. Perhaps you have not forgotten either what I said when I consented to our engagement? I ventured to tell you that my father's influence and advice had mainly decided me to give you my promise. I was guided by my father, because I had always found him the truest of all advisers, the best and fondest of all protectors and friends. I have lost him now—I have only his memory to love, but my faith in that dear dead friend has never been shaken. I believe at this moment, as truly as I ever believed, that he knew what was best, and that his hopes and wishes ought to be my hopes and wishes too."

Her voice trembled for the first time. Her restless fingers stole their way into my lap, and held fast by one of my hands. There was another moment of silence, and then Sir Percival spoke.

"May I ask," he said, "if I have ever proved myself unworthy of the trust which it has been hitherto my greatest honour and greatest happiness to possess?"

"I have found nothing in your conduct to blame," she answered. "You have always treated me with the same delicacy and the same forbearance. You have deserved my trust, and, what is of far more importance in my estimation, you have deserved my father's trust, out of which mine grew. You have given me no excuse, even if I had wanted to find one, for asking to be released from my pledge. What I have said so far has been spoken with the wish to acknowledge my whole obligation to you. My regard for that obligation, my regard for my father's memory, and my regard for my own promise, all forbid me to set the example, on my side, of withdrawing from our present position. The breaking of our engagement must be entirely your wish and your act, Sir Percival—not mine."

The uneasy beating of his foot suddenly stopped, and he leaned forward eagerly across the table.

"My act?" he said. "What reason can there be on my side for withdrawing?"

I heard her breath quickening—I felt her hand growing cold. In spite of what she had said to me when we were alone, I began to be afraid of her. I was wrong.

"A reason that it is very hard to tell you," she answered. "There is a change in me, Sir Percival—a change which is serious enough to justify you, to yourself and to me, in breaking off our engagement."

His face turned so pale again that even his lips lost their colour. He raised the arm which lay on the table, turned a little away in his chair, and supported his head on his hand, so that his profile only was presented to us.

"What change?" he asked. The tone in which he put the question jarred on me — there was something painfully suppressed in it.

She sighed heavily, and leaned towards me a little, so as to rest her shoulder against mine. I felt her trembling, and tried to spare her by speaking myself. She stopped me by a warning pressure of her hand, and then addressed Sir Percival one more, but this time without looking at him.

"I have heard," she said, "and I believe it, that the fondest and truest of all affections is the affection which a woman ought to bear to her husband. When our engagement began that affection was mine to give, if I could, and yours to win, if you could. Will you pardon me, and spare me, Sir Percival, if I acknowledge that it is not so any longer?"

A few tears gathered in her eyes, and dropped over her cheeks slowly as she paused and waited for his answer. He did not utter a word. At the beginning of her reply he had moved the hand on which his head rested, so that it hid his face. I saw nothing but the upper part of his figure at the table. Not a muscle of him moved. The fingers of the hand which supported his head were dented deep in his hair. They might have expressed hidden anger or hidden grief — it was hard to say which — there was no significant trembling in them. There was nothing, absolutely nothing, to tell the secret of his thoughts at that moment — the moment which was the crisis of his life and the crisis of hers.

I was determined to make him declare himself, for Laura's sake.

"Sir Percival!" I interposed sharply, "have you nothing to say when my sister has said so much? More, in my opinion," I added, my unlucky temper getting the better of me, "than any man alive, in your position, has a right to hear from her."

That last rash sentence opened a way for him by which to escape me if he chose, and he instantly took advantage of it.

"Pardon me, Miss Halcombe," he said, still keeping his hand over his face, "pardon me if I remind you that I have claimed no such right."

The few plain words which would have brought him back to the point from which he had wandered were just on my lips, when Laura checked me by speaking again.

"I hope I have not made my painful acknowledgment in vain," she continued. "I hope it has secured me your entire confidence in what I have still to say?"

"Pray be assured of it." He made that brief reply warmly, dropping his hand on the table while he spoke, and turning towards us again. Whatever outward change had passed over him was gone now. His face was eager and expectant—it expressed nothing but the most intense anxiety to hear her next words.

"I wish you to understand that I have not spoken from any selfish motive," she said. "If you leave me, Sir Percival, after what you have just heard, you do not leave me to marry another man, you only allow me to remain a single woman for the rest of my life. My fault towards you has begun and ended in my own thoughts. It can never go any farther. No word has passed—" She hesitated, in doubt about the expression she should use next, hesitated in a momentary confusion which it was very sad and very painful to see. "No word has passed," she patiently and resolutely resumed, "between myself and the person to whom I am now referring for the first and last time in your presence of my feelings towards him, or of his feelings towards me—no word ever can pass—neither he nor I are likely, in this world, to meet again. I earnestly beg you to spare me from saying any more, and to believe me, on my word, in what I have just told you. It is the truth, Sir Percival—the truth which I think my promised husband has a claim to hear, at any sacrifice of my own feelings. I trust to his generosity to pardon me, and to his honour to keep my secret."

"Both those trusts are sacred to me," he said, "and both shall be sacredly kept."

After answering in those terms he paused, and looked at her as if he was waiting to hear more.

"I have said all I wish to say," she added quietly—"I have said more than enough to justify you in withdrawing from your engagement."

The Woman in White

"You have said more than enough," he answered, "to make it the dearest object of my life to keep the engagement." With those words he rose from his chair, and advanced a few steps towards the place where she was sitting.

She started violently, and a faint cry of surprise escaped her. Every word she had spoken had innocently betrayed her purity and truth to a man who thoroughly understood the priceless value of a pure and true woman. Her own noble conduct had been the hidden enemy, throughout, of all the hopes she had trusted to it. I had dreaded this from the first. I would have prevented it, if she had allowed me the smallest chance of doing so. I even waited and watched now, when the harm was done, for a word from Sir Percival that would give me the opportunity of putting him in the wrong.

"You have left it to me, Miss Fairlie, to resign you," he continued. "I am not heartless enough to resign a woman who has just shown herself to be the noblest of her sex."

He spoke with such warmth and feeling, with such passionate enthusiasm, and yet with such perfect delicacy, that she raised her head, flushed up a little, and looked at him with sudden animation and spirit.

"No!" she said firmly. "The most wretched of her sex, if she must give herself in marriage when she cannot give her love."

"May she not give it in the future," he asked, "if the one object of her husband's life is to deserve it?"

"Never!" she answered. "If you still persist in maintaining our engagement, I may be your true and faithful wife, Sir Percival—your loving wife, if I know my own heart, never!"

She looked so irresistibly beautiful as she said those brave words that no man alive could have steeled his heart against her. I tried hard to feel that Sir Percival was to blame, and to say so, but my womanhood would pity him, in spite of myself.

"I gratefully accept your faith and truth," he said. "The least that you can offer is more to me than the utmost that I could hope for from any other woman in the world."

Her left hand still held mine, but her right hand hung listlessly at her side. He raised it gently to his lips—touched it with them, rather than kissed it—bowed to me—and then, with perfect delicacy and discretion, silently quitted the room.

She neither moved nor said a word when he was gone—she sat by me, cold and still, with her eyes fixed on the ground. I saw it was hopeless and useless to speak, and I only put my arm round her, and held her to me in silence. We remained together so for what seemed a long and weary time—so long and so weary, that I grew uneasy and spoke to her softly, in the hope of producing a change.

The sound of my voice seemed to startle her into consciousness. She suddenly drew herself away from me and rose to her feet.

"I must submit, Marian, as well as I can," she said. "My new life has its hard duties, and one of them begins to-day."

As she spoke she went to a side-table near the window, on which her sketching materials were placed, gathered them together carefully, and put them in a drawer of her cabinet. She locked the drawer and brought the key to me.

"I must part from everything that reminds me of him," she said. "Keep the key wherever you please—I shall never want it again."

Before I could say a word she had turned away to her bookcase, and had taken from it the album that contained Walter Hartright's drawings. She hesitated for a moment, holding the little volume fondly in her hands—then lifted it to her lips and kissed it.

"Oh, Laura! Laura!" I said, not angrily, not reprovingly—with nothing but sorrow in my voice, and nothing but sorrow in my heart.

"It is the last time, Marian," she pleaded. "I am bidding it good-bye for ever."

She laid the book on the table and drew out the comb that fastened her hair. It fell, in its matchless beauty, over her back and shoulders, and dropped round her, far below her waist. She separated one long, thin lock from the rest, cut it off, and pinned it carefully, in the form of a circle, on the first blank page of the album. The moment it was fastened she closed the volume hurriedly, and placed it in my hands.

"You write to him and he writes to you," she said. "While I am alive, if he asks after me always tell him I am well, and never say I am unhappy. Don't distress him, Marian, for my sake, don't distress him. If I die first, promise you will give him this little book of his drawings, with my hair in it. There can be no harm, when I am gone, in telling him that I put it there with my own hands. And say — oh, Marian, say for me, then, what I can never say for myself — say I loved him!"

She flung her arms round my neck, and whispered the last words in my ear with a passionate delight in uttering them which it almost broke my heart to hear. All the long restraint she had imposed on herself gave way in that first last outburst of tenderness. She broke from me with hysterical vehemence, and threw herself on the sofa in a paroxysm of sobs and tears that shook her from head to foot.

I tried vainly to soothe her and reason with her — she was past being soothed, and past being reasoned with. It was the sad, sudden end for us two of this memorable day. When the fit had worn itself out she was too exhausted to speak. She slumbered towards the afternoon, and I put away the book of drawings so that she might not see it when she woke. My face was calm, whatever my heart might be, when she opened her eyes again and looked at me. We said no more to each other about the distressing interview of the morning. Sir Percival's name was not mentioned. Walter Hartright was not alluded to again by either of us for the remainder of the day.

10th. — Finding that she was composed and like herself this morning, I returned to the painful subject of yesterday, for the sole purpose of imploring her to let me speak to Sir Percival and Mr. Fairlie, more plainly and strongly than she could speak to either of them herself, about this lamentable marriage. She interposed, gently but firmly, in the middle of my remonstrances.

"I left yesterday to decide," she said; "and yesterday has decided. It is too late to go back."

Sir Percival spoke to me this afternoon about what had passed in Laura's room. He assured me that the unparalleled trust she had placed in him had awakened such an answering conviction of her innocence and integrity in his mind, that he was guiltless of having felt even a moment's unworthy jealousy, either at the time when he was in her presence, or afterwards when he had withdrawn from it. Deeply as he lamented the unfortunate attachment which had hindered the progress he might otherwise have made in her esteem and regard, he firmly believed that it had remained unacknowledged in the past, and that it would remain, under all changes of circumstance which it was possible to contemplate, unacknowledged in the future. This was his absolute conviction; and the strongest proof he could give of it was the assurance, which he now offered, that he felt no curiosity to know whether the attachment was of recent date or not, or who had been the object of it. His implicit confidence in Miss Fairlie made him satisfied with what she had thought fit to say to him, and he was honestly innocent of the slightest feeling of anxiety to hear more.

He waited after saying those words and looked at me. I was so conscious of my unreasonable prejudice against him—so conscious of an unworthy suspicion that he might be speculating on my impulsively answering the very questions which he had just described himself as resolved not to ask—that I evaded all reference to this part of the subject with something like a feeling of confusion on my own part. At the same time I was resolved not to lose even the smallest opportunity of trying to plead Laura's cause, and I told him boldly that I regretted his generosity had not carried him one step farther, and induced him to withdraw from the engagement altogether.

Here, again, he disarmed me by not attempting to defend himself. He would merely beg me to remember the difference there was between his allowing Miss Fairlie to give him up, which was a matter of submission only, and his forcing himself to give up Miss Fairlie, which was, in other words, asking him to be the suicide of his own hopes. Her conduct of the day before had so strengthened the unchangeable love and admiration of two long years, that all active contention against those feelings, on his part, was henceforth entirely out of his power. I must think him weak, selfish, unfeeling towards the very woman whom he idolised, and he must bow to my opinion as resignedly as he could—only putting it to me, at the same time, whether her future as a single woman, pining under an unhappily placed attachment which she could never acknowledge, could be said to promise her a much brighter prospect than her future as the wife of a man who worshipped the very ground she walked on? In the last case there was hope from time, however slight it might be—in the first case, on her own showing, there was no hope at all.

I answered him—more because my tongue is a woman's, and must answer, than because I had anything convincing to say. It was only too plain that the course Laura had adopted the day before had offered him the advantage if he chose to take it—and that he had chosen to take it. I felt this at the time, and I feel it just as strongly now, while I write these lines, in my own room. The one hope left is that his motives really spring, as he says they do, from the irresistible strength of his attachment to Laura.

Before I close my diary for to-night I must record that I wrote to-day, in poor Hartright's interest, to two of my mother's old friends in London — both men of influence and position. If they can do anything for him, I am quite sure they will. Except Laura, I never was more anxious about any one than I am now about Walter. All that has happened since he left us has only increased my strong regard and sympathy for him. I hope I am doing right in trying to help him to employment abroad — I hope, most earnestly and anxiously, that it will end well.

11th. — Sir Percival had an interview with Mr. Fairlie, and I was sent for to join them.

I found Mr. Fairlie greatly relieved at the prospect of the "family worry" (as he was pleased to describe his niece's marriage) being settled at last. So far, I did not feel called on to say anything to him about my own opinion, but when he proceeded, in his most aggravatingly languid manner, to suggest that the time for the marriage had better be settled next, in accordance with Sir Percival's wishes, I enjoyed the satisfaction of assailing Mr. Fairlie's nerves with as strong a protest against hurrying Laura's decision as I could put into words. Sir Percival immediately assured me that he felt the force of my objection, and begged me to believe that the proposal had not been made in consequence of any interference on his part. Mr. Fairlie leaned back in his chair, closed his eyes, said we both of us did honour to human nature, and then repeated his suggestion as coolly as if neither Sir Percival nor I had said a word in opposition to it. It ended in my flatly declining to mention the subject to Laura, unless she first approached it of her own accord. I left the room at once after making that declaration. Sir Percival looked seriously embarrassed and distressed, Mr. Fairlie stretched out his lazy legs on his velvet footstool, and said, "Dear Marian! how I envy you your robust nervous system! Don't bang the door!"

On going to Laura's room I found that she had asked for me, and that Mrs. Vesey had informed her that I was with Mr. Fairlie. She inquired at once what I had been wanted for, and I told her all that had passed, without attempting to conceal the vexation and annoyance that I really felt. Her answer surprised and distressed me inexpressibly—it was the very last reply that I should have expected her to make.

"My uncle is right," she said. "I have caused trouble and anxiety enough to you, and to all about me. Let me cause no more, Marian—let Sir Percival decide."

I remonstrated warmly, but nothing that I could say moved her.

"I am held to my engagement," she replied; "I have broken with my old life. The evil day will not come the less surely because I put it off. No, Marian! once again my uncle is right. I have caused trouble enough and anxiety enough, and I will cause no more."

She used to be pliability itself, but she was now inflexibly passive in her resignation—I might almost say in her despair. Dearly as I love her, I should have been less pained if she had been violently agitated—it was so shockingly unlike her natural character to see her as cold and insensible as I saw her now.

12th.—Sir Percival put some questions to me at breakfast about Laura, which left me no choice but to tell him what she had said.

While we were talking she herself came down and joined us. She was just as unnaturally composed in Sir Percival's presence as she had been in mine. When breakfast was over he had an opportunity of saying a few words to her privately, in a recess of one of the windows. They were not more than two or three minutes together, and on their separating she left the room with Mrs. Vesey, while Sir Percival came to me. He said he had entreated her to favour him by maintaining her privilege of fixing the time for the marriage at her own will and pleasure. In reply she had merely expressed her acknowledgments, and had desired him to mention what his wishes were to Miss Halcombe.

I have no patience to write more. In this instance, as in every other, Sir Percival has carried his point with the utmost possible credit to himself, in spite of everything that I can say or do. His wishes are now, what they were, of course, when he first came here; and Laura having resigned herself to the one inevitable sacrifice of the marriage, remains as coldly hopeless and enduring as ever. In parting with the little occupations and relics that reminded her of Hartright, she seems to have parted with all her tenderness and all her impressibility. It is only three o'clock in the afternoon while I write these lines, and Sir Percival has left us already, in the happy hurry of a bridegroom, to prepare for the bride's reception at his house in Hampshire. Unless some extraordinary event happens to prevent it they will be married exactly at the time when he wished to be married — before the end of the year. My very fingers burn as I write it!

13th. — A sleepless night, through uneasiness about Laura. Towards the morning I came to a resolution to try what change of scene would do to rouse her. She cannot surely remain in her present torpor of insensibility, if I take her away from Limmeridge and surround her with the pleasant faces of old friends? After some consideration I decided on writing to the Arnolds, in Yorkshire. They are simple, kind-hearted, hospitable people, and she has known them from her childhood. When I had put the letter in the post-bag I told her what I had done. It would have been a relief to me if she had shown the spirit to resist and object. But no — she only said, "I will go anywhere with you, Marian. I dare say you are right — I dare say the change will do me good."

14th. — I wrote to Mr. Gilmore, informing him that there was really a prospect of this miserable marriage taking place, and also mentioning my idea of trying what change of scene would do for Laura. I had no heart to go into particulars. Time enough for them when we get nearer to the end of the year.

15th. — Three letters for me. The first, from the Arnolds, full of delight at the prospect of seeing Laura and me. The second, from one of the gentlemen to whom I wrote on Walter Hartright's behalf, informing me that he has been fortunate enough to find an opportunity of complying with my request. The third, from Walter himself, thanking me, poor fellow, in the warmest terms, for giving him an opportunity of leaving his home, his country, and his friends. A private expedition to make excavations among the ruined cities of Central America is, it seems, about to sail from Liverpool. The draughtsman who had been already appointed to accompany it has lost heart, and withdrawn at the eleventh hour, and Walter is to fill his place. He is to be engaged for six months certain, from the time of the landing in Honduras, and for a year afterwards, if the excavations are successful, and if the funds hold out. His letter ends with a promise to write me a farewell line when they are all on board ship, and when the pilot leaves them. I can only hope and pray earnestly that he and I are both acting in this matter for the best. It seems such a serious step for him to take, that the mere contemplation of it startles me. And yet, in his unhappy position, how can I expect him or wish him to remain at home?

16th. — The carriage is at the door. Laura and I set out on our visit to the Arnolds to-day.

POLESDEAN LODGE, YORKSHIRE.

23rd. — A week in these new scenes and among these kind-hearted people has done her some good, though not so much as I had hoped. I have resolved to prolong our stay for another week at least. It is useless to go back to Limmeridge till there is an absolute necessity for our return.

24th. — Sad news by this morning's post. The expedition to Central America sailed on the twenty-first. We have parted with a true man — we have lost a faithful friend. Water Hartright has left England.

25th. — Sad news yesterday — ominous news to-day. Sir Percival Glyde has written to Mr. Fairlie, and Mr. Fairlie has written to Laura and me, to recall us to Limmeridge immediately.

What can this mean? Has the day for the marriage been fixed in our absence?

II

LIMMERIDGE HOUSE.

November 27th. — My forebodings are realised. The marriage is fixed for the twenty-second of December.

The day after we left for Polesdean Lodge Sir Percival wrote, it seems, to Mr. Fairlie, to say that the necessary repairs and alterations in his house in Hampshire would occupy a much longer time in completion than he had originally anticipated. The proper estimates were to be submitted to him as soon as possible, and it would greatly facilitate his entering into definite arrangements with the workpeople, if he could be informed of the exact period at which the wedding ceremony might be expected to take place. He could then make all his calculations in reference to time, besides writing the necessary apologies to friends who had been engaged to visit him that winter, and who could not, of course, be received when the house was in the hands of the workmen.

To this letter Mr. Fairlie had replied by requesting Sir Percival himself to suggest a day for the marriage, subject to Miss Fairlie's approval, which her guardian willingly undertook to do his best to obtain. Sir Percival wrote back by the next post, and proposed (in accordance with his own views and wishes from the first?) the latter part of December — perhaps the twenty-second, or twenty-fourth, or any other day that the lady and her guardian might prefer. The lady not being at hand to speak for herself, her guardian had decided, in her absence, on the earliest day mentioned — the twenty-second of December, and had written to recall us to Limmeridge in consequence.

After explaining these particulars to me at a private interview yesterday, Mr. Fairlie suggested, in his most amiable manner, that I should open the necessary negotiations to-day. Feeling that resistance was useless, unless I could first obtain Laura's authority to make it, I consented to speak to her, but declared, at the same time, that I would on no consideration undertake to gain her consent to Sir Percival's wishes. Mr. Fairlie complimented me on my "excellent conscience," much as he would have complimented me, if he had been out walking, on my "excellent constitution," and seemed perfectly satisfied, so far, with having simply shifted one more family responsibility from his own shoulders to mine.

This morning I spoke to Laura as I had promised. The composure — I may almost say, the insensibility — which she has so strangely and so resolutely maintained ever since Sir Percival left us, was not proof against the shock of the news I had to tell her. She turned pale and trembled violently.

"Not so soon!" she pleaded. "Oh, Marian, not so soon!"

The slightest hint she could give was enough for me. I rose to leave the room, and fight her battle for her at once with Mr. Fairlie.

Just as my hand was on the door, she caught fast hold of my dress and stopped me.

"Let me go!" I said. "My tongue burns to tell your uncle that he and Sir Percival are not to have it all their own way."

She sighed bitterly, and still held my dress.

"No!" she said faintly. "Too late, Marian, too late!"

"Not a minute too late," I retorted. "The question of time is our question—and trust me, Laura, to take a woman's full advantage of it."

I unclasped her hand from my gown while I spoke; but she slipped both her arms round my waist at the same moment, and held me more effectually than ever.

"It will only involve us in more trouble and more confusion," she said. "It will set you and my uncle at variance, and bring Sir Percival here again with fresh causes of complaint—"

"So much the better!" I cried out passionately. "Who cares for his causes of complaint? Are you to break your heart to set his mind at ease? No man under heaven deserves these sacrifices from us women. Men! They are the enemies of our innocence and our peace—they drag us away from our parents' love and our sisters' friendship—they take us body and soul to themselves, and fasten our helpless lives to theirs as they chain up a dog to his kennel. And what does the best of them give us in return? Let me go, Laura—I'm mad when I think of it!"

The tears—miserable, weak, women's tears of vexation and rage—started to my eyes. She smiled sadly, and put her handkerchief over my face to hide for me the betrayal of my own weakness—the weakness of all others which she knew that I most despised.

"Oh, Marian!" she said. "You crying! Think what you would say to me, if the places were changed, and if those tears were mine. All your love and courage and devotion will not alter what must happen, sooner or later. Let my uncle have his way. Let us have no more troubles and heart-burnings that any sacrifice of mine can prevent. Say you will live with me, Marian, when I am married — and say no more."

But I did say more. I forced back the contemptible tears that were no relief to me, and that only distressed her, and reasoned and pleaded as calmly as I could. It was of no avail. She made me twice repeat the promise to live with her when she was married, and then suddenly asked a question which turned my sorrow and my sympathy for her into a new direction.

"While we were at Polesdean," she said, "you had a letter, Marian — —"

Her altered tone — the abrupt manner in which she looked away from me and hid her face on my shoulder — the hesitation which silenced her before she had completed her question, all told me, but too plainly, to whom the half-expressed inquiry pointed.

"I thought, Laura, that you and I were never to refer to him again," I said gently.

"You had a letter from him?" she persisted.

"Yes," I replied, "if you must know it."

"Do you mean to write to him again?"

I hesitated. I had been afraid to tell her of his absence from England, or of the manner in which my exertions to serve his new hopes and projects had connected me with his departure. What answer could I make? He was gone where no letters could reach him for months, perhaps for years, to come.

"Suppose I do mean to write to him again," I said at last. "What then, Laura?"

Her cheek grew burning hot against my neck, and her arms trembled and tightened round me.

"Don't tell him about the twenty-second," she whispered. "Promise, Marian — pray promise you will not even mention my name to him when you write next."

I gave the promise. No words can say how sorrowfully I gave it. She instantly took her arm from my waist, walked away to the window, and stood looking out with her back to me. After a moment she spoke once more, but without turning round, without allowing me to catch the smallest glimpse of her face.

"Are you going to my uncle's room?" she asked. "Will you say that I consent to whatever arrangement he may think best? Never mind leaving me, Marian. I shall be better alone for a little while."

I went out. If, as soon as I got into the passage, I could have transported Mr. Fairlie and Sir Percival Glyde to the uttermost ends of the earth by lifting one of my fingers, that finger would have been raised without an instant's hesitation. For once my unhappy temper now stood my friend. I should have broken down altogether and burst into a violent fit of crying, if my tears had not been all burnt up in the heat of my anger. As it was, I dashed into Mr. Fairlie's room—called to him as harshly as possible, "Laura consents to the twenty-second"—and dashed out again without waiting for a word of answer. I banged the door after me, and I hope I shattered Mr. Fairlie's nervous system for the rest of the day.

28th.—This morning I read poor Hartright's farewell letter over again, a doubt having crossed my mind since yesterday, whether I am acting wisely in concealing the fact of his departure from Laura.

On reflection, I still think I am right. The allusions in his letter to the preparations made for the expedition to Central America, all show that the leaders of it know it to be dangerous. If the discovery of this makes me uneasy, what would it make her? It is bad enough to feel that his departure has deprived us of the friend of all others to whose devotion we could trust in the hour of need, if ever that hour comes and finds us helpless; but it is far worse to know that he has gone from us to face the perils of a bad climate, a wild country, and a disturbed population. Surely it would be a cruel candour to tell Laura this, without a pressing and a positive necessity for it?

I almost doubt whether I ought not to go a step farther, and burn the letter at once, for fear of its one day falling into wrong hands. It not only refers to Laura in terms which ought to remain a secret for ever between the writer and me, but it reiterates his suspicion—so obstinate, so unaccountable, and so alarming—that he has been secretly watched since he left Limmeridge. He declares that he saw the faces of the two strange men who followed him about the streets of London, watching him among the crowd which gathered at Liverpool to see the expedition embark, and he positively asserts that he heard the name of Anne Catherick pronounced behind him as he got into the boat. His own words are, "These events have a meaning, these events must lead to a result. The mystery of Anne Catherick is not cleared up yet. She may never cross my path again, but if ever she crosses yours, make better use of the opportunity, Miss Halcombe, than I made of it. I speak on strong conviction—I entreat you to remember what I say." These are his own expressions. There is no danger of my forgetting them—my memory is only too ready to dwell on any words of Hartright's that refer to Anne Catherick. But there is danger in my keeping the letter. The merest accident might place it at the mercy of strangers. I may fall ill—I may die. Better to burn it at once, and have one anxiety the less.

It is burnt. The ashes of his farewell letter—the last he may ever write to me—lie in a few black fragments on the hearth. Is this the sad end to all that sad story? Oh, not the end—surely, surely not the end already!

29th.—The preparations for the marriage have begun. The dressmaker has come to receive her orders. Laura is perfectly impassive, perfectly careless about the question of all others in which a woman's personal interests are most closely bound up. She has left it all to the dressmaker and to me. If poor Hartright had been the baronet, and the husband of her father's choice, how differently she would have behaved! How anxious and capricious she would have been, and what a hard task the best of dressmakers would have found it to please her!

30th.—We hear every day from Sir Percival. The last news is that the alterations in his house will occupy from four to six months before they can be properly completed. If painters, paperhangers, and upholsterers could make happiness as well as splendour, I should be interested about their proceedings in Laura's future home. As it is, the only part of Sir Percival's last letter which does not leave me as it found me, perfectly indifferent to all his plans and projects, is the part which refers to the wedding tour. He proposes, as Laura is delicate, and as the winter threatens to be unusually severe, to take her to Rome, and to remain in Italy until the early part of next summer. If this plan should not be approved, he is equally ready, although he has no establishment of his own in town, to spend the season in London, in the most suitable furnished house that can be obtained for the purpose.

Putting myself and my own feelings entirely out of the question (which it is my duty to do, and which I have done), I, for one, have no doubt of the propriety of adopting the first of these proposals. In either case a separation between Laura and me is inevitable. It will be a longer separation, in the event of their going abroad, than it would be in the event of their remaining in London — but we must set against this disadvantage the benefit to Laura, on the other side, of passing the winter in a mild climate, and more than that, the immense assistance in raising her spirits, and reconciling her to her new existence, which the mere wonder and excitement of travelling for the first time in her life in the most interesting country in the world, must surely afford. She is not of a disposition to find resources in the conventional gaieties and excitements of London. They would only make the first oppression of this lamentable marriage fall the heavier on her. I dread the beginning of her new life more than words can tell, but I see some hope for her if she travels — none if she remains at home.

It is strange to look back at this latest entry in my journal, and to find that I am writing of the marriage and the parting with Laura, as people write of a settled thing. It seems so cold and so unfeeling to be looking at the future already in this cruelly composed way. But what other way is possible, now that the time is drawing so near? Before another month is over our heads she will be his Laura instead of mine! His Laura! I am as little able to realise the idea which those two words convey — my mind feels almost as dulled and stunned by it — as if writing of her marriage were like writing of her death.

December 1st. — A sad, sad day — a day that I have no heart to describe at any length. After weakly putting it off last night, I was obliged to speak to her this morning of Sir Percival's proposal about the wedding tour.

In the full conviction that I should be with her wherever she went, the poor child — for a child she is still in many things — was almost happy at the prospect of seeing the wonders of Florence and Rome and Naples. It nearly broke my heart to dispel her delusion, and to bring her face to face with the hard truth. I was obliged to tell her that no man tolerates a rival — not even a woman rival — in his wife's affections, when he first marries, whatever he may do afterwards. I was obliged to warn her that my chance of living with her permanently under her own roof, depended entirely on my not arousing Sir Percival's jealousy and distrust by standing between them at the beginning of their marriage, in the position of the chosen depositary of his wife's closest secrets. Drop by drop I poured the profaning bitterness of this world's wisdom into that pure heart and that innocent mind, while every higher and better feeling within me recoiled from my miserable task. It is over now. She has learnt her hard, her inevitable lesson. The simple illusions of her girlhood are gone, and my hand has stripped them off. Better mine than his — that is all my consolation — better mine than his.

So the first proposal is the proposal accepted. They are to go to Italy, and I am to arrange, with Sir Percival's permission, for meeting them and staying with them when they return to England. In other words, I am to ask a personal favour, for the first time in my life, and to ask it of the man of all others to whom I least desire to owe a serious obligation of any kind. Well! I think I could do even more than that, for Laura's sake.

2nd. — On looking back, I find myself always referring to Sir Percival in disparaging terms. In the turn affairs have now taken, I must and will root out my prejudice against him. I cannot think how it first got into my mind. It certainly never existed in former times.

Is it Laura's reluctance to become his wife that has set me against him? Have Hartright's perfectly intelligible prejudices infected me without my suspecting their influence? Does that letter of Anne Catherick's still leave a lurking distrust in my mind, in spite of Sir Percival's explanation, and of the proof in my possession of the truth of it? I cannot account for the state of my own feelings; the one thing I am certain of is, that it is my duty — doubly my duty now — not to wrong Sir Percival by unjustly distrusting him. If it has got to be a habit with me always to write of him in the same unfavourable manner, I must and will break myself of this unworthy tendency, even though the effort should force me to close the pages of my journal till the marriage is over! I am seriously dissatisfied with myself — I will write no more to-day.

December 16th. — A whole fortnight has passed, and I have not once opened these pages. I have been long enough away from my journal to come back to it with a healthier and better mind, I hope, so far as Sir Percival is concerned.

There is not much to record of the past two weeks. The dresses are almost all finished, and the new travelling trunks have been sent here from London. Poor dear Laura hardly leaves me for a moment all day, and last night, when neither of us could sleep, she came and crept into my bed to talk to me there. "I shall lose you so soon, Marian," she said; "I must make the most of you while I can."

They are to be married at Limmeridge Church, and thank Heaven, not one of the neighbours is to be invited to the ceremony. The only visitor will be our old friend, Mr. Arnold, who is to come from Polesdean to give Laura away, her uncle being far too delicate to trust himself outside the door in such inclement weather as we now have. If I were not determined, from this day forth, to see nothing but the bright side of our prospects, the melancholy absence of any male relative of Laura's, at the most important moment of her life, would make me very gloomy and very distrustful of the future. But I have done with gloom and distrust — that is to say, I have done with writing about either the one or the other in this journal.

Sir Percival is to arrive to-morrow. He offered, in case we wished to treat him on terms of rigid etiquette, to write and ask our clergyman to grant him the hospitality of the rectory, during the short period of his sojourn at Limmeridge, before the marriage. Under the circumstances, neither Mr. Fairlie nor I thought it at all necessary for us to trouble ourselves about attending to trifling forms and ceremonies. In our wild moorland country, and in this great lonely house, we may well claim to be beyond the reach of the trivial conventionalities which hamper people in other places. I wrote to Sir Percival to thank him for his polite offer, and to beg that he would occupy his old rooms, just as usual, at Limmeridge House.

17th. — He arrived to-day, looking, as I thought, a little worn and anxious, but still talking and laughing like a man in the best possible spirits. He brought with him some really beautiful presents in jewellery, which Laura received with her best grace, and, outwardly at least, with perfect self-possession. The only sign I can detect of the struggle it must cost her to preserve appearances at this trying time, expresses itself in a sudden unwillingness, on her part, ever to be left alone. Instead of retreating to her own room, as usual, she seems to dread going there. When I went upstairs to-day, after lunch, to put on my bonnet for a walk, she volunteered to join me, and again, before dinner, she threw the door open between our two rooms, so that we might talk to each other while we were dressing. "Keep me always doing something," she said; "keep me always in company with somebody. Don't let me think—that is all I ask now, Marian—don't let me think."

This sad change in her only increases her attractions for Sir Percival. He interprets it, I can see, to his own advantage. There is a feverish flush in her cheeks, a feverish brightness in her eyes, which he welcomes as the return of her beauty and the recovery of her spirits. She talked to-day at dinner with a gaiety and carelessness so false, so shockingly out of her character, that I secretly longed to silence her and take her away. Sir Percival's delight and surprise appeared to be beyond all expression. The anxiety which I had noticed on his face when he arrived totally disappeared from it, and he looked, even to my eyes, a good ten years younger than he really is.

There can be no doubt—though some strange perversity prevents me from seeing it myself—there can be no doubt that Laura's future husband is a very handsome man. Regular features form a personal advantage to begin with—and he has them. Bright brown eyes, either in man or woman, are a great attraction—and he has them. Even baldness, when it is only baldness over the forehead (as in his case), is rather becoming than not in a man, for it heightens the head and adds to the intelligence of the face. Grace and ease of movement, untiring animation of manner, ready, pliant, conversational powers—all these are unquestionable merits, and all these he certainly possesses. Surely Mr. Gilmore, ignorant as he is of Laura's secret, was not to blame for feeling surprised that she should repent of her marriage engagement? Any one else in his place would have shared our good old friend's opinion. If I were asked, at this moment, to say plainly what defects I have discovered in Sir Percival, I could only point out two. One, his incessant restlessness and excitability—which may be caused, naturally enough, by unusual energy of character. The other, his short, sharp, ill-tempered manner of speaking to the servants—which may be only a bad habit after all. No, I cannot dispute it, and I will not dispute it—Sir Percival is a very handsome and a very agreeable man. There! I have written it down at last, and I am glad it's over.

18th.—Feeling weary and depressed this morning, I left Laura with Mrs. Vesey, and went out alone for one of my brisk midday walks, which I have discontinued too much of late. I took the dry airy road over the moor that leads to Todd's Corner. After having been out half an hour, I was excessively surprised to see Sir Percival approaching me from the direction of the farm. He was walking rapidly, swinging his stick, his head erect as usual, and his shooting jacket flying open in the wind. When we met he did not wait for me to ask any questions—he told me at once that he had been to the farm to inquire if Mr. or Mrs. Todd had received any tidings, since his last visit to Limmeridge, of Anne Catherick.

"You found, of course, that they had heard nothing?" I said.

"Nothing whatever," he replied. "I begin to be seriously afraid that we have lost her. Do you happen to know," he continued, looking me in the face very attentively "if the artist—Mr. Hartright—is in a position to give us any further information?"

"He has neither heard of her, nor seen her, since he left Cumberland," I answered.

"Very sad," said Sir Percival, speaking like a man who was disappointed, and yet, oddly enough, looking at the same time like a man who was relieved. "It is impossible to say what misfortunes may not have happened to the miserable creature. I am inexpressibly annoyed at the failure of all my efforts to restore her to the care and protection which she so urgently needs."

This time he really looked annoyed. I said a few sympathising words, and we then talked of other subjects on our way back to the house. Surely my chance meeting with him on the moor has disclosed another favourable trait in his character? Surely it was singularly considerate and unselfish of him to think of Anne Catherick on the eve of his marriage, and to go all the way to Todd's Corner to make inquiries about her, when he might have passed the time so much more agreeably in Laura's society? Considering that he can only have acted from motives of pure charity, his conduct, under the circumstances, shows unusual good feeling and deserves extraordinary praise. Well! I give him extraordinary praise—and there's an end of it.

The Woman in White

19th.—More discoveries in the inexhaustible mine of Sir Percival's virtues.

To-day I approached the subject of my proposed sojourn under his wife's roof when he brings her back to England. I had hardly dropped my first hint in this direction before he caught me warmly by the hand, and said I had made the very offer to him which he had been, on his side, most anxious to make to me. I was the companion of all others whom he most sincerely longed to secure for his wife, and he begged me to believe that I had conferred a lasting favour on him by making the proposal to live with Laura after her marriage, exactly as I had always lived with her before it.

When I had thanked him in her name and mine for his considerate kindness to both of us, we passed next to the subject of his wedding tour, and began to talk of the English society in Rome to which Laura was to be introduced. He ran over the names of several friends whom he expected to meet abroad this winter. They were all English, as well as I can remember, with one exception. The one exception was Count Fosco.

The mention of the Count's name, and the discovery that he and his wife are likely to meet the bride and bridegroom on the continent, puts Laura's marriage, for the first time, in a distinctly favourable light. It is likely to be the means of healing a family feud. Hitherto Madame Fosco has chosen to forget her obligations as Laura's aunt out of sheer spite against the late Mr. Fairlie for his conduct in the affair of the legacy. Now however, she can persist in this course of conduct no longer. Sir Percival and Count Fosco are old and fast friends, and their wives will have no choice but to meet on civil terms. Madame Fosco in her maiden days was one of the most impertinent women I ever met with—capricious, exacting, and vain to the last degree of absurdity. If her husband has succeeded in bringing her to her senses, he deserves the gratitude of every member of the family, and he may have mine to begin with.

I am becoming anxious to know the Count. He is the most intimate friend of Laura's husband, and in that capacity he excites my strongest interest. Neither Laura nor I have ever seen him. All I know of him is that his accidental presence, years ago, on the steps of the Trinita del Monte at Rome, assisted Sir Percival's escape from robbery and assassination at the critical moment when he was wounded in the hand, and might the next instant have been wounded in the heart. I remember also that, at the time of the late Mr. Fairlie's absurd objections to his sister's marriage, the Count wrote him a very temperate and sensible letter on the subject, which, I am ashamed to say, remained unanswered. This is all I know of Sir Percival's friend. I wonder if he will ever come to England? I wonder if I shall like him?

My pen is running away into mere speculation. Let me return to sober matter of fact. It is certain that Sir Percival's reception of my venturesome proposal to live with his wife was more than kind, it was almost affectionate. I am sure Laura's husband will have no reason to complain of me if I can only go on as I have begun. I have already declared him to be handsome, agreeable, full of good feeling towards the unfortunate and full of affectionate kindness towards me. Really, I hardly know myself again, in my new character of Sir Percival's warmest friend.

20th.—I hate Sir Percival! I flatly deny his good looks. I consider him to be eminently ill-tempered and disagreeable, and totally wanting in kindness and good feeling. Last night the cards for the married couple were sent home. Laura opened the packet and saw her future name in print for the first time. Sir Percival looked over her shoulder familiarly at the new card which had already transformed Miss Fairlie into Lady Glyde—smiled with the most odious self-complacency, and whispered something in her ear. I don't know what it was—Laura has refused to tell me—but I saw her face turn to such a deadly whiteness that I thought she would have fainted. He took no notice of the change—he seemed to be barbarously unconscious that he had said anything to pain her. All my old feelings of hostility towards him revived on the instant, and all the hours that have passed since have done nothing to dissipate them. I am more unreasonable and more unjust than ever. In three words—how glibly my pen writes them!—in three words, I hate him.

21st.—Have the anxieties of this anxious time shaken me a little, at last? I have been writing, for the last few days, in a tone of levity which, Heaven knows, is far enough from my heart, and which it has rather shocked me to discover on looking back at the entries in my journal.

Perhaps I may have caught the feverish excitement of Laura's spirits for the last week. If so, the fit has already passed away from me, and has left me in a very strange state of mind.

The Woman in White

A persistent idea has been forcing itself on my attention, ever since last night, that something will yet happen to prevent the marriage. What has produced this singular fancy? Is it the indirect result of my apprehensions for Laura's future? Or has it been unconsciously suggested to me by the increasing restlessness and irritability which I have certainly observed in Sir Percival's manner as the wedding-day draws nearer and nearer? Impossible to say. I know that I have the idea—surely the wildest idea, under the circumstances, that ever entered a woman's head?—but try as I may, I cannot trace it back to its source.

This last day has been all confusion and wretchedness. How can I write about it?—and yet, I must write. Anything is better than brooding over my own gloomy thoughts.

Kind Mrs. Vesey, whom we have all too much overlooked and forgotten of late, innocently caused us a sad morning to begin with. She has been, for months past, secretly making a warm Shetland shawl for her dear pupil—a most beautiful and surprising piece of work to be done by a woman at her age and with her habits. The gift was presented this morning, and poor warm-hearted Laura completely broke down when the shawl was put proudly on her shoulders by the loving old friend and guardian of her motherless childhood. I was hardly allowed time to quiet them both, or even to dry my own eyes, when I was sent for by Mr. Fairlie, to be favoured with a long recital of his arrangements for the preservation of his own tranquillity on the wedding-day.

"Dear Laura" was to receive his present—a shabby ring, with her affectionate uncle's hair for an ornament, instead of a precious stone, and with a heartless French inscription inside, about congenial sentiments and eternal friendship—"dear Laura" was to receive this tender tribute from my hands immediately, so that she might have plenty of time to recover from the agitation produced by the gift before she appeared in Mr. Fairlie's presence. "Dear Laura" was to pay him a little visit that evening, and to be kind enough not to make a scene. "Dear Laura" was to pay him another little visit in her wedding-dress the next morning, and to be kind enough, again, not to make a scene. "Dear Laura" was to look in once more, for the third time, before going away, but without harrowing his feelings by saying when she was going away, and without tears—"in the name of pity, in the name of everything, dear Marian, that is most affectionate and most domestic, and most delightfully and charmingly self-composed, without tears!" I was so exasperated by this miserable selfish trifling, at such a time, that I should certainly have shocked Mr. Fairlie by some of the hardest and rudest truths he has ever heard in his life, if the arrival of Mr. Arnold from Polesdean had not called me away to new duties downstairs.

The rest of the day is indescribable. I believe no one in the house really knew how it passed. The confusion of small events, all huddled together one on the other, bewildered everybody. There were dresses sent home that had been forgotten—there were trunks to be packed and unpacked and packed again—there were presents from friends far and near, friends high and low. We were all needlessly hurried, all nervously expectant of the morrow. Sir Percival, especially, was too restless now to remain five minutes together in the same place. That short, sharp cough of his troubled him more than ever. He was in and out of doors all day long, and he seemed to grow so inquisitive on a sudden, that he questioned the very strangers who came on small errands to the house. Add to all this, the one perpetual thought in Laura's mind and mine, that we were to part the next day, and the haunting dread, unexpressed by either of us, and yet ever present to both, that this deplorable marriage might prove to be the one fatal error of her life and the one hopeless sorrow of mine. For the first time in all the years of our close and happy intercourse we almost avoided looking each other in the face, and we refrained, by common consent, from speaking together in private through the whole evening. I can dwell on it no longer. Whatever future sorrows may be in store for me, I shall always look back on this twenty-first of December as the most comfortless and most miserable day of my life.

I am writing these lines in the solitude of my own room, long after midnight, having just come back from a stolen look at Laura in her pretty little white bed—the bed she has occupied since the days of her girlhood.

There she lay, unconscious that I was looking at her—quiet, more quiet than I had dared to hope, but not sleeping. The glimmer of the night-light showed me that her eyes were only partially closed—the traces of tears glistened between her eyelids. My little keepsake—only a brooch—lay on the table at her bedside, with her prayer-book, and the miniature portrait of her father which she takes with her wherever she goes. I waited a moment, looking at her from behind her pillow, as she lay beneath me, with one arm and hand resting on the white coverlid, so still, so quietly breathing, that the frill on her night-dress never moved—I waited, looking at her, as I have seen her thousands of times, as I shall never see her again—and then stole back to my room. My own love! with all your wealth, and all your beauty, how friendless you are! The one man who would give his heart's life to serve you is far away, tossing, this stormy night, on the awful sea. Who else is left to you? No father, no brother—no living creature but the helpless, useless woman who writes these sad lines, and watches by you for the morning, in sorrow that she cannot compose, in doubt that she cannot conquer. Oh, what a trust is to be placed in that man's hands to-morrow! If ever he forgets it—if ever he injures a hair of her head!— —

THE TWENTY-SECOND OF DECEMBER. Seven o'clock. A wild, unsettled morning. She has just risen—better and calmer, now that the time has come, than she was yesterday.

Ten o'clock. She is dressed. We have kissed each other—we have promised each other not to lose courage. I am away for a moment in my own room. In the whirl and confusion of my thoughts, I can detect that strange fancy of some hindrance happening to stop the marriage still hanging about my mind. Is it hanging about his mind too? I see him from the window, moving hither and thither uneasily among the carriages at the door.—How can I write such folly! The marriage is a certainty. In less than half an hour we start for the church.

Eleven o'clock. It is all over. They are married.

Three o'clock. They are gone! I am blind with crying—I can write no more— —

[The First Epoch of the Story closes here.]

THE SECOND EPOCH

THE STORY CONTINUED BY MARIAN HALCOMBE.

I

BLACKWATER PARK, HAMPSHIRE.

June 11th, 1850.—Six months to look back on—six long, lonely months since Laura and I last saw each other!

How many days have I still to wait? Only one! To-morrow, the twelfth, the travellers return to England. I can hardly realise my own happiness—I can hardly believe that the next four-and-twenty hours will complete the last day of separation between Laura and me.

She and her husband have been in Italy all the winter, and afterwards in the Tyrol. They come back, accompanied by Count Fosco and his wife, who propose to settle somewhere in the neighbourhood of London, and who have engaged to stay at Blackwater Park for the summer months before deciding on a place of residence. So long as Laura returns, no matter who returns with her. Sir Percival may fill the house from floor to ceiling, if he likes, on condition that his wife and I inhabit it together.

Meanwhile, here I am, established at Blackwater Park, "the ancient and interesting seat" (as the county history obligingly informs me) "of Sir Percival Glyde, Bart.," and the future abiding-place (as I may now venture to add on my account) of plain Marian Halcombe, spinster, now settled in a snug little sitting-room, with a cup of tea by her side, and all her earthly possessions ranged round her in three boxes and a bag.

I left Limmeridge yesterday, having received Laura's delightful letter from Paris the day before. I had been previously uncertain whether I was to meet them in London or in Hampshire, but this last letter informed me that Sir Percival proposed to land at Southampton, and to travel straight on to his country-house. He has spent so much money abroad that he has none left to defray the expenses of living in London for the

The Woman in White

remainder of the season, and he is economically resolved to pass the summer and autumn quietly at Blackwater. Laura has had more than enough of excitement and change of scene, and is pleased at the prospect of country tranquillity and retirement which her husband's prudence provides for her. As for me, I am ready to be happy anywhere in her society. We are all, therefore, well contented in our various ways, to begin with.

Last night I slept in London, and was delayed there so long to-day by various calls and commissions, that I did not reach Blackwater this evening till after dusk.

Judging by my vague impressions of the place thus far, it is the exact opposite of Limmeridge.

The house is situated on a dead flat, and seems to be shut in — almost suffocated, to my north-country notions, by trees. I have seen nobody but the man-servant who opened the door to me, and the housekeeper, a very civil person, who showed me the way to my own room, and got me my tea. I have a nice little boudoir and bedroom, at the end of a long passage on the first floor. The servants and some of the spare rooms are on the second floor, and all the living rooms are on the ground floor. I have not seen one of them yet, and I know nothing about the house, except that one wing of it is said to be five hundred years old, that it had a moat round it once, and that it gets its name of Blackwater from a lake in the park.

Eleven o'clock has just struck, in a ghostly and solemn manner, from a turret over the centre of the house, which I saw when I came in. A large dog has been woke, apparently by the sound of the bell, and is howling and yawning drearily, somewhere round a corner. I hear echoing footsteps in the passages below, and the iron thumping of bolts and bars at the house door. The servants are evidently going to bed. Shall I follow their example?

No, I am not half sleepy enough. Sleepy, did I say? I feel as if I should never close my eyes again. The bare anticipation of seeing that dear face, and hearing that well-known voice to-morrow, keeps me in a perpetual fever of excitement. If I only had the privileges of a man, I would order out Sir Percival's best horse instantly, and tear away on a night-gallop, eastward, to meet the rising sun — a long, hard, heavy, ceaseless gallop of hours and hours, like the famous highwayman's ride to York. Being, however, nothing but a woman, condemned to patience, propriety, and petticoats for life, I must respect the house-keeper's opinions, and try to compose myself in some feeble and feminine way.

Reading is out of the question—I can't fix my attention on books. Let me try if I can write myself into sleepiness and fatigue. My journal has been very much neglected of late. What can I recall—standing, as I now do, on the threshold of a new life—of persons and events, of chances and changes, during the past six months—the long, weary, empty interval since Laura's wedding-day?

Walter Hartright is uppermost in my memory, and he passes first in the shadowy procession of my absent friends. I received a few lines from him, after the landing of the expedition in Honduras, written more cheerfully and hopefully than he has written yet. A month or six weeks later I saw an extract from an American newspaper, describing the departure of the adventurers on their inland journey. They were last seen entering a wild primeval forest, each man with his rifle on his shoulder and his baggage at his back. Since that time, civilisation has lost all trace of them. Not a line more have I received from Walter, not a fragment of news from the expedition has appeared in any of the public journals.

The same dense, disheartening obscurity hangs over the fate and fortunes of Anne Catherick, and her companion, Mrs. Clements. Nothing whatever has been heard of either of them. Whether they are in the country or out of it, whether they are living or dead, no one knows. Even Sir Percival's solicitor has lost all hope, and has ordered the useless search after the fugitives to be finally given up.

Our good old friend Mr. Gilmore has met with a sad check in his active professional career. Early in the spring we were alarmed by hearing that he had been found insensible at his desk, and that the seizure was pronounced to be an apoplectic fit. He had been long complaining of fulness and oppression in the head, and his doctor had warned him of the consequences that would follow his persistency in continuing to work, early and late, as if he were still a young man. The result now is that he has been positively ordered to keep out of his office for a year to come, at least, and to seek repose of body and relief of mind by altogether changing his usual mode of life. The business is left, accordingly, to be carried on by his partner, and he is himself, at this moment, away in Germany, visiting some relations who are settled there in mercantile pursuits. Thus another true friend and trustworthy adviser is lost to us—lost, I earnestly hope and trust, for a time only.

Poor Mrs. Vesey travelled with me as far as London. It was impossible to abandon her to solitude at Limmeridge after Laura and I had both left the house, and we have arranged that she is to live with an unmarried younger sister of hers, who keeps a school at Clapham. She is to come here this autumn to visit her pupil—I might almost say her adopted child. I saw the good old lady safe to her destination, and left her in the care of her relative, quietly happy at the prospect of seeing Laura again in a few months' time.

As for Mr. Fairlie, I believe I am guilty of no injustice if I describe him as being unutterably relieved by having the house clear of us women. The idea of his missing his niece is simply preposterous—he used to let months pass in the old times without attempting to see her—and in my case and Mrs. Vesey's, I take leave to consider his telling us both that he was half heart-broken at our departure, to be equivalent to a confession that he was secretly rejoiced to get rid of us. His last caprice has led him to keep two photographers incessantly employed in producing sun-pictures of all the treasures and curiosities in his possession. One complete copy of the collection of the photographs is to be presented to the Mechanics' Institution of Carlisle, mounted on the finest cardboard, with ostentatious red-letter inscriptions underneath, "Madonna and Child by Raphael. In the possession of Frederick Fairlie, Esquire." "Copper coin of the period of Tiglath Pileser. In the possession of Frederick Fairlie, Esquire." "Unique Rembrandt etching. Known all over Europe as The Smudge, from a printer's blot in the corner which exists in no other copy. Valued at three hundred guineas. In the possession of Frederick Fairlie, Esq." Dozens of photographs of this sort, and all inscribed in this manner, were completed before I left Cumberland, and hundreds more remain to be done. With this new interest to occupy him, Mr. Fairlie will be a happy man for months and months to come, and the two unfortunate photographers will share the social martyrdom which he has hitherto inflicted on his valet alone.

So much for the persons and events which hold the foremost place in my memory. What next of the one person who holds the foremost place in my heart? Laura has been present to my thoughts all the while I have been writing these lines. What can I recall of her during the past six months, before I close my journal for the night?

I have only her letters to guide me, and on the most

important of all the questions which our correspondence can discuss, every one of those letters leaves me in the dark.

Does he treat her kindly? Is she happier now than she was when I parted with her on the wedding-day? All my letters have contained these two inquiries, put more or less directly, now in one form, and now in another, and all, on that point only, have remained without reply, or have been answered as if my questions merely related to the state of her health. She informs me, over and over again, that she is perfectly well—that travelling agrees with her—that she is getting through the winter, for the first time in her life, without catching cold—but not a word can I find anywhere which tells me plainly that she is reconciled to her marriage, and that she can now look back to the twenty-second of December without any bitter feelings of repentance and regret. The name of her husband is only mentioned in her letters, as she might mention the name of a friend who was travelling with them, and who had undertaken to make all the arrangements for the journey. "Sir Percival" has settled that we leave on such a day—"Sir Percival" has decided that we travel by such a road. Sometimes she writes "Percival" only, but very seldom—in nine cases out of ten she gives him his title.

I cannot find that his habits and opinions have changed and coloured hers in any single particular. The usual moral transformation which is insensibly wrought in a young, fresh, sensitive woman by her marriage, seems never to have taken place in Laura. She writes of her own thoughts and impressions, amid all the wonders she has seen, exactly as she might have written to some one else, if I had been travelling with her instead of her husband. I see no betrayal anywhere of sympathy of any kind existing between them. Even when she wanders from the subject of her travels, and occupies herself with the prospects that await her in England, her speculations are busied with her future as my sister, and persistently neglect to notice her future as Sir Percival's wife. In all this there is no undertone of complaint to warn me that she is absolutely unhappy in her married life. The impression I have derived from our correspondence does not, thank God, lead me to any such distressing conclusion as that. I only see a sad torpor, an unchangeable indifference, when I turn my mind from her in the old character of a sister, and look at her, through the medium of her letters, in the new character of a wife. In other words, it is always Laura Fairlie who has been writing to me for the last six months, and never Lady Glyde.

The strange silence which she maintains on the subject of her husband's character and conduct, she preserves with almost equal resolution in the few references which her later letters contain to the name of her husband's bosom friend, Count Fosco.

For some unexplained reason the Count and his wife appear to have changed their plans abruptly, at the end of last autumn, and to have gone to Vienna instead of going to Rome, at which latter place Sir Percival had expected to find them when he left England. They only quitted Vienna in the spring, and travelled as far as the Tyrol to meet the bride and bridegroom on their homeward journey. Laura writes readily enough about the meeting with Madame Fosco, and assures me that she has found her aunt so much changed for the better—so much quieter, and so much more sensible as a wife than she was as a single woman—that I shall hardly know her again when I see her here. But on the subject of Count Fosco (who interests me infinitely more than his wife), Laura is provokingly circumspect and silent. She only says that he puzzles her, and that she will not tell me what her impression of him is until I have seen him, and formed my own opinion first.

This, to my mind, looks ill for the Count. Laura has preserved, far more perfectly than most people do in later life, the child's subtle faculty of knowing a friend by instinct, and if I am right in assuming that her first impression of Count Fosco has not been favourable, I for one am in some danger of doubting and distrusting that illustrious foreigner before I have so much as set eyes on him. But, patience, patience—this uncertainty, and many uncertainties more, cannot last much longer. To-morrow will see all my doubts in a fair way of being cleared up, sooner or later.

Twelve o'clock has struck, and I have just come back to close these pages, after looking out at my open window.

It is a still, sultry, moonless night. The stars are dull and few. The trees that shut out the view on all sides look dimly black and solid in the distance, like a great wall of rock. I hear the croaking of frogs, faint and far off, and the echoes of the great clock hum in the airless calm long after the strokes have ceased. I wonder how Blackwater Park will look in the daytime? I don't altogether like it by night.

12th.—A day of investigations and discoveries—a more interesting day, for many reasons, than I had ventured to anticipate.

I began my sight-seeing, of course, with the house.

The main body of the building is of the time of that highly-overrated woman, Queen Elizabeth. On the ground floor there are two hugely long galleries, with low ceilings lying parallel with each other, and rendered additionally dark and dismal by hideous family portraits—every one of which I should like to burn. The rooms on the floor above the two galleries are kept in tolerable repair, but are very seldom used. The civil housekeeper, who acted as my guide, offered to show me over them, but considerately added that she feared I should find them rather out of order. My respect for the integrity of my own petticoats and stockings infinitely exceeds my respect for all the Elizabethan bedrooms in the kingdom, so I positively declined exploring the upper regions of dust and dirt at the risk of soiling my nice clean clothes. The housekeeper said, "I am quite of your opinion, miss," and appeared to think me the most sensible woman she had met with for a long time past.

So much, then, for the main building. Two wings are added at either end of it. The half-ruined wing on the left (as you approach the house) was once a place of residence standing by itself, and was built in the fourteenth century. One of Sir Percival's maternal ancestors—I don't remember, and don't care which—tacked on the main building, at right angles to it, in the aforesaid Queen Elizabeth's time. The housekeeper told me that the architecture of "the old wing," both outside and inside, was considered remarkably fine by good judges. On further investigation I discovered that good judges could only exercise their abilities on Sir Percival's piece of antiquity by previously dismissing from their minds all fear of damp, darkness, and rats. Under these circumstances, I unhesitatingly acknowledged myself to be no judge at all, and suggested that we should treat "the old wing" precisely as we had previously treated the Elizabethan bedrooms. Once more the housekeeper said, "I am quite of your opinion, miss," and once more she looked at me with undisguised admiration of my extraordinary common-sense.

We went next to the wing on the right, which was built, by way of completing the wonderful architectural jumble at Blackwater Park, in the time of George the Second.

This is the habitable part of the house, which has been repaired and redecorated inside on Laura's account. My two rooms, and all the good bedrooms besides, are on the first floor, and the basement contains a drawing-room, a dining-room, a morning-room, a library, and a pretty little boudoir for Laura, all very nicely ornamented in the bright modern way, and all very elegantly furnished with the delightful modern luxuries. None of the rooms are anything like so large and airy as our rooms at Limmeridge, but they all look pleasant to live in. I was terribly afraid, from what I had heard of Blackwater Park, of fatiguing antique chairs, and dismal stained glass, and musty, frouzy hangings, and all the barbarous lumber which people born without a sense of comfort accumulate about them, in defiance of the consideration due to the convenience of their friends. It is an inexpressible relief to find that the nineteenth century has invaded this strange future home of mine, and has swept the dirty "good old times" out of the way of our daily life.

I dawdled away the morning—part of the time in the rooms downstairs, and part out of doors in the great square which is formed by the three sides of the house, and by the lofty iron railings and gates which protect it in front. A large circular fish-pond with stone sides, and an allegorical leaden monster in the middle, occupies the centre of the square. The pond itself is full of gold and silver fish, and is encircled by a broad belt of the softest turf I ever walked on. I loitered here on the shady side pleasantly enough till luncheon-time, and after that took my broad straw hat and wandered out alone in the warm lovely sunlight to explore the grounds.

Daylight confirmed the impression which I had felt the night before, of there being too many trees at Blackwater. The house is stifled by them. They are, for the most part, young, and planted far too thickly. I suspect there must have been a ruinous cutting down of timber all over the estate before Sir Percival's time, and an angry anxiety on the part of the next possessor to fill up all the gaps as thickly and rapidly as possible. After looking about me in front of the house, I observed a flower-garden on my left hand, and walked towards it to see what I could discover in that direction.

On a nearer view the garden proved to be small and poor and ill kept. I left it behind me, opened a little gate in a ring fence, and found myself in a plantation of fir-trees.

A pretty winding path, artificially made, led me on among the trees, and my north-country experience soon informed me that I was approaching sandy, heathy ground. After a walk of more than half a mile, I should think, among the firs, the path took a sharp turn—the trees abruptly ceased to appear on either side of me, and I found myself standing suddenly on the margin of a vast open space, and looking down at the Blackwater lake from which the house takes its name.

The ground, shelving away below me, was all sand, with a few little heathy hillocks to break the monotony of it in certain places. The lake itself had evidently once flowed to the spot on which I stood, and had been gradually wasted and dried up to less than a third of its former size. I saw its still, stagnant waters, a quarter of a mile away from me in the hollow, separated into pools and ponds by twining reeds and rushes, and little knolls of earth. On the farther bank from me the trees rose thickly again, and shut out the view, and cast their black shadows on the sluggish, shallow water. As I walked down to the lake, I saw that the ground on its farther side was damp and marshy, overgrown with rank grass and dismal willows. The water, which was clear enough on the open sandy side, where the sun shone, looked black and poisonous opposite to me, where it lay deeper under the shade of the spongy banks, and the rank overhanging thickets and tangled trees. The frogs were croaking, and the rats were slipping in and out of the shadowy water, like live shadows themselves, as I got nearer to the marshy side of the lake. I saw here, lying half in and half out of the water, the rotten wreck of an old overturned boat, with a sickly spot of sunlight glimmering through a gap in the trees on its dry surface, and a snake basking in the midst of the spot, fantastically coiled and treacherously still. Far and near the view suggested the same dreary impressions of solitude and decay, and the glorious brightness of the summer sky overhead seemed only to deepen and harden the gloom and barrenness of the wilderness on which it shone. I turned and retraced my steps to the high heathy ground, directing them a little aside from my former path towards a shabby old wooden shed, which stood on the outer skirt of the fir plantation, and which had hitherto been too unimportant to share my notice with the wide, wild prospect of the lake.

On approaching the shed I found that it had once been a boat-house, and that an attempt had apparently been made to convert it afterwards into a sort of rude arbour, by placing inside it a firwood seat, a few stools, and a table. I entered the place, and sat down for a little while to rest and get my breath again.

I had not been in the boat-house more than a minute when it struck me that the sound of my own quick breathing was very strangely echoed by something beneath me. I listened intently for a moment, and heard a low, thick, sobbing breath that seemed to come from the ground under the seat which I was occupying. My nerves are not easily shaken by trifles, but on this occasion I started to my feet in a fright—called out—received no answer—summoned back my recreant courage, and looked under the seat.

There, crouched up in the farthest corner, lay the forlorn cause of my terror, in the shape of a poor little dog—a black and white spaniel. The creature moaned feebly when I looked at it and called to it, but never stirred. I moved away the seat and looked closer. The poor little dog's eyes were glazing fast, and there were spots of blood on its glossy white side. The misery of a weak, helpless, dumb creature is surely one of the saddest of all the mournful sights which this world can show. I lifted the poor dog in my arms as gently as I could, and contrived a sort of make-shift hammock for him to lie in, by gathering up the front of my dress all round him. In this way I took the creature, as painlessly as possible, and as fast as possible, back to the house.

Finding no one in the hall I went up at once to my own sitting-room, made a bed for the dog with one of my old shawls, and rang the bell. The largest and fattest of all possible housemaids answered it, in a state of cheerful stupidity which would have provoked the patience of a saint. The girl's fat, shapeless face actually stretched into a broad grin at the sight of the wounded creature on the floor.

"What do you see there to laugh at?" I asked, as angrily as if she had been a servant of my own. "Do you know whose dog it is?"

"No, miss, that I certainly don't." She stooped, and looked down at the spaniel's injured side—brightened suddenly with the irradiation of a new idea—and pointing to the wound with a chuckle of satisfaction, said, "That's Baxter's doings, that is."

I was so exasperated that I could have boxed her ears. "Baxter?" I said. "Who is the brute you call Baxter?"

The girl grinned again more cheerfully than ever. "Bless you, miss! Baxter's the keeper, and when he finds strange dogs hunting about, he takes and shoots 'em. It's keeper's dooty, miss. I think that dog will die. Here's where he's been shot, ain't it? That's Baxter's doings, that is. Baxter's doings, miss, and Baxter's dooty."

I was almost wicked enough to wish that Baxter had shot the

housemaid instead of the dog. Seeing that it was quite useless to expect this densely impenetrable personage to give me any help in relieving the suffering creature at our feet, I told her to request the housekeeper's attendance with my compliments. She went out exactly as she had come in, grinning from ear to ear. As the door closed on her she said to herself softly, "It's Baxter's doings and Baxter's dooty—that's what it is."

The housekeeper, a person of some education and intelligence, thoughtfully brought upstairs with her some milk and some warm water. The instant she saw the dog on the floor she started and changed colour.

"Why, Lord bless me," cried the housekeeper, "that must be Mrs. Catherick's dog!"

"Whose?" I asked, in the utmost astonishment.

"Mrs. Catherick's. You seem to know Mrs. Catherick, Miss Halcombe?"

"Not personally, but I have heard of her. Does she live here? Has she had any news of her daughter?"

"No, Miss Halcombe, she came here to ask for news."

"When?"

"Only yesterday. She said some one had reported that a stranger answering to the description of her daughter had been seen in our neighbourhood. No such report has reached us here, and no such report was known in the village, when I sent to make inquiries there on Mrs. Catherick's account. She certainly brought this poor little dog with her when she came, and I saw it trot out after her when she went away. I suppose the creature strayed into the plantations, and got shot. Where did you find it, Miss Halcombe?"

"In the old shed that looks out on the lake."

"Ah, yes, that is the plantation side, and the poor thing dragged itself, I suppose, to the nearest shelter, as dogs will, to die. If you can moisten its lips with the milk, Miss Halcombe, I will wash the clotted hair from the wound. I am very much afraid it is too late to do any good. However, we can but try."

Mrs. Catherick! The name still rang in my ears, as if the housekeeper had only that moment surprised me by uttering it.

The Woman in White

While we were attending to the dog, the words of Walter Hartright's caution to me returned to my memory: "If ever Anne Catherick crosses your path, make better use of the opportunity, Miss Halcombe, than I made of it." The finding of the wounded spaniel had led me already to the discovery of Mrs. Catherick's visit to Blackwater Park, and that event might lead in its turn, to something more. I determined to make the most of the chance which was now offered to me, and to gain as much information as I could.

"Did you say that Mrs. Catherick lived anywhere in this neighbourhood?" I asked.

"Oh dear, no," said the housekeeper. "She lives at Welmingham, quite at the other end of the county—five-and-twenty miles off, at least."

"I suppose you have known Mrs. Catherick for some years?"

"On the contrary, Miss Halcombe, I never saw her before she came here yesterday. I had heard of her, of course, because I had heard of Sir Percival's kindness in putting her daughter under medical care. Mrs. Catherick is rather a strange person in her manners, but extremely respectable-looking. She seemed sorely put out when she found that there was no foundation—none, at least, that any of us could discover—for the report of her daughter having been seen in this neighbourhood."

"I am rather interested about Mrs. Catherick," I went on, continuing the conversation as long as possible. "I wish I had arrived here soon enough to see her yesterday. Did she stay for any length of time?"

"Yes," said the housekeeper, "she stayed for some time; and I think she would have remained longer, if I had not been called away to speak to a strange gentleman—a gentleman who came to ask when Sir Percival was expected back. Mrs. Catherick got up and left at once, when she heard the maid tell me what the visitor's errand was. She said to me, at parting, that there was no need to tell Sir Percival of her coming here. I thought that rather an odd remark to make, especially to a person in my responsible situation."

I thought it an odd remark too. Sir Percival had certainly led me to believe, at Limmeridge, that the most perfect confidence existed between himself and Mrs. Catherick. If that was the case, why should she be anxious to have her visit at Blackwater Park kept a secret from him?

"Probably," I said, seeing that the housekeeper expected me to give my opinion on Mrs. Catherick's parting words, "probably she thought the announcement of her visit might vex Sir Percival to no purpose, by reminding him that her lost daughter was not found yet. Did she talk much on that subject?"

"Very little," replied the housekeeper. "She talked principally of Sir Percival, and asked a great many questions about where he had been travelling, and what sort of lady his new wife was. She seemed to be more soured and put out than distressed, by failing to find any traces of her daughter in these parts. 'I give her up,' were the last words she said that I can remember; 'I give her up, ma'am, for lost.' And from that she passed at once to her questions about Lady Glyde, wanting to know if she was a handsome, amiable lady, comely and healthy and young— — Ah, dear! I thought how it would end. Look, Miss Halcombe, the poor thing is out of its misery at last!"

The dog was dead. It had given a faint, sobbing cry, it had suffered an instant's convulsion of the limbs, just as those last words, "comely and healthy and young," dropped from the housekeeper's lips. The change had happened with startling suddenness—in one moment the creature lay lifeless under our hands.

Eight o'clock. I have just returned from dining downstairs, in solitary state. The sunset is burning redly on the wilderness of trees that I see from my window, and I am poring over my journal again, to calm my impatience for the return of the travellers. They ought to have arrived, by my calculations, before this. How still and lonely the house is in the drowsy evening quiet! Oh me! how many minutes more before I hear the carriage wheels and run downstairs to find myself in Laura's arms?

The poor little dog! I wish my first day at Blackwater Park had not been associated with death, though it is only the death of a stray animal.

Welmingham—I see, on looking back through these private pages of mine, that Welmingham is the name of the place where Mrs. Catherick lives. Her note is still in my possession, the note in answer to that letter about her unhappy daughter which Sir Percival obliged me to write. One of these days, when I can find a safe opportunity, I will take the note with me by way of introduction, and try what I can make of Mrs. Catherick at a personal interview. I don't understand her wishing to conceal

The Woman in White

her visit to this place from Sir Percival's knowledge, and I don't feel half so sure, as the housekeeper seems to do, that her daughter Anne is not in the neighbourhood after all. What would Walter Hartright have said in this emergency? Poor, dear Hartright! I am beginning to feel the want of his honest advice and his willing help already.

Surely I heard something. Was it a bustle of footsteps below stairs? Yes! I hear the horses' feet—I hear the rolling wheels— —

II

June 15th. — The confusion of their arrival has had time to subside. Two days have elapsed since the return of the travellers, and that interval has sufficed to put the new machinery of our lives at Blackwater Park in fair working order. I may now return to my journal, with some little chance of being able to continue the entries in it as collectedly as usual.

I think I must begin by putting down an odd remark which has suggested itself to me since Laura came back.

When two members of a family or two intimate friends are separated, and one goes abroad and one remains at home, the return of the relative or friend who has been travelling always seems to place the relative or friend who has been staying at home at a painful disadvantage when the two first meet. The sudden encounter of the new thoughts and new habits eagerly gained in the one case, with the old thoughts and old habits passively preserved in the other, seems at first to part the sympathies of the most loving relatives and the fondest friends, and to set a sudden strangeness, unexpected by both and uncontrollable by both, between them on either side. After the first happiness of my meeting with Laura was over, after we had sat down together hand in hand to recover breath enough and calmness enough to talk, I felt this strangeness instantly, and I could see that she felt it too. It has partially worn away, now that we have fallen back into most of our old habits, and it will probably disappear before long. But it has certainly had an influence over the first impressions that I have formed of her, now that we are living together again — for which reason only I have thought fit to mention it here.

She has found me unaltered, but I have found her changed.

Changed in person, and in one respect changed in character. I cannot absolutely say that she is less beautiful than she used to be — I can only say that she is less beautiful to me.

Others, who do not look at her with my eyes and my recollections, would probably think her improved. There is more colour and more decision and roundness of outline in her face than there used to be, and her figure seems more firmly set and more sure and easy in all its movements than it was in her maiden days. But I miss something when I look at her — something that once belonged to the happy, innocent life of Laura Fairlie, and that I cannot find in Lady Glyde. There was in the old times a freshness, a softness, an ever-varying and yet ever-remaining tenderness of beauty in her face, the charm of which it is not possible to express in words, or, as poor Hartright used often to say, in painting either. This is gone. I thought I saw the faint reflection of it for a moment when she turned pale under the agitation of our sudden meeting on the evening of her return, but it has never reappeared since. None of her letters had prepared me for a personal change in her. On the contrary, they had led me to expect that her marriage had left her, in appearance at least, quite unaltered. Perhaps I read her letters wrongly in the past, and am now reading her face wrongly in the present? No matter! Whether her beauty has gained or whether it has lost in the last six months, the separation either way has made her own dear self more precious to me than ever, and that is one good result of her marriage, at any rate!

The second change, the change that I have observed in her character, has not surprised me, because I was prepared for it in this case by the tone of her letters. Now that she is at home again, I find her just as unwilling to enter into any details on the subject of her married life as I had previously found her all through the time of our separation, when we could only communicate with each other by writing. At the first approach I made to the forbidden topic she put her hand on my lips with a look and gesture which touchingly, almost painfully, recalled to my memory the days of her girlhood and the happy bygone time when there were no secrets between us.

"Whenever you and I are together, Marian," she said, "we shall both be happier and easier with one another, if we accept my married life for what it is, and say and think as little about it as possible. I would tell you everything, darling, about myself," she went on, nervously buckling and unbuckling the ribbon round my waist, "if my confidences could only end there. But they could not—they would lead me into confidences about my husband too; and now I am married, I think I had better avoid them, for his sake, and for your sake, and for mine. I don't say that they would distress you, or distress me—I wouldn't have you think that for the world. But—I want to be so happy, now I have got you back again, and I want you to be so happy too—
—" She broke off abruptly, and looked round the room, my own sitting-room, in which we were talking. "Ah!" she cried, clapping her hands with a bright smile of recognition, "another old friend found already! Your book-case, Marian—your dear-little-shabby-old-satin-wood book-case—how glad I am you brought it with you from Limmeridge! And the horrid heavy man's umbrella, that you always would walk out with when it rained! And first and foremost of all, your own dear, dark,

clever, gipsy-face, looking at me just as usual! It is so like home again to be here. How can we make it more like home still? I will put my father's portrait in your room instead of in mine—and I will keep all my little treasures from Limmeridge here—and we will pass hours and hours every day with these four friendly walls round us. Oh, Marian!" she said, suddenly seating herself on a footstool at my knees, and looking up earnestly in my face, "promise you will never marry, and leave me. It is selfish to say so, but you are so much better off as a single woman—unless—unless you are very fond of your husband—but you won't be very fond of anybody but me, will you?" She stopped again, crossed my hands on my lap, and laid her face on them. "Have you been writing many letters, and receiving many letters lately?" she asked, in low, suddenly-altered tones. I understood what the question meant, but I thought it my duty not to encourage her by meeting her half way. "Have you heard from him?" she went on, coaxing me to forgive the more direct appeal on which she now ventured, by kissing my hands, upon which her face still rested. "Is he well and happy, and getting on in his profession? Has he recovered himself—and forgotten me?"

She should not have asked those questions. She should have remembered her own resolution, on the morning when Sir Percival held her to her marriage engagement, and when she resigned the book of Hartright's drawings into my hands for ever. But, ah me! where is the faultless human creature who can persevere in a good resolution, without sometimes failing and falling back? Where is the woman who has ever really torn from her heart the image that has been once fixed in it by a true love? Books tell us that such unearthly creatures have existed—but what does our own experience say in answer to books?

I made no attempt to remonstrate with her: perhaps, because I sincerely appreciated the fearless candour which let me see, what other women in her position might have had reasons for concealing even from their dearest friends—perhaps, because I felt, in my own heart and conscience, that in her place I should have asked the same questions and had the same thoughts. All I could honestly do was to reply that I had not written to him or heard from him lately, and then to turn the conversation to less dangerous topics.

There has been much to sadden me in our interview—my first confidential interview with her since her return. The change which her marriage has produced in our relations towards each other, by placing a forbidden subject between us, for the first time in our lives; the melancholy conviction of the dearth of all warmth of feeling, of all close sympathy, between her husband and herself, which her own unwilling words now force on my mind; the distressing discovery that the influence of that ill-fated attachment still remains (no matter how innocently, how harmlessly) rooted as deeply as ever in her heart — all these are disclosures to sadden any woman who loves her as dearly, and feels for her as acutely, as I do.

There is only one consolation to set against them — a consolation that ought to comfort me, and that does comfort me. All the graces and gentleness of her character — all the frank affection of her nature — all the sweet, simple, womanly charms which used to make her the darling and delight of every one who approached her, have come back to me with herself. Of my other impressions I am sometimes a little inclined to doubt. Of this last, best, happiest of all impressions, I grow more and more certain every hour in the day.

Let me turn, now, from her to her travelling companions. Her husband must engage my attention first. What have I observed in Sir Percival, since his return, to improve my opinion of him?

I can hardly say. Small vexations and annoyances seem to have beset him since he came back, and no man, under those circumstances, is ever presented at his best. He looks, as I think, thinner than he was when he left England. His wearisome cough and his comfortless restlessness have certainly increased. His manner — at least his manner towards me — is much more abrupt than it used to be. He greeted me, on the evening of his return, with little or nothing of the ceremony and civility of former times — no polite speeches of welcome — no appearance of extraordinary gratification at seeing me — nothing but a short shake of the hand, and a sharp "How-d'ye-do, Miss Halcombe — glad to see you again." He seemed to accept me as one of the necessary fixtures of Blackwater Park, to be satisfied at finding me established in my proper place, and then to pass me over altogether.

Most men show something of their disposition in their own houses, which they have concealed elsewhere, and Sir Percival has already displayed a mania for order and regularity, which is quite a new revelation of him, so far as my previous knowledge of his character is concerned. If I take a book from the library and leave it on the table, he follows me and puts it back again. If I rise from a chair, and let it remain where I have been sitting, he carefully restores it to its proper place against the wall. He picks up stray flower-blossoms from the carpet, and mutters to himself as discontentedly as if they were hot cinders burning holes in it, and he storms at the servants if there is a crease in the tablecloth, or a knife missing from its place at the dinner-table, as fiercely as if they had personally insulted him.

I have already referred to the small annoyances which appear to have troubled him since his return. Much of the alteration for the worse which I have noticed in him may be due to these. I try to persuade myself that it is so, because I am anxious not to be disheartened already about the future. It is certainly trying to any man's temper to be met by a vexation the moment he sets foot in his own house again, after a long absence, and this annoying circumstance did really happen to Sir Percival in my presence.

On the evening of their arrival the housekeeper followed me into the hall to receive her master and mistress and their guests. The instant he saw her, Sir Percival asked if any one had called lately. The housekeeper mentioned to him, in reply, what she had previously mentioned to me, the visit of the strange gentleman to make inquiries about the time of her master's return. He asked immediately for the gentleman's name. No name had been left. The gentleman's business? No business had been mentioned. What was the gentleman like? The housekeeper tried to describe him, but failed to distinguish the nameless visitor by any personal peculiarity which her master could recognise. Sir Percival frowned, stamped angrily on the floor, and walked on into the house, taking no notice of anybody. Why he should have been so discomposed by a trifle I cannot say—but he was seriously discomposed, beyond all doubt.

Upon the whole, it will be best, perhaps, if I abstain from forming a decisive opinion of his manners, language, and conduct in his own house, until time has enabled him to shake off the anxieties, whatever they may be, which now evidently troubled his mind in secret. I will turn over to a new page, and my pen shall let Laura's husband alone for the present.

The two guests—the Count and Countess Fosco—come next in my catalogue. I will dispose of the Countess first, so as to have done with the woman as soon as possible.

Laura was certainly not chargeable with any exaggeration, in writing me word that I should hardly recognise her aunt again when we met. Never before have I beheld such a change produced in a woman by her marriage as has been produced in Madame Fosco.

The Woman in White

As Eleanor Fairlie (aged seven-and-thirty), she was always talking pretentious nonsense, and always worrying the unfortunate men with every small exaction which a vain and foolish woman can impose on long-suffering male humanity. As Madame Fosco (aged three-and-forty), she sits for hours together without saying a word, frozen up in the strangest manner in herself. The hideously ridiculous love-locks which used to hang on either side of her face are now replaced by stiff little rows of very short curls, of the sort one sees in old-fashioned wigs. A plain, matronly cap covers her head, and makes her look, for the first time in her life since I remember her, like a decent woman. Nobody (putting her husband out of the question, of course) now sees in her, what everybody once saw—I mean the structure of the female skeleton, in the upper regions of the collar-bones and the shoulder-blades. Clad in quiet black or grey gowns, made high round the throat—dresses that she would have laughed at, or screamed at, as the whim of the moment inclined her, in her maiden days—she sits speechless in corners; her dry white hands (so dry that the pores of her skin look chalky) incessantly engaged, either in monotonous embroidery work or in rolling up endless cigarettes for the Count's own particular smoking. On the few occasions when her cold blue eyes are off her work, they are generally turned on her husband, with the look of mute submissive inquiry which we are all familiar with in the eyes of a faithful dog. The only approach to an inward thaw which I have yet detected under her outer covering of icy constraint, has betrayed itself, once or twice, in the form of a suppressed tigerish jealousy of any woman in the house (the maids included) to whom the Count speaks, or on whom he looks with anything approaching to special interest or attention. Except in this one particular, she is always, morning, noon, and night, indoors and out, fair weather or foul, as cold as a statue, and as impenetrable as the stone out of which it is cut. For the common purposes of society the extraordinary change thus produced in her is, beyond all doubt, a change for the better, seeing that it has transformed her into a civil, silent, unobtrusive woman, who is never in the way. How far she is really reformed or deteriorated in her secret self, is another question. I have once or twice seen sudden changes of expression on her pinched lips, and heard sudden inflexions of tone in her calm voice, which have led me to suspect that her present state of suppression may have sealed up something dangerous in her nature, which used to evaporate harmlessly in the freedom of her former life. It is quite possible that I may be altogether wrong in this idea. My own impression, however, is, that I am right. Time will show.

And the magician who has wrought this wonderful transformation—the foreign husband who has tamed this once wayward English woman till her own relations hardly know her again—the Count himself? What of the Count?

This in two words: He looks like a man who could tame anything. If he had married a tigress, instead of a woman, he would have tamed the tigress. If he had married me, I should have made his cigarettes, as his wife does—I should have held my tongue when he looked at me, as she holds hers.

I am almost afraid to confess it, even to these secret pages. The man has interested me, has attracted me, has forced me to like him. In two short days he has made his way straight into my favourable estimation, and how he has worked the miracle is more than I can tell.

It absolutely startles me, now he is in my mind, to find how plainly I see him!—how much more plainly than I see Sir Percival, or Mr. Fairlie, or Walter Hartright, or any other absent person of whom I think, with the one exception of Laura herself! I can hear his voice, as if he was speaking at this moment. I know what his conversation was yesterday, as well as if I was hearing it now. How am I to describe him? There are peculiarities in his personal appearance, his habits, and his amusements, which I should blame in the boldest terms, or ridicule in the most merciless manner, if I had seen them in another man. What is it that makes me unable to blame them, or to ridicule them in him?

For example, he is immensely fat. Before this time I have always especially disliked corpulent humanity. I have always maintained that the popular notion of connecting excessive grossness of size and excessive good-humour as inseparable allies was equivalent to declaring, either that no people but amiable people ever get fat, or that the accidental addition of so many pounds of flesh has a directly favourable influence over the disposition of the person on whose body they accumulate. I have invariably combated both these absurd assertions by quoting examples of fat people who were as mean, vicious, and cruel as the leanest and the worst of their neighbours. I have asked whether Henry the Eighth was an amiable character? Whether Pope Alexander the Sixth was a good man? Whether Mr. Murderer and Mrs. Murderess Manning were not both unusually stout people? Whether hired nurses, proverbially as cruel a set of women as are to be found in all England, were not, for the most part, also as fat a set of women as are to be found in all England?—and so on, through dozens of other examples, modern and ancient, native and foreign, high and low. Holding these strong opinions on the subject with might and main as I do at this moment, here, nevertheless, is Count Fosco, as fat as Henry the Eighth himself, established in my favour, at one day's notice, without let or hindrance from his own odious corpulence. Marvellous indeed!

Is it his face that has recommended him?

It may be his face. He is a most remarkable likeness, on a large scale, of the great Napoleon. His features have Napoleon's magnificent regularity—his expression recalls the grandly calm, immovable power of the Great Soldier's face. This striking resemblance certainly impressed me, to begin with; but there is something in him besides the resemblance, which has impressed me more. I think the influence I am now trying to find is in his eyes. They are the most unfathomable grey eyes I ever saw, and they have at times a cold, clear, beautiful, irresistible glitter in them which forces me to look at him, and yet causes me sensations, when I do look, which I would rather not feel. Other parts of his face and head have their strange peculiarities. His complexion, for instance, has a singular sallow-fairness, so much at variance with the dark-brown colour of his hair, that I suspect the hair of being a wig, and his face, closely shaven all over, is smoother and freer from all marks and wrinkles than mine, though (according to Sir Percival's account of him) he is close on sixty years of age. But these are not the prominent personal characteristics which distinguish him, to my mind, from all the other men I have ever seen. The marked peculiarity which singles him out from the rank and file of humanity lies entirely, so far as I can tell at present, in the extraordinary expression and extraordinary power of his eyes.

His manner and his command of our language may also have assisted him, in some degree, to establish himself in my good opinion. He has that quiet deference, that look of pleased, attentive interest in listening to a woman, and that secret gentleness in his voice in speaking to a woman, which, say what we may, we can none of us resist. Here, too, his unusual command of the English language necessarily helps him. I had often heard of the extraordinary aptitude which many Italians show in mastering our strong, hard, Northern speech; but, until I saw Count Fosco, I had never supposed it possible that any foreigner could have spoken English as he speaks it. There are times when it is almost impossible to detect by his accent that he is not a countryman of our own, and as for fluency, there are very few born Englishmen who can talk with as few stoppages and repetitions as the Count. He may construct his sentences more or less in the foreign way, but I have never yet heard him use a wrong expression, or hesitate for a moment in his choice of a word.

All the smallest characteristics of this strange man have something strikingly original and perplexingly contradictory in them. Fat as he is and old as he is, his movements are astonishingly light and easy. He is as noiseless in a room as any of us women, and more than that, with all his look of unmistakable mental firmness and power, he is as nervously sensitive as the weakest of us. He starts at chance noises as inveterately as Laura herself. He winced and shuddered yesterday, when Sir Percival beat one of the spaniels, so that I felt ashamed of my own want of tenderness and sensibility by comparison with the Count.

The relation of this last incident reminds me of one of his most curious peculiarities, which I have not yet mentioned — his extraordinary fondness for pet animals.

Some of these he has left on the Continent, but he has brought with him to this house a cockatoo, two canary-birds, and a whole family of white mice. He attends to all the necessities of these strange favourites himself, and he has taught the creatures to be surprisingly fond of him and familiar with him. The cockatoo, a most vicious and treacherous bird towards every one else, absolutely seems to love him. When he lets it out of its cage, it hops on to his knee, and claws its way up his great big body, and rubs its top-knot against his sallow double chin in the most caressing manner imaginable. He has only to set the doors of the canaries' cages open, and to call them, and the pretty little cleverly trained creatures perch fearlessly on his hand, mount his fat outstretched fingers one by one, when he tells them to "go upstairs," and sing together as if they would burst their throats with delight when they get to the top finger. His white mice live in a little pagoda of gaily-painted wirework, designed and made by himself. They are almost as tame as the canaries, and they are perpetually let out like the canaries. They crawl all over him, popping in and out of his waistcoat, and sitting in couples, white as snow, on his capacious shoulders. He seems to be even fonder of his mice than of his other pets, smiles at them, and kisses them, and calls them by all sorts of endearing names. If it be possible to suppose an Englishman with any taste for such childish interests and amusements as these, that Englishman would certainly feel rather ashamed of them, and would be anxious to apologise for them, in the company of grown-up people. But the Count, apparently, sees nothing ridiculous in the amazing contrast between his colossal self and his frail little pets. He would blandly kiss his white mice and twitter to his canary-birds amid an assembly of English fox-hunters, and would only pity them as barbarians when they were all laughing their loudest at him.

It seems hardly credible while I am writing it down, but it is certainly true, that this same man, who has all the fondness of an old maid for his cockatoo, and all the small dexterities of an organ-boy in managing his white mice, can talk, when anything happens to rouse him, with a daring independence of thought, a knowledge of books in every language, and an experience of society in half the capitals of Europe, which would make him the prominent personage of any assembly in the civilised world. This trainer of canary-birds, this architect of a pagoda for white mice, is (as Sir Percival himself has told me) one of the first experimental chemists living, and has discovered, among other wonderful inventions, a means of petrifying the body after death, so as to preserve it, as hard as marble, to the end of time. This fat, indolent, elderly man, whose nerves are so finely strung that he starts at chance noises, and winces when he sees a house-spaniel get a whipping, went into the stable-yard on the morning after his arrival, and put his hand on the head of a chained bloodhound—a beast so savage that the very groom who feeds him keeps out of his reach. His wife and I were present, and I shall not forget the scene that followed, short as it was.

"Mind that dog, sir," said the groom; "he flies at everybody!" "He does that, my friend," replied the Count quietly, "because everybody is afraid of him. Let us see if he flies at me." And he laid his plump, yellow-white fingers, on which the canary-birds had been perching ten minutes before, upon the formidable brute's head, and looked him straight in the eyes. "You big dogs are all cowards," he said, addressing the animal contemptuously, with his face and the dog's within an inch of each other. "You would kill a poor cat, you infernal coward. You would fly at a starving beggar, you infernal coward. Anything that you can surprise unawares—anything that is afraid of your big body, and your wicked white teeth, and your slobbering, bloodthirsty mouth, is the thing you like to fly at. You could throttle me at this moment, you mean, miserable bully, and you daren't so much as look me in the face, because I'm not afraid of you. Will you think better of it, and try your teeth in my fat neck? Bah! not you!" He turned away, laughing at the astonishment of the men in the yard, and the dog crept back meekly to his kennel. "Ah! my nice waistcoat!" he said pathetically. "I am sorry I came here. Some of that brute's slobber has got on my pretty clean waistcoat." Those words express another of his incomprehensible oddities. He is as fond of fine clothes as the veriest fool in existence, and has appeared in four magnificent waistcoats already—all of light garish colours, and all immensely large even for him—in the two days of his residence at Blackwater Park.

His tact and cleverness in small things are quite as noticeable as the singular inconsistencies in his character, and the childish triviality of his ordinary tastes and pursuits.

I can see already that he means to live on excellent terms with all of us during the period of his sojourn in this place. He has evidently discovered that Laura secretly dislikes him (she confessed as much to me when I pressed her on the subject)—but he has also found out that she is extravagantly fond of flowers. Whenever she wants a nosegay he has got one to give her, gathered and arranged by himself, and greatly to my amusement, he is always cunningly provided with a duplicate, composed of exactly the same flowers, grouped in exactly the same way, to appease his icily jealous wife before she can so much as think herself aggrieved. His management of the Countess (in public) is a sight to see. He bows to her, he habitually addresses her as "my angel," he carries his canaries to pay her little visits on his fingers and to sing to her, he kisses her hand when she gives him his cigarettes; he presents her with sugar-plums in return, which he puts into her mouth playfully, from a box in his pocket. The rod of iron with which he rules her never appears in company—it is a private rod, and is always kept upstairs.

His method of recommending himself to me is entirely different. He flatters my vanity by talking to me as seriously and sensibly as if I was a man. Yes! I can find him out when I am away from him—I know he flatters my vanity, when I think of him up here in my own room—and yet, when I go downstairs, and get into his company again, he will blind me again, and I shall be flattered again, just as if I had never found him out at all! He can manage me as he manages his wife and Laura, as he managed the bloodhound in the stable-yard, as he manages Sir Percival himself, every hour in the day. "My good Percival! how I like your rough English humour!"—"My good Percival! how I enjoy your solid English sense!" He puts the rudest remarks Sir Percival can make on his effeminate tastes and amusements quietly away from him in that manner—always calling the baronet by his Christian name, smiling at him with the calmest superiority, patting him on the shoulder, and bearing with him benignantly, as a good-humoured father bears with a wayward son.

The interest which I really cannot help feeling in this strangely original man has led me to question Sir Percival about his past life.

Sir Percival either knows little, or will tell me little, about it. He and the Count first met many years ago, at Rome, under the dangerous circumstances to which I have alluded elsewhere. Since that time they have been perpetually together in London, in Paris, and in Vienna — but never in Italy again; the Count having, oddly enough, not crossed the frontiers of his native country for years past. Perhaps he has been made the victim of some political persecution? At all events, he seems to be patriotically anxious not to lose sight of any of his own countrymen who may happen to be in England. On the evening of his arrival he asked how far we were from the nearest town, and whether we knew of any Italian gentlemen who might happen to be settled there. He is certainly in correspondence with people on the Continent, for his letters have all sorts of odd stamps on them, and I saw one for him this morning, waiting in his place at the breakfast-table, with a huge, official-looking seal on it. Perhaps he is in correspondence with his government? And yet, that is hardly to be reconciled either with my other idea that he may be a political exile.

How much I seem to have written about Count Fosco! And what does it all amount to? — as poor, dear Mr. Gilmore would ask, in his impenetrable business-like way I can only repeat that I do assuredly feel, even on this short acquaintance, a strange, half-willing, half-unwilling liking for the Count. He seems to have established over me the same sort of ascendency which he has evidently gained over Sir Percival. Free, and even rude, as he may occasionally be in his manner towards his fat friend, Sir Percival is nevertheless afraid, as I can plainly see, of giving any serious offence to the Count. I wonder whether I am afraid too? I certainly never saw a man, in all my experience, whom I should be so sorry to have for an enemy. Is this because I like him, or because I am afraid of him? Chi sa? — as Count Fosco might say in his own language. Who knows?

June 16th. — Something to chronicle to-day besides my own ideas and impressions. A visitor has arrived — quite unknown to Laura and to me, and apparently quite unexpected by Sir Percival.

We were all at lunch, in the room with the new French windows that open into the verandah, and the Count (who devours pastry as I have never yet seen it devoured by any human beings but girls at boarding-schools) had just amused us by asking gravely for his fourth tart—when the servant entered to announce the visitor.

"Mr. Merriman has just come, Sir Percival, and wishes to see you immediately."

Sir Percival started, and looked at the man with an expression of angry alarm.

"Mr. Merriman!" he repeated, as if he thought his own ears must have deceived him.

"Yes, Sir Percival—Mr. Merriman, from London."

"Where is he?"

"In the library, Sir Percival."

He left the table the instant the last answer was given, and hurried out of the room without saying a word to any of us.

"Who is Mr. Merriman?" asked Laura, appealing to me.

"I have not the least idea," was all I could say in reply.

The Count had finished his fourth tart, and had gone to a side-table to look after his vicious cockatoo. He turned round to us with the bird perched on his shoulder.

"Mr. Merriman is Sir Percival's solicitor," he said quietly.

Sir Percival's solicitor. It was a perfectly straightforward answer to Laura's question, and yet, under the circumstances, it was not satisfactory. If Mr. Merriman had been specially sent for by his client, there would have been nothing very wonderful in his leaving town to obey the summons. But when a lawyer travels from London to Hampshire without being sent for, and when his arrival at a gentleman's house seriously startles the gentleman himself, it may be safely taken for granted that the legal visitor is the bearer of some very important and very unexpected news—news which may be either very good or very bad, but which cannot, in either case, be of the common everyday kind.

The Woman in White

Laura and I sat silent at the table for a quarter of an hour or more, wondering uneasily what had happened, and waiting for the chance of Sir Percival's speedy return. There were no signs of his return, and we rose to leave the room.

The Count, attentive as usual, advanced from the corner in which he had been feeding his cockatoo, with the bird still perched on his shoulder, and opened the door for us. Laura and Madame Fosco went out first. Just as I was on the point of following them he made a sign with his hand, and spoke to me, before I passed him, in the oddest manner.

"Yes," he said, quietly answering the unexpressed idea at that moment in my mind, as if I had plainly confided it to him in so many words—"yes, Miss Halcombe, something has happened."

I was on the point of answering, "I never said so," but the vicious cockatoo ruffled his clipped wings and gave a screech that set all my nerves on edge in an instant, and made me only too glad to get out of the room.

I joined Laura at the foot of the stairs. The thought in her mind was the same as the thought in mine, which Count Fosco had surprised, and when she spoke her words were almost the echo of his. She, too, said to me secretly that she was afraid something had happened.

III

June 16th. — I have a few lines more to add to this day's entry before I go to bed to-night.

About two hours after Sir Percival rose from the luncheon-table to receive his solicitor, Mr. Merriman, in the library, I left my room alone to take a walk in the plantations. Just as I was at the end of the landing the library door opened and the two gentlemen came out. Thinking it best not to disturb them by appearing on the stairs, I resolved to defer going down till they had crossed the hall. Although they spoke to each other in guarded tones, their words were pronounced with sufficient distinctness of utterance to reach my ears.

"Make your mind easy, Sir Percival," I heard the lawyer say; "it all rests with Lady Glyde."

I had turned to go back to my own room for a minute or two, but the sound of Laura's name on the lips of a stranger stopped me instantly. I daresay it was very wrong and very discreditable to listen, but where is the woman, in the whole range of our sex, who can regulate her actions by the abstract principles of honour, when those principles point one way, and when her affections, and the interests which grow out of them, point the other?

I listened — and under similar circumstances I would listen again — yes! with my ear at the keyhole, if I could not possibly manage it in any other way.

"You quite understand, Sir Percival," the lawyer went on. "Lady Glyde is to sign her name in the presence of a witness — or of two witnesses, if you wish to be particularly careful — and is then to put her finger on the seal and say, 'I deliver this as my act and deed.' If that is done in a week's time the arrangement will be perfectly successful, and the anxiety will be all over. If not — —"

"What do you mean by 'if not'?" asked Sir Percival angrily. "If the thing must be done it shall be done. I promise you that, Merriman."

"Just so, Sir Percival — just so; but there are two alternatives in all transactions, and we lawyers like to look both of them in the face boldly. If through any extraordinary circumstance the arrangement should not be made, I think I may be able to get the parties to accept bills at three months. But how the money is to be raised when the bills fall due— —"

"Damn the bills! The money is only to be got in one way, and in that way, I tell you again, it shall be got. Take a glass of wine, Merriman, before you go."

"Much obliged, Sir Percival; I have not a moment to lose if I am to catch the up-train. You will let me know as soon as the arrangement is complete? and you will not forget the caution I recommended— —"

"Of course I won't. There's the dog-cart at the door for you. My groom will get you to the station in no time. Benjamin, drive like mad! Jump in. If Mr. Merriman misses the train you lose your place. Hold fast, Merriman, and if you are upset trust to the devil to save his own." With that parting benediction the baronet turned about and walked back to the library.

I had not heard much, but the little that had reached my ears was enough to make me feel uneasy. The "something" that "had happened" was but too plainly a serious money embarrassment, and Sir Percival's relief from it depended upon Laura. The prospect of seeing her involved in her husband's secret difficulties filled me with dismay, exaggerated, no doubt, by my ignorance of business and my settled distrust of Sir Percival. Instead of going out, as I proposed, I went back immediately to Laura's room to tell her what I had heard.

She received my bad news so composedly as to surprise me. She evidently knows more of her husband's character and her husband's embarrassments than I have suspected up to this time.

"I feared as much," she said, "when I heard of that strange gentleman who called, and declined to leave his name."

"Who do you think the gentleman was, then?" I asked.

"Some person who has heavy claims on Sir Percival," she answered, "and who has been the cause of Mr. Merriman's visit here to-day."

"Do you know anything about those claims?"

"No, I know no particulars."

"You will sign nothing, Laura, without first looking at it?"

"Certainly not, Marian. Whatever I can harmlessly and honestly do to help him I will do—for the sake of making your life and mine, love, as easy and as happy as possible. But I will do nothing ignorantly, which we might, one day, have reason to feel ashamed of. Let us say no more about it now. You have got your hat on—suppose we go and dream away the afternoon in the grounds?"

On leaving the house we directed our steps to the nearest shade.

As we passed an open space among the trees in front of the house, there was Count Fosco, slowly walking backwards and forwards on the grass, sunning himself in the full blaze of the hot June afternoon. He had a broad straw hat on, with a violet-coloured ribbon round it. A blue blouse, with profuse white fancy-work over the bosom, covered his prodigious body, and was girt about the place where his waist might once have been with a broad scarlet leather belt. Nankeen trousers, displaying more white fancy-work over the ankles, and purple morocco slippers, adorned his lower extremities. He was singing Figaro's famous song in the Barber of Seville, with that crisply fluent vocalisation which is never heard from any other than an Italian throat, accompanying himself on the concertina, which he played with ecstatic throwings-up of his arms, and graceful twistings and turnings of his head, like a fat St. Cecilia masquerading in male attire. "Figaro qua! Figaro la! Figaro su! Figaro giu!" sang the Count, jauntily tossing up the concertina at arm's length, and bowing to us, on one side of the instrument, with the airy grace and elegance of Figaro himself at twenty years of age.

"Take my word for it, Laura, that man knows something of Sir Percival's embarrassments," I said, as we returned the Count's salutation from a safe distance.

"What makes you think that?" she asked.

"How should he have known, otherwise, that Mr. Merriman was Sir Percival's solicitor?" I rejoined. "Besides, when I followed you out of the luncheon-room, he told me, without a single word of inquiry on my part, that something had happened. Depend upon it, he knows more than we do."

"Don't ask him any questions if he does. Don't take him into our confidence!"

"You seem to dislike him, Laura, in a very determined

The Woman in White

manner. What has he said or done to justify you?"

"Nothing, Marian. On the contrary, he was all kindness and attention on our journey home, and he several times checked Sir Percival's outbreaks of temper, in the most considerate manner towards me. Perhaps I dislike him because he has so much more power over my husband than I have. Perhaps it hurts my pride to be under any obligations to his interference. All I know is, that I do dislike him."

The rest of the day and evening passed quietly enough. The Count and I played at chess. For the first two games he politely allowed me to conquer him, and then, when he saw that I had found him out, begged my pardon, and at the third game checkmated me in ten minutes. Sir Percival never once referred, all through the evening, to the lawyer's visit. But either that event, or something else, had produced a singular alteration for the better in him. He was as polite and agreeable to all of us, as he used to be in the days of his probation at Limmeridge, and he was so amazingly attentive and kind to his wife, that even icy Madame Fosco was roused into looking at him with a grave surprise. What does this mean? I think I can guess — I am afraid Laura can guess — and I am sure Count Fosco knows. I caught Sir Percival looking at him for approval more than once in the course of the evening.

June 17th. — A day of events. I most fervently hope I may not have to add, a day of disasters as well.

Sir Percival was as silent at breakfast as he had been the evening before, on the subject of the mysterious "arrangement" (as the lawyer called it) which is hanging over our heads. An hour afterwards, however, he suddenly entered the morning-room, where his wife and I were waiting, with our hats on, for Madame Fosco to join us, and inquired for the Count.

"We expect to see him here directly," I said.

"The fact is," Sir Percival went on, walking nervously about the room, "I want Fosco and his wife in the library, for a mere business formality, and I want you there, Laura, for a minute too." He stopped, and appeared to notice, for the first time, that we were in our walking costume. "Have you just come in?" he asked, "or were you just going out?"

"We were all thinking of going to the lake this morning,"

said Laura. "But if you have any other arrangement to propose——"

"No, no," he answered hastily. "My arrangement can wait. After lunch will do as well for it as after breakfast. All going to the lake, eh? A good idea. Let's have an idle morning—I'll be one of the party."

There was no mistaking his manner, even if it had been possible to mistake the uncharacteristic readiness which his words expressed, to submit his own plans and projects to the convenience of others. He was evidently relieved at finding any excuse for delaying the business formality in the library, to which his own words had referred. My heart sank within me as I drew the inevitable inference.

The Count and his wife joined us at that moment. The lady had her husband's embroidered tobacco-pouch, and her store of paper in her hand, for the manufacture of the eternal cigarettes. The gentleman, dressed, as usual, in his blouse and straw hat, carried the gay little pagoda-cage, with his darling white mice in it, and smiled on them, and on us, with a bland amiability which it was impossible to resist.

"With your kind permission," said the Count, "I will take my small family here—my poor-little-harmless-pretty-Mouseys, out for an airing along with us. There are dogs about the house, and shall I leave my forlorn white children at the mercies of the dogs? Ah, never!"

He chirruped paternally at his small white children through the bars of the pagoda, and we all left the house for the lake.

In the plantation Sir Percival strayed away from us. It seems to be part of his restless disposition always to separate himself from his companions on these occasions, and always to occupy himself when he is alone in cutting new walking-sticks for his own use. The mere act of cutting and lopping at hazard appears to please him. He has filled the house with walking-sticks of his own making, not one of which he ever takes up for a second time. When they have been once used his interest in them is all exhausted, and he thinks of nothing but going on and making more.

At the old boat-house he joined us again. I will put down the conversation that ensued when we were all settled in our places exactly as it passed. It is an important conversation, so far as I am concerned, for it has seriously disposed me to distrust the

The Woman in White

influence which Count Fosco has exercised over my thoughts and feelings, and to resist it for the future as resolutely as I can.

The boat-house was large enough to hold us all, but Sir Percival remained outside trimming the last new stick with his pocket-axe. We three women found plenty of room on the large seat. Laura took her work, and Madame Fosco began her cigarettes. I, as usual, had nothing to do. My hands always were, and always will be, as awkward as a man's. The Count good-humouredly took a stool many sizes too small for him, and balanced himself on it with his back against the side of the shed, which creaked and groaned under his weight. He put the pagoda-cage on his lap, and let out the mice to crawl over him as usual. They are pretty, innocent-looking little creatures, but the sight of them creeping about a man's body is for some reason not pleasant to me. It excites a strange responsive creeping in my own nerves, and suggests hideous ideas of men dying in prison with the crawling creatures of the dungeon preying on them undisturbed.

The morning was windy and cloudy, and the rapid alternations of shadow and sunlight over the waste of the lake made the view look doubly wild, weird, and gloomy.

"Some people call that picturesque," said Sir Percival, pointing over the wide prospect with his half-finished walking-stick. "I call it a blot on a gentleman's property. In my great-grandfather's time the lake flowed to this place. Look at it now! It is not four feet deep anywhere, and it is all puddles and pools. I wish I could afford to drain it, and plant it all over. My bailiff (a superstitious idiot) says he is quite sure the lake has a curse on it, like the Dead Sea. What do you think, Fosco? It looks just the place for a murder, doesn't it?"

"My good Percival," remonstrated the Count. "What is your solid English sense thinking of? The water is too shallow to hide the body, and there is sand everywhere to print off the murderer's footsteps. It is, upon the whole, the very worst place for a murder that I ever set my eyes on."

"Humbug!" said Sir Percival, cutting away fiercely at his stick. "You know what I mean. The dreary scenery, the lonely situation. If you choose to understand me, you can—if you don't choose, I am not going to trouble myself to explain my meaning."

"And why not," asked the Count, "when your meaning can be explained by anybody in two words? If a fool was going to commit a murder, your lake is the first place he would choose for it. If a wise man was going to commit a murder, your lake is the last place he would choose for it. Is that your meaning? If it is, there is your explanation for you ready made. Take it, Percival, with your good Fosco's blessing."

Laura looked at the Count with her dislike for him appearing a little too plainly in her face. He was so busy with his mice that he did not notice her.

"I am sorry to hear the lake-view connected with anything so horrible as the idea of murder," she said. "And if Count Fosco must divide murderers into classes, I think he has been very unfortunate in his choice of expressions. To describe them as fools only seems like treating them with an indulgence to which they have no claim. And to describe them as wise men sounds to me like a downright contradiction in terms. I have always heard that truly wise men are truly good men, and have a horror of crime."

"My dear lady," said the Count, "those are admirable sentiments, and I have seen them stated at the tops of copy-books." He lifted one of the white mice in the palm of his hand, and spoke to it in his whimsical way. "My pretty little smooth white rascal," he said, "here is a moral lesson for you. A truly wise mouse is a truly good mouse. Mention that, if you please, to your companions, and never gnaw at the bars of your cage again as long as you live."

"It is easy to turn everything into ridicule," said Laura resolutely; "but you will not find it quite so easy, Count Fosco, to give me an instance of a wise man who has been a great criminal."

The Count shrugged his huge shoulders, and smiled on Laura in the friendliest manner.

"Most true!" he said. "The fool's crime is the crime that is found out, and the wise man's crime is the crime that is not found out. If I could give you an instance, it would not be the instance of a wise man. Dear Lady Glyde, your sound English common sense has been too much for me. It is checkmate for me this time, Miss Halcombe — ha?"

"Stand to your guns, Laura," sneered Sir Percival, who had been listening in his place at the door. "Tell him next, that crimes cause their own detection. There's another bit of copy-book morality for you, Fosco. Crimes cause their own detection.

The Woman in White

What infernal humbug!"

"I believe it to be true," said Laura quietly.

Sir Percival burst out laughing, so violently, so outrageously, that he quite startled us all—the Count more than any of us.

"I believe it too," I said, coming to Laura's rescue.

Sir Percival, who had been unaccountably amused at his wife's remark, was just as unaccountably irritated by mine. He struck the new stick savagely on the sand, and walked away from us.

"Poor dear Percival!" cried Count Fosco, looking after him gaily, "he is the victim of English spleen. But, my dear Miss Halcombe, my dear Lady Glyde, do you really believe that crimes cause their own detection? And you, my angel," he continued, turning to his wife, who had not uttered a word yet, "do you think so too?"

"I wait to be instructed," replied the Countess, in tones of freezing reproof, intended for Laura and me, "before I venture on giving my opinion in the presence of well-informed men."

"Do you, indeed?" I said. "I remember the time, Countess, when you advocated the Rights of Women, and freedom of female opinion was one of them."

"What is your view of the subject, Count?" asked Madame Fosco, calmly proceeding with her cigarettes, and not taking the least notice of me.

The Count stroked one of his white mice reflectively with his chubby little finger before he answered.

"It is truly wonderful," he said, "how easily Society can console itself for the worst of its shortcomings with a little bit of clap-trap. The machinery it has set up for the detection of crime is miserably ineffective—and yet only invent a moral epigram, saying that it works well, and you blind everybody to its blunders from that moment. Crimes cause their own detection, do they? And murder will out (another moral epigram), will it? Ask Coroners who sit at inquests in large towns if that is true, Lady Glyde. Ask secretaries of life-assurance companies if that is true, Miss Halcombe. Read your own public journals. In the few cases that get into the newspapers, are there not instances of slain bodies found, and no murderers ever discovered?

Multiply the cases that are reported by the cases that are not reported, and the bodies that are found by the bodies that are not found, and what conclusion do you come to? This. That there are foolish criminals who are discovered, and wise criminals who escape. The hiding of a crime, or the detection of a crime, what is it? A trial of skill between the police on one side, and the individual on the other. When the criminal is a brutal, ignorant fool, the police in nine cases out of ten win. When the criminal is a resolute, educated, highly-intelligent man, the police in nine cases out of ten lose. If the police win, you generally hear all about it. If the police lose, you generally hear nothing. And on this tottering foundation you build up your comfortable moral maxim that Crime causes its own detection! Yes—all the crime you know of. And what of the rest?"

"Devilish true, and very well put," cried a voice at the entrance of the boat-house. Sir Percival had recovered his equanimity, and had come back while we were listening to the Count.

"Some of it may be true," I said, "and all of it may be very well put. But I don't see why Count Fosco should celebrate the victory of the criminal over Society with so much exultation, or why you, Sir Percival, should applaud him so loudly for doing it."

"Do you hear that, Fosco?" asked Sir Percival. "Take my advice, and make your peace with your audience. Tell them virtue's a fine thing—they like that, I can promise you."

The Count laughed inwardly and silently, and two of the white mice in his waistcoat, alarmed by the internal convulsion going on beneath them, darted out in a violent hurry, and scrambled into their cage again.

"The ladies, my good Percival, shall tell me about virtue," he said. "They are better authorities than I am, for they know what virtue is, and I don't."

"You hear him?" said Sir Percival. "Isn't it awful?"

"It is true," said the Count quietly. "I am a citizen of the world, and I have met, in my time, with so many different sorts of virtue, that I am puzzled, in my old age, to say which is the right sort and which is the wrong. Here, in England, there is one virtue. And there, in China, there is another virtue. And John Englishman says my virtue is the genuine virtue. And John

The Woman in White

Chinaman says my virtue is the genuine virtue. And I say Yes to one, or No to the other, and am just as much bewildered about it in the case of John with the top-boots as I am in the case of John with the pigtail. Ah, nice little Mousey! come, kiss me. What is your own private notion of a virtuous man, my pret-pret-pretty? A man who keeps you warm, and gives you plenty to eat. And a good notion, too, for it is intelligible, at the least."

"Stay a minute, Count," I interposed. "Accepting your illustration, surely we have one unquestionable virtue in England which is wanting in China. The Chinese authorities kill thousands of innocent people on the most frivolous pretexts. We in England are free from all guilt of that kind — we commit no such dreadful crime — we abhor reckless bloodshed with all our hearts."

"Quite right, Marian," said Laura. "Well thought of, and well expressed."

"Pray allow the Count to proceed," said Madame Fosco, with stern civility. "You will find, young ladies, that he never speaks without having excellent reasons for all that he says."

"Thank you, my angel," replied the Count. "Have a bon-bon?" He took out of his pocket a pretty little inlaid box, and placed it open on the table. "Chocolat à la Vanille," cried the impenetrable man, cheerfully rattling the sweetmeats in the box, and bowing all round. "Offered by Fosco as an act of homage to the charming society."

"Be good enough to go on, Count," said his wife, with a spiteful reference to myself. "Oblige me by answering Miss Halcombe."

"Miss Halcombe is unanswerable," replied the polite Italian; "that is to say, so far as she goes. Yes! I agree with her. John Bull does abhor the crimes of John Chinaman. He is the quickest old gentleman at finding out faults that are his neighbours', and the slowest old gentleman at finding out the faults that are his own, who exists on the face of creation. Is he so very much better in this way than the people whom he condemns in their way? English Society, Miss Halcombe, is as often the accomplice as it is the enemy of crime. Yes! yes! Crime is in this country what crime is in other countries — a good friend to a man and to those about him as often as it is an enemy. A great rascal provides for his wife and family. The worse he is the more he makes them the objects for your sympathy. He often provides also for himself. A profligate spendthrift who is always borrowing money will get more from his friends than the rigidly honest man who only borrows of them once, under pressure of the direst want. In the one case the friends will not be at all surprised, and they will give. In the other case they will be very much surprised, and they will hesitate. Is the prison that Mr. Scoundrel lives in at the end of his career a more uncomfortable place than the workhouse that Mr. Honesty lives in at the end of his career? When John-Howard-Philanthropist wants to relieve misery he goes to find it in prisons, where crime is wretched — not in huts and hovels, where virtue is wretched too. Who is the English poet who has won the most universal sympathy — who makes the easiest of all subjects for pathetic writing and pathetic painting? That nice young person who began life with a forgery, and ended it by a suicide — your dear, romantic, interesting Chatterton. Which gets on best, do you think, of two poor starving dressmakers — the woman who resists temptation and is honest, or the woman who falls under temptation and steals? You all know that the stealing is the making of that second woman's fortune — it advertises her from length to breadth of good-humoured, charitable England — and she is relieved, as the breaker of a commandment, when she would have been left to starve, as the keeper of it. Come here, my jolly little Mouse! Hey! presto! pass! I transform you, for the time being, into a respectable lady. Stop there, in the palm of my great big hand, my dear, and listen. You marry the poor man whom you love, Mouse, and one half your friends pity, and the other half blame you. And now, on the contrary, you sell yourself for gold to a man you don't care for, and all your friends rejoice over you, and a minister of public worship sanctions the base horror of the vilest of all human bargains, and smiles and smirks afterwards at your table, if you are polite enough to ask him to breakfast. Hey! presto! pass! Be a mouse again, and squeak. If you continue to be a lady much longer, I shall have you telling me that Society abhors crime — and then, Mouse, I shall doubt if your own eyes and ears are really of any use to you. Ah! I am a bad man, Lady Glyde, am I not? I say what other people only think, and when all the rest of the world is in a conspiracy to accept the mask for the true face, mine is the rash hand that tears off the plump pasteboard, and shows the bare bones beneath. I will get up on my big elephant's legs, before I do myself any more harm in your amiable estimations — I will get up and take a little airy walk of my own. Dear ladies, as your excellent Sheridan said, I go — and leave my character behind me."

He got up, put the cage on the table, and paused for a moment to count the mice in it. "One, two, three, four — — Ha!" he cried, with a look of horror, "where, in the name of Heaven, is the fifth — the youngest, the whitest, the most amiable of all — my Benjamin of mice!"

Neither Laura nor I were in any favorable disposition to be amused. The Count's glib cynicism had revealed a new aspect of his nature from which we both recoiled. But it was impossible to resist the comical distress of so very large a man at the loss of so very small a mouse. We laughed in spite of ourselves; and when Madame Fosco rose to set the example of leaving the boat-house empty, so that her husband might search it to its remotest corners, we rose also to follow her out.

Before we had taken three steps, the Count's quick eye discovered the lost mouse under the seat that we had been occupying. He pulled aside the bench, took the little animal up in his hand, and then suddenly stopped, on his knees, looking intently at a particular place on the ground just beneath him.

When he rose to his feet again, his hand shook so that he could hardly put the mouse back in the cage, and his face was of a faint livid yellow hue all over.

"Percival!" he said, in a whisper. "Percival! come here."

Sir Percival had paid no attention to any of us for the last ten minutes. He had been entirely absorbed in writing figures on the sand, and then rubbing them out again with the point of his stick.

"What's the matter now?" he asked, lounging carelessly into the boat-house.

"Do you see nothing there?" said the Count, catching him nervously by the collar with one hand, and pointing with the other to the place near which he had found the mouse.

"I see plenty of dry sand," answered Sir Percival, "and a spot of dirt in the middle of it."

"Not dirt," whispered the Count, fastening the other hand suddenly on Sir Percival's collar, and shaking it in his agitation. "Blood."

Laura was near enough to hear the last word, softly as he whispered it. She turned to me with a look of terror.

"Nonsense, my dear," I said. "There is no need to be alarmed. It is only the blood of a poor little stray dog."

Everybody was astonished, and everybody's eyes were fixed on me inquiringly.

"How do you know that?" asked Sir Percival, speaking first.

"I found the dog here, dying, on the day when you all returned from abroad," I replied. "The poor creature had strayed into the plantation, and had been shot by your keeper."

"Whose dog was it?" inquired Sir Percival. "Not one of mine?"

"Did you try to save the poor thing?" asked Laura earnestly. "Surely you tried to save it, Marian?"

"Yes," I said, "the housekeeper and I both did our best—but the dog was mortally wounded, and he died under our hands."

"Whose dog was it?" persisted Sir Percival, repeating his question a little irritably. "One of mine?"

"No, not one of yours."

"Whose then? Did the housekeeper know?"

The housekeeper's report of Mrs. Catherick's desire to conceal her visit to Blackwater Park from Sir Percival's knowledge recurred to my memory the moment he put that last question, and I half doubted the discretion of answering it; but in my anxiety to quiet the general alarm, I had thoughtlessly advanced too far to draw back, except at the risk of exciting suspicion, which might only make matters worse. There was nothing for it but to answer at once, without reference to results.

"Yes," I said. "The housekeeper knew. She told me it was Mrs. Catherick's dog."

Sir Percival had hitherto remained at the inner end of the boat-house with Count Fosco, while I spoke to him from the door. But the instant Mrs. Catherick's name passed my lips he pushed by the Count roughly, and placed himself face to face with me under the open daylight.

"How came the housekeeper to know it was Mrs. Catherick's dog?" he asked, fixing his eyes on mine with a frowning interest and attention, which half angered, half startled me.

The Woman in White

"She knew it," I said quietly, "because Mrs. Catherick brought the dog with her."

"Brought it with her? Where did she bring it with her?"

"To this house."

"What the devil did Mrs. Catherick want at this house?"

The manner in which he put the question was even more offensive than the language in which he expressed it. I marked my sense of his want of common politeness by silently turning away from him.

Just as I moved the Count's persuasive hand was laid on his shoulder, and the Count's mellifluous voice interposed to quiet him.

"My dear Percival! — gently — gently!"

Sir Percival looked round in his angriest manner. The Count only smiled and repeated the soothing application.

"Gently, my good friend — gently!"

Sir Percival hesitated, followed me a few steps, and, to my great surprise, offered me an apology.

"I beg your pardon, Miss Halcombe," he said. "I have been out of order lately, and I am afraid I am a little irritable. But I should like to know what Mrs. Catherick could possibly want here. When did she come? Was the housekeeper the only person who saw her?"

"The only person," I answered, "so far as I know."

The Count interposed again.

"In that case why not question the housekeeper?" he said. "Why not go, Percival, to the fountain-head of information at once?"

"Quite right!" said Sir Percival. "Of course the housekeeper is the first person to question. Excessively stupid of me not to see it myself." With those words he instantly left us to return to the house.

The motive of the Count's interference, which had puzzled

me at first, betrayed itself when Sir Percival's back was turned. He had a host of questions to put to me about Mrs. Catherick, and the cause of her visit to Blackwater Park, which he could scarcely have asked in his friend's presence. I made my answers as short as I civilly could, for I had already determined to check the least approach to any exchanging of confidences between Count Fosco and myself. Laura, however, unconsciously helped him to extract all my information, by making inquiries herself, which left me no alternative but to reply to her, or to appear in the very unenviable and very false character of a depositary of Sir Percival's secrets. The end of it was, that, in about ten minutes' time, the Count knew as much as I know of Mrs. Catherick, and of the events which have so strangely connected us with her daughter, Anne, from the time when Hartright met with her to this day.

The effect of my information on him was, in one respect, curious enough.

Intimately as he knows Sir Percival, and closely as he appears to be associated with Sir Percival's private affairs in general, he is certainly as far as I am from knowing anything of the true story of Anne Catherick. The unsolved mystery in connection with this unhappy woman is now rendered doubly suspicious, in my eyes, by the absolute conviction which I feel, that the clue to it has been hidden by Sir Percival from the most intimate friend he has in the world. It was impossible to mistake the eager curiosity of the Count's look and manner while he drank in greedily every word that fell from my lips. There are many kinds of curiosity, I know—but there is no misinterpreting the curiosity of blank surprise: if I ever saw it in my life I saw it in the Count's face.

While the questions and answers were going on, we had all been strolling quietly back through the plantation. As soon as we reached the house the first object that we saw in front of it was Sir Percival's dog-cart, with the horse put to and the groom waiting by it in his stable-jacket. If these unexpected appearances were to be trusted, the examination of the housekeeper had produced important results already.

"A fine horse, my friend," said the Count, addressing the groom with the most engaging familiarity of manner, "You are going to drive out?"

"I am not going, sir," replied the man, looking at his stable-jacket, and evidently wondering whether the foreign gentleman took it for his livery. "My master drives himself."

The Woman in White

"Aha!" said the Count, "does he indeed? I wonder he gives himself the trouble when he has got you to drive for him. Is he going to fatigue that nice, shining, pretty horse by taking him very far to-day?"

"I don't know, sir," answered the man. "The horse is a mare, if you please, sir. She's the highest-couraged thing we've got in the stables. Her name's Brown Molly, sir, and she'll go till she drops. Sir Percival usually takes Isaac of York for the short distances."

"And your shining courageous Brown Molly for the long?"

"Yes, sir."

"Logical inference, Miss Halcombe," continued the Count, wheeling round briskly, and addressing me. "Sir Percival is going a long distance to-day."

I made no reply. I had my own inferences to draw, from what I knew through the housekeeper and from what I saw before me, and I did not choose to share them with Count Fosco.

When Sir Percival was in Cumberland (I thought to myself), he walked away a long distance, on Anne's account, to question the family at Todd's Corner. Now he is in Hampshire, is he going to drive away a long distance, on Anne's account again, to question Mrs. Catherick at Welmingham?

We all entered the house. As we crossed the hall Sir Percival came out from the library to meet us. He looked hurried and pale and anxious—but for all that, he was in his most polite mood when he spoke to us.

"I am sorry to say I am obliged to leave you," he began—"a long drive—a matter that I can't very well put off. I shall be back in good time to-morrow—but before I go I should like that little business-formality, which I spoke of this morning, to be settled. Laura, will you come into the library? It won't take a minute—a mere formality. Countess, may I trouble you also? I want you and the Countess, Fosco, to be witnesses to a signature—nothing more. Come in at once and get it over."

He held the library door open until they had passed in, followed them, and shut it softly.

I remained, for a moment afterwards, standing alone in the

hall, with my heart beating fast and my mind misgiving me sadly. Then I went on to the staircase, and ascended slowly to my own room.

IV

June 17th. — Just as my hand was on the door of my room, I heard Sir Percival's voice calling to me from below.

"I must beg you to come downstairs again," he said. "It is Fosco's fault, Miss Halcombe, not mine. He has started some nonsensical objection to his wife being one of the witnesses, and has obliged me to ask you to join us in the library."

I entered the room immediately with Sir Percival. Laura was waiting by the writing-table, twisting and turning her garden hat uneasily in her hands. Madame Fosco sat near her, in an arm-chair, imperturbably admiring her husband, who stood by himself at the other end of the library, picking off the dead leaves from the flowers in the window.

The moment I appeared the Count advanced to meet me, and to offer his explanations.

"A thousand pardons, Miss Halcombe," he said. "You know the character which is given to my countrymen by the English? We Italians are all wily and suspicious by nature, in the estimation of the good John Bull. Set me down, if you please, as being no better than the rest of my race. I am a wily Italian and a suspicious Italian. You have thought so yourself, dear lady, have you not? Well! it is part of my wiliness and part of my suspicion to object to Madame Fosco being a witness to Lady Glyde's signature, when I am also a witness myself."

"There is not the shadow of a reason for his objection," interposed Sir Percival. "I have explained to him that the law of England allows Madame Fosco to witness a signature as well as her husband."

"I admit it," resumed the Count. "The law of England says, Yes, but the conscience of Fosco says, No." He spread out his fat fingers on the bosom of his blouse, and bowed solemnly, as if he wished to introduce his conscience to us all, in the character of an illustrious addition to the society. "What this document which Lady Glyde is about to sign may be," he continued, "I neither know nor desire to know. I only say this, circumstances may happen in the future which may oblige Percival, or his representatives, to appeal to the two witnesses, in which case it is certainly desirable that those witnesses should represent two opinions which are perfectly independent the one of the other. This cannot be if my wife signs as well as myself, because we have but one opinion between us, and that opinion is mine. I will not have it cast in my teeth, at some future day, that Madame Fosco acted under my coercion, and was, in plain fact, no witness at all. I speak in Percival's interest, when I propose that my name shall appear (as the nearest friend of the husband), and your name, Miss Halcombe (as the nearest friend of the wife). I am a Jesuit, if you please to think so—a splitter of straws—a man of trifles and crochets and scruples—but you will humour me, I hope, in merciful consideration for my suspicious Italian character, and my uneasy Italian conscience." He bowed again, stepped back a few paces, and withdrew his conscience from our society as politely as he had introduced it.

The Count's scruples might have been honourable and reasonable enough, but there was something in his manner of expressing them which increased my unwillingness to be concerned in the business of the signature. No consideration of less importance than my consideration for Laura would have induced me to consent to be a witness at all. One look, however, at her anxious face decided me to risk anything rather than desert her.

"I will readily remain in the room," I said. "And if I find no reason for starting any small scruples on my side, you may rely on me as a witness."

Sir Percival looked at me sharply, as if he was about to say something. But at the same moment, Madame Fosco attracted his attention by rising from her chair. She had caught her husband's eye, and had evidently received her orders to leave the room.

"You needn't go," said Sir Percival.

Madame Fosco looked for her orders again, got them again, said she would prefer leaving us to our business, and resolutely walked out. The Count lit a cigarette, went back to the flowers in the window, and puffed little jets of smoke at the leaves, in a state of the deepest anxiety about killing the insects.

Meanwhile Sir Percival unlocked a cupboard beneath one of the book-cases, and produced from it a piece of parchment, folded longwise, many times over. He placed it on the table, opened the last fold only, and kept his hand on the rest. The last fold displayed a strip of blank parchment with little wafers stuck on it at certain places. Every line of the writing was hidden in the part which he still held folded up under his hand. Laura and I looked at each other. Her face was pale, but it showed no indecision and no fear.

The Woman in White

Sir Percival dipped a pen in ink, and handed it to his wife. "Sign your name there," he said, pointing to the place. "You and Fosco are to sign afterwards, Miss Halcombe, opposite those two wafers. Come here, Fosco! witnessing a signature is not to be done by mooning out of window and smoking into the flowers."

The Count threw away his cigarette, and joined us at the table, with his hands carelessly thrust into the scarlet belt of his blouse, and his eyes steadily fixed on Sir Percival's face. Laura, who was on the other side of her husband, with the pen in her hand, looked at him too. He stood between them holding the folded parchment down firmly on the table, and glancing across at me, as I sat opposite to him, with such a sinister mixture of suspicion and embarrassment on his face that he looked more like a prisoner at the bar than a gentleman in his own house.

"Sign there," he repeated, turning suddenly on Laura, and pointing once more to the place on the parchment.

"What is it I am to sign?" she asked quietly.

"I have no time to explain," he answered. "The dog-cart is at the door, and I must go directly. Besides, if I had time, you wouldn't understand. It is a purely formal document, full of legal technicalities, and all that sort of thing. Come! come! sign your name, and let us have done as soon as possible."

"I ought surely to know what I am signing, Sir Percival, before I write my name?"

"Nonsense! What have women to do with business? I tell you again, you can't understand it."

"At any rate, let me try to understand it. Whenever Mr. Gilmore had any business for me to do, he always explained it first, and I always understood him."

"I dare say he did. He was your servant, and was obliged to explain. I am your husband, and am not obliged. How much longer do you mean to keep me here? I tell you again, there is no time for reading anything—the dog-cart is waiting at the door. Once for all, will you sign or will you not?"

She still had the pen in her hand, but she made no approach to signing her name with it.

"If my signature pledges me to anything," she said, "surely I have some claim to know what that pledge is?"

He lifted up the parchment, and struck it angrily on the table.

"Speak out!" he said. "You were always famous for telling the truth. Never mind Miss Halcombe, never mind Fosco—say, in plain terms, you distrust me."

The Count took one of his hands out of his belt and laid it on Sir Percival's shoulder. Sir Percival shook it off irritably. The Count put it on again with unruffled composure.

"Control your unfortunate temper, Percival," he said, "Lady Glyde is right."

"Right!" cried Sir Percival. "A wife right in distrusting her husband!"

"It is unjust and cruel to accuse me of distrusting you," said Laura. "Ask Marian if I am not justified in wanting to know what this writing requires of me before I sign it."

"I won't have any appeals made to Miss Halcombe," retorted Sir Percival. "Miss Halcombe has nothing to do with the matter."

I had not spoken hitherto, and I would much rather not have spoken now. But the expression of distress in Laura's face when she turned it towards me, and the insolent injustice of her husband's conduct, left me no other alternative than to give my opinion, for her sake, as soon as I was asked for it.

"Excuse me, Sir Percival," I said—"but as one of the witnesses to the signature, I venture to think that I have something to do with the matter. Laura's objection seems to me a perfectly fair one, and speaking for myself only, I cannot assume the responsibility of witnessing her signature, unless she first understands what the writing is which you wish her to sign."

"A cool declaration, upon my soul!" cried Sir Percival. "The next time you invite yourself to a man's house, Miss Halcombe, I recommend you not to repay his hospitality by taking his wife's side against him in a matter that doesn't concern you."

I started to my feet as suddenly as if he had struck me. If I had been a man, I would have knocked him down on the threshold of his own door, and have left his house, never on any earthly consideration to enter it again. But I was only a woman—and I loved his wife so dearly!

Thank God, that faithful love helped me, and I sat down again without saying a word. She knew what I had suffered and what I had suppressed. She ran round to me, with the tears streaming from her eyes. "Oh, Marian!" she whispered softly. "If my mother had been alive, she could have done no more for me!"

"Come back and sign!" cried Sir Percival from the other side of the table.

"Shall I?" she asked in my ear; "I will, if you tell me."

"No," I answered. "The right and the truth are with you—sign nothing, unless you have read it first."

"Come back and sign!" he reiterated, in his loudest and angriest tones.

The Count, who had watched Laura and me with a close and silent attention, interposed for the second time.

"Percival!" he said. "I remember that I am in the presence of ladies. Be good enough, if you please, to remember it too."

Sir Percival turned on him speechless with passion. The Count's firm hand slowly tightened its grasp on his shoulder, and the Count's steady voice quietly repeated, "Be good enough, if you please, to remember it too."

They both looked at each other. Sir Percival slowly drew his shoulder from under the Count's hand, slowly turned his face away from the Count's eyes, doggedly looked down for a little while at the parchment on the table, and then spoke, with the sullen submission of a tamed animal, rather than the becoming resignation of a convinced man.

"I don't want to offend anybody," he said, "but my wife's obstinacy is enough to try the patience of a saint. I have told her this is merely a formal document—and what more can she want? You may say what you please, but it is no part of a woman's duty to set her husband at defiance. Once more, Lady Glyde, and for the last time, will you sign or will you not?"

Laura returned to his side of the table, and took up the pen again.

"I will sign with pleasure," she said, "if you will only treat me as a responsible being. I care little what sacrifice is required of me, if it will affect no one else, and lead to no ill results—"

"Who talked of a sacrifice being required of you?" he broke in, with a half-suppressed return of his former violence.

"I only meant," she resumed, "that I would refuse no concession which I could honourably make. If I have a scruple about signing my name to an engagement of which I know nothing, why should you visit it on me so severely? It is rather hard, I think, to treat Count Fosco's scruples so much more indulgently than you have treated mine."

This unfortunate, yet most natural, reference to the Count's extraordinary power over her husband, indirect as it was, set Sir Percival's smouldering temper on fire again in an instant.

"Scruples!" he repeated. "Your scruples! It is rather late in the day for you to be scrupulous. I should have thought you had got over all weakness of that sort, when you made a virtue of necessity by marrying me."

The instant he spoke those words, Laura threw down the pen—looked at him with an expression in her eyes which, throughout all my experience of her, I had never seen in them before, and turned her back on him in dead silence.

This strong expression of the most open and the most bitter contempt was so entirely unlike herself, so utterly out of her character, that it silenced us all. There was something hidden, beyond a doubt, under the mere surface-brutality of the words which her husband had just addressed to her. There was some lurking insult beneath them, of which I was wholly ignorant, but which had left the mark of its profanation so plainly on her face that even a stranger might have seen it.

The Count, who was no stranger, saw it as distinctly as I did. When I left my chair to join Laura, I heard him whisper under his breath to Sir Percival, "You idiot!"

Laura walked before me to the door as I advanced, and at the same time her husband spoke to her once more.

"You positively refuse, then, to give me your signature?" he said, in the altered tone of a man who was conscious that he had let his own licence of language seriously injure him.

"After what you have just said to me," she replied firmly, "I refuse my signature until I have read every line in that parchment from the first word to the last. Come away, Marian, we have remained here long enough."

"One moment!" interposed the Count before Sir Percival could speak again—"one moment, Lady Glyde, I implore you!"

Laura would have left the room without noticing him, but I stopped her.

"Don't make an enemy of the Count!" I whispered. "Whatever you do, don't make an enemy of the Count!"

She yielded to me. I closed the door again, and we stood near it waiting. Sir Percival sat down at the table, with his elbow on the folded parchment, and his head resting on his clenched fist. The Count stood between us—master of the dreadful position in which we were placed, as he was master of everything else.

"Lady Glyde," he said, with a gentleness which seemed to address itself to our forlorn situation instead of to ourselves, "pray pardon me if I venture to offer one suggestion, and pray believe that I speak out of my profound respect and my friendly regard for the mistress of this house." He turned sharply towards Sir Percival. "Is it absolutely necessary," he asked, "that this thing here, under your elbow, should be signed to-day?"

"It is necessary to my plans and wishes," returned the other sulkily. "But that consideration, as you may have noticed, has no influence with Lady Glyde."

"Answer my plain question plainly. Can the business of the signature be put off till to-morrow—Yes or No?"

"Yes, if you will have it so."

"Then what are you wasting your time for here? Let the signature wait till to-morrow—let it wait till you come back."

Sir Percival looked up with a frown and an oath.

"You are taking a tone with me that I don't like," he said. "A tone I won't bear from any man."

"I am advising you for your good," returned the Count, with a smile of quiet contempt. "Give yourself time — give Lady Glyde time. Have you forgotten that your dog-cart is waiting at the door? My tone surprises you — ha? I dare say it does — it is the tone of a man who can keep his temper. How many doses of good advice have I given you in my time? More than you can count. Have I ever been wrong? I defy you to quote me an instance of it. Go! take your drive. The matter of the signature can wait till to-morrow. Let it wait — and renew it when you come back."

Sir Percival hesitated and looked at his watch. His anxiety about the secret journey which he was to take that day, revived by the Count's words, was now evidently disputing possession of his mind with his anxiety to obtain Laura's signature. He considered for a little while, and then got up from his chair.

"It is easy to argue me down," he said, "when I have no time to answer you. I will take your advice, Fosco — not because I want it, or believe in it, but because I can't stop here any longer." He paused, and looked round darkly at his wife. "If you don't give me your signature when I come back to-morrow — !" The rest was lost in the noise of his opening the book-case cupboard again, and locking up the parchment once more. He took his hat and gloves off the table, and made for the door. Laura and I drew back to let him pass. "Remember to-morrow!" he said to his wife, and went out.

We waited to give him time to cross the hall and drive away. The Count approached us while we were standing near the door.

"You have just seen Percival at his worst, Miss Halcombe," he said. "As his old friend, I am sorry for him and ashamed of him. As his old friend, I promise you that he shall not break out to-morrow in the same disgraceful manner in which he has broken out to-day."

Laura had taken my arm while he was speaking and she pressed it significantly when he had done. It would have been a hard trial to any woman to stand by and see the office of apologist for her husband's misconduct quietly assumed by his male friend in her own house — and it was a trial to her. I thanked the Count civilly, and let her out. Yes! I thanked him: for I felt already, with a sense of inexpressible helplessness and humiliation, that it was either his interest or his caprice to make sure of my continuing to reside at Blackwater Park, and I knew after Sir Percival's conduct to me, that without the support of the Count's influence, I could not hope to remain there. His influence, the influence of all others that I dreaded most, was actually the one tie which now held me to Laura in the hour of her utmost need!

We heard the wheels of the dog-cart crashing on the gravel of the drive as we came into the hall. Sir Percival had started on his journey.

"Where is he going to, Marian?" Laura whispered. "Every fresh thing he does seems to terrify me about the future. Have you any suspicions?"

After what she had undergone that morning, I was unwilling to tell her my suspicions.

"How should I know his secrets?" I said evasively.

"I wonder if the housekeeper knows?" she persisted.

"Certainly not," I replied. "She must be quite as ignorant as we are."

Laura shook her head doubtfully.

"Did you not hear from the housekeeper that there was a report of Anne Catherick having been seen in this neighbourhood? Don't you think he may have gone away to look for her?"

"I would rather compose myself, Laura, by not thinking about it at all, and after what has happened, you had better follow my example. Come into my room, and rest and quiet yourself a little."

We sat down together close to the window, and let the fragrant summer air breathe over our faces.

"I am ashamed to look at you, Marian," she said, "after what you submitted to downstairs, for my sake. Oh, my own love, I am almost heartbroken when I think of it! But I will try to make it up to you — I will indeed!"

"Hush! hush!" I replied; "don't talk so. What is the trifling mortification of my pride compared to the dreadful sacrifice of your happiness?"

"You heard what he said to me?" she went on quickly and

vehemently. "You heard the words—but you don't know what they meant—you don't know why I threw down the pen and turned my back on him." She rose in sudden agitation, and walked about the room. "I have kept many things from your knowledge, Marian, for fear of distressing you, and making you unhappy at the outset of our new lives. You don't know how he has used me. And yet you ought to know, for you saw how he used me to-day. You heard him sneer at my presuming to be scrupulous—you heard him say I had made a virtue of necessity in marrying him." She sat down again, her face flushed deeply, and her hands twisted and twined together in her lap. "I can't tell you about it now," she said; "I shall burst out crying if I tell you now—later, Marian, when I am more sure of myself. My poor head aches, darling—aches, aches, aches. Where is your smelling-bottle? Let me talk to you about yourself. I wish I had given him my signature, for your sake. Shall I give it to him to-morrow? I would rather compromise myself than compromise you. After your taking my part against him, he will lay all the blame on you if I refuse again. What shall we do? Oh, for a friend to help us and advise us!—a friend we could really trust!"

She sighed bitterly. I saw in her face that she was thinking of Hartright—saw it the more plainly because her last words set me thinking of him too. In six months only from her marriage we wanted the faithful service he had offered to us in his farewell words. How little I once thought that we should ever want it at all!

"We must do what we can to help ourselves," I said. "Let us try to talk it over calmly, Laura—let us do all in our power to decide for the best."

Putting what she knew of her husband's embarrassments and what I had heard of his conversation with the lawyer together, we arrived necessarily at the conclusion that the parchment in the library had been drawn up for the purpose of borrowing money, and that Laura's signature was absolutely necessary to fit it for the attainment of Sir Percival's object.

The second question, concerning the nature of the legal contract by which the money was to be obtained, and the degree of personal responsibility to which Laura might subject herself if she signed it in the dark, involved considerations which lay far beyond any knowledge and experience that either of us possessed. My own convictions led me to believe that the hidden contents of the parchment concealed a transaction of the meanest and the most fraudulent kind.

I had not formed this conclusion in consequence of Sir Percival's refusal to show the writing or to explain it, for that refusal might well have proceeded from his obstinate disposition and his domineering temper alone. My sole motive for distrusting his honesty sprang from the change which I had observed in his language and his manners at Blackwater Park, a change which convinced me that he had been acting a part throughout the whole period of his probation at Limmeridge House. His elaborate delicacy, his ceremonious politeness which harmonised so agreeably with Mr. Gilmore's old-fashioned notions, his modesty with Laura, his candour with me, his moderation with Mr. Fairlie—all these were the artifices of a mean, cunning, and brutal man, who had dropped his disguise when his practised duplicity had gained its end, and had openly shown himself in the library on that very day. I say nothing of the grief which this discovery caused me on Laura's account, for it is not to be expressed by any words of mine. I only refer to it at all, because it decided me to oppose her signing the parchment, whatever the consequences might be, unless she was first made acquainted with the contents.

Under these circumstances, the one chance for us when to-morrow came was to be provided with an objection to giving the signature, which might rest on sufficiently firm commercial or legal grounds to shake Sir Percival's resolution, and to make him suspect that we two women understood the laws and obligations of business as well as himself.

After some pondering, I determined to write to the only honest man within reach whom we could trust to help us discreetly in our forlorn situation. That man was Mr. Gilmore's partner, Mr. Kyrle, who conducted the business now that our old friend had been obliged to withdraw from it, and to leave London on account of his health. I explained to Laura that I had Mr. Gilmore's own authority for placing implicit confidence in his partner's integrity, discretion, and accurate knowledge of all her affairs, and with her full approval I sat down at once to write the letter, I began by stating our position to Mr. Kyrle exactly as it was, and then asked for his advice in return, expressed in plain, downright terms which he could comprehend without any danger of misinterpretations and mistakes. My letter was as short as I could possibly make it, and was, I hope, unencumbered by needless apologies and needless details.

Just as I was about to put the address on the envelope an obstacle was discovered by Laura, which in the effort and preoccupation of writing had escaped my mind altogether.

"How are we to get the answer in time?" she asked. "Your letter will not be delivered in London before to-morrow morning, and the post will not bring the reply here till the morning after."

The only way of overcoming this difficulty was to have the answer brought to us from the lawyer's office by a special messenger. I wrote a postscript to that effect, begging that the messenger might be despatched with the reply by the eleven o'clock morning train, which would bring him to our station at twenty minutes past one, and so enable him to reach Blackwater Park by two o'clock at the latest. He was to be directed to ask for me, to answer no questions addressed to him by any one else, and to deliver his letter into no hands but mine.

"In case Sir Percival should come back to-morrow before two o'clock," I said to Laura, "the wisest plan for you to adopt is to be out in the grounds all the morning with your book or your work, and not to appear at the house till the messenger has had time to arrive with the letter. I will wait here for him all the morning, to guard against any misadventures or mistakes. By following this arrangement I hope and believe we shall avoid being taken by surprise. Let us go down to the drawing-room now. We may excite suspicion if we remain shut up together too long."

"Suspicion?" she repeated. "Whose suspicion can we excite, now that Sir Percival has left the house? Do you mean Count Fosco?"

"Perhaps I do, Laura."

"You are beginning to dislike him as much as I do, Marian."

"No, not to dislike him. Dislike is always more or less associated with contempt—I can see nothing in the Count to despise."

"You are not afraid of him, are you?"

"Perhaps I am—a little."

"Afraid of him, after his interference in our favour to-day!"

"Yes. I am more afraid of his interference than I am of Sir Percival's violence. Remember what I said to you in the library. Whatever you do, Laura, don't make an enemy of the Count!"

The Woman in White

We went downstairs. Laura entered the drawing-room, while I proceeded across the hall, with my letter in my hand, to put it into the post-bag, which hung against the wall opposite to me.

The house door was open, and as I crossed past it, I saw Count Fosco and his wife standing talking together on the steps outside, with their faces turned towards me.

The Countess came into the hall rather hastily, and asked if I had leisure enough for five minutes' private conversation. Feeling a little surprised by such an appeal from such a person, I put my letter into the bag, and replied that I was quite at her disposal. She took my arm with unaccustomed friendliness and familiarity, and instead of leading me into an empty room, drew me out with her to the belt of turf which surrounded the large fish-pond.

As we passed the Count on the steps he bowed and smiled, and then went at once into the house, pushing the hall door to after him, but not actually closing it.

The Countess walked me gently round the fish-pond. I expected to be made the depositary of some extraordinary confidence, and I was astonished to find that Madame Fosco's communication for my private ear was nothing more than a polite assurance of her sympathy for me, after what had happened in the library. Her husband had told her of all that had passed, and of the insolent manner in which Sir Percival had spoken to me. This information had so shocked and distressed her, on my account and on Laura's, that she had made up her mind, if anything of the sort happened again, to mark her sense of Sir Percival's outrageous conduct by leaving the house. The Count had approved of her idea, and she now hoped that I approved of it too.

I thought this a very strange proceeding on the part of such a remarkably reserved woman as Madame Fosco, especially after the interchange of sharp speeches which had passed between us during the conversation in the boat-house on that very morning. However, it was my plain duty to meet a polite and friendly advance on the part of one of my elders with a polite and friendly reply. I answered the Countess accordingly in her own tone, and then, thinking we had said all that was necessary on either side, made an attempt to get back to the house.

But Madame Fosco seemed resolved not to part with me, and to my unspeakable amazement, resolved also to talk.

Hitherto the most silent of women, she now persecuted me with fluent conventionalities on the subject of married life, on the subject of Sir Percival and Laura, on the subject of her own happiness, on the subject of the late Mr. Fairlie's conduct to her in the matter of her legacy, and on half a dozen other subjects besides, until she had detained me walking round and round the fish-pond for more than half an hour, and had quite wearied me out. Whether she discovered this or not, I cannot say, but she stopped as abruptly as she had begun—looked towards the house door, resumed her icy manner in a moment, and dropped my arm of her own accord before I could think of an excuse for accomplishing my own release from her.

As I pushed open the door and entered the hall, I found myself suddenly face to face with the Count again. He was just putting a letter into the post-bag.

After he had dropped it in and had closed the bag, he asked me where I had left Madame Fosco. I told him, and he went out at the hall door immediately to join his wife. His manner when he spoke to me was so unusually quiet and subdued that I turned and looked after him, wondering if he were ill or out of spirits.

Why my next proceeding was to go straight up to the post-bag and take out my own letter and look at it again, with a vague distrust on me, and why the looking at it for the second time instantly suggested the idea to my mind of sealing the envelope for its greater security—are mysteries which are either too deep or too shallow for me to fathom. Women, as everybody knows, constantly act on impulses which they cannot explain even to themselves, and I can only suppose that one of those impulses was the hidden cause of my unaccountable conduct on this occasion.

Whatever influence animated me, I found cause to congratulate myself on having obeyed it as soon as I prepared to seal the letter in my own room. I had originally closed the envelope in the usual way by moistening the adhesive point and pressing it on the paper beneath, and when I now tried it with my finger, after a lapse of full three-quarters of an hour, the envelope opened on the instant, without sticking or tearing. Perhaps I had fastened it insufficiently? Perhaps there might have been some defect in the adhesive gum?

Or, perhaps——No! it is quite revolting enough to feel that third conjecture stirring in my mind. I would rather not see it confronting me in plain black and white.

The Woman in White

I almost dread to-morrow — so much depends on my discretion and self-control. There are two precautions, at all events, which I am sure not to forget. I must be careful to keep up friendly appearances with the Count, and I must be well on my guard when the messenger from the office comes here with the answer to my letter.

V

June 17th.—When the dinner hour brought us together again, Count Fosco was in his usual excellent spirits. He exerted himself to interest and amuse us, as if he was determined to efface from our memories all recollection of what had passed in the library that afternoon. Lively descriptions of his adventures in travelling, amusing anecdotes of remarkable people whom he had met with abroad, quaint comparisons between the social customs of various nations, illustrated by examples drawn from men and women indiscriminately all over Europe, humorous confessions of the innocent follies of his own early life, when he ruled the fashions of a second-rate Italian town, and wrote preposterous romances on the French model for a second-rate Italian newspaper—all flowed in succession so easily and so gaily from his lips, and all addressed our various curiosities and various interests so directly and so delicately, that Laura and I listened to him with as much attention and, inconsistent as it may seem, with as much admiration also, as Madame Fosco herself. Women can resist a man's love, a man's fame, a man's personal appearance, and a man's money, but they cannot resist a man's tongue when he knows how to talk to them.

After dinner, while the favourable impression which he had produced on us was still vivid in our minds, the Count modestly withdrew to read in the library.

Laura proposed a stroll in the grounds to enjoy the close of the long evening. It was necessary in common politeness to ask Madame Fosco to join us, but this time she had apparently received her orders beforehand, and she begged we would kindly excuse her. "The Count will probably want a fresh supply of cigarettes," she remarked by way of apology, "and nobody can make them to his satisfaction but myself." Her cold blue eyes almost warmed as she spoke the words—she looked actually proud of being the officiating medium through which her lord and master composed himself with tobacco-smoke!

Laura and I went out together alone.

It was a misty, heavy evening. There was a sense of blight in the air; the flowers were drooping in the garden, and the ground was parched and dewless. The western heaven, as we saw it over the quiet trees, was of a pale yellow hue, and the sun was setting faintly in a haze. Coming rain seemed near—it would fall probably with the fall of night.

"Which way shall we go?" I asked

"Towards the lake, Marian, if you like," she answered.

"You seem unaccountably fond, Laura, of that dismal lake."

"No, not of the lake but of the scenery about it. The sand and heath and the fir-trees are the only objects I can discover, in all this large place, to remind me of Limmeridge. But we will walk in some other direction if you prefer it."

"I have no favourite walks at Blackwater Park, my love. One is the same as another to me. Let us go to the lake—we may find it cooler in the open space than we find it here."

We walked through the shadowy plantation in silence. The heaviness in the evening air oppressed us both, and when we reached the boat-house we were glad to sit down and rest inside.

A white fog hung low over the lake. The dense brown line of the trees on the opposite bank appeared above it, like a dwarf forest floating in the sky. The sandy ground, shelving downward from where we sat, was lost mysteriously in the outward layers of the fog. The silence was horrible. No rustling of the leaves—no bird's note in the wood—no cry of water-fowl from the pools of the hidden lake. Even the croaking of the frogs had ceased to-night.

"It is very desolate and gloomy," said Laura. "But we can be more alone here than anywhere else."

She spoke quietly and looked at the wilderness of sand and mist with steady, thoughtful eyes. I could see that her mind was too much occupied to feel the dreary impressions from without which had fastened themselves already on mine.

"I promised, Marian, to tell you the truth about my married life, instead of leaving you any longer to guess it for yourself," she began. "That secret is the first I have ever had from you, love, and I am determined it shall be the last. I was silent, as you know, for your sake—and perhaps a little for my own sake as well. It is very hard for a woman to confess that the man to whom she has given her whole life is the man of all others who cares least for the gift. If you were married yourself, Marian—and especially if you were happily married—you would feel for me as no single woman can feel, however kind and true she may be."

What answer could I make? I could only take her hand and

look at her with my whole heart as well as my eyes would let me.

"How often," she went on, "I have heard you laughing over what you used to call your 'poverty!' how often you have made me mock-speeches of congratulation on my wealth! Oh, Marian, never laugh again. Thank God for your poverty—it has made you your own mistress, and has saved you from the lot that has fallen on me."

A sad beginning on the lips of a young wife!—sad in its quiet plain-spoken truth. The few days we had all passed together at Blackwater Park had been many enough to show me—to show any one—what her husband had married her for.

"You shall not be distressed," she said, "by hearing how soon my disappointments and my trials began—or even by knowing what they were. It is bad enough to have them on my memory. If I tell you how he received the first and last attempt at remonstrance that I ever made, you will know how he has always treated me, as well as if I had described it in so many words. It was one day at Rome when we had ridden out together to the tomb of Cecilia Metella. The sky was calm and lovely, and the grand old ruin looked beautiful, and the remembrance that a husband's love had raised it in the old time to a wife's memory, made me feel more tenderly and more anxiously towards my husband than I had ever felt yet. 'Would you build such a tomb for me, Percival?' I asked him. 'You said you loved me dearly before we were married, and yet, since that time——' I could get no farther. Marian! he was not even looking at me! I pulled down my veil, thinking it best not to let him see that the tears were in my eyes. I fancied he had not paid any attention to me, but he had. He said, 'Come away,' and laughed to himself as he helped me on to my horse. He mounted his own horse and laughed again as we rode away. 'If I do build you a tomb,' he said, 'it will be done with your own money. I wonder whether Cecilia Metella had a fortune and paid for hers.' I made no reply—how could I, when I was crying behind my veil? 'Ah, you light-complexioned women are all sulky,' he said. 'What do you want? compliments and soft speeches? Well! I'm in a good humour this morning. Consider the compliments paid and the speeches said.' Men little know when they say hard things to us how well we remember them, and how much harm they do us. It would have been better for me if I had gone on crying, but his contempt dried up my tears and hardened my heart. From that time, Marian, I never checked myself again in thinking of Walter Hartright. I let the memory of those happy days, when we were so fond of each other in secret, come back and comfort me. What else had I to look to for consolation? If we had been together you would have helped me to better things. I know it was wrong, darling, but tell me if I was wrong without any excuse."

I was obliged to turn my face from her. "Don't ask me!" I said. "Have I suffered as you have suffered? What right have I to decide?"

"I used to think of him," she pursued, dropping her voice and moving closer to me, "I used to think of him when Percival left me alone at night to go among the Opera people. I used to fancy what I might have been if it had pleased God to bless me with poverty, and if I had been his wife. I used to see myself in my neat cheap gown, sitting at home and waiting for him while he was earning our bread—sitting at home and working for him and loving him all the better because I had to work for him—seeing him come in tired and taking off his hat and coat for him, and, Marian, pleasing him with little dishes at dinner that I had learnt to make for his sake. Oh! I hope he is never lonely enough and sad enough to think of me and see me as I have thought of him and see him!"

As she said those melancholy words, all the lost tenderness returned to her voice, and all the lost beauty trembled back into her face. Her eyes rested as lovingly on the blighted, solitary, ill-omened view before us, as if they saw the friendly hills of Cumberland in the dim and threatening sky.

"Don't speak of Walter any more," I said, as soon as I could control myself. "Oh, Laura, spare us both the wretchedness of talking of him now!"

She roused herself, and looked at me tenderly.

"I would rather be silent about him for ever," she answered, "than cause you a moment's pain."

"It is in your interests," I pleaded; "it is for your sake that I speak. If your husband heard you——"

"It would not surprise him if he did hear me."

She made that strange reply with a weary calmness and coldness. The change in her manner, when she gave the answer, startled me almost as much as the answer itself.

"Not surprise him!" I repeated. "Laura! remember what you

are saying—you frighten me!"

"It is true," she said; "it is what I wanted to tell you to-day, when we were talking in your room. My only secret when I opened my heart to him at Limmeridge was a harmless secret, Marian—you said so yourself. The name was all I kept from him, and he has discovered it."

I heard her, but I could say nothing. Her last words had killed the little hope that still lived in me.

"It happened at Rome," she went on, as wearily calm and cold as ever. "We were at a little party given to the English by some friends of Sir Percival's—Mr. and Mrs. Markland. Mrs. Markland had the reputation of sketching very beautifully, and some of the guests prevailed on her to show us her drawings. We all admired them, but something I said attracted her attention particularly to me. 'Surely you draw yourself?' she asked. 'I used to draw a little once,' I answered, 'but I have given it up.' 'If you have once drawn,' she said, 'you may take to it again one of these days, and if you do, I wish you would let me recommend you a master.' I said nothing—you know why, Marian—and tried to change the conversation. But Mrs. Markland persisted. 'I have had all sorts of teachers,' she went on, 'but the best of all, the most intelligent and the most attentive, was a Mr. Hartright. If you ever take up your drawing again, do try him as a master. He is a young man—modest and gentlemanlike—I am sure you will like him.' Think of those words being spoken to me publicly, in the presence of strangers—strangers who had been invited to meet the bride and bridegroom! I did all I could to control myself—I said nothing, and looked down close at the drawings. When I ventured to raise my head again, my eyes and my husband's eyes met, and I knew, by his look, that my face had betrayed me. 'We will see about Mr. Hartright,' he said, looking at me all the time, 'when we get back to England. I agree with you, Mrs. Markland—I think Lady Glyde is sure to like him.' He laid an emphasis on the last words which made my cheeks burn, and set my heart beating as if it would stifle me. Nothing more was said. We came away early. He was silent in the carriage driving back to the hotel. He helped me out, and followed me upstairs as usual. But the moment we were in the drawing-room, he locked the door, pushed me down into a chair, and stood over me with his hands on my shoulders. 'Ever since that morning when you made your audacious confession to me at Limmeridge,' he said, 'I have wanted to find out the man, and I found him in your face to-night. Your drawing-master was the man, and his name is Hartright. You shall repent it, and he shall repent it, to the last hour of your lives. Now go to bed and dream of him if you like, with the marks of my horsewhip on his shoulders.' Whenever he is angry with me now he refers to what I acknowledged to him in your presence with a sneer or a threat. I have no power to prevent him from putting his own horrible construction on the confidence I placed in him. I have no influence to make him believe me, or to keep him silent. You looked surprised to-day when you heard him tell me that I had made a virtue of necessity in marrying him. You will not be surprised again when you hear him repeat it, the next time he is out of temper — — Oh, Marian! don't! don't! you hurt me!"

I had caught her in my arms, and the sting and torment of my remorse had closed them round her like a vice. Yes! my remorse. The white despair of Walter's face, when my cruel words struck him to the heart in the summer-house at Limmeridge, rose before me in mute, unendurable reproach. My hand had pointed the way which led the man my sister loved, step by step, far from his country and his friends. Between those two young hearts I had stood, to sunder them for ever, the one from the other, and his life and her life lay wasted before me alike in witness of the deed. I had done this, and done it for Sir Percival Glyde.

For Sir Percival Glyde.

I heard her speaking, and I knew by the tone of her voice that she was comforting me — I, who deserved nothing but the reproach of her silence! How long it was before I mastered the absorbing misery of my own thoughts, I cannot tell. I was first conscious that she was kissing me, and then my eyes seemed to wake on a sudden to their sense of outward things, and I knew that I was looking mechanically straight before me at the prospect of the lake.

"It is late," I heard her whisper. "It will be dark in the plantation." She shook my arm and repeated, "Marian! it will be dark in the plantation."

"Give me a minute longer," I said — "a minute, to get better in."

I was afraid to trust myself to look at her yet, and I kept my eyes fixed on the view.

It was late. The dense brown line of trees in the sky had

faded in the gathering darkness to the faint resemblance of a long wreath of smoke. The mist over the lake below had stealthily enlarged, and advanced on us. The silence was as breathless as ever, but the horror of it had gone, and the solemn mystery of its stillness was all that remained.

"We are far from the house," she whispered. "Let us go back."

She stopped suddenly, and turned her face from me towards the entrance of the boat-house.

"Marian!" she said, trembling violently. "Do you see nothing? Look!"

"Where?"

"Down there, below us."

She pointed. My eyes followed her hand, and I saw it too.

A living figure was moving over the waste of heath in the distance. It crossed our range of view from the boat-house, and passed darkly along the outer edge of the mist. It stopped far off, in front of us—waited—and passed on; moving slowly, with the white cloud of mist behind it and above it—slowly, slowly, till it glided by the edge of the boat-house, and we saw it no more.

We were both unnerved by what had passed between us that evening. Some minutes elapsed before Laura would venture into the plantation, and before I could make up my mind to lead her back to the house.

"Was it a man or a woman?" she asked in a whisper, as we moved at last into the dark dampness of the outer air.

"I am not certain."

"Which do you think?"

"It looked like a woman."

"I was afraid it was a man in a long cloak."

"It may be a man. In this dim light it is not possible to be certain."

The Woman in White

"Wait, Marian! I'm frightened — I don't see the path. Suppose the figure should follow us?"

"Not at all likely, Laura. There is really nothing to be alarmed about. The shores of the lake are not far from the village, and they are free to any one to walk on by day or night. It is only wonderful we have seen no living creature there before."

We were now in the plantation. It was very dark — so dark, that we found some difficulty in keeping the path. I gave Laura my arm, and we walked as fast as we could on our way back.

Before we were half-way through she stopped, and forced me to stop with her. She was listening.

"Hush," she whispered. "I hear something behind us."

"Dead leaves," I said to cheer her, "or a twig blown off the trees."

"It is summer time, Marian, and there is not a breath of wind. Listen!"

I heard the sound too — a sound like a light footstep following us.

"No matter who it is, or what it is," I said, "let us walk on. In another minute, if there is anything to alarm us, we shall be near enough to the house to be heard."

We went on quickly — so quickly, that Laura was breathless by the time we were nearly through the plantation, and within sight of the lighted windows.

I waited a moment to give her breathing-time. Just as we were about to proceed she stopped me again, and signed to me with her hand to listen once more. We both heard distinctly a long, heavy sigh behind us, in the black depths of the trees.

"Who's there?" I called out.

There was no answer.

"Who's there?" I repeated.

An instant of silence followed, and then we heard the light fall of the footsteps again, fainter and fainter — sinking away into the darkness—sinking, sinking, sinking—till they were lost in the silence.

We hurried out from the trees to the open lawn beyond, crossed it rapidly; and without another word passing between us, reached the house.

In the light of the hall-lamp Laura looked at me, with white cheeks and startled eyes.

"I am half dead with fear," she said. "Who could it have been?"

"We will try to guess to-morrow," I replied. "In the meantime say nothing to any one of what we have heard and seen."

"Why not?"

"Because silence is safe, and we have need of safety in this house."

I sent Laura upstairs immediately, waited a minute to take off my hat and put my hair smooth, and then went at once to make my first investigations in the library, on pretence of searching for a book.

There sat the Count, filling out the largest easy-chair in the house, smoking and reading calmly, with his feet on an ottoman, his cravat across his knees, and his shirt collar wide open. And there sat Madame Fosco, like a quiet child, on a stool by his side, making cigarettes. Neither husband nor wife could, by any possibility, have been out late that evening, and have just got back to the house in a hurry. I felt that my object in visiting the library was answered the moment I set eyes on them.

Count Fosco rose in polite confusion and tied his cravat on when I entered the room.

"Pray don't let me disturb you," I said. "I have only come here to get a book."

"All unfortunate men of my size suffer from the heat," said the Count, refreshing himself gravely with a large green fan. "I wish I could change places with my excellent wife. She is as cool at this moment as a fish in the pond outside."

The Woman in White

The Countess allowed herself to thaw under the influence of her husband's quaint comparison. "I am never warm, Miss Halcombe," she remarked, with the modest air of a woman who was confessing to one of her own merits.

"Have you and Lady Glyde been out this evening?" asked the Count, while I was taking a book from the shelves to preserve appearances.

"Yes, we went out to get a little air."

"May I ask in what direction?"

"In the direction of the lake — as far as the boat-house."

"Aha? As far as the boat-house?"

Under other circumstances I might have resented his curiosity. But to-night I hailed it as another proof that neither he nor his wife were connected with the mysterious appearance at the lake.

"No more adventures, I suppose, this evening?" he went on. "No more discoveries, like your discovery of the wounded dog?"

He fixed his unfathomable grey eyes on me, with that cold, clear, irresistible glitter in them which always forces me to look at him, and always makes me uneasy while I do look. An unutterable suspicion that his mind is prying into mine overcomes me at these times, and it overcame me now.

"No," I said shortly; "no adventures — no discoveries."

I tried to look away from him and leave the room. Strange as it seems, I hardly think I should have succeeded in the attempt if Madame Fosco had not helped me by causing him to move and look away first.

"Count, you are keeping Miss Halcombe standing," she said.

The moment he turned round to get me a chair, I seized my opportunity — thanked him — made my excuses — and slipped out.

An hour later, when Laura's maid happened to be in her mistress's room, I took occasion to refer to the closeness of the night, with a view to ascertaining next how the servants had been passing their time.

"Have you been suffering much from the heat downstairs?" I asked.

"No, miss," said the girl, "we have not felt it to speak of."

"You have been out in the woods then, I suppose?"

"Some of us thought of going, miss. But cook said she should take her chair into the cool court-yard, outside the kitchen door, and on second thoughts, all the rest of us took our chairs out there too."

The housekeeper was now the only person who remained to be accounted for.

"Is Mrs. Michelson gone to bed yet?" I inquired.

"I should think not, miss," said the girl, smiling. "Mrs. Michelson is more likely to be getting up just now than going to bed."

"Why? What do you mean? Has Mrs. Michelson been taking to her bed in the daytime?"

"No, miss, not exactly, but the next thing to it. She's been asleep all the evening on the sofa in her own room."

Putting together what I observed for myself in the library, and what I have just heard from Laura's maid, one conclusion seems inevitable. The figure we saw at the lake was not the figure of Madame Fosco, of her husband, or of any of the servants. The footsteps we heard behind us were not the footsteps of any one belonging to the house.

Who could it have been?

It seems useless to inquire. I cannot even decide whether the figure was a man's or a woman's. I can only say that I think it was a woman's.

VI

June 18th. — The misery of self-reproach which I suffered yesterday evening, on hearing what Laura told me in the boat-house, returned in the loneliness of the night, and kept me waking and wretched for hours.

I lighted my candle at last, and searched through my old journals to see what my share in the fatal error of her marriage had really been, and what I might have once done to save her from it. The result soothed me a little for it showed that, however blindly and ignorantly I acted, I acted for the best. Crying generally does me harm; but it was not so last night — I think it relieved me. I rose this morning with a settled resolution and a quiet mind. Nothing Sir Percival can say or do shall ever irritate me again, or make me forget for one moment that I am staying here in defiance of mortifications, insults, and threats, for Laura's service and for Laura's sake.

The speculations in which we might have indulged this morning, on the subject of the figure at the lake and the footsteps in the plantation, have been all suspended by a trifling accident which has caused Laura great regret. She has lost the little brooch I gave her for a keepsake on the day before her marriage. As she wore it when we went out yesterday evening we can only suppose that it must have dropped from her dress, either in the boat-house or on our way back. The servants have been sent to search, and have returned unsuccessful. And now Laura herself has gone to look for it. Whether she finds it or not the loss will help to excuse her absence from the house, if Sir Percival returns before the letter from Mr. Gilmore's partner is placed in my hands.

One o'clock has just struck. I am considering whether I had better wait here for the arrival of the messenger from London, or slip away quietly, and watch for him outside the lodge gate.

My suspicion of everybody and everything in this house inclines me to think that the second plan may be the best. The Count is safe in the breakfast-room. I heard him, through the door, as I ran upstairs ten minutes since, exercising his canary-birds at their tricks: — "Come out on my little finger, my pret-pret-pretties! Come out, and hop upstairs! One, two, three — and up! Three, two, one — and down! One, two, three — twit-twit-twit-tweet!" The birds burst into their usual ecstasy of singing, and the Count chirruped and whistled at them in return, as if he was a bird himself. My room door is open, and I can hear the shrill singing and whistling at this very moment. If I am really to slip out without being observed, now is my time.

Four o'clock. The three hours that have passed since I made my last entry have turned the whole march of events at Blackwater Park in a new direction. Whether for good or for evil, I cannot and dare not decide.

Let me get back first to the place at which I left off, or I shall lose myself in the confusion of my own thoughts.

I went out, as I had proposed, to meet the messenger with my letter from London at the lodge gate. On the stairs I saw no one. In the hall I heard the Count still exercising his birds. But on crossing the quadrangle outside, I passed Madame Fosco, walking by herself in her favourite circle, round and round the great fish-pond. I at once slackened my pace, so as to avoid all appearance of being in a hurry, and even went the length, for caution's sake, of inquiring if she thought of going out before lunch. She smiled at me in the friendliest manner—said she preferred remaining near the house, nodded pleasantly, and re-entered the hall. I looked back, and saw that she had closed the door before I had opened the wicket by the side of the carriage gates.

In less than a quarter of an hour I reached the lodge.

The lane outside took a sudden turn to the left, ran on straight for a hundred yards or so, and then took another sharp turn to the right to join the high-road. Between these two turns, hidden from the lodge on one side, and from the way to the station on the other, I waited, walking backwards and forwards. High hedges were on either side of me, and for twenty minutes, by my watch, I neither saw nor heard anything. At the end of that time the sound of a carriage caught my ear, and I was met, as I advanced towards the second turning, by a fly from the railway. I made a sign to the driver to stop. As he obeyed me a respectable-looking man put his head out of the window to see what was the matter.

"I beg your pardon," I said, "but am I right in supposing that you are going to Blackwater Park?"

"Yes, ma'am."

"With a letter for any one?"

"With a letter for Miss Halcombe, ma'am."

"You may give me the letter. I am Miss Halcombe."

The man touched his hat, got out of the fly immediately, and gave me the letter.

I opened it at once and read these lines. I copy them here, thinking it best to destroy the original for caution's sake.

"DEAR MADAM,—Your letter received this morning has caused me very great anxiety. I will reply to it as briefly and plainly as possible.

"My careful consideration of the statement made by yourself, and my knowledge of Lady Glyde's position, as defined in the settlement, lead me, I regret to say, to the conclusion that a loan of the trust money to Sir Percival (or, in other words, a loan of some portion of the twenty thousand pounds of Lady Glyde's fortune) is in contemplation, and that she is made a party to the deed, in order to secure her approval of a flagrant breach of trust, and to have her signature produced against her if she should complain hereafter. It is impossible, on any other supposition, to account, situated as she is, for her execution to a deed of any kind being wanted at all.

"In the event of Lady Glyde's signing such a document, as I am compelled to suppose the deed in question to be, her trustees would be at liberty to advance money to Sir Percival out of her twenty thousand pounds. If the amount so lent should not be paid back, and if Lady Glyde should have children, their fortune will then be diminished by the sum, large or small, so advanced. In plainer terms still, the transaction, for anything that Lady Glyde knows to the contrary, may be a fraud upon her unborn children.

"Under these serious circumstances, I would recommend Lady Glyde to assign as a reason for withholding her signature, that she wishes the deed to be first submitted to myself, as her family solicitor (in the absence of my partner, Mr. Gilmore). No reasonable objection can be made to taking this course—for, if the transaction is an honourable one, there will necessarily be no difficulty in my giving my approval.

"Sincerely assuring you of my readiness to afford any additional help or advice that may be wanted, I beg to remain,

Madam, your faithful servant,

"WILLIAM KYRLE."

I read this kind and sensible letter very thankfully. It supplied Laura with a reason for objecting to the signature which was unanswerable, and which we could both of us understand. The messenger waited near me while I was reading to receive his directions when I had done.

"Will you be good enough to say that I understand the letter, and that I am very much obliged?" I said. "There is no other reply necessary at present."

Exactly at the moment when I was speaking those words, holding the letter open in my hand, Count Fosco turned the corner of the lane from the high-road, and stood before me as if he had sprung up out of the earth.

The suddenness of his appearance, in the very last place under heaven in which I should have expected to see him, took me completely by surprise. The messenger wished me good-morning, and got into the fly again. I could not say a word to him — I was not even able to return his bow. The conviction that I was discovered — and by that man, of all others — absolutely petrified me.

"Are you going back to the house, Miss Halcombe?" he inquired, without showing the least surprise on his side, and without even looking after the fly, which drove off while he was speaking to me.

I collected myself sufficiently to make a sign in the affirmative.

"I am going back too," he said. "Pray allow me the pleasure of accompanying you. Will you take my arm? You look surprised at seeing me!"

I took his arm. The first of my scattered senses that came back was the sense that warned me to sacrifice anything rather than make an enemy of him.

"You look surprised at seeing me!" he repeated in his quietly pertinacious way.

"I thought, Count, I heard you with your birds in the breakfast-room," I answered, as quietly and firmly as I could.

"Surely. But my little feathered children, dear lady, are only too like other children. They have their days of perversity, and this morning was one of them. My wife came in as I was putting them back in their cage, and said she had left you going out alone for a walk. You told her so, did you not?"

"Certainly."

"Well, Miss Halcombe, the pleasure of accompanying you was too great a temptation for me to resist. At my age there is no harm in confessing so much as that, is there? I seized my hat, and set off to offer myself as your escort. Even so fat an old man as Fosco is surely better than no escort at all? I took the wrong path—I came back in despair, and here I am, arrived (may I say it?) at the height of my wishes."

He talked on in this complimentary strain with a fluency which left me no exertion to make beyond the effort of maintaining my composure. He never referred in the most distant manner to what he had seen in the lane, or to the letter which I still had in my hand. This ominous discretion helped to convince me that he must have surprised, by the most dishonourable means, the secret of my application in Laura's interest to the lawyer; and that, having now assured himself of the private manner in which I had received the answer, he had discovered enough to suit his purposes, and was only bent on trying to quiet the suspicions which he knew he must have aroused in my mind. I was wise enough, under these circumstances, not to attempt to deceive him by plausible explanations, and woman enough, notwithstanding my dread of him, to feel as if my hand was tainted by resting on his arm.

On the drive in front of the house we met the dog-cart being taken round to the stables. Sir Percival had just returned. He came out to meet us at the house-door. Whatever other results his journey might have had, it had not ended in softening his savage temper.

"Oh! here are two of you come back," he said, with a lowering face. "What is the meaning of the house being deserted in this way? Where is Lady Glyde?"

I told him of the loss of the brooch, and said that Laura had gone into the plantation to look for it.

"Brooch or no brooch," he growled sulkily, "I recommend her not to forget her appointment in the library this afternoon. I shall expect to see her in half an hour."

I took my hand from the Count's arm, and slowly ascended the steps. He honoured me with one of his magnificent bows, and then addressed himself gaily to the scowling master of the house.

"Tell me, Percival," he said, "have you had a pleasant drive? And has your pretty shining Brown Molly come back at all tired?"

"Brown Molly be hanged — and the drive too! I want my lunch."

"And I want five minutes' talk with you, Percival, first," returned the Count. "Five minutes' talk, my friend, here on the grass."

"What about?"

"About business that very much concerns you."

I lingered long enough in passing through the hall-door to hear this question and answer, and to see Sir Percival thrust his hands into his pockets in sullen hesitation.

"If you want to badger me with any more of your infernal scruples," he said, "I for one won't hear them. I want my lunch."

"Come out here and speak to me," repeated the Count, still perfectly uninfluenced by the rudest speech that his friend could make to him.

Sir Percival descended the steps. The Count took him by the arm, and walked him away gently. The "business," I was sure, referred to the question of the signature. They were speaking of Laura and of me beyond a doubt. I felt heart-sick and faint with anxiety. It might be of the last importance to both of us to know what they were saying to each other at that moment, and not one word of it could by any possibility reach my ears.

I walked about the house, from room to room, with the lawyer's letter in my bosom (I was afraid by this time even to trust it under lock and key), till the oppression of my suspense half maddened me. There were no signs of Laura's return, and I

The Woman in White

thought of going out to look for her. But my strength was so exhausted by the trials and anxieties of the morning that the heat of the day quite overpowered me, and after an attempt to get to the door I was obliged to return to the drawing-room and lie down on the nearest sofa to recover.

I was just composing myself when the door opened softly and the Count looked in.

"A thousand pardons, Miss Halcombe," he said; "I only venture to disturb you because I am the bearer of good news. Percival—who is capricious in everything, as you know—has seen fit to alter his mind at the last moment, and the business of the signature is put off for the present. A great relief to all of us, Miss Halcombe, as I see with pleasure in your face. Pray present my best respects and felicitations, when you mention this pleasant change of circumstances to Lady Glyde."

He left me before I had recovered my astonishment. There could be no doubt that this extraordinary alteration of purpose in the matter of the signature was due to his influence, and that his discovery of my application to London yesterday, and of my having received an answer to it to-day, had offered him the means of interfering with certain success.

I felt these impressions, but my mind seemed to share the exhaustion of my body, and I was in no condition to dwell on them with any useful reference to the doubtful present or the threatening future. I tried a second time to run out and find Laura, but my head was giddy and my knees trembled under me. There was no choice but to give it up again and return to the sofa, sorely against my will.

The quiet in the house, and the low murmuring hum of summer insects outside the open window, soothed me. My eyes closed of themselves, and I passed gradually into a strange condition, which was not waking—for I knew nothing of what was going on about me, and not sleeping—for I was conscious of my own repose. In this state my fevered mind broke loose from me, while my weary body was at rest, and in a trance, or day-dream of my fancy—I know not what to call it—I saw Walter Hartright. I had not thought of him since I rose that morning—Laura had not said one word to me either directly or indirectly referring to him—and yet I saw him now as plainly as if the past time had returned, and we were both together again at Limmeridge House.

He appeared to me as one among many other men, none of

whose faces I could plainly discern. They were all lying on the steps of an immense ruined temple. Colossal tropical trees—with rank creepers twining endlessly about their trunks, and hideous stone idols glimmering and grinning at intervals behind leaves and stalks and branches—surrounded the temple and shut out the sky, and threw a dismal shadow over the forlorn band of men on the steps. White exhalations twisted and curled up stealthily from the ground, approached the men in wreaths like smoke, touched them, and stretched them out dead, one by one, in the places where they lay. An agony of pity and fear for Walter loosened my tongue, and I implored him to escape. "Come back, come back!" I said. "Remember your promise to her and to me. Come back to us before the Pestilence reaches you and lays you dead like the rest!"

He looked at me with an unearthly quiet in his face. "Wait," he said, "I shall come back. The night when I met the lost Woman on the highway was the night which set my life apart to be the instrument of a Design that is yet unseen. Here, lost in the wilderness, or there, welcomed back in the land of my birth, I am still walking on the dark road which leads me, and you, and the sister of your love and mine, to the unknown Retribution and the inevitable End. Wait and look. The Pestilence which touches the rest will pass me."

I saw him again. He was still in the forest, and the numbers of his lost companions had dwindled to very few. The temple was gone, and the idols were gone—and in their place the figures of dark, dwarfish men lurked murderously among the trees, with bows in their hands, and arrows fitted to the string. Once more I feared for Walter, and cried out to warn him. Once more he turned to me, with the immovable quiet in his face.

"Another step," he said, "on the dark road. Wait and look. The arrows that strike the rest will spare me."

I saw him for the third time in a wrecked ship, stranded on a wild, sandy shore. The overloaded boats were making away from him for the land, and he alone was left to sink with the ship. I cried to him to hail the hindmost boat, and to make a last effort for his life. The quiet face looked at me in return, and the unmoved voice gave me back the changeless reply. "Another step on the journey. Wait and look. The Sea which drowns the rest will spare me."

I saw him for the last time. He was kneeling by a tomb of white marble, and the shadow of a veiled woman rose out of the grave beneath and waited by his side. The unearthly quiet of his face had changed to an unearthly sorrow. But the terrible certainty of his words remained the same. "Darker and darker," he said; "farther and farther yet. Death takes the good, the beautiful, and the young—and spares me. The Pestilence that wastes, the Arrow that strikes, the Sea that drowns, the Grave that closes over Love and Hope, are steps of my journey, and take me nearer and nearer to the End."

My heart sank under a dread beyond words, under a grief beyond tears. The darkness closed round the pilgrim at the marble tomb—closed round the veiled woman from the grave—closed round the dreamer who looked on them. I saw and heard no more.

I was aroused by a hand laid on my shoulder. It was Laura's.

She had dropped on her knees by the side of the sofa. Her face was flushed and agitated, and her eyes met mine in a wild bewildered manner. I started the instant I saw her.

"What has happened?" I asked. "What has frightened you?"

She looked round at the half-open door, put her lips close to my ear, and answered in a whisper—

"Marian!—the figure at the lake—the footsteps last night—I've just seen her! I've just spoken to her!"

"Who, for Heaven's sake?"

"Anne Catherick."

I was so startled by the disturbance in Laura's face and manner, and so dismayed by the first waking impressions of my dream, that I was not fit to bear the revelation which burst upon me when that name passed her lips. I could only stand rooted to the floor, looking at her in breathless silence.

She was too much absorbed by what had happened to notice the effect which her reply had produced on me. "I have seen Anne Catherick! I have spoken to Anne Catherick!" she repeated as if I had not heard her. "Oh, Marian, I have such things to tell you! Come away—we may be interrupted here—come at once into my room."

With those eager words she caught me by the hand, and led me through the library, to the end room on the ground floor, which had been fitted up for her own especial use. No third person, except her maid, could have any excuse for surprising us here. She pushed me in before her, locked the door, and drew the chintz curtains that hung over the inside.

The strange, stunned feeling which had taken possession of me still remained. But a growing conviction that the complications which had long threatened to gather about her, and to gather about me, had suddenly closed fast round us both, was now beginning to penetrate my mind. I could not express it in words—I could hardly even realise it dimly in my own thoughts. "Anne Catherick!" I whispered to myself, with useless, helpless reiteration—"Anne Catherick!"

Laura drew me to the nearest seat, an ottoman in the middle of the room. "Look!" she said, "look here!"—and pointed to the bosom of her dress.

I saw, for the first time, that the lost brooch was pinned in its place again. There was something real in the sight of it, something real in the touching of it afterwards, which seemed to steady the whirl and confusion in my thoughts, and to help me to compose myself.

"Where did you find your brooch?" The first words I could say to her were the words which put that trivial question at that important moment.

"She found it, Marian."

"Where?"

"On the floor of the boat-house. Oh, how shall I begin—how shall I tell you about it! She talked to me so strangely—she looked so fearfully ill—she left me so suddenly!"

Her voice rose as the tumult of her recollections pressed upon her mind. The inveterate distrust which weighs, night and day, on my spirits in this house, instantly roused me to warn her—just as the sight of the brooch had roused me to question her, the moment before.

"Speak low," I said. "The window is open, and the garden path runs beneath it. Begin at the beginning, Laura. Tell me, word for word, what passed between that woman and you."

"Shall I close the window?"

"No, only speak low—only remember that Anne Catherick

The Woman in White

is a dangerous subject under your husband's roof. Where did you first see her?"

"At the boat-house, Marian. I went out, as you know, to find my brooch, and I walked along the path through the plantation, looking down on the ground carefully at every step. In that way I got on, after a long time, to the boat-house, and as soon as I was inside it, I went on my knees to hunt over the floor. I was still searching with my back to the doorway, when I heard a soft, strange voice behind me say, 'Miss Fairlie.'"

"Miss Fairlie!"

"Yes, my old name—the dear, familiar name that I thought I had parted from for ever. I started up—not frightened, the voice was too kind and gentle to frighten anybody—but very much surprised. There, looking at me from the doorway, stood a woman, whose face I never remembered to have seen before—"

"How was she dressed?"

"She had a neat, pretty white gown on, and over it a poor worn thin dark shawl. Her bonnet was of brown straw, as poor and worn as the shawl. I was struck by the difference between her gown and the rest of her dress, and she saw that I noticed it. 'Don't look at my bonnet and shawl,' she said, speaking in a quick, breathless, sudden way; 'if I mustn't wear white, I don't care what I wear. Look at my gown as much as you please—I'm not ashamed of that.' Very strange, was it not? Before I could say anything to soothe her, she held out one of her hands, and I saw my brooch in it. I was so pleased and so grateful, that I went quite close to her to say what I really felt. 'Are you thankful enough to do me one little kindness?' she asked. 'Yes, indeed,' I answered, 'any kindness in my power I shall be glad to show you.' 'Then let me pin your brooch on for you, now I have found it.' Her request was so unexpected, Marian, and she made it with such extraordinary eagerness, that I drew back a step or two, not well knowing what to do. 'Ah!' she said, 'your mother would have let me pin on the brooch.' There was something in her voice and her look, as well as in her mentioning my mother in that reproachful manner, which made me ashamed of my distrust. I took her hand with the brooch in it, and put it up gently on the bosom of my dress. 'You knew my mother?' I said. 'Was it very long ago? have I ever seen you before?' Her hands were busy fastening the brooch: she stopped and pressed them against my breast. 'You don't remember a fine spring day at Limmeridge,' she said, 'and your mother walking down the path that led to the school, with a little girl on each side of her? I have had nothing else to think of since, and I remember it. You were one of the little girls, and I was the other. Pretty, clever Miss Fairlie, and poor dazed Anne Catherick were nearer to each other then than they are now!'"

"Did you remember her, Laura, when she told you her name?"

"Yes, I remembered your asking me about Anne Catherick at Limmeridge, and your saying that she had once been considered like me."

"What reminded you of that, Laura?"

"She reminded me. While I was looking at her, while she was very close to me, it came over my mind suddenly that we were like each other! Her face was pale and thin and weary — but the sight of it startled me, as if it had been the sight of my own face in the glass after a long illness. The discovery — I don't know why — gave me such a shock, that I was perfectly incapable of speaking to her for the moment."

"Did she seem hurt by your silence?"

"I am afraid she was hurt by it. 'You have not got your mother's face,' she said, 'or your mother's heart. Your mother's face was dark, and your mother's heart, Miss Fairlie, was the heart of an angel.' 'I am sure I feel kindly towards you,' I said, 'though I may not be able to express it as I ought. Why do you call me Miss Fairlie? — —' 'Because I love the name of Fairlie and hate the name of Glyde,' she broke out violently. I had seen nothing like madness in her before this, but I fancied I saw it now in her eyes. 'I only thought you might not know I was married,' I said, remembering the wild letter she wrote to me at Limmeridge, and trying to quiet her. She sighed bitterly, and turned away from me. 'Not know you were married?' she repeated. 'I am here because you are married. I am here to make atonement to you, before I meet your mother in the world beyond the grave.' She drew farther and farther away from me, till she was out of the boat-house, and then she watched and listened for a little while. When she turned round to speak again, instead of coming back, she stopped where she was, looking in at me, with a hand on each side of the entrance. 'Did you see me at the lake last night?' she said. 'Did you hear me following you in the wood? I have been waiting for days together to speak to you alone — I have left the only friend I have in the world, anxious and frightened about me — I have risked being shut up again in the mad-house — and all for your sake, Miss Fairlie, all for your sake.' Her words alarmed me, Marian, and yet there was something in the way she spoke that made me pity her with all my heart. I am sure my pity must have been sincere, for it made me bold enough to ask the poor creature to come in, and sit down in the boat-house, by my side."

"Did she do so?"

"No. She shook her head, and told me she must stop where she was, to watch and listen, and see that no third person surprised us. And from first to last, there she waited at the entrance, with a hand on each side of it, sometimes bending in suddenly to speak to me, sometimes drawing back suddenly to look about her. 'I was here yesterday,' she said, 'before it came dark, and I heard you, and the lady with you, talking together. I heard you tell her about your husband. I heard you say you had no influence to make him believe you, and no influence to keep him silent. Ah! I knew what those words meant—my conscience told me while I was listening. Why did I ever let you marry him! Oh, my fear—my mad, miserable, wicked fear!' She covered up her face in her poor worn shawl, and moaned and murmured to herself behind it. I began to be afraid she might break out into some terrible despair which neither she nor I could master. 'Try to quiet yourself,' I said; 'try to tell me how you might have prevented my marriage.' She took the shawl from her face, and looked at me vacantly. 'I ought to have had heart enough to stop at Limmeridge,' she answered. 'I ought never to have let the news of his coming there frighten me away. I ought to have warned you and saved you before it was too late. Why did I only have courage enough to write you that letter? Why did I only do harm, when I wanted and meant to do good? Oh, my fear—my mad, miserable, wicked fear!' She repeated those words again, and hid her face again in the end of her poor worn shawl. It was dreadful to see her, and dreadful to hear her."

"Surely, Laura, you asked what the fear was which she dwelt on so earnestly?"

"Yes, I asked that."

"And what did she say?"

"She asked me in return, if I should not be afraid of a man who had shut me up in a mad-house, and who would shut me up again, if he could? I said, 'Are you afraid still? Surely you would not be here if you were afraid now?' 'No,' she said, 'I am not afraid now.' I asked why not. She suddenly bent forward into the boat-house, and said, 'Can't you guess why?' I shook my head. 'Look at me,' she went on. I told her I was grieved to see that she looked very sorrowful and very ill. She smiled for the first time. 'Ill?' she repeated; 'I'm dying. You know why I'm not afraid of him now. Do you think I shall meet your mother in heaven? Will she forgive me if I do?' I was so shocked and so startled, that I could make no reply. 'I have been thinking of it,' she went on, 'all the time I have been in hiding from your husband, all the time I lay ill. My thoughts have driven me here—I want to make atonement—I want to undo all I can of the harm I once did.' I begged her as earnestly as I could to tell me what she meant. She still looked at me with fixed vacant eyes. 'Shall I undo the harm?' she said to herself doubtfully. 'You have friends to take your part. If you know his Secret, he will be afraid of you, he won't dare use you as he used me. He must treat you mercifully for his own sake, if he is afraid of you and your friends. And if he treats you mercifully, and if I can say it was my doing——' I listened eagerly for more, but she stopped at those words."

"You tried to make her go on?"

"I tried, but she only drew herself away from me again, and leaned her face and arms against the side of the boat-house. 'Oh!' I heard her say, with a dreadful, distracted tenderness in her voice, 'oh! if I could only be buried with your mother! If I could only wake at her side, when the angel's trumpet sounds, and the graves give up their dead at the resurrection!'—Marian! I trembled from head to foot—it was horrible to hear her. 'But there is no hope of that,' she said, moving a little, so as to look at me again, 'no hope for a poor stranger like me. I shall not rest under the marble cross that I washed with my own hands, and made so white and pure for her sake. Oh no! oh no! God's mercy, not man's, will take me to her, where the wicked cease from troubling and the weary are at rest.' She spoke those words quietly and sorrowfully, with a heavy, hopeless sigh, and then waited a little. Her face was confused and troubled, she seemed to be thinking, or trying to think. 'What was it I said just now?' she asked after a while. 'When your mother is in my mind, everything else goes out of it. What was I saying? what was I saying?' I reminded the poor creature, as kindly and delicately as I could. 'Ah, yes, yes,' she said, still in a vacant, perplexed manner. 'You are helpless with your wicked husband. Yes. And I must do what I have come to do here—I must make it up to you for having been afraid to speak out at a better time.' 'What is it you have to tell me?' I asked. 'The Secret that your cruel husband is afraid of,' she answered. 'I once threatened him with the Secret, and frightened him. You shall

The Woman in White

threaten him with the Secret, and frighten him too.' Her face darkened, and a hard, angry stare fixed itself in her eyes. She began waving her hand at me in a vacant, unmeaning manner. 'My mother knows the Secret,' she said. 'My mother has wasted under the Secret half her lifetime. One day, when I was grown up, she said something to me. And the next day your husband— —'"

"Yes! yes! Go on. What did she tell you about your husband?"

"She stopped again, Marian, at that point— —"

"And said no more?"

"And listened eagerly. 'Hush!' she whispered, still waving her hand at me. 'Hush!' She moved aside out of the doorway, moved slowly and stealthily, step by step, till I lost her past the edge of the boat-house."

"Surely you followed her?"

"Yes, my anxiety made me bold enough to rise and follow her. Just as I reached the entrance, she appeared again suddenly, round the side of the boat-house. 'The Secret,' I whispered to her—'wait and tell me the Secret!' She caught hold of my arm, and looked at me with wild frightened eyes. 'Not now,' she said, 'we are not alone—we are watched. Come here to-morrow at this time—by yourself—mind—by yourself.' She pushed me roughly into the boat-house again, and I saw her no more."

"Oh, Laura, Laura, another chance lost! If I had only been near you she should not have escaped us. On which side did you lose sight of her?"

"On the left side, where the ground sinks and the wood is thickest."

"Did you run out again? did you call after her?"

"How could I? I was too terrified to move or speak."

"But when you did move—when you came out?"

"I ran back here, to tell you what had happened."

"Did you see any one, or hear any one, in the plantation?"

"No, it seemed to be all still and quiet when I passed through it."

I waited for a moment to consider. Was this third person, supposed to have been secretly present at the interview, a reality, or the creature of Anne Catherick's excited fancy? It was impossible to determine. The one thing certain was, that we had failed again on the very brink of discovery—failed utterly and irretrievably, unless Anne Catherick kept her appointment at the boat-house for the next day.

"Are you quite sure you have told me everything that passed? Every word that was said?" I inquired.

"I think so," she answered. "My powers of memory, Marian, are not like yours. But I was so strongly impressed, so deeply interested, that nothing of any importance can possibly have escaped me."

"My dear Laura, the merest trifles are of importance where Anne Catherick is concerned. Think again. Did no chance reference escape her as to the place in which she is living at the present time?"

"None that I can remember."

"Did she not mention a companion and friend—a woman named Mrs. Clements?"

"Oh yes! yes! I forgot that. She told me Mrs. Clements wanted sadly to go with her to the lake and take care of her, and begged and prayed that she would not venture into this neighbourhood alone."

"Was that all she said about Mrs. Clements?"

"Yes, that was all."

"She told you nothing about the place in which she took refuge after leaving Todd's Corner?"

"Nothing—I am quite sure."

"Nor where she has lived since? Nor what her illness had been?"

"No, Marian, not a word. Tell me, pray tell me, what you think about it. I don't know what to think, or what to do next."

The Woman in White

"You must do this, my love: You must carefully keep the appointment at the boat-house to-morrow. It is impossible to say what interests may not depend on your seeing that woman again. You shall not be left to yourself a second time. I will follow you at a safe distance. Nobody shall see me, but I will keep within hearing of your voice, if anything happens. Anne Catherick has escaped Walter Hartright, and has escaped you. Whatever happens, she shall not escape me."

Laura's eyes read mine attentively.

"You believe," she said, "in this secret that my husband is afraid of? Suppose, Marian, it should only exist after all in Anne Catherick's fancy? Suppose she only wanted to see me and to speak to me, for the sake of old remembrances? Her manner was so strange—I almost doubted her. Would you trust her in other things?"

"I trust nothing, Laura, but my own observation of your husband's conduct. I judge Anne Catherick's words by his actions, and I believe there is a secret."

I said no more, and got up to leave the room. Thoughts were troubling me which I might have told her if we had spoken together longer, and which it might have been dangerous for her to know. The influence of the terrible dream from which she had awakened me hung darkly and heavily over every fresh impression which the progress of her narrative produced on my mind. I felt the ominous future coming close, chilling me with an unutterable awe, forcing on me the conviction of an unseen design in the long series of complications which had now fastened round us. I thought of Hartright—as I saw him in the body when he said farewell; as I saw him in the spirit in my dream—and I too began to doubt now whether we were not advancing blindfold to an appointed and an inevitable end.

Leaving Laura to go upstairs alone, I went out to look about me in the walks near the house. The circumstances under which Anne Catherick had parted from her had made me secretly anxious to know how Count Fosco was passing the afternoon, and had rendered me secretly distrustful of the results of that solitary journey from which Sir Percival had returned but a few hours since.

After looking for them in every direction and discovering nothing, I returned to the house, and entered the different rooms on the ground floor one after another. They were all empty. I came out again into the hall, and went upstairs to return to Laura. Madame Fosco opened her door as I passed it in my way along the passage, and I stopped to see if she could inform me of the whereabouts of her husband and Sir Percival. Yes, she had seen them both from her window more than an hour since. The Count had looked up with his customary kindness, and had mentioned with his habitual attention to her in the smallest trifles, that he and his friend were going out together for a long walk.

For a long walk! They had never yet been in each other's company with that object in my experience of them. Sir Percival cared for no exercise but riding, and the Count (except when he was polite enough to be my escort) cared for no exercise at all.

When I joined Laura again, I found that she had called to mind in my absence the impending question of the signature to the deed, which, in the interest of discussing her interview with Anne Catherick, we had hitherto overlooked. Her first words when I saw her expressed her surprise at the absence of the expected summons to attend Sir Percival in the library.

"You may make your mind easy on that subject," I said. "For the present, at least, neither your resolution nor mine will be exposed to any further trial. Sir Percival has altered his plans — the business of the signature is put off."

"Put off?" Laura repeated amazedly. "Who told you so?"

"My authority is Count Fosco. I believe it is to his interference that we are indebted for your husband's sudden change of purpose."

"It seems impossible, Marian. If the object of my signing was, as we suppose, to obtain money for Sir Percival that he urgently wanted, how can the matter be put off?"

"I think, Laura, we have the means at hand of setting that doubt at rest. Have you forgotten the conversation that I heard between Sir Percival and the lawyer as they were crossing the hall?"

"No, but I don't remember — —"

"I do. There were two alternatives proposed. One was to obtain your signature to the parchment. The other was to gain time by giving bills at three months. The last resource is evidently the resource now adopted, and we may fairly hope to be relieved from our share in Sir Percival's embarrassments for some time to come."

"Oh, Marian, it sounds too good to be true!"

"Does it, my love? You complimented me on my ready memory not long since, but you seem to doubt it now. I will get my journal, and you shall see if I am right or wrong."

I went away and got the book at once.

On looking back to the entry referring to the lawyer's visit, we found that my recollection of the two alternatives presented was accurately correct. It was almost as great a relief to my mind as to Laura's, to find that my memory had served me, on this occasion, as faithfully as usual. In the perilous uncertainty of our present situation, it is hard to say what future interests may not depend upon the regularity of the entries in my journal, and upon the reliability of my recollection at the time when I make them.

Laura's face and manner suggested to me that this last consideration had occurred to her as well as to myself. Anyway, it is only a trifling matter, and I am almost ashamed to put it down here in writing — it seems to set the forlornness of our situation in such a miserably vivid light. We must have little indeed to depend on, when the discovery that my memory can still be trusted to serve us is hailed as if it was the discovery of a new friend!

The first bell for dinner separated us. Just as it had done ringing, Sir Percival and the Count returned from their walk. We heard the master of the house storming at the servants for being five minutes late, and the master's guest interposing, as usual, in the interests of propriety, patience, and peace.

The evening has come and gone. No extraordinary event has happened. But I have noticed certain peculiarities in the conduct of Sir Percival and the Count, which have sent me to my bed feeling very anxious and uneasy about Anne Catherick, and about the results which to-morrow may produce.

I know enough by this time, to be sure, that the aspect of Sir Percival which is the most false, and which, therefore, means the worst, is his polite aspect. That long walk with his friend had ended in improving his manners, especially towards his wife. To Laura's secret surprise and to my secret alarm, he called her by her Christian name, asked if she had heard lately from her uncle, inquired when Mrs. Vesey was to receive her invitation to Blackwater, and showed her so many other little attentions that he almost recalled the days of his hateful courtship at Limmeridge House. This was a bad sign to begin with, and I thought it more ominous still that he should pretend after dinner to fall asleep in the drawing-room, and that his eyes should cunningly follow Laura and me when he thought we neither of us suspected him. I have never had any doubt that his sudden journey by himself took him to Welmingham to question Mrs. Catherick—but the experience of to-night has made me fear that the expedition was not undertaken in vain, and that he has got the information which he unquestionably left us to collect. If I knew where Anne Catherick was to be found, I would be up to-morrow with sunrise and warn her.

While the aspect under which Sir Percival presented himself to-night was unhappily but too familiar to me, the aspect under which the Count appeared was, on the other hand, entirely new in my experience of him. He permitted me, this evening, to make his acquaintance, for the first time, in the character of a Man of Sentiment—of sentiment, as I believe, really felt, not assumed for the occasion.

For instance, he was quiet and subdued—his eyes and his voice expressed a restrained sensibility. He wore (as if there was some hidden connection between his showiest finery and his deepest feeling) the most magnificent waistcoat he has yet appeared in—it was made of pale sea-green silk, and delicately trimmed with fine silver braid. His voice sank into the tenderest inflections, his smile expressed a thoughtful, fatherly admiration, whenever he spoke to Laura or to me. He pressed his wife's hand under the table when she thanked him for trifling little attentions at dinner. He took wine with her. "Your health and happiness, my angel!" he said, with fond glistening eyes. He ate little or nothing, and sighed, and said "Good Percival!" when his friend laughed at him. After dinner, he took Laura by the hand, and asked her if she would be "so sweet as to play to him." She complied, through sheer astonishment. He sat by the piano, with his watch-chain resting in folds, like a golden serpent, on the sea-green protuberance of his waistcoat. His immense head lay languidly on one side, and he gently beat time with two of his yellow-white fingers. He highly approved of the music, and tenderly admired Laura's manner of playing—not as poor Hartright used to praise it, with an innocent enjoyment of the sweet sounds, but with a clear, cultivated, practical knowledge of the merits of the composition, in the first place, and of the merits of the player's touch in the second. As the evening closed in, he begged that the lovely dying light might not be profaned, just yet, by the appearance of the lamps. He came, with his horribly silent tread, to the distant window at which I was standing, to be out of his way and to avoid the very sight of him—he came to ask me to support his protest against the lamps. If any one of them could only have burnt him up at that moment, I would have gone down to the kitchen and fetched it myself.

"Surely you like this modest, trembling English twilight?" he said softly. "Ah! I love it. I feel my inborn admiration of all that is noble, and great, and good, purified by the breath of heaven on an evening like this. Nature has such imperishable charms, such inextinguishable tenderness for me!—I am an old, fat man—talk which would become your lips, Miss Halcombe, sounds like a derision and a mockery on mine. It is hard to be laughed at in my moments of sentiment, as if my soul was like myself, old and overgrown. Observe, dear lady, what a light is dying on the trees! Does it penetrate your heart, as it penetrates mine?"

He paused, looked at me, and repeated the famous lines of Dante on the Evening-time, with a melody and tenderness which added a charm of their own to the matchless beauty of the poetry itself.

"Bah!" he cried suddenly, as the last cadence of those noble Italian words died away on his lips; "I make an old fool of myself, and only weary you all! Let us shut up the window in our bosoms and get back to the matter-of-fact world. Percival! I sanction the admission of the lamps. Lady Glyde—Miss Halcombe—Eleanor, my good wife—which of you will indulge me with a game at dominoes?"

He addressed us all, but he looked especially at Laura.

She had learnt to feel my dread of offending him, and she accepted his proposal. It was more than I could have done at that moment. I could not have sat down at the same table with him for any consideration. His eyes seemed to reach my inmost soul through the thickening obscurity of the twilight. His voice trembled along every nerve in my body, and turned me hot and cold alternately. The mystery and terror of my dream, which had haunted me at intervals all through the evening, now oppressed my mind with an unendurable foreboding and an unutterable awe. I saw the white tomb again, and the veiled woman rising out of it by Hartright's side. The thought of Laura welled up like a spring in the depths of my heart, and filled it with waters of bitterness, never, never known to it before. I caught her by the hand as she passed me on her way to the table, and kissed her as if that night was to part us for ever. While they were all gazing at me in astonishment, I ran out through the low window which was open before me to the ground—ran out to hide from them in the darkness, to hide even from myself.

We separated that evening later than usual. Towards midnight the summer silence was broken by the shuddering of a low, melancholy wind among the trees. We all felt the sudden chill in the atmosphere, but the Count was the first to notice the stealthy rising of the wind. He stopped while he was lighting my candle for me, and held up his hand warningly—

"Listen!" he said. "There will be a change to-morrow."

VII

June 19th.—The events of yesterday warned me to be ready, sooner or later, to meet the worst. To-day is not yet at an end, and the worst has come.

Judging by the closest calculation of time that Laura and I could make, we arrived at the conclusion that Anne Catherick must have appeared at the boat-house at half-past two o'clock on the afternoon of yesterday. I accordingly arranged that Laura should just show herself at the luncheon-table to-day, and should then slip out at the first opportunity, leaving me behind to preserve appearances, and to follow her as soon as I could safely do so. This mode of proceeding, if no obstacles occurred to thwart us, would enable her to be at the boat-house before half-past two, and (when I left the table, in my turn) would take me to a safe position in the plantation before three.

The change in the weather, which last night's wind warned us to expect, came with the morning. It was raining heavily when I got up, and it continued to rain until twelve o'clock—when the clouds dispersed, the blue sky appeared, and the sun shone again with the bright promise of a fine afternoon.

My anxiety to know how Sir Percival and the Count would occupy the early part of the day was by no means set at rest, so far as Sir Percival was concerned, by his leaving us immediately after breakfast, and going out by himself, in spite of the rain. He neither told us where he was going nor when we might expect him back. We saw him pass the breakfast-room window hastily, with his high boots and his waterproof coat on—and that was all.

The Count passed the morning quietly indoors, some part of it in the library, some part in the drawing-room, playing odds and ends of music on the piano, and humming to himself. Judging by appearances, the sentimental side of his character was persistently inclined to betray itself still. He was silent and sensitive, and ready to sigh and languish ponderously (as only fat men can sigh and languish) on the smallest provocation.

Luncheon-time came and Sir Percival did not return. The Count took his friend's place at the table, plaintively devoured the greater part of a fruit tart, submerged under a whole jugful of cream, and explained the full merit of the achievement to us as soon as he had done. "A taste for sweets," he said in his softest tones and his tenderest manner, "is the innocent taste of women and children. I love to share it with them—it is another bond, dear ladies, between you and me."

Laura left the table in ten minutes' time. I was sorely tempted to accompany her. But if we had both gone out together we must have excited suspicion, and worse still, if we allowed Anne Catherick to see Laura, accompanied by a second person who was a stranger to her, we should in all probability forfeit her confidence from that moment, never to regain it again.

I waited, therefore, as patiently as I could, until the servant came in to clear the table. When I quitted the room, there were no signs, in the house or out of it, of Sir Percival's return. I left the Count with a piece of sugar between his lips, and the vicious cockatoo scrambling up his waistcoat to get at it, while Madame Fosco, sitting opposite to her husband, watched the proceedings of his bird and himself as attentively as if she had never seen anything of the sort before in her life. On my way to the plantation I kept carefully beyond the range of view from the luncheon-room window. Nobody saw me and nobody followed me. It was then a quarter to three o'clock by my watch.

Once among the trees I walked rapidly, until I had advanced more than half-way through the plantation. At that point I slackened my pace and proceeded cautiously, but I saw no one, and heard no voices. By little and little I came within view of the back of the boat-house—stopped and listened—then went on, till I was close behind it, and must have heard any persons who were talking inside. Still the silence was unbroken—still far and near no sign of a living creature appeared anywhere.

After skirting round by the back of the building, first on one side and then on the other, and making no discoveries, I ventured in front of it, and fairly looked in. The place was empty.

I called, "Laura!"—at first softly, then louder and louder. No one answered and no one appeared. For all that I could see and hear, the only human creature in the neighbourhood of the lake and the plantation was myself.

My heart began to beat violently, but I kept my resolution, and searched, first the boat-house and then the ground in front of it, for any signs which might show me whether Laura had really reached the place or not. No mark of her presence appeared inside the building, but I found traces of her outside it, in footsteps on the sand.

I detected the footsteps of two persons—large footsteps like a man's, and small footsteps, which, by putting my own feet into them and testing their size in that manner, I felt certain were Laura's. The ground was confusedly marked in this way just before the boat-house. Close against one side of it, under shelter of the projecting roof, I discovered a little hole in the sand—a hole artificially made, beyond a doubt. I just noticed it, and then turned away immediately to trace the footsteps as far as I could, and to follow the direction in which they might lead me.

They led me, starting from the left-hand side of the boat-house, along the edge of the trees, a distance, I should think, of between two and three hundred yards, and then the sandy ground showed no further trace of them. Feeling that the persons whose course I was tracking must necessarily have entered the plantation at this point, I entered it too. At first I could find no path, but I discovered one afterwards, just faintly traced among the trees, and followed it. It took me, for some distance, in the direction of the village, until I stopped at a point where another foot-track crossed it. The brambles grew thickly on either side of this second path. I stood looking down it, uncertain which way to take next, and while I looked I saw on one thorny branch some fragments of fringe from a woman's shawl. A closer examination of the fringe satisfied me that it had been torn from a shawl of Laura's, and I instantly followed the second path. It brought me out at last, to my great relief, at the back of the house. I say to my great relief, because I inferred that

The Woman in White

Laura must, for some unknown reason, have returned before me by this roundabout way. I went in by the court-yard and the offices. The first person whom I met in crossing the servants' hall was Mrs. Michelson, the housekeeper.

"Do you know," I asked, "whether Lady Glyde has come in from her walk or not?"

"My lady came in a little while ago with Sir Percival," answered the housekeeper. "I am afraid, Miss Halcombe, something very distressing has happened."

My heart sank within me. "You don't mean an accident?" I said faintly.

"No, no—thank God, no accident. But my lady ran upstairs to her own room in tears, and Sir Percival has ordered me to give Fanny warning to leave in an hour's time."

Fanny was Laura's maid—a good affectionate girl who had been with her for years—the only person in the house whose fidelity and devotion we could both depend upon.

"Where is Fanny?" I inquired.

"In my room, Miss Halcombe. The young woman is quite overcome, and I told her to sit down and try to recover herself."

I went to Mrs. Michelson's room, and found Fanny in a corner, with her box by her side, crying bitterly.

She could give me no explanation whatever of her sudden dismissal. Sir Percival had ordered that she should have a month's wages, in place of a month's warning, and go. No reason had been assigned—no objection had been made to her conduct. She had been forbidden to appeal to her mistress, forbidden even to see her for a moment to say good-bye. She was to go without explanations or farewells, and to go at once.

After soothing the poor girl by a few friendly words, I asked where she proposed to sleep that night. She replied that she thought of going to the little inn in the village, the landlady of which was a respectable woman, known to the servants at Blackwater Park. The next morning, by leaving early, she might get back to her friends in Cumberland without stopping in London, where she was a total stranger.

I felt directly that Fanny's departure offered us a safe means of communication with London and with Limmeridge House, of which it might be very important to avail ourselves. Accordingly, I told her that she might expect to hear from her mistress or from me in the course of the evening, and that she might depend on our both doing all that lay in our power to help her, under the trial of leaving us for the present. Those words said, I shook hands with her and went upstairs.

The door which led to Laura's room was the door of an antechamber opening on to the passage. When I tried it, it was bolted on the inside.

I knocked, and the door was opened by the same heavy, overgrown housemaid whose lumpish insensibility had tried my patience so severely on the day when I found the wounded dog.

I had, since that time, discovered that her name was Margaret Porcher, and that she was the most awkward, slatternly, and obstinate servant in the house.

On opening the door she instantly stepped out to the threshold, and stood grinning at me in stolid silence.

"Why do you stand there?" I said. "Don't you see that I want to come in?"

"Ah, but you mustn't come in," was the answer, with another and a broader grin still.

"How dare you talk to me in that way? Stand back instantly!"

She stretched out a great red hand and arm on each side of her, so as to bar the doorway, and slowly nodded her addle head at me.

"Master's orders," she said, and nodded again.

I had need of all my self-control to warn me against contesting the matter with her, and to remind me that the next words I had to say must be addressed to her master. I turned my back on her, and instantly went downstairs to find him. My resolution to keep my temper under all the irritations that Sir Percival could offer was, by this time, as completely forgotten — I say so to my shame — as if I had never made it. It did me good, after all I had suffered and suppressed in that house — it actually did me good to feel how angry I was.

The Woman in White

The drawing-room and the breakfast-room were both empty. I went on to the library, and there I found Sir Percival, the Count, and Madame Fosco. They were all three standing up, close together, and Sir Percival had a little slip of paper in his hand. As I opened the door I heard the Count say to him, "No—a thousand times over, no."

I walked straight up to him, and looked him full in the face.

"Am I to understand, Sir Percival, that your wife's room is a prison, and that your housemaid is the gaoler who keeps it?" I asked.

"Yes, that is what you are to understand," he answered. "Take care my gaoler hasn't got double duty to do—take care your room is not a prison too."

"Take you care how you treat your wife, and how you threaten me," I broke out in the heat of my anger. "There are laws in England to protect women from cruelty and outrage. If you hurt a hair of Laura's head, if you dare to interfere with my freedom, come what may, to those laws I will appeal."

Instead of answering me he turned round to the Count.

"What did I tell you?" he asked. "What do you say now?"

"What I said before," replied the Count—"No."

Even in the vehemence of my anger I felt his calm, cold, grey eyes on my face. They turned away from me as soon as he had spoken, and looked significantly at his wife. Madame Fosco immediately moved close to my side, and in that position addressed Sir Percival before either of us could speak again.

"Favour me with your attention for one moment," she said, in her clear icily-suppressed tones. "I have to thank you, Sir Percival, for your hospitality, and to decline taking advantage of it any longer. I remain in no house in which ladies are treated as your wife and Miss Halcombe have been treated here to-day!"

Sir Percival drew back a step, and stared at her in dead silence. The declaration he had just heard—a declaration which he well knew, as I well knew, Madame Fosco would not have ventured to make without her husband's permission—seemed to petrify him with surprise. The Count stood by, and looked at his wife with the most enthusiastic admiration.

"She is sublime!" he said to himself. He approached her while he spoke, and drew her hand through his arm. "I am at your service, Eleanor," he went on, with a quiet dignity that I had never noticed in him before. "And at Miss Halcombe's service, if she will honour me by accepting all the assistance I can offer her."

"Damn it! what do you mean?" cried Sir Percival, as the Count quietly moved away with his wife to the door.

"At other times I mean what I say, but at this time I mean what my wife says," replied the impenetrable Italian. "We have changed places, Percival, for once, and Madame Fosco's opinion is—mine."

Sir Percival crumpled up the paper in his hand, and pushing past the Count, with another oath, stood between him and the door.

"Have your own way," he said, with baffled rage in his low, half-whispering tones. "Have your own way—and see what comes of it." With those words he left the room.

Madame Fosco glanced inquiringly at her husband. "He has gone away very suddenly," she said. "What does it mean?"

"It means that you and I together have brought the worst-tempered man in all England to his senses," answered the Count. "It means, Miss Halcombe, that Lady Glyde is relieved from a gross indignity, and you from the repetition of an unpardonable insult. Suffer me to express my admiration of your conduct and your courage at a very trying moment."

"Sincere admiration," suggested Madame Fosco.

"Sincere admiration," echoed the Count.

I had no longer the strength of my first angry resistance to outrage and injury to support me. My heart-sick anxiety to see Laura, my sense of my own helpless ignorance of what had happened at the boat-house, pressed on me with an intolerable weight. I tried to keep up appearances by speaking to the Count and his wife in the tone which they had chosen to adopt in speaking to me, but the words failed on my lips—my breath came short and thick—my eyes looked longingly, in silence, at the door. The Count, understanding my anxiety, opened it, went out, and pulled it to after him. At the same time Sir Percival's heavy step descended the stairs. I heard them whispering together outside, while Madame Fosco was assuring me, in her calmest and most conventional manner, that she rejoiced, for all our sakes, that Sir Percival's conduct had not obliged her husband and herself to leave Blackwater Park. Before she had done speaking the whispering ceased, the door opened, and the Count looked in.

"Miss Halcombe," he said, "I am happy to inform you that Lady Glyde is mistress again in her own house. I thought it might be more agreeable to you to hear of this change for the better from me than from Sir Percival, and I have therefore expressly returned to mention it."

"Admirable delicacy!" said Madame Fosco, paying back her husband's tribute of admiration with the Count's own coin, in the Count's own manner. He smiled and bowed as if he had received a formal compliment from a polite stranger, and drew back to let me pass out first.

Sir Percival was standing in the hall. As I hurried to the stairs I heard him call impatiently to the Count to come out of the library.

"What are you waiting there for?" he said. "I want to speak to you."

"And I want to think a little by myself," replied the other. "Wait till later, Percival, wait till later."

Neither he nor his friend said any more. I gained the top of the stairs and ran along the passage. In my haste and my agitation I left the door of the ante-chamber open, but I closed the door of the bedroom the moment I was inside it.

Laura was sitting alone at the far end of the room, her arms resting wearily on a table, and her face hidden in her hands. She started up with a cry of delight when she saw me.

"How did you get here?" she asked. "Who gave you leave? Not Sir Percival?"

In my overpowering anxiety to hear what she had to tell me, I could not answer her — I could only put questions on my side. Laura's eagerness to know what had passed downstairs proved, however, too strong to be resisted. She persistently repeated her inquiries.

"The Count, of course," I answered impatiently. "Whose

influence in the house— —"

She stopped me with a gesture of disgust.

"Don't speak of him," she cried. "The Count is the vilest creature breathing! The Count is a miserable Spy— —!"

Before we could either of us say another word we were alarmed by a soft knocking at the door of the bedroom.

I had not yet sat down, and I went first to see who it was. When I opened the door Madame Fosco confronted me with my handkerchief in her hand.

"You dropped this downstairs, Miss Halcombe," she said, "and I thought I could bring it to you, as I was passing by to my own room."

Her face, naturally pale, had turned to such a ghastly whiteness that I started at the sight of it. Her hands, so sure and steady at all other times, trembled violently, and her eyes looked wolfishly past me through the open door, and fixed on Laura.

She had been listening before she knocked! I saw it in her white face, I saw it in her trembling hands, I saw it in her look at Laura.

After waiting an instant she turned from me in silence, and slowly walked away.

I closed the door again. "Oh, Laura! Laura! We shall both rue the day when you called the Count a Spy!"

"You would have called him so yourself, Marian, if you had known what I know. Anne Catherick was right. There was a third person watching us in the plantation yesterday, and that third person— —"

"Are you sure it was the Count?"

"I am absolutely certain. He was Sir Percival's spy—he was Sir Percival's informer—he set Sir Percival watching and waiting, all the morning through, for Anne Catherick and for me."

"Is Anne found? Did you see her at the lake?"

"No. She has saved herself by keeping away from the place. When I got to the boat-house no one was there."

"Yes? Yes?"

"I went in and sat waiting for a few minutes. But my restlessness made me get up again, to walk about a little. As I passed out I saw some marks on the sand, close under the front of the boat-house. I stooped down to examine them, and discovered a word written in large letters on the sand. The word was—LOOK."

"And you scraped away the sand, and dug a hollow place in it?"

"How do you know that, Marian?"

"I saw the hollow place myself when I followed you to the boat-house. Go on—go on!"

"Yes, I scraped away the sand on the surface, and in a little while I came to a strip of paper hidden beneath, which had writing on it. The writing was signed with Anne Catherick's initials."

"Where is it?"

"Sir Percival has taken it from me."

"Can you remember what the writing was? Do you think you can repeat it to me?"

"In substance I can, Marian. It was very short. You would have remembered it, word for word."

"Try to tell me what the substance was before we go any further."

She complied. I write the lines down here exactly as she repeated them to me. They ran thus—

"I was seen with you, yesterday, by a tall, stout old man, and had to run to save myself. He was not quick enough on his feet to follow me, and he lost me among the trees. I dare not risk coming back here to-day at the same time. I write this, and hide it in the sand, at six in the morning, to tell you so. When we speak next of your wicked husband's Secret we must speak safely, or not at all. Try to have patience. I promise you shall see me again and that soon. — A. C."

The reference to the "tall, stout old man" (the terms of which Laura was certain that she had repeated to me correctly) left no doubt as to who the intruder had been. I called to mind that I had told Sir Percival, in the Count's presence the day before, that Laura had gone to the boat-house to look for her brooch. In all probability he had followed her there, in his officious way, to relieve her mind about the matter of the signature, immediately after he had mentioned the change in Sir Percival's plans to me in the drawing-room. In this case he could only have got to the neighbourhood of the boat-house at the very moment when Anne Catherick discovered him. The suspiciously hurried manner in which she parted from Laura had no doubt prompted his useless attempt to follow her. Of the conversation which had previously taken place between them he could have heard nothing. The distance between the house and the lake, and the time at which he left me in the drawing-room, as compared with the time at which Laura and Anne Catherick had been speaking together, proved that fact to us at any rate, beyond a doubt.

Having arrived at something like a conclusion so far, my next great interest was to know what discoveries Sir Percival had made after Count Fosco had given him his information.

"How came you to lose possession of the letter?" I asked. "What did you do with it when you found it in the sand?"

"After reading it once through," she replied, "I took it into the boat-house with me to sit down and look over it a second time. While I was reading a shadow fell across the paper. I looked up, and saw Sir Percival standing in the doorway watching me."

"Did you try to hide the letter?"

"I tried, but he stopped me. 'You needn't trouble to hide that,' he said. 'I happen to have read it.' I could only look at him helplessly — I could say nothing. 'You understand?' he went on; 'I have read it. I dug it up out of the sand two hours since, and buried it again, and wrote the word above it again, and left it ready to your hands. You can't lie yourself out of the scrape now. You saw Anne Catherick in secret yesterday, and you have got her letter in your hand at this moment. I have not caught her yet, but I have caught you. Give me the letter.' He stepped close up to me—I was alone with him, Marian—what could I do?—I gave him the letter."

"What did he say when you gave it to him?"

"At first he said nothing. He took me by the arm, and led me out of the boat-house, and looked about him on all sides, as if he was afraid of our being seen or heard. Then he clasped his hand fast round my arm, and whispered to me, 'What did Anne Catherick say to you yesterday? I insist on hearing every word, from first to last.'"

"Did you tell him?"

"I was alone with him, Marian—his cruel hand was bruising my arm—what could I do?"

"Is the mark on your arm still? Let me see it."

"Why do you want to see it?"

"I want to see it, Laura, because our endurance must end, and our resistance must begin to-day. That mark is a weapon to strike him with. Let me see it now—I may have to swear to it at some future time."

"Oh, Marian, don't look so—don't talk so! It doesn't hurt me now!"

"Let me see it!"

She showed me the marks. I was past grieving over them, past crying over them, past shuddering over them. They say we are either better than men, or worse. If the temptation that has fallen in some women's way, and made them worse, had fallen in mine at that moment—Thank God! my face betrayed nothing that his wife could read. The gentle, innocent, affectionate creature thought I was frightened for her and sorry for her, and thought no more.

"Don't think too seriously of it, Marian," she said simply, as she pulled her sleeve down again. "It doesn't hurt me now."

"I will try to think quietly of it, my love, for your sake.—Well! well! And you told him all that Anne Catherick had said to you—all that you told me?"

"Yes, all. He insisted on it—I was alone with him—I could conceal nothing."

"Did he say anything when you had done?"

"He looked at me, and laughed to himself in a mocking, bitter way. 'I mean to have the rest out of you,' he said, 'do you hear?—the rest.' I declared to him solemnly that I had told him everything I knew. 'Not you,' he answered, 'you know more than you choose to tell. Won't you tell it? You shall! I'll wring it out of you at home if I can't wring it out of you here.' He led me away by a strange path through the plantation—a path where there was no hope of our meeting you—and he spoke no more till we came within sight of the house. Then he stopped again, and said, 'Will you take a second chance, if I give it to you? Will you think better of it, and tell me the rest?' I could only repeat the same words I had spoken before. He cursed my obstinacy, and went on, and took me with him to the house. 'You can't deceive me,' he said, 'you know more than you choose to tell. I'll have your secret out of you, and I'll have it out of that sister of yours as well. There shall be no more plotting and whispering between you. Neither you nor she shall see each other again till you have confessed the truth. I'll have you watched morning, noon, and night, till you confess the truth.' He was deaf to everything I could say. He took me straight upstairs into my own room. Fanny was sitting there, doing some work for me, and he instantly ordered her out. 'I'll take good care you're not mixed up in the conspiracy,' he said. 'You shall leave this house to-day. If your mistress wants a maid, she shall have one of my choosing.' He pushed me into the room, and locked the door on me. He set that senseless woman to watch me outside, Marian! He looked and spoke like a madman. You may hardly understand it—he did indeed."

"I do understand it, Laura. He is mad—mad with the terrors of a guilty conscience. Every word you have said makes me positively certain that when Anne Catherick left you yesterday you were on the eve of discovering a secret which might have been your vile husband's ruin, and he thinks you have discovered it. Nothing you can say or do will quiet that guilty distrust, and convince his false nature of your truth. I don't say this, my love, to alarm you. I say it to open your eyes to your position, and to convince you of the urgent necessity of letting me act, as I best can, for your protection while the chance is our own. Count Fosco's interference has secured me access to you to-day, but he may withdraw that interference to-morrow. Sir Percival has already dismissed Fanny because she is a quick-witted girl, and devotedly attached to you, and has chosen a woman to take her place who cares nothing for your interests, and whose dull intelligence lowers her to the level of the watch-dog in the yard. It is impossible to say what violent measures he may take next, unless we make the most of our opportunities while we have them."

"What can we do, Marian? Oh, if we could only leave this house, never to see it again!"

"Listen to me, my love, and try to think that you are not quite helpless so long as I am here with you."

"I will think so—I do think so. Don't altogether forget poor Fanny in thinking of me. She wants help and comfort too."

"I will not forget her. I saw her before I came up here, and I have arranged to communicate with her to-night. Letters are not safe in the post-bag at Blackwater Park, and I shall have two to write to-day, in your interests, which must pass through no hands but Fanny's."

"What letters?"

"I mean to write first, Laura, to Mr. Gilmore's partner, who has offered to help us in any fresh emergency. Little as I know of the law, I am certain that it can protect a woman from such treatment as that ruffian has inflicted on you to-day. I will go into no details about Anne Catherick, because I have no certain information to give. But the lawyer shall know of those bruises on your arm, and of the violence offered to you in this room—he shall, before I rest to-night!"

"But think of the exposure, Marian!"

"I am calculating on the exposure. Sir Percival has more to dread from it than you have. The prospect of an exposure may bring him to terms when nothing else will."

I rose as I spoke, but Laura entreated me not to leave her. "You will drive him to desperation," she said, "and increase our dangers tenfold."

I felt the truth—the disheartening truth—of those words. But I could not bring myself plainly to acknowledge it to her. In our dreadful position there was no help and no hope for us but in risking the worst. I said so in guarded terms. She sighed bitterly, but did not contest the matter. She only asked about the second letter that I had proposed writing. To whom was it to be addressed?

"To Mr. Fairlie," I said. "Your uncle is your nearest male relative, and the head of the family. He must and shall interfere."

Laura shook her head sorrowfully.

"Yes, yes," I went on, "your uncle is a weak, selfish, worldly man, I know, but he is not Sir Percival Glyde, and he has no such friend about him as Count Fosco. I expect nothing from his kindness or his tenderness of feeling towards you or towards me, but he will do anything to pamper his own indolence, and to secure his own quiet. Let me only persuade him that his interference at this moment will save him inevitable trouble and wretchedness and responsibility hereafter, and he will bestir himself for his own sake. I know how to deal with him, Laura — I have had some practice."

"If you could only prevail on him to let me go back to Limmeridge for a little while and stay there quietly with you, Marian, I could be almost as happy again as I was before I was married!"

Those words set me thinking in a new direction. Would it be possible to place Sir Percival between the two alternatives of either exposing himself to the scandal of legal interference on his wife's behalf, or of allowing her to be quietly separated from him for a time under pretext of a visit to her uncle's house? And could he, in that case, be reckoned on as likely to accept the last resource? It was doubtful — more than doubtful. And yet, hopeless as the experiment seemed, surely it was worth trying. I resolved to try it in sheer despair of knowing what better to do.

"Your uncle shall know the wish you have just expressed," I said, "and I will ask the lawyer's advice on the subject as well. Good may come of it — and will come of it, I hope."

Saying that I rose again, and again Laura tried to make me resume my seat.

"Don't leave me," she said uneasily. "My desk is on that table. You can write here."

It tried me to the quick to refuse her, even in her own interests. But we had been too long shut up alone together already. Our chance of seeing each other again might entirely depend on our not exciting any fresh suspicions. It was full time to show myself, quietly and unconcernedly, among the wretches who were at that very moment, perhaps, thinking of us and talking of us downstairs. I explained the miserable necessity to Laura, and prevailed on her to recognise it as I did.

"I will come back again, love, in an hour or less," I said. "The worst is over for to-day. Keep yourself quiet and fear nothing."

"Is the key in the door, Marian? Can I lock it on the inside?"

"Yes, here is the key. Lock the door, and open it to nobody until I come upstairs again."

I kissed her and left her. It was a relief to me as I walked away to hear the key turned in the lock, and to know that the door was at her own command.

VIII

June 19th. — I had only got as far as the top of the stairs when the locking of Laura's door suggested to me the precaution of also locking my own door, and keeping the key safely about me while I was out of the room. My journal was already secured with other papers in the table drawer, but my writing materials were left out. These included a seal bearing the common device of two doves drinking out of the same cup, and some sheets of blotting-paper, which had the impression on them of the closing lines of my writing in these pages traced during the past night. Distorted by the suspicion which had now become a part of myself, even such trifles as these looked too dangerous to be trusted without a guard — even the locked table drawer seemed to be not sufficiently protected in my absence until the means of access to it had been carefully secured as well.

I found no appearance of any one having entered the room while I had been talking with Laura. My writing materials (which I had given the servant instructions never to meddle with) were scattered over the table much as usual. The only circumstance in connection with them that at all struck me was that the seal lay tidily in the tray with the pencils and the wax. It was not in my careless habits (I am sorry to say) to put it there, neither did I remember putting it there. But as I could not call to mind, on the other hand, where else I had thrown it down, and as I was also doubtful whether I might not for once have laid it mechanically in the right place, I abstained from adding to the perplexity with which the day's events had filled my mind by troubling it afresh about a trifle. I locked the door, put the key in my pocket, and went downstairs.

Madame Fosco was alone in the hall looking at the weather-glass.

"Still falling," she said. "I am afraid we must expect more rain."

Her face was composed again to its customary expression and its customary colour. But the hand with which she pointed to the dial of the weather-glass still trembled.

Could she have told her husband already that she had overheard Laura reviling him, in my company, as a "spy?" My strong suspicion that she must have told him, my irresistible dread (all the more overpowering from its very vagueness) of the consequences which might follow, my fixed conviction, derived from various little self-betrayals which women notice in each other, that Madame Fosco, in spite of her well-assumed external civility, had not forgiven her niece for innocently standing between her and the legacy of ten thousand pounds — all rushed upon my mind together, all impelled me to speak in the vain hope of using my own influence and my own powers of persuasion for the atonement of Laura's offence.

"May I trust to your kindness to excuse me, Madame Fosco, if I venture to speak to you on an exceedingly painful subject?"

She crossed her hands in front of her and bowed her head solemnly, without uttering a word, and without taking her eyes off mine for a moment.

"When you were so good as to bring me back my handkerchief," I went on, "I am very, very much afraid you must have accidentally heard Laura say something which I am unwilling to repeat, and which I will not attempt to defend. I will only venture to hope that you have not thought it of sufficient importance to be mentioned to the Count?"

"I think it of no importance whatever," said Madame Fosco sharply and suddenly. "But," she added, resuming her icy manner in a moment, "I have no secrets from my husband even in trifles. When he noticed just now that I looked distressed, it was my painful duty to tell him why I was distressed, and I frankly acknowledge to you, Miss Halcombe, that I have told him."

I was prepared to hear it, and yet she turned me cold all over when she said those words.

"Let me earnestly entreat you, Madame Fosco — let me earnestly entreat the Count — to make some allowances for the sad position in which my sister is placed. She spoke while she was smarting under the insult and injustice inflicted on her by her husband, and she was not herself when she said those rash words. May I hope that they will be considerately and generously forgiven?"

"Most assuredly," said the Count's quiet voice behind me. He had stolen on us with his noiseless tread and his book in his hand from the library.

"When Lady Glyde said those hasty words," he went on, "she did me an injustice which I lament — and forgive. Let us never return to the subject, Miss Halcombe; let us all comfortably combine to forget it from this moment."

"You are very kind," I said, "you relieve me inexpressibly."

I tried to continue, but his eyes were on me; his deadly smile that hides everything was set, hard, and unwavering on his broad, smooth face. My distrust of his unfathomable falseness, my sense of my own degradation in stooping to conciliate his wife and himself, so disturbed and confused me, that the next words failed on my lips, and I stood there in silence.

"I beg you on my knees to say no more, Miss Halcombe—I am truly shocked that you should have thought it necessary to say so much." With that polite speech he took my hand—oh, how I despise myself! oh, how little comfort there is even in knowing that I submitted to it for Laura's sake!—he took my hand and put it to his poisonous lips. Never did I know all my horror of him till then. That innocent familiarity turned my blood as if it had been the vilest insult that a man could offer me. Yet I hid my disgust from him—I tried to smile—I, who once mercilessly despised deceit in other women, was as false as the worst of them, as false as the Judas whose lips had touched my hand.

I could not have maintained my degrading self-control—it is all that redeems me in my own estimation to know that I could not—if he had still continued to keep his eyes on my face. His wife's tigerish jealousy came to my rescue and forced his attention away from me the moment he possessed himself of my hand. Her cold blue eyes caught light, her dull white cheeks flushed into bright colour, she looked years younger than her age in an instant.

"Count!" she said. "Your foreign forms of politeness are not understood by Englishwomen."

"Pardon me, my angel! The best and dearest Englishwoman in the world understands them." With those words he dropped my hand and quietly raised his wife's hand to his lips in place of it.

I ran back up the stairs to take refuge in my own room. If there had been time to think, my thoughts, when I was alone again, would have caused me bitter suffering. But there was no time to think. Happily for the preservation of my calmness and my courage there was time for nothing but action.

The letters to the lawyer and to Mr. Fairlie were still to be written, and I sat down at once without a moment's hesitation to devote myself to them.

The Woman in White

There was no multitude of resources to perplex me — there was absolutely no one to depend on, in the first instance, but myself. Sir Percival had neither friends nor relatives in the neighbourhood whose intercession I could attempt to employ. He was on the coldest terms — in some cases on the worst terms — with the families of his own rank and station who lived near him. We two women had neither father nor brother to come to the house and take our parts. There was no choice but to write those two doubtful letters, or to put Laura in the wrong and myself in the wrong, and to make all peaceable negotiation in the future impossible by secretly escaping from Blackwater Park. Nothing but the most imminent personal peril could justify our taking that second course. The letters must be tried first, and I wrote them.

I said nothing to the lawyer about Anne Catherick, because (as I had already hinted to Laura) that topic was connected with a mystery which we could not yet explain, and which it would therefore be useless to write about to a professional man. I left my correspondent to attribute Sir Percival's disgraceful conduct, if he pleased, to fresh disputes about money matters, and simply consulted him on the possibility of taking legal proceedings for Laura's protection in the event of her husband's refusal to allow her to leave Blackwater Park for a time and return with me to Limmeridge. I referred him to Mr. Fairlie for the details of this last arrangement — I assured him that I wrote with Laura's authority — and I ended by entreating him to act in her name to the utmost extent of his power and with the least possible loss of time.

The letter to Mr. Fairlie occupied me next. I appealed to him on the terms which I had mentioned to Laura as the most likely to make him bestir himself; I enclosed a copy of my letter to the lawyer to show him how serious the case was, and I represented our removal to Limmeridge as the only compromise which would prevent the danger and distress of Laura's present position from inevitably affecting her uncle as well as herself at no very distant time.

When I had done, and had sealed and directed the two envelopes, I went back with the letters to Laura's room, to show her that they were written.

"Has anybody disturbed you?" I asked, when she opened the door to me.

"Nobody has knocked," she replied. "But I heard some one in the outer room."

"Was it a man or a woman?"

"A woman. I heard the rustling of her gown."

"A rustling like silk?"

"Yes, like silk."

Madame Fosco had evidently been watching outside. The mischief she might do by herself was little to be feared. But the mischief she might do, as a willing instrument in her husband's hands, was too formidable to be overlooked.

"What became of the rustling of the gown when you no longer heard it in the ante-room?" I inquired. "Did you hear it go past your wall, along the passage?"

"Yes. I kept still and listened, and just heard it."

"Which way did it go?"

"Towards your room."

I considered again. The sound had not caught my ears. But I was then deeply absorbed in my letters, and I write with a heavy hand and a quill pen, scraping and scratching noisily over the paper. It was more likely that Madame Fosco would hear the scraping of my pen than that I should hear the rustling of her dress. Another reason (if I had wanted one) for not trusting my letters to the post-bag in the hall.

Laura saw me thinking. "More difficulties!" she said wearily; "more difficulties and more dangers!"

"No dangers," I replied. "Some little difficulty, perhaps. I am thinking of the safest way of putting my two letters into Fanny's hands."

"You have really written them, then? Oh, Marian, run no risks—pray, pray run no risks!"

"No, no—no fear. Let me see—what o'clock is it now?"

It was a quarter to six. There would be time for me to get to the village inn, and to come back again before dinner. If I waited till the evening I might find no second opportunity of safely leaving the house.

The Woman in White

"Keep the key turned in the lock, Laura," I said, "and don't be afraid about me. If you hear any inquiries made, call through the door, and say that I am gone out for a walk."

"When shall you be back?"

"Before dinner, without fail. Courage, my love. By this time to-morrow you will have a clear-headed, trustworthy man acting for your good. Mr. Gilmore's partner is our next best friend to Mr. Gilmore himself."

A moment's reflection, as soon as I was alone, convinced me that I had better not appear in my walking-dress until I had first discovered what was going on in the lower part of the house. I had not ascertained yet whether Sir Percival was indoors or out.

The singing of the canaries in the library, and the smell of tobacco-smoke that came through the door, which was not closed, told me at once where the Count was. I looked over my shoulder as I passed the doorway, and saw to my surprise that he was exhibiting the docility of the birds in his most engagingly polite manner to the housekeeper. He must have specially invited her to see them — for she would never have thought of going into the library of her own accord. The man's slightest actions had a purpose of some kind at the bottom of every one of them. What could be his purpose here?

It was no time then to inquire into his motives. I looked about for Madame Fosco next, and found her following her favourite circle round and round the fish-pond.

I was a little doubtful how she would meet me, after the outbreak of jealousy of which I had been the cause so short a time since. But her husband had tamed her in the interval, and she now spoke to me with the same civility as usual. My only object in addressing myself to her was to ascertain if she knew what had become of Sir Percival. I contrived to refer to him indirectly, and after a little fencing on either side she at last mentioned that he had gone out.

"Which of the horses has he taken?" I asked carelessly.

"None of them," she replied. "He went away two hours since on foot. As I understood it, his object was to make fresh inquiries about the woman named Anne Catherick. He appears to be unreasonably anxious about tracing her. Do you happen to know if she is dangerously mad, Miss Halcombe?"

"I do not, Countess."

"Are you going in?"

"Yes, I think so. I suppose it will soon be time to dress for dinner."

We entered the house together. Madame Fosco strolled into the library, and closed the door. I went at once to fetch my hat and shawl. Every moment was of importance, if I was to get to Fanny at the inn and be back before dinner.

When I crossed the hall again no one was there, and the singing of the birds in the library had ceased. I could not stop to make any fresh investigations. I could only assure myself that the way was clear, and then leave the house with the two letters safe in my pocket.

On my way to the village I prepared myself for the possibility of meeting Sir Percival. As long as I had him to deal with alone I felt certain of not losing my presence of mind. Any woman who is sure of her own wits is a match at any time for a man who is not sure of his own temper. I had no such fear of Sir Percival as I had of the Count. Instead of fluttering, it had composed me, to hear of the errand on which he had gone out. While the tracing of Anne Catherick was the great anxiety that occupied him, Laura and I might hope for some cessation of any active persecution at his hands. For our sakes now, as well as for Anne's, I hoped and prayed fervently that she might still escape him.

I walked on as briskly as the heat would let me till I reached the cross-road which led to the village, looking back from time to time to make sure that I was not followed by any one.

Nothing was behind me all the way but an empty country waggon. The noise made by the lumbering wheels annoyed me, and when I found that the waggon took the road to the village, as well as myself, I stopped to let it go by and pass out of hearing. As I looked toward it, more attentively than before, I thought I detected at intervals the feet of a man walking close behind it, the carter being in front, by the side of his horses. The part of the cross-road which I had just passed over was so narrow that the waggon coming after me brushed the trees and thickets on either side, and I had to wait until it went by before I could test the correctness of my impression. Apparently that impression was wrong, for when the waggon had passed me the road behind it was quite clear.

I reached the inn without meeting Sir Percival, and without noticing anything more, and was glad to find that the landlady had received Fanny with all possible kindness. The girl had a little parlour to sit in, away from the noise of the taproom, and a clean bedchamber at the top of the house. She began crying again at the sight of me, and said, poor soul, truly enough, that it was dreadful to feel herself turned out into the world as if she had committed some unpardonable fault, when no blame could be laid at her door by anybody—not even by her master, who had sent her away.

"Try to make the best of it, Fanny," I said. "Your mistress and I will stand your friends, and will take care that your character shall not suffer. Now, listen to me. I have very little time to spare, and I am going to put a great trust in your hands. I wish you to take care of these two letters. The one with the stamp on it you are to put into the post when you reach London to-morrow. The other, directed to Mr. Fairlie, you are to deliver to him yourself as soon as you get home. Keep both the letters about you and give them up to no one. They are of the last importance to your mistress's interests."

Fanny put the letters into the bosom of her dress. "There they shall stop, miss," she said, "till I have done what you tell me."

"Mind you are at the station in good time to-morrow morning," I continued. "And when you see the housekeeper at Limmeridge give her my compliments, and say that you are in my service until Lady Glyde is able to take you back. We may meet again sooner than you think. So keep a good heart, and don't miss the seven o'clock train."

"Thank you, miss—thank you kindly. It gives one courage to hear your voice again. Please to offer my duty to my lady, and say I left all the things as tidy as I could in the time. Oh, dear! dear! who will dress her for dinner to-day? It really breaks my heart, miss, to think of it."

When I got back to the house I had only a quarter of an hour to spare to put myself in order for dinner, and to say two words to Laura before I went downstairs.

"The letters are in Fanny's hands," I whispered to her at the door. "Do you mean to join us at dinner?"

"Oh, no, no — not for the world."

"Has anything happened? Has any one disturbed you?"

"Yes — just now — Sir Percival — —"

"Did he come in?"

"No, he frightened me by a thump on the door outside. I said, 'Who's there?' 'You know,' he answered. 'Will you alter your mind, and tell me the rest? You shall! Sooner or later I'll wring it out of you. You know where Anne Catherick is at this moment.' 'Indeed, indeed,' I said, 'I don't.' 'You do!' he called back. 'I'll crush your obstinacy — mind that! — I'll wring it out of you!' He went away with those words — went away, Marian, hardly five minutes ago."

He had not found Anne! We were safe for that night — he had not found her yet.

"You are going downstairs, Marian? Come up again in the evening."

"Yes, yes. Don't be uneasy if I am a little late — I must be careful not to give offence by leaving them too soon."

The dinner-bell rang and I hastened away.

Sir Percival took Madame Fosco into the dining-room, and the Count gave me his arm. He was hot and flushed, and was not dressed with his customary care and completeness. Had he, too, been out before dinner, and been late in getting back? or was he only suffering from the heat a little more severely than usual?

However this might be, he was unquestionably troubled by some secret annoyance or anxiety, which, with all his powers of deception, he was not able entirely to conceal. Through the whole of dinner he was almost as silent as Sir Percival himself, and he, every now and then, looked at his wife with an expression of furtive uneasiness which was quite new in my experience of him. The one social obligation which he seemed to be self-possessed enough to perform as carefully as ever was the obligation of being persistently civil and attentive to me. What vile object he has in view I cannot still discover, but be the design what it may, invariable politeness towards myself, invariable humility towards Laura, and invariable suppression (at any cost) of Sir Percival's clumsy violence, have been the means he has resolutely and impenetrably used to get to his end ever since he set foot in this house. I suspected it when he first interfered in our favour, on the day when the deed was produced in the library, and I feel certain of it now.

When Madame Fosco and I rose to leave the table, the Count rose also to accompany us back to the drawing-room.

"What are you going away for?" asked Sir Percival—"I mean you, Fosco."

"I am going away because I have had dinner enough, and wine enough," answered the Count. "Be so kind, Percival, as to make allowances for my foreign habit of going out with the ladies, as well as coming in with them."

"Nonsense! Another glass of claret won't hurt you. Sit down again like an Englishman. I want half an hour's quiet talk with you over our wine."

"A quiet talk, Percival, with all my heart, but not now, and not over the wine. Later in the evening, if you please—later in the evening."

"Civil!" said Sir Percival savagely. "Civil behaviour, upon my soul, to a man in his own house!"

I had more than once seen him look at the Count uneasily during dinner-time, and had observed that the Count carefully abstained from looking at him in return. This circumstance, coupled with the host's anxiety for a little quiet talk over the wine, and the guest's obstinate resolution not to sit down again at the table, revived in my memory the request which Sir Percival had vainly addressed to his friend earlier in the day to come out of the library and speak to him. The Count had deferred granting that private interview, when it was first asked for in the afternoon, and had again deferred granting it, when it was a second time asked for at the dinner-table. Whatever the coming subject of discussion between them might be, it was clearly an important subject in Sir Percival's estimation—and perhaps (judging from his evident reluctance to approach it) a dangerous subject as well, in the estimation of the Count.

These considerations occurred to me while we were passing from the dining-room to the drawing-room. Sir Percival's angry commentary on his friend's desertion of him had not produced the slightest effect. The Count obstinately accompanied us to the tea-table—waited a minute or two in the room—went out into the hall—and returned with the post-bag in his hands. It was then eight o'clock—the hour at which the letters were always despatched from Blackwater Park.

"Have you any letter for the post, Miss Halcombe?" he asked, approaching me with the bag.

I saw Madame Fosco, who was making the tea, pause, with the sugar-tongs in her hand, to listen for my answer.

"No, Count, thank you. No letters to-day."

He gave the bag to the servant, who was then in the room; sat down at the piano, and played the air of the lively Neapolitan street-song, "La mia Carolina," twice over. His wife, who was usually the most deliberate of women in all her movements, made the tea as quickly as I could have made it myself—finished her own cup in two minutes, and quietly glided out of the room.

I rose to follow her example—partly because I suspected her of attempting some treachery upstairs with Laura, partly because I was resolved not to remain alone in the same room with her husband.

Before I could get to the door the Count stopped me, by a request for a cup of tea. I gave him the cup of tea, and tried a second time to get away. He stopped me again—this time by going back to the piano, and suddenly appealing to me on a musical question in which he declared that the honour of his country was concerned.

I vainly pleaded my own total ignorance of music, and total want of taste in that direction. He only appealed to me again with a vehemence which set all further protest on my part at defiance. "The English and the Germans (he indignantly declared) were always reviling the Italians for their inability to cultivate the higher kinds of music. We were perpetually talking of our Oratorios, and they were perpetually talking of their Symphonies. Did we forget and did they forget his immortal friend and countryman, Rossini? What was Moses in Egypt but a sublime oratorio, which was acted on the stage instead of being coldly sung in a concert-room? What was the overture to Guillaume Tell but a symphony under another name? Had I heard Moses in Egypt? Would I listen to this, and this, and this, and say if anything more sublimely sacred and grand had ever been composed by mortal man?"—And without waiting for a word of assent or dissent on my part, looking me hard in the face all the time, he began thundering on the piano, and singing to it with loud and lofty enthusiasm—only interrupting himself, at intervals, to announce to me fiercely the titles of the different pieces of music: "Chorus of Egyptians in the Plague of Darkness, Miss Halcombe!"—"Recitativo of Moses with the tables of the Law."—"Prayer of Israelites, at the passage of the Red Sea. Aha! Aha! Is that sacred? is that sublime?" The piano trembled under his powerful hands, and the teacups on the table rattled, as his big bass voice thundered out the notes, and his heavy foot beat time on the floor.

There was something horrible—something fierce and devilish—in the outburst of his delight at his own singing and playing, and in the triumph with which he watched its effect upon me as I shrank nearer and nearer to the door. I was released at last, not by my own efforts, but by Sir Percival's interposition. He opened the dining-room door, and called out angrily to know what "that infernal noise" meant. The Count instantly got up from the piano. "Ah! if Percival is coming," he said, "harmony and melody are both at an end. The Muse of Music, Miss Halcombe, deserts us in dismay, and I, the fat old minstrel, exhale the rest of my enthusiasm in the open air!" He stalked out into the verandah, put his hands in his pockets, and resumed the Recitativo of Moses", sotto voce, in the garden.

I heard Sir Percival call after him from the dining-room window. But he took no notice—he seemed determined not to hear. That long-deferred quiet talk between them was still to be put off, was still to wait for the Count's absolute will and pleasure.

He had detained me in the drawing-room nearly half an hour from the time when his wife left us. Where had she been, and what had she been doing in that interval?

I went upstairs to ascertain, but I made no discoveries, and when I questioned Laura, I found that she had not heard anything. Nobody had disturbed her, no faint rustling of the silk dress had been audible, either in the ante-room or in the passage.

It was then twenty minutes to nine. After going to my room to get my journal, I returned, and sat with Laura, sometimes writing, sometimes stopping to talk with her. Nobody came near us, and nothing happened. We remained together till ten o'clock. I then rose, said my last cheering words, and wished her good-night. She locked her door again after we had arranged that I should come in and see her the first thing in the morning.

I had a few sentences more to add to my diary before going to bed myself, and as I went down again to the drawing-room after leaving Laura for the last time that weary day, I resolved merely to show myself there, to make my excuses, and then to retire an hour earlier than usual for the night.

Sir Percival, and the Count and his wife, were sitting together. Sir Percival was yawning in an easy-chair, the Count was reading, Madame Fosco was fanning herself. Strange to say, her face was flushed now. She, who never suffered from the heat, was most undoubtedly suffering from it to-night.

"I am afraid, Countess, you are not quite so well as usual?" I said.

"The very remark I was about to make to you," she replied. "You are looking pale, my dear."

My dear! It was the first time she had ever addressed me with that familiarity! There was an insolent smile too on her face when she said the words.

"I am suffering from one of my bad headaches," I answered coldly.

"Ah, indeed? Want of exercise, I suppose? A walk before dinner would have been just the thing for you." She referred to the "walk" with a strange emphasis. Had she seen me go out? No matter if she had. The letters were safe now in Fanny's hands.

"Come and have a smoke, Fosco," said Sir Percival, rising, with another uneasy look at his friend.

"With pleasure, Percival, when the ladies have gone to bed," replied the Count.

"Excuse me, Countess, if I set you the example of retiring," I said. "The only remedy for such a headache as mine is going to bed."

I took my leave. There was the same insolent smile on the woman's face when I shook hands with her. Sir Percival paid no attention to me. He was looking impatiently at Madame Fosco, who showed no signs of leaving the room with me. The Count smiled to himself behind his book. There was yet another delay to that quiet talk with Sir Percival — and the Countess was the impediment this time.

IX

June 19th. — Once safely shut into my own room, I opened these pages, and prepared to go on with that part of the day's record which was still left to write.

For ten minutes or more I sat idle, with the pen in my hand, thinking over the events of the last twelve hours. When I at last addressed myself to my task, I found a difficulty in proceeding with it which I had never experienced before. In spite of my efforts to fix my thoughts on the matter in hand, they wandered away with the strangest persistency in the one direction of Sir Percival and the Count, and all the interest which I tried to concentrate on my journal centred instead in that private interview between them which had been put off all through the day, and which was now to take place in the silence and solitude of the night.

In this perverse state of my mind, the recollection of what had passed since the morning would not come back to me, and there was no resource but to close my journal and to get away from it for a little while.

I opened the door which led from my bedroom into my sitting-room, and having passed through, pulled it to again, to prevent any accident in case of draught with the candle left on the dressing-table. My sitting-room window was wide open, and I leaned out listlessly to look at the night.

It was dark and quiet. Neither moon nor stars were visible. There was a smell like rain in the still, heavy air, and I put my hand out of window. No. The rain was only threatening, it had not come yet.

I remained leaning on the window-sill for nearly a quarter of an hour, looking out absently into the black darkness, and hearing nothing, except now and then the voices of the servants, or the distant sound of a closing door, in the lower part of the house.

Just as I was turning away wearily from the window to go back to the bedroom and make a second attempt to complete the unfinished entry in my journal, I smelt the odour of tobacco-smoke stealing towards me on the heavy night air. The next moment I saw a tiny red spark advancing from the farther end of the house in the pitch darkness. I heard no footsteps, and I could see nothing but the spark. It travelled along in the night, passed the window at which I was standing, and stopped opposite my bedroom window, inside which I had left the light burning on the dressing-table.

The spark remained stationary for a moment, then moved back again in the direction from which it had advanced. As I followed its progress I saw a second red spark, larger than the first, approaching from the distance. The two met together in the darkness. Remembering who smoked cigarettes and who smoked cigars, I inferred immediately that the Count had come out first to look and listen under my window, and that Sir Percival had afterwards joined him. They must both have been walking on the lawn — or I should certainly have heard Sir Percival's heavy footfall, though the Count's soft step might have escaped me, even on the gravel walk.

I waited quietly at the window, certain that they could neither of them see me in the darkness of the room.

"What's the matter?" I heard Sir Percival say in a low voice. "Why don't you come in and sit down?"

"I want to see the light out of that window," replied the Count softly.

"What harm does the light do?"

"It shows she is not in bed yet. She is sharp enough to suspect something, and bold enough to come downstairs and listen, if she can get the chance. Patience, Percival — patience."

"Humbug! You're always talking of patience."

"I shall talk of something else presently. My good friend, you are on the edge of your domestic precipice, and if I let you give the women one other chance, on my sacred word of honour they will push you over it!"

"What the devil do you mean?"

"We will come to our explanations, Percival, when the light is out of that window, and when I have had one little look at the rooms on each side of the library, and a peep at the staircase as well."

They slowly moved away, and the rest of the conversation between them (which had been conducted throughout in the same low tones) ceased to be audible. It was no matter. I had heard enough to determine me on justifying the Count's opinion of my sharpness and my courage. Before the red sparks were out of sight in the darkness I had made up my mind that there should be a listener when those two men sat down to their talk—and that the listener, in spite of all the Count's precautions to the contrary, should be myself. I wanted but one motive to sanction the act to my own conscience, and to give me courage enough for performing it—and that motive I had. Laura's honour, Laura's happiness—Laura's life itself—might depend on my quick ears and my faithful memory to-night.

I had heard the Count say that he meant to examine the rooms on each side of the library, and the staircase as well, before he entered on any explanation with Sir Percival. This expression of his intentions was necessarily sufficient to inform me that the library was the room in which he proposed that the conversation should take place. The one moment of time which was long enough to bring me to that conclusion was also the moment which showed me a means of baffling his precautions—or, in other words, of hearing what he and Sir Percival said to each other, without the risk of descending at all into the lower regions of the house.

In speaking of the rooms on the ground floor I have mentioned incidentally the verandah outside them, on which they all opened by means of French windows, extending from the cornice to the floor. The top of this verandah was flat, the rain-water being carried off from it by pipes into tanks which helped to supply the house. On the narrow leaden roof, which ran along past the bedrooms, and which was rather less, I should think, than three feet below the sills of the window, a row of flower-pots was ranged, with wide intervals between each pot—the whole being protected from falling in high winds by an ornamental iron railing along the edge of the roof.

The plan which had now occurred to me was to get out at my sitting-room window on to this roof, to creep along noiselessly till I reached that part of it which was immediately over the library window, and to crouch down between the flower-pots, with my ear against the outer railing. If Sir Percival and the Count sat and smoked to-night, as I had seen them sitting and smoking many nights before, with their chairs close at the open window, and their feet stretched on the zinc garden seats which were placed under the verandah, every word they said to each other above a whisper (and no long conversation, as we all know by experience, can be carried on in a whisper) must inevitably reach my ears. If, on the other hand, they chose to-night to sit far back inside the room, then the chances were that I should hear little or nothing—and in that case, I must run

The Woman in White

the far more serious risk of trying to outwit them downstairs.

Strongly as I was fortified in my resolution by the desperate nature of our situation, I hoped most fervently that I might escape this last emergency. My courage was only a woman's courage after all, and it was very near to failing me when I thought of trusting myself on the ground floor, at the dead of night, within reach of Sir Percival and the Count.

I went softly back to my bedroom to try the safer experiment of the verandah roof first.

A complete change in my dress was imperatively necessary for many reasons. I took off my silk gown to begin with, because the slightest noise from it on that still night might have betrayed me. I next removed the white and cumbersome parts of my underclothing, and replaced them by a petticoat of dark flannel. Over this I put my black travelling cloak, and pulled the hood on to my head. In my ordinary evening costume I took up the room of three men at least. In my present dress, when it was held close about me, no man could have passed through the narrowest spaces more easily than I. The little breadth left on the roof of the verandah, between the flower-pots on one side and the wall and the windows of the house on the other, made this a serious consideration. If I knocked anything down, if I made the least noise, who could say what the consequences might be?

I only waited to put the matches near the candle before I extinguished it, and groped my way back into the sitting-room. I locked that door, as I had locked my bedroom door—then quietly got out of the window, and cautiously set my feet on the leaden roof of the verandah.

My two rooms were at the inner extremity of the new wing of the house in which we all lived, and I had five windows to pass before I could reach the position it was necessary to take up immediately over the library. The first window belonged to a spare room which was empty. The second and third windows belonged to Laura's room. The fourth window belonged to Sir Percival's room. The fifth belonged to the Countess's room. The others, by which it was not necessary for me to pass, were the windows of the Count's dressing-room, of the bathroom, and of the second empty spare room.

No sound reached my ears—the black blinding darkness of the night was all round me when I first stood on the verandah, except at that part of it which Madame Fosco's window overlooked. There, at the very place above the library to which my course was directed — there I saw a gleam of light! The Countess was not yet in bed.

It was too late to draw back — it was no time to wait. I determined to go on at all hazards, and trust for security to my own caution and to the darkness of the night. "For Laura's sake!" I thought to myself, as I took the first step forward on the roof, with one hand holding my cloak close round me, and the other groping against the wall of the house. It was better to brush close by the wall than to risk striking my feet against the flower-pots within a few inches of me, on the other side.

I passed the dark window of the spare room, trying the leaden roof at each step with my foot before I risked resting my weight on it. I passed the dark windows of Laura's room ("God bless her and keep her to-night!"). I passed the dark window of Sir Percival's room. Then I waited a moment, knelt down with my hands to support me, and so crept to my position, under the protection of the low wall between the bottom of the lighted window and the verandah roof.

When I ventured to look up at the window itself I found that the top of it only was open, and that the blind inside was drawn down. While I was looking I saw the shadow of Madame Fosco pass across the white field of the blind — then pass slowly back again. Thus far she could not have heard me, or the shadow would surely have stopped at the blind, even if she had wanted courage enough to open the window and look out?

I placed myself sideways against the railing of the verandah — first ascertaining, by touching them, the position of the flower-pots on either side of me. There was room enough for me to sit between them and no more. The sweet-scented leaves of the flower on my left hand just brushed my cheek as I lightly rested my head against the railing.

The first sounds that reached me from below were caused by the opening or closing (most probably the latter) of three doors in succession — the doors, no doubt, leading into the hall and into the rooms on each side of the library, which the Count had pledged himself to examine. The first object that I saw was the red spark again travelling out into the night from under the verandah, moving away towards my window, waiting a moment, and then returning to the place from which it had set out.

"The devil take your restlessness! When do you mean to sit

The Woman in White

down?" growled Sir Percival's voice beneath me.

"Ouf! how hot it is!" said the Count, sighing and puffing wearily.

His exclamation was followed by the scraping of the garden chairs on the tiled pavement under the verandah—the welcome sound which told me they were going to sit close at the window as usual. So far the chance was mine. The clock in the turret struck the quarter to twelve as they settled themselves in their chairs. I heard Madame Fosco through the open window yawning, and saw her shadow pass once more across the white field of the blind.

Meanwhile, Sir Percival and the Count began talking together below, now and then dropping their voices a little lower than usual, but never sinking them to a whisper. The strangeness and peril of my situation, the dread, which I could not master, of Madame Fosco's lighted window, made it difficult, almost impossible, for me, at first, to keep my presence of mind, and to fix my attention solely on the conversation beneath. For some minutes I could only succeed in gathering the general substance of it. I understood the Count to say that the one window alight was his wife's, that the ground floor of the house was quite clear, and that they might now speak to each other without fear of accidents. Sir Percival merely answered by upbraiding his friend with having unjustifiably slighted his wishes and neglected his interests all through the day. The Count thereupon defended himself by declaring that he had been beset by certain troubles and anxieties which had absorbed all his attention, and that the only safe time to come to an explanation was a time when they could feel certain of being neither interrupted nor overheard. "We are at a serious crisis in our affairs, Percival," he said, "and if we are to decide on the future at all, we must decide secretly to-night."

That sentence of the Count's was the first which my attention was ready enough to master exactly as it was spoken. From this point, with certain breaks and interruptions, my whole interest fixed breathlessly on the conversation, and I followed it word for word.

"Crisis?" repeated Sir Percival. "It's a worse crisis than you think for, I can tell you."

"So I should suppose, from your behaviour for the last day or two," returned the other coolly. "But wait a little. Before we advance to what I do not know, let us be quite certain of what I do know. Let us first see if I am right about the time that is past, before I make any proposal to you for the time that is to come."

"Stop till I get the brandy and water. Have some yourself."

"Thank you, Percival. The cold water with pleasure, a spoon, and the basin of sugar. Eau sucrée, my friend—nothing more."

"Sugar-and-water for a man of your age!—There! mix your sickly mess. You foreigners are all alike."

"Now listen, Percival. I will put our position plainly before you, as I understand it, and you shall say if I am right or wrong. You and I both came back to this house from the Continent with our affairs very seriously embarrassed—"

"Cut it short! I wanted some thousands and you some hundreds, and without the money we were both in a fair way to go to the dogs together. There's the situation. Make what you can of it. Go on."

"Well, Percival, in your own solid English words, you wanted some thousands and I wanted some hundreds, and the only way of getting them was for you to raise the money for your own necessity (with a small margin beyond for my poor little hundreds) by the help of your wife. What did I tell you about your wife on our way to England?—and what did I tell you again when we had come here, and when I had seen for myself the sort of woman Miss Halcombe was?"

"How should I know? You talked nineteen to the dozen, I suppose, just as usual."

"I said this: Human ingenuity, my friend, has hitherto only discovered two ways in which a man can manage a woman. One way is to knock her down—a method largely adopted by the brutal lower orders of the people, but utterly abhorrent to the refined and educated classes above them. The other way (much longer, much more difficult, but in the end not less certain) is never to accept a provocation at a woman's hands. It holds with animals, it holds with children, and it holds with women, who are nothing but children grown up. Quiet resolution is the one quality the animals, the children, and the women all fail in. If they can once shake this superior quality in their master, they get the better of him. If they can never succeed in disturbing it, he gets the better of them. I said to you, Remember that plain truth when you want your wife to help you to the money. I said, Remember it doubly and trebly in the presence of your wife's sister, Miss Halcombe. Have you remembered it? Not once in all the implications that have twisted themselves about us in this house. Every provocation that your wife and her sister could offer to you, you instantly accepted from them. Your mad temper lost the signature to the deed, lost the ready money, set Miss Halcombe writing to the lawyer for the first time."

"First time! Has she written again?"

"Yes, she has written again to-day."

A chair fell on the pavement of the verandah—fell with a crash, as if it had been kicked down.

It was well for me that the Count's revelation roused Sir Percival's anger as it did. On hearing that I had been once more discovered I started so that the railing against which I leaned cracked again. Had he followed me to the inn? Did he infer that I must have given my letters to Fanny when I told him I had none for the post-bag? Even if it was so, how could he have examined the letters when they had gone straight from my hand to the bosom of the girl's dress?

"Thank your lucky star," I heard the Count say next, "that you have me in the house to undo the harm as fast as you do it. Thank your lucky star that I said No when you were mad enough to talk of turning the key to-day on Miss Halcombe, as you turned it in your mischievous folly on your wife. Where are your eyes? Can you look at Miss Halcombe and not see that she has the foresight and the resolution of a man? With that woman for my friend I would snap these fingers of mine at the world. With that woman for my enemy, I, with all my brains and experience—I, Fosco, cunning as the devil himself, as you have told me a hundred times—I walk, in your English phrase, upon egg-shells! And this grand creature—I drink her health in my sugar-and-water—this grand creature, who stands in the strength of her love and her courage, firm as a rock, between us two and that poor, flimsy, pretty blonde wife of yours—this magnificent woman, whom I admire with all my soul, though I oppose her in your interests and in mine, you drive to extremities as if she was no sharper and no bolder than the rest of her sex. Percival! Percival! you deserve to fail, and you have failed."

There was a pause. I write the villain's words about myself because I mean to remember them—because I hope yet for the day when I may speak out once for all in his presence, and cast them back one by one in his teeth.

Sir Percival was the first to break the silence again.

"Yes, yes, bully and bluster as much as you like," he said sulkily; "the difficulty about the money is not the only difficulty. You would be for taking strong measures with the women yourself — if you knew as much as I do."

"We will come to that second difficulty all in good time," rejoined the Count. "You may confuse yourself, Percival, as much as you please, but you shall not confuse me. Let the question of the money be settled first. Have I convinced your obstinacy? have I shown you that your temper will not let you help yourself? — Or must I go back, and (as you put it in your dear straightforward English) bully and bluster a little more?"

"Pooh! It's easy enough to grumble at me. Say what is to be done — that's a little harder."

"Is it? Bah! This is what is to be done: You give up all direction in the business from to-night — you leave it for the future in my hands only. I am talking to a Practical British man — ha? Well, Practical, will that do for you?"

"What do you propose if I leave it all to you?"

"Answer me first. Is it to be in my hands or not?"

"Say it is in your hands — what then?"

"A few questions, Percival, to begin with. I must wait a little yet, to let circumstances guide me, and I must know, in every possible way, what those circumstances are likely to be. There is no time to lose. I have told you already that Miss Halcombe has written to the lawyer to-day for the second time."

"How did you find it out? What did she say?"

"If I told you, Percival, we should only come back at the end to where we are now. Enough that I have found it out — and the finding has caused that trouble and anxiety which made me so inaccessible to you all through to-day. Now, to refresh my memory about your affairs — it is some time since I talked them over with you. The money has been raised, in the absence of your wife's signature, by means of bills at three months — raised at a cost that makes my poverty-stricken foreign hair stand on end to think of it! When the bills are due, is there really and truly no earthly way of paying them but by the help of your wife?"

"None."

"What! You have no money at the bankers?"

"A few hundreds, when I want as many thousands."

"Have you no other security to borrow upon?"

"Not a shred."

"What have you actually got with your wife at the present moment?"

"Nothing but the interest of her twenty thousand pounds—barely enough to pay our daily expenses."

"What do you expect from your wife?"

"Three thousand a year when her uncle dies."

"A fine fortune, Percival. What sort of a man is this uncle? Old?"

"No—neither old nor young."

"A good-tempered, freely-living man? Married? No—I think my wife told me, not married."

"Of course not. If he was married, and had a son, Lady Glyde would not be next heir to the property. I'll tell you what he is. He's a maudlin, twaddling, selfish fool, and bores everybody who comes near him about the state of his health."

"Men of that sort, Percival, live long, and marry malevolently when you least expect it. I don't give you much, my friend, for your chance of the three thousand a year. Is there nothing more that comes to you from your wife?"

"Nothing."

"Absolutely nothing?"

"Absolutely nothing—except in case of her death."

"Aha! in the case of her death."

There was another pause. The Count moved from the verandah to the gravel walk outside. I knew that he had moved by his voice. "The rain has come at last," I heard him say. It had come. The state of my cloak showed that it had been falling thickly for some little time.

The Count went back under the verandah—I heard the chair creak beneath his weight as he sat down in it again.

"Well, Percival," he said, "and in the case of Lady Glyde's death, what do you get then?"

"If she leaves no children— —"

"Which she is likely to do?"

"Which she is not in the least likely to do— —"

"Yes?"

"Why, then I get her twenty thousand pounds."

"Paid down?"

"Paid down."

They were silent once more. As their voices ceased Madame Fosco's shadow darkened the blind again. Instead of passing this time, it remained, for a moment, quite still. I saw her fingers steal round the corner of the blind, and draw it on one side. The dim white outline of her face, looking out straight over me, appeared behind the window. I kept still, shrouded from head to foot in my black cloak. The rain, which was fast wetting me, dripped over the glass, blurred it, and prevented her from seeing anything. "More rain!" I heard her say to herself. She dropped the blind, and I breathed again freely.

The talk went on below me, the Count resuming it this time.

"Percival! do you care about your wife?"

"Fosco! that's rather a downright question."

"I am a downright man, and I repeat it."

"Why the devil do you look at me in that way?"

"You won't answer me? Well, then, let us say your wife dies

before the summer is out— —"

"Drop it, Fosco!"

"Let us say your wife dies— —"

"Drop it, I tell you!"

"In that case, you would gain twenty thousand pounds, and you would lose— —"

"I should lose the chance of three thousand a year."

"The remote chance, Percival—the remote chance only. And you want money, at once. In your position the gain is certain—the loss doubtful."

"Speak for yourself as well as for me. Some of the money I want has been borrowed for you. And if you come to gain, my wife's death would be ten thousand pounds in your wife's pocket. Sharp as you are, you seem to have conveniently forgotten Madame Fosco's legacy. Don't look at me in that way! I won't have it! What with your looks and your questions, upon my soul, you make my flesh creep!"

"Your flesh? Does flesh mean conscience in English? I speak of your wife's death as I speak of a possibility. Why not? The respectable lawyers who scribble-scrabble your deeds and your wills look the deaths of living people in the face. Do lawyers make your flesh creep? Why should I? It is my business to-night to clear up your position beyond the possibility of mistake, and I have now done it. Here is your position. If your wife lives, you pay those bills with her signature to the parchment. If your wife dies, you pay them with her death."

As he spoke the light in Madame Fosco's room was extinguished, and the whole second floor of the house was now sunk in darkness.

"Talk! talk!" grumbled Sir Percival. "One would think, to hear you, that my wife's signature to the deed was got already."

"You have left the matter in my hands," retorted the Count, "and I have more than two months before me to turn round in. Say no more about it, if you please, for the present. When the bills are due, you will see for yourself if my 'talk! talk!' is worth something, or if it is not. And now, Percival, having done with the money matters for to-night, I can place my attention at your disposal, if you wish to consult me on that second difficulty which has mixed itself up with our little embarrassments, and which has so altered you for the worse, that I hardly know you again. Speak, my friend—and pardon me if I shock your fiery national tastes by mixing myself a second glass of sugar-and-water."

"It's very well to say speak," replied Sir Percival, in a far more quiet and more polite tone than he had yet adopted, "but it's not so easy to know how to begin."

"Shall I help you?" suggested the Count. "Shall I give this private difficulty of yours a name? What if I call it—Anne Catherick?"

"Look here, Fosco, you and I have known each other for a long time, and if you have helped me out of one or two scrapes before this, I have done the best I could to help you in return, as far as money would go. We have made as many friendly sacrifices, on both sides, as men could, but we have had our secrets from each other, of course—haven't we?"

"You have had a secret from me, Percival. There is a skeleton in your cupboard here at Blackwater Park that has peeped out in these last few days at other people besides yourself."

"Well, suppose it has. If it doesn't concern you, you needn't be curious about it, need you?"

"Do I look curious about it?"

"Yes, you do."

"So! so! my face speaks the truth, then? What an immense foundation of good there must be in the nature of a man who arrives at my age, and whose face has not yet lost the habit of speaking the truth!—Come, Glyde! let us be candid one with the other. This secret of yours has sought me: I have not sought it. Let us say I am curious—do you ask me, as your old friend, to respect your secret, and to leave it, once for all, in your own keeping?"

"Yes—that's just what I do ask."

"Then my curiosity is at an end. It dies in me from this moment."

"Do you really mean that?"

The Woman in White

"What makes you doubt me?"

"I have had some experience, Fosco, of your roundabout ways, and I am not so sure that you won't worm it out of me after all."

The chair below suddenly creaked again—I felt the trellis-work pillar under me shake from top to bottom. The Count had started to his feet, and had struck it with his hand in indignation.

"Percival! Percival!" he cried passionately, "do you know me no better than that? Has all your experience shown you nothing of my character yet? I am a man of the antique type! I am capable of the most exalted acts of virtue—when I have the chance of performing them. It has been the misfortune of my life that I have had few chances. My conception of friendship is sublime! Is it my fault that your skeleton has peeped out at me? Why do I confess my curiosity? You poor superficial Englishman, it is to magnify my own self-control. I could draw your secret out of you, if I liked, as I draw this finger out of the palm of my hand—you know I could! But you have appealed to my friendship, and the duties of friendship are sacred to me. See! I trample my base curiosity under my feet. My exalted sentiments lift me above it. Recognise them, Percival! imitate them, Percival! Shake hands—I forgive you."

His voice faltered over the last words—faltered, as if he were actually shedding tears!

Sir Percival confusedly attempted to excuse himself, but the Count was too magnanimous to listen to him.

"No!" he said. "When my friend has wounded me, I can pardon him without apologies. Tell me, in plain words, do you want my help?"

"Yes, badly enough."

"And you can ask for it without compromising yourself?"

"I can try, at any rate."

"Try, then."

"Well, this is how it stands:—I told you to-day that I had done my best to find Anne Catherick, and failed."

"Yes, you did."

"Fosco! I'm a lost man if I don't find her."

"Ha! Is it so serious as that?"

A little stream of light travelled out under the verandah, and fell over the gravel-walk. The Count had taken the lamp from the inner part of the room to see his friend clearly by the light of it.

"Yes!" he said. "Your face speaks the truth this time. Serious, indeed—as serious as the money matters themselves."

"More serious. As true as I sit here, more serious!"

The light disappeared again and the talk went on.

"I showed you the letter to my wife that Anne Catherick hid in the sand," Sir Percival continued. "There's no boasting in that letter, Fosco—she does know the Secret."

"Say as little as possible, Percival, in my presence, of the Secret. Does she know it from you?"

"No, from her mother."

"Two women in possession of your private mind—bad, bad, bad, my friend! One question here, before we go any farther. The motive of your shutting up the daughter in the asylum is now plain enough to me, but the manner of her escape is not quite so clear. Do you suspect the people in charge of her of closing their eyes purposely, at the instance of some enemy who could afford to make it worth their while?"

"No, she was the best-behaved patient they had—and, like fools, they trusted her. She's just mad enough to be shut up, and just sane enough to ruin me when she's at large—if you understand that?"

"I do understand it. Now, Percival, come at once to the point, and then I shall know what to do. Where is the danger of your position at the present moment?"

"Anne Catherick is in this neighbourhood, and in communication with Lady Glyde—there's the danger, plain enough. Who can read the letter she hid in the sand, and not see that my wife is in possession of the Secret, deny it as she may?"

"One moment, Percival. If Lady Glyde does know the Secret, she must know also that it is a compromising secret for you. As your wife, surely it is her interest to keep it?"

"Is it? I'm coming to that. It might be her interest if she cared two straws about me. But I happen to be an encumbrance in the way of another man. She was in love with him before she married me—she's in love with him now—an infernal vagabond of a drawing-master, named Hartright."

"My dear friend! what is there extraordinary in that? They are all in love with some other man. Who gets the first of a woman's heart? In all my experience I have never yet met with the man who was Number One. Number Two, sometimes. Number Three, Four, Five, often. Number One, never! He exists, of course—but I have not met with him."

"Wait! I haven't done yet. Who do you think helped Anne Catherick to get the start, when the people from the mad-house were after her? Hartright. Who do you think saw her again in Cumberland? Hartright. Both times he spoke to her alone. Stop! don't interrupt me. The scoundrel's as sweet on my wife as she is on him. He knows the Secret, and she knows the Secret. Once let them both get together again, and it's her interest and his interest to turn their information against me."

"Gently, Percival—gently! Are you insensible to the virtue of Lady Glyde?"

"That for the virtue of Lady Glyde! I believe in nothing about her but her money. Don't you see how the case stands? She might be harmless enough by herself; but if she and that vagabond Hartright——"

"Yes, yes, I see. Where is Mr. Hartright?"

"Out of the country. If he means to keep a whole skin on his bones, I recommend him not to come back in a hurry."

"Are you sure he is out of the country?"

"Certain. I had him watched from the time he left Cumberland to the time he sailed. Oh, I've been careful, I can tell you! Anne Catherick lived with some people at a farmhouse near Limmeridge. I went there myself, after she had given me the slip, and made sure that they knew nothing. I gave her mother a form of letter to write to Miss Halcombe, exonerating me from any bad motive in putting her under restraint. I've spent, I'm afraid to say how much, in trying to trace her, and in spite of it all, she turns up here and escapes me on my own property! How do I know who else may see her, who else may speak to her? That prying scoundrel, Hartright, may come back without my knowing it, and may make use of her to-morrow——"

"Not he, Percival! While I am on the spot, and while that woman is in the neighbourhood, I will answer for our laying hands on her before Mr. Hartright—even if he does come back. I see! yes, yes, I see! The finding of Anne Catherick is the first necessity—make your mind easy about the rest. Your wife is here, under your thumb—Miss Halcombe is inseparable from her, and is, therefore, under your thumb also—and Mr. Hartright is out of the country. This invisible Anne of yours is all we have to think of for the present. You have made your inquiries?"

"Yes. I have been to her mother, I have ransacked the village—and all to no purpose."

"Is her mother to be depended on?"

"Yes."

"She has told your secret once."

"She won't tell it again."

"Why not? Are her own interests concerned in keeping it, as well as yours?"

"Yes—deeply concerned."

"I am glad to hear it, Percival, for your sake. Don't be discouraged, my friend. Our money matters, as I told you, leave me plenty of time to turn round in, and I may search for Anne Catherick to-morrow to better purpose than you. One last question before we go to bed."

"What is it?"

"It is this. When I went to the boat-house to tell Lady Glyde that the little difficulty of her signature was put off, accident took me there in time to see a strange woman parting in a very suspicious manner from your wife. But accident did not bring me near enough to see this same woman's face plainly. I must know how to recognise our invisible Anne. What is she like?"

"Like? Come! I'll tell you in two words. She's a sickly likeness of my wife."

The chair creaked, and the pillar shook once more. The Count was on his feet again—this time in astonishment.

"What!!!" he exclaimed eagerly.

"Fancy my wife, after a bad illness, with a touch of something wrong in her head—and there is Anne Catherick for you," answered Sir Percival.

"Are they related to each other?"

"Not a bit of it."

"And yet so like?"

"Yes, so like. What are you laughing about?"

There was no answer, and no sound of any kind. The Count was laughing in his smooth silent internal way.

"What are you laughing about?" reiterated Sir Percival.

"Perhaps at my own fancies, my good friend. Allow me my Italian humour—do I not come of the illustrious nation which invented the exhibition of Punch? Well, well, well, I shall know Anne Catherick when I see her—and so enough for to-night. Make your mind easy, Percival. Sleep, my son, the sleep of the just, and see what I will do for you when daylight comes to help us both. I have my projects and my plans here in my big head. You shall pay those bills and find Anne Catherick—my sacred word of honour on it, but you shall! Am I a friend to be treasured in the best corner of your heart, or am I not? Am I worth those loans of money which you so delicately reminded me of a little while since? Whatever you do, never wound me in my sentiments any more. Recognise them, Percival! imitate them, Percival! I forgive you again—I shake hands again. Good-night!"

Not another word was spoken. I heard the Count close the library door. I heard Sir Percival barring up the window-shutters. It had been raining, raining all the time. I was cramped by my position and chilled to the bones. When I first tried to move, the effort was so painful to me that I was obliged to desist. I tried a second time, and succeeded in rising to my knees on the wet roof.

As I crept to the wall, and raised myself against it, I looked back, and saw the window of the Count's dressing-room gleam into light. My sinking courage flickered up in me again, and kept my eyes fixed on his window, as I stole my way back, step by step, past the wall of the house.

The clock struck the quarter after one, when I laid my hands on the window-sill of my own room. I had seen nothing and heard nothing which could lead me to suppose that my retreat had been discovered.

X

June 20th. — Eight o'clock. The sun is shining in a clear sky. I have not been near my bed — I have not once closed my weary wakeful eyes. From the same window at which I looked out into the darkness of last night, I look out now at the bright stillness of the morning.

I count the hours that have passed since I escaped to the shelter of this room by my own sensations — and those hours seem like weeks.

How short a time, and yet how long to me — since I sank down in the darkness, here, on the floor — drenched to the skin, cramped in every limb, cold to the bones, a useless, helpless, panic-stricken creature.

I hardly know when I roused myself. I hardly know when I groped my way back to the bedroom, and lighted the candle, and searched (with a strange ignorance, at first, of where to look for them) for dry clothes to warm me. The doing of these things is in my mind, but not the time when they were done.

Can I even remember when the chilled, cramped feeling left me, and the throbbing heat came in its place?

Surely it was before the sun rose? Yes, I heard the clock strike three. I remember the time by the sudden brightness and clearness, the feverish strain and excitement of all my faculties which came with it. I remember my resolution to control myself, to wait patiently hour after hour, till the chance offered of removing Laura from this horrible place, without the danger of immediate discovery and pursuit. I remember the persuasion settling itself in my mind that the words those two men had said to each other would furnish us, not only with our justification for leaving the house, but with our weapons of defence against them as well. I recall the impulse that awakened in me to preserve those words in writing, exactly as they were spoken, while the time was my own, and while my memory vividly retained them. All this I remember plainly: there is no confusion in my head yet. The coming in here from the bedroom, with my pen and ink and paper, before sunrise — the sitting down at the widely-opened window to get all the air I could to cool me — the ceaseless writing, faster and faster, hotter and hotter, driving on more and more wakefully, all through the dreadful interval before the house was astir again — how clearly I recall it, from the beginning by candle-light, to the end on the page before this, in the sunshine of the new day!

Why do I sit here still? Why do I weary my hot eyes and my burning head by writing more? Why not lie down and rest myself, and try to quench the fever that consumes me, in sleep?

I dare not attempt it. A fear beyond all other fears has got possession of me. I am afraid of this heat that parches my skin. I am afraid of the creeping and throbbing that I feel in my head. If I lie down now, how do I know that I may have the sense and the strength to rise again?

Oh, the rain, the rain — the cruel rain that chilled me last night!

Nine o'clock. Was it nine struck, or eight? Nine, surely? I am shivering again — shivering, from head to foot, in the summer air. Have I been sitting here asleep? I don't know what I have been doing.

Oh, my God! am I going to be ill?

Ill, at such a time as this!

My head — I am sadly afraid of my head. I can write, but the lines all run together. I see the words. Laura — I can write Laura, and see I write it. Eight or nine — which was it?

So cold, so cold — oh, that rain last night! — and the strokes of the clock, the strokes I can't count, keep striking in my head — —

Note [At this place the entry in the Diary ceases to be legible. The two or three lines which follow contain fragments of words only, mingled with blots and scratches of the pen. The last marks on the paper bear some resemblance to the first two letters (L and A) of the name of Lady Glyde.

On the next page of the Diary, another entry appears. It is in a man's handwriting, large, bold, and firmly regular, and the date is "June the 21st." It contains these lines —]

POSTSCRIPT BY A SINCERE FRIEND

The illness of our excellent Miss Halcombe has afforded me

the opportunity of enjoying an unexpected intellectual pleasure.

I refer to the perusal (which I have just completed) of this interesting Diary.

There are many hundred pages here. I can lay my hand on my heart, and declare that every page has charmed, refreshed, delighted me.

To a man of my sentiments it is unspeakably gratifying to be able to say this.

Admirable woman!

I allude to Miss Halcombe.

Stupendous effort!

I refer to the Diary.

Yes! these pages are amazing. The tact which I find here, the discretion, the rare courage, the wonderful power of memory, the accurate observation of character, the easy grace of style, the charming outbursts of womanly feeling, have all inexpressibly increased my admiration of this sublime creature, of this magnificent Marian. The presentation of my own character is masterly in the extreme. I certify, with my whole heart, to the fidelity of the portrait. I feel how vivid an impression I must have produced to have been painted in such strong, such rich, such massive colours as these. I lament afresh the cruel necessity which sets our interests at variance, and opposes us to each other. Under happier circumstances how worthy I should have been of Miss Halcombe — how worthy Miss Halcombe would have been of ME.

The sentiments which animate my heart assure me that the lines I have just written express a Profound Truth.

Those sentiments exalt me above all merely personal considerations. I bear witness, in the most disinterested manner, to the excellence of the stratagem by which this unparalleled woman surprised the private interview between Percival and myself — also to the marvellous accuracy of her report of the whole conversation from its beginning to its end.

Those sentiments have induced me to offer to the unimpressionable doctor who attends on her my vast knowledge of chemistry, and my luminous experience of the more subtle resources which medical and magnetic science have placed at the disposal of mankind. He has hitherto declined to avail himself of my assistance. Miserable man!

Finally, those sentiments dictate the lines—grateful, sympathetic, paternal lines—which appear in this place. I close the book. My strict sense of propriety restores it (by the hands of my wife) to its place on the writer's table. Events are hurrying me away. Circumstances are guiding me to serious issues. Vast perspectives of success unroll themselves before my eyes. I accomplish my destiny with a calmness which is terrible to myself. Nothing but the homage of my admiration is my own. I deposit it with respectful tenderness at the feet of Miss Halcombe.

I breathe my wishes for her recovery.

I condole with her on the inevitable failure of every plan that she has formed for her sister's benefit. At the same time, I entreat her to believe that the information which I have derived from her Diary will in no respect help me to contribute to that failure. It simply confirms the plan of conduct which I had previously arranged. I have to thank these pages for awakening the finest sensibilities in my nature—nothing more.

To a person of similar sensibility this simple assertion will explain and excuse everything.

Miss Halcombe is a person of similar sensibility.

In that persuasion I sign myself,

Fosco.

The Woman in White

THE STORY CONTINUED BY FREDERICK FAIRLIE, ESQ., OF LIMMERIDGE HOUSE[2]

[2] The manner in which Mr. Fairlie's Narrative, and other Narratives that are shortly to follow it, were originally obtained, forms the subject of an explanation which will appear at a later period.

It is the grand misfortune of my life that nobody will let me alone.

Why — I ask everybody — why worry me? Nobody answers that question, and nobody lets me alone. Relatives, friends, and strangers all combine to annoy me. What have I done? I ask myself, I ask my servant, Louis, fifty times a day — what have I done? Neither of us can tell. Most extraordinary!

The last annoyance that has assailed me is the annoyance of being called upon to write this Narrative. Is a man in my state of nervous wretchedness capable of writing narratives? When I put this extremely reasonable objection, I am told that certain very serious events relating to my niece have happened within my experience, and that I am the fit person to describe them on that account. I am threatened if I fail to exert myself in the manner required, with consequences which I cannot so much as think of without perfect prostration. There is really no need to threaten me. Shattered by my miserable health and my family troubles, I am incapable of resistance. If you insist, you take your unjust advantage of me, and I give way immediately. I will endeavour to remember what I can (under protest), and to write what I can (also under protest), and what I can't remember and can't write, Louis must remember and write for me. He is an ass, and I am an invalid, and we are likely to make all sorts of mistakes between us. How humiliating!

I am told to remember dates. Good heavens! I never did such a thing in my life — how am I to begin now?

I have asked Louis. He is not quite such an ass as I have hitherto supposed. He remembers the date of the event, within a week or two — and I remember the name of the person. The date was towards the end of June, or the beginning of July, and the name (in my opinion a remarkably vulgar one) was Fanny.

At the end of June, or the beginning of July, then, I was

reclining in my customary state, surrounded by the various objects of Art which I have collected about me to improve the taste of the barbarous people in my neighbourhood. That is to say, I had the photographs of my pictures, and prints, and coins, and so forth, all about me, which I intend, one of these days, to present (the photographs, I mean, if the clumsy English language will let me mean anything) to present to the institution at Carlisle (horrid place!), with a view to improving the tastes of the members (Goths and Vandals to a man). It might be supposed that a gentleman who was in course of conferring a great national benefit on his countrymen was the last gentleman in the world to be unfeelingly worried about private difficulties and family affairs. Quite a mistake, I assure you, in my case.

However, there I was, reclining, with my art-treasures about me, and wanting a quiet morning. Because I wanted a quiet morning, of course Louis came in. It was perfectly natural that I should inquire what the deuce he meant by making his appearance when I had not rung my bell. I seldom swear—it is such an ungentlemanlike habit—but when Louis answered by a grin, I think it was also perfectly natural that I should damn him for grinning. At any rate, I did.

This rigorous mode of treatment, I have observed, invariably brings persons in the lower class of life to their senses. It brought Louis to his senses. He was so obliging as to leave off grinning, and inform me that a Young Person was outside wanting to see me. He added (with the odious talkativeness of servants), that her name was Fanny.

"Who is Fanny?"

"Lady Glyde's maid, sir."

"What does Lady Glyde's maid want with me?"

"A letter, sir— —"

"Take it."

"She refuses to give it to anybody but you, sir."

"Who sends the letter?"

"Miss Halcombe, sir."

The moment I heard Miss Halcombe's name I gave up. It is a habit of mine always to give up to Miss Halcombe. I find, by experience, that it saves noise. I gave up on this occasion. Dear Marian!

"Let Lady Glyde's maid come in, Louis. Stop! Do her shoes creak?"

I was obliged to ask the question. Creaking shoes invariably upset me for the day. I was resigned to see the Young Person, but I was not resigned to let the Young Person's shoes upset me. There is a limit even to my endurance.

Louis affirmed distinctly that her shoes were to be depended upon. I waved my hand. He introduced her. Is it necessary to say that she expressed her sense of embarrassment by shutting up her mouth and breathing through her nose? To the student of female human nature in the lower orders, surely not.

Let me do the girl justice. Her shoes did not creak. But why do Young Persons in service all perspire at the hands? Why have they all got fat noses and hard cheeks? And why are their faces so sadly unfinished, especially about the corners of the eyelids? I am not strong enough to think deeply myself on any subject, but I appeal to professional men, who are. Why have we no variety in our breed of Young Persons?

"You have a letter for me, from Miss Halcombe? Put it down on the table, please, and don't upset anything. How is Miss Halcombe?"

"Very well, thank you, sir."

"And Lady Glyde?"

I received no answer. The Young Person's face became more unfinished than ever, and I think she began to cry. I certainly saw something moist about her eyes. Tears or perspiration? Louis (whom I have just consulted) is inclined to think, tears. He is in her class of life, and he ought to know best. Let us say, tears.

Except when the refining process of Art judiciously removes from them all resemblance to Nature, I distinctly object to tears. Tears are scientifically described as a Secretion. I can understand that a secretion may be healthy or unhealthy, but I cannot see the interest of a secretion from a sentimental point of view. Perhaps my own secretions being all wrong together, I am a little prejudiced on the subject. No matter. I behaved, on this occasion, with all possible propriety and feeling. I closed my eyes and said to Louis—

"Endeavour to ascertain what she means."

Louis endeavoured, and the Young Person endeavoured. They succeeded in confusing each other to such an extent that I am bound in common gratitude to say, they really amused me. I think I shall send for them again when I am in low spirits. I have just mentioned this idea to Louis. Strange to say, it seems to make him uncomfortable. Poor devil!

Surely I am not expected to repeat my niece's maid's explanation of her tears, interpreted in the English of my Swiss valet? The thing is manifestly impossible. I can give my own impressions and feelings perhaps. Will that do as well? Please say, Yes.

My idea is that she began by telling me (through Louis) that her master had dismissed her from her mistress's service. (Observe, throughout, the strange irrelevancy of the Young Person. Was it my fault that she had lost her place?) On her dismissal, she had gone to the inn to sleep. (I don't keep the inn—why mention it to me?) Between six o'clock and seven Miss Halcombe had come to say good-bye, and had given her two letters, one for me, and one for a gentleman in London. (I am not a gentleman in London—hang the gentleman in London!) She had carefully put the two letters into her bosom (what have I to do with her bosom?); she had been very unhappy, when Miss Halcombe had gone away again; she had not had the heart to put bit or drop between her lips till it was near bedtime, and then, when it was close on nine o'clock, she had thought she should like a cup of tea. (Am I responsible for any of these vulgar fluctuations, which begin with unhappiness and end with tea?) Just as she was warming the pot (I give the words on the authority of Louis, who says he knows what they mean, and wishes to explain, but I snub him on principle)—just as she was warming the pot the door opened, and she was struck of a heap (her own words again, and perfectly unintelligible this time to Louis, as well as to myself) by the appearance in the inn parlour of her ladyship the Countess. I give my niece's maid's description of my sister's title with a sense of the highest relish. My poor dear sister is a tiresome woman who married a foreigner. To resume: the door opened, her ladyship the Countess appeared in the parlour, and the Young Person was struck of a heap. Most remarkable!

The Woman in White

I must really rest a little before I can get on any farther. When I have reclined for a few minutes, with my eyes closed, and when Louis has refreshed my poor aching temples with a little eau-de-Cologne, I may be able to proceed.

Her ladyship the Countess — —

No. I am able to proceed, but not to sit up. I will recline and dictate. Louis has a horrid accent, but he knows the language, and can write. How very convenient!

Her ladyship, the Countess, explained her unexpected appearance at the inn by telling Fanny that she had come to bring one or two little messages which Miss Halcombe in her hurry had forgotten. The Young Person thereupon waited anxiously to hear what the messages were, but the Countess seemed disinclined to mention them (so like my sister's tiresome way!) until Fanny had had her tea. Her ladyship was surprisingly kind and thoughtful about it (extremely unlike my sister), and said, "I am sure, my poor girl, you must want your tea. We can let the messages wait till afterwards. Come, come, if nothing else will put you at your ease, I'll make the tea and have a cup with you." I think those were the words, as reported excitably, in my presence, by the Young Person. At any rate, the Countess insisted on making the tea, and carried her ridiculous ostentation of humility so far as to take one cup herself, and to insist on the girl's taking the other. The girl drank the tea, and according to her own account, solemnised the extraordinary occasion five minutes afterwards by fainting dead away for the first time in her life. Here again I use her own words. Louis thinks they were accompanied by an increased secretion of tears. I can't say myself. The effort of listening being quite as much as I could manage, my eyes were closed.

Where did I leave off? Ah, yes — she fainted after drinking a cup of tea with the Countess — a proceeding which might have interested me if I had been her medical man, but being nothing of the sort I felt bored by hearing of it, nothing more. When she came to herself in half an hour's time she was on the sofa, and nobody was with her but the landlady. The Countess, finding it too late to remain any longer at the inn, had gone away as soon as the girl showed signs of recovering, and the landlady had been good enough to help her upstairs to bed.

Left by herself, she had felt in her bosom (I regret the necessity of referring to this part of the subject a second time), and had found the two letters there quite safe, but strangely crumpled. She had been giddy in the night, but had got up well enough to travel in the morning. She had put the letter addressed to that obtrusive stranger, the gentleman in London into the post, and had now delivered the other letter into my hands as she was told. This was the plain truth, and though she could not blame herself for any intentional neglect, she was sadly troubled in her mind, and sadly in want of a word of advice. At this point Louis thinks the secretions appeared again. Perhaps they did, but it is of infinitely greater importance to mention that at this point also I lost my patience, opened my eyes, and interfered.

"What is the purport of all this?" I inquired.

My niece's irrelevant maid stared, and stood speechless.

"Endeavour to explain," I said to my servant. "Translate me, Louis."

Louis endeavoured and translated. In other words, he descended immediately into a bottomless pit of confusion, and the Young Person followed him down. I really don't know when I have been so amused. I left them at the bottom of the pit as long as they diverted me. When they ceased to divert me, I exerted my intelligence, and pulled them up again.

It is unnecessary to say that my interference enabled me, in due course of time, to ascertain the purport of the Young Person's remarks.

I discovered that she was uneasy in her mind, because the train of events that she had just described to me had prevented her from receiving those supplementary messages which Miss Halcombe had intrusted to the Countess to deliver. She was afraid the messages might have been of great importance to her mistress's interests. Her dread of Sir Percival had deterred her from going to Blackwater Park late at night to inquire about them, and Miss Halcombe's own directions to her, on no account to miss the train in the morning, had prevented her from waiting at the inn the next day. She was most anxious that the misfortune of her fainting-fit should not lead to the second misfortune of making her mistress think her neglectful, and she would humbly beg to ask me whether I would advise her to write her explanations and excuses to Miss Halcombe, requesting to receive the messages by letter, if it was not too late. I make no apologies for this extremely prosy paragraph. I have been ordered to write it. There are people, unaccountable as it may appear, who actually take more interest in what my niece's maid said to me on this occasion than in what I said to my niece's maid. Amusing perversity!

"I should feel very much obliged to you, sir, if you would kindly tell me what I had better do," remarked the Young Person.

"Let things stop as they are," I said, adapting my language to my listener. "I invariably let things stop as they are. Yes. Is that all?"

"If you think it would be a liberty in me, sir, to write, of course I wouldn't venture to do so. But I am so very anxious to do all I can to serve my mistress faithfully — —"

People in the lower class of life never know when or how to go out of a room. They invariably require to be helped out by their betters. I thought it high time to help the Young Person out. I did it with two judicious words —

"Good-morning."

Something outside or inside this singular girl suddenly creaked. Louis, who was looking at her (which I was not), says she creaked when she curtseyed. Curious. Was it her shoes, her stays, or her bones? Louis thinks it was her stays. Most extraordinary!

As soon as I was left by myself I had a little nap — I really wanted it. When I awoke again I noticed dear Marian's letter. If I had had the least idea of what it contained I should certainly not have attempted to open it. Being, unfortunately for myself, quite innocent of all suspicion, I read the letter. It immediately upset me for the day.

I am, by nature, one of the most easy-tempered creatures that ever lived — I make allowances for everybody, and I take offence at nothing. But as I have before remarked, there are limits to my endurance. I laid down Marian's letter, and felt myself — justly felt myself — an injured man.

I am about to make a remark. It is, of course, applicable to the very serious matter now under notice, or I should not allow it to appear in this place.

Nothing, in my opinion, sets the odious selfishness of mankind in such a repulsively vivid light as the treatment, in all classes of society, which the Single people receive at the hands of the Married people. When you have once shown yourself too considerate and self-denying to add a family of your own to an already overcrowded population, you are vindictively marked out by your married friends, who have no similar consideration and no similar self-denial, as the recipient of half their conjugal troubles, and the born friend of all their children. Husbands and wives talk of the cares of matrimony, and bachelors and spinsters bear them. Take my own case. I considerately remain single, and my poor dear brother Philip inconsiderately marries. What does he do when he dies? He leaves his daughter to me. She is a sweet girl — she is also a dreadful responsibility. Why lay her on my shoulders? Because I am bound, in the harmless character of a single man, to relieve my married connections of all their own troubles. I do my best with my brother's responsibility — I marry my niece, with infinite fuss and difficulty, to the man her father wanted her to marry. She and her husband disagree, and unpleasant consequences follow. What does she do with those consequences? She transfers them to me. Why transfer them to me? Because I am bound, in the harmless character of a single man, to relieve my married connections of all their own troubles. Poor single people! Poor human nature!

It is quite unnecessary to say that Marian's letter threatened me. Everybody threatens me. All sorts of horrors were to fall on my devoted head if I hesitated to turn Limmeridge House into an asylum for my niece and her misfortunes. I did hesitate, nevertheless.

I have mentioned that my usual course, hitherto, had been to submit to dear Marian, and save noise. But on this occasion, the consequences involved in her extremely inconsiderate proposal were of a nature to make me pause. If I opened Limmeridge House as an asylum to Lady Glyde, what security had I against Sir Percival Glyde's following her here in a state of violent resentment against me for harbouring his wife? I saw such a perfect labyrinth of troubles involved in this proceeding that I determined to feel my ground, as it were. I wrote, therefore, to dear Marian to beg (as she had no husband to lay claim to her) that she would come here by herself, first, and talk the matter over with me. If she could answer my objections to my own perfect satisfaction, then I assured her that I would receive our sweet Laura with the greatest pleasure, but not otherwise.

I felt, of course, at the time, that this temporising on my part would probably end in bringing Marian here in a state of virtuous indignation, banging doors. But then, the other course of proceeding might end in bringing Sir Percival here in a state of virtuous indignation, banging doors also, and of the two indignations and bangings I preferred Marian's, because I was used to her. Accordingly I despatched the letter by return of post. It gained me time, at all events — and, oh dear me! what a point that was to begin with.

When I am totally prostrated (did I mention that I was totally prostrated by Marian's letter?) it always takes me three days to get up again. I was very unreasonable — I expected three days of quiet. Of course I didn't get them.

The third day's post brought me a most impertinent letter from a person with whom I was totally unacquainted. He described himself as the acting partner of our man of business — our dear, pig-headed old Gilmore — and he informed me that he had lately received, by the post, a letter addressed to him in Miss Halcombe's handwriting. On opening the envelope, he had discovered, to his astonishment, that it contained nothing but a blank sheet of note-paper. This circumstance appeared to him so suspicious (as suggesting to his restless legal mind that the letter had been tampered with) that he had at once written to Miss Halcombe, and had received no answer by return of post. In this difficulty, instead of acting like a sensible man and letting things take their proper course, his next absurd proceeding, on his own showing, was to pester me by writing to inquire if I knew anything about it. What the deuce should I know about it? Why alarm me as well as himself? I wrote back to that effect. It was one of my keenest letters. I have produced nothing with a sharper epistolary edge to it since I tendered his dismissal in writing to that extremely troublesome person, Mr. Walter Hartright.

My letter produced its effect. I heard nothing more from the lawyer.

This perhaps was not altogether surprising. But it was certainly a remarkable circumstance that no second letter reached me from Marian, and that no warning signs appeared of her arrival. Her unexpected absence did me amazing good. It was so very soothing and pleasant to infer (as I did of course) that my married connections had made it up again. Five days of undisturbed tranquillity, of delicious single blessedness, quite restored me. On the sixth day I felt strong enough to send for my photographer, and to set him at work again on the presentation copies of my art-treasures, with a view, as I have already mentioned, to the improvement of taste in this barbarous neighbourhood. I had just dismissed him to his workshop, and had just begun coquetting with my coins, when Louis suddenly made his appearance with a card in his hand.

"Another Young Person?" I said. "I won't see her. In my state of health Young Persons disagree with me. Not at home."

"It is a gentleman this time, sir."

A gentleman of course made a difference. I looked at the card.

Gracious Heaven! my tiresome sister's foreign husband, Count Fosco.

Is it necessary to say what my first impression was when I looked at my visitor's card? Surely not! My sister having married a foreigner, there was but one impression that any man in his senses could possibly feel. Of course the Count had come to borrow money of me.

"Louis," I said, "do you think he would go away if you gave him five shillings?"

Louis looked quite shocked. He surprised me inexpressibly by declaring that my sister's foreign husband was dressed superbly, and looked the picture of prosperity. Under these circumstances my first impression altered to a certain extent. I now took it for granted that the Count had matrimonial difficulties of his own to contend with, and that he had come, like the rest of the family, to cast them all on my shoulders.

"Did he mention his business?" I asked.

"Count Fosco said he had come here, sir, because Miss Halcombe was unable to leave Blackwater Park."

Fresh troubles, apparently. Not exactly his own, as I had supposed, but dear Marian's. Troubles, anyway. Oh dear!

"Show him in," I said resignedly.

The Count's first appearance really startled me. He was such an alarmingly large person that I quite trembled. I felt certain that he would shake the floor and knock down my art-treasures.

The Woman in White

He did neither the one nor the other. He was refreshingly dressed in summer costume—his manner was delightfully self-possessed and quiet—he had a charming smile. My first impression of him was highly favourable. It is not creditable to my penetration—as the sequel will show—to acknowledge this, but I am a naturally candid man, and I do acknowledge it notwithstanding.

"Allow me to present myself, Mr. Fairlie," he said. "I come from Blackwater Park, and I have the honour and the happiness of being Madame Fosco's husband. Let me take my first and last advantage of that circumstance by entreating you not to make a stranger of me. I beg you will not disturb yourself—I beg you will not move."

"You are very good," I replied. "I wish I was strong enough to get up. Charmed to see you at Limmeridge. Please take a chair."

"I am afraid you are suffering to-day," said the Count.

"As usual," I said. "I am nothing but a bundle of nerves dressed up to look like a man."

"I have studied many subjects in my time," remarked this sympathetic person. "Among others the inexhaustible subject of nerves. May I make a suggestion, at once the simplest and the most profound? Will you let me alter the light in your room?"

"Certainly—if you will be so very kind as not to let any of it in on me."

He walked to the window. Such a contrast to dear Marian! so extremely considerate in all his movements!

"Light," he said, in that delightfully confidential tone which is so soothing to an invalid, "is the first essential. Light stimulates, nourishes, preserves. You can no more do without it, Mr. Fairlie, than if you were a flower. Observe. Here, where you sit, I close the shutters to compose you. There, where you do not sit, I draw up the blind and let in the invigorating sun. Admit the light into your room if you cannot bear it on yourself. Light, sir, is the grand decree of Providence. You accept Providence with your own restrictions. Accept light on the same terms."

I thought this very convincing and attentive. He had taken me in up to that point about the light, he had certainly taken me in.

"You see me confused," he said, returning to his place—"on my word of honour, Mr. Fairlie, you see me confused in your presence."

"Shocked to hear it, I am sure. May I inquire why?"

"Sir, can I enter this room (where you sit a sufferer), and see you surrounded by these admirable objects of Art, without discovering that you are a man whose feelings are acutely impressionable, whose sympathies are perpetually alive? Tell me, can I do this?"

If I had been strong enough to sit up in my chair I should, of course, have bowed. Not being strong enough, I smiled my acknowledgments instead. It did just as well, we both understood one another.

"Pray follow my train of thought," continued the Count. "I sit here, a man of refined sympathies myself, in the presence of another man of refined sympathies also. I am conscious of a terrible necessity for lacerating those sympathies by referring to domestic events of a very melancholy kind. What is the inevitable consequence? I have done myself the honour of pointing it out to you already. I sit confused."

Was it at this point that I began to suspect he was going to bore me? I rather think it was.

"Is it absolutely necessary to refer to these unpleasant matters?" I inquired. "In our homely English phrase, Count Fosco, won't they keep?"

The Count, with the most alarming solemnity, sighed and shook his head.

"Must I really hear them?"

He shrugged his shoulders (it was the first foreign thing he had done since he had been in the room), and looked at me in an unpleasantly penetrating manner. My instincts told me that I had better close my eyes. I obeyed my instincts.

"Please break it gently," I pleaded. "Anybody dead?"

"Dead!" cried the Count, with unnecessary foreign fierceness. "Mr. Fairlie, your national composure terrifies me. In the name of Heaven, what have I said or done to make you think me the messenger of death?"

"Pray accept my apologies," I answered. "You have said and done nothing. I make it a rule in these distressing cases always to anticipate the worst. It breaks the blow by meeting it half-way, and so on. Inexpressibly relieved, I am sure, to hear that nobody is dead. Anybody ill?"

I opened my eyes and looked at him. Was he very yellow when he came in, or had he turned very yellow in the last minute or two? I really can't say, and I can't ask Louis, because he was not in the room at the time.

"Anybody ill?" I repeated, observing that my national composure still appeared to affect him.

"That is part of my bad news, Mr. Fairlie. Yes. Somebody is ill."

"Grieved, I am sure. Which of them is it?"

"To my profound sorrow, Miss Halcombe. Perhaps you were in some degree prepared to hear this? Perhaps when you found that Miss Halcombe did not come here by herself, as you proposed, and did not write a second time, your affectionate anxiety may have made you fear that she was ill?"

I have no doubt my affectionate anxiety had led to that melancholy apprehension at some time or other, but at the moment my wretched memory entirely failed to remind me of the circumstance. However, I said yes, in justice to myself. I was much shocked. It was so very uncharacteristic of such a robust person as dear Marian to be ill, that I could only suppose she had met with an accident. A horse, or a false step on the stairs, or something of that sort.

"Is it serious?" I asked.

"Serious—beyond a doubt," he replied. "Dangerous—I hope and trust not. Miss Halcombe unhappily exposed herself to be wetted through by a heavy rain. The cold that followed was of an aggravated kind, and it has now brought with it the worst consequence—fever."

When I heard the word fever, and when I remembered at the same moment that the unscrupulous person who was now addressing me had just come from Blackwater Park, I thought I should have fainted on the spot.

"Good God!" I said. "Is it infectious?"

"Not at present," he answered, with detestable composure. "It may turn to infection—but no such deplorable complication had taken place when I left Blackwater Park. I have felt the deepest interest in the case, Mr. Fairlie—I have endeavoured to assist the regular medical attendant in watching it—accept my personal assurances of the uninfectious nature of the fever when I last saw it."

Accept his assurances! I never was farther from accepting anything in my life. I would not have believed him on his oath. He was too yellow to be believed. He looked like a walking-West-Indian-epidemic. He was big enough to carry typhus by the ton, and to dye the very carpet he walked on with scarlet fever. In certain emergencies my mind is remarkably soon made up. I instantly determined to get rid of him.

"You will kindly excuse an invalid," I said—"but long conferences of any kind invariably upset me. May I beg to know exactly what the object is to which I am indebted for the honour of your visit?"

I fervently hoped that this remarkably broad hint would throw him off his balance—confuse him—reduce him to polite apologies—in short, get him out of the room. On the contrary, it only settled him in his chair. He became additionally solemn, and dignified, and confidential. He held up two of his horrid fingers and gave me another of his unpleasantly penetrating looks. What was I to do? I was not strong enough to quarrel with him. Conceive my situation, if you please. Is language adequate to describe it? I think not.

"The objects of my visit," he went on, quite irrepressibly, "are numbered on my fingers. They are two. First, I come to bear my testimony, with profound sorrow, to the lamentable disagreements between Sir Percival and Lady Glyde. I am Sir Percival's oldest friend—I am related to Lady Glyde by marriage—I am an eye-witness of all that has happened at Blackwater Park. In those three capacities I speak with authority, with confidence, with honourable regret. Sir, I inform you, as the head of Lady Glyde's family, that Miss Halcombe has exaggerated nothing in the letter which she wrote to your address. I affirm that the remedy which that admirable lady has proposed is the only remedy that will spare you the horrors of public scandal. A temporary separation between husband and wife is the one peaceable solution of this difficulty. Part them for the present, and when all causes of irritation are removed, I, who have now the honour of addressing you—I will undertake to bring Sir Percival to reason. Lady Glyde is innocent, Lady

Glyde is injured, but—follow my thought here!—she is, on that very account (I say it with shame), the cause of irritation while she remains under her husband's roof. No other house can receive her with propriety but yours. I invite you to open it."

Cool. Here was a matrimonial hailstorm pouring in the South of England, and I was invited, by a man with fever in every fold of his coat, to come out from the North of England and take my share of the pelting. I tried to put the point forcibly, just as I have put it here. The Count deliberately lowered one of his horrid fingers, kept the other up, and went on—rode over me, as it were, without even the common coachmanlike attention of crying "Hi!" before he knocked me down.

"Follow my thought once more, if you please," he resumed. "My first object you have heard. My second object in coming to this house is to do what Miss Halcombe's illness has prevented her from doing for herself. My large experience is consulted on all difficult matters at Blackwater Park, and my friendly advice was requested on the interesting subject of your letter to Miss Halcombe. I understood at once—for my sympathies are your sympathies—why you wished to see her here before you pledged yourself to inviting Lady Glyde. You are most right, sir, in hesitating to receive the wife until you are quite certain that the husband will not exert his authority to reclaim her. I agree to that. I also agree that such delicate explanations as this difficulty involves are not explanations which can be properly disposed of by writing only. My presence here (to my own great inconvenience) is the proof that I speak sincerely. As for the explanations themselves, I—Fosco—I, who know Sir Percival much better than Miss Halcombe knows him, affirm to you, on my honour and my word, that he will not come near this house, or attempt to communicate with this house, while his wife is living in it. His affairs are embarrassed. Offer him his freedom by means of the absence of Lady Glyde. I promise you he will take his freedom, and go back to the Continent at the earliest moment when he can get away. Is this clear to you as crystal? Yes, it is. Have you questions to address to me? Be it so, I am here to answer. Ask, Mr. Fairlie—oblige me by asking to your heart's content."

He had said so much already in spite of me, and he looked so dreadfully capable of saying a great deal more also in spite of me, that I declined his amiable invitation in pure self-defence.

"Many thanks," I replied. "I am sinking fast. In my state of health I must take things for granted. Allow me to do so on this occasion. We quite understand each other. Yes. Much obliged, I am sure, for your kind interference. If I ever get better, and ever have a second opportunity of improving our acquaintance—"

He got up. I thought he was going. No. More talk, more time for the development of infectious influences—in my room, too—remember that, in my room!

"One moment yet," he said, "one moment before I take my leave. I ask permission at parting to impress on you an urgent necessity. It is this, sir. You must not think of waiting till Miss Halcombe recovers before you receive Lady Glyde. Miss Halcombe has the attendance of the doctor, of the housekeeper at Blackwater Park, and of an experienced nurse as well—three persons for whose capacity and devotion I answer with my life. I tell you that. I tell you, also, that the anxiety and alarm of her sister's illness has already affected the health and spirits of Lady Glyde, and has made her totally unfit to be of use in the sick-room. Her position with her husband grows more and more deplorable and dangerous every day. If you leave her any longer at Blackwater Park, you do nothing whatever to hasten her sister's recovery, and at the same time, you risk the public scandal, which you and I, and all of us, are bound in the sacred interests of the family to avoid. With all my soul, I advise you to remove the serious responsibility of delay from your own shoulders by writing to Lady Glyde to come here at once. Do your affectionate, your honourable, your inevitable duty, and whatever happens in the future, no one can lay the blame on you. I speak from my large experience—I offer my friendly advice. Is it accepted—Yes, or No?"

I looked at him—merely looked at him—with my sense of his amazing assurance, and my dawning resolution to ring for Louis and have him shown out of the room expressed in every line of my face. It is perfectly incredible, but quite true, that my face did not appear to produce the slightest impression on him. Born without nerves—evidently born without nerves.

"You hesitate?" he said. "Mr. Fairlie! I understand that hesitation. You object—see, sir, how my sympathies look straight down into your thoughts!—you object that Lady Glyde is not in health and not in spirits to take the long journey, from Hampshire to this place, by herself. Her own maid is removed from her, as you know, and of other servants fit to travel with her, from one end of England to another, there are none at Blackwater Park. You object, again, that she cannot comfortably stop and rest in London, on her way here, because she cannot comfortably go alone to a public hotel where she is a total stranger. In one breath, I grant both objections—in another breath, I remove them. Follow me, if you please, for the last time. It was my intention, when I returned to England with Sir Percival, to settle myself in the neighbourhood of London. That purpose has just been happily accomplished. I have taken, for six months, a little furnished house in the quarter called St. John's Wood. Be so obliging as to keep this fact in your mind, and observe the programme I now propose. Lady Glyde travels to London (a short journey) — I myself meet her at the station — I take her to rest and sleep at my house, which is also the house of her aunt — when she is restored I escort her to the station again — she travels to this place, and her own maid (who is now under your roof) receives her at the carriage-door. Here is comfort consulted — here are the interests of propriety consulted — here is your own duty — duty of hospitality, sympathy, protection, to an unhappy lady in need of all three — smoothed and made easy, from the beginning to the end. I cordially invite you, sir, to second my efforts in the sacred interests of the family. I seriously advise you to write, by my hands, offering the hospitality of your house (and heart), and the hospitality of my house (and heart), to that injured and unfortunate lady whose cause I plead to-day."

He waved his horrid hand at me — he struck his infectious breast — he addressed me oratorically, as if I was laid up in the House of Commons. It was high time to take a desperate course of some sort. It was also high time to send for Louis, and adopt the precaution of fumigating the room.

In this trying emergency an idea occurred to me — an inestimable idea which, so to speak, killed two intrusive birds with one stone. I determined to get rid of the Count's tiresome eloquence, and of Lady Glyde's tiresome troubles, by complying with this odious foreigner's request, and writing the letter at once. There was not the least danger of the invitation being accepted, for there was not the least chance that Laura would consent to leave Blackwater Park while Marian was lying there ill. How this charmingly convenient obstacle could have escaped the officious penetration of the Count, it was impossible to conceive — but it had escaped him. My dread that he might yet discover it, if I allowed him any more time to think, stimulated me to such an amazing degree, that I struggled into a sitting position — seized, really seized, the writing materials by my side, and produced the letter as rapidly as if I had been a common clerk in an office. "Dearest Laura, Please come, whenever you like. Break the journey by sleeping in London at your aunt's house. Grieved to hear of dear Marian's illness. Ever affectionately yours." I handed these lines, at arm's length, to the Count — I sank back in my chair — I said, "Excuse me—I am entirely prostrated—I can do no more. Will you rest and lunch downstairs? Love to all, and sympathy, and so on. Good-morning."

He made another speech—the man was absolutely inexhaustible. I closed my eyes—I endeavoured to hear as little as possible. In spite of my endeavours I was obliged to hear a great deal. My sister's endless husband congratulated himself, and congratulated me, on the result of our interview—he mentioned a great deal more about his sympathies and mine—he deplored my miserable health—he offered to write me a prescription—he impressed on me the necessity of not forgetting what he had said about the importance of light—he accepted my obliging invitation to rest and lunch—he recommended me to expect Lady Glyde in two or three days' time—he begged my permission to look forward to our next meeting, instead of paining himself and paining me, by saying farewell—he added a great deal more, which, I rejoice to think, I did not attend to at the time, and do not remember now. I heard his sympathetic voice travelling away from me by degrees—but, large as he was, I never heard him. He had the negative merit of being absolutely noiseless. I don't know when he opened the door, or when he shut it. I ventured to make use of my eyes again, after an interval of silence—and he was gone.

I rang for Louis, and retired to my bathroom. Tepid water, strengthened with aromatic vinegar, for myself, and copious fumigation for my study, were the obvious precautions to take, and of course I adopted them. I rejoice to say they proved successful. I enjoyed my customary siesta. I awoke moist and cool.

My first inquiries were for the Count. Had we really got rid of him? Yes—he had gone away by the afternoon train. Had he lunched, and if so, upon what? Entirely upon fruit-tart and cream. What a man! What a digestion!

Am I expected to say anything more? I believe not. I believe I have reached the limits assigned to me. The shocking circumstances which happened at a later period did not, I am thankful to say, happen in my presence. I do beg and entreat that nobody will be so very unfeeling as to lay any part of the blame of those circumstances on me. I did everything for the best. I am not answerable for a deplorable calamity, which it was quite impossible to foresee. I am shattered by it—I have suffered under it, as nobody else has suffered. My servant,

Louis (who is really attached to me in his unintelligent way), thinks I shall never get over it. He sees me dictating at this moment, with my handkerchief to my eyes. I wish to mention, in justice to myself, that it was not my fault, and that I am quite exhausted and heartbroken. Need I say more?

THE STORY CONTINUED
BY ELIZA MICHELSON

(Housekeeper at Blackwater Park)

I

I am asked to state plainly what I know of the progress of Miss Halcombe's illness and of the circumstances under which Lady Glyde left Blackwater Park for London.

The reason given for making this demand on me is, that my testimony is wanted in the interests of truth. As the widow of a clergyman of the Church of England (reduced by misfortune to the necessity of accepting a situation), I have been taught to place the claims of truth above all other considerations. I therefore comply with a request which I might otherwise, through reluctance to connect myself with distressing family affairs, have hesitated to grant.

I made no memorandum at the time, and I cannot therefore be sure to a day of the date, but I believe I am correct in stating that Miss Halcombe's serious illness began during the last fortnight or ten days in June. The breakfast hour was late at Blackwater Park—sometimes as late as ten, never earlier than half-past nine. On the morning to which I am now referring, Miss Halcombe (who was usually the first to come down) did not make her appearance at the table. After the family had waited a quarter of an hour, the upper housemaid was sent to see after her, and came running out of the room dreadfully frightened. I met the servant on the stairs, and went at once to Miss Halcombe to see what was the matter. The poor lady was incapable of telling me. She was walking about her room with a pen in her hand, quite light-headed, in a state of burning fever.

Lady Glyde (being no longer in Sir Percival's service, I may, without impropriety, mention my former mistress by her name, instead of calling her my lady) was the first to come in from her own bedroom. She was so dreadfully alarmed and distressed that she was quite useless. The Count Fosco, and his lady, who came upstairs immediately afterwards, were both most serviceable and kind. Her ladyship assisted me to get Miss Halcombe to her bed. His lordship the Count remained in the sitting-room, and having sent for my medicine-chest, made a mixture for Miss Halcombe, and a cooling lotion to be applied

The Woman in White

to her head, so as to lose no time before the doctor came. We applied the lotion, but we could not get her to take the mixture. Sir Percival undertook to send for the doctor. He despatched a groom, on horseback, for the nearest medical man, Mr. Dawson, of Oak Lodge.

Mr. Dawson arrived in less than an hour's time. He was a respectable elderly man, well known all round the country, and we were much alarmed when we found that he considered the case to be a very serious one.

His lordship the Count affably entered into conversation with Mr. Dawson, and gave his opinions with a judicious freedom. Mr. Dawson, not over-courteously, inquired if his lordship's advice was the advice of a doctor, and being informed that it was the advice of one who had studied medicine unprofessionally, replied that he was not accustomed to consult with amateur physicians. The Count, with truly Christian meekness of temper, smiled and left the room. Before he went out he told me that he might be found, in case he was wanted in the course of the day, at the boat-house on the banks of the lake. Why he should have gone there, I cannot say. But he did go, remaining away the whole day till seven o'clock, which was dinner-time. Perhaps he wished to set the example of keeping the house as quiet as possible. It was entirely in his character to do so. He was a most considerate nobleman.

Miss Halcombe passed a very bad night, the fever coming and going, and getting worse towards the morning instead of better. No nurse fit to wait on her being at hand in the neighbourhood, her ladyship the Countess and myself undertook the duty, relieving each other. Lady Glyde, most unwisely, insisted on sitting up with us. She was much too nervous and too delicate in health to bear the anxiety of Miss Halcombe's illness calmly. She only did herself harm, without being of the least real assistance. A more gentle and affectionate lady never lived—but she cried, and she was frightened, two weaknesses which made her entirely unfit to be present in a sick-room.

Sir Percival and the Count came in the morning to make their inquiries.

Sir Percival (from distress, I presume, at his lady's affliction and at Miss Halcombe's illness) appeared much confused and unsettled in his mind. His lordship testified, on the contrary, a becoming composure and interest. He had his straw hat in one hand, and his book in the other, and he mentioned to Sir

Percival in my hearing that he would go out again and study at the lake. "Let us keep the house quiet," he said. "Let us not smoke indoors, my friend, now Miss Halcombe is ill. You go your way, and I will go mine. When I study I like to be alone. Good-morning, Mrs. Michelson."

Sir Percival was not civil enough—perhaps I ought in justice to say, not composed enough—to take leave of me with the same polite attention. The only person in the house, indeed, who treated me, at that time or at any other, on the footing of a lady in distressed circumstances, was the Count. He had the manners of a true nobleman—he was considerate towards every one. Even the young person (Fanny by name) who attended on Lady Glyde was not beneath his notice. When she was sent away by Sir Percival, his lordship (showing me his sweet little birds at the time) was most kindly anxious to know what had become of her, where she was to go the day she left Blackwater Park, and so on. It is in such little delicate attentions that the advantages of aristocratic birth always show themselves. I make no apology for introducing these particulars—they are brought forward in justice to his lordship, whose character, I have reason to know, is viewed rather harshly in certain quarters. A nobleman who can respect a lady in distressed circumstances, and can take a fatherly interest in the fortunes of an humble servant girl, shows principles and feelings of too high an order to be lightly called in question. I advance no opinions—I offer facts only. My endeavour through life is to judge not that I be not judged. One of my beloved husband's finest sermons was on that text. I read it constantly—in my own copy of the edition printed by subscription, in the first days of my widowhood—and at every fresh perusal I derive an increase of spiritual benefit and edification.

There was no improvement in Miss Halcombe, and the second night was even worse than the first. Mr. Dawson was constant in his attendance. The practical duties of nursing were still divided between the Countess and myself, Lady Glyde persisting in sitting up with us, though we both entreated her to take some rest. "My place is by Marian's bedside," was her only answer. "Whether I am ill, or well, nothing will induce me to lose sight of her."

Towards midday I went downstairs to attend to some of my regular duties. An hour afterwards, on my way back to the sick-room, I saw the Count (who had gone out again early, for the third time) entering the hall, to all appearance in the highest good spirits. Sir Percival, at the same moment, put his head out of the library door, and addressed his noble friend, with extreme eagerness, in these words—

"Have you found her?"

His lordship's large face became dimpled all over with placid smiles, but he made no reply in words. At the same time Sir Percival turned his head, observed that I was approaching the stairs, and looked at me in the most rudely angry manner possible.

"Come in here and tell me about it," he said to the Count. "Whenever there are women in a house they're always sure to be going up or down stairs."

"My dear Percival," observed his lordship kindly, "Mrs. Michelson has duties. Pray recognise her admirable performance of them as sincerely as I do! How is the sufferer, Mrs. Michelson?"

"No better, my lord, I regret to say."

"Sad—most sad!" remarked the Count. "You look fatigued, Mrs. Michelson. It is certainly time you and my wife had some help in nursing. I think I may be the means of offering you that help. Circumstances have happened which will oblige Madame Fosco to travel to London either to-morrow or the day after. She will go away in the morning and return at night, and she will bring back with her, to relieve you, a nurse of excellent conduct and capacity, who is now disengaged. The woman is known to my wife as a person to be trusted. Before she comes here say nothing about her, if you please, to the doctor, because he will look with an evil eye on any nurse of my providing. When she appears in this house she will speak for herself, and Mr. Dawson will be obliged to acknowledge that there is no excuse for not employing her. Lady Glyde will say the same. Pray present my best respects and sympathies to Lady Glyde."

I expressed my grateful acknowledgments for his lordship's kind consideration. Sir Percival cut them short by calling to his noble friend (using, I regret to say, a profane expression) to come into the library, and not to keep him waiting there any longer.

I proceeded upstairs. We are poor erring creatures, and however well established a woman's principles may be she cannot always keep on her guard against the temptation to exercise an idle curiosity. I am ashamed to say that an idle curiosity, on this occasion, got the better of my principles, and made me unduly inquisitive about the question which Sir Percival had addressed to his noble friend at the library door. Who was the Count expected to find in the course of his studious morning rambles at Blackwater Park? A woman, it was to be presumed, from the terms of Sir Percival's inquiry. I did not suspect the Count of any impropriety — I knew his moral character too well. The only question I asked myself was — Had he found her?

To resume. The night passed as usual without producing any change for the better in Miss Halcombe. The next day she seemed to improve a little. The day after that her ladyship the Countess, without mentioning the object of her journey to any one in my hearing, proceeded by the morning train to London — her noble husband, with his customary attention, accompanying her to the station.

I was now left in sole charge of Miss Halcombe, with every apparent chance, in consequence of her sister's resolution not to leave the bedside, of having Lady Glyde herself to nurse next.

The only circumstance of any importance that happened in the course of the day was the occurrence of another unpleasant meeting between the doctor and the Count.

His lordship, on returning from the station, stepped up into Miss Halcombe's sitting-room to make his inquiries. I went out from the bedroom to speak to him, Mr. Dawson and Lady Glyde being both with the patient at the time. The Count asked me many questions about the treatment and the symptoms. I informed him that the treatment was of the kind described as "saline," and that the symptoms, between the attacks of fever, were certainly those of increasing weakness and exhaustion. Just as I was mentioning these last particulars, Mr. Dawson came out from the bedroom.

"Good-morning, sir," said his lordship, stepping forward in the most urbane manner, and stopping the doctor, with a high-bred resolution impossible to resist, "I greatly fear you find no improvement in the symptoms to-day?"

"I find decided improvement," answered Mr. Dawson.

"You still persist in your lowering treatment of this case of fever?" continued his lordship.

"I persist in the treatment which is justified by my own professional experience," said Mr. Dawson.

The Woman in White

"Permit me to put one question to you on the vast subject of professional experience," observed the Count. "I presume to offer no more advice—I only presume to make an inquiry. You live at some distance, sir, from the gigantic centres of scientific activity—London and Paris. Have you ever heard of the wasting effects of fever being reasonably and intelligibly repaired by fortifying the exhausted patient with brandy, wine, ammonia, and quinine? Has that new heresy of the highest medical authorities ever reached your ears—Yes or No?"

"When a professional man puts that question to me I shall be glad to answer him," said the doctor, opening the door to go out. "You are not a professional man, and I beg to decline answering you."

Buffeted in this inexcusably uncivil way on one cheek, the Count, like a practical Christian, immediately turned the other, and said, in the sweetest manner, "Good-morning, Mr. Dawson."

If my late beloved husband had been so fortunate as to know his lordship, how highly he and the Count would have esteemed each other!

Her ladyship the Countess returned by the last train that night, and brought with her the nurse from London. I was instructed that this person's name was Mrs. Rubelle. Her personal appearance, and her imperfect English when she spoke, informed me that she was a foreigner.

I have always cultivated a feeling of humane indulgence for foreigners. They do not possess our blessings and advantages, and they are, for the most part, brought up in the blind errors of Popery. It has also always been my precept and practice, as it was my dear husband's precept and practice before me (see Sermon XXIX. in the Collection by the late Rev. Samuel Michelson, M.A.), to do as I would be done by. On both these accounts I will not say that Mrs. Rubelle struck me as being a small, wiry, sly person, of fifty or thereabouts, with a dark brown or Creole complexion and watchful light grey eyes. Nor will I mention, for the reasons just alleged, that I thought her dress, though it was of the plainest black silk, inappropriately costly in texture and unnecessarily refined in trimming and finish, for a person in her position in life. I should not like these things to be said of me, and therefore it is my duty not to say them of Mrs. Rubelle. I will merely mention that her manners were, not perhaps unpleasantly reserved, but only remarkably quiet and retiring—that she looked about her a great deal, and said very little, which might have arisen quite as much from her own modesty as from distrust of her position at Blackwater Park; and that she declined to partake of supper (which was curious perhaps, but surely not suspicious?), although I myself politely invited her to that meal in my own room.

At the Count's particular suggestion (so like his lordship's forgiving kindness!), it was arranged that Mrs. Rubelle should not enter on her duties until she had been seen and approved by the doctor the next morning. I sat up that night. Lady Glyde appeared to be very unwilling that the new nurse should be employed to attend on Miss Halcombe. Such want of liberality towards a foreigner on the part of a lady of her education and refinement surprised me. I ventured to say, "My lady, we must all remember not to be hasty in our judgments on our inferiors—especially when they come from foreign parts." Lady Glyde did not appear to attend to me. She only sighed, and kissed Miss Halcombe's hand as it lay on the counterpane. Scarcely a judicious proceeding in a sick-room, with a patient whom it was highly desirable not to excite. But poor Lady Glyde knew nothing of nursing—nothing whatever, I am sorry to say.

The next morning Mrs. Rubelle was sent to the sitting-room, to be approved by the doctor on his way through to the bedroom.

I left Lady Glyde with Miss Halcombe, who was slumbering at the time, and joined Mrs. Rubelle, with the object of kindly preventing her from feeling strange and nervous in consequence of the uncertainty of her situation. She did not appear to see it in that light. She seemed to be quite satisfied, beforehand, that Mr. Dawson would approve of her, and she sat calmly looking out of window, with every appearance of enjoying the country air. Some people might have thought such conduct suggestive of brazen assurance. I beg to say that I more liberally set it down to extraordinary strength of mind.

Instead of the doctor coming up to us, I was sent for to see the doctor. I thought this change of affairs rather odd, but Mrs. Rubelle did not appear to be affected by it in any way. I left her still calmly looking out of the window, and still silently enjoying the country air.

Mr. Dawson was waiting for me by himself in the breakfast-room.

"About this new nurse, Mrs. Michelson," said the doctor.

"Yes, sir?"

"I find that she has been brought here from London by the wife of that fat old foreigner, who is always trying to interfere with me. Mrs. Michelson, the fat old foreigner is a quack."

This was very rude. I was naturally shocked at it.

"Are you aware, sir," I said, "that you are talking of a nobleman?"

"Pooh! He isn't the first quack with a handle to his name. They're all Counts—hang 'em!"

"He would not be a friend of Sir Percival Glyde's, sir, if he was not a member of the highest aristocracy—excepting the English aristocracy, of course."

"Very well, Mrs. Michelson, call him what you like, and let us get back to the nurse. I have been objecting to her already."

"Without having seen her, sir?"

"Yes, without having seen her. She may be the best nurse in existence, but she is not a nurse of my providing. I have put that objection to Sir Percival, as the master of the house. He doesn't support me. He says a nurse of my providing would have been a stranger from London also, and he thinks the woman ought to have a trial, after his wife's aunt has taken the trouble to fetch her from London. There is some justice in that, and I can't decently say No. But I have made it a condition that she is to go at once, if I find reason to complain of her. This proposal being one which I have some right to make, as medical attendant, Sir Percival has consented to it. Now, Mrs. Michelson, I know I can depend on you, and I want you to keep a sharp eye on the nurse for the first day or two, and to see that she gives Miss Halcombe no medicines but mine. This foreign nobleman of yours is dying to try his quack remedies (mesmerism included) on my patient, and a nurse who is brought here by his wife may be a little too willing to help him. You understand? Very well, then, we may go upstairs. Is the nurse there? I'll say a word to her before she goes into the sick-room."

We found Mrs. Rubelle still enjoying herself at the window. When I introduced her to Mr. Dawson, neither the doctor's doubtful looks nor the doctor's searching questions appeared to confuse her in the least. She answered him quietly in her broken English, and though he tried hard to puzzle her, she never betrayed the least ignorance, so far, about any part of her duties. This was doubtless the result of strength of mind, as I said before, and not of brazen assurance, by any means.

We all went into the bedroom.

Mrs. Rubelle looked very attentively at the patient, curtseyed to Lady Glyde, set one or two little things right in the room, and sat down quietly in a corner to wait until she was wanted. Her ladyship seemed startled and annoyed by the appearance of the strange nurse. No one said anything, for fear of rousing Miss Halcombe, who was still slumbering, except the doctor, who whispered a question about the night. I softly answered, "Much as usual," and then Mr. Dawson went out. Lady Glyde followed him, I suppose to speak about Mrs. Rubelle. For my own part, I had made up my mind already that this quiet foreign person would keep her situation. She had all her wits about her, and she certainly understood her business. So far, I could hardly have done much better by the bedside myself.

Remembering Mr. Dawson's caution to me, I subjected Mrs. Rubelle to a severe scrutiny at certain intervals for the next three or four days. I over and over again entered the room softly and suddenly, but I never found her out in any suspicious action. Lady Glyde, who watched her as attentively as I did, discovered nothing either. I never detected a sign of the medicine bottles being tampered with, I never saw Mrs. Rubelle say a word to the Count, or the Count to her. She managed Miss Halcombe with unquestionable care and discretion. The poor lady wavered backwards and forwards between a sort of sleepy exhaustion, which was half faintness and half slumbering, and attacks of fever which brought with them more or less of wandering in her mind. Mrs. Rubelle never disturbed her in the first case, and never startled her in the second, by appearing too suddenly at the bedside in the character of a stranger. Honour to whom honour is due (whether foreign or English) — and I give her privilege impartially to Mrs. Rubelle. She was remarkably uncommunicative about herself, and she was too quietly independent of all advice from experienced persons who understood the duties of a sick-room — but with these drawbacks, she was a good nurse, and she never gave either Lady Glyde or Mr. Dawson the shadow of a reason for complaining of her.

The next circumstance of importance that occurred in the house was the temporary absence of the Count, occasioned by business which took him to London. He went away (I think) on the morning of the fourth day after the arrival of Mrs. Rubelle, and at parting he spoke to Lady Glyde very seriously, in my presence, on the subject of Miss Halcombe.

"Trust Mr. Dawson," he said, "for a few days more, if you please. But if there is not some change for the better in that time, send for advice from London, which this mule of a doctor must accept in spite of himself. Offend Mr. Dawson, and save Miss Halcombe. I say this seriously, on my word of honour and from the bottom of my heart."

His lordship spoke with extreme feeling and kindness. But poor Lady Glyde's nerves were so completely broken down that she seemed quite frightened at him. She trembled from head to foot, and allowed him to take his leave without uttering a word on her side. She turned to me when he had gone, and said, "Oh, Mrs. Michelson, I am heartbroken about my sister, and I have no friend to advise me! Do you think Mr. Dawson is wrong? He told me himself this morning that there was no fear, and no need to send for another doctor."

"With all respect to Mr. Dawson," I answered, "in your ladyship's place I should remember the Count's advice."

Lady Glyde turned away from me suddenly, with an appearance of despair, for which I was quite unable to account.

"His advice!" she said to herself. "God help us—his advice!"

The Count was away from Blackwater Park, as nearly as I remember, a week.

Sir Percival seemed to feel the loss of his lordship in various ways, and appeared also, I thought, much depressed and altered by the sickness and sorrow in the house. Occasionally he was so very restless that I could not help noticing it, coming and going, and wandering here and there and everywhere in the grounds. His inquiries about Miss Halcombe, and about his lady (whose failing health seemed to cause him sincere anxiety), were most attentive. I think his heart was much softened. If some kind clerical friend—some such friend as he might have found in my late excellent husband—had been near him at this time, cheering moral progress might have been made with Sir Percival. I seldom find myself mistaken on a point of this sort, having had experience to guide me in my happy married days.

Her ladyship the Countess, who was now the only company for Sir Percival downstairs, rather neglected him, as I considered—or, perhaps, it might have been that he neglected her. A stranger might almost have supposed that they were bent, now they were left together alone, on actually avoiding one another. This, of course, could not be. But it did so happen, nevertheless, that the Countess made her dinner at luncheon-time, and that she always came upstairs towards evening, although Mrs. Rubelle had taken the nursing duties entirely off her hands. Sir Percival dined by himself, and William (the man out of livery) made the remark, in my hearing, that his master had put himself on half rations of food and on a double allowance of drink. I attach no importance to such an insolent observation as this on the part of a servant. I reprobated it at the time, and I wish to be understood as reprobating it once more on this occasion.

In the course of the next few days Miss Halcombe did certainly seem to all of us to be mending a little. Our faith in Mr. Dawson revived. He appeared to be very confident about the case, and he assured Lady Glyde, when she spoke to him on the subject, that he would himself propose to send for a physician the moment he felt so much as the shadow of a doubt crossing his own mind.

The only person among us who did not appear to be relieved by these words was the Countess. She said to me privately, that she could not feel easy about Miss Halcombe on Mr. Dawson's authority, and that she should wait anxiously for her husband's opinion on his return. That return, his letters informed her, would take place in three days' time. The Count and Countess corresponded regularly every morning during his lordship's absence. They were in that respect, as in all others, a pattern to married people.

On the evening of the third day I noticed a change in Miss Halcombe, which caused me serious apprehension. Mrs. Rubelle noticed it too. We said nothing on the subject to Lady Glyde, who was then lying asleep, completely overpowered by exhaustion, on the sofa in the sitting-room.

Mr. Dawson did not pay his evening visit till later than usual. As soon as he set eyes on his patient I saw his face alter. He tried to hide it, but he looked both confused and alarmed. A messenger was sent to his residence for his medicine-chest, disinfecting preparations were used in the room, and a bed was made up for him in the house by his own directions. "Has the fever turned to infection?" I whispered to him. "I am afraid it

The Woman in White

has," he answered; "we shall know better to-morrow morning."

By Mr. Dawson's own directions Lady Glyde was kept in ignorance of this change for the worse. He himself absolutely forbade her, on account of her health, to join us in the bedroom that night. She tried to resist—there was a sad scene—but he had his medical authority to support him, and he carried his point.

The next morning one of the men-servants was sent to London at eleven o'clock, with a letter to a physician in town, and with orders to bring the new doctor back with him by the earliest possible train. Half an hour after the messenger had gone the Count returned to Blackwater Park.

The Countess, on her own responsibility, immediately brought him in to see the patient. There was no impropriety that I could discover in her taking this course. His lordship was a married man, he was old enough to be Miss Halcombe's father, and he saw her in the presence of a female relative, Lady Glyde's aunt. Mr. Dawson nevertheless protested against his presence in the room, but I could plainly remark the doctor was too much alarmed to make any serious resistance on this occasion.

The poor suffering lady was past knowing any one about her. She seemed to take her friends for enemies. When the Count approached her bedside her eyes, which had been wandering incessantly round and round the room before, settled on his face with a dreadful stare of terror, which I shall remember to my dying day. The Count sat down by her, felt her pulse and her temples, looked at her very attentively, and then turned round upon the doctor with such an expression of indignation and contempt in his face, that the words failed on Mr. Dawson's lips, and he stood for a moment, pale with anger and alarm—pale and perfectly speechless.

His lordship looked next at me.

"When did the change happen?" he asked.

I told him the time.

"Has Lady Glyde been in the room since?"

I replied that she had not. The doctor had absolutely forbidden her to come into the room on the evening before, and had repeated the order again in the morning.

"Have you and Mrs. Rubelle been made aware of the full extent of the mischief?" was his next question.

We were aware, I answered, that the malady was considered infectious. He stopped me before I could add anything more.

"It is typhus fever," he said.

In the minute that passed, while these questions and answers were going on, Mr. Dawson recovered himself, and addressed the Count with his customary firmness.

"It is not typhus fever," he remarked sharply. "I protest against this intrusion, sir. No one has a right to put questions here but me. I have done my duty to the best of my ability—"

The Count interrupted him—not by words, but only by pointing to the bed. Mr. Dawson seemed to feel that silent contradiction to his assertion of his own ability, and to grow only the more angry under it.

"I say I have done my duty," he reiterated. "A physician has been sent for from London. I will consult on the nature of the fever with him, and with no one else. I insist on your leaving the room."

"I entered this room, sir, in the sacred interests of humanity," said the Count. "And in the same interests, if the coming of the physician is delayed, I will enter it again. I warn you once more that the fever has turned to typhus, and that your treatment is responsible for this lamentable change. If that unhappy lady dies, I will give my testimony in a court of justice that your ignorance and obstinacy have been the cause of her death."

Before Mr. Dawson could answer, before the Count could leave us, the door was opened from the sitting-room, and we saw Lady Glyde on the threshold.

"I must and will come in," she said, with extraordinary firmness.

Instead of stopping her, the Count moved into the sitting-room, and made way for her to go in. On all other occasions he was the last man in the world to forget anything, but in the surprise of the moment he apparently forgot the danger of infection from typhus, and the urgent necessity of forcing Lady Glyde to take proper care of herself.

To my astonishment Mr. Dawson showed more presence of mind. He stopped her ladyship at the first step she took towards the bedside. "I am sincerely sorry, I am sincerely grieved," he said. "The fever may, I fear, be infectious. Until I am certain that it is not, I entreat you to keep out of the room."

She struggled for a moment, then suddenly dropped her arms and sank forward. She had fainted. The Countess and I took her from the doctor and carried her into her own room. The Count preceded us, and waited in the passage till I came out and told him that we had recovered her from the swoon.

I went back to the doctor to tell him, by Lady Glyde's desire, that she insisted on speaking to him immediately. He withdrew at once to quiet her ladyship's agitation, and to assure her of the physician's arrival in the course of a few hours. Those hours passed very slowly. Sir Percival and the Count were together downstairs, and sent up from time to time to make their inquiries. At last, between five and six o'clock, to our great relief, the physician came.

He was a younger man than Mr. Dawson, very serious and very decided. What he thought of the previous treatment I cannot say, but it struck me as curious that he put many more questions to myself and to Mrs. Rubelle than he put to the doctor, and that he did not appear to listen with much interest to what Mr. Dawson said, while he was examining Mr. Dawson's patient. I began to suspect, from what I observed in this way, that the Count had been right about the illness all the way through, and I was naturally confirmed in that idea when Mr. Dawson, after some little delay, asked the one important question which the London doctor had been sent for to set at rest.

"What is your opinion of the fever?" he inquired.

"Typhus," replied the physician. "Typhus fever beyond all doubt."

That quiet foreign person, Mrs. Rubelle, crossed her thin brown hands in front of her, and looked at me with a very significant smile. The Count himself could hardly have appeared more gratified if he had been present in the room and had heard the confirmation of his own opinion.

After giving us some useful directions about the management of the patient, and mentioning that he would come again in five days' time, the physician withdrew to consult in private with Mr. Dawson. He would offer no opinion on Miss Halcombe's chances of recovery—he said it was impossible at that stage of the illness to pronounce one way or the other.

The five days passed anxiously.

Countess Fosco and myself took it by turns to relieve Mrs. Rubelle, Miss Halcombe's condition growing worse and worse, and requiring our utmost care and attention. It was a terribly trying time. Lady Glyde (supported, as Mr. Dawson said, by the constant strain of her suspense on her sister's account) rallied in the most extraordinary manner, and showed a firmness and determination for which I should myself never have given her credit. She insisted on coming into the sick-room two or three times every day, to look at Miss Halcombe with her own eyes, promising not to go too close to the bed, if the doctor would consent to her wishes so far. Mr. Dawson very unwillingly made the concession required of him—I think he saw that it was hopeless to dispute with her. She came in every day, and she self-denyingly kept her promise. I felt it personally so distressing (as reminding me of my own affliction during my husband's last illness) to see how she suffered under these circumstances, that I must beg not to dwell on this part of the subject any longer. It is more agreeable to me to mention that no fresh disputes took place between Mr. Dawson and the Count. His lordship made all his inquiries by deputy, and remained continually in company with Sir Percival downstairs.

On the fifth day the physician came again and gave us a little hope. He said the tenth day from the first appearance of the typhus would probably decide the result of the illness, and he arranged for his third visit to take place on that date. The interval passed as before—except that the Count went to London again one morning and returned at night.

On the tenth day it pleased a merciful Providence to relieve our household from all further anxiety and alarm. The physician positively assured us that Miss Halcombe was out of danger. "She wants no doctor now—all she requires is careful watching and nursing for some time to come, and that I see she has." Those were his own words. That evening I read my husband's touching sermon on Recovery from Sickness, with more happiness and advantage (in a spiritual point of view) than I ever remember to have derived from it before.

The effect of the good news on poor Lady Glyde was, I

grieve to say, quite overpowering. She was too weak to bear the violent reaction, and in another day or two she sank into a state of debility and depression which obliged her to keep her room. Rest and quiet, and change of air afterwards, were the best remedies which Mr. Dawson could suggest for her benefit. It was fortunate that matters were no worse, for, on the very day after she took to her room, the Count and the doctor had another disagreement — and this time the dispute between them was of so serious a nature that Mr. Dawson left the house.

I was not present at the time, but I understood that the subject of dispute was the amount of nourishment which it was necessary to give to assist Miss Halcombe's convalescence after the exhaustion of the fever. Mr. Dawson, now that his patient was safe, was less inclined than ever to submit to unprofessional interference, and the Count (I cannot imagine why) lost all the self-control which he had so judiciously preserved on former occasions, and taunted the doctor, over and over again, with his mistake about the fever when it changed to typhus. The unfortunate affair ended in Mr. Dawson's appealing to Sir Percival, and threatening (now that he could leave without absolute danger to Miss Halcombe) to withdraw from his attendance at Blackwater Park if the Count's interference was not peremptorily suppressed from that moment. Sir Percival's reply (though not designedly uncivil) had only resulted in making matters worse, and Mr. Dawson had thereupon withdrawn from the house in a state of extreme indignation at Count Fosco's usage of him, and had sent in his bill the next morning.

We were now, therefore, left without the attendance of a medical man. Although there was no actual necessity for another doctor — nursing and watching being, as the physician had observed, all that Miss Halcombe required — I should still, if my authority had been consulted, have obtained professional assistance from some other quarter, for form's sake.

The matter did not seem to strike Sir Percival in that light. He said it would be time enough to send for another doctor if Miss Halcombe showed any signs of a relapse. In the meanwhile we had the Count to consult in any minor difficulty, and we need not unnecessarily disturb our patient in her present weak and nervous condition by the presence of a stranger at her bedside. There was much that was reasonable, no doubt, in these considerations, but they left me a little anxious nevertheless. Nor was I quite satisfied in my own mind of the propriety of our concealing the doctor's absence as we did from Lady Glyde. It was a merciful deception, I admit — for she was in no state to bear any fresh anxieties. But still it was a deception, and, as such, to a person of my principles, at best a doubtful proceeding.

A second perplexing circumstance which happened on the same day, and which took me completely by surprise, added greatly to the sense of uneasiness that was now weighing on my mind.

I was sent for to see Sir Percival in the library. The Count, who was with him when I went in, immediately rose and left us alone together. Sir Percival civilly asked me to take a seat, and then, to my great astonishment, addressed me in these terms—

"I want to speak to you, Mrs. Michelson, about a matter which I decided on some time ago, and which I should have mentioned before, but for the sickness and trouble in the house. In plain words, I have reasons for wishing to break up my establishment immediately at this place—leaving you in charge, of course, as usual. As soon as Lady Glyde and Miss Halcombe can travel they must both have change of air. My friends, Count Fosco and the Countess, will leave us before that time to live in the neighbourhood of London, and I have reasons for not opening the house to any more company, with a view to economising as carefully as I can. I don't blame you, but my expenses here are a great deal too heavy. In short, I shall sell the horses, and get rid of all the servants at once. I never do things by halves, as you know, and I mean to have the house clear of a pack of useless people by this time to-morrow."

I listened to him, perfectly aghast with astonishment.

"Do you mean, Sir Percival, that I am to dismiss the indoor servants under my charge without the usual month's warning?" I asked.

"Certainly I do. We may all be out of the house before another month, and I am not going to leave the servants here in idleness, with no master to wait on."

"Who is to do the cooking, Sir Percival, while you are still staying here?"

"Margaret Porcher can roast and boil—keep her. What do I want with a cook if I don't mean to give any dinner-parties?"

"The servant you have mentioned is the most unintelligent servant in the house, Sir Percival."

"Keep her, I tell you, and have a woman in from the village to do the cleaning and go away again. My weekly expenses must and shall be lowered immediately. I don't send for you to make objections, Mrs. Michelson—I send for you to carry out my plans of economy. Dismiss the whole lazy pack of indoor servants to-morrow, except Porcher. She is as strong as a horse—and we'll make her work like a horse."

"You will excuse me for reminding you, Sir Percival, that if the servants go to-morrow they must have a month's wages in lieu of a month's warning."

"Let them! A month's wages saves a month's waste and gluttony in the servants' hall."

This last remark conveyed an aspersion of the most offensive kind on my management. I had too much self-respect to defend myself under so gross an imputation. Christian consideration for the helpless position of Miss Halcombe and Lady Glyde, and for the serious inconvenience which my sudden absence might inflict on them, alone prevented me from resigning my situation on the spot. I rose immediately. It would have lowered me in my own estimation to have permitted the interview to continue a moment longer.

"After that last remark, Sir Percival, I have nothing more to say. Your directions shall be attended to." Pronouncing those words, I bowed my head with the most distant respect, and went out of the room.

The next day the servants left in a body. Sir Percival himself dismissed the grooms and stablemen, sending them, with all the horses but one, to London. Of the whole domestic establishment, indoors and out, there now remained only myself, Margaret Porcher, and the gardener—this last living in his own cottage, and being wanted to take care of the one horse that remained in the stables.

With the house left in this strange and lonely condition—with the mistress of it ill in her room—with Miss Halcombe still as helpless as a child—and with the doctor's attendance withdrawn from us in enmity—it was surely not unnatural that my spirits should sink, and my customary composure be very hard to maintain. My mind was ill at ease. I wished the poor ladies both well again, and I wished myself away from Blackwater Park.

II

The next event that occurred was of so singular a nature that it might have caused me a feeling of superstitious surprise, if my mind had not been fortified by principle against any pagan weakness of that sort. The uneasy sense of something wrong in the family which had made me wish myself away from Blackwater Park, was actually followed, strange to say, by my departure from the house. It is true that my absence was for a temporary period only, but the coincidence was, in my opinion, not the less remarkable on that account.

My departure took place under the following circumstances—

A day or two after the servants all left I was again sent for to see Sir Percival. The undeserved slur which he had cast on my management of the household did not, I am happy to say, prevent me from returning good for evil to the best of my ability, by complying with his request as readily and respectfully as ever. It cost me a struggle with that fallen nature, which we all share in common, before I could suppress my feelings. Being accustomed to self-discipline, I accomplished the sacrifice.

I found Sir Percival and Count Fosco sitting together again. On this occasion his lordship remained present at the interview, and assisted in the development of Sir Percival's views.

The subject to which they now requested my attention related to the healthy change of air by which we all hoped that Miss Halcombe and Lady Glyde might soon be enabled to profit. Sir Percival mentioned that both the ladies would probably pass the autumn (by invitation of Frederick Fairlie, Esquire) at Limmeridge House, Cumberland. But before they went there, it was his opinion, confirmed by Count Fosco (who here took up the conversation and continued it to the end), that they would benefit by a short residence first in the genial climate of Torquay. The great object, therefore, was to engage lodgings at that place, affording all the comforts and advantages of which they stood in need, and the great difficulty was to find an experienced person capable of choosing the sort of residence which they wanted. In this emergency the Count begged to inquire, on Sir Percival's behalf, whether I would object to give the ladies the benefit of my assistance, by proceeding myself to Torquay in their interests.

It was impossible for a person in my situation to meet any

proposal, made in these terms, with a positive objection.

I could only venture to represent the serious inconvenience of my leaving Blackwater Park in the extraordinary absence of all the indoor servants, with the one exception of Margaret Porcher. But Sir Percival and his lordship declared that they were both willing to put up with inconvenience for the sake of the invalids. I next respectfully suggested writing to an agent at Torquay, but I was met here by being reminded of the imprudence of taking lodgings without first seeing them. I was also informed that the Countess (who would otherwise have gone to Devonshire herself) could not, in Lady Glyde's present condition, leave her niece, and that Sir Percival and the Count had business to transact together which would oblige them to remain at Blackwater Park. In short, it was clearly shown me that if I did not undertake the errand, no one else could be trusted with it. Under these circumstances, I could only inform Sir Percival that my services were at the disposal of Miss Halcombe and Lady Glyde.

It was thereupon arranged that I should leave the next morning, that I should occupy one or two days in examining all the most convenient houses in Torquay, and that I should return with my report as soon as I conveniently could. A memorandum was written for me by his lordship, stating the requisites which the place I was sent to take must be found to possess, and a note of the pecuniary limit assigned to me was added by Sir Percival.

My own idea on reading over these instructions was, that no such residence as I saw described could be found at any watering-place in England, and that, even if it could by chance be discovered, it would certainly not be parted with for any period on such terms as I was permitted to offer. I hinted at these difficulties to both the gentlemen, but Sir Percival (who undertook to answer me) did not appear to feel them. It was not for me to dispute the question. I said no more, but I felt a very strong conviction that the business on which I was sent away was so beset by difficulties that my errand was almost hopeless at starting.

Before I left I took care to satisfy myself that Miss Halcombe was going on favourably.

There was a painful expression of anxiety in her face which made me fear that her mind, on first recovering itself, was not at ease. But she was certainly strengthening more rapidly than I could have ventured to anticipate, and she was able to send kind messages to Lady Glyde, saying that she was fast getting well, and entreating her ladyship not to exert herself again too soon. I left her in charge of Mrs. Rubelle, who was still as quietly independent of every one else in the house as ever. When I knocked at Lady Glyde's door before going away, I was told that she was still sadly weak and depressed, my informant being the Countess, who was then keeping her company in her room. Sir Percival and the Count were walking on the road to the lodge as I was driven by in the chaise. I bowed to them and quitted the house, with not a living soul left in the servants' offices but Margaret Porcher.

Every one must feel what I have felt myself since that time, that these circumstances were more than unusual — they were almost suspicious. Let me, however, say again that it was impossible for me, in my dependent position, to act otherwise than I did.

The result of my errand at Torquay was exactly what I had foreseen. No such lodgings as I was instructed to take could be found in the whole place, and the terms I was permitted to give were much too low for the purpose, even if I had been able to discover what I wanted. I accordingly returned to Blackwater Park, and informed Sir Percival, who met me at the door, that my journey had been taken in vain. He seemed too much occupied with some other subject to care about the failure of my errand, and his first words informed me that even in the short time of my absence another remarkable change had taken place in the house.

The Count and Countess Fosco had left Blackwater Park for their new residence in St. John's Wood.

I was not made aware of the motive for this sudden departure — I was only told that the Count had been very particular in leaving his kind compliments to me. When I ventured on asking Sir Percival whether Lady Glyde had any one to attend to her comforts in the absence of the Countess, he replied that she had Margaret Porcher to wait on her, and he added that a woman from the village had been sent for to do the work downstairs.

The answer really shocked me — there was such a glaring impropriety in permitting an under-housemaid to fill the place of confidential attendant on Lady Glyde. I went upstairs at once, and met Margaret on the bedroom landing. Her services had not been required (naturally enough), her mistress having sufficiently recovered that morning to be able to leave her bed. I asked next after Miss Halcombe, but I was answered in a slouching, sulky way, which left me no wiser than I was before.

I did not choose to repeat the question, and perhaps provoke an impertinent reply. It was in every respect more becoming to a person in my position to present myself immediately in Lady Glyde's room.

I found that her ladyship had certainly gained in health during the last few days. Although still sadly weak and nervous, she was able to get up without assistance, and to walk slowly about her room, feeling no worse effect from the exertion than a slight sensation of fatigue. She had been made a little anxious that morning about Miss Halcombe, through having received no news of her from any one. I thought this seemed to imply a blamable want of attention on the part of Mrs. Rubelle, but I said nothing, and remained with Lady Glyde to assist her to dress. When she was ready we both left the room together to go to Miss Halcombe.

We were stopped in the passage by the appearance of Sir Percival. He looked as if he had been purposely waiting there to see us.

"Where are you going?" he said to Lady Glyde.

"To Marian's room," she answered.

"It may spare you a disappointment," remarked Sir Percival, "if I tell you at once that you will not find her there."

"Not find her there!"

"No. She left the house yesterday morning with Fosco and his wife."

Lady Glyde was not strong enough to bear the surprise of this extraordinary statement. She turned fearfully pale, and leaned back against the wall, looking at her husband in dead silence.

I was so astonished myself that I hardly knew what to say. I asked Sir Percival if he really meant that Miss Halcombe had left Blackwater Park.

"I certainly mean it," he answered.

"In her state, Sir Percival! Without mentioning her intentions to Lady Glyde!"

Before he could reply her ladyship recovered herself a little and spoke.

"Impossible!" she cried out in a loud, frightened manner, taking a step or two forward from the wall. "Where was the doctor? where was Mr. Dawson when Marian went away?"

"Mr. Dawson wasn't wanted, and wasn't here," said Sir Percival. "He left of his own accord, which is enough of itself to show that she was strong enough to travel. How you stare! If you don't believe she has gone, look for yourself. Open her room door, and all the other room doors if you like."

She took him at his word, and I followed her. There was no one in Miss Halcombe's room but Margaret Porcher, who was busy setting it to rights. There was no one in the spare rooms or the dressing-rooms when we looked into them afterwards. Sir Percival still waited for us in the passage. As we were leaving the last room that we had examined Lady Glyde whispered, "Don't go, Mrs. Michelson! don't leave me, for God's sake!" Before I could say anything in return she was out again in the passage, speaking to her husband.

"What does it mean, Sir Percival? I insist—I beg and pray you will tell me what it means."

"It means," he answered, "that Miss Halcombe was strong enough yesterday morning to sit up and be dressed, and that she insisted on taking advantage of Fosco's going to London to go there too."

"To London!"

"Yes—on her way to Limmeridge."

Lady Glyde turned and appealed to me.

"You saw Miss Halcombe last," she said. "Tell me plainly, Mrs. Michelson, did you think she looked fit to travel?"

"Not in my opinion, your ladyship."

Sir Percival, on his side, instantly turned and appealed to me also.

"Before you went away," he said, "did you, or did you not,

The Woman in White

tell the nurse that Miss Halcombe looked much stronger and better?"

"I certainly made the remark, Sir Percival."

He addressed her ladyship again the moment I offered that reply.

"Set one of Mrs. Michelson's opinions fairly against the other," he said, "and try to be reasonable about a perfectly plain matter. If she had not been well enough to be moved do you think we should any of us have risked letting her go? She has got three competent people to look after her—Fosco and your aunt, and Mrs. Rubelle, who went away with them expressly for that purpose. They took a whole carriage yesterday, and made a bed for her on the seat in case she felt tired. To-day, Fosco and Mrs. Rubelle go on with her themselves to Cumberland."

"Why does Marian go to Limmeridge and leave me here by myself?" said her ladyship, interrupting Sir Percival.

"Because your uncle won't receive you till he has seen your sister first," he replied. "Have you forgotten the letter he wrote to her at the beginning of her illness? It was shown to you, you read it yourself, and you ought to remember it."

"I do remember it."

"If you do, why should you be surprised at her leaving you? You want to be back at Limmeridge, and she has gone there to get your uncle's leave for you on his own terms."

Poor Lady Glyde's eyes filled with tears.

"Marian never left me before," she said, "without bidding me good-bye."

"She would have bid you good-bye this time," returned Sir Percival, "if she had not been afraid of herself and of you. She knew you would try to stop her, she knew you would distress her by crying. Do you want to make any more objections? If you do, you must come downstairs and ask questions in the dining-room. These worries upset me. I want a glass of wine."

He left us suddenly.

His manner all through this strange conversation had been very unlike what it usually was. He seemed to be almost as

375

nervous and fluttered, every now and then, as his lady herself. I should never have supposed that his health had been so delicate, or his composure so easy to upset.

I tried to prevail on Lady Glyde to go back to her room, but it was useless. She stopped in the passage, with the look of a woman whose mind was panic-stricken.

"Something has happened to my sister!" she said.

"Remember, my lady, what surprising energy there is in Miss Halcombe," I suggested. "She might well make an effort which other ladies in her situation would be unfit for. I hope and believe there is nothing wrong — I do indeed."

"I must follow Marian," said her ladyship, with the same panic-stricken look. "I must go where she has gone, I must see that she is alive and well with my own eyes. Come! come down with me to Sir Percival."

I hesitated, fearing that my presence might be considered an intrusion. I attempted to represent this to her ladyship, but she was deaf to me. She held my arm fast enough to force me to go downstairs with her, and she still clung to me with all the little strength she had at the moment when I opened the dining-room door.

Sir Percival was sitting at the table with a decanter of wine before him. He raised the glass to his lips as we went in and drained it at a draught. Seeing that he looked at me angrily when he put it down again, I attempted to make some apology for my accidental presence in the room.

"Do you suppose there are any secrets going on here?" he broke out suddenly; "there are none — there is nothing underhand, nothing kept from you or from any one." After speaking those strange words loudly and sternly, he filled himself another glass of wine and asked Lady Glyde what she wanted of him.

"If my sister is fit to travel, I am fit to travel," said her ladyship, with more firmness than she had yet shown. "I come to beg you will make allowances for my anxiety about Marian, and let me follow her at once by the afternoon train."

"You must wait till to-morrow," replied Sir Percival, "and then if you don't hear to the contrary you can go. I don't suppose you are at all likely to hear to the contrary, so I shall write to Fosco by to-night's post."

He said those last words holding his glass up to the light, and looking at the wine in it instead of at Lady Glyde. Indeed he never once looked at her throughout the conversation. Such a singular want of good breeding in a gentleman of his rank impressed me, I own, very painfully.

"Why should you write to Count Fosco?" she asked, in extreme surprise.

"To tell him to expect you by the midday train," said Sir Percival. "He will meet you at the station when you get to London, and take you on to sleep at your aunt's in St. John's Wood."

Lady Glyde's hand began to tremble violently round my arm—why I could not imagine.

"There is no necessity for Count Fosco to meet me," she said. "I would rather not stay in London to sleep."

"You must. You can't take the whole journey to Cumberland in one day. You must rest a night in London—and I don't choose you to go by yourself to an hotel. Fosco made the offer to your uncle to give you house-room on the way down, and your uncle has accepted it. Here! here is a letter from him addressed to yourself. I ought to have sent it up this morning, but I forgot. Read it and see what Mr. Fairlie himself says to you."

Lady Glyde looked at the letter for a moment and then placed it in my hands.

"Read it," she said faintly. "I don't know what is the matter with me. I can't read it myself."

It was a note of only four lines—so short and so careless that it quite struck me. If I remember correctly it contained no more than these words—

"Dearest Laura, Please come whenever you like. Break the journey by sleeping at your aunt's house. Grieved to hear of dear Marian's illness. Affectionately yours, Frederick Fairlie."

"I would rather not go there—I would rather not stay a night in London," said her ladyship, breaking out eagerly with those words before I had quite done reading the note, short as it was. "Don't write to Count Fosco! Pray, pray don't write to him!"

Sir Percival filled another glass from the decanter so awkwardly that he upset it and spilt all the wine over the table. "My sight seems to be failing me," he muttered to himself, in an odd, muffled voice. He slowly set the glass up again, refilled it, and drained it once more at a draught. I began to fear, from his look and manner, that the wine was getting into his head.

"Pray don't write to Count Fosco," persisted Lady Glyde, more earnestly than ever.

"Why not, I should like to know?" cried Sir Percival, with a sudden burst of anger that startled us both. "Where can you stay more properly in London than at the place your uncle himself chooses for you — at your aunt's house? Ask Mrs. Michelson."

The arrangement proposed was so unquestionably the right and the proper one, that I could make no possible objection to it. Much as I sympathised with Lady Glyde in other respects, I could not sympathise with her in her unjust prejudices against Count Fosco. I never before met with any lady of her rank and station who was so lamentably narrow-minded on the subject of foreigners. Neither her uncle's note nor Sir Percival's increasing impatience seemed to have the least effect on her. She still objected to staying a night in London, she still implored her husband not to write to the Count.

"Drop it!" said Sir Percival, rudely turning his back on us. "If you haven't sense enough to know what is best for yourself other people must know it for you. The arrangement is made and there is an end of it. You are only wanted to do what Miss Halcombe has done before you — —"

"Marian?" repeated her Ladyship, in a bewildered manner; "Marian sleeping in Count Fosco's house!"

"Yes, in Count Fosco's house. She slept there last night to break the journey, and you are to follow her example, and do what your uncle tells you. You are to sleep at Fosco's to-morrow night, as your sister did, to break the journey. Don't throw too many obstacles in my way! don't make me repent of letting you go at all!"

He started to his feet, and suddenly walked out into the verandah through the open glass doors.

"Will your ladyship excuse me," I whispered, "if I suggest that we had better not wait here till Sir Percival comes back? I am very much afraid he is over-excited with wine."

She consented to leave the room in a weary, absent manner.

As soon as we were safe upstairs again, I did all I could to compose her ladyship's spirits. I reminded her that Mr. Fairlie's letters to Miss Halcombe and to herself did certainly sanction, and even render necessary, sooner or later, the course that had been taken. She agreed to this, and even admitted, of her own accord, that both letters were strictly in character with her uncle's peculiar disposition—but her fears about Miss Halcombe, and her unaccountable dread of sleeping at the Count's house in London, still remained unshaken in spite of every consideration that I could urge. I thought it my duty to protest against Lady Glyde's unfavourable opinion of his lordship, and I did so, with becoming forbearance and respect.

"Your ladyship will pardon my freedom," I remarked, in conclusion, "but it is said, 'by their fruits ye shall know them.' I am sure the Count's constant kindness and constant attention, from the very beginning of Miss Halcombe's illness, merit our best confidence and esteem. Even his lordship's serious misunderstanding with Mr. Dawson was entirely attributable to his anxiety on Miss Halcombe's account."

"What misunderstanding?" inquired her ladyship, with a look of sudden interest.

I related the unhappy circumstances under which Mr. Dawson had withdrawn his attendance—mentioning them all the more readily because I disapproved of Sir Percival's continuing to conceal what had happened (as he had done in my presence) from the knowledge of Lady Glyde.

Her ladyship started up, with every appearance of being additionally agitated and alarmed by what I had told her.

"Worse! worse than I thought!" she said, walking about the room, in a bewildered manner. "The Count knew Mr. Dawson would never consent to Marian's taking a journey—he purposely insulted the doctor to get him out of the house."

"Oh, my lady! my lady!" I remonstrated.

"Mrs. Michelson!" she went on vehemently, "no words that ever were spoken will persuade me that my sister is in that man's power and in that man's house with her own consent. My horror of him is such, that nothing Sir Percival could say and no letters my uncle could write, would induce me, if I had only my own feelings to consult, to eat, drink, or sleep under his roof. But my misery of suspense about Marian gives me the courage to follow her anywhere, to follow her even into Count Fosco's house."

I thought it right, at this point, to mention that Miss Halcombe had already gone on to Cumberland, according to Sir Percival's account of the matter.

"I am afraid to believe it!" answered her ladyship. "I am afraid she is still in that man's house. If I am wrong, if she has really gone on to Limmeridge, I am resolved I will not sleep to-morrow night under Count Fosco's roof. My dearest friend in the world, next to my sister, lives near London. You have heard me, you have heard Miss Halcombe, speak of Mrs. Vesey? I mean to write, and propose to sleep at her house. I don't know how I shall get there—I don't know how I shall avoid the Count—but to that refuge I will escape in some way, if my sister has gone to Cumberland. All I ask of you to do, is to see yourself that my letter to Mrs. Vesey goes to London to-night, as certainly as Sir Percival's letter goes to Count Fosco. I have reasons for not trusting the post-bag downstairs. Will you keep my secret, and help me in this? it is the last favour, perhaps, that I shall ever ask of you."

I hesitated, I thought it all very strange, I almost feared that her ladyship's mind had been a little affected by recent anxiety and suffering. At my own risk, however, I ended by giving my consent. If the letter had been addressed to a stranger, or to any one but a lady so well known to me by report as Mrs. Vesey, I might have refused. I thank God—looking to what happened afterwards—I thank God I never thwarted that wish, or any other, which Lady Glyde expressed to me, on the last day of her residence at Blackwater Park.

The letter was written and given into my hands. I myself put it into the post-box in the village that evening.

We saw nothing more of Sir Percival for the rest of the day.

I slept, by Lady Glyde's own desire, in the next room to hers, with the door open between us. There was something so strange and dreadful in the loneliness and emptiness of the house, that I was glad, on my side, to have a companion near me. Her ladyship sat up late, reading letters and burning them, and emptying her drawers and cabinets of little things she prized, as if she never expected to return to Blackwater Park. Her sleep was sadly disturbed when she at last went to bed—she cried out in it several times, once so loud that she woke herself. Whatever her dreams were, she did not think fit to communicate them to me. Perhaps, in my situation, I had no right to expect that she should do so. It matters little now. I was sorry for her, I was indeed heartily sorry for her all the same.

The next day was fine and sunny. Sir Percival came up, after breakfast, to tell us that the chaise would be at the door at a quarter to twelve—the train to London stopping at our station at twenty minutes after. He informed Lady Glyde that he was obliged to go out, but added that he hoped to be back before she left. If any unforeseen accident delayed him, I was to accompany her to the station, and to take special care that she was in time for the train. Sir Percival communicated these directions very hastily—walking here and there about the room all the time. Her ladyship looked attentively after him wherever he went. He never once looked at her in return.

She only spoke when he had done, and then she stopped him as he approached the door, by holding out her hand.

"I shall see you no more," she said, in a very marked manner. "This is our parting—our parting, it may be for ever. Will you try to forgive me, Percival, as heartily as I forgive you?"

His face turned of an awful whiteness all over, and great beads of perspiration broke out on his bald forehead. "I shall come back," he said, and made for the door, as hastily as if his wife's farewell words had frightened him out of the room.

I had never liked Sir Percival, but the manner in which he left Lady Glyde made me feel ashamed of having eaten his bread and lived in his service. I thought of saying a few comforting and Christian words to the poor lady, but there was something in her face, as she looked after her husband when the door closed on him, that made me alter my mind and keep silence.

At the time named the chaise drew up at the gates. Her ladyship was right—Sir Percival never came back. I waited for him till the last moment, and waited in vain.

No positive responsibility lay on my shoulders, and yet I did not feel easy in my mind. "It is of your own free will," I said, as the chaise drove through the lodge-gates, "that your ladyship goes to London?"

"I will go anywhere," she answered, "to end the dreadful suspense that I am suffering at this moment."

She had made me feel almost as anxious and as uncertain about Miss Halcombe as she felt herself. I presumed to ask her to write me a line, if all went well in London. She answered, "Most willingly, Mrs. Michelson."

"We all have our crosses to bear, my lady," I said, seeing her silent and thoughtful, after she had promised to write.

She made no reply — she seemed to be too much wrapped up in her own thoughts to attend to me.

"I fear your ladyship rested badly last night," I remarked, after waiting a little.

"Yes," she said, "I was terribly disturbed by dreams."

"Indeed, my lady?" I thought she was going to tell me her dreams, but no, when she spoke next it was only to ask a question.

"You posted the letter to Mrs. Vesey with your own hands?"

"Yes, my lady."

"Did Sir Percival say, yesterday, that Count Fosco was to meet me at the terminus in London?"

"He did, my lady."

She sighed heavily when I answered that last question, and said no more.

We arrived at the station, with hardly two minutes to spare. The gardener (who had driven us) managed about the luggage, while I took the ticket. The whistle of the train was sounding when I joined her ladyship on the platform. She looked very strangely, and pressed her hand over her heart, as if some sudden pain or fright had overcome her at that moment.

"I wish you were going with me!" she said, catching eagerly at my arm when I gave her the ticket.

If there had been time, if I had felt the day before as I felt then, I would have made my arrangements to accompany her, even though the doing so had obliged me to give Sir Percival warning on the spot. As it was, her wishes, expressed at the last moment only, were expressed too late for me to comply with them. She seemed to understand this herself before I could explain it, and did not repeat her desire to have me for a travelling companion. The train drew up at the platform. She gave the gardener a present for his children, and took my hand, in her simple hearty manner, before she got into the carriage.

"You have been very kind to me and to my sister," she said—"kind when we were both friendless. I shall remember you gratefully, as long as I live to remember any one. Good-bye—and God bless you!"

She spoke those words with a tone and a look which brought the tears into my eyes—she spoke them as if she was bidding me farewell for ever.

"Good-bye, my lady," I said, putting her into the carriage, and trying to cheer her; "good-bye, for the present only; good-bye, with my best and kindest wishes for happier times."

She shook her head, and shuddered as she settled herself in the carriage. The guard closed the door. "Do you believe in dreams?" she whispered to me at the window. "My dreams, last night, were dreams I have never had before. The terror of them is hanging over me still." The whistle sounded before I could answer, and the train moved. Her pale quiet face looked at me for the last time—looked sorrowfully and solemnly from the window. She waved her hand, and I saw her no more.

Towards five o'clock on the afternoon of that same day, having a little time to myself in the midst of the household duties which now pressed upon me, I sat down alone in my own room, to try and compose my mind with the volume of my husband's Sermons. For the first time in my life I found my attention wandering over those pious and cheering words. Concluding that Lady Glyde's departure must have disturbed me far more seriously than I had myself supposed, I put the book aside, and went out to take a turn in the garden. Sir Percival had not yet returned, to my knowledge, so I could feel no hesitation about showing myself in the grounds.

On turning the corner of the house, and gaining a view of the garden, I was startled by seeing a stranger walking in it. The stranger was a woman—she was lounging along the path with her back to me, and was gathering the flowers.

As I approached she heard me, and turned round.

My blood curdled in my veins. The strange woman in the garden was Mrs. Rubelle!

I could neither move nor speak. She came up to me, as composedly as ever, with her flowers in her hand.

"What is the matter, ma'am?" she said quietly.

"You here!" I gasped out. "Not gone to London! Not gone to Cumberland!"

Mrs. Rubelle smelt at her flowers with a smile of malicious pity.

"Certainly not," she said. "I have never left Blackwater Park."

I summoned breath enough and courage enough for another question.

"Where is Miss Halcombe?"

Mrs. Rubelle fairly laughed at me this time, and replied in these words—

"Miss Halcombe, ma'am, has not left Blackwater Park either."

When I heard that astounding answer, all my thoughts were startled back on the instant to my parting with Lady Glyde. I can hardly say I reproached myself, but at that moment I think I would have given many a year's hard savings to have known four hours earlier what I knew now.

Mrs. Rubelle waited, quietly arranging her nosegay, as if she expected me to say something.

I could say nothing. I thought of Lady Glyde's worn-out energies and weakly health, and I trembled for the time when the shock of the discovery that I had made would fall on her. For a minute or more my fears for the poor ladies silenced me. At the end of that time Mrs. Rubelle looked up sideways from her flowers, and said, "Here is Sir Percival, ma'am, returned from his ride."

I saw him as soon as she did. He came towards us, slashing

viciously at the flowers with his riding-whip. When he was near enough to see my face he stopped, struck at his boot with the whip, and burst out laughing, so harshly and so violently that the birds flew away, startled, from the tree by which he stood.

"Well, Mrs. Michelson," he said, "you have found it out at last, have you?"

I made no reply. He turned to Mrs. Rubelle.

"When did you show yourself in the garden?"

"I showed myself about half an hour ago, sir. You said I might take my liberty again as soon as Lady Glyde had gone away to London."

"Quite right. I don't blame you — I only asked the question." He waited a moment, and then addressed himself once more to me. "You can't believe it, can you?" he said mockingly. "Here! come along and see for yourself."

He led the way round to the front of the house. I followed him, and Mrs. Rubelle followed me. After passing through the iron gates he stopped, and pointed with his whip to the disused middle wing of the building.

"There!" he said. "Look up at the first floor. You know the old Elizabethan bedrooms? Miss Halcombe is snug and safe in one of the best of them at this moment. Take her in, Mrs. Rubelle (you have got your key?); take Mrs. Michelson in, and let her own eyes satisfy her that there is no deception this time."

The tone in which he spoke to me, and the minute or two that had passed since we left the garden, helped me to recover my spirits a little. What I might have done at this critical moment, if all my life had been passed in service, I cannot say. As it was, possessing the feelings, the principles, and the bringing up of a lady, I could not hesitate about the right course to pursue. My duty to myself, and my duty to Lady Glyde, alike forbade me to remain in the employment of a man who had shamefully deceived us both by a series of atrocious falsehoods.

"I must beg permission, Sir Percival, to speak a few words to you in private," I said. "Having done so, I shall be ready to proceed with this person to Miss Halcombe's room."

Mrs. Rubelle, whom I had indicated by a slight turn of my head, insolently sniffed at her nosegay and walked away, with great deliberation, towards the house door.

"Well," said Sir Percival sharply, "what is it now?"

"I wish to mention, sir, that I am desirous of resigning the situation I now hold at Blackwater Park." That was literally how I put it. I was resolved that the first words spoken in his presence should be words which expressed my intention to leave his service.

He eyed me with one of his blackest looks, and thrust his hands savagely into the pockets of his riding-coat.

"Why?" he said; "why, I should like to know?"

"It is not for me, Sir Percival, to express an opinion on what has taken place in this house. I desire to give no offence. I merely wish to say that I do not feel it consistent with my duty to Lady Glyde and to myself to remain any longer in your service."

"Is it consistent with your duty to me to stand there, casting suspicion on me to my face?" he broke out in his most violent manner. "I see what you're driving at. You have taken your own mean, underhand view of an innocent deception practised on Lady Glyde for her own good. It was essential to her health that she should have a change of air immediately, and you know as well as I do she would never have gone away if she had been told Miss Halcombe was still left here. She has been deceived in her own interests—and I don't care who knows it. Go, if you like—there are plenty of housekeepers as good as you to be had for the asking. Go when you please—but take care how you spread scandals about me and my affairs when you're out of my service. Tell the truth, and nothing but the truth, or it will be the worse for you! See Miss Halcombe for yourself—see if she hasn't been as well taken care of in one part of the house as in the other. Remember the doctor's own orders that Lady Glyde was to have a change of air at the earliest possible opportunity. Bear all that well in mind, and then say anything against me and my proceedings if you dare!"

He poured out these words fiercely, all in a breath, walking backwards and forwards, and striking about him in the air with his whip.

Nothing that he said or did shook my opinion of the disgraceful series of falsehoods that he had told in my presence the day before, or of the cruel deception by which he had separated Lady Glyde from her sister, and had sent her uselessly to London, when she was half distracted with anxiety on Miss Halcombe's account. I naturally kept these thoughts to myself, and said nothing more to irritate him; but I was not the less resolved to persist in my purpose. A soft answer turneth away wrath, and I suppressed my own feelings accordingly when it was my turn to reply.

"While I am in your service, Sir Percival," I said, "I hope I know my duty well enough not to inquire into your motives. When I am out of your service, I hope I know my own place well enough not to speak of matters which don't concern me—"

"When do you want to go?" he asked, interrupting me without ceremony. "Don't suppose I am anxious to keep you—don't suppose I care about your leaving the house. I am perfectly fair and open in this matter, from first to last. When do you want to go?"

"I should wish to leave at your earliest convenience, Sir Percival."

"My convenience has nothing to do with it. I shall be out of the house for good and all to-morrow morning, and I can settle your accounts to-night. If you want to study anybody's convenience, it had better be Miss Halcombe's. Mrs. Rubelle's time is up to-day, and she has reasons for wishing to be in London to-night. If you go at once, Miss Halcombe won't have a soul left here to look after her."

I hope it is unnecessary for me to say that I was quite incapable of deserting Miss Halcombe in such an emergency as had now befallen Lady Glyde and herself. After first distinctly ascertaining from Sir Percival that Mrs. Rubelle was certain to leave at once if I took her place, and after also obtaining permission to arrange for Mr. Dawson's resuming his attendance on his patient, I willingly consented to remain at Blackwater Park until Miss Halcombe no longer required my services. It was settled that I should give Sir Percival's solicitor a week's notice before I left, and that he was to undertake the necessary arrangements for appointing my successor. The matter was discussed in very few words. At its conclusion Sir Percival abruptly turned on his heel, and left me free to join Mrs. Rubelle. That singular foreign person had been sitting composedly on the door-step all this time, waiting till I could follow her to Miss Halcombe's room.

I had hardly walked half-way towards the house when Sir

Percival, who had withdrawn in the opposite direction, suddenly stopped and called me back.

"Why are you leaving my service?" he asked.

The question was so extraordinary, after what had just passed between us, that I hardly knew what to say in answer to it.

"Mind! I don't know why you are going," he went on. "You must give a reason for leaving me, I suppose, when you get another situation. What reason? The breaking up of the family? Is that it?"

"There can be no positive objection, Sir Percival, to that reason — —"

"Very well! That's all I want to know. If people apply for your character, that's your reason, stated by yourself. You go in consequence of the breaking up of the family."

He turned away again before I could say another word, and walked out rapidly into the grounds. His manner was as strange as his language. I acknowledge he alarmed me.

Even the patience of Mrs. Rubelle was getting exhausted, when I joined her at the house door.

"At last!" she said, with a shrug of her lean foreign shoulders. She led the way into the inhabited side of the house, ascended the stairs, and opened with her key the door at the end of the passage, which communicated with the old Elizabethan rooms — a door never previously used, in my time, at Blackwater Park. The rooms themselves I knew well, having entered them myself on various occasions from the other side of the house. Mrs. Rubelle stopped at the third door along the old gallery, handed me the key of it, with the key of the door of communication, and told me I should find Miss Halcombe in that room. Before I went in I thought it desirable to make her understand that her attendance had ceased. Accordingly, I told her in plain words that the charge of the sick lady henceforth devolved entirely on myself.

"I am glad to hear it, ma'am," said Mrs. Rubelle. "I want to go very much."

"Do you leave to-day?" I asked, to make sure of her.

"Now that you have taken charge, ma'am, I leave in half an hour's time. Sir Percival has kindly placed at my disposition the gardener, and the chaise, whenever I want them. I shall want them in half an hour's time to go to the station. I am packed up in anticipation already. I wish you good-day, ma'am."

She dropped a brisk curtsey, and walked back along the gallery, humming a little tune, and keeping time to it cheerfully with the nosegay in her hand. I am sincerely thankful to say that was the last I saw of Mrs. Rubelle.

When I went into the room Miss Halcombe was asleep. I looked at her anxiously, as she lay in the dismal, high, old-fashioned bed. She was certainly not in any respect altered for the worse since I had seen her last. She had not been neglected, I am bound to admit, in any way that I could perceive. The room was dreary, and dusty, and dark, but the window (looking on a solitary court-yard at the back of the house) was opened to let in the fresh air, and all that could be done to make the place comfortable had been done. The whole cruelty of Sir Percival's deception had fallen on poor Lady Glyde. The only ill-usage which either he or Mrs. Rubelle had inflicted on Miss Halcombe consisted, so far as I could see, in the first offence of hiding her away.

I stole back, leaving the sick lady still peacefully asleep, to give the gardener instructions about bringing the doctor. I begged the man, after he had taken Mrs. Rubelle to the station, to drive round by Mr. Dawson's, and leave a message in my name, asking him to call and see me. I knew he would come on my account, and I knew he would remain when he found Count Fosco had left the house.

In due course of time the gardener returned, and said that he had driven round by Mr. Dawson's residence, after leaving Mrs. Rubelle at the station. The doctor sent me word that he was poorly in health himself, but that he would call, if possible, the next morning.

Having delivered his message the gardener was about to withdraw, but I stopped him to request that he would come back before dark, and sit up that night, in one of the empty bedrooms, so as to be within call in case I wanted him. He understood readily enough my unwillingness to be left alone all night in the most desolate part of that desolate house, and we arranged that he should come in between eight and nine.

He came punctually, and I found cause to be thankful that I

had adopted the precaution of calling him in. Before midnight Sir Percival's strange temper broke out in the most violent and most alarming manner, and if the gardener had not been on the spot to pacify him on the instant, I am afraid to think what might have happened.

Almost all the afternoon and evening he had been walking about the house and grounds in an unsettled, excitable manner, having, in all probability, as I thought, taken an excessive quantity of wine at his solitary dinner. However that may be, I heard his voice calling loudly and angrily in the new wing of the house, as I was taking a turn backwards and forwards along the gallery the last thing at night. The gardener immediately ran down to him, and I closed the door of communication, to keep the alarm, if possible, from reaching Miss Halcombe's ears. It was full half an hour before the gardener came back. He declared that his master was quite out of his senses—not through the excitement of drink, as I had supposed, but through a kind of panic or frenzy of mind, for which it was impossible to account. He had found Sir Percival walking backwards and forwards by himself in the hall, swearing, with every appearance of the most violent passion, that he would not stop another minute alone in such a dungeon as his own house, and that he would take the first stage of his journey immediately in the middle of the night. The gardener, on approaching him, had been hunted out, with oaths and threats, to get the horse and chaise ready instantly. In a quarter of an hour Sir Percival had joined him in the yard, had jumped into the chaise, and, lashing the horse into a gallop, had driven himself away, with his face as pale as ashes in the moonlight. The gardener had heard him shouting and cursing at the lodge-keeper to get up and open the gate—had heard the wheels roll furiously on again in the still night, when the gate was unlocked—and knew no more.

The next day, or a day or two after, I forget which, the chaise was brought back from Knowlesbury, our nearest town, by the ostler at the old inn. Sir Percival had stopped there, and had afterwards left by the train—for what destination the man could not tell. I never received any further information, either from himself or from any one else, of Sir Percival's proceedings, and I am not even aware, at this moment, whether he is in England or out of it. He and I have not met since he drove away like an escaped criminal from his own house, and it is my fervent hope and prayer that we may never meet again.

My own part of this sad family story is now drawing to an

end.

I have been informed that the particulars of Miss Halcombe's waking, and of what passed between us when she found me sitting by her bedside, are not material to the purpose which is to be answered by the present narrative. It will be sufficient for me to say in this place, that she was not herself conscious of the means adopted to remove her from the inhabited to the uninhabited part of the house. She was in a deep sleep at the time, whether naturally or artificially produced she could not say. In my absence at Torquay, and in the absence of all the resident servants except Margaret Porcher (who was perpetually eating, drinking, or sleeping, when she was not at work), the secret transfer of Miss Halcombe from one part of the house to the other was no doubt easily performed. Mrs. Rubelle (as I discovered for myself, in looking about the room) had provisions, and all other necessaries, together with the means of heating water, broth, and so on, without kindling a fire, placed at her disposal during the few days of her imprisonment with the sick lady. She had declined to answer the questions which Miss Halcombe naturally put, but had not, in other respects, treated her with unkindness or neglect. The disgrace of lending herself to a vile deception is the only disgrace with which I can conscientiously charge Mrs. Rubelle.

I need write no particulars (and I am relieved to know it) of the effect produced on Miss Halcombe by the news of Lady Glyde's departure, or by the far more melancholy tidings which reached us only too soon afterwards at Blackwater Park. In both cases I prepared her mind beforehand as gently and as carefully as possible, having the doctor's advice to guide me, in the last case only, through Mr. Dawson's being too unwell to come to the house for some days after I had sent for him. It was a sad time, a time which it afflicts me to think of or to write of now. The precious blessings of religious consolation which I endeavoured to convey were long in reaching Miss Halcombe's heart, but I hope and believe they came home to her at last. I never left her till her strength was restored. The train which took me away from that miserable house was the train which took her away also. We parted very mournfully in London. I remained with a relative at Islington, and she went on to Mr. Fairlie's house in Cumberland.

I have only a few lines more to write before I close this painful statement. They are dictated by a sense of duty.

In the first place, I wish to record my own personal conviction that no blame whatever, in connection with the events which I have now related, attaches to Count Fosco. I am informed that a dreadful suspicion has been raised, and that some very serious constructions are placed upon his lordship's conduct. My persuasion of the Count's innocence remains, however, quite unshaken. If he assisted Sir Percival in sending me to Torquay, he assisted under a delusion, for which, as a foreigner and a stranger, he was not to blame. If he was concerned in bringing Mrs. Rubelle to Blackwater Park, it was his misfortune and not his fault, when that foreign person was base enough to assist a deception planned and carried out by the master of the house. I protest, in the interests of morality, against blame being gratuitously and wantonly attached to the proceedings of the Count.

In the second place, I desire to express my regret at my own inability to remember the precise day on which Lady Glyde left Blackwater Park for London. I am told that it is of the last importance to ascertain the exact date of that lamentable journey, and I have anxiously taxed my memory to recall it. The effort has been in vain. I can only remember now that it was towards the latter part of July. We all know the difficulty, after a lapse of time, of fixing precisely on a past date unless it has been previously written down. That difficulty is greatly increased in my case by the alarming and confusing events which took place about the period of Lady Glyde's departure. I heartily wish I had made a memorandum at the time. I heartily wish my memory of the date was as vivid as my memory of that poor lady's face, when it looked at me sorrowfully for the last time from the carriage window.

THE STORY CONTINUED IN SEVERAL NARRATIVES

1. THE NARRATIVE OF HESTER PINHORN, COOK IN THE SERVICE OF COUNT FOSCO

[Taken down from her own statement]

I am sorry to say that I have never learnt to read or write. I have been a hard-working woman all my life, and have kept a good character. I know that it is a sin and wickedness to say the thing which is not, and I will truly beware of doing so on this occasion. All that I know I will tell, and I humbly beg the gentleman who takes this down to put my language right as he goes on, and to make allowances for my being no scholar.

In this last summer I happened to be out of place (through no fault of my own), and I heard of a situation as plain cook, at Number Five, Forest Road, St. John's Wood. I took the place on trial. My master's name was Fosco. My mistress was an English lady. He was Count and she was Countess. There was a girl to do housemaid's work when I got there. She was not over-clean or tidy, but there was no harm in her. I and she were the only servants in the house.

Our master and mistress came after we got in; and as soon as they did come we were told, downstairs, that company was expected from the country.

The company was my mistress's niece, and the back bedroom on the first floor was got ready for her. My mistress mentioned to me that Lady Glyde (that was her name) was in poor health, and that I must be particular in my cooking accordingly. She was to come that day, as well as I can remember — but whatever you do, don't trust my memory in the matter. I am sorry to say it's no use asking me about days of the month, and such-like. Except Sundays, half my time I take no heed of them, being a hard-working woman and no scholar. All I know is Lady Glyde came, and when she did come, a fine fright she gave us all surely. I don't know how master brought her to the house, being hard at work at the time. But he did bring her in the afternoon, I think, and the housemaid opened the door to them, and showed them into the parlour. Before she had been long down in the kitchen again with me, we heard a hurry-skurry upstairs, and the parlour bell ringing like mad, and my mistress's voice calling out for help.

We both ran up, and there we saw the lady laid on the sofa, with her face ghastly white, and her hands fast clenched, and her head drawn down to one side. She had been taken with a sudden fright, my mistress said, and master he told us she was in a fit of convulsions. I ran out, knowing the neighbourhood a little better than the rest of them, to fetch the nearest doctor's help. The nearest help was at Goodricke's and Garth's, who worked together as partners, and had a good name and connection, as I have heard, all round St. John's Wood. Mr. Goodricke was in, and he came back with me directly.

It was some time before he could make himself of much use. The poor unfortunate lady fell out of one fit into another, and went on so till she was quite wearied out, and as helpless as a new-born babe. We then got her to bed. Mr. Goodricke went away to his house for medicine, and came back again in a quarter of an hour or less. Besides the medicine he brought a bit of hollow mahogany wood with him, shaped like a kind of trumpet, and after waiting a little while, he put one end over the lady's heart and the other to his ear, and listened carefully.

When he had done he says to my mistress, who was in the room, "This is a very serious case," he says, "I recommend you to write to Lady Glyde's friends directly." My mistress says to him, "Is it heart-disease?" And he says, "Yes, heart-disease of a most dangerous kind." He told her exactly what he thought was the matter, which I was not clever enough to understand. But I know this, he ended by saying that he was afraid neither his help nor any other doctor's help was likely to be of much service.

My mistress took this ill news more quietly than my master. He was a big, fat, odd sort of elderly man, who kept birds and white mice, and spoke to them as if they were so many Christian children. He seemed terribly cut up by what had happened. "Ah! poor Lady Glyde! poor dear Lady Glyde!" he says, and went stalking about, wringing his fat hands more like a play-actor than a gentleman. For one question my mistress asked the doctor about the lady's chances of getting round, he asked a good fifty at least. I declare he quite tormented us all, and when he was quiet at last, out he went into the bit of back garden, picking trumpery little nosegays, and asking me to take them upstairs and make the sick-room look pretty with them. As if that did any good. I think he must have been, at times, a little soft in his head. But he was not a bad master—he had a monstrous civil tongue of his own, and a jolly, easy, coaxing way with him. I liked him a deal better than my mistress. She was a hard one, if ever there was a hard one yet.

The Woman in White

Towards night-time the lady roused up a little. She had been so wearied out, before that, by the convulsions, that she never stirred hand or foot, or spoke a word to anybody. She moved in the bed now, and stared about her at the room and us in it. She must have been a nice-looking lady when well, with light hair, and blue eyes and all that. Her rest was troubled at night — at least so I heard from my mistress, who sat up alone with her. I only went in once before going to bed to see if I could be of any use, and then she was talking to herself in a confused, rambling manner. She seemed to want sadly to speak to somebody who was absent from her somewhere. I couldn't catch the name the first time, and the second time master knocked at the door, with his regular mouthful of questions, and another of his trumpery nosegays.

When I went in early the next morning, the lady was clean worn out again, and lay in a kind of faint sleep. Mr. Goodricke brought his partner, Mr. Garth, with him to advise. They said she must not be disturbed out of her rest on any account. They asked my mistress many questions, at the other end of the room, about what the lady's health had been in past times, and who had attended her, and whether she had ever suffered much and long together under distress of mind. I remember my mistress said "Yes" to that last question. And Mr. Goodricke looked at Mr. Garth, and shook his head; and Mr. Garth looked at Mr. Goodricke, and shook his head. They seemed to think that the distress might have something to do with the mischief at the lady's heart. She was but a frail thing to look at, poor creature! Very little strength at any time, I should say — very little strength.

Later on the same morning, when she woke, the lady took a sudden turn, and got seemingly a great deal better. I was not let in again to see her, no more was the housemaid, for the reason that she was not to be disturbed by strangers. What I heard of her being better was through my master. He was in wonderful good spirits about the change, and looked in at the kitchen window from the garden, with his great big curly-brimmed white hat on, to go out.

"Good Mrs. Cook," says he, "Lady Glyde is better. My mind is more easy than it was, and I am going out to stretch my big legs with a sunny little summer walk. Shall I order for you, shall I market for you, Mrs. Cook? What are you making there? A nice tart for dinner? Much crust, if you please — much crisp crust, my dear, that melts and crumbles delicious in the mouth." That was his way. He was past sixty, and fond of pastry. Just think of that!

The doctor came again in the forenoon, and saw for himself that Lady Glyde had woke up better. He forbid us to talk to her, or to let her talk to us, in case she was that way disposed, saying she must be kept quiet before all things, and encouraged to sleep as much as possible. She did not seem to want to talk whenever I saw her, except overnight, when I couldn't make out what she was saying—she seemed too much worn down. Mr. Goodricke was not nearly in such good spirits about her as master. He said nothing when he came downstairs, except that he would call again at five o'clock.

About that time (which was before master came home again) the bell rang hard from the bedroom, and my mistress ran out into the landing, and called to me to go for Mr. Goodricke, and tell him the lady had fainted. I got on my bonnet and shawl, when, as good luck would have it, the doctor himself came to the house for his promised visit.

I let him in, and went upstairs along with him. "Lady Glyde was just as usual," says my mistress to him at the door; "she was awake, and looking about her in a strange, forlorn manner, when I heard her give a sort of half cry, and she fainted in a moment." The doctor went up to the bed, and stooped down over the sick lady. He looked very serious, all on a sudden, at the sight of her, and put his hand on her heart.

My mistress stared hard in Mr. Goodricke's face. "Not dead!" says she, whispering, and turning all of a tremble from head to foot.

"Yes," says the doctor, very quiet and grave. "Dead. I was afraid it would happen suddenly when I examined her heart yesterday." My mistress stepped back from the bedside while he was speaking, and trembled and trembled again. "Dead!" she whispers to herself; "dead so suddenly! dead so soon! What will the Count say?" Mr. Goodricke advised her to go downstairs, and quiet herself a little. "You have been sitting up all night," says he, "and your nerves are shaken. This person," says he, meaning me, "this person will stay in the room till I can send for the necessary assistance." My mistress did as he told her. "I must prepare the Count," she says. "I must carefully prepare the Count." And so she left us, shaking from head to foot, and went out.

"Your master is a foreigner," says Mr. Goodricke, when my mistress had left us. "Does he understand about registering the death?" "I can't rightly tell, sir," says I, "but I should think not." The doctor considered a minute, and then says he, "I don't

The Woman in White

usually do such things," says he, "but it may save the family trouble in this case if I register the death myself. I shall pass the district office in half an hour's time, and I can easily look in. Mention, if you please, that I will do so." "Yes, sir," says I, "with thanks, I'm sure, for your kindness in thinking of it." "You don't mind staying here till I can send you the proper person?" says he. "No, sir," says I; "I'll stay with the poor lady till then. I suppose nothing more could be done, sir, than was done?" says I. "No," says he, "nothing; she must have suffered sadly before ever I saw her—the case was hopeless when I was called in." "Ah, dear me! we all come to it, sooner or later, don't we, sir?" says I. He gave no answer to that—he didn't seem to care about talking. He said, "Good-day," and went out.

I stopped by the bedside from that time till the time when Mr. Goodricke sent the person in, as he had promised. She was, by name, Jane Gould. I considered her to be a respectable-looking woman. She made no remark, except to say that she understood what was wanted of her, and that she had winded a many of them in her time.

How master bore the news, when he first heard it, is more than I can tell, not having been present. When I did see him he looked awfully overcome by it, to be sure. He sat quiet in a corner, with his fat hands hanging over his thick knees, and his head down, and his eyes looking at nothing. He seemed not so much sorry, as scared and dazed like, by what had happened. My mistress managed all that was to be done about the funeral. It must have cost a sight of money—the coffin, in particular, being most beautiful. The dead lady's husband was away, as we heard, in foreign parts. But my mistress (being her aunt) settled it with her friends in the country (Cumberland, I think) that she should be buried there, in the same grave along with her mother. Everything was done handsomely, in respect of the funeral, I say again, and master went down to attend the burying in the country himself. He looked grand in his deep mourning, with his big solemn face, and his slow walk, and his broad hatband—that he did!

In conclusion. I have to say, in answer to questions put to me—

(1) That neither I nor my fellow-servant ever saw my master give Lady Glyde any medicine himself.

(2) That he was never, to my knowledge and belief, left alone in the room with Lady Glyde.

(3) That I am not able to say what caused the sudden fright, which my mistress informed me had seized the lady on her first coming into the house. The cause was never explained, either to me or to my fellow-servant.

The above statement has been read over in my presence. I have nothing to add to it, or to take away from it. I say, on my oath as a Christian woman, this is the truth.

(Signed) HESTER PINHORN, Her + Mark.

2. THE NARRATIVE OF THE DOCTOR

To the Registrar of the Sub-District in which the undermentioned death took place.—I hereby certify that I attended Lady Glyde, aged Twenty-One last Birthday; that I last saw her on Thursday the 25th July 1850; that she died on the same day at No. 5 Forest Road, St. John's Wood, and that the cause of her death was Aneurism. Duration of disease not known.

(Signed) ALFRED GOODRICKE.

Prof. Title. M.R.C.S. Eng., L.S.A.

Address, 12 Croydon Gardens

St. John's Wood.

3. THE NARRATIVE OF JANE GOULD

I was the person sent in by Mr. Goodricke to do what was right and needful by the remains of a lady who had died at the house named in the certificate which precedes this. I found the body in charge of the servant, Hester Pinhorn. I remained with it, and prepared it at the proper time for the grave. It was laid in the coffin in my presence, and I afterwards saw the coffin screwed down previous to its removal. When that had been done, and not before, I received what was due to me and left the house. I refer persons who may wish to investigate my character to Mr. Goodricke. He will bear witness that I can be trusted to tell the truth.

(Signed) JANE GOULD.

4. THE NARRATIVE OF THE TOMBSTONE

Sacred to the Memory of Laura, Lady Glyde, wife of Sir Percival Glyde, Bart., of Blackwater Park, Hampshire, and daughter of the late Philip Fairlie, Esq., of Limmeridge House, in this parish. Born March 27th, 1829; married December 22nd, 1849; died July 25th, 1850.

5. THE NARRATIVE OF WALTER HARTRIGHT

Early in the summer of 1850 I and my surviving companions left the wilds and forests of Central America for home. Arrived at the coast, we took ship there for England. The vessel was wrecked in the Gulf of Mexico—I was among the few saved from the sea. It was my third escape from peril of death. Death by disease, death by the Indians, death by drowning—all three had approached me; all three had passed me by.

The survivors of the wreck were rescued by an American vessel bound for Liverpool. The ship reached her port on the thirteenth day of October 1850. We landed late in the afternoon, and I arrived in London the same night.

These pages are not the record of my wanderings and my dangers away from home. The motives which led me from my country and my friends to a new world of adventure and peril are known. From that self-imposed exile I came back, as I had hoped, prayed, believed I should come back—a changed man. In the waters of a new life I had tempered my nature afresh. In the stern school of extremity and danger my will had learnt to be strong, my heart to be resolute, my mind to rely on itself. I had gone out to fly from my own future. I came back to face it, as a man should.

To face it with that inevitable suppression of myself which I knew it would demand from me. I had parted with the worst bitterness of the past, but not with my heart's remembrance of the sorrow and the tenderness of that memorable time. I had not ceased to feel the one irreparable disappointment of my life—I had only learnt to bear it. Laura Fairlie was in all my thoughts when the ship bore me away, and I looked my last at England. Laura Fairlie was in all my thoughts when the ship brought me back, and the morning light showed the friendly shore in view.

My pen traces the old letters as my heart goes back to the old love. I write of her as Laura Fairlie still. It is hard to think of her, it is hard to speak of her, by her husband's name.

There are no more words of explanation to add on my appearance for the second time in these pages. This narrative, if I have the strength and the courage to write it, may now go on.

My first anxieties and first hopes when the morning came centred in my mother and my sister. I felt the necessity of preparing them for the joy and surprise of my return, after an absence during which it had been impossible for them to receive any tidings of me for months past. Early in the morning I sent a letter to the Hampstead Cottage, and followed it myself in an hour's time.

When the first meeting was over, when our quiet and composure of other days began gradually to return to us, I saw something in my mother's face which told me that a secret oppression lay heavy on her heart. There was more than love—there was sorrow in the anxious eyes that looked on me so tenderly—there was pity in the kind hand that slowly and fondly strengthened its hold on mine. We had no concealments from each other. She knew how the hope of my life had been wrecked—she knew why I had left her. It was on my lips to ask as composedly as I could if any letter had come for me from Miss Halcombe, if there was any news of her sister that I might hear. But when I looked in my mother's face I lost courage to put the question even in that guarded form. I could only say, doubtingly and restrainedly—

"You have something to tell me."

My sister, who had been sitting opposite to us, rose

suddenly without a word of explanation—rose and left the room.

My mother moved closer to me on the sofa and put her arms round my neck. Those fond arms trembled—the tears flowed fast over the faithful loving face.

"Walter!" she whispered, "my own darling! my heart is heavy for you. Oh, my son! my son! try to remember that I am still left!"

My head sank on her bosom. She had said all in saying those words.

It was the morning of the third day since my return—the morning of the sixteenth of October.

I had remained with them at the cottage—I had tried hard not to embitter the happiness of my return to them as it was embittered to me. I had done all man could to rise after the shock, and accept my life resignedly—to let my great sorrow come in tenderness to my heart, and not in despair. It was useless and hopeless. No tears soothed my aching eyes, no relief came to me from my sister's sympathy or my mother's love.

On that third morning I opened my heart to them. At last the words passed my lips which I had longed to speak on the day when my mother told me of her death.

"Let me go away alone for a little while," I said. "I shall bear it better when I have looked once more at the place where I first saw her—when I have knelt and prayed by the grave where they have laid her to rest."

I departed on my journey—my journey to the grave of Laura Fairlie.

It was a quiet autumn afternoon when I stopped at the solitary station, and set forth alone on foot by the well-remembered road. The waning sun was shining faintly through thin white clouds—the air was warm and still—the peacefulness of the lonely country was overshadowed and saddened by the influence of the falling year.

I reached the moor—I stood again on the brow of the hill—I looked on along the path—and there were the familiar garden trees in the distance, the clear sweeping semicircle of the drive, the high white walls of Limmeridge House. The chances and changes, the wanderings and dangers of months and months past, all shrank and shrivelled to nothing in my mind. It was like yesterday since my feet had last trodden the fragrant heathy ground. I thought I should see her coming to meet me, with her little straw hat shading her face, her simple dress fluttering in the air, and her well-filled sketch-book ready in her hand.

Oh death, thou hast thy sting! oh, grave, thou hast thy victory!

I turned aside, and there below me in the glen was the lonesome grey church, the porch where I had waited for the coming of the woman in white, the hills encircling the quiet burial-ground, the brook bubbling cold over its stony bed. There was the marble cross, fair and white, at the head of the tomb—the tomb that now rose over mother and daughter alike.

I approached the grave. I crossed once more the low stone stile, and bared my head as I touched the sacred ground. Sacred to gentleness and goodness, sacred to reverence and grief.

I stopped before the pedestal from which the cross rose. On one side of it, on the side nearest to me, the newly-cut inscription met my eyes—the hard, clear, cruel black letters which told the story of her life and death. I tried to read them. I did read as far as the name. "Sacred to the Memory of Laura——" The kind blue eyes dim with tears—the fair head drooping wearily—the innocent parting words which implored me to leave her—oh, for a happier last memory of her than this; the memory I took away with me, the memory I bring back with me to her grave!

A second time I tried to read the inscription. I saw at the end the date of her death, and above it——

Above it there were lines on the marble—there was a name among them which disturbed my thoughts of her. I went round to the other side of the grave, where there was nothing to read, nothing of earthly vileness to force its way between her spirit and mine.

I knelt down by the tomb. I laid my hands, I laid my head on the broad white stone, and closed my weary eyes on the earth around, on the light above. I let her come back to me. Oh, my love! my love! my heart may speak to you now! It is yesterday again since we parted—yesterday, since your dear hand lay in mine—yesterday, since my eyes looked their last on you. My

The Woman in White

love! my love!

Time had flowed on, and silence had fallen like thick night over its course.

The first sound that came after the heavenly peace rustled faintly like a passing breath of air over the grass of the burial-ground. I heard it nearing me slowly, until it came changed to my ear—came like footsteps moving onward—then stopped.

I looked up.

The sunset was near at hand. The clouds had parted—the slanting light fell mellow over the hills. The last of the day was cold and clear and still in the quiet valley of the dead.

Beyond me, in the burial-ground, standing together in the cold clearness of the lower light, I saw two women. They were looking towards the tomb, looking towards me.

Two.

They came a little on, and stopped again. Their veils were down, and hid their faces from me. When they stopped, one of them raised her veil. In the still evening light I saw the face of Marian Halcombe.

Changed, changed as if years had passed over it! The eyes large and wild, and looking at me with a strange terror in them. The face worn and wasted piteously. Pain and fear and grief written on her as with a brand.

I took one step towards her from the grave. She never moved—she never spoke. The veiled woman with her cried out faintly. I stopped. The springs of my life fell low, and the shuddering of an unutterable dread crept over me from head to foot.

The woman with the veiled face moved away from her companion, and came towards me slowly. Left by herself, standing by herself, Marian Halcombe spoke. It was the voice that I remembered—the voice not changed, like the frightened eyes and the wasted face.

"My dream! my dream!" I heard her say those words softly in the awful silence. She sank on her knees, and raised her clasped hands to heaven. "Father! strengthen him. Father! help him in his hour of need."

The woman came on, slowly and silently came on. I looked at her—at her, and at none other, from that moment.

The voice that was praying for me faltered and sank low—then rose on a sudden, and called affrightedly, called despairingly to me to come away.

But the veiled woman had possession of me, body and soul. She stopped on one side of the grave. We stood face to face with the tombstone between us. She was close to the inscription on the side of the pedestal. Her gown touched the black letters.

The voice came nearer, and rose and rose more passionately still. "Hide your face! don't look at her! Oh, for God's sake, spare him——"

The woman lifted her veil.

"Sacred to the Memory of Laura, Lady Glyde——"

Laura, Lady Glyde, was standing by the inscription, and was looking at me over the grave.

[The Second Epoch of the Story closes here.]

THE THIRD EPOCH

THE STORY CONTINUED BY WALTER HARTRIGHT.

I

I open a new page. I advance my narrative by one week.

The history of the interval which I thus pass over must remain unrecorded. My heart turns faint, my mind sinks in darkness and confusion when I think of it. This must not be, if I who write am to guide, as I ought, you who read. This must not be, if the clue that leads through the windings of the story is to remain from end to end untangled in my hands.

A life suddenly changed — its whole purpose created afresh, its hopes and fears, its struggles, its interests, and its sacrifices all turned at once and for ever into a new direction — this is the prospect which now opens before me, like the burst of view from a mountain's top. I left my narrative in the quiet shadow of Limmeridge church — I resume it, one week later, in the stir and turmoil of a London street.

The street is in a populous and a poor neighbourhood. The ground floor of one of the houses in it is occupied by a small newsvendor's shop, and the first floor and the second are let as furnished lodgings of the humblest kind.

I have taken those two floors in an assumed name. On the upper floor I live, with a room to work in, a room to sleep in. On the lower floor, under the same assumed name, two women live, who are described as my sisters. I get my bread by drawing and engraving on wood for the cheap periodicals. My sisters are supposed to help me by taking in a little needle-work. Our poor place of abode, our humble calling, our assumed relationship, and our assumed name, are all used alike as a means of hiding us in the house-forest of London. We are numbered no longer with the people whose lives are open and known. I am an obscure, unnoticed man, without patron or friend to help me. Marian Halcombe is nothing now but my eldest sister, who provides for our household wants by the toil of her own hands.

We two, in the estimation of others, are at once the dupes and the agents of a daring imposture. We are supposed to be the accomplices of mad Anne Catherick, who claims the name, the place, and the living personality of dead Lady Glyde.

That is our situation. That is the changed aspect in which we three must appear, henceforth, in this narrative, for many and many a page to come.

In the eye of reason and of law, in the estimation of relatives and friends, according to every received formality of civilised society, "Laura, Lady Glyde," lay buried with her mother in Limmeridge churchyard. Torn in her own lifetime from the list of the living, the daughter of Philip Fairlie and the wife of Percival Glyde might still exist for her sister, might still exist for me, but to all the world besides she was dead. Dead to her uncle, who had renounced her; dead to the servants of the house, who had failed to recognise her; dead to the persons in authority, who had transmitted her fortune to her husband and her aunt; dead to my mother and my sister, who believed me to be the dupe of an adventuress and the victim of a fraud; socially, morally, legally—dead.

And yet alive! Alive in poverty and in hiding. Alive, with the poor drawing-master to fight her battle, and to win the way back for her to her place in the world of living beings.

Did no suspicion, excited by my own knowledge of Anne Catherick's resemblance to her, cross my mind, when her face was first revealed to me? Not the shadow of a suspicion, from the moment when she lifted her veil by the side of the inscription which recorded her death.

Before the sun of that day had set, before the last glimpse of the home which was closed against her had passed from our view, the farewell words I spoke, when we parted at Limmeridge House, had been recalled by both of us—repeated by me, recognised by her. "If ever the time comes, when the devotion of my whole heart and soul and strength will give you a moment's happiness, or spare you a moment's sorrow, will you try to remember the poor drawing-master who has taught you?" She, who now remembered so little of the trouble and terror of a later time, remembered those words, and laid her poor head innocently and trustingly on the bosom of the man who had spoken them. In that moment, when she called me by my name, when she said, "They have tried to make me forget everything, Walter; but I remember Marian, and I remember you"—in that moment, I, who had long since given her my love, gave her my life, and thanked God that it was mine to bestow on her. Yes! the time had come. From thousands on thousands of miles away — through forest and wilderness, where companions stronger than I had fallen by my side, through peril of death thrice renewed, and thrice escaped, the Hand that leads men on the dark road to the future had led me to meet that time. Forlorn and disowned, sorely tried and sadly changed — her beauty faded, her mind clouded — robbed of her station in the world, of her place among living creatures — the devotion I had promised, the devotion of my whole heart and soul and strength, might be laid blamelessly now at those dear feet. In the right of her calamity, in the right of her friendlessness, she was mine at last! Mine to support, to protect, to cherish, to restore. Mine to love and honour as father and brother both. Mine to vindicate through all risks and all sacrifices — through the hopeless struggle against Rank and Power, through the long fight with armed deceit and fortified Success, through the waste of my reputation, through the loss of my friends, through the hazard of my life.

II

My position is defined—my motives are acknowledged. The story of Marian and the story of Laura must come next.

I shall relate both narratives, not in the words (often interrupted, often inevitably confused) of the speakers themselves, but in the words of the brief, plain, studiously simple abstract which I committed to writing for my own guidance, and for the guidance of my legal adviser. So the tangled web will be most speedily and most intelligibly unrolled.

The story of Marian begins where the narrative of the housekeeper at Blackwater Park left off.

On Lady Glyde's departure from her husband's house, the fact of that departure, and the necessary statement of the circumstances under which it had taken place, were communicated to Miss Halcombe by the housekeeper. It was not till some days afterwards (how many days exactly, Mrs. Michelson, in the absence of any written memorandum on the subject, could not undertake to say) that a letter arrived from Madame Fosco announcing Lady Glyde's sudden death in Count Fosco's house. The letter avoided mentioning dates, and left it to Mrs. Michelson's discretion to break the news at once to Miss Halcombe, or to defer doing so until that lady's health should be more firmly established.

Having consulted Mr. Dawson (who had been himself delayed, by ill health, in resuming his attendance at Blackwater Park), Mrs. Michelson, by the doctor's advice, and in the doctor's presence, communicated the news, either on the day when the letter was received, or on the day after. It is not necessary to dwell here upon the effect which the intelligence of Lady Glyde's sudden death produced on her sister. It is only useful to the present purpose to say that she was not able to travel for more than three weeks afterwards. At the end of that time she proceeded to London accompanied by the housekeeper. They parted there—Mrs. Michelson previously informing Miss Halcombe of her address, in case they might wish to communicate at a future period.

On parting with the housekeeper Miss Halcombe went at once to the office of Messrs. Gilmore & Kyrle to consult with the latter gentleman in Mr. Gilmore's absence. She mentioned to

The Woman in White

Mr. Kyrle what she had thought it desirable to conceal from every one else (Mrs. Michelson included) — her suspicion of the circumstances under which Lady Glyde was said to have met her death. Mr. Kyrle, who had previously given friendly proof of his anxiety to serve Miss Halcombe, at once undertook to make such inquiries as the delicate and dangerous nature of the investigation proposed to him would permit.

To exhaust this part of the subject before going farther, it may be mentioned that Count Fosco offered every facility to Mr. Kyrle, on that gentleman's stating that he was sent by Miss Halcombe to collect such particulars as had not yet reached her of Lady Glyde's decease. Mr. Kyrle was placed in communication with the medical man, Mr. Goodricke, and with the two servants. In the absence of any means of ascertaining the exact date of Lady Glyde's departure from Blackwater Park, the result of the doctor's and the servants' evidence, and of the volunteered statements of Count Fosco and his wife, was conclusive to the mind of Mr. Kyrle. He could only assume that the intensity of Miss Halcombe's suffering, under the loss of her sister, had misled her judgment in a most deplorable manner, and he wrote her word that the shocking suspicion to which she had alluded in his presence was, in his opinion, destitute of the smallest fragment of foundation in truth. Thus the investigation by Mr. Gilmore's partner began and ended.

Meanwhile, Miss Halcombe had returned to Limmeridge House, and had there collected all the additional information which she was able to obtain.

Mr. Fairlie had received his first intimation of his niece's death from his sister, Madame Fosco, this letter also not containing any exact reference to dates. He had sanctioned his sister's proposal that the deceased lady should be laid in her mother's grave in Limmeridge churchyard. Count Fosco had accompanied the remains to Cumberland, and had attended the funeral at Limmeridge, which took place on the 30th of July. It was followed, as a mark of respect, by all the inhabitants of the village and the neighbourhood. On the next day the inscription (originally drawn out, it was said, by the aunt of the deceased lady, and submitted for approval to her brother, Mr. Fairlie) was engraved on one side of the monument over the tomb.

On the day of the funeral, and for one day after it, Count Fosco had been received as a guest at Limmeridge House, but no interview had taken place between Mr. Fairlie and himself, by the former gentleman's desire. They had communicated by writing, and through this medium Count Fosco had made Mr.

Fairlie acquainted with the details of his niece's last illness and death. The letter presenting this information added no new facts to the facts already known, but one very remarkable paragraph was contained in the postscript. It referred to Anne Catherick.

The substance of the paragraph in question was as follows—

It first informed Mr. Fairlie that Anne Catherick (of whom he might hear full particulars from Miss Halcombe when she reached Limmeridge) had been traced and recovered in the neighbourhood of Blackwater Park, and had been for the second time placed under the charge of the medical man from whose custody she had once escaped.

This was the first part of the postscript. The second part warned Mr. Fairlie that Anne Catherick's mental malady had been aggravated by her long freedom from control, and that the insane hatred and distrust of Sir Percival Glyde, which had been one of her most marked delusions in former times, still existed under a newly-acquired form. The unfortunate woman's last idea in connection with Sir Percival was the idea of annoying and distressing him, and of elevating herself, as she supposed, in the estimation of the patients and nurses, by assuming the character of his deceased wife, the scheme of this personation having evidently occurred to her after a stolen interview which she had succeeded in obtaining with Lady Glyde, and at which she had observed the extraordinary accidental likeness between the deceased lady and herself. It was to the last degree improbable that she would succeed a second time in escaping from the Asylum, but it was just possible she might find some means of annoying the late Lady Glyde's relatives with letters, and in that case Mr. Fairlie was warned beforehand how to receive them.

The postscript, expressed in these terms, was shown to Miss Halcombe when she arrived at Limmeridge. There were also placed in her possession the clothes Lady Glyde had worn, and the other effects she had brought with her to her aunt's house. They had been carefully collected and sent to Cumberland by Madame Fosco.

Such was the posture of affairs when Miss Halcombe reached Limmeridge in the early part of September.

Shortly afterwards she was confined to her room by a relapse, her weakened physical energies giving way under the severe mental affliction from which she was now suffering. On getting stronger again, in a month's time, her suspicion of the

The Woman in White

circumstances described as attending her sister's death still remained unshaken. She had heard nothing in the interim of Sir Percival Glyde, but letters had reached her from Madame Fosco, making the most affectionate inquiries on the part of her husband and herself. Instead of answering these letters, Miss Halcombe caused the house in St. John's Wood, and the proceedings of its inmates, to be privately watched.

Nothing doubtful was discovered. The same result attended the next investigations, which were secretly instituted on the subject of Mrs. Rubelle. She had arrived in London about six months before with her husband. They had come from Lyons, and they had taken a house in the neighbourhood of Leicester Square, to be fitted up as a boarding-house for foreigners, who were expected to visit England in large numbers to see the Exhibition of 1851. Nothing was known against husband or wife in the neighbourhood. They were quiet people, and they had paid their way honestly up to the present time. The final inquiries related to Sir Percival Glyde. He was settled in Paris, and living there quietly in a small circle of English and French friends.

Foiled at all points, but still not able to rest, Miss Halcombe next determined to visit the Asylum in which she then supposed Anne Catherick to be for the second time confined. She had felt a strong curiosity about the woman in former days, and she was now doubly interested—first, in ascertaining whether the report of Anne Catherick's attempted personation of Lady Glyde was true, and secondly (if it proved to be true), in discovering for herself what the poor creature's real motives were for attempting the deceit.

Although Count Fosco's letter to Mr. Fairlie did not mention the address of the Asylum, that important omission cast no difficulties in Miss Halcombe's way. When Mr. Hartright had met Anne Catherick at Limmeridge, she had informed him of the locality in which the house was situated, and Miss Halcombe had noted down the direction in her diary, with all the other particulars of the interview exactly as she heard them from Mr. Hartright's own lips. Accordingly she looked back at the entry and extracted the address—furnished herself with the Count's letter to Mr. Fairlie as a species of credential which might be useful to her, and started by herself for the Asylum on the eleventh of October.

She passed the night of the eleventh in London. It had been her intention to sleep at the house inhabited by Lady Glyde's old governess, but Mrs. Vesey's agitation at the sight of her lost pupil's nearest and dearest friend was so distressing that Miss Halcombe considerately refrained from remaining in her presence, and removed to a respectable boarding-house in the neighbourhood, recommended by Mrs. Vesey's married sister. The next day she proceeded to the Asylum, which was situated not far from London on the northern side of the metropolis.

She was immediately admitted to see the proprietor.

At first he appeared to be decidedly unwilling to let her communicate with his patient. But on her showing him the postscript to Count Fosco's letter — on her reminding him that she was the "Miss Halcombe" there referred to — that she was a near relative of the deceased Lady Glyde — and that she was therefore naturally interested, for family reasons, in observing for herself the extent of Anne Catherick's delusion in relation to her late sister — the tone and manner of the owner of the Asylum altered, and he withdrew his objections. He probably felt that a continued refusal, under these circumstances, would not only be an act of discourtesy in itself, but would also imply that the proceedings in his establishment were not of a nature to bear investigation by respectable strangers.

Miss Halcombe's own impression was that the owner of the Asylum had not been received into the confidence of Sir Percival and the Count. His consenting at all to let her visit his patient seemed to afford one proof of this, and his readiness in making admissions which could scarcely have escaped the lips of an accomplice, certainly appeared to furnish another.

For example, in the course of the introductory conversation which took place, he informed Miss Halcombe that Anne Catherick had been brought back to him with the necessary order and certificates by Count Fosco on the twenty-seventh of July — the Count also producing a letter of explanations and instructions signed by Sir Percival Glyde. On receiving his inmate again, the proprietor of the Asylum acknowledged that he had observed some curious personal changes in her. Such changes no doubt were not without precedent in his experience of persons mentally afflicted. Insane people were often at one time, outwardly as well as inwardly, unlike what they were at another — the change from better to worse, or from worse to better, in the madness having a necessary tendency to produce alterations of appearance externally. He allowed for these, and he allowed also for the modification in the form of Anne Catherick's delusion, which was reflected no doubt in her manner and expression. But he was still perplexed at times by certain differences between his patient before she had escaped

The Woman in White

and his patient since she had been brought back. Those differences were too minute to be described. He could not say of course that she was absolutely altered in height or shape or complexion, or in the colour of her hair and eyes, or in the general form of her face — the change was something that he felt more than something that he saw. In short, the case had been a puzzle from the first, and one more perplexity was added to it now.

It cannot be said that this conversation led to the result of even partially preparing Miss Halcombe's mind for what was to come. But it produced, nevertheless, a very serious effect upon her. She was so completely unnerved by it, that some little time elapsed before she could summon composure enough to follow the proprietor of the Asylum to that part of the house in which the inmates were confined.

On inquiry, it turned out that the supposed Anne Catherick was then taking exercise in the grounds attached to the establishment. One of the nurses volunteered to conduct Miss Halcombe to the place, the proprietor of the Asylum remaining in the house for a few minutes to attend to a case which required his services, and then engaging to join his visitor in the grounds.

The nurse led Miss Halcombe to a distant part of the property, which was prettily laid out, and after looking about her a little, turned into a turf walk, shaded by a shrubbery on either side. About half-way down this walk two women were slowly approaching. The nurse pointed to them and said, "There is Anne Catherick, ma'am, with the attendant who waits on her. The attendant will answer any questions you wish to put." With those words the nurse left her to return to the duties of the house.

Miss Halcombe advanced on her side, and the women advanced on theirs. When they were within a dozen paces of each other, one of the women stopped for an instant, looked eagerly at the strange lady, shook off the nurse's grasp on her, and the next moment rushed into Miss Halcombe's arms. In that moment Miss Halcombe recognised her sister — recognised the dead-alive.

Fortunately for the success of the measures taken subsequently, no one was present at that moment but the nurse. She was a young woman, and she was so startled that she was at first quite incapable of interfering. When she was able to do so her whole services were required by Miss Halcombe, who had for the moment sunk altogether in the effort to keep her own senses under the shock of the discovery. After waiting a few minutes in the fresh air and the cool shade, her natural energy and courage helped her a little, and she became sufficiently mistress of herself to feel the necessity of recalling her presence of mind for her unfortunate sister's sake.

She obtained permission to speak alone with the patient, on condition that they both remained well within the nurse's view. There was no time for questions—there was only time for Miss Halcombe to impress on the unhappy lady the necessity of controlling herself, and to assure her of immediate help and rescue if she did so. The prospect of escaping from the Asylum by obedience to her sister's directions was sufficient to quiet Lady Glyde, and to make her understand what was required of her. Miss Halcombe next returned to the nurse, placed all the gold she then had in her pocket (three sovereigns) in the nurse's hands, and asked when and where she could speak to her alone.

The woman was at first surprised and distrustful. But on Miss Halcombe's declaring that she only wanted to put some questions which she was too much agitated to ask at that moment, and that she had no intention of misleading the nurse into any dereliction of duty, the woman took the money, and proposed three o'clock on the next day as the time for the interview. She might then slip out for half an hour, after the patients had dined, and she would meet the lady in a retired place, outside the high north wall which screened the grounds of the house. Miss Halcombe had only time to assent, and to whisper to her sister that she should hear from her on the next day, when the proprietor of the Asylum joined them. He noticed his visitor's agitation, which Miss Halcombe accounted for by saying that her interview with Anne Catherick had a little startled her at first. She took her leave as soon after as possible—that is to say, as soon as she could summon courage to force herself from the presence of her unfortunate sister.

A very little reflection, when the capacity to reflect returned, convinced her that any attempt to identify Lady Glyde and to rescue her by legal means, would, even if successful, involve a delay that might be fatal to her sister's intellects, which were shaken already by the horror of the situation to which she had been consigned. By the time Miss Halcombe had got back to London, she had determined to effect Lady Glyde's escape privately, by means of the nurse.

She went at once to her stockbroker, and sold out of the funds all the little property she possessed, amounting to rather less than seven hundred pounds. Determined, if necessary, to pay the price of her sister's liberty with every farthing she had in the world, she repaired the next day, having the whole sum about her in bank-notes, to her appointment outside the Asylum wall.

The nurse was there. Miss Halcombe approached the subject cautiously by many preliminary questions. She discovered, among other particulars, that the nurse who had in former times attended on the true Anne Catherick had been held responsible (although she was not to blame for it) for the patient's escape, and had lost her place in consequence. The same penalty, it was added, would attach to the person then speaking to her, if the supposed Anne Catherick was missing a second time; and, moreover, the nurse in this case had an especial interest in keeping her place. She was engaged to be married, and she and her future husband were waiting till they could save, together, between two and three hundred pounds to start in business. The nurse's wages were good, and she might succeed, by strict economy, in contributing her small share towards the sum required in two years' time.

On this hint Miss Halcombe spoke. She declared that the supposed Anne Catherick was nearly related to her, that she had been placed in the Asylum under a fatal mistake, and that the nurse would be doing a good and a Christian action in being the means of restoring them to one another. Before there was time to start a single objection, Miss Halcombe took four bank-notes of a hundred pounds each from her pocket-book, and offered them to the woman, as a compensation for the risk she was to run, and for the loss of her place.

The nurse hesitated, through sheer incredulity and surprise. Miss Halcombe pressed the point on her firmly.

"You will be doing a good action," she repeated; "you will be helping the most injured and unhappy woman alive. There is your marriage portion for a reward. Bring her safely to me here, and I will put these four bank-notes into your hand before I claim her."

"Will you give me a letter saying those words, which I can show to my sweetheart when he asks how I got the money?" inquired the woman.

"I will bring the letter with me, ready written and signed," answered Miss Halcombe.

"Then I'll risk it," said the nurse.

"When?"

"To-morrow."

It was hastily agreed between them that Miss Halcombe should return early the next morning and wait out of sight among the trees—always, however, keeping near the quiet spot of ground under the north wall. The nurse could fix no time for her appearance, caution requiring that she should wait and be guided by circumstances. On that understanding they separated.

Miss Halcombe was at her place, with the promised letter and the promised bank-notes, before ten the next morning. She waited more than an hour and a half. At the end of that time the nurse came quickly round the corner of the wall holding Lady Glyde by the arm. The moment they met Miss Halcombe put the bank-notes and the letter into her hand, and the sisters were united again.

The nurse had dressed Lady Glyde, with excellent forethought, in a bonnet, veil, and shawl of her own. Miss Halcombe only detained her to suggest a means of turning the pursuit in a false direction, when the escape was discovered at the Asylum. She was to go back to the house, to mention in the hearing of the other nurses that Anne Catherick had been inquiring latterly about the distance from London to Hampshire, to wait till the last moment, before discovery was inevitable, and then to give the alarm that Anne was missing. The supposed inquiries about Hampshire, when communicated to the owner of the Asylum, would lead him to imagine that his patient had returned to Blackwater Park, under the influence of the delusion which made her persist in asserting herself to be Lady Glyde, and the first pursuit would, in all probability, be turned in that direction.

The nurse consented to follow these suggestions, the more readily as they offered her the means of securing herself against any worse consequences than the loss of her place, by remaining in the Asylum, and so maintaining the appearance of innocence, at least. She at once returned to the house, and Miss Halcombe lost no time in taking her sister back with her to London. They caught the afternoon train to Carlisle the same afternoon, and arrived at Limmeridge, without accident or difficulty of any kind, that night.

The Woman in White

During the latter part of their journey they were alone in the carriage, and Miss Halcombe was able to collect such remembrances of the past as her sister's confused and weakened memory was able to recall. The terrible story of the conspiracy so obtained was presented in fragments, sadly incoherent in themselves, and widely detached from each other. Imperfect as the revelation was, it must nevertheless be recorded here before this explanatory narrative closes with the events of the next day at Limmeridge House.

Lady Glyde's recollection of the events which followed her departure from Blackwater Park began with her arrival at the London terminus of the South Western Railway. She had omitted to make a memorandum beforehand of the day on which she took the journey. All hope of fixing that important date by any evidence of hers, or of Mrs. Michelson's, must be given up for lost.

On the arrival of the train at the platform Lady Glyde found Count Fosco waiting for her. He was at the carriage door as soon as the porter could open it. The train was unusually crowded, and there was great confusion in getting the luggage. Some person whom Count Fosco brought with him procured the luggage which belonged to Lady Glyde. It was marked with her name. She drove away alone with the Count in a vehicle which she did not particularly notice at the time.

Her first question, on leaving the terminus, referred to Miss Halcombe. The Count informed her that Miss Halcombe had not yet gone to Cumberland, after-consideration having caused him to doubt the prudence of her taking so long a journey without some days' previous rest.

Lady Glyde next inquired whether her sister was then staying in the Count's house. Her recollection of the answer was confused, her only distinct impression in relation to it being that the Count declared he was then taking her to see Miss Halcombe. Lady Glyde's experience of London was so limited that she could not tell, at the time, through what streets they were driving. But they never left the streets, and they never passed any gardens or trees. When the carriage stopped, it stopped in a small street behind a square—a square in which there were shops, and public buildings, and many people. From these recollections (of which Lady Glyde was certain) it seems quite clear that Count Fosco did not take her to his own residence in the suburb of St. John's Wood.

They entered the house, and went upstairs to a back room, either on the first or second floor. The luggage was carefully brought in. A female servant opened the door, and a man with a dark beard, apparently a foreigner, met them in the hall, and with great politeness showed them the way upstairs. In answer to Lady Glyde's inquiries, the Count assured her that Miss Halcombe was in the house, and that she should be immediately informed of her sister's arrival. He and the foreigner then went away and left her by herself in the room. It was poorly furnished as a sitting-room, and it looked out on the backs of houses.

The place was remarkably quiet—no footsteps went up or down the stairs—she only heard in the room beneath her a dull, rumbling sound of men's voices talking. Before she had been long left alone the Count returned, to explain that Miss Halcombe was then taking rest, and could not be disturbed for a little while. He was accompanied into the room by a gentleman (an Englishman), whom he begged to present as a friend of his.

After this singular introduction—in the course of which no names, to the best of Lady Glyde's recollection, had been mentioned—she was left alone with the stranger. He was perfectly civil, but he startled and confused her by some odd questions about herself, and by looking at her, while he asked them, in a strange manner. After remaining a short time he went out, and a minute or two afterwards a second stranger—also an Englishman—came in. This person introduced himself as another friend of Count Fosco's, and he, in his turn, looked at her very oddly, and asked some curious questions—never, as well as she could remember, addressing her by name, and going out again, after a little while, like the first man. By this time she was so frightened about herself, and so uneasy about her sister, that she had thoughts of venturing downstairs again, and claiming the protection and assistance of the only woman she had seen in the house—the servant who answered the door.

Just as she had risen from her chair, the Count came back into the room.

The moment he appeared she asked anxiously how long the meeting between her sister and herself was to be still delayed. At first he returned an evasive answer, but on being pressed, he acknowledged, with great apparent reluctance, that Miss Halcombe was by no means so well as he had hitherto represented her to be. His tone and manner, in making this reply, so alarmed Lady Glyde, or rather so painfully increased the uneasiness which she had felt in the company of the two

The Woman in White

strangers, that a sudden faintness overcame her, and she was obliged to ask for a glass of water. The Count called from the door for water, and for a bottle of smelling-salts. Both were brought in by the foreign-looking man with the beard. The water, when Lady Glyde attempted to drink it, had so strange a taste that it increased her faintness, and she hastily took the bottle of salts from Count Fosco, and smelt at it. Her head became giddy on the instant. The Count caught the bottle as it dropped out of her hand, and the last impression of which she was conscious was that he held it to her nostrils again.

From this point her recollections were found to be confused, fragmentary, and difficult to reconcile with any reasonable probability.

Her own impression was that she recovered her senses later in the evening, that she then left the house, that she went (as she had previously arranged to go, at Blackwater Park) to Mrs. Vesey's — that she drank tea there, and that she passed the night under Mrs. Vesey's roof. She was totally unable to say how, or when, or in what company she left the house to which Count Fosco had brought her. But she persisted in asserting that she had been to Mrs. Vesey's, and still more extraordinary, that she had been helped to undress and get to bed by Mrs. Rubelle! She could not remember what the conversation was at Mrs. Vesey's or whom she saw there besides that lady, or why Mrs. Rubelle should have been present in the house to help her.

Her recollection of what happened to her the next morning was still more vague and unreliable.

She had some dim idea of driving out (at what hour she could not say) with Count Fosco, and with Mrs. Rubelle again for a female attendant. But when, and why, she left Mrs. Vesey she could not tell; neither did she know what direction the carriage drove in, or where it set her down, or whether the Count and Mrs. Rubelle did or did not remain with her all the time she was out. At this point in her sad story there was a total blank. She had no impressions of the faintest kind to communicate — no idea whether one day, or more than one day, had passed — until she came to herself suddenly in a strange place, surrounded by women who were all unknown to her.

This was the Asylum. Here she first heard herself called by Anne Catherick's name, and here, as a last remarkable circumstance in the story of the conspiracy, her own eyes informed her that she had Anne Catherick's clothes on. The nurse, on the first night in the Asylum, had shown her the marks on each article of her underclothing as it was taken off, and had said, not at all irritably or unkindly, "Look at your own name on your own clothes, and don't worry us all any more about being Lady Glyde. She's dead and buried, and you're alive and hearty. Do look at your clothes now! There it is, in good marking ink, and there you will find it on all your old things, which we have kept in the house—Anne Catherick, as plain as print!" And there it was, when Miss Halcombe examined the linen her sister wore, on the night of their arrival at Limmeridge House.

These were the only recollections—all of them uncertain, and some of them contradictory—which could be extracted from Lady Glyde by careful questioning on the journey to Cumberland. Miss Halcombe abstained from pressing her with any inquiries relating to events in the Asylum—her mind being but too evidently unfit to bear the trial of reverting to them. It was known, by the voluntary admission of the owner of the mad-house, that she was received there on the twenty-seventh of July. From that date until the fifteenth of October (the day of her rescue) she had been under restraint, her identity with Anne Catherick systematically asserted, and her sanity, from first to last, practically denied. Faculties less delicately balanced, constitutions less tenderly organised, must have suffered under such an ordeal as this. No man could have gone through it and come out of it unchanged.

Arriving at Limmeridge late on the evening of the fifteenth, Miss Halcombe wisely resolved not to attempt the assertion of Lady Glyde's identity until the next day.

The first thing in the morning she went to Mr. Fairlie's room, and using all possible cautions and preparations beforehand, at last told him in so many words what had happened. As soon as his first astonishment and alarm had subsided, he angrily declared that Miss Halcombe had allowed herself to be duped by Anne Catherick. He referred her to Count Fosco's letter, and to what she had herself told him of the personal resemblance between Anne and his deceased niece, and he positively declined to admit to his presence, even for one minute only, a madwoman, whom it was an insult and an outrage to have brought into his house at all.

Miss Halcombe left the room—waited till the first heat of her indignation had passed away—decided on reflection that Mr. Fairlie should see his niece in the interests of common humanity before he closed his doors on her as a stranger—and thereupon, without a word of previous warning, took Lady Glyde with her to his room. The servant was posted at the door to prevent their entrance, but Miss Halcombe insisted on passing him, and made her way into Mr. Fairlie's presence, leading her sister by the hand.

The scene that followed, though it only lasted for a few minutes, was too painful to be described—Miss Halcombe herself shrank from referring to it. Let it be enough to say that Mr. Fairlie declared, in the most positive terms, that he did not recognise the woman who had been brought into his room—that he saw nothing in her face and manner to make him doubt for a moment that his niece lay buried in Limmeridge churchyard, and that he would call on the law to protect him if before the day was over she was not removed from the house.

Taking the very worst view of Mr. Fairlie's selfishness, indolence, and habitual want of feeling, it was manifestly impossible to suppose that he was capable of such infamy as secretly recognising and openly disowning his brother's child. Miss Halcombe humanely and sensibly allowed all due force to the influence of prejudice and alarm in preventing him from fairly exercising his perceptions, and accounted for what had happened in that way. But when she next put the servants to the test, and found that they too were, in every case, uncertain, to say the least of it, whether the lady presented to them was their young mistress or Anne Catherick, of whose resemblance to her they had all heard, the sad conclusion was inevitable that the change produced in Lady Glyde's face and manner by her imprisonment in the Asylum was far more serious than Miss Halcombe had at first supposed. The vile deception which had asserted her death defied exposure even in the house where she was born, and among the people with whom she had lived.

In a less critical situation the effort need not have been given up as hopeless even yet.

For example, the maid, Fanny, who happened to be then absent from Limmeridge, was expected back in two days, and there would be a chance of gaining her recognition to start with, seeing that she had been in much more constant communication with her mistress, and had been much more heartily attached to her than the other servants. Again, Lady Glyde might have been privately kept in the house or in the village to wait until her health was a little recovered and her mind was a little steadied again. When her memory could be once more trusted to serve her, she would naturally refer to persons and events in the past with a certainty and a familiarity which no impostor could simulate, and so the fact of her identity, which her own appearance had failed to establish, might subsequently be proved, with time to help her, by the surer test of her own words.

But the circumstances under which she had regained her freedom rendered all recourse to such means as these simply impracticable. The pursuit from the Asylum, diverted to Hampshire for the time only, would infallibly next take the direction of Cumberland. The persons appointed to seek the fugitive might arrive at Limmeridge House at a few hours' notice, and in Mr. Fairlie's present temper of mind they might count on the immediate exertion of his local influence and authority to assist them. The commonest consideration for Lady Glyde's safety forced on Miss Halcombe the necessity of resigning the struggle to do her justice, and of removing her at once from the place of all others that was now most dangerous to her—the neighbourhood of her own home.

An immediate return to London was the first and wisest measure of security which suggested itself. In the great city all traces of them might be most speedily and most surely effaced. There were no preparations to make—no farewell words of kindness to exchange with any one. On the afternoon of that memorable day of the sixteenth Miss Halcombe roused her sister to a last exertion of courage, and without a living soul to wish them well at parting, the two took their way into the world alone, and turned their backs for ever on Limmeridge House.

They had passed the hill above the churchyard, when Lady Glyde insisted on turning back to look her last at her mother's grave. Miss Halcombe tried to shake her resolution, but, in this one instance, tried in vain. She was immovable. Her dim eyes lit with a sudden fire, and flashed through the veil that hung over them—her wasted fingers strengthened moment by moment round the friendly arm by which they had held so listlessly till this time. I believe in my soul that the hand of God was pointing their way back to them, and that the most innocent and the most afflicted of His creatures was chosen in that dread moment to see it.

They retraced their steps to the burial-ground, and by that act sealed the future of our three lives.

III

This was the story of the past — the story so far as we knew it then.

Two obvious conclusions presented themselves to my mind after hearing it. In the first place, I saw darkly what the nature of the conspiracy had been, how chances had been watched, and how circumstances had been handled to ensure impunity to a daring and an intricate crime. While all details were still a mystery to me, the vile manner in which the personal resemblance between the woman in white and Lady Glyde had been turned to account was clear beyond a doubt. It was plain that Anne Catherick had been introduced into Count Fosco's house as Lady Glyde — it was plain that Lady Glyde had taken the dead woman's place in the Asylum — the substitution having been so managed as to make innocent people (the doctor and the two servants certainly, and the owner of the mad-house in all probability) accomplices in the crime.

The second conclusion came as the necessary consequence of the first. We three had no mercy to expect from Count Fosco and Sir Percival Glyde. The success of the conspiracy had brought with it a clear gain to those two men of thirty thousand pounds — twenty thousand to one, ten thousand to the other through his wife. They had that interest, as well as other interests, in ensuring their impunity from exposure, and they would leave no stone unturned, no sacrifice unattempted, no treachery untried, to discover the place in which their victim was concealed, and to part her from the only friends she had in the world — Marian Halcombe and myself.

The sense of this serious peril — a peril which every day and every hour might bring nearer and nearer to us — was the one influence that guided me in fixing the place of our retreat. I chose it in the far east of London, where there were fewest idle people to lounge and look about them in the streets. I chose it in a poor and a populous neighbourhood — because the harder the struggle for existence among the men and women about us, the less the risk of their having the time or taking the pains to notice chance strangers who came among them. These were the great advantages I looked to, but our locality was a gain to us also in another and a hardly less important respect. We could live cheaply by the daily work of my hands, and could save every farthing we possessed to forward the purpose, the righteous purpose, of redressing an infamous wrong — which, from first to last, I now kept steadily in view.

In a week's time Marian Halcombe and I had settled how the course of our new lives should be directed.

There were no other lodgers in the house, and we had the means of going in and out without passing through the shop. I arranged, for the present at least, that neither Marian nor Laura should stir outside the door without my being with them, and that in my absence from home they should let no one into their rooms on any pretence whatever. This rule established, I went to a friend whom I had known in former days—a wood engraver in large practice—to seek for employment, telling him, at the same time, that I had reasons for wishing to remain unknown.

He at once concluded that I was in debt, expressed his regret in the usual forms, and then promised to do what he could to assist me. I left his false impression undisturbed, and accepted the work he had to give. He knew that he could trust my experience and my industry. I had what he wanted, steadiness and facility, and though my earnings were but small, they sufficed for our necessities. As soon as we could feel certain of this, Marian Halcombe and I put together what we possessed. She had between two and three hundred pounds left of her own property, and I had nearly as much remaining from the purchase-money obtained by the sale of my drawing-master's practice before I left England. Together we made up between us more than four hundred pounds. I deposited this little fortune in a bank, to be kept for the expense of those secret inquiries and investigations which I was determined to set on foot, and to carry on by myself if I could find no one to help me. We calculated our weekly expenditure to the last farthing, and we never touched our little fund except in Laura's interests and for Laura's sake.

The house-work, which, if we had dared trust a stranger near us, would have been done by a servant, was taken on the first day, taken as her own right, by Marian Halcombe. "What a woman's hands are fit for," she said, "early and late, these hands of mine shall do." They trembled as she held them out. The wasted arms told their sad story of the past, as she turned up the sleeves of the poor plain dress that she wore for safety's sake; but the unquenchable spirit of the woman burnt bright in her even yet. I saw the big tears rise thick in her eyes, and fall slowly over her cheeks as she looked at me. She dashed them away with a touch of her old energy, and smiled with a faint reflection of her old good spirits. "Don't doubt my courage, Walter," she pleaded, "it's my weakness that cries, not me. The house-work shall conquer it if I can't." And she kept her word—

the victory was won when we met in the evening, and she sat down to rest. Her large steady black eyes looked at me with a flash of their bright firmness of bygone days. "I am not quite broken down yet," she said. "I am worth trusting with my share of the work." Before I could answer, she added in a whisper, "And worth trusting with my share in the risk and the danger too. Remember that, if the time comes!"

I did remember it when the time came.

As early as the end of October the daily course of our lives had assumed its settled direction, and we three were as completely isolated in our place of concealment as if the house we lived in had been a desert island, and the great network of streets and the thousands of our fellow-creatures all round us the waters of an illimitable sea. I could now reckon on some leisure time for considering what my future plan of action should be, and how I might arm myself most securely at the outset for the coming struggle with Sir Percival and the Count.

I gave up all hope of appealing to my recognition of Laura, or to Marian's recognition of her, in proof of her identity. If we had loved her less dearly, if the instinct implanted in us by that love had not been far more certain than any exercise of reasoning, far keener than any process of observation, even we might have hesitated on first seeing her.

The outward changes wrought by the suffering and the terror of the past had fearfully, almost hopelessly, strengthened the fatal resemblance between Anne Catherick and herself. In my narrative of events at the time of my residence in Limmeridge House, I have recorded, from my own observation of the two, how the likeness, striking as it was when viewed generally, failed in many important points of similarity when tested in detail. In those former days, if they had both been seen together side by side, no person could for a moment have mistaken them one for the other—as has happened often in the instances of twins. I could not say this now. The sorrow and suffering which I had once blamed myself for associating even by a passing thought with the future of Laura Fairlie, had set their profaning marks on the youth and beauty of her face; and the fatal resemblance which I had once seen and shuddered at seeing, in idea only, was now a real and living resemblance which asserted itself before my own eyes. Strangers, acquaintances, friends even who could not look at her as we looked, if she had been shown to them in the first days of her rescue from the Asylum, might have doubted if she were the Laura Fairlie they had once seen, and doubted without blame.

The one remaining chance, which I had at first thought might be trusted to serve us — the chance of appealing to her recollection of persons and events with which no impostor could be familiar, was proved, by the sad test of our later experience, to be hopeless. Every little caution that Marian and I practised towards her — every little remedy we tried, to strengthen and steady slowly the weakened, shaken faculties, was a fresh protest in itself against the risk of turning her mind back on the troubled and the terrible past.

The only events of former days which we ventured on encouraging her to recall were the little trivial domestic events of that happy time at Limmeridge, when I first went there and taught her to draw. The day when I roused those remembrances by showing her the sketch of the summer-house which she had given me on the morning of our farewell, and which had never been separated from me since, was the birthday of our first hope. Tenderly and gradually, the memory of the old walks and drives dawned upon her, and the poor weary pining eyes looked at Marian and at me with a new interest, with a faltering thoughtfulness in them, which from that moment we cherished and kept alive. I bought her a little box of colours, and a sketch-book like the old sketch-book which I had seen in her hands on the morning that we first met. Once again — oh me, once again! — at spare hours saved from my work, in the dull London light, in the poor London room, I sat by her side to guide the faltering touch, to help the feeble hand. Day by day I raised and raised the new interest till its place in the blank of her existence was at last assured — till she could think of her drawing and talk of it, and patiently practise it by herself, with some faint reflection of the innocent pleasure in my encouragement, the growing enjoyment in her own progress, which belonged to the lost life and the lost happiness of past days.

We helped her mind slowly by this simple means, we took her out between us to walk on fine days, in a quiet old City square near at hand, where there was nothing to confuse or alarm her — we spared a few pounds from the fund at the banker's to get her wine, and the delicate strengthening food that she required — we amused her in the evenings with children's games at cards, with scrap-books full of prints which I borrowed from the engraver who employed me — by these, and other trifling attentions like them, we composed her and steadied her, and hoped all things, as cheerfully as we could from time and care, and love that never neglected and never despaired of her. But to take her mercilessly from seclusion and repose — to confront her with strangers, or with acquaintances who were little better than strangers — to rouse the painful impressions of her past life which we had so carefully hushed to rest — this, even in her own interests, we dared not do. Whatever sacrifices it cost, whatever long, weary, heartbreaking delays it involved, the wrong that had been inflicted on her, if mortal means could grapple it, must be redressed without her knowledge and without her help.

This resolution settled, it was next necessary to decide how the first risk should be ventured, and what the first proceedings should be.

After consulting with Marian, I resolved to begin by gathering together as many facts as could be collected — then to ask the advice of Mr. Kyrle (whom we knew we could trust), and to ascertain from him, in the first instance, if the legal remedy lay fairly within our reach. I owed it to Laura's interests not to stake her whole future on my own unaided exertions, so long as there was the faintest prospect of strengthening our position by obtaining reliable assistance of any kind.

The first source of information to which I applied was the journal kept at Blackwater Park by Marian Halcombe. There were passages in this diary relating to myself which she thought it best that I should not see. Accordingly, she read to me from the manuscript, and I took the notes I wanted as she went on. We could only find time to pursue this occupation by sitting up late at night. Three nights were devoted to the purpose, and were enough to put me in possession of all that Marian could tell.

My next proceeding was to gain as much additional evidence as I could procure from other people without exciting suspicion. I went myself to Mrs. Vesey to ascertain if Laura's impression of having slept there was correct or not. In this case, from consideration for Mrs. Vesey's age and infirmity, and in all subsequent cases of the same kind from considerations of caution, I kept our real position a secret, and was always careful to speak of Laura as "the late Lady Glyde."

Mrs. Vesey's answer to my inquiries only confirmed the apprehensions which I had previously felt. Laura had certainly written to say she would pass the night under the roof of her old friend — but she had never been near the house.

Her mind in this instance, and, as I feared, in other instances besides, confusedly presented to her something which she had only intended to do in the false light of something which she had really done. The unconscious contradiction of herself was easy to account for in this way—but it was likely to lead to serious results. It was a stumble on the threshold at starting—it was a flaw in the evidence which told fatally against us.

When I next asked for the letter which Laura had written to Mrs. Vesey from Blackwater Park, it was given to me without the envelope, which had been thrown into the wastepaper basket, and long since destroyed. In the letter itself no date was mentioned—not even the day of the week. It only contained these lines:—"Dearest Mrs. Vesey, I am in sad distress and anxiety, and I may come to your house to-morrow night, and ask for a bed. I can't tell you what is the matter in this letter—I write it in such fear of being found out that I can fix my mind on nothing. Pray be at home to see me. I will give you a thousand kisses, and tell you everything. Your affectionate Laura." What help was there in those lines? None.

On returning from Mrs. Vesey's, I instructed Marian to write (observing the same caution which I practised myself) to Mrs. Michelson. She was to express, if she pleased, some general suspicion of Count Fosco's conduct, and she was to ask the housekeeper to supply us with a plain statement of events, in the interests of truth. While we were waiting for the answer, which reached us in a week's time, I went to the doctor in St. John's Wood, introducing myself as sent by Miss Halcombe to collect, if possible, more particulars of her sister's last illness than Mr. Kyrle had found the time to procure. By Mr. Goodricke's assistance, I obtained a copy of the certificate of death, and an interview with the woman (Jane Gould) who had been employed to prepare the body for the grave. Through this person I also discovered a means of communicating with the servant, Hester Pinhorn. She had recently left her place in consequence of a disagreement with her mistress, and she was lodging with some people in the neighbourhood whom Mrs. Gould knew. In the manner here indicated I obtained the Narratives of the housekeeper, of the doctor, of Jane Gould, and of Hester Pinhorn, exactly as they are presented in these pages.

Furnished with such additional evidence as these documents afforded, I considered myself to be sufficiently prepared for a consultation with Mr. Kyrle, and Marian wrote accordingly to mention my name to him, and to specify the day and hour at which I requested to see him on private business.

There was time enough in the morning for me to take Laura

out for her walk as usual, and to see her quietly settled at her drawing afterwards. She looked up at me with a new anxiety in her face as I rose to leave the room, and her fingers began to toy doubtfully, in the old way, with the brushes and pencils on the table.

"You are not tired of me yet?" she said. "You are not going away because you are tired of me? I will try to do better — I will try to get well. Are you as fond of me, Walter, as you used to be, now I am so pale and thin, and so slow in learning to draw?"

She spoke as a child might have spoken, she showed me her thoughts as a child might have shown them. I waited a few minutes longer — waited to tell her that she was dearer to me now than she had ever been in the past times. "Try to get well again," I said, encouraging the new hope in the future which I saw dawning in her mind, "try to get well again, for Marian's sake and for mine."

"Yes," she said to herself, returning to her drawing. "I must try, because they are both so fond of me." She suddenly looked up again. "Don't be gone long! I can't get on with my drawing, Walter, when you are not here to help me."

"I shall soon be back, my darling — soon be back to see how you are getting on."

My voice faltered a little in spite of me. I forced myself from the room. It was no time, then, for parting with the self-control which might yet serve me in my need before the day was out.

As I opened the door, I beckoned to Marian to follow me to the stairs. It was necessary to prepare her for a result which I felt might sooner or later follow my showing myself openly in the streets.

"I shall, in all probability, be back in a few hours," I said, "and you will take care, as usual, to let no one inside the doors in my absence. But if anything happens— —"

"What can happen?" she interposed quickly. "Tell me plainly, Walter, if there is any danger, and I shall know how to meet it."

"The only danger," I replied, "is that Sir Percival Glyde may have been recalled to London by the news of Laura's escape. You are aware that he had me watched before I left England, and that he probably knows me by sight, although I don't know him?"

She laid her hand on my shoulder and looked at me in anxious silence. I saw she understood the serious risk that threatened us.

"It is not likely," I said, "that I shall be seen in London again so soon, either by Sir Percival himself or by the persons in his employ. But it is barely possible that an accident may happen. In that case, you will not be alarmed if I fail to return to-night, and you will satisfy any inquiry of Laura's with the best excuse that you can make for me? If I find the least reason to suspect that I am watched, I will take good care that no spy follows me back to this house. Don't doubt my return, Marian, however it may be delayed—and fear nothing."

"Nothing!" she answered firmly. "You shall not regret, Walter, that you have only a woman to help you." She paused, and detained me for a moment longer. "Take care!" she said, pressing my hand anxiously—"take care!"

I left her, and set forth to pave the way for discovery—the dark and doubtful way, which began at the lawyer's door.

IV

No circumstance of the slightest importance happened on my way to the offices of Messrs. Gilmore & Kyrle, in Chancery Lane.

While my card was being taken in to Mr. Kyrle, a consideration occurred to me which I deeply regretted not having thought of before. The information derived from Marian's diary made it a matter of certainty that Count Fosco had opened her first letter from Blackwater Park to Mr. Kyrle, and had, by means of his wife, intercepted the second. He was therefore well aware of the address of the office, and he would naturally infer that if Marian wanted advice and assistance, after Laura's escape from the Asylum, she would apply once more to the experience of Mr. Kyrle. In this case the office in Chancery Lane was the very first place which he and Sir Percival would cause to be watched, and if the same persons were chosen for the purpose who had been employed to follow me, before my departure from England, the fact of my return would in all probability be ascertained on that very day. I had thought, generally, of the chances of my being recognised in the streets, but the special risk connected with the office had never occurred to me until the present moment. It was too late now to repair this unfortunate error in judgment—too late to wish that I had made arrangements for meeting the lawyer in some place privately appointed beforehand. I could only resolve to be cautious on leaving Chancery Lane, and not to go straight home again under any circumstances whatever.

After waiting a few minutes I was shown into Mr. Kyrle's private room. He was a pale, thin, quiet, self-possessed man, with a very attentive eye, a very low voice, and a very undemonstrative manner—not (as I judged) ready with his sympathy where strangers were concerned, and not at all easy to disturb in his professional composure. A better man for my purpose could hardly have been found. If he committed himself to a decision at all, and if the decision was favourable, the strength of our case was as good as proved from that moment.

"Before I enter on the business which brings me here," I said, "I ought to warn you, Mr. Kyrle, that the shortest statement I can make of it may occupy some little time."

"My time is at Miss Halcombe's disposal," he replied. "Where any interests of hers are concerned, I represent my partner personally, as well as professionally. It was his request that I should do so, when he ceased to take an active part in business."

"May I inquire whether Mr. Gilmore is in England?"

"He is not, he is living with his relatives in Germany. His health has improved, but the period of his return is still uncertain."

While we were exchanging these few preliminary words, he had been searching among the papers before him, and he now produced from them a sealed letter. I thought he was about to hand the letter to me, but, apparently changing his mind, he placed it by itself on the table, settled himself in his chair, and silently waited to hear what I had to say.

Without wasting a moment in prefatory words of any sort, I entered on my narrative, and put him in full possession of the events which have already been related in these pages.

Lawyer as he was to the very marrow of his bones, I startled him out of his professional composure. Expressions of incredulity and surprise, which he could not repress, interrupted me several times before I had done. I persevered, however, to the end, and as soon as I reached it, boldly asked the one important question—

"What is your opinion, Mr. Kyrle?"

He was too cautious to commit himself to an answer without taking time to recover his self-possession first.

"Before I give my opinion," he said, "I must beg permission to clear the ground by a few questions."

He put the questions—sharp, suspicious, unbelieving questions, which clearly showed me, as they proceeded, that he thought I was the victim of a delusion, and that he might even have doubted, but for my introduction to him by Miss Halcombe, whether I was not attempting the perpetration of a cunningly-designed fraud.

"Do you believe that I have spoken the truth, Mr. Kyrle?" I asked, when he had done examining me.

"So far as your own convictions are concerned, I am certain you have spoken the truth," he replied. "I have the highest esteem for Miss Halcombe, and I have therefore every reason to respect a gentleman whose mediation she trusts in a matter of this kind. I will even go farther, if you like, and admit, for courtesy's sake and for argument's sake, that the identity of Lady Glyde as a living person is a proved fact to Miss Halcombe and yourself. But you come to me for a legal opinion. As a lawyer, and as a lawyer only, it is my duty to tell you, Mr. Hartright, that you have not the shadow of a case."

"You put it strongly, Mr. Kyrle."

"I will try to put it plainly as well. The evidence of Lady Glyde's death is, on the face of it, clear and satisfactory. There is her aunt's testimony to prove that she came to Count Fosco's house, that she fell ill, and that she died. There is the testimony of the medical certificate to prove the death, and to show that it took place under natural circumstances. There is the fact of the funeral at Limmeridge, and there is the assertion of the inscription on the tomb. That is the case you want to overthrow. What evidence have you to support the declaration on your side that the person who died and was buried was not Lady Glyde? Let us run through the main points of your statement and see what they are worth. Miss Halcombe goes to a certain private Asylum, and there sees a certain female patient. It is known that a woman named Anne Catherick, and bearing an extraordinary personal resemblance to Lady Glyde, escaped from the Asylum; it is known that the person received there last July was received as Anne Catherick brought back; it is known that the gentleman who brought her back warned Mr. Fairlie that it was part of her insanity to be bent on personating his dead niece; and it is known that she did repeatedly declare herself in the Asylum (where no one believed her) to be Lady Glyde. These are all facts. What have you to set against them? Miss Halcombe's recognition of the woman, which recognition after-events invalidate or contradict. Does Miss Halcombe assert her supposed sister's identity to the owner of the Asylum, and take legal means for rescuing her? No, she secretly bribes a nurse to let her escape. When the patient has been released in this doubtful manner, and is taken to Mr. Fairlie, does he recognise her? Is he staggered for one instant in his belief of his niece's death? No. Do the servants recognise her? No. Is she kept in the neighbourhood to assert her own identity, and to stand the test of further proceedings? No, she is privately taken to London. In the meantime you have recognised her also, but you are not a relative—you are not even an old friend of the family. The servants contradict you, and Mr. Fairlie contradicts Miss Halcombe, and the supposed Lady Glyde contradicts herself. She declares she passed the night in London at a certain house. Your own evidence shows that she has never been near that house, and your own admission is that her condition of mind prevents you from producing her anywhere to submit to investigation, and to speak for herself. I pass over minor points of evidence on both sides to save time, and I ask you, if this case were to go now into a court of law — to go before a jury, bound to take facts as they reasonably appear — where are your proofs?"

I was obliged to wait and collect myself before I could answer him. It was the first time the story of Laura and the story of Marian had been presented to me from a stranger's point of view — the first time the terrible obstacles that lay across our path had been made to show themselves in their true character.

"There can be no doubt," I said, "that the facts, as you have stated them, appear to tell against us, but — —"

"But you think those facts can be explained away," interposed Mr. Kyrle. "Let me tell you the result of my experience on that point. When an English jury has to choose between a plain fact on the surface and a long explanation under the surface, it always takes the fact in preference to the explanation. For example, Lady Glyde (I call the lady you represent by that name for argument's sake) declares she has slept at a certain house, and it is proved that she has not slept at that house. You explain this circumstance by entering into the state of her mind, and deducing from it a metaphysical conclusion. I don't say the conclusion is wrong — I only say that the jury will take the fact of her contradicting herself in preference to any reason for the contradiction that you can offer."

"But is it not possible," I urged, "by dint of patience and exertion, to discover additional evidence? Miss Halcombe and I have a few hundred pounds — —"

He looked at me with a half-suppressed pity, and shook his head.

"Consider the subject, Mr. Hartright, from your own point of view," he said. "If you are right about Sir Percival Glyde and Count Fosco (which I don't admit, mind), every imaginable difficulty would be thrown in the way of your getting fresh evidence. Every obstacle of litigation would be raised — every point in the case would be systematically contested — and by the time we had spent our thousands instead of our hundreds, the final result would, in all probability, be against us. Questions of identity, where instances of personal resemblance are concerned, are, in themselves, the hardest of all questions to settle—the hardest, even when they are free from the complications which beset the case we are now discussing. I really see no prospect of throwing any light whatever on this extraordinary affair. Even if the person buried in Limmeridge churchyard be not Lady Glyde, she was, in life, on your own showing, so like her, that we should gain nothing, if we applied for the necessary authority to have the body exhumed. In short, there is no case, Mr. Hartright—there is really no case."

I was determined to believe that there was a case, and in that determination shifted my ground, and appealed to him once more.

"Are there not other proofs that we might produce besides the proof of identity?" I asked.

"Not as you are situated," he replied. "The simplest and surest of all proofs, the proof by comparison of dates, is, as I understand, altogether out of your reach. If you could show a discrepancy between the date of the doctor's certificate and the date of Lady Glyde's journey to London, the matter would wear a totally different aspect, and I should be the first to say, Let us go on."

"That date may yet be recovered, Mr. Kyrle."

"On the day when it is recovered, Mr. Hartright, you will have a case. If you have any prospect, at this moment, of getting at it—tell me, and we shall see if I can advise you."

I considered. The housekeeper could not help us—Laura could not help us—Marian could not help us. In all probability, the only persons in existence who knew the date were Sir Percival and the Count.

"I can think of no means of ascertaining the date at present," I said, "because I can think of no persons who are sure to know it, but Count Fosco and Sir Percival Glyde."

Mr. Kyrle's calmly attentive face relaxed, for the first time, into a smile.

"With your opinion of the conduct of those two gentlemen," he said, "you don't expect help in that quarter, I presume? If they have combined to gain large sums of money by a conspiracy, they are not likely to confess it, at any rate."

"They may be forced to confess it, Mr. Kyrle."

"By whom?"

"By me."

We both rose. He looked me attentively in the face with more appearance of interest than he had shown yet. I could see that I had perplexed him a little.

"You are very determined," he said. "You have, no doubt, a personal motive for proceeding, into which it is not my business to inquire. If a case can be produced in the future, I can only say, my best assistance is at your service. At the same time I must warn you, as the money question always enters into the law question, that I see little hope, even if you ultimately established the fact of Lady Glyde's being alive, of recovering her fortune. The foreigner would probably leave the country before proceedings were commenced, and Sir Percival's embarrassments are numerous enough and pressing enough to transfer almost any sum of money he may possess from himself to his creditors. You are of course aware— —"

I stopped him at that point.

"Let me beg that we may not discuss Lady Glyde's affairs," I said. "I have never known anything about them in former times, and I know nothing of them now—except that her fortune is lost. You are right in assuming that I have personal motives for stirring in this matter. I wish those motives to be always as disinterested as they are at the present moment— —"

He tried to interpose and explain. I was a little heated, I suppose, by feeling that he had doubted me, and I went on bluntly, without waiting to hear him.

"There shall be no money motive," I said, "no idea of personal advantage in the service I mean to render to Lady Glyde. She has been cast out as a stranger from the house in which she was born—a lie which records her death has been written on her mother's tomb—and there are two men, alive and unpunished, who are responsible for it. That house shall open again to receive her in the presence of every soul who followed the false funeral to the grave—that lie shall be publicly erased from the tombstone by the authority of the head of the family, and those two men shall answer for their crime to ME, though the justice that sits in tribunals is powerless to pursue them. I have given my life to that purpose, and, alone as I stand, if God spares me, I will accomplish it."

He drew back towards his table, and said nothing. His face showed plainly that he thought my delusion had got the better of my reason, and that he considered it totally useless to give me any more advice.

"We each keep our opinion, Mr. Kyrle," I said, "and we must wait till the events of the future decide between us. In the meantime, I am much obliged to you for the attention you have given to my statement. You have shown me that the legal remedy lies, in every sense of the word, beyond our means. We cannot produce the law proof, and we are not rich enough to pay the law expenses. It is something gained to know that."

I bowed and walked to the door. He called me back and gave me the letter which I had seen him place on the table by itself at the beginning of our interview.

"This came by post a few days ago," he said. "Perhaps you will not mind delivering it? Pray tell Miss Halcombe, at the same time, that I sincerely regret being, thus far, unable to help her, except by advice, which will not be more welcome, I am afraid, to her than to you."

I looked at the letter while he was speaking. It was addressed to "Miss Halcombe. Care of Messrs. Gilmore & Kyrle, Chancery Lane." The handwriting was quite unknown to me.

On leaving the room I asked one last question.

"Do you happen to know," I said, "if Sir Percival Glyde is still in Paris?"

"He has returned to London," replied Mr. Kyrle. "At least I heard so from his solicitor, whom I met yesterday."

After that answer I went out.

On leaving the office the first precaution to be observed was to abstain from attracting attention by stopping to look about me. I walked towards one of the quietest of the large squares on the north of Holborn, then suddenly stopped and turned round at a place where a long stretch of pavement was left behind me.

There were two men at the corner of the square who had stopped also, and who were standing talking together. After a moment's reflection I turned back so as to pass them. One moved as I came near, and turned the corner leading from the square into the street. The other remained stationary. I looked at him as I passed and instantly recognised one of the men who had watched me before I left England.

If I had been free to follow my own instincts, I should probably have begun by speaking to the man, and have ended by knocking him down. But I was bound to consider consequences. If I once placed myself publicly in the wrong, I put the weapons at once into Sir Percival's hands. There was no choice but to oppose cunning by cunning. I turned into the street down which the second man had disappeared, and passed him, waiting in a doorway. He was a stranger to me, and I was glad to make sure of his personal appearance in case of future annoyance. Having done this, I again walked northward till I reached the New Road. There I turned aside to the west (having the men behind me all the time), and waited at a point where I knew myself to be at some distance from a cab-stand, until a fast two-wheel cab, empty, should happen to pass me. One passed in a few minutes. I jumped in and told the man to drive rapidly towards Hyde Park. There was no second fast cab for the spies behind me. I saw them dart across to the other side of the road, to follow me by running, until a cab or a cab-stand came in their way. But I had the start of them, and when I stopped the driver and got out, they were nowhere in sight. I crossed Hyde Park and made sure, on the open ground, that I was free. When I at last turned my steps homewards, it was not till many hours later — not till after dark.

I found Marian waiting for me alone in the little sitting-room. She had persuaded Laura to go to rest, after first promising to show me her drawing the moment I came in. The poor little dim faint sketch — so trifling in itself, so touching in its associations — was propped up carefully on the table with two books, and was placed where the faint light of the one candle we allowed ourselves might fall on it to the best advantage. I sat down to look at the drawing, and to tell Marian, in whispers, what had happened. The partition which divided us from the next room was so thin that we could almost hear Laura's breathing, and we might have disturbed her if we had spoken aloud.

Marian preserved her composure while I described my interview with Mr. Kyrle. But her face became troubled when I spoke next of the men who had followed me from the lawyer's office, and when I told her of the discovery of Sir Percival's return.

The Woman in White

"Bad news, Walter," she said, "the worst news you could bring. Have you nothing more to tell me?"

"I have something to give you," I replied, handing her the note which Mr. Kyrle had confided to my care.

She looked at the address and recognised the handwriting instantly.

"You know your correspondent?" I said.

"Too well," she answered. "My correspondent is Count Fosco."

With that reply she opened the note. Her face flushed deeply while she read it — her eyes brightened with anger as she handed it to me to read in my turn.

The note contained these lines —

"Impelled by honourable admiration — honourable to myself, honourable to you — I write, magnificent Marian, in the interests of your tranquillity, to say two consoling words —

"Fear nothing!

"Exercise your fine natural sense and remain in retirement. Dear and admirable woman, invite no dangerous publicity. Resignation is sublime — adopt it. The modest repose of home is eternally fresh — enjoy it. The storms of life pass harmless over the valley of Seclusion — dwell, dear lady, in the valley.

"Do this and I authorise you to fear nothing. No new calamity shall lacerate your sensibilities — sensibilities precious to me as my own. You shall not be molested, the fair companion of your retreat shall not be pursued. She has found a new asylum in your heart. Priceless asylum! — I envy her and leave her there.

"One last word of affectionate warning, of paternal caution, and I tear myself from the charm of addressing you — I close these fervent lines.

"Advance no farther than you have gone already, compromise no serious interests, threaten nobody. Do not, I implore you, force me into action — ME, the Man of Action —

439

when it is the cherished object of my ambition to be passive, to restrict the vast reach of my energies and my combinations for your sake. If you have rash friends, moderate their deplorable ardour. If Mr. Hartright returns to England, hold no communication with him. I walk on a path of my own, and Percival follows at my heels. On the day when Mr. Hartright crosses that path, he is a lost man."

The only signature to these lines was the initial letter F, surrounded by a circle of intricate flourishes. I threw the letter on the table with all the contempt that I felt for it.

"He is trying to frighten you—a sure sign that he is frightened himself," I said.

She was too genuine a woman to treat the letter as I treated it. The insolent familiarity of the language was too much for her self-control. As she looked at me across the table, her hands clenched themselves in her lap, and the old quick fiery temper flamed out again brightly in her cheeks and her eyes.

"Walter!" she said, "if ever those two men are at your mercy, and if you are obliged to spare one of them, don't let it be the Count."

"I will keep this letter, Marian, to help my memory when the time comes."

She looked at me attentively as I put the letter away in my pocket-book.

"When the time comes?" she repeated. "Can you speak of the future as if you were certain of it?—certain after what you have heard in Mr. Kyrle's office, after what has happened to you to-day?"

"I don't count the time from to-day, Marian. All I have done to-day is to ask another man to act for me. I count from to-morrow — —"

"Why from to-morrow?"

"Because to-morrow I mean to act for myself."

"How?"

The Woman in White

"I shall go to Blackwater by the first train, and return, I hope, at night."

"To Blackwater!"

"Yes. I have had time to think since I left Mr. Kyrle. His opinion on one point confirms my own. We must persist to the last in hunting down the date of Laura's journey. The one weak point in the conspiracy, and probably the one chance of proving that she is a living woman, centre in the discovery of that date."

"You mean," said Marian, "the discovery that Laura did not leave Blackwater Park till after the date of her death on the doctor's certificate?"

"Certainly."

"What makes you think it might have been after? Laura can tell us nothing of the time she was in London."

"But the owner of the Asylum told you that she was received there on the twenty-seventh of July. I doubt Count Fosco's ability to keep her in London, and to keep her insensible to all that was passing around her, more than one night. In that case, she must have started on the twenty-sixth, and must have come to London one day after the date of her own death on the doctor's certificate. If we can prove that date, we prove our case against Sir Percival and the Count."

"Yes, yes—I see! But how is the proof to be obtained?"

"Mrs. Michelson's narrative has suggested to me two ways of trying to obtain it. One of them is to question the doctor, Mr. Dawson, who must know when he resumed his attendance at Blackwater Park after Laura left the house. The other is to make inquiries at the inn to which Sir Percival drove away by himself at night. We know that his departure followed Laura's after the lapse of a few hours, and we may get at the date in that way. The attempt is at least worth making, and to-morrow I am determined it shall be made."

"And suppose it fails—I look at the worst now, Walter; but I will look at the best if disappointments come to try us—suppose no one can help you at Blackwater?"

"There are two men who can help me, and shall help me in London—Sir Percival and the Count. Innocent people may well forget the date—but they are guilty, and they know it. If I fail everywhere else, I mean to force a confession out of one or both of them on my own terms."

All the woman flushed up in Marian's face as I spoke.

"Begin with the Count," she whispered eagerly. "For my sake, begin with the Count."

"We must begin, for Laura's sake, where there is the best chance of success," I replied.

The colour faded from her face again, and she shook her head sadly.

"Yes," she said, "you are right—it was mean and miserable of me to say that. I try to be patient, Walter, and succeed better now than I did in happier times. But I have a little of my old temper still left, and it will get the better of me when I think of the Count!"

"His turn will come," I said. "But, remember, there is no weak place in his life that we know of yet." I waited a little to let her recover her self-possession, and then spoke the decisive words—

"Marian! There is a weak place we both know of in Sir Percival's life——"

"You mean the Secret!"

"Yes: the Secret. It is our only sure hold on him. I can force him from his position of security, I can drag him and his villainy into the face of day, by no other means. Whatever the Count may have done, Sir Percival has consented to the conspiracy against Laura from another motive besides the motive of gain. You heard him tell the Count that he believed his wife knew enough to ruin him? You heard him say that he was a lost man if the secret of Anne Catherick was known?"

"Yes! yes! I did."

"Well, Marian, when our other resources have failed us, I mean to know the Secret. My old superstition clings to me, even yet. I say again the woman in white is a living influence in our three lives. The End is appointed—the End is drawing us on—and Anne Catherick, dead in her grave, points the way to it still!"

V

The story of my first inquiries in Hampshire is soon told.

My early departure from London enabled me to reach Mr. Dawson's house in the forenoon. Our interview, so far as the object of my visit was concerned, led to no satisfactory result.

Mr. Dawson's books certainly showed when he had resumed his attendance on Miss Halcombe at Blackwater Park, but it was not possible to calculate back from this date with any exactness, without such help from Mrs. Michelson as I knew she was unable to afford. She could not say from memory (who, in similar cases, ever can?) how many days had elapsed between the renewal of the doctor's attendance on his patient and the previous departure of Lady Glyde. She was almost certain of having mentioned the circumstance of the departure to Miss Halcombe, on the day after it happened—but then she was no more able to fix the date of the day on which this disclosure took place, than to fix the date of the day before, when Lady Glyde had left for London. Neither could she calculate, with any nearer approach to exactness, the time that had passed from the departure of her mistress, to the period when the undated letter from Madame Fosco arrived. Lastly, as if to complete the series of difficulties, the doctor himself, having been ill at the time, had omitted to make his usual entry of the day of the week and month when the gardener from Blackwater Park had called on him to deliver Mrs. Michelson's message.

Hopeless of obtaining assistance from Mr. Dawson, I resolved to try next if I could establish the date of Sir Percival's arrival at Knowlesbury.

It seemed like a fatality! When I reached Knowlesbury the inn was shut up, and bills were posted on the walls. The speculation had been a bad one, as I was informed, ever since the time of the railway. The new hotel at the station had gradually absorbed the business, and the old inn (which we knew to be the inn at which Sir Percival had put up), had been closed about two months since. The proprietor had left the town with all his goods and chattels, and where he had gone I could not positively ascertain from any one. The four people of whom I inquired gave me four different accounts of his plans and projects when he left Knowlesbury.

There were still some hours to spare before the last train left for London, and I drove back again in a fly from the Knowlesbury station to Blackwater Park, with the purpose of questioning the gardener and the person who kept the lodge. If they, too, proved unable to assist me, my resources for the present were at an end, and I might return to town.

I dismissed the fly a mile distant from the park, and getting my directions from the driver, proceeded by myself to the house.

As I turned into the lane from the high-road, I saw a man, with a carpet-bag, walking before me rapidly on the way to the lodge. He was a little man, dressed in shabby black, and wearing a remarkably large hat. I set him down (as well as it was possible to judge) for a lawyer's clerk, and stopped at once to widen the distance between us. He had not heard me, and he walked on out of sight, without looking back. When I passed through the gates myself, a little while afterwards, he was not visible—he had evidently gone on to the house.

There were two women in the lodge. One of them was old, the other I knew at once, by Marian's description of her, to be Margaret Porcher.

I asked first if Sir Percival was at the Park, and receiving a reply in the negative, inquired next when he had left it. Neither of the women could tell me more than that he had gone away in the summer. I could extract nothing from Margaret Porcher but vacant smiles and shakings of the head. The old woman was a little more intelligent, and I managed to lead her into speaking of the manner of Sir Percival's departure, and of the alarm that it caused her. She remembered her master calling her out of bed, and remembered his frightening her by swearing—but the date at which the occurrence happened was, as she honestly acknowledged, "quite beyond her."

On leaving the lodge I saw the gardener at work not far off. When I first addressed him, he looked at me rather distrustfully, but on my using Mrs. Michelson's name, with a civil reference to himself, he entered into conversation readily enough. There is no need to describe what passed between us—it ended, as all my other attempts to discover the date had ended. The gardener knew that his master had driven away, at night, "some time in July, the last fortnight or the last ten days in the month"—and knew no more.

While we were speaking together I saw the man in black, with the large hat, come out from the house, and stand at some little distance observing us.

444

The Woman in White

Certain suspicions of his errand at Blackwater Park had already crossed my mind. They were now increased by the gardener's inability (or unwillingness) to tell me who the man was, and I determined to clear the way before me, if possible, by speaking to him. The plainest question I could put as a stranger would be to inquire if the house was allowed to be shown to visitors. I walked up to the man at once, and accosted him in those words.

His look and manner unmistakably betrayed that he knew who I was, and that he wanted to irritate me into quarrelling with him. His reply was insolent enough to have answered the purpose, if I had been less determined to control myself. As it was, I met him with the most resolute politeness, apologised for my involuntary intrusion (which he called a "trespass,") and left the grounds. It was exactly as I suspected. The recognition of me when I left Mr. Kyrle's office had been evidently communicated to Sir Percival Glyde, and the man in black had been sent to the Park in anticipation of my making inquiries at the house or in the neighbourhood. If I had given him the least chance of lodging any sort of legal complaint against me, the interference of the local magistrate would no doubt have been turned to account as a clog on my proceedings, and a means of separating me from Marian and Laura for some days at least.

I was prepared to be watched on the way from Blackwater Park to the station, exactly as I had been watched in London the day before. But I could not discover at the time, whether I was really followed on this occasion or not. The man in black might have had means of tracking me at his disposal of which I was not aware, but I certainly saw nothing of him, in his own person, either on the way to the station, or afterwards on my arrival at the London terminus in the evening. I reached home on foot, taking the precaution, before I approached our own door, of walking round by the loneliest street in the neighbourhood, and there stopping and looking back more than once over the open space behind me. I had first learnt to use this stratagem against suspected treachery in the wilds of Central America—and now I was practising it again, with the same purpose and with even greater caution, in the heart of civilised London!

Nothing had happened to alarm Marian during my absence. She asked eagerly what success I had met with. When I told her she could not conceal her surprise at the indifference with which I spoke of the failure of my investigations thus far.

The truth was, that the ill-success of my inquiries had in no sense daunted me. I had pursued them as a matter of duty, and I had expected nothing from them. In the state of my mind at that time, it was almost a relief to me to know that the struggle was now narrowed to a trial of strength between myself and Sir Percival Glyde. The vindictive motive had mingled itself all along with my other and better motives, and I confess it was a satisfaction to me to feel that the surest way, the only way left, of serving Laura's cause, was to fasten my hold firmly on the villain who had married her.

While I acknowledge that I was not strong enough to keep my motives above the reach of this instinct of revenge, I can honestly say something in my own favour on the other side. No base speculation on the future relations of Laura and myself, and on the private and personal concessions which I might force from Sir Percival if I once had him at my mercy, ever entered my mind. I never said to myself, "If I do succeed, it shall be one result of my success that I put it out of her husband's power to take her from me again." I could not look at her and think of the future with such thoughts as those. The sad sight of the change in her from her former self, made the one interest of my love an interest of tenderness and compassion which her father or her brother might have felt, and which I felt, God knows, in my inmost heart. All my hopes looked no farther on now than to the day of her recovery. There, till she was strong again and happy again—there, till she could look at me as she had once looked, and speak to me as she had once spoken—the future of my happiest thoughts and my dearest wishes ended.

These words are written under no prompting of idle self-contemplation. Passages in this narrative are soon to come which will set the minds of others in judgment on my conduct. It is right that the best and the worst of me should be fairly balanced before that time.

On the morning after my return from Hampshire I took Marian upstairs into my working-room, and there laid before her the plan that I had matured thus far, for mastering the one assailable point in the life of Sir Percival Glyde.

The way to the Secret lay through the mystery, hitherto impenetrable to all of us, of the woman in white. The approach to that in its turn might be gained by obtaining the assistance of Anne Catherick's mother, and the only ascertainable means of prevailing on Mrs. Catherick to act or to speak in the matter depended on the chance of my discovering local particulars and family particulars first of all from Mrs. Clements. After thinking the subject over carefully, I felt certain that I could only begin the new inquiries by placing myself in communication with the faithful friend and protectress of Anne Catherick.

The first difficulty then was to find Mrs. Clements.

I was indebted to Marian's quick perception for meeting this necessity at once by the best and simplest means. She proposed to write to the farm near Limmeridge (Todd's Corner), to inquire whether Mrs. Clements had communicated with Mrs. Todd during the past few months. How Mrs. Clements had been separated from Anne it was impossible for us to say, but that separation once effected, it would certainly occur to Mrs. Clements to inquire after the missing woman in the neighbourhood of all others to which she was known to be most attached — the neighbourhood of Limmeridge. I saw directly that Marian's proposal offered us a prospect of success, and she wrote to Mrs. Todd accordingly by that day's post.

While we were waiting for the reply, I made myself master of all the information Marian could afford on the subject of Sir Percival's family, and of his early life. She could only speak on these topics from hearsay, but she was reasonably certain of the truth of what little she had to tell.

Sir Percival was an only child. His father, Sir Felix Glyde, had suffered from his birth under a painful and incurable deformity, and had shunned all society from his earliest years. His sole happiness was in the enjoyment of music, and he had married a lady with tastes similar to his own, who was said to be a most accomplished musician. He inherited the Blackwater property while still a young man. Neither he nor his wife after taking possession, made advances of any sort towards the society of the neighbourhood, and no one endeavoured to tempt them into abandoning their reserve, with the one disastrous exception of the rector of the parish.

The rector was the worst of all innocent mischief-makers — an over-zealous man. He had heard that Sir Felix had left College with the character of being little better than a revolutionist in politics and an infidel in religion, and he arrived conscientiously at the conclusion that it was his bounden duty to summon the lord of the manor to hear sound views enunciated in the parish church. Sir Felix fiercely resented the clergyman's well-meant but ill-directed interference, insulting him so grossly and so publicly, that the families in the neighbourhood sent letters of indignant remonstrance to the

Park, and even the tenants of the Blackwater property expressed their opinion as strongly as they dared. The baronet, who had no country tastes of any kind, and no attachment to the estate or to any one living on it, declared that society at Blackwater should never have a second chance of annoying him, and left the place from that moment.

After a short residence in London he and his wife departed for the Continent, and never returned to England again. They lived part of the time in France and part in Germany — always keeping themselves in the strict retirement which the morbid sense of his own personal deformity had made a necessity to Sir Felix. Their son, Percival, had been born abroad, and had been educated there by private tutors. His mother was the first of his parents whom he lost. His father had died a few years after her, either in 1825 or 1826. Sir Percival had been in England, as a young man, once or twice before that period, but his acquaintance with the late Mr. Fairlie did not begin till after the time of his father's death. They soon became very intimate, although Sir Percival was seldom, or never, at Limmeridge House in those days. Mr. Frederick Fairlie might have met him once or twice in Mr. Philip Fairlie's company, but he could have known little of him at that or at any other time. Sir Percival's only intimate friend in the Fairlie family had been Laura's father.

These were all the particulars that I could gain from Marian. They suggested nothing which was useful to my present purpose, but I noted them down carefully, in the event of their proving to be of importance at any future period.

Mrs. Todd's reply (addressed, by our own wish, to a post-office at some distance from us) had arrived at its destination when I went to apply for it. The chances, which had been all against us hitherto, turned from this moment in our favour. Mrs. Todd's letter contained the first item of information of which we were in search.

Mrs. Clements, it appeared, had (as we had conjectured) written to Todd's Corner, asking pardon in the first place for the abrupt manner in which she and Anne had left their friends at the farm-house (on the morning after I had met the woman in white in Limmeridge churchyard), and then informing Mrs. Todd of Anne's disappearance, and entreating that she would cause inquiries to be made in the neighbourhood, on the chance that the lost woman might have strayed back to Limmeridge. In making this request, Mrs. Clements had been careful to add to it the address at which she might always be heard of, and that address Mrs. Todd now transmitted to Marian. It was in London, and within half an hour's walk of our own lodging.

In the words of the proverb, I was resolved not to let the grass grow under my feet. The next morning I set forth to seek an interview with Mrs. Clements. This was my first step forward in the investigation. The story of the desperate attempt to which I now stood committed begins here.

VI

The address communicated by Mrs. Todd took me to a lodging-house situated in a respectable street near the Gray's Inn Road.

When I knocked the door was opened by Mrs. Clements herself. She did not appear to remember me, and asked what my business was. I recalled to her our meeting in Limmeridge churchyard at the close of my interview there with the woman in white, taking special care to remind her that I was the person who assisted Anne Catherick (as Anne had herself declared) to escape the pursuit from the Asylum. This was my only claim to the confidence of Mrs. Clements. She remembered the circumstance the moment I spoke of it, and asked me into the parlour, in the greatest anxiety to know if I had brought her any news of Anne.

It was impossible for me to tell her the whole truth without, at the same time, entering into particulars on the subject of the conspiracy, which it would have been dangerous to confide to a stranger. I could only abstain most carefully from raising any false hopes, and then explain that the object of my visit was to discover the persons who were really responsible for Anne's disappearance. I even added, so as to exonerate myself from any after-reproach of my own conscience, that I entertained not the least hope of being able to trace her—that I believed we should never see her alive again—and that my main interest in the affair was to bring to punishment two men whom I suspected to be concerned in luring her away, and at whose hands I and some dear friends of mine had suffered a grievous wrong. With this explanation I left it to Mrs. Clements to say whether our interest in the matter (whatever difference there might be in the motives which actuated us) was not the same, and whether she felt any reluctance to forward my object by giving me such information on the subject of my inquiries as she happened to possess.

The poor woman was at first too much confused and agitated to understand thoroughly what I said to her. She could only reply that I was welcome to anything she could tell me in return for the kindness I had shown to Anne; but as she was not very quick and ready, at the best of times, in talking to strangers, she would beg me to put her in the right way, and to say where I wished her to begin.

Knowing by experience that the plainest narrative attainable from persons who are not accustomed to arrange their ideas, is the narrative which goes far enough back at the beginning to avoid all impediments of retrospection in its course, I asked Mrs. Clements to tell me first what had happened after she had left Limmeridge, and so, by watchful questioning, carried her on from point to point, till we reached the period of Anne's disappearance.

The substance of the information which I thus obtained was as follows:—

On leaving the farm at Todd's Corner, Mrs. Clements and Anne had travelled that day as far as Derby, and had remained there a week on Anne's account. They had then gone on to London, and had lived in the lodging occupied by Mrs. Clements at that time for a month or more, when circumstances connected with the house and the landlord had obliged them to change their quarters. Anne's terror of being discovered in London or its neighbourhood, whenever they ventured to walk out, had gradually communicated itself to Mrs. Clements, and she had determined on removing to one of the most out-of-the-way places in England—to the town of Grimsby in Lincolnshire, where her deceased husband had passed all his early life. His relatives were respectable people settled in the town—they had always treated Mrs. Clements with great kindness, and she thought it impossible to do better than go there and take the advice of her husband's friends. Anne would not hear of returning to her mother at Welmingham, because she had been removed to the Asylum from that place, and because Sir Percival would be certain to go back there and find her again. There was serious weight in this objection, and Mrs. Clements felt that it was not to be easily removed.

At Grimsby the first serious symptoms of illness had shown themselves in Anne. They appeared soon after the news of Lady Glyde's marriage had been made public in the newspapers, and had reached her through that medium.

The medical man who was sent for to attend the sick woman discovered at once that she was suffering from a serious affection of the heart. The illness lasted long, left her very weak, and returned at intervals, though with mitigated severity, again and again. They remained at Grimsby, in consequence, during the first half of the new year, and there they might probably have stayed much longer, but for the sudden resolution which Anne took at this time to venture back to Hampshire, for the purpose of obtaining a private interview with Lady Glyde.

Mrs. Clements did all in her power to oppose the execution

of this hazardous and unaccountable project. No explanation of her motives was offered by Anne, except that she believed the day of her death was not far off, and that she had something on her mind which must be communicated to Lady Glyde, at any risk, in secret. Her resolution to accomplish this purpose was so firmly settled that she declared her intention of going to Hampshire by herself if Mrs. Clements felt any unwillingness to go with her. The doctor, on being consulted, was of opinion that serious opposition to her wishes would, in all probability, produce another and perhaps a fatal fit of illness, and Mrs. Clements, under this advice, yielded to necessity, and once more, with sad forebodings of trouble and danger to come, allowed Anne Catherick to have her own way.

On the journey from London to Hampshire Mrs. Clements discovered that one of their fellow-passengers was well acquainted with the neighbourhood of Blackwater, and could give her all the information she needed on the subject of localities. In this way she found out that the only place they could go to, which was not dangerously near to Sir Percival's residence, was a large village called Sandon. The distance here from Blackwater Park was between three and four miles — and that distance, and back again, Anne had walked on each occasion when she had appeared in the neighbourhood of the lake.

For the few days during which they were at Sandon without being discovered they had lived a little away from the village, in the cottage of a decent widow-woman who had a bedroom to let, and whose discreet silence Mrs. Clements had done her best to secure, for the first week at least. She had also tried hard to induce Anne to be content with writing to Lady Glyde, in the first instance; but the failure of the warning contained in the anonymous letter sent to Limmeridge had made Anne resolute to speak this time, and obstinate in the determination to go on her errand alone.

Mrs. Clements, nevertheless, followed her privately on each occasion when she went to the lake, without, however, venturing near enough to the boat-house to be witness of what took place there. When Anne returned for the last time from the dangerous neighbourhood, the fatigue of walking, day after day, distances which were far too great for her strength, added to the exhausting effect of the agitation from which she had suffered, produced the result which Mrs. Clements had dreaded all along. The old pain over the heart and the other symptoms of the illness at Grimsby returned, and Anne was confined to her bed in the cottage.

The Woman in White

In this emergency the first necessity, as Mrs. Clements knew by experience, was to endeavour to quiet Anne's anxiety of mind, and for this purpose the good woman went herself the next day to the lake, to try if she could find Lady Glyde (who would be sure, as Anne said, to take her daily walk to the boat-house), and prevail on her to come back privately to the cottage near Sandon. On reaching the outskirts of the plantation Mrs. Clements encountered, not Lady Glyde, but a tall, stout, elderly gentleman, with a book in his hand — in other words, Count Fosco.

The Count, after looking at her very attentively for a moment, asked if she expected to see any one in that place, and added, before she could reply, that he was waiting there with a message from Lady Glyde, but that he was not quite certain whether the person then before him answered the description of the person with whom he was desired to communicate.

Upon this Mrs. Clements at once confided her errand to him, and entreated that he would help to allay Anne's anxiety by trusting his message to her. The Count most readily and kindly complied with her request. The message, he said, was a very important one. Lady Glyde entreated Anne and her good friend to return immediately to London, as she felt certain that Sir Percival would discover them if they remained any longer in the neighbourhood of Blackwater. She was herself going to London in a short time, and if Mrs. Clements and Anne would go there first, and would let her know what their address was, they should hear from her and see her in a fortnight or less. The Count added that he had already attempted to give a friendly warning to Anne herself, but that she had been too much startled by seeing that he was a stranger to let him approach and speak to her.

To this Mrs. Clements replied, in the greatest alarm and distress, that she asked nothing better than to take Anne safely to London, but that there was no present hope of removing her from the dangerous neighbourhood, as she lay ill in her bed at that moment. The Count inquired if Mrs. Clements had sent for medical advice, and hearing that she had hitherto hesitated to do so, from the fear of making their position publicly known in the village, informed her that he was himself a medical man, and that he would go back with her if she pleased, and see what could be done for Anne. Mrs. Clements (feeling a natural confidence in the Count, as a person trusted with a secret message from Lady Glyde) gratefully accepted the offer, and they went back together to the cottage.

Anne was asleep when they got there. The Count started at the sight of her (evidently from astonishment at her resemblance to Lady Glyde). Poor Mrs. Clements supposed that he was only shocked to see how ill she was. He would not allow her to be awakened—he was contented with putting questions to Mrs. Clements about her symptoms, with looking at her, and with lightly touching her pulse. Sandon was a large enough place to have a grocer's and druggist's shop in it, and thither the Count went to write his prescription and to get the medicine made up. He brought it back himself, and told Mrs. Clements that the medicine was a powerful stimulant, and that it would certainly give Anne strength to get up and bear the fatigue of a journey to London of only a few hours. The remedy was to be administered at stated times on that day and on the day after. On the third day she would be well enough to travel, and he arranged to meet Mrs. Clements at the Blackwater station, and to see them off by the midday train. If they did not appear he would assume that Anne was worse, and would proceed at once to the cottage.

As events turned out, no such emergency as this occurred.

This medicine had an extraordinary effect on Anne, and the good results of it were helped by the assurance Mrs. Clements could now give her that she would soon see Lady Glyde in London. At the appointed day and time (when they had not been quite so long as a week in Hampshire altogether), they arrived at the station. The Count was waiting there for them, and was talking to an elderly lady, who appeared to be going to travel by the train to London also. He most kindly assisted them, and put them into the carriage himself, begging Mrs. Clements not to forget to send her address to Lady Glyde. The elderly lady did not travel in the same compartment, and they did not notice what became of her on reaching the London terminus. Mrs. Clements secured respectable lodgings in a quiet neighbourhood, and then wrote, as she had engaged to do, to inform Lady Glyde of the address.

A little more than a fortnight passed, and no answer came.

At the end of that time a lady (the same elderly lady whom they had seen at the station) called in a cab, and said that she came from Lady Glyde, who was then at an hotel in London, and who wished to see Mrs. Clements, for the purpose of arranging a future interview with Anne. Mrs. Clements expressed her willingness (Anne being present at the time, and entreating her to do so) to forward the object in view, especially as she was not required to be away from the house for more

The Woman in White

than half an hour at the most. She and the elderly lady (clearly Madame Fosco) then left in the cab. The lady stopped the cab, after it had driven some distance, at a shop before they got to the hotel, and begged Mrs. Clements to wait for her for a few minutes while she made a purchase that had been forgotten. She never appeared again.

After waiting some time Mrs. Clements became alarmed, and ordered the cabman to drive back to her lodgings. When she got there, after an absence of rather more than half an hour, Anne was gone.

The only information to be obtained from the people of the house was derived from the servant who waited on the lodgers. She had opened the door to a boy from the street, who had left a letter for "the young woman who lived on the second floor" (the part of the house which Mrs. Clements occupied). The servant had delivered the letter, had then gone downstairs, and five minutes afterwards had observed Anne open the front door and go out, dressed in her bonnet and shawl. She had probably taken the letter with her, for it was not to be found, and it was therefore impossible to tell what inducement had been offered to make her leave the house. It must have been a strong one, for she would never stir out alone in London of her own accord. If Mrs. Clements had not known this by experience nothing would have induced her to go away in the cab, even for so short a time as half an hour only.

As soon as she could collect her thoughts, the first idea that naturally occurred to Mrs. Clements was to go and make inquiries at the Asylum, to which she dreaded that Anne had been taken back.

She went there the next day, having been informed of the locality in which the house was situated by Anne herself. The answer she received (her application having in all probability been made a day or two before the false Anne Catherick had really been consigned to safe keeping in the Asylum) was, that no such person had been brought back there. She had then written to Mrs. Catherick at Welmingham to know if she had seen or heard anything of her daughter, and had received an answer in the negative. After that reply had reached her, she was at the end of her resources, and perfectly ignorant where else to inquire or what else to do. From that time to this she had remained in total ignorance of the cause of Anne's disappearance and of the end of Anne's story.

VII

Thus far the information which I had received from Mrs. Clements—though it established facts of which I had not previously been aware—was of a preliminary character only.

It was clear that the series of deceptions which had removed Anne Catherick to London, and separated her from Mrs. Clements, had been accomplished solely by Count Fosco and the Countess, and the question whether any part of the conduct of husband or wife had been of a kind to place either of them within reach of the law might be well worthy of future consideration. But the purpose I had now in view led me in another direction than this. The immediate object of my visit to Mrs. Clements was to make some approach at least to the discovery of Sir Percival's secret, and she had said nothing as yet which advanced me on my way to that important end. I felt the necessity of trying to awaken her recollections of other times, persons, and events than those on which her memory had hitherto been employed, and when I next spoke I spoke with that object indirectly in view.

"I wish I could be of any help to you in this sad calamity," I said. "All I can do is to feel heartily for your distress. If Anne had been your own child, Mrs. Clements, you could have shown her no truer kindness—you could have made no readier sacrifices for her sake."

"There's no great merit in that, sir," said Mrs. Clements simply. "The poor thing was as good as my own child to me. I nursed her from a baby, sir, bringing her up by hand—and a hard job it was to rear her. It wouldn't go to my heart so to lose her if I hadn't made her first short clothes and taught her to walk. I always said she was sent to console me for never having chick or child of my own. And now she's lost the old times keep coming back to my mind, and even at my age I can't help crying about her—I can't indeed, sir!"

I waited a little to give Mrs. Clements time to compose herself. Was the light that I had been looking for so long glimmering on me—far off, as yet—in the good woman's recollections of Anne's early life?

"Did you know Mrs. Catherick before Anne was born?" I asked.

"Not very long, sir—not above four months. We saw a great deal of each other in that time, but we were never very friendly together."

Her voice was steadier as she made that reply. Painful as many of her recollections might be, I observed that it was unconsciously a relief to her mind to revert to the dimly-seen troubles of the past, after dwelling so long on the vivid sorrows of the present.

"Were you and Mrs. Catherick neighbours?" I inquired, leading her memory on as encouragingly as I could.

"Yes, sir — neighbours at Old Welmingham."

"Old Welmingham? There are two places of that name, then, in Hampshire?"

"Well, sir, there used to be in those days — better than three-and-twenty years ago. They built a new town about two miles off, convenient to the river — and Old Welmingham, which was never much more than a village, got in time to be deserted. The new town is the place they call Welmingham now — but the old parish church is the parish church still. It stands by itself, with the houses pulled down or gone to ruin all round it. I've lived to see sad changes. It was a pleasant, pretty place in my time."

"Did you live there before your marriage, Mrs. Clements?"

"No, sir — I'm a Norfolk woman. It wasn't the place my husband belonged to either. He was from Grimsby, as I told you, and he served his apprenticeship there. But having friends down south, and hearing of an opening, he got into business at Southampton. It was in a small way, but he made enough for a plain man to retire on, and settled at Old Welmingham. I went there with him when he married me. We were neither of us young, but we lived very happy together — happier than our neighbour, Mr. Catherick, lived along with his wife when they came to Old Welmingham a year or two afterwards."

"Was your husband acquainted with them before that?"

"With Catherick, sir — not with his wife. She was a stranger to both of us. Some gentlemen had made interest for Catherick, and he got the situation of clerk at Welmingham church, which was the reason of his coming to settle in our neighbourhood. He brought his newly-married wife along with him, and we heard in course of time she had been lady's-maid in a family that lived at Varneck Hall, near Southampton. Catherick had found it a hard matter to get her to marry him, in consequence of her holding herself uncommonly high. He had asked and asked, and given the thing up at last, seeing she was so contrary about it. When he had given it up she turned contrary just the other way, and came to him of her own accord, without rhyme or reason seemingly. My poor husband always said that was the time to have given her a lesson. But Catherick was too fond of her to do anything of the sort—he never checked her either before they were married or after. He was a quick man in his feelings, letting them carry him a deal too far, now in one way and now in another, and he would have spoilt a better wife than Mrs. Catherick if a better had married him. I don't like to speak ill of any one, sir, but she was a heartless woman, with a terrible will of her own—fond of foolish admiration and fine clothes, and not caring to show so much as decent outward respect to Catherick, kindly as he always treated her. My husband said he thought things would turn out badly when they first came to live near us, and his words proved true. Before they had been quite four months in our neighbourhood there was a dreadful scandal and a miserable break-up in their household. Both of them were in fault—I am afraid both of them were equally in fault."

"You mean both husband and wife?"

"Oh, no, sir! I don't mean Catherick—he was only to be pitied. I meant his wife and the person—"

"And the person who caused the scandal?"

"Yes, sir. A gentleman born and brought up, who ought to have set a better example. You know him, sir—and my poor dear Anne knew him only too well."

"Sir Percival Glyde?"

"Yes, Sir Percival Glyde."

My heart beat fast—I thought I had my hand on the clue. How little I knew then of the windings of the labyrinths which were still to mislead me!

"Did Sir Percival live in your neighbourhood at that time?" I asked.

"No, sir. He came among us as a stranger. His father had died not long before in foreign parts. I remember he was in mourning. He put up at the little inn on the river (they have pulled it down since that time), where gentlemen used to go to fish. He wasn't much noticed when he first came—it was a common thing enough for gentlemen to travel from all parts of England to fish in our river."

"Did he make his appearance in the village before Anne was born?"

"Yes, sir. Anne was born in the June month of eighteen hundred and twenty-seven—and I think he came at the end of April or the beginning of May."

"Came as a stranger to all of you? A stranger to Mrs. Catherick as well as to the rest of the neighbours?"

"So we thought at first, sir. But when the scandal broke out, nobody believed they were strangers. I remember how it happened as well as if it was yesterday. Catherick came into our garden one night, and woke us by throwing up a handful of gravel from the walk at our window. I heard him beg my husband, for the Lord's sake, to come down and speak to him. They were a long time together talking in the porch. When my husband came back upstairs he was all of a tremble. He sat down on the side of the bed and he says to me, 'Lizzie! I always told you that woman was a bad one—I always said she would end ill, and I'm afraid in my own mind that the end has come already. Catherick has found a lot of lace handkerchiefs, and two fine rings, and a new gold watch and chain, hid away in his wife's drawer—things that nobody but a born lady ought ever to have—and his wife won't say how she came by them.' 'Does he think she stole them?' says I. 'No,' says he, 'stealing would be bad enough. But it's worse than that, she's had no chance of stealing such things as those, and she's not a woman to take them if she had. They're gifts, Lizzie—there's her own initials engraved inside the watch—and Catherick has seen her talking privately, and carrying on as no married woman should, with that gentleman in mourning, Sir Percival Glyde. Don't you say anything about it—I've quieted Catherick for to-night. I've told him to keep his tongue to himself, and his eyes and his ears open, and to wait a day or two, till he can be quite certain.' 'I believe you are both of you wrong,' says I. 'It's not in nature, comfortable and respectable as she is here, that Mrs. Catherick should take up with a chance stranger like Sir Percival Glyde.' 'Ay, but is he a stranger to her?' says my husband. 'You forget how Catherick's wife came to marry him. She went to him of her own accord, after saying No over and over again when he asked her. There have been wicked women before her time, Lizzie, who have used honest men who loved them as a means of saving their characters, and I'm sorely afraid this Mrs.

Catherick is as wicked as the worst of them. We shall see,' says my husband, 'we shall soon see.' And only two days afterwards we did see."

Mrs. Clements waited for a moment before she went on. Even in that moment, I began to doubt whether the clue that I thought I had found was really leading me to the central mystery of the labyrinth after all. Was this common, too common, story of a man's treachery and a woman's frailty the key to a secret which had been the lifelong terror of Sir Percival Glyde?

"Well, sir, Catherick took my husband's advice and waited," Mrs. Clements continued. "And as I told you, he hadn't long to wait. On the second day he found his wife and Sir Percival whispering together quite familiar, close under the vestry of the church. I suppose they thought the neighbourhood of the vestry was the last place in the world where anybody would think of looking after them, but, however that may be, there they were. Sir Percival, being seemingly surprised and confounded, defended himself in such a guilty way that poor Catherick (whose quick temper I have told you of already) fell into a kind of frenzy at his own disgrace, and struck Sir Percival. He was no match (and I am sorry to say it) for the man who had wronged him, and he was beaten in the cruelest manner, before the neighbours, who had come to the place on hearing the disturbance, could run in to part them. All this happened towards evening, and before nightfall, when my husband went to Catherick's house, he was gone, nobody knew where. No living soul in the village ever saw him again. He knew too well, by that time, what his wife's vile reason had been for marrying him, and he felt his misery and disgrace, especially after what had happened to him with Sir Percival, too keenly. The clergyman of the parish put an advertisement in the paper begging him to come back, and saying that he should not lose his situation or his friends. But Catherick had too much pride and spirit, as some people said — too much feeling, as I think, sir — to face his neighbours again, and try to live down the memory of his disgrace. My husband heard from him when he had left England, and heard a second time, when he was settled and doing well in America. He is alive there now, as far as I know, but none of us in the old country — his wicked wife least of all — are ever likely to set eyes on him again."

"What became of Sir Percival?" I inquired. "Did he stay in the neighbourhood?"

"Not he, sir. The place was too hot to hold him. He was

heard at high words with Mrs. Catherick the same night when the scandal broke out, and the next morning he took himself off."

"And Mrs. Catherick? Surely she never remained in the village among the people who knew of her disgrace?"

"She did, sir. She was hard enough and heartless enough to set the opinions of all her neighbours at flat defiance. She declared to everybody, from the clergyman downwards, that she was the victim of a dreadful mistake, and that all the scandal-mongers in the place should not drive her out of it, as if she was a guilty woman. All through my time she lived at Old Welmingham, and after my time, when the new town was building, and the respectable neighbours began moving to it, she moved too, as if she was determined to live among them and scandalise them to the very last. There she is now, and there she will stop, in defiance of the best of them, to her dying day."

"But how has she lived through all these years?" I asked. "Was her husband able and willing to help her?"

"Both able and willing, sir," said Mrs. Clements. "In the second letter he wrote to my good man, he said she had borne his name, and lived in his home, and, wicked as she was, she must not starve like a beggar in the street. He could afford to make her some small allowance, and she might draw for it quarterly at a place in London."

"Did she accept the allowance?"

"Not a farthing of it, sir. She said she would never be beholden to Catherick for bit or drop, if she lived to be a hundred. And she has kept her word ever since. When my poor dear husband died, and left all to me, Catherick's letter was put in my possession with the other things, and I told her to let me know if she was ever in want. 'I'll let all England know I'm in want,' she said, 'before I tell Catherick, or any friend of Catherick's. Take that for your answer, and give it to him for an answer, if he ever writes again.'"

"Do you suppose that she had money of her own?"

"Very little, if any, sir. It was said, and said truly, I am afraid, that her means of living came privately from Sir Percival Glyde."

After that last reply I waited a little, to reconsider what I had heard. If I unreservedly accepted the story so far, it was now plain that no approach, direct or indirect, to the Secret had yet been revealed to me, and that the pursuit of my object had ended again in leaving me face to face with the most palpable and the most disheartening failure.

But there was one point in the narrative which made me doubt the propriety of accepting it unreservedly, and which suggested the idea of something hidden below the surface.

I could not account to myself for the circumstance of the clerk's guilty wife voluntarily living out all her after-existence on the scene of her disgrace. The woman's own reported statement that she had taken this strange course as a practical assertion of her innocence did not satisfy me. It seemed, to my mind, more natural and more probable to assume that she was not so completely a free agent in this matter as she had herself asserted. In that case, who was the likeliest person to possess the power of compelling her to remain at Welmingham? The person unquestionably from whom she derived the means of living. She had refused assistance from her husband, she had no adequate resources of her own, she was a friendless, degraded woman—from what source should she derive help but from the source at which report pointed—Sir Percival Glyde?

Reasoning on these assumptions, and always bearing in mind the one certain fact to guide me, that Mrs. Catherick was in possession of the Secret, I easily understood that it was Sir Percival's interest to keep her at Welmingham, because her character in that place was certain to isolate her from all communication with female neighbours, and to allow her no opportunities of talking incautiously in moments of free intercourse with inquisitive bosom friends. But what was the mystery to be concealed? Not Sir Percival's infamous connection with Mrs. Catherick's disgrace, for the neighbours were the very people who knew of it—not the suspicion that he was Anne's father, for Welmingham was the place in which that suspicion must inevitably exist. If I accepted the guilty appearances described to me as unreservedly as others had accepted them, if I drew from them the same superficial conclusion which Mr. Catherick and all his neighbours had drawn, where was the suggestion, in all that I had heard, of a dangerous secret between Sir Percival and Mrs. Catherick, which had been kept hidden from that time to this?

And yet, in those stolen meetings, in those familiar whisperings between the clerk's wife and "the gentleman in mourning," the clue to discovery existed beyond a doubt.

Was it possible that appearances in this case had pointed one way while the truth lay all the while unsuspected in another direction? Could Mrs. Catherick's assertion, that she was the victim of a dreadful mistake, by any possibility be true? Or, assuming it to be false, could the conclusion which associated Sir Percival with her guilt have been founded in some inconceivable error? Had Sir Percival, by any chance, courted the suspicion that was wrong for the sake of diverting from himself some other suspicion that was right? Here—if I could find it—here was the approach to the Secret, hidden deep under the surface of the apparently unpromising story which I had just heard.

My next questions were now directed to the one object of ascertaining whether Mr. Catherick had or had not arrived truly at the conviction of his wife's misconduct. The answers I received from Mrs. Clements left me in no doubt whatever on that point. Mrs. Catherick had, on the clearest evidence, compromised her reputation, while a single woman, with some person unknown, and had married to save her character. It had been positively ascertained, by calculations of time and place into which I need not enter particularly, that the daughter who bore her husband's name was not her husband's child.

The next object of inquiry, whether it was equally certain that Sir Percival must have been the father of Anne, was beset by far greater difficulties. I was in no position to try the probabilities on one side or on the other in this instance by any better test than the test of personal resemblance.

"I suppose you often saw Sir Percival when he was in your village?" I said.

"Yes, sir, very often," replied Mrs. Clements.

"Did you ever observe that Anne was like him?"

"She was not at all like him, sir."

"Was she like her mother, then?"

"Not like her mother either, sir. Mrs. Catherick was dark, and full in the face."

Not like her mother and not like her (supposed) father. I knew that the test by personal resemblance was not to be implicitly trusted, but, on the other hand, it was not to be altogether rejected on that account. Was it possible to strengthen the evidence by discovering any conclusive facts in relation to the lives of Mrs. Catherick and Sir Percival before they either of them appeared at Old Welmingham? When I asked my next questions I put them with this view.

"When Sir Percival first arrived in your neighbourhood," I said, "did you hear where he had come from last?"

"No, sir. Some said from Blackwater Park, and some said from Scotland — but nobody knew."

"Was Mrs. Catherick living in service at Varneck Hall immediately before her marriage?"

"Yes, sir."

"And had she been long in her place?"

"Three or four years, sir; I am not quite certain which."

"Did you ever hear the name of the gentleman to whom Varneck Hall belonged at that time?"

"Yes, sir. His name was Major Donthorne."

"Did Mr. Catherick, or did any one else you knew, ever hear that Sir Percival was a friend of Major Donthorne's, or ever see Sir Percival in the neighbourhood of Varneck Hall?"

"Catherick never did, sir, that I can remember — nor any one else either, that I know of."

I noted down Major Donthorne's name and address, on the chance that he might still be alive, and that it might be useful at some future time to apply to him. Meanwhile, the impression on my mind was now decidedly adverse to the opinion that Sir Percival was Anne's father, and decidedly favourable to the conclusion that the secret of his stolen interviews with Mrs. Catherick was entirely unconnected with the disgrace which the woman had inflicted on her husband's good name. I could think of no further inquiries which I might make to strengthen this impression — I could only encourage Mrs. Clements to speak next of Anne's early days, and watch for any chance-suggestion which might in this way offer itself to me.

The Woman in White

"I have not heard yet," I said, "how the poor child, born in all this sin and misery, came to be trusted, Mrs. Clements, to your care."

"There was nobody else, sir, to take the little helpless creature in hand," replied Mrs. Clements. "The wicked mother seemed to hate it—as if the poor baby was in fault!—from the day it was born. My heart was heavy for the child, and I made the offer to bring it up as tenderly as if it was my own."

"Did Anne remain entirely under your care from that time?"

"Not quite entirely, sir. Mrs. Catherick had her whims and fancies about it at times, and used now and then to lay claim to the child, as if she wanted to spite me for bringing it up. But these fits of hers never lasted for long. Poor little Anne was always returned to me, and was always glad to get back—though she led but a gloomy life in my house, having no playmates, like other children, to brighten her up. Our longest separation was when her mother took her to Limmeridge. Just at that time I lost my husband, and I felt it was as well, in that miserable affliction, that Anne should not be in the house. She was between ten and eleven years old then, slow at her lessons, poor soul, and not so cheerful as other children—but as pretty a little girl to look at as you would wish to see. I waited at home till her mother brought her back, and then I made the offer to take her with me to London—the truth being, sir, that I could not find it in my heart to stop at Old Welmingham after my husband's death, the place was so changed and so dismal to me."

"And did Mrs. Catherick consent to your proposal?"

"No, sir. She came back from the north harder and bitterer than ever. Folks did say that she had been obliged to ask Sir Percival's leave to go, to begin with; and that she only went to nurse her dying sister at Limmeridge because the poor woman was reported to have saved money—the truth being that she hardly left enough to bury her. These things may have soured Mrs. Catherick likely enough, but however that may be, she wouldn't hear of my taking the child away. She seemed to like distressing us both by parting us. All I could do was to give Anne my direction, and to tell her privately, if she was ever in trouble, to come to me. But years passed before she was free to come. I never saw her again, poor soul, till the night she escaped from the mad-house."

"You know, Mrs. Clements, why Sir Percival Glyde shut her

up?"

"I only know what Anne herself told me, sir. The poor thing used to ramble and wander about it sadly. She said her mother had got some secret of Sir Percival's to keep, and had let it out to her long after I left Hampshire—and when Sir Percival found she knew it, he shut her up. But she never could say what it was when I asked her. All she could tell me was, that her mother might be the ruin and destruction of Sir Percival if she chose. Mrs. Catherick may have let out just as much as that, and no more. I'm next to certain I should have heard the whole truth from Anne, if she had really known it as she pretended to do, and as she very likely fancied she did, poor soul."

This idea had more than once occurred to my own mind. I had already told Marian that I doubted whether Laura was really on the point of making any important discovery when she and Anne Catherick were disturbed by Count Fosco at the boat-house. It was perfectly in character with Anne's mental affliction that she should assume an absolute knowledge of the secret on no better grounds than vague suspicion, derived from hints which her mother had incautiously let drop in her presence. Sir Percival's guilty distrust would, in that case, infallibly inspire him with the false idea that Anne knew all from her mother, just as it had afterwards fixed in his mind the equally false suspicion that his wife knew all from Anne.

The time was passing, the morning was wearing away. It was doubtful, if I stayed longer, whether I should hear anything more from Mrs. Clements that would be at all useful to my purpose. I had already discovered those local and family particulars, in relation to Mrs. Catherick, of which I had been in search, and I had arrived at certain conclusions, entirely new to me, which might immensely assist in directing the course of my future proceedings. I rose to take my leave, and to thank Mrs. Clements for the friendly readiness she had shown in affording me information.

"I am afraid you must have thought me very inquisitive," I said. "I have troubled you with more questions than many people would have cared to answer."

"You are heartily welcome, sir, to anything I can tell you," answered Mrs. Clements. She stopped and looked at me wistfully. "But I do wish," said the poor woman, "you could have told me a little more about Anne, sir. I thought I saw something in your face when you came in which looked as if you could. You can't think how hard it is not even to know whether she is living or dead. I could bear it better if I was only certain. You said you never expected we should see her alive again. Do you know, sir—do you know for truth—that it has pleased God to take her?"

I was not proof against this appeal; it would have been unspeakably mean and cruel of me if I had resisted it.

"I am afraid there is no doubt of the truth," I answered gently; "I have the certainty in my own mind that her troubles in this world are over."

The poor woman dropped into her chair and hid her face from me. "Oh, sir," she said, "how do you know it? Who can have told you?"

"No one has told me, Mrs. Clements. But I have reasons for feeling sure of it—reasons which I promise you shall know as soon as I can safely explain them. I am certain she was not neglected in her last moments—I am certain the heart complaint from which she suffered so sadly was the true cause of her death. You shall feel as sure of this as I do, soon—you shall know, before long, that she is buried in a quiet country churchyard—in a pretty, peaceful place, which you might have chosen for her yourself."

"Dead!" said Mrs. Clements, "dead so young, and I am left to hear it! I made her first short frocks. I taught her to walk. The first time she ever said Mother she said it to me—and now I am left and Anne is taken! Did you say, sir," said the poor woman, removing the handkerchief from her face, and looking up at me for the first time, "did you say that she had been nicely buried? Was it the sort of funeral she might have had if she had really been my own child?"

I assured her that it was. She seemed to take an inexplicable pride in my answer—to find a comfort in it which no other and higher considerations could afford. "It would have broken my heart," she said simply, "if Anne had not been nicely buried—but how do you know it, sir? who told you?" I once more entreated her to wait until I could speak to her unreservedly. "You are sure to see me again," I said, "for I have a favour to ask when you are a little more composed—perhaps in a day or two."

"Don't keep it waiting, sir, on my account," said Mrs. Clements. "Never mind my crying if I can be of use. If you have anything on your mind to say to me, sir, please to say it now."

"I only wish to ask you one last question," I said. "I only want to know Mrs. Catherick's address at Welmingham."

My request so startled Mrs. Clements, that, for the moment, even the tidings of Anne's death seemed to be driven from her mind. Her tears suddenly ceased to flow, and she sat looking at me in blank amazement.

"For the Lord's sake, sir!" she said, "what do you want with Mrs. Catherick!"

"I want this, Mrs. Clements," I replied, "I want to know the secret of those private meetings of hers with Sir Percival Glyde. There is something more in what you have told me of that woman's past conduct, and of that man's past relations with her, than you or any of your neighbours ever suspected. There is a secret we none of us know between those two, and I am going to Mrs. Catherick with the resolution to find it out."

"Think twice about it, sir!" said Mrs. Clements, rising in her earnestness and laying her hand on my arm. "She's an awful woman—you don't know her as I do. Think twice about it."

"I am sure your warning is kindly meant, Mrs. Clements. But I am determined to see the woman, whatever comes of it."

Mrs. Clements looked me anxiously in the face.

"I see your mind is made up, sir," she said. "I will give you the address."

I wrote it down in my pocket-book and then took her hand to say farewell.

"You shall hear from me soon," I said; "you shall know all that I have promised to tell you."

Mrs. Clements sighed and shook her head doubtfully.

"An old woman's advice is sometimes worth taking, sir," she said. "Think twice before you go to Welmingham."

VIII

When I reached home again after my interview with Mrs. Clements, I was struck by the appearance of a change in Laura.

The unvarying gentleness and patience which long misfortune had tried so cruelly and had never conquered yet, seemed now to have suddenly failed her. Insensible to all Marian's attempts to soothe and amuse her, she sat, with her neglected drawing pushed away on the table, her eyes resolutely cast down, her fingers twining and untwining themselves restlessly in her lap. Marian rose when I came in, with a silent distress in her face, waited for a moment to see if Laura would look up at my approach, whispered to me, "Try if you can rouse her," and left the room.

I sat down in the vacant chair—gently unclasped the poor, worn, restless fingers, and took both her hands in mine.

"What are you thinking of, Laura? Tell me, my darling—try and tell me what it is."

She struggled with herself, and raised her eyes to mine. "I can't feel happy," she said, "I can't help thinking——" She stopped, bent forward a little, and laid her head on my shoulder, with a terrible mute helplessness that struck me to the heart.

"Try to tell me," I repeated gently; "try to tell me why you are not happy."

"I am so useless—I am such a burden on both of you," she answered, with a weary, hopeless sigh. "You work and get money, Walter, and Marian helps you. Why is there nothing I can do? You will end in liking Marian better than you like me—you will, because I am so helpless! Oh, don't, don't, don't treat me like a child!"

I raised her head, and smoothed away the tangled hair that fell over her face, and kissed her—my poor, faded flower! my lost, afflicted sister! "You shall help us, Laura," I said, "you shall begin, my darling, to-day."

She looked at me with a feverish eagerness, with a breathless interest, that made me tremble for the new life of hope which I had called into being by those few words.

I rose, and set her drawing materials in order, and placed

them near her again.

"You know that I work and get money by drawing," I said. "Now you have taken such pains, now you are so much improved, you shall begin to work and get money too. Try to finish this little sketch as nicely and prettily as you can. When it is done I will take it away with me, and the same person will buy it who buys all that I do. You shall keep your own earnings in your own purse, and Marian shall come to you to help us, as often as she comes to me. Think how useful you are going to make yourself to both of us, and you will soon be as happy, Laura, as the day is long."

Her face grew eager, and brightened into a smile. In the moment while it lasted, in the moment when she again took up the pencils that had been laid aside, she almost looked like the Laura of past days.

I had rightly interpreted the first signs of a new growth and strength in her mind, unconsciously expressing themselves in the notice she had taken of the occupations which filled her sister's life and mine. Marian (when I told her what had passed) saw, as I saw, that she was longing to assume her own little position of importance, to raise herself in her own estimation and in ours—and, from that day, we tenderly helped the new ambition which gave promise of the hopeful, happier future, that might now not be far off. Her drawings, as she finished them, or tried to finish them, were placed in my hands. Marian took them from me and hid them carefully, and I set aside a little weekly tribute from my earnings, to be offered to her as the price paid by strangers for the poor, faint, valueless sketches, of which I was the only purchaser. It was hard sometimes to maintain our innocent deception, when she proudly brought out her purse to contribute her share towards the expenses, and wondered with serious interest, whether I or she had earned the most that week. I have all those hidden drawings in my possession still—they are my treasures beyond price—the dear remembrances that I love to keep alive—the friends in past adversity that my heart will never part from, my tenderness never forget.

Am I trifling, here, with the necessities of my task? am I looking forward to the happier time which my narrative has not yet reached? Yes. Back again—back to the days of doubt and dread, when the spirit within me struggled hard for its life, in the icy stillness of perpetual suspense. I have paused and rested for a while on my forward course. It is not, perhaps, time wasted, if the friends who read these pages have paused and rested too.

I took the first opportunity I could find of speaking to Marian in private, and of communicating to her the result of the inquiries which I had made that morning. She seemed to share the opinion on the subject of my proposed journey to Welmingham, which Mrs. Clements had already expressed to me.

"Surely, Walter," she said, "you hardly know enough yet to give you any hope of claiming Mrs. Catherick's confidence? Is it wise to proceed to these extremities, before you have really exhausted all safer and simpler means of attaining your object? When you told me that Sir Percival and the Count were the only two people in existence who knew the exact date of Laura's journey, you forgot, and I forgot, that there was a third person who must surely know it—I mean Mrs. Rubelle. Would it not be far easier, and far less dangerous, to insist on a confession from her, than to force it from Sir Percival?"

"It might be easier," I replied, "but we are not aware of the full extent of Mrs. Rubelle's connivance and interest in the conspiracy, and we are therefore not certain that the date has been impressed on her mind, as it has been assuredly impressed on the minds of Sir Percival and the Count. It is too late, now, to waste the time on Mrs. Rubelle, which may be all-important to the discovery of the one assailable point in Sir Percival's life. Are you thinking a little too seriously, Marian, of the risk I may run in returning to Hampshire? Are you beginning to doubt whether Sir Percival Glyde may not in the end be more than a match for me?"

"He will not be more than your match," she replied decidedly, "because he will not be helped in resisting you by the impenetrable wickedness of the Count."

"What has led you to that conclusion?" I replied, in some surprise.

"My own knowledge of Sir Percival's obstinacy and impatience of the Count's control," she answered. "I believe he will insist on meeting you single-handed—just as he insisted at first on acting for himself at Blackwater Park. The time for suspecting the Count's interference will be the time when you have Sir Percival at your mercy. His own interests will then be directly threatened, and he will act, Walter, to terrible purpose in his own defence."

"We may deprive him of his weapons beforehand," I said. "Some of the particulars I have heard from Mrs. Clements may yet be turned to account against him, and other means of strengthening the case may be at our disposal. There are passages in Mrs. Michelson's narrative which show that the Count found it necessary to place himself in communication with Mr. Fairlie, and there may be circumstances which compromise him in that proceeding. While I am away, Marian, write to Mr. Fairlie and say that you want an answer describing exactly what passed between the Count and himself, and informing you also of any particulars that may have come to his knowledge at the same time in connection with his niece. Tell him that the statement you request will, sooner or later, be insisted on, if he shows any reluctance to furnish you with it of his own accord."

"The letter shall be written, Walter. But are you really determined to go to Welmingham?"

"Absolutely determined. I will devote the next two days to earning what we want for the week to come, and on the third day I go to Hampshire."

When the third day came I was ready for my journey.

As it was possible that I might be absent for some little time, I arranged with Marian that we were to correspond every day — of course addressing each other by assumed names, for caution's sake. As long as I heard from her regularly, I should assume that nothing was wrong. But if the morning came and brought me no letter, my return to London would take place, as a matter of course, by the first train. I contrived to reconcile Laura to my departure by telling her that I was going to the country to find new purchasers for her drawings and for mine, and I left her occupied and happy. Marian followed me downstairs to the street door.

"Remember what anxious hearts you leave here," she whispered, as we stood together in the passage. "Remember all the hopes that hang on your safe return. If strange things happen to you on this journey — if you and Sir Percival meet — —"

"What makes you think we shall meet?" I asked.

"I don't know — I have fears and fancies that I cannot

account for. Laugh at them, Walter, if you like—but, for God's sake, keep your temper if you come in contact with that man!"

"Never fear, Marian! I answer for my self-control."

With those words we parted.

I walked briskly to the station. There was a glow of hope in me. There was a growing conviction in my mind that my journey this time would not be taken in vain. It was a fine, clear, cold morning. My nerves were firmly strung, and I felt all the strength of my resolution stirring in me vigorously from head to foot.

As I crossed the railway platform, and looked right and left among the people congregated on it, to search for any faces among them that I knew, the doubt occurred to me whether it might not have been to my advantage if I had adopted a disguise before setting out for Hampshire. But there was something so repellent to me in the idea—something so meanly like the common herd of spies and informers in the mere act of adopting a disguise—that I dismissed the question from consideration almost as soon as it had risen in my mind. Even as a mere matter of expediency the proceeding was doubtful in the extreme. If I tried the experiment at home the landlord of the house would sooner or later discover me, and would have his suspicions aroused immediately. If I tried it away from home the same persons might see me, by the commonest accident, with the disguise and without it, and I should in that way be inviting the notice and distrust which it was my most pressing interest to avoid. In my own character I had acted thus far—and in my own character I was resolved to continue to the end.

The train left me at Welmingham early in the afternoon.

Is there any wilderness of sand in the deserts of Arabia, is there any prospect of desolation among the ruins of Palestine, which can rival the repelling effect on the eye, and the depressing influence on the mind, of an English country town in the first stage of its existence, and in the transition state of its prosperity? I asked myself that question as I passed through the clean desolation, the neat ugliness, the prim torpor of the streets of Welmingham. And the tradesmen who stared after me from their lonely shops—the trees that drooped helpless in their arid exile of unfinished crescents and squares—the dead housecarcasses that waited in vain for the vivifying human element to animate them with the breath of life—every creature that I saw, every object that I passed, seemed to answer with one accord: The deserts of Arabia are innocent of our civilised desolation—the ruins of Palestine are incapable of our modern gloom!

I inquired my way to the quarter of the town in which Mrs. Catherick lived, and on reaching it found myself in a square of small houses, one story high. There was a bare little plot of grass in the middle, protected by a cheap wire fence. An elderly nursemaid and two children were standing in a corner of the enclosure, looking at a lean goat tethered to the grass. Two foot-passengers were talking together on one side of the pavement before the houses, and an idle little boy was leading an idle little dog along by a string on the other. I heard the dull tinkling of a piano at a distance, accompanied by the intermittent knocking of a hammer nearer at hand. These were all the sights and sounds of life that encountered me when I entered the square.

I walked at once to the door of Number Thirteen—the number of Mrs. Catherick's house—and knocked, without waiting to consider beforehand how I might best present myself when I got in. The first necessity was to see Mrs. Catherick. I could then judge, from my own observation, of the safest and easiest manner of approaching the object of my visit.

The door was opened by a melancholy middle-aged woman servant. I gave her my card, and asked if I could see Mrs. Catherick. The card was taken into the front parlour, and the servant returned with a message requesting me to mention what my business was.

"Say, if you please, that my business relates to Mrs. Catherick's daughter," I replied. This was the best pretext I could think of, on the spur of the moment, to account for my visit.

The servant again retired to the parlour, again returned, and this time begged me, with a look of gloomy amazement, to walk in.

I entered a little room, with a flaring paper of the largest pattern on the walls. Chairs, tables, cheffonier, and sofa, all gleamed with the glutinous brightness of cheap upholstery. On the largest table, in the middle of the room, stood a smart Bible, placed exactly in the centre on a red and yellow woollen mat and at the side of the table nearest to the window, with a little knitting-basket on her lap, and a wheezing, blear-eyed old spaniel crouched at her feet, there sat an elderly woman, wearing a black net cap and a black silk gown, and having slate-coloured mittens on her hands. Her iron-grey hair hung in heavy bands on either side of her face—her dark eyes looked straight forward, with a hard, defiant, implacable stare. She had full square cheeks, a long, firm chin, and thick, sensual, colourless lips. Her figure was stout and sturdy, and her manner aggressively self-possessed. This was Mrs. Catherick.

"You have come to speak to me about my daughter," she said, before I could utter a word on my side. "Be so good as to mention what you have to say."

The tone of her voice was as hard, as defiant, as implacable as the expression of her eyes. She pointed to a chair, and looked me all over attentively, from head to foot, as I sat down in it. I saw that my only chance with this woman was to speak to her in her own tone, and to meet her, at the outset of our interview, on her own ground.

"You are aware," I said, "that your daughter has been lost?"

"I am perfectly aware of it."

"Have you felt any apprehension that the misfortune of her loss might be followed by the misfortune of her death?"

"Yes. Have you come here to tell me she is dead?"

"I have."

"Why?"

She put that extraordinary question without the slightest change in her voice, her face, or her manner. She could not have appeared more perfectly unconcerned if I had told her of the death of the goat in the enclosure outside.

"Why?" I repeated. "Do you ask why I come here to tell you of your daughter's death?"

"Yes. What interest have you in me, or in her? How do you come to know anything about my daughter?"

"In this way. I met her on the night when she escaped from the Asylum, and I assisted her in reaching a place of safety."

"You did very wrong."

"I am sorry to hear her mother say so."

"Her mother does say so. How do you know she is dead?"

"I am not at liberty to say how I know it—but I do know it."

"Are you at liberty to say how you found out my address?"

"Certainly. I got your address from Mrs. Clements."

"Mrs. Clements is a foolish woman. Did she tell you to come here?"

"She did not."

"Then, I ask you again, why did you come?"

As she was determined to have her answer, I gave it to her in the plainest possible form.

"I came," I said, "because I thought Anne Catherick's mother might have some natural interest in knowing whether she was alive or dead."

"Just so," said Mrs. Catherick, with additional self-possession. "Had you no other motive?"

I hesitated. The right answer to that question was not easy to find at a moment's notice.

"If you have no other motive," she went on, deliberately taking off her slate-coloured mittens, and rolling them up, "I have only to thank you for your visit, and to say that I will not detain you here any longer. Your information would be more satisfactory if you were willing to explain how you became possessed of it. However, it justifies me, I suppose, in going into mourning. There is not much alteration necessary in my dress, as you see. When I have changed my mittens, I shall be all in black."

She searched in the pocket of her gown, drew out a pair of black lace mittens, put them on with the stoniest and steadiest composure, and then quietly crossed her hands in her lap.

"I wish you good morning," she said.

The cool contempt of her manner irritated me into directly avowing that the purpose of my visit had not been answered yet.

"I have another motive in coming here," I said.

"Ah! I thought so," remarked Mrs. Catherick.

"Your daughter's death — —"

"What did she die of?"

"Of disease of the heart."

"Yes. Go on."

"Your daughter's death has been made the pretext for inflicting serious injury on a person who is very dear to me. Two men have been concerned, to my certain knowledge, in doing that wrong. One of them is Sir Percival Glyde."

"Indeed!"

I looked attentively to see if she flinched at the sudden mention of that name. Not a muscle of her stirred — the hard, defiant, implacable stare in her eyes never wavered for an instant.

"You may wonder," I went on, "how the event of your daughter's death can have been made the means of inflicting injury on another person."

"No," said Mrs. Catherick; "I don't wonder at all. This appears to be your affair. You are interested in my affairs. I am not interested in yours."

"You may ask, then," I persisted, "why I mention the matter in your presence."

"Yes, I do ask that."

"I mention it because I am determined to bring Sir Percival Glyde to account for the wickedness he has committed."

"What have I to do with your determination?"

"You shall hear. There are certain events in Sir Percival's past life which it is necessary for my purpose to be fully acquainted with. You know them — and for that reason I come to you."

"What events do you mean?"

"Events that occurred at Old Welmingham when your husband was parish-clerk at that place, and before the time when your daughter was born."

I had reached the woman at last through the barrier of impenetrable reserve that she had tried to set up between us. I saw her temper smouldering in her eyes—as plainly as I saw her hands grow restless, then unclasp themselves, and begin mechanically smoothing her dress over her knees.

"What do you know of those events?" she asked.

"All that Mrs. Clements could tell me," I answered.

There was a momentary flush on her firm square face, a momentary stillness in her restless hands, which seemed to betoken a coming outburst of anger that might throw her off her guard. But no—she mastered the rising irritation, leaned back in her chair, crossed her arms on her broad bosom, and with a smile of grim sarcasm on her thick lips, looked at me as steadily as ever.

"Ah! I begin to understand it all now," she said, her tamed and disciplined anger only expressing itself in the elaborate mockery of her tone and manner. "You have got a grudge of your own against Sir Percival Glyde, and I must help you to wreak it. I must tell you this, that, and the other about Sir Percival and myself, must I? Yes, indeed? You have been prying into my private affairs. You think you have found a lost woman to deal with, who lives here on sufferance, and who will do anything you ask for fear you may injure her in the opinions of the town's-people. I see through you and your precious speculation—I do! and it amuses me. Ha! ha!"

She stopped for a moment, her arms tightened over her bosom, and she laughed to herself—a hard, harsh, angry laugh.

"You don't know how I have lived in this place, and what I have done in this place, Mr. What's-your-name," she went on. "I'll tell you, before I ring the bell and have you shown out. I came here a wronged woman—I came here robbed of my character and determined to claim it back. I've been years and years about it—and I have claimed it back. I have matched the respectable people fairly and openly on their own ground. If they say anything against me now they must say it in secret— they can't say it, they daren't say it, openly. I stand high enough in this town to be out of your reach. The clergyman bows to me. Aha! you didn't bargain for that when you came here. Go to the church and inquire about me—you will find Mrs. Catherick has her sitting like the rest of them, and pays the rent on the day it's due. Go to the town-hall. There's a petition lying there—a petition of the respectable inhabitants against allowing a circus to come and perform here and corrupt our morals—yes! OUR morals. I signed that petition this morning. Go to the bookseller's shop. The clergyman's Wednesday evening Lectures on Justification by Faith are publishing there by subscription—I'm down on the list. The doctor's wife only put a shilling in the plate at our last charity sermon—I put half-a-crown. Mr. Churchwarden Soward held the plate, and bowed to me. Ten years ago he told Pigrum the chemist I ought to be whipped out of the town at the cart's tail. Is your mother alive? Has she got a better Bible on her table than I have got on mine? Does she stand better with her trades-people than I do with mine? Has she always lived within her income? I have always lived within mine. Ah! there is the clergyman coming along the square. Look, Mr. What's-your-name—look, if you please!"

She started up with the activity of a young woman, went to the window, waited till the clergyman passed, and bowed to him solemnly. The clergyman ceremoniously raised his hat, and walked on. Mrs. Catherick returned to her chair, and looked at me with a grimmer sarcasm than ever.

"There!" she said. "What do you think of that for a woman with a lost character? How does your speculation look now?"

The singular manner in which she had chosen to assert herself, the extraordinary practical vindication of her position in the town which she had just offered, had so perplexed me that I listened to her in silent surprise. I was not the less resolved, however, to make another effort to throw her off her guard. If the woman's fierce temper once got beyond her control, and once flamed out on me, she might yet say the words which would put the clue in my hands.

"How does your speculation look now?" she repeated.

"Exactly as it looked when I first came in," I answered. "I don't doubt the position you have gained in the town, and I don't wish to assail it even if I could. I came here because Sir Percival Glyde is, to my certain knowledge, your enemy, as well as mine. If I have a grudge against him, you have a grudge against him too. You may deny it if you like, you may distrust me as much as you please, you may be as angry as you will—

but, of all the women in England, you, if you have any sense of injury, are the woman who ought to help me to crush that man."

"Crush him for yourself," she said; "then come back here, and see what I say to you."

She spoke those words as she had not spoken yet, quickly, fiercely, vindictively. I had stirred in its lair the serpent-hatred of years, but only for a moment. Like a lurking reptile it leaped up at me as she eagerly bent forward towards the place in which I was sitting. Like a lurking reptile it dropped out of sight again as she instantly resumed her former position in the chair.

"You won't trust me?" I said.

"No."

"You are afraid?"

"Do I look as if I was?"

"You are afraid of Sir Percival Glyde?"

"Am I?"

Her colour was rising, and her hands were at work again smoothing her gown. I pressed the point farther and farther home, I went on without allowing her a moment of delay.

"Sir Percival has a high position in the world," I said; "it would be no wonder if you were afraid of him. Sir Percival is a powerful man, a baronet, the possessor of a fine estate, the descendant of a great family — —"

She amazed me beyond expression by suddenly bursting out laughing.

"Yes," she repeated, in tones of the bitterest, steadiest contempt. "A baronet, the possessor of a fine estate, the descendant of a great family. Yes, indeed! A great family — especially by the mother's side."

There was no time to reflect on the words that had just escaped her, there was only time to feel that they were well worth thinking over the moment I left the house.

"I am not here to dispute with you about family questions,"

The Woman in White

I said. "I know nothing of Sir Percival's mother——"

"And you know as little of Sir Percival himself," she interposed sharply.

"I advise you not to be too sure of that," I rejoined. "I know some things about him, and I suspect many more."

"What do you suspect?"

"I'll tell you what I don't suspect. I don't suspect him of being Anne's father."

She started to her feet, and came close up to me with a look of fury.

"How dare you talk to me about Anne's father! How dare you say who was her father, or who wasn't!" she broke out, her face quivering, her voice trembling with passion.

"The secret between you and Sir Percival is not that secret," I persisted. "The mystery which darkens Sir Percival's life was not born with your daughter's birth, and has not died with your daughter's death."

She drew back a step. "Go!" she said, and pointed sternly to the door.

"There was no thought of the child in your heart or in his," I went on, determined to press her back to her last defences. "There was no bond of guilty love between you and him when you held those stolen meetings, when your husband found you whispering together under the vestry of the church."

Her pointing hand instantly dropped to her side, and the deep flush of anger faded from her face while I spoke. I saw the change pass over her—I saw that hard, firm, fearless, self-possessed woman quail under a terror which her utmost resolution was not strong enough to resist when I said those five last words, "the vestry of the church."

For a minute or more we stood looking at each other in silence. I spoke first.

"Do you still refuse to trust me?" I asked.

She could not call the colour that had left it back to her face, but she had steadied her voice, she had recovered the defiant self-possession of her manner when she answered me.

"I do refuse," she said.

"Do you still tell me to go?"

"Yes. Go—and never come back."

I walked to the door, waited a moment before I opened it, and turned round to look at her again.

"I may have news to bring you of Sir Percival which you don't expect," I said, "and in that case I shall come back."

"There is no news of Sir Percival that I don't expect, except——"

She stopped, her pale face darkened, and she stole back with a quiet, stealthy, cat-like step to her chair.

"Except the news of his death," she said, sitting down again, with the mockery of a smile just hovering on her cruel lips, and the furtive light of hatred lurking deep in her steady eyes.

As I opened the door of the room to go out, she looked round at me quickly. The cruel smile slowly widened her lips—she eyed me, with a strange stealthy interest, from head to foot—an unutterable expectation showed itself wickedly all over her face. Was she speculating, in the secrecy of her own heart, on my youth and strength, on the force of my sense of injury and the limits of my self-control, and was she considering the lengths to which they might carry me, if Sir Percival and I ever chanced to meet? The bare doubt that it might be so drove me from her presence, and silenced even the common forms of farewell on my lips. Without a word more, on my side or on hers, I left the room.

As I opened the outer door, I saw the same clergyman who had already passed the house once, about to pass it again, on his way back through the square. I waited on the door-step to let him go by, and looked round, as I did so, at the parlour window.

Mrs. Catherick had heard his footsteps approaching, in the silence of that lonely place, and she was on her feet at the window again, waiting for him. Not all the strength of all the terrible passions I had roused in that woman's heart, could loosen her desperate hold on the one fragment of social consideration which years of resolute effort had just dragged within her grasp. There she was again, not a minute after I had left her, placed purposely in a position which made it a matter of common courtesy on the part of the clergyman to bow to her for a second time. He raised his hat once more. I saw the hard ghastly face behind the window soften, and light up with gratified pride—I saw the head with the grim black cap bend ceremoniously in return. The clergyman had bowed to her, and in my presence, twice in one day!

IX

I left the house, feeling that Mrs. Catherick had helped me a step forward, in spite of herself. Before I had reached the turning which led out of the square, my attention was suddenly aroused by the sound of a closing door behind me.

I looked round, and saw an undersized man in black on the door-step of a house, which, as well as I could judge, stood next to Mrs. Catherick's place of abode—next to it, on the side nearest to me. The man did not hesitate a moment about the direction he should take. He advanced rapidly towards the turning at which I had stopped. I recognised him as the lawyer's clerk, who had preceded me in my visit to Blackwater Park, and who had tried to pick a quarrel with me, when I asked him if I could see the house.

I waited where I was, to ascertain whether his object was to come to close quarters and speak on this occasion. To my surprise he passed on rapidly, without saying a word, without even looking up in my face as he went by. This was such a complete inversion of the course of proceeding which I had every reason to expect on his part, that my curiosity, or rather my suspicion, was aroused, and I determined on my side to keep him cautiously in view, and to discover what the business might be in which he was now employed. Without caring whether he saw me or not, I walked after him. He never looked back, and he led me straight through the streets to the railway station.

The train was on the point of starting, and two or three passengers who were late were clustering round the small opening through which the tickets were issued. I joined them, and distinctly heard the lawyer's clerk demand a ticket for the Blackwater station. I satisfied myself that he had actually left by the train before I came away.

There was only one interpretation that I could place on what I had just seen and heard. I had unquestionably observed the man leaving a house which closely adjoined Mrs. Catherick's residence. He had been probably placed there, by Sir Percival's directions, as a lodger, in anticipation of my inquiries leading me, sooner or later, to communicate with Mrs. Catherick. He had doubtless seen me go in and come out, and he had hurried away by the first train to make his report at Blackwater Park, to which place Sir Percival would naturally betake himself (knowing what he evidently knew of my movements), in order to be ready on the spot, if I returned to Hampshire. Before many days were over, there seemed every likelihood now that he and I might meet.

Whatever result events might be destined to produce, I resolved to pursue my own course, straight to the end in view, without stopping or turning aside for Sir Percival or for any one. The great responsibility which weighed on me heavily in London—the responsibility of so guiding my slightest actions as to prevent them from leading accidentally to the discovery of Laura's place of refuge—was removed, now that I was in Hampshire. I could go and come as I pleased at Welmingham, and if I chanced to fail in observing any necessary precautions, the immediate results, at least, would affect no one but myself.

When I left the station the winter evening was beginning to close in. There was little hope of continuing my inquiries after dark to any useful purpose in a neighbourhood that was strange to me. Accordingly, I made my way to the nearest hotel, and ordered my dinner and my bed. This done, I wrote to Marian, to tell her that I was safe and well, and that I had fair prospects of success. I had directed her, on leaving home, to address the first letter she wrote to me (the letter I expected to receive the next morning) to "The Post-Office, Welmingham," and I now begged her to send her second day's letter to the same address.

I could easily receive it by writing to the postmaster if I happened to be away from the town when it arrived.

The coffee-room of the hotel, as it grew late in the evening, became a perfect solitude. I was left to reflect on what I had accomplished that afternoon as uninterruptedly as if the house had been my own. Before I retired to rest I had attentively thought over my extraordinary interview with Mrs. Catherick from beginning to end, and had verified at my leisure the conclusions which I had hastily drawn in the earlier part of the day.

The vestry of Old Welmingham church was the starting-point from which my mind slowly worked its way back through all that I had heard Mrs. Catherick say, and through all I had seen Mrs. Catherick do.

At the time when the neighbourhood of the vestry was first referred to in my presence by Mrs. Clements, I had thought it the strangest and most unaccountable of all places for Sir Percival to select for a clandestine meeting with the clerk's wife. Influenced by this impression, and by no other, I had mentioned "the vestry of the church" before Mrs. Catherick on pure speculation—it represented one of the minor peculiarities of the story which occurred to me while I was speaking. I was prepared for her answering me confusedly or angrily, but the blank terror that seized her when I said the words took me completely by surprise. I had long before associated Sir Percival's Secret with the concealment of a serious crime which Mrs. Catherick knew of, but I had gone no further than this. Now the woman's paroxysm of terror associated the crime, either directly or indirectly, with the vestry, and convinced me that she had been more than the mere witness of it—she was also the accomplice, beyond a doubt.

What had been the nature of the crime? Surely there was a contemptible side to it, as well as a dangerous side, or Mrs. Catherick would not have repeated my own words, referring to Sir Percival's rank and power, with such marked disdain as she had certainly displayed. It was a contemptible crime then and a dangerous crime, and she had shared in it, and it was associated with the vestry of the church.

The next consideration to be disposed of led me a step farther from this point.

Mrs. Catherick's undisguised contempt for Sir Percival plainly extended to his mother as well. She had referred with the bitterest sarcasm to the great family he had descended from—"especially by the mother's side." What did this mean?

There appeared to be only two explanations of it. Either his mother's birth had been low, or his mother's reputation was damaged by some hidden flaw with which Mrs. Catherick and Sir Percival were both privately acquainted? I could only put the first explanation to the test by looking at the register of her marriage, and so ascertaining her maiden name and her parentage as a preliminary to further inquiries.

On the other hand, if the second case supposed were the true one, what had been the flaw in her reputation? Remembering the account which Marian had given me of Sir Percival's father and mother, and of the suspiciously unsocial secluded life they had both led, I now asked myself whether it might not be possible that his mother had never been married at all. Here again the register might, by offering written evidence of the marriage, prove to me, at any rate, that this doubt had no foundation in truth. But where was the register to be found? At this point I took up the conclusions which I had previously formed, and the same mental process which had discovered the locality of the concealed crime, now lodged the register also in the vestry of Old Welmingham church.

These were the results of my interview with Mrs. Catherick—these were the various considerations, all steadily converging to one point, which decided the course of my proceedings on the next day.

The morning was cloudy and lowering, but no rain fell. I left my bag at the hotel to wait there till I called for it, and, after inquiring the way, set forth on foot for Old Welmingham church.

It was a walk of rather more than two miles, the ground rising slowly all the way.

On the highest point stood the church—an ancient, weather-beaten building, with heavy buttresses at its sides, and a clumsy square tower in front. The vestry at the back was built out from the church, and seemed to be of the same age. Round the building at intervals appeared the remains of the village which Mrs. Clements had described to me as her husband's place of abode in former years, and which the principal inhabitants had long since deserted for the new town. Some of the empty houses had been dismantled to their outer walls, some had been left to decay with time, and some were still inhabited by persons evidently of the poorest class. It was a dreary scene, and yet, in the worst aspect of its ruin, not so dreary as the modern town that I had just left. Here there was the brown, breezy sweep of surrounding fields for the eye to repose on—here the trees, leafless as they were, still varied the monotony of the prospect, and helped the mind to look forward to summer-time and shade.

As I moved away from the back of the church, and passed some of the dismantled cottages in search of a person who might direct me to the clerk, I saw two men saunter out after me from behind a wall. The tallest of the two—a stout muscular man in the dress of a gamekeeper—was a stranger to me. The other was one of the men who had followed me in London on the day when I left Mr. Kyrle's office. I had taken particular notice of him at the time; and I felt sure that I was not mistaken in identifying the fellow on this occasion.

Neither he nor his companion attempted to speak to me, and both kept themselves at a respectful distance, but the motive of their presence in the neighbourhood of the church was plainly apparent. It was exactly as I had supposed—Sir Percival was already prepared for me. My visit to Mrs. Catherick had been reported to him the evening before, and those two men had been placed on the look-out near the church in anticipation of my appearance at Old Welmingham. If I had wanted any further proof that my investigations had taken the right direction at last, the plan now adopted for watching me would have supplied it.

I walked on away from the church till I reached one of the inhabited houses, with a patch of kitchen garden attached to it on which a labourer was at work. He directed me to the clerk's abode, a cottage at some little distance off, standing by itself on the outskirts of the forsaken village. The clerk was indoors, and was just putting on his greatcoat. He was a cheerful, familiar, loudly-talkative old man, with a very poor opinion (as I soon discovered) of the place in which he lived, and a happy sense of superiority to his neighbours in virtue of the great personal distinction of having once been in London.

"It's well you came so early, sir," said the old man, when I had mentioned the object of my visit. "I should have been away in ten minutes more. Parish business, sir, and a goodish long trot before it's all done for a man at my age. But, bless you, I'm strong on my legs still! As long as a man don't give at his legs, there's a deal of work left in him. Don't you think so yourself, sir?"

He took his keys down while he was talking from a hook behind the fireplace, and locked his cottage door behind us.

"Nobody at home to keep house for me," said the clerk, with a cheerful sense of perfect freedom from all family encumbrances. "My wife's in the churchyard there, and my children are all married. A wretched place this, isn't it, sir? But the parish is a large one—every man couldn't get through the business as I do. It's learning does it, and I've had my share, and a little more. I can talk the Queen's English (God bless the Queen!), and that's more than most of the people about here can do. You're from London, I suppose, sir? I've been in London a matter of five-and-twenty year ago. What's the news there now, if you please?"

Chattering on in this way, he led me back to the vestry. I looked about to see if the two spies were still in sight. They were not visible anywhere. After having discovered my application to the clerk, they had probably concealed themselves where they could watch my next proceedings in perfect freedom.

The vestry door was of stout old oak, studded with strong nails, and the clerk put his large heavy key into the lock with the air of a man who knew that he had a difficulty to encounter, and who was not quite certain of creditably conquering it.

"I'm obliged to bring you this way, sir," he said, "because the door from the vestry to the church is bolted on the vestry side. We might have got in through the church otherwise. This is a perverse lock, if ever there was one yet. It's big enough for a prison-door—it's been hampered over and over again, and it ought to be changed for a new one. I've mentioned that to the churchwarden fifty times over at least—he's always saying, 'I'll see about it'—and he never does see. Ah, it's a sort of lost corner, this place. Not like London—is it, sir? Bless you, we are all asleep here! We don't march with the times."

After some twisting and turning of the key, the heavy lock yielded, and he opened the door.

The vestry was larger than I should have supposed it to be, judging from the outside only. It was a dim, mouldy, melancholy old room, with a low, raftered ceiling. Round two sides of it, the sides nearest to the interior of the church, ran heavy wooden presses, worm-eaten and gaping with age. Hooked to the inner corner of one of these presses hung several surplices, all bulging out at their lower ends in an irreverent-looking bundle of limp drapery. Below the surplices, on the floor, stood three packing-cases, with the lids half off, half on, and the straw profusely bursting out of their cracks and crevices in every direction. Behind them, in a corner, was a litter of dusty papers, some large and rolled up like architects' plans, some loosely strung together on files like bills or letters. The room had once been lighted by a small side window, but this had been bricked up, and a lantern skylight was now substituted for it. The atmosphere of the place was heavy and mouldy, being rendered additionally oppressive by the closing of the door which led into the church. This door also was composed of solid oak, and was bolted at the top and bottom on the vestry side.

"We might be tidier, mightn't we, sir?" said the cheerful clerk; "but when you're in a lost corner of a place like this, what are you to do? Why, look here now, just look at these packing-cases. There they've been, for a year or more, ready to go down to London—there they are, littering the place, and there they'll stop as long as the nails hold them together. I'll tell you what, sir, as I said before, this is not London. We are all asleep here.

Bless you, we don't march with the times!"

"What is there in the packing-cases?" I asked.

"Bits of old wood carvings from the pulpit, and panels from the chancel, and images from the organ-loft," said the clerk. "Portraits of the twelve apostles in wood, and not a whole nose among 'em. All broken, and worm-eaten, and crumbling to dust at the edges. As brittle as crockery, sir, and as old as the church, if not older."

"And why were they going to London? To be repaired?"

"That's it, sir, to be repaired, and where they were past repair, to be copied in sound wood. But, bless you, the money fell short, and there they are, waiting for new subscriptions, and nobody to subscribe. It was all done a year ago, sir. Six gentlemen dined together about it, at the hotel in the new town. They made speeches, and passed resolutions, and put their names down, and printed off thousands of prospectuses. Beautiful prospectuses, sir, all flourished over with Gothic devices in red ink, saying it was a disgrace not to restore the church and repair the famous carvings, and so on. There are the prospectuses that couldn't be distributed, and the architect's plans and estimates, and the whole correspondence which set everybody at loggerheads and ended in a dispute, all down together in that corner, behind the packing-cases. The money dribbled in a little at first—but what can you expect out of London? There was just enough, you know, to pack the broken carvings, and get the estimates, and pay the printer's bill, and after that there wasn't a halfpenny left. There the things are, as I said before. We have nowhere else to put them—nobody in the new town cares about accommodating us—we're in a lost corner—and this is an untidy vestry—and who's to help it?—that's what I want to know."

My anxiety to examine the register did not dispose me to offer much encouragement to the old man's talkativeness. I agreed with him that nobody could help the untidiness of the vestry, and then suggested that we should proceed to our business without more delay.

"Ay, ay, the marriage-register, to be sure," said the clerk, taking a little bunch of keys from his pocket. "How far do you want to look back, sir?"

Marian had informed me of Sir Percival's age at the time when we had spoken together of his marriage engagement with

Laura. She had then described him as being forty-five years old. Calculating back from this, and making due allowance for the year that had passed since I had gained my information, I found that he must have been born in eighteen hundred and four, and that I might safely start on my search through the register from that date.

"I want to begin with the year eighteen hundred and four," I said.

"Which way after that, sir?" asked the clerk. "Forwards to our time or backwards away from us?"

"Backwards from eighteen hundred and four."

He opened the door of one of the presses—the press from the side of which the surplices were hanging—and produced a large volume bound in greasy brown leather. I was struck by the insecurity of the place in which the register was kept. The door of the press was warped and cracked with age, and the lock was of the smallest and commonest kind. I could have forced it easily with the walking-stick I carried in my hand.

"Is that considered a sufficiently secure place for the register?" I inquired. "Surely a book of such importance as this ought to be protected by a better lock, and kept carefully in an iron safe?"

"Well, now, that's curious!" said the clerk, shutting up the book again, just after he had opened it, and smacking his hand cheerfully on the cover. "Those were the very words my old master was always saying years and years ago, when I was a lad. 'Why isn't the register' (meaning this register here, under my hand)—'why isn't it kept in an iron safe?' If I've heard him say that once, I've heard him say it a hundred times. He was the solicitor in those days, sir, who had the appointment of vestry-clerk to this church. A fine hearty old gentleman, and the most particular man breathing. As long as he lived he kept a copy of this book in his office at Knowlesbury, and had it posted up regular, from time to time, to correspond with the fresh entries here. You would hardly think it, but he had his own appointed days, once or twice in every quarter, for riding over to this church on his old white pony, to check the copy, by the register, with his own eyes and hands. 'How do I know?' (he used to say) 'how do I know that the register in this vestry may not be stolen or destroyed? Why isn't it kept in an iron safe? Why can't I make other people as careful as I am myself? Some of these days there will be an accident happen, and when the register's lost, then the parish will find out the value of my copy.' He used to take his pinch of snuff after that, and look about him as bold as a lord. Ah! the like of him for doing business isn't easy to find now. You may go to London and not match him, even there. Which year did you say, sir? Eighteen hundred and what?"

"Eighteen hundred and four," I replied, mentally resolving to give the old man no more opportunities of talking, until my examination of the register was over.

The clerk put on his spectacles, and turned over the leaves of the register, carefully wetting his finger and thumb at every third page. "There it is, sir," said he, with another cheerful smack on the open volume. "There's the year you want."

As I was ignorant of the month in which Sir Percival was born, I began my backward search with the early part of the year. The register-book was of the old-fashioned kind, the entries being all made on blank pages in manuscript, and the divisions which separated them being indicated by ink lines drawn across the page at the close of each entry.

I reached the beginning of the year eighteen hundred and four without encountering the marriage, and then travelled back through December eighteen hundred and three—through November and October—through——

No! not through September also. Under the heading of that month in the year I found the marriage.

I looked carefully at the entry. It was at the bottom of a page, and was for want of room compressed into a smaller space than that occupied by the marriages above. The marriage immediately before it was impressed on my attention by the circumstance of the bridegroom's Christian name being the same as my own. The entry immediately following it (on the top of the next page) was noticeable in another way from the large space it occupied, the record in this case registering the marriages of two brothers at the same time. The register of the marriage of Sir Felix Glyde was in no respect remarkable except for the narrowness of the space into which it was compressed at the bottom of the page. The information about his wife was the usual information given in such cases. She was described as "Cecilia Jane Elster, of Park-View Cottages, Knowlesbury, only daughter of the late Patrick Elster, Esq., formerly of Bath."

I noted down these particulars in my pocket-book, feeling as I did so both doubtful and disheartened about my next proceedings. The Secret which I had believed until this moment to be within my grasp seemed now farther from my reach than ever.

What suggestions of any mystery unexplained had arisen out of my visit to the vestry? I saw no suggestions anywhere. What progress had I made towards discovering the suspected stain on the reputation of Sir Percival's mother? The one fact I had ascertained vindicated her reputation. Fresh doubts, fresh difficulties, fresh delays began to open before me in interminable prospect. What was I to do next? The one immediate resource left to me appeared to be this. I might institute inquiries about "Miss Elster of Knowlesbury," on the chance of advancing towards the main object of my investigation, by first discovering the secret of Mrs. Catherick's contempt for Sir Percival's mother.

"Have you found what you wanted, sir?" said the clerk, as I closed the register-book.

"Yes," I replied, "but I have some inquiries still to make. I suppose the clergyman who officiated here in the year eighteen hundred and three is no longer alive?"

"No, no, sir, he was dead three or four years before I came here, and that was as long ago as the year twenty-seven. I got this place, sir," persisted my talkative old friend, "through the clerk before me leaving it. They say he was driven out of house and home by his wife—and she's living still down in the new town there. I don't know the rights of the story myself—all I know is I got the place. Mr. Wansborough got it for me—the son of my old master that I was telling you of. He's a free, pleasant gentleman as ever lived—rides to the hounds, keeps his pointers and all that. He's vestry-clerk here now as his father was before him."

"Did you not tell me your former master lived at Knowlesbury?" I asked, calling to mind the long story about the precise gentleman of the old school with which my talkative friend had wearied me before he opened the register-book.

"Yes, to be sure, sir," replied the clerk. "Old Mr. Wansborough lived at Knowlesbury, and young Mr. Wansborough lives there too."

"You said just now he was vestry-clerk, like his father before him. I am not quite sure that I know what a vestry-clerk is."

"Don't you indeed, sir?—and you come from London too! Every parish church, you know, has a vestry-clerk and a parish-clerk. The parish-clerk is a man like me (except that I've got a deal more learning than most of them—though I don't boast of it). The vestry-clerk is a sort of an appointment that the lawyers get, and if there's any business to be done for the vestry, why there they are to do it. It's just the same in London. Every parish church there has got its vestry-clerk—and you may take my word for it he's sure to be a lawyer."

"Then young Mr. Wansborough is a lawyer, I suppose?"

"Of course he is, sir! A lawyer in High Street, Knowlesbury—the old offices that his father had before him. The number of times I've swept those offices out, and seen the old gentleman come trotting in to business on his white pony, looking right and left all down the street and nodding to everybody! Bless you, he was a popular character!—he'd have done in London!"

"How far is it to Knowlesbury from this place?"

"A long stretch, sir," said the clerk, with that exaggerated idea of distances, and that vivid perception of difficulties in getting from place to place, which is peculiar to all country people. "Nigh on five mile, I can tell you!"

It was still early in the forenoon. There was plenty of time for a walk to Knowlesbury and back again to Welmingham; and there was no person probably in the town who was fitter to assist my inquiries about the character and position of Sir Percival's mother before her marriage than the local solicitor. Resolving to go at once to Knowlesbury on foot, I led the way out of the vestry.

"Thank you kindly, sir," said the clerk, as I slipped my little present into his hand. "Are you really going to walk all the way to Knowlesbury and back? Well! you're strong on your legs, too—and what a blessing that is, isn't it? There's the road, you can't miss it. I wish I was going your way—it's pleasant to meet with gentlemen from London in a lost corner like this. One hears the news. Wish you good-morning, sir, and thank you kindly once more."

We parted. As I left the church behind me I looked back, and there were the two men again on the road below, with a third in their company, that third person being the short man in black whom I had traced to the railway the evening before.

The Woman in White

The three stood talking together for a little while, then separated. The man in black went away by himself towards Welmingham — the other two remained together, evidently waiting to follow me as soon as I walked on.

I proceeded on my way without letting the fellows see that I took any special notice of them. They caused me no conscious irritation of feeling at that moment — on the contrary, they rather revived my sinking hopes. In the surprise of discovering the evidence of the marriage, I had forgotten the inference I had drawn on first perceiving the men in the neighbourhood of the vestry. Their reappearance reminded me that Sir Percival had anticipated my visit to Old Welmingham church as the next result of my interview with Mrs. Catherick — otherwise he would never have placed his spies there to wait for me. Smoothly and fairly as appearances looked in the vestry, there was something wrong beneath them — there was something in the register-book, for aught I knew, that I had not discovered yet.

X

Once out of sight of the church, I pressed forward briskly on my way to Knowlesbury.

The road was, for the most part, straight and level. Whenever I looked back over it I saw the two spies steadily following me. For the greater part of the way they kept at a safe distance behind. But once or twice they quickened their pace, as if with the purpose of overtaking me, then stopped, consulted together, and fell back again to their former position. They had some special object evidently in view, and they seemed to be hesitating or differing about the best means of accomplishing it. I could not guess exactly what their design might be, but I felt serious doubts of reaching Knowlesbury without some mischance happening to me on the way. These doubts were realised.

I had just entered on a lonely part of the road, with a sharp turn at some distance ahead, and had just concluded (calculating by time) that I must be getting near to the town, when I suddenly heard the steps of the men close behind me.

Before I could look round, one of them (the man by whom I had been followed in London) passed rapidly on my left side and hustled me with his shoulder. I had been more irritated by the manner in which he and his companion had dogged my steps all the way from Old Welmingham than I was myself aware of, and I unfortunately pushed the fellow away smartly with my open hand. He instantly shouted for help. His companion, the tall man in the gamekeeper's clothes, sprang to my right side, and the next moment the two scoundrels held me pinioned between them in the middle of the road.

The conviction that a trap had been laid for me, and the vexation of knowing that I had fallen into it, fortunately restrained me from making my position still worse by an unavailing struggle with two men, one of whom would, in all probability, have been more than a match for me single-handed. I repressed the first natural movement by which I had attempted to shake them off, and looked about to see if there was any person near to whom I could appeal.

A labourer was at work in an adjoining field who must have witnessed all that had passed. I called to him to follow us to the town. He shook his head with stolid obstinacy, and walked away in the direction of a cottage which stood back from the high-road. At the same time the men who held me between them declared their intention of charging me with an assault. I was cool enough and wise enough now to make no opposition. "Drop your hold of my arms," I said, "and I will go with you to the town." The man in the gamekeeper's dress roughly refused. But the shorter man was sharp enough to look to consequences, and not to let his companion commit himself by unnecessary violence. He made a sign to the other, and I walked on between them with my arms free.

We reached the turning in the road, and there, close before us, were the suburbs of Knowlesbury. One of the local policemen was walking along the path by the roadside. The men at once appealed to him. He replied that the magistrate was then sitting at the town-hall, and recommended that we should appear before him immediately.

We went on to the town-hall. The clerk made out a formal summons, and the charge was preferred against me, with the customary exaggeration and the customary perversion of the truth on such occasions. The magistrate (an ill-tempered man, with a sour enjoyment in the exercise of his own power) inquired if any one on or near the road had witnessed the assault, and, greatly to my surprise, the complainant admitted the presence of the labourer in the field. I was enlightened, however, as to the object of the admission by the magistrate's next words. He remanded me at once for the production of the witness, expressing, at the same time, his willingness to take bail for my reappearance if I could produce one responsible surety to offer it. If I had been known in the town he would have liberated me on my own recognisances, but as I was a total stranger it was necessary that I should find responsible bail.

The whole object of the stratagem was now disclosed to me. It had been so managed as to make a remand necessary in a town where I was a perfect stranger, and where I could not hope to get my liberty on bail. The remand merely extended over three days, until the next sitting of the magistrate. But in that time, while I was in confinement, Sir Percival might use any means he pleased to embarrass my future proceedings — perhaps to screen himself from detection altogether — without the slightest fear of any hindrance on my part. At the end of the three days the charge would, no doubt, be withdrawn, and the attendance of the witness would be perfectly useless.

My indignation, I may almost say, my despair, at this mischievous check to all further progress — so base and trifling in itself, and yet so disheartening and so serious in its probable results — quite unfitted me at first to reflect on the best means of extricating myself from the dilemma in which I now stood. I had the folly to call for writing materials, and to think of privately communicating my real position to the magistrate. The hopelessness and the imprudence of this proceeding failed to strike me before I had actually written the opening lines of the letter. It was not till I had pushed the paper away—not till, I am ashamed to say, I had almost allowed the vexation of my helpless position to conquer me—that a course of action suddenly occurred to my mind, which Sir Percival had probably not anticipated, and which might set me free again in a few hours. I determined to communicate the situation in which I was placed to Mr. Dawson, of Oak Lodge.

I had visited this gentleman's house, it may be remembered, at the time of my first inquiries in the Blackwater Park neighbourhood, and I had presented to him a letter of introduction from Miss Halcombe, in which she recommended me to his friendly attention in the strongest terms. I now wrote, referring to this letter, and to what I had previously told Mr. Dawson of the delicate and dangerous nature of my inquiries. I had not revealed to him the truth about Laura, having merely described my errand as being of the utmost importance to private family interests with which Miss Halcombe was concerned. Using the same caution still, I now accounted for my presence at Knowlesbury in the same manner, and I put it to the doctor to say whether the trust reposed in me by a lady whom he well knew, and the hospitality I had myself received in his house, justified me or not in asking him to come to my assistance in a place where I was quite friendless.

I obtained permission to hire a messenger to drive away at once with my letter in a conveyance which might be used to bring the doctor back immediately. Oak Lodge was on the Knowlesbury side of Blackwater. The man declared he could drive there in forty minutes, and could bring Mr. Dawson back in forty more. I directed him to follow the doctor wherever he might happen to be, if he was not at home, and then sat down to wait for the result with all the patience and all the hope that I could summon to help me.

It was not quite half-past one when the messenger departed. Before half-past three he returned, and brought the doctor with him. Mr. Dawson's kindness, and the delicacy with which he treated his prompt assistance quite as a matter of course, almost overpowered me. The bail required was offered, and accepted immediately. Before four o'clock, on that afternoon, I was shaking hands warmly with the good old doctor—a free man again—in the streets of Knowlesbury.

The Woman in White

Mr. Dawson hospitably invited me to go back with him to Oak Lodge, and take up my quarters there for the night. I could only reply that my time was not my own, and I could only ask him to let me pay my visit in a few days, when I might repeat my thanks, and offer to him all the explanations which I felt to be only his due, but which I was not then in a position to make. We parted with friendly assurances on both sides, and I turned my steps at once to Mr. Wansborough's office in the High Street.

Time was now of the last importance.

The news of my being free on bail would reach Sir Percival, to an absolute certainty, before night. If the next few hours did not put me in a position to justify his worst fears, and to hold him helpless at my mercy, I might lose every inch of the ground I had gained, never to recover it again. The unscrupulous nature of the man, the local influence he possessed, the desperate peril of exposure with which my blindfold inquiries threatened him — all warned me to press on to positive discovery, without the useless waste of a single minute. I had found time to think while I was waiting for Mr. Dawson's arrival, and I had well employed it. Certain portions of the conversation of the talkative old clerk, which had wearied me at the time, now recurred to my memory with a new significance, and a suspicion crossed my mind darkly which had not occurred to me while I was in the vestry. On my way to Knowlesbury, I had only proposed to apply to Mr. Wansborough for information on the subject of Sir Percival's mother. My object now was to examine the duplicate register of Old Welmingham Church.

Mr. Wansborough was in his office when I inquired for him.

He was a jovial, red-faced, easy-looking man — more like a country squire than a lawyer — and he seemed to be both surprised and amused by my application. He had heard of his father's copy of the register, but had not even seen it himself. It had never been inquired after, and it was no doubt in the strong room among other papers that had not been disturbed since his father's death. It was a pity (Mr. Wansborough said) that the old gentleman was not alive to hear his precious copy asked for at last. He would have ridden his favourite hobby harder than ever now. How had I come to hear of the copy? was it through anybody in the town?

I parried the question as well as I could. It was impossible at this stage of the investigation to be too cautious, and it was just as well not to let Mr. Wansborough know prematurely that I had already examined the original register. I described myself,

499

therefore, as pursuing a family inquiry, to the object of which every possible saving of time was of great importance. I was anxious to send certain particulars to London by that day's post, and one look at the duplicate register (paying, of course, the necessary fees) might supply what I required, and save me a further journey to Old Welmingham. I added that, in the event of my subsequently requiring a copy of the original register, I should make application to Mr. Wansborough's office to furnish me with the document.

After this explanation no objection was made to producing the copy. A clerk was sent to the strong room, and after some delay returned with the volume. It was of exactly the same size as the volume in the vestry, the only difference being that the copy was more smartly bound. I took it with me to an unoccupied desk. My hands were trembling—my head was burning hot—I felt the necessity of concealing my agitation as well as I could from the persons about me in the room, before I ventured on opening the book.

On the blank page at the beginning, to which I first turned, were traced some lines in faded ink. They contained these words—

"Copy of the Marriage Register of Welmingham Parish Church. Executed under my orders, and afterwards compared, entry by entry, with the original, by myself. (Signed) Robert Wansborough, vestry-clerk." Below this note there was a line added, in another handwriting, as follows: "Extending from the first of January, 1800, to the thirtieth of June, 1815."

I turned to the month of September, eighteen hundred and three. I found the marriage of the man whose Christian name was the same as my own. I found the double register of the marriages of the two brothers. And between these entries, at the bottom of the page?

Nothing! Not a vestige of the entry which recorded the marriage of Sir Felix Glyde and Cecilia Jane Elster in the register of the church!

My heart gave a great bound, and throbbed as if it would stifle me. I looked again—I was afraid to believe the evidence of my own eyes. No! not a doubt. The marriage was not there. The entries on the copy occupied exactly the same places on the page as the entries in the original. The last entry on one page recorded the marriage of the man with my Christian name. Below it there was a blank space—a space evidently left because it was too narrow to contain the entry of the marriages of the two brothers, which in the copy, as in the original, occupied the top of the next page. That space told the whole story! There it must have remained in the church register from eighteen hundred and three (when the marriages had been solemnised and the copy had been made) to eighteen hundred and twenty-seven, when Sir Percival appeared at Old Welmingham. Here, at Knowlesbury, was the chance of committing the forgery shown to me in the copy, and there, at Old Welmingham, was the forgery committed in the register of the church.

My head turned giddy—I held by the desk to keep myself from falling. Of all the suspicions which had struck me in relation to that desperate man, not one had been near the truth.

The idea that he was not Sir Percival Glyde at all, that he had no more claim to the baronetcy and to Blackwater Park than the poorest labourer who worked on the estate, had never once occurred to my mind. At one time I had thought he might be Anne Catherick's father—at another time I had thought he might have been Anne Catherick's husband—the offence of which he was really guilty had been, from first to last, beyond the widest reach of my imagination.

The paltry means by which the fraud had been effected, the magnitude and daring of the crime that it represented, the horror of the consequences involved in its discovery, overwhelmed me. Who could wonder now at the brute-restlessness of the wretch's life—at his desperate alternations between abject duplicity and reckless violence—at the madness of guilty distrust which had made him imprison Anne Catherick in the Asylum, and had given him over to the vile conspiracy against his wife, on the bare suspicion that the one and the other knew his terrible secret? The disclosure of that secret might, in past years, have hanged him—might now transport him for life. The disclosure of that secret, even if the sufferers by his deception spared him the penalties of the law, would deprive him at one blow of the name, the rank, the estate, the whole social existence that he had usurped. This was the Secret, and it was mine! A word from me, and house, lands, baronetcy, were gone from him for ever—a word from me, and he was driven out into the world, a nameless, penniless, friendless outcast! The man's whole future hung on my lips—and he knew it by this time as certainly as I did!

That last thought steadied me. Interests far more precious than my own depended on the caution which must now guide my slightest actions. There was no possible treachery which Sir

Percival might not attempt against me. In the danger and desperation of his position he would be staggered by no risks, he would recoil at no crime — he would literally hesitate at nothing to save himself.

I considered for a minute. My first necessity was to secure positive evidence in writing of the discovery that I had just made, and in the event of any personal misadventure happening to me, to place that evidence beyond Sir Percival's reach. The copy of the register was sure to be safe in Mr. Wansborough's strong room. But the position of the original in the vestry was, as I had seen with my own eyes, anything but secure.

In this emergency I resolved to return to the church, to apply again to the clerk, and to take the necessary extract from the register before I slept that night. I was not then aware that a legally-certified copy was necessary, and that no document merely drawn out by myself could claim the proper importance as a proof. I was not aware of this, and my determination to keep my present proceedings a secret prevented me from asking any questions which might have procured the necessary information. My one anxiety was the anxiety to get back to Old Welmingham. I made the best excuses I could for the discomposure in my face and manner which Mr. Wansborough had already noticed, laid the necessary fee on his table, arranged that I should write to him in a day or two, and left the office, with my head in a whirl and my blood throbbing through my veins at fever heat.

It was just getting dark. The idea occurred to me that I might be followed again and attacked on the high-road.

My walking-stick was a light one, of little or no use for purposes of defence. I stopped before leaving Knowlesbury and bought a stout country cudgel, short, and heavy at the head. With this homely weapon, if any one man tried to stop me I was a match for him. If more than one attacked me I could trust to my heels. In my school-days I had been a noted runner, and I had not wanted for practice since in the later time of my experience in Central America.

I started from the town at a brisk pace, and kept the middle of the road.

A small misty rain was falling, and it was impossible for the first half of the way to make sure whether I was followed or not. But at the last half of my journey, when I supposed myself to be about two miles from the church, I saw a man run by me in the rain, and then heard the gate of a field by the roadside shut to sharply. I kept straight on, with my cudgel ready in my hand, my ears on the alert, and my eyes straining to see through the mist and the darkness. Before I had advanced a hundred yards there was a rustling in the hedge on my right, and three men sprang out into the road.

I drew aside on the instant to the footpath. The two foremost men were carried beyond me before they could check themselves. The third was as quick as lightning. He stopped, half turned, and struck at me with his stick. The blow was aimed at hazard, and was not a severe one. It fell on my left shoulder. I returned it heavily on his head. He staggered back and jostled his two companions just as they were both rushing at me. This circumstance gave me a moment's start. I slipped by them, and took to the middle of the road again at the top of my speed.

The two unhurt men pursued me. They were both good runners — the road was smooth and level, and for the first five minutes or more I was conscious that I did not gain on them. It was perilous work to run for long in the darkness. I could barely see the dim black line of the hedges on either side, and any chance obstacle in the road would have thrown me down to a certainty. Ere long I felt the ground changing — it descended from the level at a turn, and then rose again beyond. Downhill the men rather gained on me, but uphill I began to distance them. The rapid, regular thump of their feet grew fainter on my ear, and I calculated by the sound that I was far enough in advance to take to the fields with a good chance of their passing me in the darkness. Diverging to the footpath, I made for the first break that I could guess at, rather than see, in the hedge. It proved to be a closed gate. I vaulted over, and finding myself in a field, kept across it steadily with my back to the road. I heard the men pass the gate, still running, then in a minute more heard one of them call to the other to come back. It was no matter what they did now, I was out of their sight and out of their hearing. I kept straight across the field, and when I had reached the farther extremity of it, waited there for a minute to recover my breath.

It was impossible to venture back to the road, but I was determined nevertheless to get to Old Welmingham that evening.

Neither moon nor stars appeared to guide me. I only knew that I had kept the wind and rain at my back on leaving

Knowlesbury, and if I now kept them at my back still, I might at least be certain of not advancing altogether in the wrong direction.

Proceeding on this plan, I crossed the country—meeting with no worse obstacles than hedges, ditches, and thickets, which every now and then obliged me to alter my course for a little while—until I found myself on a hill-side, with the ground sloping away steeply before me. I descended to the bottom of the hollow, squeezed my way through a hedge, and got out into a lane. Having turned to the right on leaving the road, I now turned to the left, on the chance of regaining the line from which I had wandered. After following the muddy windings of the lane for ten minutes or more, I saw a cottage with a light in one of the windows. The garden gate was open to the lane, and I went in at once to inquire my way.

Before I could knock at the door it was suddenly opened, and a man came running out with a lighted lantern in his hand. He stopped and held it up at the sight of me. We both started as we saw each other. My wanderings had led me round the outskirts of the village, and had brought me out at the lower end of it. I was back at Old Welmingham, and the man with the lantern was no other than my acquaintance of the morning, the parish clerk.

His manner appeared to have altered strangely in the interval since I had last seen him. He looked suspicious and confused—his ruddy cheeks were deeply flushed—and his first words, when he spoke, were quite unintelligible to me.

"Where are the keys?" he asked. "Have you taken them?"

"What keys?" I repeated. "I have this moment come from Knowlesbury. What keys do you mean?"

"The keys of the vestry. Lord save us and help us! what shall I do? The keys are gone! Do you hear?" cried the old man, shaking the lantern at me in his agitation, "the keys are gone!"

"How? When? Who can have taken them?"

"I don't know," said the clerk, staring about him wildly in the darkness. "I've only just got back. I told you I had a long day's work this morning—I locked the door and shut the window down—it's open now, the window's open. Look! somebody has got in there and taken the keys."

The Woman in White

He turned to the casement window to show me that it was wide open. The door of the lantern came loose from its fastening as he swayed it round, and the wind blew the candle out instantly.

"Get another light," I said, "and let us both go to the vestry together. Quick! quick!"

I hurried him into the house. The treachery that I had every reason to expect, the treachery that might deprive me of every advantage I had gained, was at that moment, perhaps, in process of accomplishment. My impatience to reach the church was so great that I could not remain inactive in the cottage while the clerk lit the lantern again. I walked out, down the garden path, into the lane.

Before I had advanced ten paces a man approached me from the direction leading to the church. He spoke respectfully as we met. I could not see his face, but judging by his voice only, he was a perfect stranger to me.

"I beg your pardon, Sir Percival— —" he began.

I stopped him before he could say more.

"The darkness misleads you," I said. "I am not Sir Percival."

The man drew back directly.

"I thought it was my master," he muttered, in a confused, doubtful way.

"You expected to meet your master here?"

"I was told to wait in the lane."

With that answer he retraced his steps. I looked back at the cottage and saw the clerk coming out, with the lantern lighted once more. I took the old man's arm to help him on the more quickly. We hastened along the lane, and passed the person who had accosted me. As well as I could see by the light of the lantern, he was a servant out of livery.

"Who's that?" whispered the clerk. "Does he know anything about the keys?"

"We won't wait to ask him," I replied. "We will go on to the vestry first."

The church was not visible, even by daytime, until the end of the lane was reached. As we mounted the rising ground which led to the building from that point, one of the village children—a boy—came close up to us, attracted by the light we carried, and recognised the clerk.

"I say, measter," said the boy, pulling officiously at the clerk's coat, "there be summun up yander in the church. I heerd un lock the door on hisself—I heerd un strike a loight wi' a match."

The clerk trembled and leaned against me heavily.

"Come! come!" I said encouragingly. "We are not too late. We will catch the man, whoever he is. Keep the lantern, and follow me as fast as you can."

I mounted the hill rapidly. The dark mass of the church-tower was the first object I discerned dimly against the night sky. As I turned aside to get round to the vestry, I heard heavy footsteps close to me. The servant had ascended to the church after us. "I don't mean any harm," he said, when I turned round on him, "I'm only looking for my master." The tones in which he spoke betrayed unmistakable fear. I took no notice of him and went on.

The instant I turned the corner and came in view of the vestry, I saw the lantern-skylight on the roof brilliantly lit up from within. It shone out with dazzling brightness against the murky, starless sky.

I hurried through the churchyard to the door.

As I got near there was a strange smell stealing out on the damp night air. I heard a snapping noise inside—I saw the light above grow brighter and brighter—a pane of the glass cracked—I ran to the door and put my hand on it. The vestry was on fire!

Before I could move, before I could draw my breath after that discovery, I was horror-struck by a heavy thump against the door from the inside. I heard the key worked violently in the lock—I heard a man's voice behind the door, raised to a dreadful shrillness, screaming for help.

The servant who had followed me staggered back shuddering, and dropped to his knees. "Oh, my God!" he said, "it's Sir Percival!"

The Woman in White

As the words passed his lips the clerk joined us, and at the same moment there was another and a last grating turn of the key in the lock.

"The Lord have mercy on his soul!" said the old man. "He is doomed and dead. He has hampered the lock."

I rushed to the door. The one absorbing purpose that had filled all my thoughts, that had controlled all my actions, for weeks and weeks past, vanished in an instant from my mind. All remembrance of the heartless injury the man's crimes had inflicted—of the love, the innocence, the happiness he had pitilessly laid waste—of the oath I had sworn in my own heart to summon him to the terrible reckoning that he deserved—passed from my memory like a dream. I remembered nothing but the horror of his situation. I felt nothing but the natural human impulse to save him from a frightful death.

"Try the other door!" I shouted. "Try the door into the church! The lock's hampered. You're a dead man if you waste another moment on it."

There had been no renewed cry for help when the key was turned for the last time. There was no sound now of any kind, to give token that he was still alive. I heard nothing but the quickening crackle of the flames, and the sharp snap of the glass in the skylight above.

I looked round at my two companions. The servant had risen to his feet—he had taken the lantern, and was holding it up vacantly at the door. Terror seemed to have struck him with downright idiocy—he waited at my heels, he followed me about when I moved like a dog. The clerk sat crouched up on one of the tombstones, shivering, and moaning to himself. The one moment in which I looked at them was enough to show me that they were both helpless.

Hardly knowing what I did, acting desperately on the first impulse that occurred to me, I seized the servant and pushed him against the vestry wall. "Stoop!" I said, "and hold by the stones. I am going to climb over you to the roof—I am going to break the skylight, and give him some air!"

The man trembled from head to foot, but he held firm. I got on his back, with my cudgel in my mouth, seized the parapet with both hands, and was instantly on the roof. In the frantic hurry and agitation of the moment, it never struck me that I might let out the flame instead of letting in the air. I struck at the skylight, and battered in the cracked, loosened glass at a blow. The fire leaped out like a wild beast from its lair. If the wind had not chanced, in the position I occupied, to set it away from me, my exertions might have ended then and there. I crouched on the roof as the smoke poured out above me with the flame. The gleams and flashes of the light showed me the servant's face staring up vacantly under the wall — the clerk risen to his feet on the tombstone, wringing his hands in despair — and the scanty population of the village, haggard men and terrified women, clustered beyond in the churchyard — all appearing and disappearing, in the red of the dreadful glare, in the black of the choking smoke. And the man beneath my feet! — the man, suffocating, burning, dying so near us all, so utterly beyond our reach!

The thought half maddened me. I lowered myself from the roof, by my hands, and dropped to the ground.

"The key of the church!" I shouted to the clerk. "We must try it that way — we may save him yet if we can burst open the inner door."

"No, no, no!" cried the old man. "No hope! the church key and the vestry key are on the same ring — both inside there! Oh, sir, he's past saving — he's dust and ashes by this time!"

"They'll see the fire from the town," said a voice from among the men behind me. "There's a ingine in the town. They'll save the church."

I called to that man — he had his wits about him — I called to him to come and speak to me. It would be a quarter of an hour at least before the town engine could reach us. The horror of remaining inactive all that time was more than I could face. In defiance of my own reason I persuaded myself that the doomed and lost wretch in the vestry might still be lying senseless on the floor, might not be dead yet. If we broke open the door, might we save him? I knew the strength of the heavy lock — I knew the thickness of the nailed oak — I knew the hopelessness of assailing the one and the other by ordinary means. But surely there were beams still left in the dismantled cottages near the church? What if we got one, and used it as a battering-ram against the door?

The thought leaped through me like the fire leaping out of the shattered skylight. I appealed to the man who had spoken first of the fire-engine in the town. "Have you got your pickaxes handy?" Yes, they had. "And a hatchet, and a saw, and a bit of

The Woman in White

rope?" Yes! yes! yes! I ran down among the villagers, with the lantern in my hand. "Five shillings apiece to every man who helps me!" They started into life at the words. That ravenous second hunger of poverty—the hunger for money—roused them into tumult and activity in a moment. "Two of you for more lanterns, if you have them! Two of you for the pickaxes and the tools! The rest after me to find the beam!" They cheered—with shrill starveling voices they cheered. The women and the children fled back on either side. We rushed in a body down the churchyard path to the first empty cottage. Not a man was left behind but the clerk—the poor old clerk standing on the flat tombstone sobbing and wailing over the church. The servant was still at my heels—his white, helpless, panic-stricken face was close over my shoulder as we pushed into the cottage. There were rafters from the torn-down floor above, lying loose on the ground—but they were too light. A beam ran across over our heads, but not out of reach of our arms and our pickaxes—a beam fast at each end in the ruined wall, with ceiling and flooring all ripped away, and a great gap in the roof above, open to the sky. We attacked the beam at both ends at once. God! how it held—how the brick and mortar of the wall resisted us! We struck, and tugged, and tore. The beam gave at one end—it came down with a lump of brickwork after it. There was a scream from the women all huddled in the doorway to look at us—a shout from the men—two of them down but not hurt. Another tug all together—and the beam was loose at both ends. We raised it, and gave the word to clear the doorway. Now for the work! now for the rush at the door! There is the fire streaming into the sky, streaming brighter than ever to light us! Steady along the churchyard path—steady with the beam for a rush at the door. One, two, three—and off. Out rings the cheering again, irrepressibly. We have shaken it already, the hinges must give if the lock won't. Another run with the beam! One, two, three—and off. It's loose! the stealthy fire darts at us through the crevice all round it. Another, and a last rush! The door falls in with a crash. A great hush of awe, a stillness of breathless expectation, possesses every living soul of us. We look for the body. The scorching heat on our faces drives us back: we see nothing—above, below, all through the room, we see nothing but a sheet of living fire.

"Where is he?" whispered the servant, staring vacantly at the flames.

"He's dust and ashes," said the clerk. "And the books are dust and ashes—and oh, sirs! the church will be dust and ashes soon."

Those were the only two who spoke. When they were silent again, nothing stirred in the stillness but the bubble and the crackle of the flames.

Hark!

A harsh rattling sound in the distance—then the hollow beat of horses' hoofs at full gallop—then the low roar, the all-predominant tumult of hundreds of human voices clamouring and shouting together. The engine at last.

The people about me all turned from the fire, and ran eagerly to the brow of the hill. The old clerk tried to go with the rest, but his strength was exhausted. I saw him holding by one of the tombstones. "Save the church!" he cried out faintly, as if the firemen could hear him already.

"Save the church!"

The only man who never moved was the servant. There he stood, his eyes still fastened on the flames in a changeless, vacant stare. I spoke to him, I shook him by the arm. He was past rousing. He only whispered once more, "Where is he?"

In ten minutes the engine was in position, the well at the back of the church was feeding it, and the hose was carried to the doorway of the vestry. If help had been wanted from me I could not have afforded it now. My energy of will was gone—my strength was exhausted—the turmoil of my thoughts was fearfully and suddenly stilled, now I knew that he was dead.

I stood useless and helpless—looking, looking, looking into the burning room.

I saw the fire slowly conquered. The brightness of the glare faded—the steam rose in white clouds, and the smouldering heaps of embers showed red and black through it on the floor. There was a pause—then an advance all together of the firemen and the police which blocked up the doorway—then a consultation in low voices—and then two men were detached from the rest, and sent out of the churchyard through the crowd. The crowd drew back on either side in dead silence to let them pass.

After a while a great shudder ran through the people, and the living lane widened slowly. The men came back along it with a door from one of the empty houses. They carried it to the vestry and went in. The police closed again round the doorway, and men stole out from among the crowd by twos and threes and stood behind them to be the first to see. Others waited near to be the first to hear. Women and children were among these last.

The tidings from the vestry began to flow out among the crowd—they dropped slowly from mouth to mouth till they reached the place where I was standing. I heard the questions and answers repeated again and again in low, eager tones all round me.

"Have they found him?" "Yes."—"Where?" "Against the door, on his face."—"Which door?" "The door that goes into the church. His head was against it—he was down on his face."—"Is his face burnt?" "No." "Yes, it is." "No, scorched, not burnt—he lay on his face, I tell you."—"Who was he? A lord, they say." "No, not a lord. Sir Something; Sir means Knight." "And Baronight, too." "No." "Yes, it does."—"What did he want in there?" "No good, you may depend on it."—"Did he do it on purpose?"—"Burn himself on purpose!"—"I don't mean himself, I mean the vestry."—"Is he dreadful to look at?" "Dreadful!"—"Not about the face, though?" "No, no, not so much about the face. Don't anybody know him?" "There's a man says he does."—"Who?" "A servant, they say. But he's struck stupid-like, and the police don't believe him."—"Don't anybody else know who it is?" "Hush— —!"

The loud, clear voice of a man in authority silenced the low hum of talking all round me in an instant.

"Where is the gentleman who tried to save him?" said the voice.

"Here, sir—here he is!" Dozens of eager faces pressed about me—dozens of eager arms parted the crowd. The man in authority came up to me with a lantern in his hand.

"This way, sir, if you please," he said quietly.

I was unable to speak to him, I was unable to resist him when he took my arm. I tried to say that I had never seen the dead man in his lifetime—that there was no hope of identifying him by means of a stranger like me. But the words failed on my lips. I was faint, and silent, and helpless.

"Do you know him, sir?"

I was standing inside a circle of men. Three of them opposite to me were holding lanterns low down to the ground. Their eyes, and the eyes of all the rest, were fixed silently and expectantly on my face. I knew what was at my feet—I knew why they were holding the lanterns so low to the ground.

"Can you identify him, sir?"

My eyes dropped slowly. At first I saw nothing under them but a coarse canvas cloth. The dripping of the rain on it was audible in the dreadful silence. I looked up, along the cloth, and there at the end, stark and grim and black, in the yellow light—there was his dead face.

So, for the first and last time, I saw him. So the Visitation of God ruled it that he and I should meet.

XI

The inquest was hurried for certain local reasons which weighed with the coroner and the town authorities. It was held on the afternoon of the next day. I was necessarily one among the witnesses summoned to assist the objects of the investigation.

My first proceeding in the morning was to go to the post-office, and inquire for the letter which I expected from Marian. No change of circumstances, however extraordinary, could affect the one great anxiety which weighed on my mind while I was away from London. The morning's letter, which was the only assurance I could receive that no misfortune had happened in my absence, was still the absorbing interest with which my day began.

To my relief, the letter from Marian was at the office waiting for me.

Nothing had happened—they were both as safe and as well as when I had left them. Laura sent her love, and begged that I would let her know of my return a day beforehand. Her sister added, in explanation of this message, that she had saved "nearly a sovereign" out of her own private purse, and that she had claimed the privilege of ordering the dinner and giving the dinner which was to celebrate the day of my return. I read these little domestic confidences in the bright morning with the terrible recollection of what had happened the evening before vivid in my memory. The necessity of sparing Laura any sudden knowledge of the truth was the first consideration which the letter suggested to me. I wrote at once to Marian to tell her what I have told in these pages—presenting the tidings as gradually and gently as I could, and warning her not to let any such thing as a newspaper fall in Laura's way while I was absent. In the case of any other woman, less courageous and less reliable, I might have hesitated before I ventured on unreservedly disclosing the whole truth. But I owed it to Marian to be faithful to my past experience of her, and to trust her as I trusted myself.

My letter was necessarily a long one. It occupied me until the time came for proceeding to the inquest.

The objects of the legal inquiry were necessarily beset by peculiar complications and difficulties. Besides the investigation into the manner in which the deceased had met his death, there were serious questions to be settled relating to the cause of the fire, to the abstraction of the keys, and to the presence of a stranger in the vestry at the time when the flames broke out. Even the identification of the dead man had not yet been accomplished. The helpless condition of the servant had made the police distrustful of his asserted recognition of his master. They had sent to Knowlesbury overnight to secure the attendance of witnesses who were well acquainted with the personal appearance of Sir Percival Glyde, and they had communicated, the first thing in the morning, with Blackwater Park. These precautions enabled the coroner and jury to settle the question of identity, and to confirm the correctness of the servant's assertion; the evidence offered by competent witnesses, and by the discovery of certain facts, being subsequently strengthened by an examination of the dead man's watch. The crest and the name of Sir Percival Glyde were engraved inside it.

The next inquiries related to the fire.

The servant and I, and the boy who had heard the light struck in the vestry, were the first witnesses called. The boy gave his evidence clearly enough, but the servant's mind had not yet recovered the shock inflicted on it — he was plainly incapable of assisting the objects of the inquiry, and he was desired to stand down.

To my own relief, my examination was not a long one. I had not known the deceased — I had never seen him — I was not aware of his presence at Old Welmingham — and I had not been in the vestry at the finding of the body. All I could prove was that I had stopped at the clerk's cottage to ask my way — that I had heard from him of the loss of the keys — that I had accompanied him to the church to render what help I could — that I had seen the fire — that I had heard some person unknown, inside the vestry, trying vainly to unlock the door — and that I had done what I could, from motives of humanity, to save the man. Other witnesses, who had been acquainted with the deceased, were asked if they could explain the mystery of his presumed abstraction of the keys, and his presence in the burning room. But the coroner seemed to take it for granted, naturally enough, that I, as a total stranger in the neighbourhood, and a total stranger to Sir Percival Glyde, could not be in a position to offer any evidence on these two points.

The course that I was myself bound to take, when my formal examination had closed, seemed clear to me. I did not feel called on to volunteer any statement of my own private convictions; in the first place, because my doing so could serve no practical purpose, now that all proof in support of any surmises of mine was burnt with the burnt register; in the second place, because I could not have intelligibly stated my opinion—my unsupported opinion—without disclosing the whole story of the conspiracy, and producing beyond a doubt the same unsatisfactory effect an the minds of the coroner and the jury, which I had already produced on the mind of Mr. Kyrle.

In these pages, however, and after the time that has now elapsed, no such cautions and restraints as are here described need fetter the free expression of my opinion. I will state briefly, before my pen occupies itself with other events, how my own convictions lead me to account for the abstraction of the keys, for the outbreak of the fire, and for the death of the man.

The news of my being free on bail drove Sir Percival, as I believe, to his last resources. The attempted attack on the road was one of those resources, and the suppression of all practical proof of his crime, by destroying the page of the register on which the forgery had been committed, was the other, and the surest of the two. If I could produce no extract from the original book to compare with the certified copy at Knowlesbury, I could produce no positive evidence, and could threaten him with no fatal exposure. All that was necessary to the attainment of his end was, that he should get into the vestry unperceived, that he should tear out the page in the register, and that he should leave the vestry again as privately as he had entered it.

On this supposition, it is easy to understand why he waited until nightfall before he made the attempt, and why he took advantage of the clerk's absence to possess himself of the keys. Necessity would oblige him to strike a light to find his way to the right register, and common caution would suggest his locking the door on the inside in case of intrusion on the part of any inquisitive stranger, or on my part, if I happened to be in the neighbourhood at the time.

I cannot believe that it was any part of his intention to make the destruction of the register appear to be the result of accident, by purposely setting the vestry on fire. The bare chance that prompt assistance might arrive, and that the books might, by the remotest possibility, be saved, would have been enough, on a moment's consideration, to dismiss any idea of this sort from his mind. Remembering the quantity of combustible objects in the vestry—the straw, the papers, the packing-cases, the dry wood, the old worm-eaten presses—all the probabilities, in my estimation, point to the fire as the result of an accident with his matches or his light.

His first impulse, under these circumstances, was doubtless to try to extinguish the flames, and failing in that, his second impulse (ignorant as he was of the state of the lock) had been to attempt to escape by the door which had given him entrance. When I had called to him, the flames must have reached across the door leading into the church, on either side of which the presses extended, and close to which the other combustible objects were placed. In all probability, the smoke and flame (confined as they were to the room) had been too much for him when he tried to escape by the inner door. He must have dropped in his death-swoon—he must have sunk in the place where he was found—just as I got on the roof to break the skylight window. Even if we had been able, afterwards, to get into the church, and to burst open the door from that side, the delay must have been fatal. He would have been past saving, long past saving, by that time. We should only have given the flames free ingress into the church—the church, which was now preserved, but which, in that event, would have shared the fate of the vestry. There is no doubt in my mind, there can be no doubt in the mind of any one, that he was a dead man before ever we got to the empty cottage, and worked with might and main to tear down the beam.

This is the nearest approach that any theory of mine can make towards accounting for a result which was visible matter of fact. As I have described them, so events passed to us outside. As I have related it, so his body was found.

The inquest was adjourned over one day—no explanation that the eye of the law could recognise having been discovered thus far to account for the mysterious circumstances of the case.

It was arranged that more witnesses should be summoned, and that the London solicitor of the deceased should be invited to attend. A medical man was also charged with the duty of reporting on the mental condition of the servant, which appeared at present to debar him from giving any evidence of the least importance. He could only declare, in a dazed way, that he had been ordered, on the night of the fire, to wait in the lane, and that he knew nothing else, except that the deceased was certainly his master.

My own impression was, that he had been first used (without any guilty knowledge on his own part) to ascertain the fact of the clerk's absence from home on the previous day, and that he had been afterwards ordered to wait near the church (but out of sight of the vestry) to assist his master, in the event of my escaping the attack on the road, and of a collision occurring between Sir Percival and myself. It is necessary to add, that the man's own testimony was never obtained to confirm this view. The medical report of him declared that what little mental faculty he possessed was seriously shaken; nothing satisfactory was extracted from him at the adjourned inquest, and for aught I know to the contrary, he may never have recovered to this day.

I returned to the hotel at Welmingham so jaded in body and mind, so weakened and depressed by all that I had gone through, as to be quite unfit to endure the local gossip about the inquest, and to answer the trivial questions that the talkers addressed to me in the coffee-room. I withdrew from my scanty dinner to my cheap garret-chamber to secure myself a little quiet, and to think undisturbed of Laura and Marian.

If I had been a richer man I would have gone back to London, and would have comforted myself with a sight of the two dear faces again that night. But I was bound to appear, if called on, at the adjourned inquest, and doubly bound to answer my bail before the magistrate at Knowlesbury. Our slender resources had suffered already, and the doubtful future—more doubtful than ever now—made me dread decreasing our means unnecessarily by allowing myself an indulgence even at the small cost of a double railway journey in the carriages of the second class.

The next day—the day immediately following the inquest—was left at my own disposal. I began the morning by again applying at the post-office for my regular report from Marian. It was waiting for me as before, and it was written throughout in good spirits. I read the letter thankfully, and then set forth with my mind at ease for the day to go to Old Welmingham, and to view the scene of the fire by the morning light.

What changes met me when I got there!

Through all the ways of our unintelligible world the trivial and the terrible walk hand in hand together. The irony of circumstances holds no mortal catastrophe in respect. When I reached the church, the trampled condition of the burial-ground was the only serious trace left to tell of the fire and the death. A rough hoarding of boards had been knocked up before the vestry doorway. Rude caricatures were scrawled on it already, and the village children were fighting and shouting for the possession of the best peep-hole to see through. On the spot where I had heard the cry for help from the burning room, on the spot where the panic-stricken servant had dropped on his knees, a fussy flock of poultry was now scrambling for the first choice of worms after the rain; and on the ground at my feet, where the door and its dreadful burden had been laid, a workman's dinner was waiting for him, tied up in a yellow basin, and his faithful cur in charge was yelping at me for coming near the food. The old clerk, looking idly at the slow commencement of the repairs, had only one interest that he could talk about now—the interest of escaping all blame for his own part on account of the accident that had happened. One of the village women, whose white wild face I remembered the picture of terror when we pulled down the beam, was giggling with another woman, the picture of inanity, over an old washing-tub. There is nothing serious in mortality! Solomon in all his glory was Solomon with the elements of the contemptible lurking in every fold of his robes and in every corner of his palace.

As I left the place, my thoughts turned, not for the first time, to the complete overthrow that all present hope of establishing Laura's identity had now suffered through Sir Percival's death. He was gone—and with him the chance was gone which had been the one object of all my labours and all my hopes.

Could I look at my failure from no truer point of view than this?

Suppose he had lived, would that change of circumstance have altered the result? Could I have made my discovery a marketable commodity, even for Laura's sake, after I had found out that robbery of the rights of others was the essence of Sir Percival's crime? Could I have offered the price of my silence for his confession of the conspiracy, when the effect of that silence must have been to keep the right heir from the estates, and the right owner from the name? Impossible! If Sir Percival had lived, the discovery, from which (in my ignorance of the true nature of the Secret) I had hoped so much, could not have been mine to suppress or to make public, as I thought best, for the vindication of Laura's rights. In common honesty and common honour I must have gone at once to the stranger whose birthright had been usurped—I must have renounced the victory at the moment when it was mine by placing my discovery unreservedly in that stranger's hands—and I must have faced afresh all the difficulties which stood between me and the one object of my life, exactly as I was resolved in my heart of hearts to face them now!

The Woman in White

I returned to Welmingham with my mind composed, feeling more sure of myself and my resolution than I had felt yet.

On my way to the hotel I passed the end of the square in which Mrs. Catherick lived. Should I go back to the house, and make another attempt to see her? No. That news of Sir Percival's death, which was the last news she ever expected to hear, must have reached her hours since. All the proceedings at the inquest had been reported in the local paper that morning — there was nothing I could tell her which she did not know already. My interest in making her speak had slackened. I remembered the furtive hatred in her face when she said, "There is no news of Sir Percival that I don't expect — except the news of his death." I remembered the stealthy interest in her eyes when they settled on me at parting, after she had spoken those words. Some instinct, deep in my heart, which I felt to be a true one, made the prospect of again entering her presence repulsive to me — I turned away from the square, and went straight back to the hotel.

Some hours later, while I was resting in the coffee-room, a letter was placed in my hands by the waiter. It was addressed to me by name, and I found on inquiry that it had been left at the bar by a woman just as it was near dusk, and just before the gas was lighted. She had said nothing, and she had gone away again before there was time to speak to her, or even to notice who she was.

I opened the letter. It was neither dated nor signed, and the handwriting was palpably disguised. Before I had read the first sentence, however, I knew who my correspondent was — Mrs. Catherick.

The letter ran as follows — I copy it exactly, word for word: —

THE STORY CONTINUED BY MRS. CATHERICK

SIR,—You have not come back, as you said you would. No matter—I know the news, and I write to tell you so. Did you see anything particular in my face when you left me? I was wondering, in my own mind, whether the day of his downfall had come at last, and whether you were the chosen instrument for working it. You were, and you have worked it.

You were weak enough, as I have heard, to try and save his life. If you had succeeded, I should have looked upon you as my enemy. Now you have failed, I hold you as my friend. Your inquiries frightened him into the vestry by night—your inquiries, without your privity and against your will, have served the hatred and wreaked the vengeance of three-and-twenty years. Thank you, sir, in spite of yourself.

I owe something to the man who has done this. How can I pay my debt? If I was a young woman still I might say, "Come, put your arm round my waist, and kiss me, if you like." I should have been fond enough of you even to go that length, and you would have accepted my invitation—you would, sir, twenty years ago! But I am an old woman now. Well! I can satisfy your curiosity, and pay my debt in that way. You had a great curiosity to know certain private affairs of mine when you came to see me—private affairs which all your sharpness could not look into without my help—private affairs which you have not discovered, even now. You shall discover them—your curiosity shall be satisfied. I will take any trouble to please you, my estimable young friend!

You were a little boy, I suppose, in the year twenty-seven? I was a handsome young woman at that time, living at Old Welmingham. I had a contemptible fool for a husband. I had also the honour of being acquainted (never mind how) with a certain gentleman (never mind whom). I shall not call him by his name. Why should I? It was not his own. He never had a name: you know that, by this time, as well as I do.

It will be more to the purpose to tell you how he worked himself into my good graces. I was born with the tastes of a lady, and he gratified them—in other words, he admired me, and he made me presents. No woman can resist admiration and presents—especially presents, provided they happen to be just the thing she wants. He was sharp enough to know that—most men are. Naturally he wanted something in return—all men do.

And what do you think was the something? The merest trifle. Nothing but the key of the vestry, and the key of the press inside it, when my husband's back was turned. Of course he lied when I asked him why he wished me to get him the keys in that private way. He might have saved himself the trouble—I didn't believe him. But I liked my presents, and I wanted more. So I got him the keys, without my husband's knowledge, and I watched him, without his own knowledge. Once, twice, four times I watched him, and the fourth time I found him out.

I was never over-scrupulous where other people's affairs were concerned, and I was not over-scrupulous about his adding one to the marriages in the register on his own account.

Of course I knew it was wrong, but it did no harm to me, which was one good reason for not making a fuss about it. And I had not got a gold watch and chain, which was another, still better—and he had promised me one from London only the day before, which was a third, best of all. If I had known what the law considered the crime to be, and how the law punished it, I should have taken proper care of myself, and have exposed him then and there. But I knew nothing, and I longed for the gold watch. All the conditions I insisted on were that he should take me into his confidence and tell me everything. I was as curious about his affairs then as you are about mine now. He granted my conditions—why, you will see presently.

This, put in short, is what I heard from him. He did not willingly tell me all that I tell you here. I drew some of it from him by persuasion and some of it by questions. I was determined to have all the truth, and I believe I got it.

He knew no more than any one else of what the state of things really was between his father and mother till after his mother's death. Then his father confessed it, and promised to do what he could for his son. He died having done nothing—not having even made a will. The son (who can blame him?) wisely provided for himself. He came to England at once, and took possession of the property. There was no one to suspect him, and no one to say him nay. His father and mother had always lived as man and wife—none of the few people who were acquainted with them ever supposed them to be anything else. The right person to claim the property (if the truth had been known) was a distant relation, who had no idea of ever getting it, and who was away at sea when his father died. He had no difficulty so far—he took possession, as a matter of course. But he could not borrow money on the property as a matter of course. There were two things wanted of him before he could do this. One was a certificate of his birth, and the other was a certificate of his parents' marriage. The certificate of his birth was easily got—he was born abroad, and the certificate was there in due form. The other matter was a difficulty, and that difficulty brought him to Old Welmingham.

But for one consideration he might have gone to Knowlesbury instead.

His mother had been living there just before she met with his father—living under her maiden name, the truth being that she was really a married woman, married in Ireland, where her husband had ill-used her, and had afterwards gone off with some other person. I give you this fact on good authority—Sir Felix mentioned it to his son as the reason why he had not married. You may wonder why the son, knowing that his parents had met each other at Knowlesbury, did not play his first tricks with the register of that church, where it might have been fairly presumed his father and mother were married. The reason was that the clergyman who did duty at Knowlesbury church, in the year eighteen hundred and three (when, according to his birth certificate, his father and mother ought to have been married), was alive still when he took possession of the property in the New Year of eighteen hundred and twenty-seven. This awkward circumstance forced him to extend his inquiries to our neighbourhood. There no such danger existed, the former clergyman at our church having been dead for some years.

Old Welmingham suited his purpose as well as Knowlesbury. His father had removed his mother from Knowlesbury, and had lived with her at a cottage on the river, a little distance from our village. People who had known his solitary ways when he was single did not wonder at his solitary ways when he was supposed to be married. If he had not been a hideous creature to look at, his retired life with the lady might have raised suspicions; but, as things were, his hiding his ugliness and his deformity in the strictest privacy surprised nobody. He lived in our neighbourhood till he came in possession of the Park. After three or four and twenty years had passed, who was to say (the clergyman being dead) that his marriage had not been as private as the rest of his life, and that it had not taken place at Old Welmingham church?

So, as I told you, the son found our neighbourhood the surest place he could choose to set things right secretly in his own interests. It may surprise you to hear that what he really did to the marriage register was done on the spur of the moment—done on second thoughts.

His first notion was only to tear the leaf out (in the right year and month), to destroy it privately, to go back to London, and to tell the lawyers to get him the necessary certificate of his father's marriage, innocently referring them of course to the date on the leaf that was gone. Nobody could say his father and mother had not been married after that, and whether, under the circumstances, they would stretch a point or not about lending him the money (he thought they would), he had his answer ready at all events, if a question was ever raised about his right to the name and the estate.

But when he came to look privately at the register for himself, he found at the bottom of one of the pages for the year eighteen hundred and three a blank space left, seemingly through there being no room to make a long entry there, which was made instead at the top of the next page. The sight of this chance altered all his plans. It was an opportunity he had never hoped for, or thought of—and he took it—you know how. The blank space, to have exactly tallied with his birth certificate, ought to have occurred in the July part of the register. It occurred in the September part instead. However, in this case, if suspicious questions were asked, the answer was not hard to find. He had only to describe himself as a seven months' child.

I was fool enough, when he told me his story, to feel some interest and some pity for him—which was just what he calculated on, as you will see. I thought him hardly used. It was not his fault that his father and mother were not married, and it was not his father's and mother's fault either. A more scrupulous woman than I was—a woman who had not set her heart on a gold watch and chain—would have found some excuses for him. At all events, I held my tongue, and helped to screen what he was about.

He was some time getting the ink the right colour (mixing it over and over again in pots and bottles of mine), and some time afterwards in practising the handwriting. But he succeeded in the end, and made an honest woman of his mother after she was dead in her grave! So far, I don't deny that he behaved honourably enough to myself. He gave me my watch and chain, and spared no expense in buying them; both were of superior workmanship, and very expensive. I have got them still—the watch goes beautifully.

You said the other day that Mrs. Clements had told you everything she knew. In that case there is no need for me to write about the trumpery scandal by which I was the sufferer—the innocent sufferer, I positively assert. You must know as well as I do what the notion was which my husband took into his head when he found me and my fine-gentleman acquaintance meeting each other privately and talking secrets together. But what you don't know is how it ended between that same gentleman and myself. You shall read and see how he behaved to me.

The first words I said to him, when I saw the turn things had taken, were, "Do me justice—clear my character of a stain on it which you know I don't deserve. I don't want you to make a clean breast of it to my husband—only tell him, on your word of honour as a gentleman, that he is wrong, and that I am not to blame in the way he thinks I am. Do me that justice, at least, after all I have done for you." He flatly refused, in so many words. He told me plainly that it was his interest to let my husband and all my neighbours believe the falsehood—because, as long as they did so they were quite certain never to suspect the truth. I had a spirit of my own, and I told him they should know the truth from my lips. His reply was short, and to the point. If I spoke, I was a lost woman, as certainly as he was a lost man.

Yes! it had come to that. He had deceived me about the risk I ran in helping him. He had practised on my ignorance, he had tempted me with his gifts, he had interested me with his story—and the result of it was that he made me his accomplice. He owned this coolly, and he ended by telling me, for the first time, what the frightful punishment really was for his offence, and for any one who helped him to commit it. In those days the law was not so tender-hearted as I hear it is now. Murderers were not the only people liable to be hanged, and women convicts were not treated like ladies in undeserved distress. I confess he frightened me—the mean impostor! the cowardly blackguard! Do you understand now how I hated him? Do you understand why I am taking all this trouble—thankfully taking it—to gratify the curiosity of the meritorious young gentleman who hunted him down?

Well, to go on. He was hardly fool enough to drive me to downright desperation. I was not the sort of woman whom it was quite safe to hunt into a corner—he knew that, and wisely quieted me with proposals for the future.

I deserved some reward (he was kind enough to say) for the service I had done him, and some compensation (he was so obliging as to add) for what I had suffered. He was quite

The Woman in White

willing—generous scoundrel!—to make me a handsome yearly allowance, payable quarterly, on two conditions. First, I was to hold my tongue—in my own interests as well as in his. Secondly, I was not to stir away from Welmingham without first letting him know, and waiting till I had obtained his permission. In my own neighbourhood, no virtuous female friends would tempt me into dangerous gossiping at the tea-table. In my own neighbourhood, he would always know where to find me. A hard condition, that second one—but I accepted it.

What else was I to do? I was left helpless, with the prospect of a coming incumbrance in the shape of a child. What else was I to do? Cast myself on the mercy of my runaway idiot of a husband who had raised the scandal against me? I would have died first. Besides, the allowance was a handsome one. I had a better income, a better house over my head, better carpets on my floors, than half the women who turned up the whites of their eyes at the sight of me. The dress of Virtue, in our parts, was cotton print. I had silk.

So I accepted the conditions he offered me, and made the best of them, and fought my battle with my respectable neighbours on their own ground, and won it in course of time—as you saw yourself. How I kept his Secret (and mine) through all the years that have passed from that time to this, and whether my late daughter, Anne, ever really crept into my confidence, and got the keeping of the Secret too—are questions, I dare say, to which you are curious to find an answer. Well! my gratitude refuses you nothing. I will turn to a fresh page and give you the answer immediately. But you must excuse one thing—you must excuse my beginning, Mr. Hartright, with an expression of surprise at the interest which you appear to have felt in my late daughter. It is quite unaccountable to me. If that interest makes you anxious for any particulars of her early life, I must refer you to Mrs. Clements, who knows more of the subject than I do. Pray understand that I do not profess to have been at all overfond of my late daughter. She was a worry to me from first to last, with the additional disadvantage of being always weak in the head. You like candour, and I hope this satisfies you.

There is no need to trouble you with many personal particulars relating to those past times. It will be enough to say that I observed the terms of the bargain on my side, and that I enjoyed my comfortable income in return, paid quarterly.

Now and then I got away and changed the scene for a short time, always asking leave of my lord and master first, and generally getting it. He was not, as I have already told you, fool enough to drive me too hard, and he could reasonably rely on my holding my tongue for my own sake, if not for his. One of my longest trips away from home was the trip I took to Limmeridge to nurse a half-sister there, who was dying. She was reported to have saved money, and I thought it as well (in case any accident happened to stop my allowance) to look after my own interests in that direction. As things turned out, however, my pains were all thrown away, and I got nothing, because nothing was to be had.

I had taken Anne to the north with me, having my whims and fancies, occasionally, about my child, and getting, at such times, jealous of Mrs. Clements' influence over her. I never liked Mrs. Clements. She was a poor, empty-headed, spiritless woman — what you call a born drudge — and I was now and then not averse to plaguing her by taking Anne away. Not knowing what else to do with my girl while I was nursing in Cumberland, I put her to school at Limmeridge. The lady of the manor, Mrs. Fairlie (a remarkably plain-looking woman, who had entrapped one of the handsomest men in England into marrying her), amused me wonderfully by taking a violent fancy to my girl. The consequence was, she learnt nothing at school, and was petted and spoilt at Limmeridge House. Among other whims and fancies which they taught her there, they put some nonsense into her head about always wearing white. Hating white and liking colours myself, I determined to take the nonsense out of her head as soon as we got home again.

Strange to say, my daughter resolutely resisted me. When she had got a notion once fixed in her mind she was, like other half-witted people, as obstinate as a mule in keeping it. We quarrelled finely, and Mrs. Clements, not liking to see it, I suppose, offered to take Anne away to live in London with her. I should have said Yes, if Mrs. Clements had not sided with my daughter about her dressing herself in white. But being determined she should not dress herself in white, and disliking Mrs. Clements more than ever for taking part against me, I said No, and meant No, and stuck to No. The consequence was, my daughter remained with me, and the consequence of that, in its turn, was the first serious quarrel that happened about the Secret.

The circumstance took place long after the time I have just been writing of. I had been settled for years in the new town, and was steadily living down my bad character and slowly gaining ground among the respectable inhabitants. It helped me forward greatly towards this object to have my daughter with me. Her harmlessness and her fancy for dressing in white excited a certain amount of sympathy. I left off opposing her favourite whim on that account, because some of the sympathy was sure, in course of time, to fall to my share. Some of it did fall. I date my getting a choice of the two best sittings to let in the church from that time, and I date the clergyman's first bow from my getting the sittings.

Well, being settled in this way, I received a letter one morning from that highly born gentleman (now deceased) in answer to one of mine, warning him, according to agreement, of my wishing to leave the town for a little change of air and scene.

The ruffianly side of him must have been uppermost, I suppose, when he got my letter, for he wrote back, refusing me in such abominably insolent language, that I lost all command over myself, and abused him, in my daughter's presence, as "a low impostor whom I could ruin for life if I chose to open my lips and let out his Secret." I said no more about him than that, being brought to my senses as soon as those words had escaped me by the sight of my daughter's face looking eagerly and curiously at mine. I instantly ordered her out of the room until I had composed myself again.

My sensations were not pleasant, I can tell you, when I came to reflect on my own folly. Anne had been more than usually crazy and queer that year, and when I thought of the chance there might be of her repeating my words in the town, and mentioning his name in connection with them, if inquisitive people got hold of her, I was finely terrified at the possible consequences. My worst fears for myself, my worst dread of what he might do, led me no farther than this. I was quite unprepared for what really did happen only the next day.

On that next day, without any warning to me to expect him, he came to the house.

His first words, and the tone in which he spoke them, surly as it was, showed me plainly enough that he had repented already of his insolent answer to my application, and that he had come in a mighty bad temper to try and set matters right again before it was too late. Seeing my daughter in the room with me (I had been afraid to let her out of my sight after what had happened the day before) he ordered her away. They neither of them liked each other, and he vented the ill-temper on her which he was afraid to show to me.

"Leave us," he said, looking at her over his shoulder. She

looked back over her shoulder and waited as if she didn't care to go. "Do you hear?" he roared out, "leave the room." "Speak to me civilly," says she, getting red in the face. "Turn the idiot out," says he, looking my way. She had always had crazy notions of her own about her dignity, and that word "idiot" upset her in a moment. Before I could interfere she stepped up to him in a fine passion. "Beg my pardon, directly," says she, "or I'll make it the worse for you. I'll let out your Secret. I can ruin you for life if I choose to open my lips." My own words!—repeated exactly from what I had said the day before—repeated, in his presence, as if they had come from herself. He sat speechless, as white as the paper I am writing on, while I pushed her out of the room. When he recovered himself — —

No! I am too respectable a woman to mention what he said when he recovered himself. My pen is the pen of a member of the rector's congregation, and a subscriber to the "Wednesday Lectures on Justification by Faith"—how can you expect me to employ it in writing bad language? Suppose, for yourself, the raging, swearing frenzy of the lowest ruffian in England, and let us get on together, as fast as may be, to the way in which it all ended.

It ended, as you probably guess by this time, in his insisting on securing his own safety by shutting her up.

I tried to set things right. I told him that she had merely repeated, like a parrot, the words she had heard me say and that she knew no particulars whatever, because I had mentioned none. I explained that she had affected, out of crazy spite against him, to know what she really did not know—that she only wanted to threaten him and aggravate him for speaking to her as he had just spoken—and that my unlucky words gave her just the chance of doing mischief of which she was in search. I referred him to other queer ways of hers, and to his own experience of the vagaries of half-witted people—it was all to no purpose—he would not believe me on my oath—he was absolutely certain I had betrayed the whole Secret. In short, he would hear of nothing but shutting her up.

Under these circumstances, I did my duty as a mother. "No pauper Asylum," I said, "I won't have her put in a pauper Asylum. A Private Establishment, if you please. I have my feelings as a mother, and my character to preserve in the town, and I will submit to nothing but a Private Establishment, of the sort which my genteel neighbours would choose for afflicted relatives of their own." Those were my words. It is gratifying to me to reflect that I did my duty. Though never overfond of my late daughter, I had a proper pride about her. No pauper stain—thanks to my firmness and resolution—ever rested on MY child.

Having carried my point (which I did the more easily, in consequence of the facilities offered by private Asylums), I could not refuse to admit that there were certain advantages gained by shutting her up. In the first place, she was taken excellent care of—being treated (as I took care to mention in the town) on the footing of a lady. In the second place, she was kept away from Welmingham, where she might have set people suspecting and inquiring, by repeating my own incautious words.

The only drawback of putting her under restraint was a very slight one. We merely turned her empty boast about knowing the Secret into a fixed delusion. Having first spoken in sheer crazy spitefulness against the man who had offended her, she was cunning enough to see that she had seriously frightened him, and sharp enough afterwards to discover that he was concerned in shutting her up. The consequence was she flamed out into a perfect frenzy of passion against him, going to the Asylum, and the first words she said to the nurses, after they had quieted her, were, that she was put in confinement for knowing his Secret, and that she meant to open her lips and ruin him, when the right time came.

She may have said the same thing to you, when you thoughtlessly assisted her escape. She certainly said it (as I heard last summer) to the unfortunate woman who married our sweet-tempered, nameless gentleman lately deceased. If either you, or that unlucky lady, had questioned my daughter closely, and had insisted on her explaining what she really meant, you would have found her lose all her self-importance suddenly, and get vacant, and restless, and confused—you would have discovered that I am writing nothing here but the plain truth. She knew that there was a Secret—she knew who was connected with it—she knew who would suffer by its being known—and beyond that, whatever airs of importance she may have given herself, whatever crazy boasting she may have indulged in with strangers, she never to her dying day knew more.

Have I satisfied your curiosity? I have taken pains enough to satisfy it at any rate. There is really nothing else I have to tell you about myself or my daughter. My worst responsibilities, so far as she was concerned, were all over when she was secured in the Asylum. I had a form of letter relating to the circumstances under which she was shut up, given me to write, in answer to one Miss Halcombe, who was curious in the matter, and who must have heard plenty of lies about me from a certain tongue well accustomed to the telling of the same. And I did what I could afterwards to trace my runaway daughter, and prevent her from doing mischief by making inquiries myself in the neighbourhood where she was falsely reported to have been seen. But these, and other trifles like them, are of little or no interest to you after what you have heard already.

So far, I have written in the friendliest possible spirit. But I cannot close this letter without adding a word here of serious remonstrance and reproof, addressed to yourself.

In the course of your personal interview with me, you audaciously referred to my late daughter's parentage on the father's side, as if that parentage was a matter of doubt. This was highly improper and very ungentlemanlike on your part! If we see each other again, remember, if you please, that I will allow no liberties to be taken with my reputation, and that the moral atmosphere of Welmingham (to use a favourite expression of my friend the rector's) must not be tainted by loose conversation of any kind. If you allow yourself to doubt that my husband was Anne's father, you personally insult me in the grossest manner. If you have felt, and if you still continue to feel, an unhallowed curiosity on this subject, I recommend you, in your own interests, to check it at once, and for ever. On this side of the grave, Mr. Hartright, whatever may happen on the other, that curiosity will never be gratified.

Perhaps, after what I have just said, you will see the necessity of writing me an apology. Do so, and I will willingly receive it. I will, afterwards, if your wishes point to a second interview with me, go a step farther, and receive you. My circumstances only enable me to invite you to tea—not that they are at all altered for the worse by what has happened. I have always lived, as I think I told you, well within my income, and I have saved enough, in the last twenty years, to make me quite comfortable for the rest of my life. It is not my intention to leave Welmingham. There are one or two little advantages which I have still to gain in the town. The clergyman bows to me—as you saw. He is married, and his wife is not quite so civil. I propose to join the Dorcas Society, and I mean to make the clergyman's wife bow to me next.

If you favour me with your company, pray understand that the conversation must be entirely on general subjects. Any attempted reference to this letter will be quite useless—I am determined not to acknowledge having written it. The evidence has been destroyed in the fire, I know, but I think it desirable to err on the side of caution, nevertheless.

On this account no names are mentioned here, nor is any signature attached to these lines: the handwriting is disguised throughout, and I mean to deliver the letter myself, under circumstances which will prevent all fear of its being traced to my house. You can have no possible cause to complain of these precautions, seeing that they do not affect the information I here communicate, in consideration of the special indulgence which you have deserved at my hands. My hour for tea is half-past five, and my buttered toast waits for nobody.

THE STORY CONTINUED BY WALTER HARTRIGHT

I

My first impulse, after reading Mrs. Catherick's extraordinary narrative, was to destroy it. The hardened shameless depravity of the whole composition, from beginning to end — the atrocious perversity of mind which persistently associated me with a calamity for which I was in no sense answerable, and with a death which I had risked my life in trying to avert — so disgusted me, that I was on the point of tearing the letter, when a consideration suggested itself which warned me to wait a little before I destroyed it.

This consideration was entirely unconnected with Sir Percival. The information communicated to me, so far as it concerned him, did little more than confirm the conclusions at which I had already arrived.

He had committed his offence, as I had supposed him to have committed it, and the absence of all reference, on Mrs. Catherick's part, to the duplicate register at Knowlesbury, strengthened my previous conviction that the existence of the book, and the risk of detection which it implied, must have been necessarily unknown to Sir Percival. My interest in the question of the forgery was now at an end, and my only object in keeping the letter was to make it of some future service in clearing up the last mystery that still remained to baffle me — the parentage of Anne Catherick on the father's side. There were one or two sentences dropped in her mother's narrative, which it might be useful to refer to again, when matters of more immediate importance allowed me leisure to search for the missing evidence. I did not despair of still finding that evidence, and I had lost none of my anxiety to discover it, for I had lost none of my interest in tracing the father of the poor creature who now lay at rest in Mrs. Fairlie's grave.

Accordingly, I sealed up the letter and put it away carefully in my pocket-book, to be referred to again when the time came.

The next day was my last in Hampshire. When I had appeared again before the magistrate at Knowlesbury, and when I had attended at the adjourned inquest, I should be free to return to London by the afternoon or the evening train.

The Woman in White

My first errand in the morning was, as usual, to the post-office. The letter from Marian was there, but I thought when it was handed to me that it felt unusually light. I anxiously opened the envelope. There was nothing inside but a small strip of paper folded in two. The few blotted hurriedly-written lines which were traced on it contained these words:

"Come back as soon as you can. I have been obliged to move. Come to Gower's Walk, Fulham (number five). I will be on the look-out for you. Don't be alarmed about us, we are both safe and well. But come back. — Marian."

The news which those lines contained — news which I instantly associated with some attempted treachery on the part of Count Fosco — fairly overwhelmed me. I stood breathless with the paper crumpled up in my hand. What had happened? What subtle wickedness had the Count planned and executed in my absence? A night had passed since Marian's note was written — hours must elapse still before I could get back to them — some new disaster might have happened already of which I was ignorant. And here, miles and miles away from them, here I must remain — held, doubly held, at the disposal of the law!

I hardly know to what forgetfulness of my obligations anxiety and alarm might not have tempted me, but for the quieting influence of my faith in Marian. My absolute reliance on her was the one earthly consideration which helped me to restrain myself, and gave me courage to wait. The inquest was the first of the impediments in the way of my freedom of action. I attended it at the appointed time, the legal formalities requiring my presence in the room, but as it turned out, not calling on me to repeat my evidence. This useless delay was a hard trial, although I did my best to quiet my impatience by following the course of the proceedings as closely as I could.

The London solicitor of the deceased (Mr. Merriman) was among the persons present. But he was quite unable to assist the objects of the inquiry. He could only say that he was inexpressibly shocked and astonished, and that he could throw no light whatever on the mysterious circumstances of the case. At intervals during the adjourned investigation, he suggested questions which the Coroner put, but which led to no results. After a patient inquiry, which lasted nearly three hours, and which exhausted every available source of information, the jury pronounced the customary verdict in cases of sudden death by accident. They added to the formal decision a statement, that there had been no evidence to show how the keys had been abstracted, how the fire had been caused, or what the purpose was for which the deceased had entered the vestry. This act closed the proceedings. The legal representative of the dead man was left to provide for the necessities of the interment, and the witnesses were free to retire.

Resolved not to lose a minute in getting to Knowlesbury, I paid my bill at the hotel, and hired a fly to take me to the town. A gentleman who heard me give the order, and who saw that I was going alone, informed me that he lived in the neighbourhood of Knowlesbury, and asked if I would have any objection to his getting home by sharing the fly with me. I accepted his proposal as a matter of course.

Our conversation during the drive was naturally occupied by the one absorbing subject of local interest.

My new acquaintance had some knowledge of the late Sir Percival's solicitor, and he and Mr. Merriman had been discussing the state of the deceased gentleman's affairs and the succession to the property. Sir Percival's embarrassments were so well known all over the county that his solicitor could only make a virtue of necessity and plainly acknowledge them. He had died without leaving a will, and he had no personal property to bequeath, even if he had made one, the whole fortune which he had derived from his wife having been swallowed up by his creditors. The heir to the estate (Sir Percival having left no issue) was a son of Sir Felix Glyde's first cousin, an officer in command of an East Indiaman. He would find his unexpected inheritance sadly encumbered, but the property would recover with time, and, if "the captain" was careful, he might be a rich man yet before he died.

Absorbed as I was in the one idea of getting to London, this information (which events proved to be perfectly correct) had an interest of its own to attract my attention. I thought it justified me in keeping secret my discovery of Sir Percival's fraud. The heir, whose rights he had usurped, was the heir who would now have the estate. The income from it, for the last three-and-twenty years, which should properly have been his, and which the dead man had squandered to the last farthing, was gone beyond recall. If I spoke, my speaking would confer advantage on no one. If I kept the secret, my silence concealed the character of the man who had cheated Laura into marrying him. For her sake, I wished to conceal it—for her sake, still, I tell this story under feigned names.

I parted with my chance companion at Knowlesbury, and

The Woman in White

went at once to the town-hall. As I had anticipated, no one was present to prosecute the case against me—the necessary formalities were observed, and I was discharged. On leaving the court a letter from Mr. Dawson was put into my hand. It informed me that he was absent on professional duty, and it reiterated the offer I had already received from him of any assistance which I might require at his hands. I wrote back, warmly acknowledging my obligations to his kindness, and apologising for not expressing my thanks personally, in consequence of my immediate recall on pressing business to town.

Half an hour later I was speeding back to London by the express train.

II

It was between nine and ten o'clock before I reached Fulham, and found my way to Gower's Walk.

Both Laura and Marian came to the door to let me in. I think we had hardly known how close the tie was which bound us three together, until the evening came which united us again. We met as if we had been parted for months instead of for a few days only. Marian's face was sadly worn and anxious. I saw who had known all the danger and borne all the trouble in my absence the moment I looked at her. Laura's brighter looks and better spirits told me how carefully she had been spared all knowledge of the dreadful death at Welmingham, and of the true reason of our change of abode.

The stir of the removal seemed to have cheered and interested her. She only spoke of it as a happy thought of Marian's to surprise me on my return with a change from the close, noisy street to the pleasant neighbourhood of trees and fields and the river. She was full of projects for the future—of the drawings she was to finish—of the purchasers I had found in the country who were to buy them—of the shillings and sixpences she had saved, till her purse was so heavy that she proudly asked me to weigh it in my own hand. The change for the better which had been wrought in her during the few days of my absence was a surprise to me for which I was quite unprepared—and for all the unspeakable happiness of seeing it, I was indebted to Marian's courage and to Marian's love.

When Laura had left us, and when we could speak to one another without restraint, I tried to give some expression to the gratitude and the admiration which filled my heart. But the generous creature would not wait to hear me. That sublime self-forgetfulness of women, which yields so much and asks so little, turned all her thoughts from herself to me.

"I had only a moment left before post-time," she said, "or I should have written less abruptly. You look worn and weary, Walter. I am afraid my letter must have seriously alarmed you?"

"Only at first," I replied. "My mind was quieted, Marian, by my trust in you. Was I right in attributing this sudden change of place to some threatened annoyance on the part of Count Fosco?"

"Perfectly right," she said. "I saw him yesterday, and worse than that, Walter—I spoke to him."

"Spoke to him? Did he know where we lived? Did he come to the house?"

"He did. To the house—but not upstairs. Laura never saw him—Laura suspects nothing. I will tell you how it happened: the danger, I believe and hope, is over now. Yesterday, I was in the sitting-room, at our old lodgings. Laura was drawing at the table, and I was walking about and setting things to rights. I passed the window, and as I passed it, looked out into the street. There, on the opposite side of the way, I saw the Count, with a man talking to him——"

"Did he notice you at the window?"

"No—at least, I thought not. I was too violently startled to be quite sure."

"Who was the other man? A stranger?"

"Not a stranger, Walter. As soon as I could draw my breath again, I recognised him. He was the owner of the Lunatic Asylum."

"Was the Count pointing out the house to him?"

"No, they were talking together as if they had accidentally met in the street. I remained at the window looking at them from behind the curtain. If I had turned round, and if Laura had seen my face at that moment——Thank God, she was absorbed over her drawing! They soon parted. The man from the Asylum went one way, and the Count the other. I began to hope they were in the street by chance, till I saw the Count come back, stop opposite to us again, take out his card-case and pencil, write something, and then cross the road to the shop below us. I ran past Laura before she could see me, and said I had forgotten something upstairs. As soon as I was out of the room I went down to the first landing and waited—I was determined to stop him if he tried to come upstairs. He made no such attempt. The girl from the shop came through the door into the passage, with his card in her hand—a large gilt card with his name, and a coronet above it, and these lines underneath in pencil: 'Dear lady' (yes! the villain could address me in that way still)—'dear lady, one word, I implore you, on a matter serious to us both.' If one can think at all, in serious difficulties, one thinks quick. I felt directly that it might be a fatal mistake to leave myself and to leave you in the dark, where such a man as the Count was concerned. I felt that the doubt of what he might do, in your absence, would be ten times more trying to me if I declined to see him than if I consented. 'Ask the gentleman to wait in the shop,' I said. 'I will be with him in a moment.' I ran upstairs for my bonnet, being determined not to let him speak to me indoors. I knew his deep ringing voice, and I was afraid Laura might hear it, even in the shop. In less than a minute I was down again in the passage, and had opened the door into the street. He came round to meet me from the shop. There he was in deep mourning, with his smooth bow and his deadly smile, and some idle boys and women near him, staring at his great size, his fine black clothes, and his large cane with the gold knob to it. All the horrible time at Blackwater came back to me the moment I set eyes on him. All the old loathing crept and crawled through me, when he took off his hat with a flourish and spoke to me, as if we had parted on the friendliest terms hardly a day since."

"You remember what he said?"

"I can't repeat it, Walter. You shall know directly what he said about you — — but I can't repeat what he said to me. It was worse than the polite insolence of his letter. My hands tingled to strike him, as if I had been a man! I only kept them quiet by tearing his card to pieces under my shawl. Without saying a word on my side, I walked away from the house (for fear of Laura seeing us), and he followed, protesting softly all the way. In the first by-street I turned, and asked him what he wanted with me. He wanted two things. First, if I had no objection, to express his sentiments. I declined to hear them. Secondly, to repeat the warning in his letter. I asked, what occasion there was for repeating it. He bowed and smiled, and said he would explain. The explanation exactly confirmed the fears I expressed before you left us. I told you, if you remember, that Sir Percival would be too headstrong to take his friend's advice where you were concerned, and that there was no danger to be dreaded from the Count till his own interests were threatened, and he was roused into acting for himself?"

"I recollect, Marian."

"Well, so it has really turned out. The Count offered his advice, but it was refused. Sir Percival would only take counsel of his own violence, his own obstinacy, and his own hatred of you. The Count let him have his way, first privately ascertaining, in case of his own interests being threatened next, where we lived. You were followed, Walter, on returning here, after your first journey to Hampshire, by the lawyer's men for some distance from the railway, and by the Count himself to the door of the house. How he contrived to escape being seen by you he did not tell me, but he found us out on that occasion, and in that way. Having made the discovery, he took no advantage of it till the news reached him of Sir Percival's death, and then, as I told you, he acted for himself, because he believed you would next proceed against the dead man's partner in the conspiracy. He at once made his arrangements to meet the owner of the Asylum in London, and to take him to the place where his runaway patient was hidden, believing that the results, whichever way they ended, would be to involve you in interminable legal disputes and difficulties, and to tie your hands for all purposes of offence, so far as he was concerned. That was his purpose, on his own confession to me. The only consideration which made him hesitate, at the last moment—"

"Yes?"

"It is hard to acknowledge it, Walter, and yet I must. I was the only consideration. No words can say how degraded I feel in my own estimation when I think of it, but the one weak point in that man's iron character is the horrible admiration he feels for me. I have tried, for the sake of my own self-respect, to disbelieve it as long as I could; but his looks, his actions, force on me the shameful conviction of the truth. The eyes of that monster of wickedness moistened while he was speaking to me—they did, Walter! He declared that at the moment of pointing out the house to the doctor, he thought of my misery if I was separated from Laura, of my responsibility if I was called on to answer for effecting her escape, and he risked the worst that you could do to him, the second time, for my sake. All he asked was that I would remember the sacrifice, and restrain your rashness, in my own interests—interests which he might never be able to consult again. I made no such bargain with him—I would have died first. But believe him or not, whether it is true or false that he sent the doctor away with an excuse, one thing is certain, I saw the man leave him without so much as a glance at our window, or even at our side of the way."

"I believe it, Marian. The best men are not consistent in good—why should the worst men be consistent in evil? At the same time, I suspect him of merely attempting to frighten you, by threatening what he cannot really do. I doubt his power of annoying us, by means of the owner of the Asylum, now that Sir Percival is dead, and Mrs. Catherick is free from all control. But let me hear more. What did the Count say of me?"

"He spoke last of you. His eyes brightened and hardened, and his manner changed to what I remember it in past times — to that mixture of pitiless resolution and mountebank mockery which makes it so impossible to fathom him. 'Warn Mr. Hartright!' he said in his loftiest manner. 'He has a man of brains to deal with, a man who snaps his big fingers at the laws and conventions of society, when he measures himself with ME. If my lamented friend had taken my advice, the business of the inquest would have been with the body of Mr. Hartright. But my lamented friend was obstinate. See! I mourn his loss — inwardly in my soul, outwardly on my hat. This trivial crape expresses sensibilities which I summon Mr. Hartright to respect. They may be transformed to immeasurable enmities if he ventures to disturb them. Let him be content with what he has got — with what I leave unmolested, for your sake, to him and to you. Say to him (with my compliments), if he stirs me, he has Fosco to deal with. In the English of the Popular Tongue, I inform him — Fosco sticks at nothing. Dear lady, good morning.' His cold grey eyes settled on my face — he took off his hat solemnly — bowed, bare-headed — and left me."

"Without returning? without saying more last words?"

"He turned at the corner of the street, and waved his hand, and then struck it theatrically on his breast. I lost sight of him after that. He disappeared in the opposite direction to our house, and I ran back to Laura. Before I was indoors again, I had made up my mind that we must go. The house (especially in your absence) was a place of danger instead of a place of safety, now that the Count had discovered it. If I could have felt certain of your return, I should have risked waiting till you came back. But I was certain of nothing, and I acted at once on my own impulse. You had spoken, before leaving us, of moving into a quieter neighbourhood and purer air, for the sake of Laura's health. I had only to remind her of that, and to suggest surprising you and saving you trouble by managing the move in your absence, to make her quite as anxious for the change as I was. She helped me to pack up your things, and she has arranged them all for you in your new working-room here."

"What made you think of coming to this place?"

"My ignorance of other localities in the neighbourhood of London. I felt the necessity of getting as far away as possible from our old lodgings, and I knew something of Fulham, because I had once been at school there. I despatched a messenger with a note, on the chance that the school might still be in existence. It was in existence — the daughters of my old mistress were carrying it on for her, and they engaged this place from the instructions I had sent. It was just post-time when the messenger returned to me with the address of the house. We moved after dark—we came here quite unobserved. Have I done right, Walter? Have I justified your trust in me?"

I answered her warmly and gratefully, as I really felt. But the anxious look still remained on her face while I was speaking, and the first question she asked, when I had done, related to Count Fosco.

I saw that she was thinking of him now with a changed mind. No fresh outbreak of anger against him, no new appeal to me to hasten the day of reckoning escaped her. Her conviction that the man's hateful admiration of herself was really sincere, seemed to have increased a hundredfold her distrust of his unfathomable cunning, her inborn dread of the wicked energy and vigilance of all his faculties. Her voice fell low, her manner was hesitating, her eyes searched into mine with an eager fear when she asked me what I thought of his message, and what I meant to do next after hearing it.

"Not many weeks have passed, Marian," I answered, "since my interview with Mr. Kyrle. When he and I parted, the last words I said to him about Laura were these: 'Her uncle's house shall open to receive her, in the presence of every soul who followed the false funeral to the grave; the lie that records her death shall be publicly erased from the tombstone by the authority of the head of the family, and the two men who have wronged her shall answer for their crime to ME, though the justice that sits in tribunals is powerless to pursue them.' One of those men is beyond mortal reach. The other remains, and my resolution remains."

Her eyes lit up—her colour rose. She said nothing, but I saw all her sympathies gathering to mine in her face.

"I don't disguise from myself, or from you," I went on, "that the prospect before us is more than doubtful. The risks we have run already are, it may be, trifles compared with the risks that threaten us in the future, but the venture shall be tried, Marian, for all that. I am not rash enough to measure myself against such a man as the Count before I am well prepared for him. I have learnt patience—I can wait my time. Let him believe that his message has produced its effect—let him know nothing of us, and hear nothing of us—let us give him full time to feel secure—his own boastful nature, unless I seriously mistake him, will hasten that result. This is one reason for waiting, but there is another more important still. My position, Marian, towards you and towards Laura ought to be a stronger one than it is now before I try our last chance."

She leaned near to me, with a look of surprise.

"How can it be stronger?" she asked.

"I will tell you," I replied, "when the time comes. It has not come yet—it may never come at all. I may be silent about it to Laura for ever—I must be silent now, even to you, till I see for myself that I can harmlessly and honourably speak. Let us leave that subject. There is another which has more pressing claims on our attention. You have kept Laura, mercifully kept her, in ignorance of her husband's death——"

"Oh, Walter, surely it must be long yet before we tell her of it?"

"No, Marian. Better that you should reveal it to her now, than that accident, which no one can guard against, should reveal it to her at some future time. Spare her all the details—break it to her very tenderly, but tell her that he is dead."

"You have a reason, Walter, for wishing her to know of her husband's death besides the reason you have just mentioned?"

"I have."

"A reason connected with that subject which must not be mentioned between us yet?—which may never be mentioned to Laura at all?"

She dwelt on the last words meaningly. When I answered her in the affirmative, I dwelt on them too.

Her face grew pale. For a while she looked at me with a sad, hesitating interest. An unaccustomed tenderness trembled in her dark eyes and softened her firm lips, as she glanced aside at the empty chair in which the dear companion of all our joys and sorrows had been sitting.

"I think I understand," she said. "I think I owe it to her and to you, Walter, to tell her of her husband's death."

She sighed, and held my hand fast for a moment—then dropped it abruptly, and left the room. On the next day Laura knew that his death had released her, and that the error and the calamity of her life lay buried in his tomb.

His name was mentioned among us no more. Thenceforward, we shrank from the slightest approach to the subject of his death, and in the same scrupulous manner, Marian and I avoided all further reference to that other subject, which, by her consent and mine, was not to be mentioned between us yet. It was not the less present in our minds — it was rather kept alive in them by the restraint which we had imposed on ourselves. We both watched Laura more anxiously than ever, sometimes waiting and hoping, sometimes waiting and fearing, till the time came.

By degrees we returned to our accustomed way of life. I resumed the daily work, which had been suspended during my absence in Hampshire. Our new lodgings cost us more than the smaller and less convenient rooms which we had left, and the claim thus implied on my increased exertions was strengthened by the doubtfulness of our future prospects. Emergencies might yet happen which would exhaust our little fund at the banker's, and the work of my hands might be, ultimately, all we had to look to for support. More permanent and more lucrative employment than had yet been offered to me was a necessity of our position — a necessity for which I now diligently set myself to provide.

It must not be supposed that the interval of rest and seclusion of which I am now writing, entirely suspended, on my part, all pursuit of the one absorbing purpose with which my thoughts and actions are associated in these pages. That purpose was, for months and months yet, never to relax its claims on me. The slow ripening of it still left me a measure of precaution to take, an obligation of gratitude to perform, and a doubtful question to solve.

The measure of precaution related, necessarily, to the Count. It was of the last importance to ascertain, if possible, whether his plans committed him to remaining in England — or, in other words, to remaining within my reach. I contrived to set this doubt at rest by very simple means. His address in St. John's Wood being known to me, I inquired in the neighbourhood, and having found out the agent who had the disposal of the furnished house in which he lived, I asked if number five, Forest Road, was likely to be let within a reasonable time. The reply was in the negative. I was informed that the foreign gentleman then residing in the house had renewed his term of occupation for another six months, and would remain in possession until the end of June in the following year. We were then at the beginning of December only. I left the agent with my mind relieved from all present fear of the Count's escaping me.

The obligation I had to perform took me once more into the presence of Mrs. Clements. I had promised to return, and to confide to her those particulars relating to the death and burial of Anne Catherick which I had been obliged to withhold at our first interview. Changed as circumstances now were, there was no hindrance to my trusting the good woman with as much of the story of the conspiracy as it was necessary to tell. I had every reason that sympathy and friendly feeling could suggest to urge on me the speedy performance of my promise, and I did conscientiously and carefully perform it. There is no need to burden these pages with any statement of what passed at the interview. It will be more to the purpose to say, that the interview itself necessarily brought to my mind the one doubtful question still remaining to be solved — the question of Anne Catherick's parentage on the father's side.

A multitude of small considerations in connection with this subject — trifling enough in themselves, but strikingly important when massed together — had latterly led my mind to a conclusion which I resolved to verify. I obtained Marian's permission to write to Major Donthorne, of Varneck Hall (where Mrs. Catherick had lived in service for some years previous to her marriage), to ask him certain questions. I made the inquiries in Marian's name, and described them as relating to matters of personal history in her family, which might explain and excuse my application. When I wrote the letter I had no certain knowledge that Major Donthorne was still alive — I despatched it on the chance that he might be living, and able and willing to reply.

After a lapse of two days proof came, in the shape of a letter, that the Major was living, and that he was ready to help us.

The idea in my mind when I wrote to him, and the nature of my inquiries will be easily inferred from his reply. His letter answered my questions by communicating these important facts —

In the first place, "the late Sir Percival Glyde, of Blackwater Park," had never set foot in Varneck Hall. The deceased gentleman was a total stranger to Major Donthorne, and to all his family.

In the second place, "the late Mr. Philip Fairlie, of Limmeridge House," had been, in his younger days, the intimate friend and constant guest of Major Donthorne. Having refreshed his memory by looking back to old letters and other papers, the Major was in a position to say positively that Mr. Philip Fairlie was staying at Varneck Hall in the month of August, eighteen hundred and twenty-six, and that he remained there for the shooting during the month of September and part of October following. He then left, to the best of the Major's belief, for Scotland, and did not return to Varneck Hall till after a lapse of time, when he reappeared in the character of a newly-married man.

Taken by itself, this statement was, perhaps, of little positive value, but taken in connection with certain facts, every one of which either Marian or I knew to be true, it suggested one plain conclusion that was, to our minds, irresistible.

Knowing, now, that Mr. Philip Fairlie had been at Varneck Hall in the autumn of eighteen hundred and twenty-six, and that Mrs. Catherick had been living there in service at the same time, we knew also—first, that Anne had been born in June, eighteen hundred and twenty-seven; secondly, that she had always presented an extraordinary personal resemblance to Laura; and, thirdly, that Laura herself was strikingly like her father. Mr. Philip Fairlie had been one of the notoriously handsome men of his time. In disposition entirely unlike his brother Frederick, he was the spoilt darling of society, especially of the women—an easy, light-hearted, impulsive, affectionate man—generous to a fault—constitutionally lax in his principles, and notoriously thoughtless of moral obligations where women were concerned. Such were the facts we knew—such was the character of the man. Surely the plain inference that follows needs no pointing out?

Read by the new light which had now broken upon me, even Mrs. Catherick's letter, in despite of herself, rendered its mite of assistance towards strengthening the conclusion at which I had arrived. She had described Mrs. Fairlie (in writing to me) as "plain-looking," and as having "entrapped the handsomest man in England into marrying her." Both assertions were gratuitously made, and both were false. Jealous dislike (which, in such a woman as Mrs. Catherick, would express itself in petty malice rather than not express itself at all) appeared to me to be the only assignable cause for the peculiar insolence of her reference to Mrs. Fairlie, under circumstances which did not necessitate any reference at all.

The mention here of Mrs. Fairlie's name naturally suggests one other question. Did she ever suspect whose child the little girl brought to her at Limmeridge might be?

Marian's testimony was positive on this point. Mrs. Fairlie's letter to her husband, which had been read to me in former days — the letter describing Anne's resemblance to Laura, and acknowledging her affectionate interest in the little stranger — had been written, beyond all question, in perfect innocence of heart. It even seemed doubtful, on consideration, whether Mr. Philip Fairlie himself had been nearer than his wife to any suspicion of the truth. The disgracefully deceitful circumstances under which Mrs. Catherick had married, the purpose of concealment which the marriage was intended to answer, might well keep her silent for caution's sake, perhaps for her own pride's sake also, even assuming that she had the means, in his absence, of communicating with the father of her unborn child.

As this surmise floated through my mind, there rose on my memory the remembrance of the Scripture denunciation which we have all thought of in our time with wonder and with awe: "The sins of the fathers shall be visited on the children." But for the fatal resemblance between the two daughters of one father, the conspiracy of which Anne had been the innocent instrument and Laura the innocent victim could never have been planned. With what unerring and terrible directness the long chain of circumstances led down from the thoughtless wrong committed by the father to the heartless injury inflicted on the child!

These thoughts came to me, and others with them, which drew my mind away to the little Cumberland churchyard where Anne Catherick now lay buried. I thought of the bygone days when I had met her by Mrs. Fairlie's grave, and met her for the last time. I thought of her poor helpless hands beating on the tombstone, and her weary, yearning words, murmured to the dead remains of her protectress and her friend: "Oh, if I could die, and be hidden and at rest with you!" Little more than a year had passed since she breathed that wish; and how inscrutably, how awfully, it had been fulfilled! The words she had spoken to Laura by the shores of the lake, the very words had now come true. "Oh, if I could only be buried with your mother! If I could only wake at her side when the angel's trumpet sounds and the graves give up their dead at the resurrection!" Through what mortal crime and horror, through what darkest windings of the way down to death — the lost creature had wandered in God's leading to the last home that, living, she never hoped to reach! In that sacred rest I leave her — in that dread companionship let her remain undisturbed.

The Woman in White

So the ghostly figure which has haunted these pages, as it haunted my life, goes down into the impenetrable gloom. Like a shadow she first came to me in the loneliness of the night. Like a shadow she passes away in the loneliness of the dead.

III

Four months elapsed. April came — the month of spring — the month of change.

The course of time had flowed through the interval since the winter peacefully and happily in our new home. I had turned my long leisure to good account, had largely increased my sources of employment, and had placed our means of subsistence on surer grounds. Freed from the suspense and the anxiety which had tried her so sorely and hung over her so long, Marian's spirits rallied, and her natural energy of character began to assert itself again, with something, if not all, of the freedom and the vigour of former times.

More pliable under change than her sister, Laura showed more plainly the progress made by the healing influences of her new life. The worn and wasted look which had prematurely aged her face was fast leaving it, and the expression which had been the first of its charms in past days was the first of its beauties that now returned. My closest observations of her detected but one serious result of the conspiracy which had once threatened her reason and her life. Her memory of events, from the period of her leaving Blackwater Park to the period of our meeting in the burial-ground of Limmeridge Church, was lost beyond all hope of recovery. At the slightest reference to that time she changed and trembled still, her words became confused, her memory wandered and lost itself as helplessly as ever. Here, and here only, the traces of the past lay deep — too deep to be effaced.

In all else she was now so far on the way to recovery that, on her best and brightest days, she sometimes looked and spoke like the Laura of old times. The happy change wrought its natural result in us both. From their long slumber, on her side and on mine, those imperishable memories of our past life in Cumberland now awoke, which were one and all alike, the memories of our love.

Gradually and insensibly our daily relations towards each other became constrained. The fond words which I had spoken to her so naturally, in the days of her sorrow and her suffering, faltered strangely on my lips. In the time when my dread of losing her was most present to my mind, I had always kissed her when she left me at night and when she met me in the morning. The kiss seemed now to have dropped between us — to be lost out of our lives. Our hands began to tremble again when they met. We hardly ever looked long at one another out of

Marian's presence. The talk often flagged between us when we were alone. When I touched her by accident I felt my heart beating fast, as it used to beat at Limmeridge House—I saw the lovely answering flush glowing again in her cheeks, as if we were back among the Cumberland Hills in our past characters of master and pupil once more. She had long intervals of silence and thoughtfulness, and denied she had been thinking when Marian asked her the question. I surprised myself one day neglecting my work to dream over the little water-colour portrait of her which I had taken in the summer-house where we first met—just as I used to neglect Mr. Fairlie's drawings to dream over the same likeness when it was newly finished in the bygone time. Changed as all the circumstances now were, our position towards each other in the golden days of our first companionship seemed to be revived with the revival of our love. It was as if Time had drifted us back on the wreck of our early hopes to the old familiar shore!

To any other woman I could have spoken the decisive words which I still hesitated to speak to her. The utter helplessness of her position—her friendless dependence on all the forbearing gentleness that I could show her—my fear of touching too soon some secret sensitiveness in her which my instinct as a man might not have been fine enough to discover—these considerations, and others like them, kept me self-distrustfully silent. And yet I knew that the restraint on both sides must be ended, that the relations in which we stood towards one another must be altered in some settled manner for the future, and that it rested with me, in the first instance, to recognise the necessity for a change.

The more I thought of our position, the harder the attempt to alter it appeared, while the domestic conditions on which we three had been living together since the winter remained undisturbed. I cannot account for the capricious state of mind in which this feeling originated, but the idea nevertheless possessed me that some previous change of place and circumstances, some sudden break in the quiet monotony of our lives, so managed as to vary the home aspect under which we had been accustomed to see each other, might prepare the way for me to speak, and might make it easier and less embarrassing for Laura and Marian to hear.

With this purpose in view, I said, one morning, that I thought we had all earned a little holiday and a change of scene. After some consideration, it was decided that we should go for a fortnight to the sea-side.

On the next day we left Fulham for a quiet town on the south coast. At that early season of the year we were the only visitors in the place. The cliffs, the beach, and the walks inland were all in the solitary condition which was most welcome to us. The air was mild—the prospects over hill and wood and down were beautifully varied by the shifting April light and shade, and the restless sea leapt under our windows, as if it felt, like the land, the glow and freshness of spring.

I owed it to Marian to consult her before I spoke to Laura, and to be guided afterwards by her advice.

On the third day from our arrival I found a fit opportunity of speaking to her alone. The moment we looked at one another, her quick instinct detected the thought in my mind before I could give it expression. With her customary energy and directness she spoke at once, and spoke first.

"You are thinking of that subject which was mentioned between us on the evening of your return from Hampshire," she said. "I have been expecting you to allude to it for some time past. There must be a change in our little household, Walter, we cannot go on much longer as we are now. I see it as plainly as you do—as plainly as Laura sees it, though she says nothing. How strangely the old times in Cumberland seem to have come back! You and I are together again, and the one subject of interest between us is Laura once more. I could almost fancy that this room is the summer-house at Limmeridge, and that those waves beyond us are beating on our sea-shore."

"I was guided by your advice in those past days," I said, "and now, Marian, with reliance tenfold greater I will be guided by it again."

She answered by pressing my hand. I saw that she was deeply touched by my reference to the past. We sat together near the window, and while I spoke and she listened, we looked at the glory of the sunlight shining on the majesty of the sea.

"Whatever comes of this confidence between us," I said, "whether it ends happily or sorrowfully for me, Laura's interests will still be the interests of my life. When we leave this place, on whatever terms we leave it, my determination to wrest from Count Fosco the confession which I failed to obtain from his accomplice, goes back with me to London, as certainly as I go back myself. Neither you nor I can tell how that man may turn on me, if I bring him to bay; we only know, by his own words and actions, that he is capable of striking at me through

Laura, without a moment's hesitation, or a moment's remorse. In our present position I have no claim on her which society sanctions, which the law allows, to strengthen me in resisting him, and in protecting her. This places me at a serious disadvantage. If I am to fight our cause with the Count, strong in the consciousness of Laura's safety, I must fight it for my Wife. Do you agree to that, Marian, so far?"

"To every word of it," she answered.

"I will not plead out of my own heart," I went on; "I will not appeal to the love which has survived all changes and all shocks — I will rest my only vindication of myself for thinking of her, and speaking of her as my wife, on what I have just said. If the chance of forcing a confession from the Count is, as I believe it to be, the last chance left of publicly establishing the fact of Laura's existence, the least selfish reason that I can advance for our marriage is recognised by us both. But I may be wrong in my conviction — other means of achieving our purpose may be in our power, which are less uncertain and less dangerous. I have searched anxiously, in my own mind, for those means, and I have not found them. Have you?"

"No. I have thought about it too, and thought in vain."

"In all likelihood," I continued, "the same questions have occurred to you, in considering this difficult subject, which have occurred to me. Ought we to return with her to Limmeridge, now that she is like herself again, and trust to the recognition of her by the people of the village, or by the children at the school? Ought we to appeal to the practical test of her handwriting? Suppose we did so. Suppose the recognition of her obtained, and the identity of the handwriting established. Would success in both those cases do more than supply an excellent foundation for a trial in a court of law? Would the recognition and the handwriting prove her identity to Mr. Fairlie and take her back to Limmeridge House, against the evidence of her aunt, against the evidence of the medical certificate, against the fact of the funeral and the fact of the inscription on the tomb? No! We could only hope to succeed in throwing a serious doubt on the assertion of her death, a doubt which nothing short of a legal inquiry can settle. I will assume that we possess (what we have certainly not got) money enough to carry this inquiry on through all its stages. I will assume that Mr. Fairlie's prejudices might be reasoned away — that the false testimony of the Count and his wife, and all the rest of the false testimony, might be confuted — that the recognition could not possibly be ascribed to a mistake between Laura and Anne Catherick, or the handwriting be declared by our enemies to be a clever fraud—all these are assumptions which, more or less, set plain probabilities at defiance; but let them pass—and let us ask ourselves what would be the first consequence or the first questions put to Laura herself on the subject of the conspiracy. We know only too well what the consequence would be, for we know that she has never recovered her memory of what happened to her in London. Examine her privately, or examine her publicly, she is utterly incapable of assisting the assertion of her own case. If you don't see this, Marian, as plainly as I see it, we will go to Limmeridge and try the experiment to-morrow."

"I do see it, Walter. Even if we had the means of paying all the law expenses, even if we succeeded in the end, the delays would be unendurable, the perpetual suspense, after what we have suffered already, would be heartbreaking. You are right about the hopelessness of going to Limmeridge. I wish I could feel sure that you are right also in determining to try that last chance with the Count. Is it a chance at all?"

"Beyond a doubt, Yes. It is the chance of recovering the lost date of Laura's journey to London. Without returning to the reasons I gave you some time since, I am still as firmly persuaded as ever that there is a discrepancy between the date of that journey and the date on the certificate of death. There lies the weak point of the whole conspiracy—it crumbles to pieces if we attack it in that way, and the means of attacking it are in possession of the Count. If I succeed in wresting them from him, the object of your life and mine is fulfilled. If I fail, the wrong that Laura has suffered will, in this world, never be redressed."

"Do you fear failure yourself, Walter?"

"I dare not anticipate success, and for that very reason, Marian, I speak openly and plainly as I have spoken now. In my heart and my conscience I can say it, Laura's hopes for the future are at their lowest ebb. I know that her fortune is gone—I know that the last chance of restoring her to her place in the world lies at the mercy of her worst enemy, of a man who is now absolutely unassailable, and who may remain unassailable to the end. With every worldly advantage gone from her, with all prospect of recovering her rank and station more than doubtful, with no clearer future before her than the future which her husband can provide, the poor drawing-master may harmlessly open his heart at last. In the days of her prosperity, Marian, I was only the teacher who guided her hand—I ask for it, in her adversity, as the hand of my wife!"

Marian's eyes met mine affectionately—I could say no more. My heart was full, my lips were trembling. In spite of myself I was in danger of appealing to her pity. I got up to leave the room. She rose at the same moment, laid her hand gently on my shoulder, and stopped me.

"Walter!" she said, "I once parted you both, for your good and for hers. Wait here, my brother!—wait, my dearest, best friend, till Laura comes, and tells you what I have done now!"

For the first time since the farewell morning at Limmeridge she touched my forehead with her lips. A tear dropped on my face as she kissed me. She turned quickly, pointed to the chair from which I had risen, and left the room.

I sat down alone at the window to wait through the crisis of my life. My mind in that breathless interval felt like a total blank. I was conscious of nothing but a painful intensity of all familiar perceptions. The sun grew blinding bright, the white sea birds chasing each other far beyond me seemed to be flitting before my face, the mellow murmur of the waves on the beach was like thunder in my ears.

The door opened, and Laura came in alone. So she had entered the breakfast-room at Limmeridge House on the morning when we parted. Slowly and falteringly, in sorrow and in hesitation, she had once approached me. Now she came with the haste of happiness in her feet, with the light of happiness radiant in her face. Of their own accord those dear arms clasped themselves round me, of their own accord the sweet lips came to meet mine. "My darling!" she whispered, "we may own we love each other now?" Her head nestled with a tender contentedness on my bosom. "Oh," she said innocently, "I am so happy at last!"

Ten days later we were happier still. We were married.

IV

The course of this narrative, steadily flowing on, bears me away from the morning-time of our married life, and carries me forward to the end.

In a fortnight more we three were back in London, and the shadow was stealing over us of the struggle to come.

Marian and I were careful to keep Laura in ignorance of the cause that had hurried us back — the necessity of making sure of the Count. It was now the beginning of May, and his term of occupation at the house in Forest Road expired in June. If he renewed it (and I had reasons, shortly to be mentioned, for anticipating that he would), I might be certain of his not escaping me. But if by any chance he disappointed my expectations and left the country, then I had no time to lose in arming myself to meet him as I best might.

In the first fulness of my new happiness, there had been moments when my resolution faltered — moments when I was tempted to be safely content, now that the dearest aspiration of my life was fulfilled in the possession of Laura's love. For the first time I thought faint-heartedly of the greatness of the risk, of the adverse chances arrayed against me, of the fair promise of our new life, and of the peril in which I might place the happiness which we had so hardly earned. Yes! let me own it honestly. For a brief time I wandered, in the sweet guiding of love, far from the purpose to which I had been true under sterner discipline and in darker days. Innocently Laura had tempted me aside from the hard path — innocently she was destined to lead me back again.

At times, dreams of the terrible past still disconnectedly recalled to her, in the mystery of sleep, the events of which her waking memory had lost all trace. One night (barely two weeks after our marriage), when I was watching her at rest, I saw the tears come slowly through her closed eyelids, I heard the faint murmuring words escape her which told me that her spirit was back again on the fatal journey from Blackwater Park. That unconscious appeal, so touching and so awful in the sacredness of her sleep, ran through me like fire. The next day was the day we came back to London — the day when my resolution returned to me with tenfold strength.

The first necessity was to know something of the man. Thus far, the true story of his life was an impenetrable mystery to me.

The Woman in White

I began with such scanty sources of information as were at my own disposal. The important narrative written by Mr. Frederick Fairlie (which Marian had obtained by following the directions I had given to her in the winter) proved to be of no service to the special object with which I now looked at it. While reading it I reconsidered the disclosure revealed to me by Mrs. Clements of the series of deceptions which had brought Anne Catherick to London, and which had there devoted her to the interests of the conspiracy. Here, again, the Count had not openly committed himself — here, again, he was, to all practical purpose, out of my reach.

I next returned to Marian's journal at Blackwater Park. At my request she read to me again a passage which referred to her past curiosity about the Count, and to the few particulars which she had discovered relating to him.

The passage to which I allude occurs in that part of her journal which delineates his character and his personal appearance. She describes him as "not having crossed the frontiers of his native country for years past" — as "anxious to know if any Italian gentlemen were settled in the nearest town to Blackwater Park" — as "receiving letters with all sorts of odd stamps on them, and one with a large official-looking seal on it." She is inclined to consider that his long absence from his native country may be accounted for by assuming that he is a political exile. But she is, on the other hand, unable to reconcile this idea with the reception of the letter from abroad bearing "the large official-looking seal" — letters from the Continent addressed to political exiles being usually the last to court attention from foreign post-offices in that way.

The considerations thus presented to me in the diary, joined to certain surmises of my own that grew out of them, suggested a conclusion which I wondered I had not arrived at before. I now said to myself — what Laura had once said to Marian at Blackwater Park, what Madame Fosco had overheard by listening at the door — the Count is a spy!

Laura had applied the word to him at hazard, in natural anger at his proceedings towards herself. I applied it to him with the deliberate conviction that his vocation in life was the vocation of a spy. On this assumption, the reason for his extraordinary stay in England so long after the objects of the conspiracy had been gained, became, to my mind, quite intelligible.

The year of which I am now writing was the year of the

famous Crystal Palace Exhibition in Hyde Park. Foreigners in unusually large numbers had arrived already, and were still arriving in England. Men were among us by hundreds whom the ceaseless distrustfulness of their governments had followed privately, by means of appointed agents, to our shores. My surmises did not for a moment class a man of the Count's abilities and social position with the ordinary rank and file of foreign spies. I suspected him of holding a position of authority, of being entrusted by the government which he secretly served with the organisation and management of agents specially employed in this country, both men and women, and I believed Mrs. Rubelle, who had been so opportunely found to act as nurse at Blackwater Park, to be, in all probability, one of the number.

Assuming that this idea of mine had a foundation in truth, the position of the Count might prove to be more assailable than I had hitherto ventured to hope. To whom could I apply to know something more of the man's history and of the man himself than I knew now?

In this emergency it naturally occurred to my mind that a countryman of his own, on whom I could rely, might be the fittest person to help me. The first man whom I thought of under these circumstances was also the only Italian with whom I was intimately acquainted — my quaint little friend, Professor Pesca.

The professor has been so long absent from these pages that he has run some risk of being forgotten altogether.

It is the necessary law of such a story as mine that the persons concerned in it only appear when the course of events takes them up — they come and go, not by favour of my personal partiality, but by right of their direct connection with the circumstances to be detailed. For this reason, not Pesca alone, but my mother and sister as well, have been left far in the background of the narrative. My visits to the Hampstead cottage, my mother's belief in the denial of Laura's identity which the conspiracy had accomplished, my vain efforts to overcome the prejudice on her part and on my sister's to which, in their jealous affection for me, they both continued to adhere, the painful necessity which that prejudice imposed on me of concealing my marriage from them till they had learnt to do justice to my wife — all these little domestic occurrences have been left unrecorded because they were not essential to the main interest of the story. It is nothing that they added to my anxieties and embittered my disappointments — the steady march of events has inexorably passed them by.

For the same reason I have said nothing here of the consolation that I found in Pesca's brotherly affection for me, when I saw him again after the sudden cessation of my residence at Limmeridge House. I have not recorded the fidelity with which my warm-hearted little friend followed me to the place of embarkation when I sailed for Central America, or the noisy transport of joy with which he received me when we next met in London. If I had felt justified in accepting the offers of service which he made to me on my return, he would have appeared again long ere this. But, though I knew that his honour and his courage were to be implicitly relied on, I was not so sure that his discretion was to be trusted, and, for that reason only, I followed the course of all my inquiries alone. It will now be sufficiently understood that Pesca was not separated from all connection with me and my interests, although he has hitherto been separated from all connection with the progress of this narrative. He was as true and as ready a friend of mine still as ever he had been in his life.

Before I summoned Pesca to my assistance it was necessary to see for myself what sort of man I had to deal with. Up to this time I had never once set eyes on Count Fosco.

Three days after my return with Laura and Marian to London, I set forth alone for Forest Road, St. John's Wood, between ten and eleven o'clock in the morning. It was a fine day — I had some hours to spare — and I thought it likely, if I waited a little for him, that the Count might be tempted out. I had no great reason to fear the chance of his recognising me in the daytime, for the only occasion when I had been seen by him was the occasion on which he had followed me home at night.

No one appeared at the windows in the front of the house. I walked down a turning which ran past the side of it, and looked over the low garden wall. One of the back windows on the lower floor was thrown up and a net was stretched across the opening. I saw nobody, but I heard, in the room, first a shrill whistling and singing of birds, then the deep ringing voice which Marian's description had made familiar to me. "Come out on my little finger, my pret-pret-pretties!" cried the voice. "Come out and hop upstairs! One, two, three — and up! Three, two, one — and down! One, two, three — twit-twit-twit-tweet!"

The Count was exercising his canaries as he used to exercise them in Marian's time at Blackwater Park.

I waited a little while, and the singing and the whistling ceased. "Come, kiss me, my pretties!" said the deep voice. There was a responsive twittering and chirping—a low, oily laugh—a silence of a minute or so, and then I heard the opening of the house door. I turned and retraced my steps. The magnificent melody of the Prayer in Rossini's Moses, sung in a sonorous bass voice, rose grandly through the suburban silence of the place. The front garden gate opened and closed. The Count had come out.

He crossed the road and walked towards the western boundary of the Regent's Park. I kept on my own side of the way, a little behind him, and walked in that direction also.

Marian had prepared me for his high stature, his monstrous corpulence, and his ostentatious mourning garments, but not for the horrible freshness and cheerfulness and vitality of the man. He carried his sixty years as if they had been fewer than forty. He sauntered along, wearing his hat a little on one side, with a light jaunty step, swinging his big stick, humming to himself, looking up from time to time at the houses and gardens on either side of him with superb, smiling patronage. If a stranger had been told that the whole neighbourhood belonged to him, that stranger would not have been surprised to hear it. He never looked back, he paid no apparent attention to me, no apparent attention to any one who passed him on his own side of the road, except now and then, when he smiled and smirked, with an easy paternal good humour, at the nursery-maids and the children whom he met. In this way he led me on, till we reached a colony of shops outside the western terraces of the Park.

Here he stopped at a pastrycook's, went in (probably to give an order), and came out again immediately with a tart in his hand. An Italian was grinding an organ before the shop, and a miserable little shrivelled monkey was sitting on the instrument. The Count stopped, bit a piece for himself out of the tart, and gravely handed the rest to the monkey. "My poor little man!" he said, with grotesque tenderness, "you look hungry. In the sacred name of humanity, I offer you some lunch!" The organ-grinder piteously put in his claim to a penny from the benevolent stranger. The Count shrugged his shoulders contemptuously, and passed on.

We reached the streets and the better class of shops between

The Woman in White

the New Road and Oxford Street. The Count stopped again and entered a small optician's shop, with an inscription in the window announcing that repairs were neatly executed inside. He came out again with an opera-glass in his hand, walked a few paces on, and stopped to look at a bill of the opera placed outside a music-seller's shop. He read the bill attentively, considered a moment, and then hailed an empty cab as it passed him. "Opera Box-office," he said to the man, and was driven away.

I crossed the road, and looked at the bill in my turn. The performance announced was Lucrezia Borgia, and it was to take place that evening. The opera-glass in the Count's hand, his careful reading of the bill, and his direction to the cabman, all suggested that he proposed making one of the audience. I had the means of getting an admission for myself and a friend to the pit by applying to one of the scene-painters attached to the theatre, with whom I had been well acquainted in past times. There was a chance at least that the Count might be easily visible among the audience to me and to any one with me, and in this case I had the means of ascertaining whether Pesca knew his countryman or not that very night.

This consideration at once decided the disposal of my evening. I procured the tickets, leaving a note at the Professor's lodgings on the way. At a quarter to eight I called to take him with me to the theatre. My little friend was in a state of the highest excitement, with a festive flower in his button-hole, and the largest opera-glass I ever saw hugged up under his arm.

"Are you ready?" I asked.

"Right-all-right," said Pesca.

We started for the theatre.

559

V

The last notes of the introduction to the opera were being played, and the seats in the pit were all filled, when Pesca and I reached the theatre.

There was plenty of room, however, in the passage that ran round the pit—precisely the position best calculated to answer the purpose for which I was attending the performance. I went first to the barrier separating us from the stalls, and looked for the Count in that part of the theatre. He was not there. Returning along the passage, on the left-hand side from the stage, and looking about me attentively, I discovered him in the pit. He occupied an excellent place, some twelve or fourteen seats from the end of a bench, within three rows of the stalls. I placed myself exactly on a line with him; Pesca standing by my side. The Professor was not yet aware of the purpose for which I had brought him to the theatre, and he was rather surprised that we did not move nearer to the stage.

The curtain rose, and the opera began.

Throughout the whole of the first act we remained in our position—the Count, absorbed by the orchestra and the stage, never casting so much as a chance glance at us. Not a note of Donizetti's delicious music was lost on him. There he sat, high above his neighbours, smiling, and nodding his great head enjoyingly from time to time. When the people near him applauded the close of an air (as an English audience in such circumstances always will applaud), without the least consideration for the orchestral movement which immediately followed it, he looked round at them with an expression of compassionate remonstrance, and held up one hand with a gesture of polite entreaty. At the more refined passages of the singing, at the more delicate phases of the music, which passed unapplauded by others, his fat hands, adorned with perfectly-fitting black kid gloves, softly patted each other, in token of the cultivated appreciation of a musical man. At such times, his oily murmur of approval, "Bravo! Bra-a-a-a!" hummed through the silence, like the purring of a great cat. His immediate neighbours on either side—hearty, ruddy-faced people from the country, basking amazedly in the sunshine of fashionable London—seeing and hearing him, began to follow his lead. Many a burst of applause from the pit that night started from the soft, comfortable patting of the black-gloved hands. The man's voracious vanity devoured this implied tribute to his local and critical supremacy with an appearance of the highest relish. Smiles rippled continuously over his fat face. He looked about him, at the pauses in the music, serenely satisfied with himself and his fellow-creatures. "Yes! yes! these barbarous English people are learning something from ME. Here, there, and everywhere, I—Fosco—am an influence that is felt, a man who sits supreme!" If ever face spoke, his face spoke then, and that was its language.

The curtain fell on the first act, and the audience rose to look about them. This was the time I had waited for—the time to try if Pesca knew him.

He rose with the rest, and surveyed the occupants of the boxes grandly with his opera-glass. At first his back was towards us, but he turned round in time, to our side of the theatre, and looked at the boxes above us, using his glass for a few minutes—then removing it, but still continuing to look up. This was the moment I chose, when his full face was in view, for directing Pesca's attention to him.

"Do you know that man?" I asked.

"Which man, my friend?"

"The tall, fat man, standing there, with his face towards us."

Pesca raised himself on tiptoe, and looked at the Count.

"No," said the Professor. "The big fat man is a stranger to me. Is he famous? Why do you point him out?"

"Because I have particular reasons for wishing to know something of him. He is a countryman of yours—his name is Count Fosco. Do you know that name?"

"Not I, Walter. Neither the name nor the man is known to me."

"Are you quite sure you don't recognise him? Look again—look carefully. I will tell you why I am so anxious about it when we leave the theatre. Stop! let me help you up here, where you can see him better."

I helped the little man to perch himself on the edge of the raised dais upon which the pit-seats were all placed. His small stature was no hindrance to him—here he could see over the heads of the ladies who were seated near the outermost part of the bench.

A slim, light-haired man standing by us, whom I had not noticed before—a man with a scar on his left cheek—looked attentively at Pesca as I helped him up, and then looked still more attentively, following the direction of Pesca's eyes, at the Count. Our conversation might have reached his ears, and might, as it struck me, have roused his curiosity.

Meanwhile, Pesca fixed his eyes earnestly on the broad, full, smiling face turned a little upward, exactly opposite to him.

"No," he said, "I have never set my two eyes on that big fat man before in all my life."

As he spoke the Count looked downwards towards the boxes behind us on the pit tier.

The eyes of the two Italians met.

The instant before I had been perfectly satisfied, from his own reiterated assertion, that Pesca did not know the Count. The instant afterwards I was equally certain that the Count knew Pesca!

Knew him, and—more surprising still—feared him as well! There was no mistaking the change that passed over the villain's face. The leaden hue that altered his yellow complexion in a moment, the sudden rigidity of all his features, the furtive scrutiny of his cold grey eyes, the motionless stillness of him from head to foot told their own tale. A mortal dread had mastered him body and soul—and his own recognition of Pesca was the cause of it!

The slim man with the scar on his cheek was still close by us. He had apparently drawn his inference from the effect produced on the Count by the sight of Pesca as I had drawn mine. He was a mild, gentlemanlike man, looking like a foreigner, and his interest in our proceedings was not expressed in anything approaching to an offensive manner.

For my own part I was so startled by the change in the Count's face, so astounded at the entirely unexpected turn which events had taken, that I knew neither what to say or do next. Pesca roused me by stepping back to his former place at my side and speaking first.

"How the fat man stares!" he exclaimed. "Is it at me? Am I famous? How can he know me when I don't know him?"

The Woman in White

I kept my eye still on the Count. I saw him move for the first time when Pesca moved, so as not to lose sight of the little man in the lower position in which he now stood. I was curious to see what would happen if Pesca's attention under these circumstances was withdrawn from him, and I accordingly asked the Professor if he recognised any of his pupils that evening among the ladies in the boxes. Pesca immediately raised the large opera-glass to his eyes, and moved it slowly all round the upper part of the theatre, searching for his pupils with the most conscientious scrutiny.

The moment he showed himself to be thus engaged the Count turned round, slipped past the persons who occupied seats on the farther side of him from where we stood, and disappeared in the middle passage down the centre of the pit. I caught Pesca by the arm, and to his inexpressible astonishment, hurried him round with me to the back of the pit to intercept the Count before he could get to the door. Somewhat to my surprise, the slim man hastened out before us, avoiding a stoppage caused by some people on our side of the pit leaving their places, by which Pesca and myself were delayed. When we reached the lobby the Count had disappeared, and the foreigner with the scar was gone too.

"Come home," I said; "come home, Pesca, to your lodgings. I must speak to you in private—I must speak directly."

"My-soul-bless-my-soul!" cried the Professor, in a state of the extremest bewilderment. "What on earth is the matter?"

I walked on rapidly without answering. The circumstances under which the Count had left the theatre suggested to me that his extraordinary anxiety to escape Pesca might carry him to further extremities still. He might escape me, too, by leaving London. I doubted the future if I allowed him so much as a day's freedom to act as he pleased. And I doubted that foreign stranger, who had got the start of us, and whom I suspected of intentionally following him out.

With this double distrust in my mind, I was not long in making Pesca understand what I wanted. As soon as we two were alone in his room, I increased his confusion and amazement a hundredfold by telling him what my purpose was as plainly and unreservedly as I have acknowledged it here.

"My friend, what can I do?" cried the Professor, piteously appealing to me with both hands. "Deuce-what-the-deuce! how can I help you, Walter, when I don't know the man?"

"He knows you — he is afraid of you — he has left the theatre to escape you. Pesca! there must be a reason for this. Look back into your own life before you came to England. You left Italy, as you have told me yourself, for political reasons. You have never mentioned those reasons to me, and I don't inquire into them now. I only ask you to consult your own recollections, and to say if they suggest no past cause for the terror which the first sight of you produced in that man."

To my unutterable surprise, these words, harmless as they appeared to me, produced the same astounding effect on Pesca which the sight of Pesca had produced on the Count. The rosy face of my little friend whitened in an instant, and he drew back from me slowly, trembling from head to foot.

"Walter!" he said. "You don't know what you ask."

He spoke in a whisper — he looked at me as if I had suddenly revealed to him some hidden danger to both of us. In less than one minute of time he was so altered from the easy, lively, quaint little man of all my past experience, that if I had met him in the street, changed as I saw him now, I should most certainly not have known him again.

"Forgive me, if I have unintentionally pained and shocked you," I replied. "Remember the cruel wrong my wife has suffered at Count Fosco's hands. Remember that the wrong can never be redressed, unless the means are in my power of forcing him to do her justice. I spoke in her interests, Pesca — I ask you again to forgive me — I can say no more."

I rose to go. He stopped me before I reached the door.

"Wait," he said. "You have shaken me from head to foot. You don't know how I left my country, and why I left my country. Let me compose myself, let me think, if I can."

I returned to my chair. He walked up and down the room, talking to himself incoherently in his own language. After several turns backwards and forwards, he suddenly came up to me, and laid his little hands with a strange tenderness and solemnity on my breast.

"On your heart and soul, Walter," he said, "is there no other way to get to that man but the chance-way through me?"

"There is no other way," I answered.

The Woman in White

He left me again, opened the door of the room and looked out cautiously into the passage, closed it once more, and came back.

"You won your right over me, Walter," he said, "on the day when you saved my life. It was yours from that moment, when you pleased to take it. Take it now. Yes! I mean what I say. My next words, as true as the good God is above us, will put my life into your hands."

The trembling earnestness with which he uttered this extraordinary warning, carried with it, to my mind, the conviction that he spoke the truth.

"Mind this!" he went on, shaking his hands at me in the vehemence of his agitation. "I hold no thread, in my own mind, between that man Fosco, and the past time which I call back to me for your sake. If you find the thread, keep it to yourself — tell me nothing — on my knees I beg and pray, let me be ignorant, let me be innocent, let me be blind to all the future as I am now!"

He said a few words more, hesitatingly and disconnectedly, then stopped again.

I saw that the effort of expressing himself in English, on an occasion too serious to permit him the use of the quaint turns and phrases of his ordinary vocabulary, was painfully increasing the difficulty he had felt from the first in speaking to me at all. Having learnt to read and understand his native language (though not to speak it), in the earlier days of our intimate companionship, I now suggested to him that he should express himself in Italian, while I used English in putting any questions which might be necessary to my enlightenment. He accepted the proposal. In his smooth-flowing language, spoken with a vehement agitation which betrayed itself in the perpetual working of his features, in the wildness and the suddenness of his foreign gesticulations, but never in the raising of his voice, I now heard the words which armed me to meet the last struggle, that is left for this story to record.[3]

[3] It is only right to mention here, that I repeat Pesco's statement to me with the careful suppressions and alterations which the serious nature of the subject and my own sense of duty to my friend demand. My first and last concealments from the reader are those which caution renders absolutely necessary in this portion of the narrative.

"You know nothing of my motive for leaving Italy," he

began, "except that it was for political reasons. If I had been driven to this country by the persecution of my government, I should not have kept those reasons a secret from you or from any one. I have concealed them because no government authority has pronounced the sentence of my exile. You have heard, Walter, of the political societies that are hidden in every great city on the continent of Europe? To one of those societies I belonged in Italy—and belong still in England. When I came to this country, I came by the direction of my chief. I was over-zealous in my younger time—I ran the risk of compromising myself and others. For those reasons I was ordered to emigrate to England and to wait. I emigrated—I have waited—I wait still. To-morrow I may be called away—ten years hence I may be called away. It is all one to me—I am here, I support myself by teaching, and I wait. I violate no oath (you shall hear why presently) in making my confidence complete by telling you the name of the society to which I belong. All I do is to put my life in your hands. If what I say to you now is ever known by others to have passed my lips, as certainly as we two sit here, I am a dead man."

He whispered the next words in my ear. I keep the secret which he thus communicated. The society to which he belonged will be sufficiently individualised for the purpose of these pages, if I call it "The Brotherhood," on the few occasions when any reference to the subject will be needed in this place.

"The object of the Brotherhood," Pesca went on, "is, briefly, the object of other political societies of the same sort—the destruction of tyranny and the assertion of the rights of the people. The principles of the Brotherhood are two. So long as a man's life is useful, or even harmless only, he has the right to enjoy it. But, if his life inflicts injury on the well-being of his fellow-men, from that moment he forfeits the right, and it is not only no crime, but a positive merit, to deprive him of it. It is not for me to say in what frightful circumstances of oppression and suffering this society took its rise. It is not for you to say—you Englishmen, who have conquered your freedom so long ago, that you have conveniently forgotten what blood you shed, and what extremities you proceeded to in the conquering—it is not for you to say how far the worst of all exasperations may, or may not, carry the maddened men of an enslaved nation. The iron that has entered into our souls has gone too deep for you to find it. Leave the refugee alone! Laugh at him, distrust him, open your eyes in wonder at that secret self which smoulders in him, sometimes under the everyday respectability and tranquillity of a man like me—sometimes under the grinding poverty, the fierce squalor, of men less lucky, less pliable, less patient than I am—but judge us not! In the time of your first Charles you might have done us justice—the long luxury of your own freedom has made you incapable of doing us justice now."

All the deepest feelings of his nature seemed to force themselves to the surface in those words—all his heart was poured out to me for the first time in our lives—but still his voice never rose, still his dread of the terrible revelation he was making to me never left him.

"So far," he resumed, "you think the society like other societies. Its object (in your English opinion) is anarchy and revolution. It takes the life of a bad king or a bad minister, as if the one and the other were dangerous wild beasts to be shot at the first opportunity. I grant you this. But the laws of the Brotherhood are the laws of no other political society on the face of the earth. The members are not known to one another. There is a president in Italy; there are presidents abroad. Each of these has his secretary. The presidents and the secretaries know the members, but the members, among themselves, are all strangers, until their chiefs see fit, in the political necessity of the time, or in the private necessity of the society, to make them known to each other. With such a safeguard as this there is no oath among us on admittance. We are identified with the Brotherhood by a secret mark, which we all bear, which lasts while our lives last. We are told to go about our ordinary business, and to report ourselves to the president, or the secretary, four times a year, in the event of our services being required. We are warned, if we betray the Brotherhood, or if we injure it by serving other interests, that we die by the principles of the Brotherhood—die by the hand of a stranger who may be sent from the other end of the world to strike the blow—or by the hand of our own bosom-friend, who may have been a member unknown to us through all the years of our intimacy. Sometimes the death is delayed—sometimes it follows close on the treachery. It is our first business to know how to wait—our second business to know how to obey when the word is spoken. Some of us may wait our lives through, and may not be wanted. Some of us may be called to the work, or to the preparation for the work, the very day of our admission. I myself—the little, easy, cheerful man you know, who, of his own accord, would hardly lift up his handkerchief to strike down the fly that buzzes about his face—I, in my younger time, under provocation so dreadful that I will not tell you of it, entered the Brotherhood by an impulse, as I might have killed myself by an impulse. I must remain in it now—it has got me, whatever I may think of it in my better circumstances and my cooler manhood, to my dying day. While I was still in Italy I was chosen secretary, and all the members of that time, who were brought face to face with my president, were brought face to face also with me."

I began to understand him—I saw the end towards which his extraordinary disclosure was now tending. He waited a moment, watching me earnestly—watching till he had evidently guessed what was passing in my mind before he resumed.

"You have drawn your own conclusion already," he said. "I see it in your face. Tell me nothing—keep me out of the secret of your thoughts. Let me make my one last sacrifice of myself, for your sake, and then have done with this subject, never to return to it again."

He signed to me not to answer him—rose—removed his coat—and rolled up the shirt-sleeve on his left arm.

"I promised you that this confidence should be complete," he whispered, speaking close at my ear, with his eyes looking watchfully at the door. "Whatever comes of it you shall not reproach me with having hidden anything from you which it was necessary to your interests to know. I have said that the Brotherhood identifies its members by a mark that lasts for life. See the place, and the mark on it for yourself."

He raised his bare arm, and showed me, high on the upper part of it and in the inner side, a brand deeply burnt in the flesh and stained of a bright blood-red colour. I abstain from describing the device which the brand represented. It will be sufficient to say that it was circular in form, and so small that it would have been completely covered by a shilling coin.

"A man who has this mark, branded in this place," he said, covering his arm again, "is a member of the Brotherhood. A man who has been false to the Brotherhood is discovered sooner or later by the chiefs who know him—presidents or secretaries, as the case may be. And a man discovered by the chiefs is dead. No human laws can protect him. Remember what you have seen and heard—draw what conclusions you like—act as you please. But, in the name of God, whatever you discover, whatever you do, tell me nothing! Let me remain free from a responsibility which it horrifies me to think of—which I know, in my conscience, is not my responsibility now. For the last time I say it—on my honour as a gentleman, on my oath as a Christian, if the man you pointed out at the Opera knows me, he is so altered, or so disguised, that I do not know him. I am ignorant of his proceedings or his purposes in England. I never saw him, I never heard the name he goes by, to my knowledge, before to-night. I say no more. Leave me a little, Walter. I am overpowered by what has happened—I am shaken by what I have said. Let me try to be like myself again when we meet next."

He dropped into a chair, and turning away from me, hid his face in his hands. I gently opened the door so as not to disturb him, and spoke my few parting words in low tones, which he might hear or not, as he pleased.

"I will keep the memory of to-night in my heart of hearts," I said. "You shall never repent the trust you have reposed in me. May I come to you to-morrow? May I come as early as nine o'clock?"

"Yes, Walter," he replied, looking up at me kindly, and speaking in English once more, as if his one anxiety now was to get back to our former relations towards each other. "Come to my little bit of breakfast before I go my ways among the pupils that I teach."

"Good-night, Pesca."

"Good-night, my friend."

VI

My first conviction as soon as I found myself outside the house, was that no alternative was left me but to act at once on the information I had received—to make sure of the Count that night, or to risk the loss, if I only delayed till the morning, of Laura's last chance. I looked at my watch—it was ten o'clock.

Not the shadow of a doubt crossed my mind of the purpose for which the Count had left the theatre. His escape from us, that evening, was beyond all question the preliminary only to his escape from London. The mark of the Brotherhood was on his arm—I felt as certain of it as if he had shown me the brand; and the betrayal of the Brotherhood was on his conscience—I had seen it in his recognition of Pesca.

It was easy to understand why that recognition had not been mutual. A man of the Count's character would never risk the terrible consequences of turning spy without looking to his personal security quite as carefully as he looked to his golden reward. The shaven face, which I had pointed out at the Opera, might have been covered by a beard in Pesca's time—his dark brown hair might be a wig—his name was evidently a false one. The accident of time might have helped him as well—his immense corpulence might have come with his later years. There was every reason why Pesca should not have known him again—every reason also why he should have known Pesca, whose singular personal appearance made a marked man of him, go where he might.

I have said that I felt certain of the purpose in the Count's mind when he escaped us at the theatre. How could I doubt it, when I saw, with my own eyes, that he believed himself, in spite of the change in his appearance, to have been recognised by Pesca, and to be therefore in danger of his life? If I could get speech of him that night, if I could show him that I, too knew of the mortal peril in which he stood, what result would follow? Plainly this. One of us must be master of the situation—one of us must inevitably be at the mercy of the other.

I owed it to myself to consider the chances against me before I confronted them. I owed it to my wife to do all that lay in my power to lessen the risk.

The chances against me wanted no reckoning up—they were all merged in one. If the Count discovered, by my own avowal, that the direct way to his safety lay through my life, he was probably the last man in existence who would shrink from

570

throwing me off my guard and taking that way, when he had me alone within his reach. The only means of defence against him on which I could at all rely to lessen the risk, presented themselves, after a little careful thinking, clearly enough. Before I made any personal acknowledgment of my discovery in his presence, I must place the discovery itself where it would be ready for instant use against him, and safe from any attempt at suppression on his part. If I laid the mine under his feet before I approached him, and if I left instructions with a third person to fire it on the expiration of a certain time, unless directions to the contrary were previously received under my own hand, or from my own lips—in that event the Count's security was absolutely dependent upon mine, and I might hold the vantage ground over him securely, even in his own house.

This idea occurred to me when I was close to the new lodgings which we had taken on returning from the sea-side. I went in without disturbing any one, by the help of my key. A light was in the hall, and I stole up with it to my workroom to make my preparations, and absolutely to commit myself to an interview with the Count, before either Laura or Marian could have the slightest suspicion of what I intended to do.

A letter addressed to Pesca represented the surest measure of precaution which it was now possible for me to take. I wrote as follows—

"The man whom I pointed out to you at the Opera is a member of the Brotherhood, and has been false to his trust. Put both these assertions to the test instantly. You know the name he goes by in England. His address is No. 5 Forest Road, St. John's Wood. On the love you once bore me, use the power entrusted to you without mercy and without delay against that man. I have risked all and lost all—and the forfeit of my failure has been paid with my life."

I signed and dated these lines, enclosed them in an envelope, and sealed it up. On the outside I wrote this direction: "Keep the enclosure unopened until nine o'clock to-morrow morning. If you do not hear from me, or see me, before that time, break the seal when the clock strikes, and read the contents." I added my initials, and protected the whole by enclosing it in a second sealed envelope, addressed to Pesca at his lodgings.

Nothing remained to be done after this but to find the means of sending my letter to its destination immediately. I should then have accomplished all that lay in my power. If anything happened to me in the Count's house, I had now provided for his answering it with his life.

That the means of preventing his escape, under any circumstances whatever, were at Pesca's disposal, if he chose to exert them, I did not for an instant doubt. The extraordinary anxiety which he had expressed to remain unenlightened as to the Count's identity — or, in other words, to be left uncertain enough about facts to justify him to his own conscience in remaining passive — betrayed plainly that the means of exercising the terrible justice of the Brotherhood were ready to his hand, although, as a naturally humane man, he had shrunk from plainly saying as much in my presence. The deadly certainty with which the vengeance of foreign political societies can hunt down a traitor to the cause, hide himself where he may, had been too often exemplified, even in my superficial experience, to allow of any doubt. Considering the subject only as a reader of newspapers, cases recurred to my memory, both in London and in Paris, of foreigners found stabbed in the streets, whose assassins could never be traced — of bodies and parts of bodies thrown into the Thames and the Seine, by hands that could never be discovered — of deaths by secret violence which could only be accounted for in one way. I have disguised nothing relating to myself in these pages, and I do not disguise here that I believed I had written Count Fosco's death-warrant, if the fatal emergency happened which authorised Pesca to open my enclosure.

I left my room to go down to the ground floor of the house, and speak to the landlord about finding me a messenger. He happened to be ascending the stairs at the time, and we met on the landing. His son, a quick lad, was the messenger he proposed to me on hearing what I wanted. We had the boy upstairs, and I gave him his directions. He was to take the letter in a cab, to put it into Professor Pesca's own hands, and to bring me back a line of acknowledgment from that gentleman — returning in the cab, and keeping it at the door for my use. It was then nearly half-past ten. I calculated that the boy might be back in twenty minutes, and that I might drive to St. John's Wood, on his return, in twenty minutes more.

When the lad had departed on his errand I returned to my own room for a little while, to put certain papers in order, so that they might be easily found in case of the worst. The key of the old-fashioned bureau in which the papers were kept I sealed up, and left it on my table, with Marian's name written on the outside of the little packet. This done, I went downstairs to the sitting-room, in which I expected to find Laura and Marian awaiting my return from the Opera. I felt my hand trembling for the first time when I laid it on the lock of the door.

No one was in the room but Marian. She was reading, and she looked at her watch, in surprise, when I came in.

"How early you are back!" she said. "You must have come away before the Opera was over."

"Yes," I replied, "neither Pesca nor I waited for the end. Where is Laura?"

"She had one of her bad headaches this evening, and I advised her to go to bed when we had done tea."

I left the room again on the pretext of wishing to see whether Laura was asleep. Marian's quick eyes were beginning to look inquiringly at my face—Marian's quick instinct was beginning to discover that I had something weighing on my mind.

When I entered the bedchamber, and softly approached the bedside by the dim flicker of the night-lamp, my wife was asleep.

We had not been married quite a month yet. If my heart was heavy, if my resolution for a moment faltered again, when I looked at her face turned faithfully to my pillow in her sleep—when I saw her hand resting open on the coverlid, as if it was waiting unconsciously for mine—surely there was some excuse for me? I only allowed myself a few minutes to kneel down at the bedside, and to look close at her—so close that her breath, as it came and went, fluttered on my face. I only touched her hand and her cheek with my lips at parting. She stirred in her sleep and murmured my name, but without waking. I lingered for an instant at the door to look at her again. "God bless and keep you, my darling!" I whispered, and left her.

Marian was at the stairhead waiting for me. She had a folded slip of paper in her hand.

"The landlord's son has brought this for you," she said. "He has got a cab at the door—he says you ordered him to keep it at your disposal."

"Quite right, Marian. I want the cab—I am going out again."

I descended the stairs as I spoke, and looked into the sitting-room to read the slip of paper by the light on the table. It contained these two sentences in Pesca's handwriting—

"Your letter is received. If I don't see you before the time you mention, I will break the seal when the clock strikes."

I placed the paper in my pocket-book, and made for the door. Marian met me on the threshold, and pushed me back into the room, where the candle-light fell full on my face. She held me by both hands, and her eyes fastened searchingly on mine.

"I see!" she said, in a low eager whisper. "You are trying the last chance to-night."

"Yes, the last chance and the best," I whispered back.

"Not alone! Oh, Walter, for God's sake, not alone! Let me go with you. Don't refuse me because I'm only a woman. I must go! I will go! I'll wait outside in the cab!"

It was my turn now to hold her. She tried to break away from me and get down first to the door.

"If you want to help me," I said, "stop here and sleep in my wife's room to-night. Only let me go away with my mind easy about Laura, and I answer for everything else. Come, Marian, give me a kiss, and show that you have the courage to wait till I come back."

I dared not allow her time to say a word more. She tried to hold me again. I unclasped her hands, and was out of the room in a moment. The boy below heard me on the stairs, and opened the hall-door. I jumped into the cab before the driver could get off the box. "Forest Road, St. John's Wood," I called to him through the front window. "Double fare if you get there in a quarter of an hour." "I'll do it, sir." I looked at my watch. Eleven o'clock. Not a minute to lose.

The rapid motion of the cab, the sense that every instant now was bringing me nearer to the Count, the conviction that I was embarked at last, without let or hindrance, on my hazardous enterprise, heated me into such a fever of excitement that I shouted to the man to go faster and faster. As we left the streets, and crossed St. John's Wood Road, my impatience so completely overpowered me that I stood up in the cab and stretched my head out of the window, to see the end of the journey before we reached it. Just as a church clock in the distance struck the quarter past, we turned into the Forest Road. I stopped the driver a little away from the Count's house, paid and dismissed him, and walked on to the door.

As I approached the garden gate, I saw another person advancing towards it also from the direction opposite to mine. We met under the gas lamp in the road, and looked at each other. I instantly recognised the light-haired foreigner with the scar on his cheek, and I thought he recognised me. He said nothing, and instead of stopping at the house, as I did, he slowly walked on. Was he in the Forest Road by accident? Or had he followed the Count home from the Opera?

I did not pursue those questions. After waiting a little till the foreigner had slowly passed out of sight, I rang the gate bell. It was then twenty minutes past eleven—late enough to make it quite easy for the Count to get rid of me by the excuse that he was in bed.

The only way of providing against this contingency was to send in my name without asking any preliminary questions, and to let him know, at the same time, that I had a serious motive for wishing to see him at that late hour. Accordingly, while I was waiting, I took out my card and wrote under my name "On important business." The maid-servant answered the door while I was writing the last word in pencil, and asked me distrustfully what I "pleased to want."

"Be so good as to take that to your master," I replied, giving her the card.

I saw, by the girl's hesitation of manner, that if I had asked for the Count in the first instance she would only have followed her instructions by telling me he was not at home. She was staggered by the confidence with which I gave her the card. After staring at me, in great perturbation, she went back into the house with my message, closing the door, and leaving me to wait in the garden.

In a minute or so she reappeared. "Her master's compliments, and would I be so obliging as to say what my business was?" "Take my compliments back," I replied, "and say that the business cannot be mentioned to any one but your master." She left me again, again returned, and this time asked me to walk in.

I followed her at once. In another moment I was inside the Count's house.

VII

There was no lamp in the hall, but by the dim light of the kitchen candle, which the girl had brought upstairs with her, I saw an elderly lady steal noiselessly out of a back room on the ground floor. She cast one viperish look at me as I entered the hall, but said nothing, and went slowly upstairs without returning my bow. My familiarity with Marian's journal sufficiently assured me that the elderly lady was Madame Fosco.

The servant led me to the room which the Countess had just left. I entered it, and found myself face to face with the Count.

He was still in his evening dress, except his coat, which he had thrown across a chair. His shirt-sleeves were turned up at the wrists, but no higher. A carpet-bag was on one side of him, and a box on the other. Books, papers, and articles of wearing apparel were scattered about the room. On a table, at one side of the door, stood the cage, so well known to me by description, which contained his white mice. The canaries and the cockatoo were probably in some other room. He was seated before the box, packing it, when I went in, and rose with some papers in his hand to receive me. His face still betrayed plain traces of the shock that had overwhelmed him at the Opera. His fat cheeks hung loose, his cold grey eyes were furtively vigilant, his voice, look, and manner were all sharply suspicious alike, as he advanced a step to meet me, and requested, with distant civility, that I would take a chair.

"You come here on business, sir?" he said. "I am at a loss to know what that business can possibly be."

The unconcealed curiosity, with which he looked hard in my face while he spoke, convinced me that I had passed unnoticed by him at the Opera. He had seen Pesca first, and from that moment till he left the theatre he had evidently seen nothing else. My name would necessarily suggest to him that I had not come into his house with other than a hostile purpose towards himself, but he appeared to be utterly ignorant thus far of the real nature of my errand.

"I am fortunate in finding you here to-night," I said. "You seem to be on the point of taking a journey?"

"Is your business connected with my journey?"

"In some degree."

The Woman in White

"In what degree? Do you know where I am going to?"

"No. I only know why you are leaving London."

He slipped by me with the quickness of thought, locked the door, and put the key in his pocket.

"You and I, Mr. Hartright, are excellently well acquainted with one another by reputation," he said. "Did it, by any chance, occur to you when you came to this house that I was not the sort of man you could trifle with?"

"It did occur to me," I replied. "And I have not come to trifle with you. I am here on a matter of life and death, and if that door which you have locked was open at this moment, nothing you could say or do would induce me to pass through it."

I walked farther into the room, and stood opposite to him on the rug before the fireplace. He drew a chair in front of the door, and sat down on it, with his left arm resting on the table. The cage with the white mice was close to him, and the little creatures scampered out of their sleeping-place as his heavy arm shook the table, and peered at him through the gaps in the smartly painted wires.

"On a matter of life and death," he repeated to himself. "Those words are more serious, perhaps, than you think. What do you mean?"

"What I say."

The perspiration broke out thickly on his broad forehead. His left hand stole over the edge of the table. There was a drawer in it, with a lock, and the key was in the lock. His finger and thumb closed over the key, but did not turn it.

"So you know why I am leaving London?" he went on. "Tell me the reason, if you please." He turned the key, and unlocked the drawer as he spoke.

"I can do better than that," I replied. "I can show you the reason, if you like."

"How can you show it?"

"You have got your coat off," I said. "Roll up the shirt-sleeve on your left arm, and you will see it there."

The same livid leaden change passed over his face which I had seen pass over it at the theatre. The deadly glitter in his eyes shone steady and straight into mine. He said nothing. But his left hand slowly opened the table-drawer, and softly slipped into it. The harsh grating noise of something heavy that he was moving unseen to me sounded for a moment, then ceased. The silence that followed was so intense that the faint ticking nibble of the white mice at their wires was distinctly audible where I stood.

My life hung by a thread, and I knew it. At that final moment I thought with his mind, I felt with his fingers—I was as certain as if I had seen it of what he kept hidden from me in the drawer.

"Wait a little," I said. "You have got the door locked—you see I don't move—you see my hands are empty. Wait a little. I have something more to say."

"You have said enough," he replied, with a sudden composure so unnatural and so ghastly that it tried my nerves as no outbreak of violence could have tried them. "I want one moment for my own thoughts, if you please. Do you guess what I am thinking about?"

"Perhaps I do."

"I am thinking," he remarked quietly, "whether I shall add to the disorder in this room by scattering your brains about the fireplace."

If I had moved at that moment, I saw in his face that he would have done it.

"I advise you to read two lines of writing which I have about me," I rejoined, "before you finally decide that question."

The proposal appeared to excite his curiosity. He nodded his head. I took Pesca's acknowledgment of the receipt of my letter out of my pocket-book, handed it to him at arm's length, and returned to my former position in front of the fireplace.

He read the lines aloud: "Your letter is received. If I don't hear from you before the time you mention, I will break the seal when the clock strikes."

Another man in his position would have needed some explanation of those words—the Count felt no such necessity.

The Woman in White

One reading of the note showed him the precaution that I had taken as plainly as if he had been present at the time when I adopted it. The expression of his face changed on the instant, and his hand came out of the drawer empty.

"I don't lock up my drawer, Mr. Hartright," he said, "and I don't say that I may not scatter your brains about the fireplace yet. But I am a just man even to my enemy, and I will acknowledge beforehand that they are cleverer brains than I thought them. Come to the point, sir! You want something of me?"

"I do, and I mean to have it."

"On conditions?"

"On no conditions."

His hand dropped into the drawer again.

"Bah! we are travelling in a circle," he said, "and those clever brains of yours are in danger again. Your tone is deplorably imprudent, sir—moderate it on the spot! The risk of shooting you on the place where you stand is less to me than the risk of letting you out of this house, except on conditions that I dictate and approve. You have not got my lamented friend to deal with now—you are face to face with Fosco! If the lives of twenty Mr. Hartrights were the stepping-stones to my safety, over all those stones I would go, sustained by my sublime indifference, self-balanced by my impenetrable calm. Respect me, if you love your own life! I summon you to answer three questions before you open your lips again. Hear them—they are necessary to this interview. Answer them—they are necessary to ME." He held up one finger of his right hand. "First question!" he said. "You come here possessed of information which may be true or may be false—where did you get it?"

"I decline to tell you."

"No matter—I shall find out. If that information is true—mind I say, with the whole force of my resolution, if—you are making your market of it here by treachery of your own or by treachery of some other man. I note that circumstance for future use in my memory, which forgets nothing, and proceed." He held up another finger. "Second question! Those lines you invited me to read are without signature. Who wrote them?"

"A man whom I have every reason to depend on, and whom

you have every reason to fear."

My answer reached him to some purpose. His left hand trembled audibly in the drawer.

"How long do you give me," he asked, putting his third question in a quieter tone, "before the clock strikes and the seal is broken?"

"Time enough for you to come to my terms," I replied.

"Give me a plainer answer, Mr. Hartright. What hour is the clock to strike?"

"Nine, to-morrow morning."

"Nine, to-morrow morning? Yes, yes — your trap is laid for me before I can get my passport regulated and leave London. It is not earlier, I suppose? We will see about that presently — I can keep you hostage here, and bargain with you to send for your letter before I let you go. In the meantime, be so good next as to mention your terms."

"You shall hear them. They are simple, and soon stated. You know whose interests I represent in coming here?"

He smiled with the most supreme composure, and carelessly waved his right hand.

"I consent to hazard a guess," he said jeeringly. "A lady's interests, of course!"

"My Wife's interests."

He looked at me with the first honest expression that had crossed his face in my presence — an expression of blank amazement. I could see that I sank in his estimation as a dangerous man from that moment. He shut up the drawer at once, folded his arms over his breast, and listened to me with a smile of satirical attention.

"You are well enough aware," I went on, "of the course which my inquiries have taken for many months past, to know that any attempted denial of plain facts will be quite useless in my presence. You are guilty of an infamous conspiracy! And the gain of a fortune of ten thousand pounds was your motive for it."

The Woman in White

He said nothing. But his face became overclouded suddenly by a lowering anxiety.

"Keep your gain," I said. (His face lightened again immediately, and his eyes opened on me in wider and wider astonishment.) "I am not here to disgrace myself by bargaining for money which has passed through your hands, and which has been the price of a vile crime— —"

"Gently, Mr. Hartright. Your moral clap-traps have an excellent effect in England—keep them for yourself and your own countrymen, if you please. The ten thousand pounds was a legacy left to my excellent wife by the late Mr. Fairlie. Place the affair on those grounds, and I will discuss it if you like. To a man of my sentiments, however, the subject is deplorably sordid. I prefer to pass it over. I invite you to resume the discussion of your terms. What do you demand?"

"In the first place, I demand a full confession of the conspiracy, written and signed in my presence by yourself."

He raised his finger again. "One!" he said, checking me off with the steady attention of a practical man.

"In the second place, I demand a plain proof, which does not depend on your personal asseveration, of the date at which my wife left Blackwater Park and travelled to London."

"So! so! you can lay your finger, I see, on the weak place," he remarked composedly. "Any more?"

"At present, no more."

"Good! you have mentioned your terms, now listen to mine. The responsibility to myself of admitting what you are pleased to call the 'conspiracy' is less, perhaps, upon the whole, than the responsibility of laying you dead on that hearthrug. Let us say that I meet your proposal—on my own conditions. The statement you demand of me shall be written, and the plain proof shall be produced. You call a letter from my late lamented friend informing me of the day and hour of his wife's arrival in London, written, signed, and dated by himself, a proof, I suppose? I can give you this. I can also send you to the man of whom I hired the carriage to fetch my visitor from the railway, on the day when she arrived—his order-book may help you to your date, even if his coachman who drove me proves to be of no use. These things I can do, and will do, on conditions. I recite them. First condition! Madame Fosco and I leave this house when and how we please, without interference of any kind on your part. Second condition! You wait here, in company with me, to see my agent, who is coming at seven o'clock in the morning to regulate my affairs. You give my agent a written order to the man who has got your sealed letter to resign his possession of it. You wait here till my agent places that letter unopened in my hands, and you then allow me one clear half-hour to leave the house—after which you resume your own freedom of action and go where you please. Third condition! You give me the satisfaction of a gentleman for your intrusion into my private affairs, and for the language you have allowed yourself to use to me at this conference. The time and place, abroad, to be fixed in a letter from my hand when I am safe on the Continent, and that letter to contain a strip of paper measuring accurately the length of my sword. Those are my terms. Inform me if you accept them—Yes or No."

The extraordinary mixture of prompt decision, far-sighted cunning, and mountebank bravado in this speech, staggered me for a moment—and only for a moment. The one question to consider was, whether I was justified or not in possessing myself of the means of establishing Laura's identity at the cost of allowing the scoundrel who had robbed her of it to escape me with impunity. I knew that the motive of securing the just recognition of my wife in the birthplace from which she had been driven out as an impostor, and of publicly erasing the lie that still profaned her mother's tombstone, was far purer, in its freedom from all taint of evil passion, than the vindictive motive which had mingled itself with my purpose from the first. And yet I cannot honestly say that my own moral convictions were strong enough to decide the struggle in me by themselves. They were helped by my remembrance of Sir Percival's death. How awfully, at the last moment, had the working of the retribution there been snatched from my feeble hands! What right had I to decide, in my poor mortal ignorance of the future, that this man, too, must escape with impunity because he escaped me? I thought of these things—perhaps with the superstition inherent in my nature, perhaps with a sense worthier of me than superstition. It was hard, when I had fastened my hold on him at last, to loosen it again of my own accord—but I forced myself to make the sacrifice. In plainer words, I determined to be guided by the one higher motive of which I was certain, the motive of serving the cause of Laura and the cause of Truth.

"I accept your conditions," I said. "With one reservation on my part."

"What reservation may that be?" he asked.

"It refers to the sealed letter," I answered. "I require you to destroy it unopened in my presence as soon as it is placed in your hands."

My object in making this stipulation was simply to prevent him from carrying away written evidence of the nature of my communication with Pesca. The fact of my communication he would necessarily discover, when I gave the address to his agent in the morning. But he could make no use of it on his own unsupported testimony — even if he really ventured to try the experiment — which need excite in me the slightest apprehension on Pesca's account.

"I grant your reservation," he replied, after considering the question gravely for a minute or two. "It is not worth dispute — the letter shall be destroyed when it comes into my hands."

He rose, as he spoke, from the chair in which he had been sitting opposite to me up to this time. With one effort he appeared to free his mind from the whole pressure on it of the interview between us thus far. "Ouf!" he cried, stretching his arms luxuriously, "the skirmish was hot while it lasted. Take a seat, Mr. Hartright. We meet as mortal enemies hereafter — let us, like gallant gentlemen, exchange polite attentions in the meantime. Permit me to take the liberty of calling for my wife."

He unlocked and opened the door. "Eleanor!" he called out in his deep voice. The lady of the viperish face came in. "Madame Fosco — Mr. Hartright," said the Count, introducing us with easy dignity. "My angel," he went on, addressing his wife, "will your labours of packing up allow you time to make me some nice strong coffee? I have writing business to transact with Mr. Hartright — and I require the full possession of my intelligence to do justice to myself."

Madame Fosco bowed her head twice — once sternly to me, once submissively to her husband, and glided out of the room.

The Count walked to a writing-table near the window, opened his desk, and took from it several quires of paper and a bundle of quill pens. He scattered the pens about the table, so that they might lie ready in all directions to be taken up when wanted, and then cut the paper into a heap of narrow slips, of the form used by professional writers for the press. "I shall make this a remarkable document," he said, looking at me over his shoulder. "Habits of literary composition are perfectly familiar to me. One of the rarest of all the intellectual accomplishments that a man can possess is the grand faculty of arranging his ideas. Immense privilege! I possess it. Do you?"

He marched backwards and forwards in the room, until the coffee appeared, humming to himself, and marking the places at which obstacles occurred in the arrangement of his ideas, by striking his forehead from time to time with the palm of his hand. The enormous audacity with which he seized on the situation in which I placed him, and made it the pedestal on which his vanity mounted for the one cherished purpose of self-display, mastered my astonishment by main force. Sincerely as I loathed the man, the prodigious strength of his character, even in its most trivial aspects, impressed me in spite of myself.

The coffee was brought in by Madame Fosco. He kissed her hand in grateful acknowledgment, and escorted her to the door; returned, poured out a cup of coffee for himself, and took it to the writing-table.

"May I offer you some coffee, Mr. Hartright?" he said, before he sat down.

I declined.

"What! you think I shall poison you?" he said gaily. "The English intellect is sound, so far as it goes," he continued, seating himself at the table; "but it has one grave defect—it is always cautious in the wrong place."

He dipped his pen in the ink, placed the first slip of paper before him with a thump of his hand on the desk, cleared his throat, and began. He wrote with great noise and rapidity, in so large and bold a hand, and with such wide spaces between the lines, that he reached the bottom of the slip in not more than two minutes certainly from the time when he started at the top. Each slip as he finished it was paged, and tossed over his shoulder out of his way on the floor. When his first pen was worn out, that went over his shoulder too, and he pounced on a second from the supply scattered about the table. Slip after slip, by dozens, by fifties, by hundreds, flew over his shoulders on either side of him till he had snowed himself up in paper all round his chair. Hour after hour passed—and there I sat watching, there he sat writing. He never stopped, except to sip his coffee, and when that was exhausted, to smack his forehead from time to time. One o'clock struck, two, three, four—and still the slips flew about all round him; still the untiring pen scraped its way ceaselessly from top to bottom of the page, still the white chaos of paper rose higher and higher all round his chair. At four o'clock I heard a sudden splutter of the pen, indicative of the flourish with which he signed his name. "Bravo!" he cried, springing to his feet with the activity of a young man, and looking me straight in the face with a smile of superb triumph.

"Done, Mr. Hartright!" he announced with a self-renovating thump of his fist on his broad breast. "Done, to my own profound satisfaction—to your profound astonishment, when you read what I have written. The subject is exhausted: the man—Fosco—is not. I proceed to the arrangement of my slips—to the revision of my slips—to the reading of my slips—addressed emphatically to your private ear. Four o'clock has just struck. Good! Arrangement, revision, reading, from four to five. Short snooze of restoration for myself from five to six. Final preparations from six to seven. Affair of agent and sealed letter from seven to eight. At eight, en route. Behold the programme!"

He sat down cross-legged on the floor among his papers, strung them together with a bodkin and a piece of string—revised them, wrote all the titles and honours by which he was personally distinguished at the head of the first page, and then read the manuscript to me with loud theatrical emphasis and profuse theatrical gesticulation. The reader will have an opportunity, ere long, of forming his own opinion of the document. It will be sufficient to mention here that it answered my purpose.

He next wrote me the address of the person from whom he had hired the fly, and handed me Sir Percival's letter. It was dated from Hampshire on the 25th of July, and it announced the journey of "Lady Glyde" to London on the 26th. Thus, on the very day (the 25th) when the doctor's certificate declared that she had died in St. John's Wood, she was alive, by Sir Percival's own showing, at Blackwater—and, on the day after, she was to take a journey! When the proof of that journey was obtained from the flyman, the evidence would be complete.

"A quarter-past five," said the Count, looking at his watch. "Time for my restorative snooze. I personally resemble Napoleon the Great, as you may have remarked, Mr. Hartright—I also resemble that immortal man in my power of commanding sleep at will. Excuse me one moment. I will summon Madame Fosco, to keep you from feeling dull."

Knowing as well as he did, that he was summoning Madame Fosco to ensure my not leaving the house while he was asleep, I made no reply, and occupied myself in tying up the papers which he had placed in my possession.

The lady came in, cool, pale, and venomous as ever. "Amuse Mr. Hartright, my angel," said the Count. He placed a chair for her, kissed her hand for the second time, withdrew to a sofa, and, in three minutes, was as peacefully and happily asleep as the most virtuous man in existence.

Madame Fosco took a book from the table, sat down, and looked at me, with the steady vindictive malice of a woman who never forgot and never forgave.

"I have been listening to your conversation with my husband," she said. "If I had been in his place—I would have laid you dead on the hearthrug."

With those words she opened her book, and never looked at me or spoke to me from that time till the time when her husband woke.

He opened his eyes and rose from the sofa, accurately to an hour from the time when he had gone to sleep.

"I feel infinitely refreshed," he remarked. "Eleanor, my good wife, are you all ready upstairs? That is well. My little packing here can be completed in ten minutes—my travelling-dress assumed in ten minutes more. What remains before the agent comes?" He looked about the room, and noticed the cage with his white mice in it. "Ah!" he cried piteously, "a last laceration of my sympathies still remains. My innocent pets! my little cherished children! what am I to do with them? For the present we are settled nowhere; for the present we travel incessantly—the less baggage we carry the better for ourselves. My cockatoo, my canaries, and my little mice—who will cherish them when their good Papa is gone?"

He walked about the room deep in thought. He had not been at all troubled about writing his confession, but he was visibly perplexed and distressed about the far more important question of the disposal of his pets. After long consideration he suddenly sat down again at the writing-table.

"An idea!" he exclaimed. "I will offer my canaries and my cockatoo to this vast Metropolis—my agent shall present them in my name to the Zoological Gardens of London. The

Document that describes them shall be drawn out on the spot."

He began to write, repeating the words as they flowed from his pen.

"Number one. Cockatoo of transcendent plumage: attraction, of himself, to all visitors of taste. Number two. Canaries of unrivalled vivacity and intelligence: worthy of the garden of Eden, worthy also of the garden in the Regent's Park. Homage to British Zoology. Offered by Fosco."

The pen spluttered again, and the flourish was attached to his signature.

"Count! you have not included the mice," said Madame Fosco.

He left the table, took her hand, and placed it on his heart.

"All human resolution, Eleanor," he said solemnly, "has its limits. My limits are inscribed on that Document. I cannot part with my white mice. Bear with me, my angel, and remove them to their travelling cage upstairs."

"Admirable tenderness!" said Madame Fosco, admiring her husband, with a last viperish look in my direction. She took up the cage carefully, and left the room.

The Count looked at his watch. In spite of his resolute assumption of composure, he was getting anxious for the agent's arrival. The candles had long since been extinguished, and the sunlight of the new morning poured into the room. It was not till five minutes past seven that the gate bell rang, and the agent made his appearance. He was a foreigner with a dark beard.

"Mr. Hartright—Monsieur Rubelle," said the Count, introducing us. He took the agent (a foreign spy, in every line of his face, if ever there was one yet) into a corner of the room, whispered some directions to him, and then left us together. "Monsieur Rubelle," as soon as we were alone, suggested with great politeness that I should favour him with his instructions. I wrote two lines to Pesca, authorising him to deliver my sealed letter "to the bearer," directed the note, and handed it to Monsieur Rubelle.

The agent waited with me till his employer returned, equipped in travelling costume. The Count examined the address of my letter before he dismissed the agent. "I thought so!" he said, turning on me with a dark look, and altering again in his manner from that moment.

He completed his packing, and then sat consulting a travelling map, making entries in his pocket-book, and looking every now and then impatiently at his watch. Not another word, addressed to myself, passed his lips. The near approach of the hour for his departure, and the proof he had seen of the communication established between Pesca and myself, had plainly recalled his whole attention to the measures that were necessary for securing his escape.

A little before eight o'clock, Monsieur Rubelle came back with my unopened letter in his hand. The Count looked carefully at the superscription and the seal, lit a candle, and burnt the letter. "I perform my promise," he said, "but this matter, Mr. Hartright, shall not end here."

The agent had kept at the door the cab in which he had returned. He and the maid-servant now busied themselves in removing the luggage. Madame Fosco came downstairs, thickly veiled, with the travelling cage of the white mice in her hand. She neither spoke to me nor looked towards me. Her husband escorted her to the cab. "Follow me as far as the passage," he whispered in my ear; "I may want to speak to you at the last moment."

I went out to the door, the agent standing below me in the front garden. The Count came back alone, and drew me a few steps inside the passage.

"Remember the Third condition!" he whispered. "You shall hear from me, Mr. Hartright—I may claim from you the satisfaction of a gentleman sooner than you think for." He caught my hand before I was aware of him, and wrung it hard—then turned to the door, stopped, and came back to me again.

"One word more," he said confidentially. "When I last saw Miss Halcombe, she looked thin and ill. I am anxious about that admirable woman. Take care of her, sir! With my hand on my heart, I solemnly implore you, take care of Miss Halcombe!"

Those were the last words he said to me before he squeezed his huge body into the cab and drove off.

The agent and I waited at the door a few moments looking

after him. While we were standing together, a second cab appeared from a turning a little way down the road. It followed the direction previously taken by the Count's cab, and as it passed the house and the open garden gate, a person inside looked at us out of the window. The stranger at the Opera again! — the foreigner with a scar on his left cheek.

"You wait here with me, sir, for half an hour more!" said Monsieur Rubelle.

"I do."

We returned to the sitting-room. I was in no humour to speak to the agent, or to allow him to speak to me. I took out the papers which the Count had placed in my hands, and read the terrible story of the conspiracy told by the man who had planned and perpetrated it.

THE STORY CONTINUED BY ISIDOR, OTTAVIO, BALDASSARE FOSCO

(Count of the Holy Roman Empire, Knight Grand Cross of the Order of the Brazen Crown, Perpetual Arch-Master of the Rosicrucian Masons of Mesopotamia; Attached (in Honorary Capacities) to Societies Musical, Societies Medical, Societies Philosophical, and Societies General Benevolent, throughout Europe; etc. etc. etc.)

THE COUNT'S NARRATIVE

In the summer of eighteen hundred and fifty I arrived in England, charged with a delicate political mission from abroad. Confidential persons were semi-officially connected with me, whose exertions I was authorised to direct, Monsieur and Madame Rubelle being among the number. Some weeks of spare time were at my disposal, before I entered on my functions by establishing myself in the suburbs of London. Curiosity may stop here to ask for some explanation of those functions on my part. I entirely sympathise with the request. I also regret that diplomatic reserve forbids me to comply with it.

I arranged to pass the preliminary period of repose, to which I have just referred, in the superb mansion of my late lamented friend, Sir Percival Glyde. He arrived from the Continent with his wife. I arrived from the Continent with mine. England is the land of domestic happiness — how appropriately we entered it under these domestic circumstances!

The bond of friendship which united Percival and myself was strengthened, on this occasion, by a touching similarity in the pecuniary position on his side and on mine. We both wanted money. Immense necessity! Universal want! Is there a civilised human being who does not feel for us? How insensible must that man be! Or how rich!

I enter into no sordid particulars, in discussing this part of the subject. My mind recoils from them. With a Roman austerity, I show my empty purse and Percival's to the shrinking public gaze. Let us allow the deplorable fact to assert itself, once for all, in that manner, and pass on.

We were received at the mansion by the magnificent creature who is inscribed on my heart as "Marian," who is known in the colder atmosphere of society as "Miss Halcombe."

Just Heaven! with what inconceivable rapidity I learnt to adore that woman. At sixty, I worshipped her with the volcanic ardour of eighteen. All the gold of my rich nature was poured hopelessly at her feet. My wife—poor angel!—my wife, who adores me, got nothing but the shillings and the pennies. Such is the World, such Man, such Love. What are we (I ask) but puppets in a show-box? Oh, omnipotent Destiny, pull our strings gently! Dance us mercifully off our miserable little stage!

The preceding lines, rightly understood, express an entire system of philosophy. It is mine.

I resume.

The domestic position at the commencement of our residence at Blackwater Park has been drawn with amazing accuracy, with profound mental insight, by the hand of Marian herself. (Pass me the intoxicating familiarity of mentioning this sublime creature by her Christian name.) Accurate knowledge of the contents of her journal—to which I obtained access by clandestine means, unspeakably precious to me in the remembrance—warns my eager pen from topics which this essentially exhaustive woman has already made her own.

The interests—interests, breathless and immense!—with which I am here concerned, begin with the deplorable calamity of Marian's illness.

The situation at this period was emphatically a serious one. Large sums of money, due at a certain time, were wanted by Percival (I say nothing of the modicum equally necessary to myself), and the one source to look to for supplying them was the fortune of his wife, of which not one farthing was at his disposal until her death. Bad so far, and worse still farther on. My lamented friend had private troubles of his own, into which the delicacy of my disinterested attachment to him forbade me from inquiring too curiously. I knew nothing but that a woman, named Anne Catherick, was hidden in the neighbourhood, that she was in communication with Lady Glyde, and that the disclosure of a secret, which would be the certain ruin of Percival, might be the result. He had told me himself that he was a lost man, unless his wife was silenced, and unless Anne Catherick was found. If he was a lost man, what would become of our pecuniary interests? Courageous as I am by nature, I absolutely trembled at the idea!

The whole force of my intelligence was now directed to the finding of Anne Catherick. Our money affairs, important as they were, admitted of delay—but the necessity of discovering the woman admitted of none. I only knew her by description, as presenting an extraordinary personal resemblance to Lady Glyde. The statement of this curious fact—intended merely to assist me in identifying the person of whom we were in search—when coupled with the additional information that Anne Catherick had escaped from a mad-house, started the first immense conception in my mind, which subsequently led to such amazing results. That conception involved nothing less than the complete transformation of two separate identities. Lady Glyde and Anne Catherick were to change names, places, and destinies, the one with the other—the prodigious consequences contemplated by the change being the gain of thirty thousand pounds, and the eternal preservation of Sir Percival's secret.

My instincts (which seldom err) suggested to me, on reviewing the circumstances, that our invisible Anne would, sooner or later, return to the boat-house at the Blackwater lake. There I posted myself, previously mentioning to Mrs. Michelson, the housekeeper, that I might be found when wanted, immersed in study, in that solitary place. It is my rule never to make unnecessary mysteries, and never to set people suspecting me for want of a little seasonable candour on my part. Mrs. Michelson believed in me from first to last. This ladylike person (widow of a Protestant priest) overflowed with faith. Touched by such superfluity of simple confidence in a woman of her mature years, I opened the ample reservoirs of my nature and absorbed it all.

I was rewarded for posting myself sentinel at the lake by the appearance—not of Anne Catherick herself, but of the person in charge of her. This individual also overflowed with simple faith, which I absorbed in myself, as in the case already mentioned. I leave her to describe the circumstances (if she has not done so already) under which she introduced me to the object of her maternal care. When I first saw Anne Catherick she was asleep. I was electrified by the likeness between this unhappy woman and Lady Glyde. The details of the grand scheme which had suggested themselves in outline only, up to that period, occurred to me, in all their masterly combination, at the sight of the sleeping face. At the same time, my heart, always accessible to tender influences, dissolved in tears at the spectacle of suffering before me. I instantly set myself to impart relief. In other words, I provided the necessary stimulant for strengthening Anne Catherick to perform the journey to London.

The best years of my life have been passed in the ardent study of medical and chemical science. Chemistry especially has always had irresistible attractions for me from the enormous, the illimitable power which the knowledge of it confers. Chemists — I assert it emphatically — might sway, if they pleased, the destinies of humanity. Let me explain this before I go further.

Mind, they say, rules the world. But what rules the mind? The body (follow me closely here) lies at the mercy of the most omnipotent of all potentates — the Chemist. Give me — Fosco — chemistry; and when Shakespeare has conceived Hamlet, and sits down to execute the conception — with a few grains of powder dropped into his daily food, I will reduce his mind, by the action of his body, till his pen pours out the most abject drivel that has ever degraded paper. Under similar circumstances, revive me the illustrious Newton. I guarantee that when he sees the apple fall he shall eat it, instead of discovering the principle of gravitation. Nero's dinner shall transform Nero into the mildest of men before he has done digesting it, and the morning draught of Alexander the Great shall make Alexander run for his life at the first sight of the enemy the same afternoon. On my sacred word of honour it is lucky for Society that modern chemists are, by incomprehensible good fortune, the most harmless of mankind. The mass are worthy fathers of families, who keep shops. The few are philosophers besotted with admiration for the sound of their own lecturing voices, visionaries who waste their lives on fantastic impossibilities, or quacks whose ambition soars no higher than our corns. Thus Society escapes, and the illimitable power of Chemistry remains the slave of the most superficial and the most insignificant ends.

Why this outburst? Why this withering eloquence?

Because my conduct has been misrepresented, because my motives have been misunderstood. It has been assumed that I used my vast chemical resources against Anne Catherick, and that I would have used them if I could against the magnificent Marian herself. Odious insinuations both! All my interests were concerned (as will be seen presently) in the preservation of Anne Catherick's life. All my anxieties were concentrated on

Marian's rescue from the hands of the licensed imbecile who attended her, and who found my advice confirmed from first to last by the physician from London. On two occasions only—both equally harmless to the individual on whom I practised—did I summon to myself the assistance of chemical knowledge. On the first of the two, after following Marian to the inn at Blackwater (studying, behind a convenient waggon which hid me from her, the poetry of motion, as embodied in her walk), I availed myself of the services of my invaluable wife, to copy one and to intercept the other of two letters which my adored enemy had entrusted to a discarded maid. In this case, the letters being in the bosom of the girl's dress, Madame Fosco could only open them, read them, perform her instructions, seal them, and put them back again by scientific assistance—which assistance I rendered in a half-ounce bottle. The second occasion, when the same means were employed, was the occasion (to which I shall soon refer) of Lady Glyde's arrival in London. Never at any other time was I indebted to my Art as distinguished from myself. To all other emergencies and complications my natural capacity for grappling, single-handed, with circumstances, was invariably equal. I affirm the all-pervading intelligence of that capacity. At the expense of the Chemist I vindicate the Man.

Respect this outburst of generous indignation. It has inexpressibly relieved me. En route! Let us proceed.

Having suggested to Mrs. Clement (or Clements, I am not sure which) that the best method of keeping Anne out of Percival's reach was to remove her to London—having found that my proposal was eagerly received, and having appointed a day to meet the travellers at the station and to see them leave it, I was at liberty to return to the house and to confront the difficulties which still remained to be met.

My first proceeding was to avail myself of the sublime devotion of my wife. I had arranged with Mrs. Clements that she should communicate her London address, in Anne's interests, to Lady Glyde. But this was not enough. Designing persons in my absence might shake the simple confidence of Mrs. Clements, and she might not write after all. Who could I find capable of travelling to London by the train she travelled by, and of privately seeing her home? I asked myself this question. The conjugal part of me immediately answered—Madame Fosco.

After deciding on my wife's mission to London, I arranged that the journey should serve a double purpose. A nurse for the suffering Marian, equally devoted to the patient and to myself, was a necessity of my position. One of the most eminently confidential and capable women in existence was by good fortune at my disposal. I refer to that respectable matron, Madame Rubelle, to whom I addressed a letter, at her residence in London, by the hands of my wife.

On the appointed day Mrs. Clements and Anne Catherick met me at the station. I politely saw them off, I politely saw Madame Fosco off by the same train. The last thing at night my wife returned to Blackwater, having followed her instructions with the most unimpeachable accuracy. She was accompanied by Madame Rubelle, and she brought me the London address of Mrs. Clements. After-events proved this last precaution to have been unnecessary. Mrs. Clements punctually informed Lady Glyde of her place of abode. With a wary eye on future emergencies, I kept the letter.

The same day I had a brief interview with the doctor, at which I protested, in the sacred interests of humanity, against his treatment of Marian's case. He was insolent, as all ignorant people are. I showed no resentment, I deferred quarrelling with him till it was necessary to quarrel to some purpose. My next proceeding was to leave Blackwater myself. I had my London residence to take in anticipation of coming events. I had also a little business of the domestic sort to transact with Mr. Frederick Fairlie. I found the house I wanted in St. John's Wood. I found Mr. Fairlie at Limmeridge, Cumberland.

My own private familiarity with the nature of Marian's correspondence had previously informed me that she had written to Mr. Fairlie, proposing, as a relief to Lady Glyde's matrimonial embarrassments, to take her on a visit to her uncle in Cumberland. This letter I had wisely allowed to reach its destination, feeling at the time that it could do no harm, and might do good. I now presented myself before Mr. Fairlie to support Marian's own proposal — with certain modifications which, happily for the success of my plans, were rendered really inevitable by her illness. It was necessary that Lady Glyde should leave Blackwater alone, by her uncle's invitation, and that she should rest a night on the journey at her aunt's house (the house I had in St. John's Wood) by her uncle's express advice. To achieve these results, and to secure a note of invitation which could be shown to Lady Glyde, were the objects of my visit to Mr. Fairlie. When I have mentioned that this gentleman was equally feeble in mind and body, and that I let loose the whole force of my character on him, I have said enough. I came, saw, and conquered Fairlie.

On my return to Blackwater Park (with the letter of invitation) I found that the doctor's imbecile treatment of Marian's case had led to the most alarming results. The fever had turned to typhus. Lady Glyde, on the day of my return, tried to force herself into the room to nurse her sister. She and I had no affinities of sympathy—she had committed the unpardonable outrage on my sensibilities of calling me a spy—she was a stumbling-block in my way and in Percival's—but, for all that, my magnanimity forbade me to put her in danger of infection with my own hand. At the same time I offered no hindrance to her putting herself in danger. If she had succeeded in doing so, the intricate knot which I was slowly and patiently operating on might perhaps have been cut by circumstances. As it was, the doctor interfered and she was kept out of the room.

I had myself previously recommended sending for advice to London. This course had been now taken. The physician, on his arrival, confirmed my view of the case. The crisis was serious. But we had hope of our charming patient on the fifth day from the appearance of the typhus. I was only once absent from Blackwater at this time—when I went to London by the morning train to make the final arrangements at my house in St. John's Wood, to assure myself by private inquiry that Mrs. Clements had not moved, and to settle one or two little preliminary matters with the husband of Madame Rubelle. I returned at night. Five days afterwards the physician pronounced our interesting Marian to be out of all danger, and to be in need of nothing but careful nursing. This was the time I had waited for. Now that medical attendance was no longer indispensable, I played the first move in the game by asserting myself against the doctor. He was one among many witnesses in my way whom it was necessary to remove. A lively altercation between us (in which Percival, previously instructed by me, refused to interfere) served the purpose in view. I descended on the miserable man in an irresistible avalanche of indignation, and swept him from the house.

The servants were the next encumbrances to get rid of. Again I instructed Percival (whose moral courage required perpetual stimulants), and Mrs. Michelson was amazed, one day, by hearing from her master that the establishment was to be broken up. We cleared the house of all the servants but one, who was kept for domestic purposes, and whose lumpish stupidity we could trust to make no embarrassing discoveries. When they were gone, nothing remained but to relieve ourselves of Mrs. Michelson—a result which was easily achieved by sending this amiable lady to find lodgings for her mistress at the sea-side.

The circumstances were now exactly what they were required to be. Lady Glyde was confined to her room by nervous illness, and the lumpish housemaid (I forget her name) was shut up there at night in attendance on her mistress. Marian, though fast recovering, still kept her bed, with Mrs. Rubelle for nurse. No other living creatures but my wife, myself, and Percival were in the house. With all the chances thus in our favour I confronted the next emergency, and played the second move in the game.

The object of the second move was to induce Lady Glyde to leave Blackwater unaccompanied by her sister. Unless we could persuade her that Marian had gone on to Cumberland first, there was no chance of removing her, of her own free will, from the house. To produce this necessary operation in her mind, we concealed our interesting invalid in one of the uninhabited bedrooms at Blackwater. At the dead of night Madame Fosco, Madame Rubelle, and myself (Percival not being cool enough to be trusted) accomplished the concealment. The scene was picturesque, mysterious, dramatic in the highest degree. By my directions the bed had been made, in the morning, on a strong movable framework of wood. We had only to lift the framework gently at the head and foot, and to transport our patient where we pleased, without disturbing herself or her bed. No chemical assistance was needed or used in this case. Our interesting Marian lay in the deep repose of convalescence. We placed the candles and opened the doors beforehand. I, in right of my great personal strength, took the head of the framework—my wife and Madame Rubelle took the foot. I bore my share of that inestimably precious burden with a manly tenderness, with a fatherly care. Where is the modern Rembrandt who could depict our midnight procession? Alas for the Arts! alas for this most pictorial of subjects! The modern Rembrandt is nowhere to be found.

The next morning my wife and I started for London, leaving Marian secluded, in the uninhabited middle of the house, under care of Madame Rubelle, who kindly consented to imprison herself with her patient for two or three days. Before taking our departure I gave Percival Mr. Fairlie's letter of invitation to his niece (instructing her to sleep on the journey to Cumberland at her aunt's house), with directions to show it to Lady Glyde on hearing from me. I also obtained from him the address of the Asylum in which Anne Catherick had been confined, and a letter to the proprietor, announcing to that gentleman the return of his runaway patient to medical care.

I had arranged, at my last visit to the metropolis, to have our modest domestic establishment ready to receive us when we arrived in London by the early train. In consequence of this wise precaution, we were enabled that same day to play the third move in the game—the getting possession of Anne Catherick.

Dates are of importance here. I combine in myself the opposite characteristics of a Man of Sentiment and a Man of Business. I have all the dates at my fingers' ends.

On Wednesday, the 24th of July 1850, I sent my wife in a cab to clear Mrs. Clements out of the way, in the first place. A supposed message from Lady Glyde in London was sufficient to obtain this result. Mrs. Clements was taken away in the cab, and was left in the cab, while my wife (on pretence of purchasing something at a shop) gave her the slip, and returned to receive her expected visitor at our house in St. John's Wood. It is hardly necessary to add that the visitor had been described to the servants as "Lady Glyde."

In the meanwhile I had followed in another cab, with a note for Anne Catherick, merely mentioning that Lady Glyde intended to keep Mrs. Clements to spend the day with her, and that she was to join them under care of the good gentleman waiting outside, who had already saved her from discovery in Hampshire by Sir Percival. The "good gentleman" sent in this note by a street boy, and paused for results a door or two farther on. At the moment when Anne appeared at the house door and closed it this excellent man had the cab door open ready for her, absorbed her into the vehicle, and drove off.

(Pass me, here, one exclamation in parenthesis. How interesting this is!)

On the way to Forest Road my companion showed no fear. I can be paternal—no man more so—when I please, and I was intensely paternal on this occasion. What titles I had to her confidence! I had compounded the medicine which had done her good—I had warned her of her danger from Sir Percival. Perhaps I trusted too implicitly to these titles—perhaps I underrated the keenness of the lower instincts in persons of weak intellect—it is certain that I neglected to prepare her sufficiently for a disappointment on entering my house. When I took her into the drawing-room—when she saw no one present but Madame Fosco, who was a stranger to her—she exhibited the most violent agitation; if she had scented danger in the air, as a dog scents the presence of some creature unseen, her alarm could not have displayed itself more suddenly and more causelessly. I interposed in vain. The fear from which she was suffering I might have soothed, but the serious heart-disease, under which she laboured, was beyond the reach of all moral palliatives. To my unspeakable horror she was seized with convulsions—a shock to the system, in her condition, which might have laid her dead at any moment at our feet.

The nearest doctor was sent for, and was told that "Lady Glyde" required his immediate services. To my infinite relief, he was a capable man. I represented my visitor to him as a person of weak intellect, and subject to delusions, and I arranged that no nurse but my wife should watch in the sick-room. The unhappy woman was too ill, however, to cause any anxiety about what she might say. The one dread which now oppressed me was the dread that the false Lady Glyde might die before the true Lady Glyde arrived in London.

I had written a note in the morning to Madame Rubelle, telling her to join me at her husband's house on the evening of Friday the 26th, with another note to Percival, warning him to show his wife her uncle's letter of invitation, to assert that Marian had gone on before her, and to despatch her to town by the midday train, on the 26th, also. On reflection I had felt the necessity, in Anne Catherick's state of health, of precipitating events, and of having Lady Glyde at my disposal earlier than I had originally contemplated. What fresh directions, in the terrible uncertainty of my position, could I now issue? I could do nothing but trust to chance and the doctor. My emotions expressed themselves in pathetic apostrophes, which I was just self-possessed enough to couple, in the hearing of other people, with the name of "Lady Glyde." In all other respects Fosco, on that memorable day, was Fosco shrouded in total eclipse.

She passed a bad night, she awoke worn out, but later in the day she revived amazingly. My elastic spirits revived with her. I could receive no answers from Percival and Madame Rubelle till the morning of the next day, the 26th. In anticipation of their following my directions, which, accident apart, I knew they would do, I went to secure a fly to fetch Lady Glyde from the railway, directing it to be at my house on the 26th, at two o'clock. After seeing the order entered in the book, I went on to arrange matters with Monsieur Rubelle. I also procured the services of two gentlemen who could furnish me with the necessary certificates of lunacy. One of them I knew personally—the other was known to Monsieur Rubelle. Both were men whose vigorous minds soared superior to narrow scruples—both were labouring under temporary embarrassments—both believed in ME.

It was past five o'clock in the afternoon before I returned from the performance of these duties. When I got back Anne Catherick was dead. Dead on the 25th, and Lady Glyde was not to arrive in London till the 26th!

I was stunned. Meditate on that. Fosco stunned!

It was too late to retrace our steps. Before my return the doctor had officiously undertaken to save me all trouble by registering the death, on the date when it happened, with his own hand. My grand scheme, unassailable hitherto, had its weak place now—no efforts on my part could alter the fatal event of the 25th. I turned manfully to the future. Percival's interests and mine being still at stake, nothing was left but to play the game through to the end. I recalled my impenetrable calm—and played it.

On the morning of the 26th Percival's letter reached me, announcing his wife's arrival by the midday train. Madame Rubelle also wrote to say she would follow in the evening. I started in the fly, leaving the false Lady Glyde dead in the house, to receive the true Lady Glyde on her arrival by the railway at three o'clock. Hidden under the seat of the carriage, I carried with me all the clothes Anne Catherick had worn on coming into my house—they were destined to assist the resurrection of the woman who was dead in the person of the woman who was living. What a situation! I suggest it to the rising romance writers of England. I offer it, as totally new, to the worn-out dramatists of France.

Lady Glyde was at the station. There was great crowding and confusion, and more delay than I liked (in case any of her friends had happened to be on the spot), in reclaiming her luggage. Her first questions, as we drove off, implored me to tell her news of her sister. I invented news of the most pacifying kind, assuring her that she was about to see her sister at my house. My house, on this occasion only, was in the neighbourhood of Leicester Square, and was in the occupation of Monsieur Rubelle, who received us in the hall.

I took my visitor upstairs into a back room, the two medical gentlemen being there in waiting on the floor beneath to see the patient, and to give me their certificates. After quieting Lady Glyde by the necessary assurances about her sister, I introduced my friends separately to her presence. They performed the formalities of the occasion briefly, intelligently, conscientiously. I entered the room again as soon as they had left it, and at once precipitated events by a reference of the alarming kind to "Miss Halcombe's" state of health.

Results followed as I had anticipated. Lady Glyde became frightened, and turned faint. For the second time, and the last, I called Science to my assistance. A medicated glass of water and a medicated bottle of smelling-salts relieved her of all further embarrassment and alarm. Additional applications later in the evening procured her the inestimable blessing of a good night's rest. Madame Rubelle arrived in time to preside at Lady Glyde's toilet. Her own clothes were taken away from her at night, and Anne Catherick's were put on her in the morning, with the strictest regard to propriety, by the matronly hands of the good Rubelle. Throughout the day I kept our patient in a state of partially-suspended consciousness, until the dexterous assistance of my medical friends enabled me to procure the necessary order rather earlier than I had ventured to hope. That evening (the evening of the 27th) Madame Rubelle and I took our revived "Anne Catherick" to the Asylum. She was received with great surprise, but without suspicion, thanks to the order and certificates, to Percival's letter, to the likeness, to the clothes, and to the patient's own confused mental condition at the time. I returned at once to assist Madame Fosco in the preparations for the burial of the False "Lady Glyde," having the clothes and luggage of the true "Lady Glyde" in my possession. They were afterwards sent to Cumberland by the conveyance which was used for the funeral. I attended the funeral, with becoming dignity, attired in the deepest mourning.

My narrative of these remarkable events, written under equally remarkable circumstances, closes here. The minor precautions which I observed in communicating with Limmeridge House are already known—so is the magnificent success of my enterprise—so are the solid pecuniary results which followed it. I have to assert, with the whole force of my conviction, that the one weak place in my scheme would never have been found out if the one weak place in my heart had not been discovered first. Nothing but my fatal admiration for Marian restrained me from stepping in to my own rescue when she effected her sister's escape. I ran the risk, and trusted in the complete destruction of Lady Glyde's identity. If either Marian or Mr. Hartright attempted to assert that identity, they would publicly expose themselves to the imputation of sustaining a rank deception, they would be distrusted and discredited accordingly, and they would therefore be powerless to place my interests or Percival's secret in jeopardy. I committed one error in trusting myself to such a blindfold calculation of chances as this. I committed another when Percival had paid the penalty of his own obstinacy and violence, by granting Lady Glyde a second reprieve from the mad-house, and allowing Mr. Hartright a second chance of escaping me. In brief, Fosco, at this serious crisis, was untrue to himself. Deplorable and uncharacteristic fault! Behold the cause, in my heart—behold, in the image of Marian Halcombe, the first and last weakness of Fosco's life!

At the ripe age of sixty, I make this unparalleled confession. Youths! I invoke your sympathy. Maidens! I claim your tears.

A word more, and the attention of the reader (concentrated breathlessly on myself) shall be released.

My own mental insight informs me that three inevitable questions will be asked here by persons of inquiring minds. They shall be stated—they shall be answered.

First question. What is the secret of Madame Fosco's unhesitating devotion of herself to the fulfilment of my boldest wishes, to the furtherance of my deepest plans? I might answer this by simply referring to my own character, and by asking, in my turn, Where, in the history of the world, has a man of my order ever been found without a woman in the background self-immolated on the altar of his life? But I remember that I am writing in England, I remember that I was married in England, and I ask if a woman's marriage obligations in this country provide for her private opinion of her husband's principles? No! They charge her unreservedly to love, honour, and obey him. That is exactly what my wife has done. I stand here on a supreme moral elevation, and I loftily assert her accurate performance of her conjugal duties. Silence, Calumny! Your sympathy, Wives of England, for Madame Fosco!

Second question. If Anne Catherick had not died when she did, what should I have done? I should, in that case, have assisted worn-out Nature in finding permanent repose. I should have opened the doors of the Prison of Life, and have extended to the captive (incurably afflicted in mind and body both) a happy release.

Third question. On a calm revision of all the circumstances—Is my conduct worthy of any serious blame? Most emphatically,

The Woman in White

No! Have I not carefully avoided exposing myself to the odium of committing unnecessary crime? With my vast resources in chemistry, I might have taken Lady Glyde's life. At immense personal sacrifice I followed the dictates of my own ingenuity, my own humanity, my own caution, and took her identity instead. Judge me by what I might have done. How comparatively innocent! how indirectly virtuous I appear in what I really did!

I announced on beginning it that this narrative would be a remarkable document. It has entirely answered my expectations. Receive these fervid lines — my last legacy to the country I leave for ever. They are worthy of the occasion, and worthy of

FOSCO.

THE STORY CONCLUDED
BY WALTER HARTRIGHT

I

When I closed the last leaf of the Count's manuscript the half-hour during which I had engaged to remain at Forest Road had expired. Monsieur Rubelle looked at his watch and bowed. I rose immediately, and left the agent in possession of the empty house. I never saw him again—I never heard more of him or of his wife. Out of the dark byways of villainy and deceit they had crawled across our path—into the same byways they crawled back secretly and were lost.

In a quarter of an hour after leaving Forest Road I was at home again.

But few words sufficed to tell Laura and Marian how my desperate venture had ended, and what the next event in our lives was likely to be. I left all details to be described later in the day, and hastened back to St. John's Wood, to see the person of whom Count Fosco had ordered the fly, when he went to meet Laura at the station.

The address in my possession led me to some "livery stables," about a quarter of a mile distant from Forest Road. The proprietor proved to be a civil and respectable man. When I explained that an important family matter obliged me to ask him to refer to his books for the purpose of ascertaining a date with which the record of his business transactions might supply me, he offered no objection to granting my request. The book was produced, and there, under the date of "July 26th, 1850," the order was entered in these words—

"Brougham to Count Fosco, 5 Forest Road. Two o'clock. (John Owen)."

I found on inquiry that the name of "John Owen," attached to the entry, referred to the man who had been employed to drive the fly. He was then at work in the stable-yard, and was sent for to see me at my request.

"Do you remember driving a gentleman, in the month of July last, from Number Five Forest Road to the Waterloo Bridge station?" I asked.

"Well, sir," said the man, "I can't exactly say I do."

"Perhaps you remember the gentleman himself? Can you call to mind driving a foreigner last summer—a tall gentleman and remarkably fat?"

The man's face brightened directly. "I remember him, sir! The fattest gentleman as ever I see, and the heaviest customer as ever I drove. Yes, yes—I call him to mind, sir! We did go to the station, and it was from Forest Road. There was a parrot, or summat like it, screeching in the window. The gentleman was in a mortal hurry about the lady's luggage, and he gave me a handsome present for looking sharp and getting the boxes."

Getting the boxes! I recollected immediately that Laura's own account of herself on her arrival in London described her luggage as being collected for her by some person whom Count Fosco brought with him to the station. This was the man.

"Did you see the lady?" I asked. "What did she look like? Was she young or old?"

"Well, sir, what with the hurry and the crowd of people pushing about, I can't rightly say what the lady looked like. I can't call nothing to mind about her that I know of excepting her name."

"You remember her name?"

"Yes, sir. Her name was Lady Glyde."

"How do you come to remember that, when you have forgotten what she looked like?"

The man smiled, and shifted his feet in some little embarrassment.

"Why, to tell you the truth, sir," he said, "I hadn't been long married at that time, and my wife's name, before she changed it for mine, was the same as the lady's—meaning the name of Glyde, sir. The lady mentioned it herself. 'Is your name on your boxes, ma'am?' says I. 'Yes,' says she, 'my name is on my luggage—it is Lady Glyde.' 'Come!' I says to myself, 'I've a bad head for gentlefolks' names in general—but this one comes like an old friend, at any rate.' I can't say nothing about the time, sir, it might be nigh on a year ago, or it mightn't. But I can swear to the stout gentleman, and swear to the lady's name."

There was no need that he should remember the time—the date was positively established by his master's order-book. I felt at once that the means were now in my power of striking down the whole conspiracy at a blow with the irresistible weapon of plain fact. Without a moment's hesitation, I took the proprietor of the livery stables aside and told him what the real importance was of the evidence of his order-book and the evidence of his driver. An arrangement to compensate him for the temporary loss of the man's services was easily made, and a copy of the entry in the book was taken by myself, and certified as true by the master's own signature. I left the livery stables, having settled that John Owen was to hold himself at my disposal for the next three days, or for a longer period if necessity required it.

I now had in my possession all the papers that I wanted—the district registrar's own copy of the certificate of death, and Sir Percival's dated letter to the Count, being safe in my pocket-book.

With this written evidence about me, and with the coachman's answers fresh in my memory, I next turned my steps, for the first time since the beginning of all my inquiries, in the direction of Mr. Kyrle's office. One of my objects in paying him this second visit was, necessarily, to tell him what I had done. The other was to warn him of my resolution to take my wife to Limmeridge the next morning, and to have her publicly received and recognised in her uncle's house. I left it to Mr. Kyrle to decide under these circumstances, and in Mr. Gilmore's absence, whether he was or was not bound, as the family solicitor, to be present on that occasion in the family interests.

I will say nothing of Mr. Kyrle's amazement, or of the terms in which he expressed his opinion of my conduct from the first stage of the investigation to the last. It is only necessary to mention that he at once decided on accompanying us to Cumberland.

We started the next morning by the early train. Laura, Marian, Mr. Kyrle, and myself in one carriage, and John Owen, with a clerk from Mr. Kyrle's office, occupying places in another. On reaching the Limmeridge station we went first to the farmhouse at Todd's Corner. It was my firm determination that Laura should not enter her uncle's house till she appeared there publicly recognised as his niece. I left Marian to settle the question of accommodation with Mrs. Todd, as soon as the good woman had recovered from the bewilderment of hearing what our errand was in Cumberland, and I arranged with her husband that John Owen was to be committed to the ready hospitality of the farm-servants. These preliminaries completed, Mr. Kyrle and I set forth together for Limmeridge House.

I cannot write at any length of our interview with Mr. Fairlie, for I cannot recall it to mind without feelings of impatience and contempt, which make the scene, even in remembrance only, utterly repulsive to me. I prefer to record simply that I carried my point. Mr. Fairlie attempted to treat us on his customary plan. We passed without notice his polite insolence at the outset of the interview. We heard without sympathy the protestations with which he tried next to persuade us that the disclosure of the conspiracy had overwhelmed him. He absolutely whined and whimpered at last like a fretful child. "How was he to know that his niece was alive when he was told that she was dead? He would welcome dear Laura with pleasure, if we would only allow him time to recover. Did we think he looked as if he wanted hurrying into his grave? No. Then, why hurry him?" He reiterated these remonstrances at every available opportunity, until I checked them once for all, by placing him firmly between two inevitable alternatives. I gave him his choice between doing his niece justice on my terms, or facing the consequence of a public assertion of her existence in a court of law. Mr. Kyrle, to whom he turned for help, told him plainly that he must decide the question then and there. Characteristically choosing the alternative which promised soonest to release him from all personal anxiety, he announced with a sudden outburst of energy, that he was not strong enough to bear any more bullying, and that we might do as we pleased.

Mr. Kyrle and I at once went downstairs, and agreed upon a form of letter which was to be sent round to the tenants who had attended the false funeral, summoning them, in Mr. Fairlie's name, to assemble in Limmeridge House on the next day but one. An order referring to the same date was also written, directing a statuary in Carlisle to send a man to Limmeridge churchyard for the purpose of erasing an inscription—Mr. Kyrle, who had arranged to sleep in the house, undertaking that Mr. Fairlie should hear these letters read to him, and should sign them with his own hand.

I occupied the interval day at the farm in writing a plain narrative of the conspiracy, and in adding to it a statement of the practical contradiction which facts offered to the assertion of Laura's death. This I submitted to Mr. Kyrle before I read it the next day to the assembled tenants. We also arranged the form in which the evidence should be presented at the close of the reading. After these matters were settled, Mr. Kyrle endeavoured to turn the conversation next to Laura's affairs. Knowing, and desiring to know nothing of those affairs, and doubting whether he would approve, as a man of business, of my conduct in relation to my wife's life-interest in the legacy left to Madame Fosco, I begged Mr. Kyrle to excuse me if I abstained from discussing the subject. It was connected, as I could truly tell him, with those sorrows and troubles of the past which we never referred to among ourselves, and which we instinctively shrank from discussing with others.

My last labour, as the evening approached, was to obtain "The Narrative of the Tombstone," by taking a copy of the false inscription on the grave before it was erased.

The day came — the day when Laura once more entered the familiar breakfast-room at Limmeridge House. All the persons assembled rose from their seats as Marian and I led her in. A perceptible shock of surprise, an audible murmur of interest ran through them, at the sight of her face. Mr. Fairlie was present (by my express stipulation), with Mr. Kyrle by his side. His valet stood behind him with a smelling-bottle ready in one hand, and a white handkerchief, saturated with eau-de-Cologne, in the other.

I opened the proceedings by publicly appealing to Mr. Fairlie to say whether I appeared there with his authority and under his express sanction. He extended an arm, on either side, to Mr. Kyrle and to his valet — was by them assisted to stand on his legs, and then expressed himself in these terms: "Allow me to present Mr. Hartright. I am as great an invalid as ever, and he is so very obliging as to speak for me. The subject is dreadfully embarrassing. Please hear him, and don't make a noise!" With those words he slowly sank back again into the chair, and took refuge in his scented pocket-handkerchief.

The disclosure of the conspiracy followed, after I had offered my preliminary explanation, first of all, in the fewest and the plainest words. I was there present (I informed my hearers) to declare, first, that my wife, then sitting by me, was the daughter of the late Mr. Philip Fairlie; secondly, to prove by positive facts, that the funeral which they had attended in Limmeridge churchyard was the funeral of another woman; thirdly, to give them a plain account of how it had all happened. Without further preface, I at once read the narrative of the conspiracy, describing it in clear outline, and dwelling only upon the pecuniary motive for it, in order to avoid complicating my statement by unnecessary reference to Sir Percival's secret. This done, I reminded my audience of the date on the inscription in the churchyard (the 25th), and confirmed its correctness by producing the certificate of death. I then read them Sir Percival's letter of the 25th, announcing his wife's intended journey from Hampshire to London on the 26th. I next showed that she had taken that journey, by the personal testimony of the driver of the fly, and I proved that she had performed it on the appointed day, by the order-book at the livery stables. Marian then added her own statement of the meeting between Laura and herself at the mad-house, and of her sister's escape. After which I closed the proceedings by informing the persons present of Sir Percival's death and of my marriage.

Mr. Kyrle rose when I resumed my seat, and declared, as the legal adviser of the family, that my case was proved by the plainest evidence he had ever heard in his life. As he spoke those words, I put my arm round Laura, and raised her so that she was plainly visible to every one in the room. "Are you all of the same opinion?" I asked, advancing towards them a few steps, and pointing to my wife.

The effect of the question was electrical. Far down at the lower end of the room one of the oldest tenants on the estate started to his feet, and led the rest with him in an instant. I see the man now, with his honest brown face and his iron-grey hair, mounted on the window-seat, waving his heavy riding-whip over his head, and leading the cheers. "There she is, alive and hearty—God bless her! Gi' it tongue, lads! Gi' it tongue!" The shout that answered him, reiterated again and again, was the sweetest music I ever heard. The labourers in the village and the boys from the school, assembled on the lawn, caught up the cheering and echoed it back on us. The farmers' wives clustered round Laura, and struggled which should be first to shake hands with her, and to implore her, with the tears pouring over their own cheeks, to bear up bravely and not to cry. She was so completely overwhelmed, that I was obliged to take her from them, and carry her to the door. There I gave her into Marian's care—Marian, who had never failed us yet, whose courageous self-control did not fail us now. Left by myself at the door, I invited all the persons present (after thanking them in Laura's name and mine) to follow me to the churchyard, and see the false inscription struck off the tombstone with their own eyes.

They all left the house, and all joined the throng of villagers collected round the grave, where the statuary's man was waiting for us. In a breathless silence, the first sharp stroke of the steel sounded on the marble. Not a voice was heard—not a soul moved, till those three words, "Laura, Lady Glyde," had vanished from sight. Then there was a great heave of relief among the crowd, as if they felt that the last fetters of the conspiracy had been struck off Laura herself, and the assembly slowly withdrew. It was late in the day before the whole inscription was erased. One line only was afterwards engraved in its place: "Anne Catherick, July 25th, 1850."

I returned to Limmeridge House early enough in the evening to take leave of Mr. Kyrle. He and his clerk, and the driver of the fly, went back to London by the night train. On their departure an insolent message was delivered to me from Mr. Fairlie—who had been carried from the room in a shattered condition, when the first outbreak of cheering answered my appeal to the tenantry. The message conveyed to us "Mr. Fairlie's best congratulations," and requested to know whether "we contemplated stopping in the house." I sent back word that the only object for which we had entered his doors was accomplished—that I contemplated stopping in no man's house but my own—and that Mr. Fairlie need not entertain the slightest apprehension of ever seeing us or hearing from us again. We went back to our friends at the farm to rest that night, and the next morning—escorted to the station, with the heartiest enthusiasm and good will, by the whole village and by all the farmers in the neighbourhood—we returned to London.

As our view of the Cumberland hills faded in the distance, I thought of the first disheartening circumstances under which the long struggle that was now past and over had been pursued. It was strange to look back and to see, now, that the poverty which had denied us all hope of assistance had been the indirect means of our success, by forcing me to act for myself. If we had been rich enough to find legal help, what would have been the result? The gain (on Mr. Kyrle's own showing) would have been more than doubtful—the loss, judging by the plain test of events as they had really happened, certain. The law would never have obtained me my interview with Mrs. Catherick. The law would never have made Pesca the means of forcing a confession from the Count.

II

Two more events remain to be added to the chain before it reaches fairly from the outset of the story to the close.

While our new sense of freedom from the long oppression of the past was still strange to us, I was sent for by the friend who had given me my first employment in wood engraving, to receive from him a fresh testimony of his regard for my welfare. He had been commissioned by his employers to go to Paris, and to examine for them a fresh discovery in the practical application of his Art, the merits of which they were anxious to ascertain. His own engagements had not allowed him leisure time to undertake the errand, and he had most kindly suggested that it should be transferred to me. I could have no hesitation in thankfully accepting the offer, for if I acquitted myself of my commission as I hoped I should, the result would be a permanent engagement on the illustrated newspaper, to which I was now only occasionally attached.

I received my instructions and packed up for the journey the next day. On leaving Laura once more (under what changed circumstances!) in her sister's care, a serious consideration recurred to me, which had more than once crossed my wife's mind, as well as my own, already—I mean the consideration of Marian's future. Had we any right to let our selfish affection accept the devotion of all that generous life? Was it not our duty, our best expression of gratitude, to forget ourselves, and to think only of her? I tried to say this when we were alone for a moment, before I went away. She took my hand, and silenced me at the first words.

"After all that we three have suffered together," she said, "there can be no parting between us till the last parting of all. My heart and my happiness, Walter, are with Laura and you. Wait a little till there are children's voices at your fireside. I will teach them to speak for me in their language, and the first lesson they say to their father and mother shall be—We can't spare our aunt!"

My journey to Paris was not undertaken alone. At the eleventh hour Pesca decided that he would accompany me. He had not recovered his customary cheerfulness since the night at the Opera, and he determined to try what a week's holiday would do to raise his spirits.

I performed the errand entrusted to me, and drew out the necessary report, on the fourth day from our arrival in Paris.

The fifth day I arranged to devote to sight-seeing and amusements in Pesca's company.

Our hotel had been too full to accommodate us both on the same floor. My room was on the second story, and Pesca's was above me, on the third. On the morning of the fifth day I went upstairs to see if the Professor was ready to go out. Just before I reached the landing I saw his door opened from the inside — a long, delicate, nervous hand (not my friend's hand certainly) held it ajar. At the same time I heard Pesca's voice saying eagerly, in low tones, and in his own language — "I remember the name, but I don't know the man. You saw at the Opera he was so changed that I could not recognise him. I will forward the report — I can do no more." "No more need be done," answered the second voice. The door opened wide, and the light-haired man with the scar on his cheek — the man I had seen following Count Fosco's cab a week before — came out. He bowed as I drew aside to let him pass — his face was fearfully pale — and he held fast by the banisters as he descended the stairs.

I pushed open the door and entered Pesca's room. He was crouched up, in the strangest manner, in a corner of the sofa. He seemed to shrink from me when I approached him.

"Am I disturbing you?" I asked. "I did not know you had a friend with you till I saw him come out."

"No friend," said Pesca eagerly. "I see him to-day for the first time and the last."

"I am afraid he has brought you bad news?"

"Horrible news, Walter! Let us go back to London — I don't want to stop here — I am sorry I ever came. The misfortunes of my youth are very hard upon me," he said, turning his face to the wall, "very hard upon me in my later time. I try to forget them — and they will not forget me!"

"We can't return, I am afraid, before the afternoon," I replied. "Would you like to come out with me in the meantime?"

"No, my friend, I will wait here. But let us go back to-day — pray let us go back."

I left him with the assurance that he should leave Paris that afternoon. We had arranged the evening before to ascend the

The Woman in White

Cathedral of Notre Dame, with Victor Hugo's noble romance for our guide. There was nothing in the French capital that I was more anxious to see, and I departed by myself for the church.

Approaching Notre Dame by the river-side, I passed on my way the terrible dead-house of Paris — the Morgue. A great crowd clamoured and heaved round the door. There was evidently something inside which excited the popular curiosity, and fed the popular appetite for horror.

I should have walked on to the church if the conversation of two men and a woman on the outskirts of the crowd had not caught my ear. They had just come out from seeing the sight in the Morgue, and the account they were giving of the dead body to their neighbours described it as the corpse of a man — a man of immense size, with a strange mark on his left arm.

The moment those words reached me I stopped and took my place with the crowd going in. Some dim foreshadowing of the truth had crossed my mind when I heard Pesca's voice through the open door, and when I saw the stranger's face as he passed me on the stairs of the hotel. Now the truth itself was revealed to me — revealed in the chance words that had just reached my ears. Other vengeance than mine had followed that fated man from the theatre to his own door — from his own door to his refuge in Paris. Other vengeance than mine had called him to the day of reckoning, and had exacted from him the penalty of his life. The moment when I had pointed him out to Pesca at the theatre in the hearing of that stranger by our side, who was looking for him too — was the moment that sealed his doom. I remembered the struggle in my own heart, when he and I stood face to face — the struggle before I could let him escape me — and shuddered as I recalled it.

Slowly, inch by inch, I pressed in with the crowd, moving nearer and nearer to the great glass screen that parts the dead from the living at the Morgue — nearer and nearer, till I was close behind the front row of spectators, and could look in.

There he lay, unowned, unknown, exposed to the flippant curiosity of a French mob! There was the dreadful end of that long life of degraded ability and heartless crime! Hushed in the sublime repose of death, the broad, firm, massive face and head fronted us so grandly that the chattering Frenchwomen about me lifted their hands in admiration, and cried in shrill chorus, "Ah, what a handsome man!" The wound that had killed him had been struck with a knife or dagger exactly over his heart. No other traces of violence appeared about the body except on the left arm, and there, exactly in the place where I had seen the brand on Pesca's arm, were two deep cuts in the shape of the letter T, which entirely obliterated the mark of the Brotherhood. His clothes, hung above him, showed that he had been himself conscious of his danger—they were clothes that had disguised him as a French artisan. For a few moments, but not for longer, I forced myself to see these things through the glass screen. I can write of them at no greater length, for I saw no more.

The few facts in connection with his death which I subsequently ascertained (partly from Pesca and partly from other sources), may be stated here before the subject is dismissed from these pages.

His body was taken out of the Seine in the disguise which I have described, nothing being found on him which revealed his name, his rank, or his place of abode. The hand that struck him was never traced, and the circumstances under which he was killed were never discovered. I leave others to draw their own conclusions in reference to the secret of the assassination as I have drawn mine. When I have intimated that the foreigner with the scar was a member of the Brotherhood (admitted in Italy after Pesca's departure from his native country), and when I have further added that the two cuts, in the form of a T, on the left arm of the dead man, signified the Italian word "Traditore," and showed that justice had been done by the Brotherhood on a traitor, I have contributed all that I know towards elucidating the mystery of Count Fosco's death.

The body was identified the day after I had seen it by means of an anonymous letter addressed to his wife. He was buried by Madame Fosco in the cemetery of Père la Chaise. Fresh funeral wreaths continue to this day to be hung on the ornamental bronze railings round the tomb by the Countess's own hand. She lives in the strictest retirement at Versailles. Not long since she published a biography of her deceased husband. The work throws no light whatever on the name that was really his own or on the secret history of his life—it is almost entirely devoted to the praise of his domestic virtues, the assertion of his rare abilities, and the enumeration of the honours conferred on him. The circumstances attending his death are very briefly noticed, and are summed up on the last page in this sentence—"His life was one long assertion of the rights of the aristocracy and the sacred principles of Order, and he died a martyr to his cause."

III

The summer and autumn passed after my return from Paris, and brought no changes with them which need be noticed here. We lived so simply and quietly that the income which I was now steadily earning sufficed for all our wants.

In the February of the new year our first child was born—a son. My mother and sister and Mrs. Vesey were our guests at the little christening party, and Mrs. Clements was present to assist my wife on the same occasion. Marian was our boy's godmother, and Pesca and Mr. Gilmore (the latter acting by proxy) were his godfathers. I may add here that when Mr. Gilmore returned to us a year later he assisted the design of these pages, at my request, by writing the Narrative which appears early in the story under his name, and which, though first in order of precedence, was thus, in order of time, the last that I received.

The only event in our lives which now remains to be recorded, occurred when our little Walter was six months old.

At that time I was sent to Ireland to make sketches for certain forthcoming illustrations in the newspaper to which I was attached. I was away for nearly a fortnight, corresponding regularly with my wife and Marian, except during the last three days of my absence, when my movements were too uncertain to enable me to receive letters. I performed the latter part of my journey back at night, and when I reached home in the morning, to my utter astonishment there was no one to receive me. Laura and Marian and the child had left the house on the day before my return.

A note from my wife, which was given to me by the servant, only increased my surprise, by informing me that they had gone to Limmeridge House. Marian had prohibited any attempt at written explanations—I was entreated to follow them the moment I came back—complete enlightenment awaited me on my arrival in Cumberland—and I was forbidden to feel the slightest anxiety in the meantime. There the note ended. It was still early enough to catch the morning train. I reached Limmeridge House the same afternoon.

My wife and Marian were both upstairs. They had established themselves (by way of completing my amazement) in the little room which had been once assigned to me for a studio, when I was employed on Mr. Fairlie's drawings. On the very chair which I used to occupy when I was at work Marian was sitting now, with the child industriously sucking his coral upon her lap — while Laura was standing by the well-remembered drawing-table which I had so often used, with the little album that I had filled for her in past times open under her hand.

"What in the name of heaven has brought you here?" I asked. "Does Mr. Fairlie know — — ?"

Marian suspended the question on my lips by telling me that Mr. Fairlie was dead. He had been struck by paralysis, and had never rallied after the shock. Mr. Kyrle had informed them of his death, and had advised them to proceed immediately to Limmeridge House.

Some dim perception of a great change dawned on my mind. Laura spoke before I had quite realised it. She stole close to me to enjoy the surprise which was still expressed in my face.

"My darling Walter," she said, "must we really account for our boldness in coming here? I am afraid, love, I can only explain it by breaking through our rule, and referring to the past."

"There is not the least necessity for doing anything of the kind," said Marian. "We can be just as explicit, and much more interesting, by referring to the future." She rose and held up the child kicking and crowing in her arms. "Do you know who this is, Walter?" she asked, with bright tears of happiness gathering in her eyes.

"Even my bewilderment has its limits," I replied. "I think I can still answer for knowing my own child."

"Child!" she exclaimed, with all her easy gaiety of old times. "Do you talk in that familiar manner of one of the landed gentry of England? Are you aware, when I present this illustrious baby to your notice, in whose presence you stand? Evidently not! Let me make two eminent personages known to one another: Mr. Walter Hartright — the Heir of Limmeridge."

So she spoke. In writing those last words, I have written all. The pen falters in my hand. The long, happy labour of many months is over. Marian was the good angel of our lives — let Marian end our Story.

The Marble Faun

By Nathaniel Hawthorne

Volume I
CHAPTER I

MIRIAM, HILDA, KENYON, DONATELLO

Four individuals, in whose fortunes we should be glad to interest the reader, happened to be standing in one of the saloons of the sculpture-gallery in the Capitol at Rome. It was that room (the first, after ascending the staircase) in the centre of which reclines the noble and most pathetic figure of the Dying Gladiator, just sinking into his death-swoon. Around the walls stand the Antinous, the Amazon, the Lycian Apollo, the Juno; all famous productions of antique sculpture, and still shining in the undiminished majesty and beauty of their ideal life, although the marble that embodies them is yellow with time, and perhaps corroded by the damp earth in which they lay buried for centuries. Here, likewise, is seen a symbol (as apt at this moment as it was two thousand years ago) of the Human Soul, with its choice of Innocence or Evil close at hand, in the pretty figure of a child, clasping a dove to her bosom, but assaulted by a snake.

From one of the windows of this saloon, we may see a flight of broad stone steps, descending alongside the antique and massive foundation of the Capitol, towards the battered triumphal arch of Septimius Severus, right below. Farther on, the eye skirts along the edge of the desolate Forum (where Roman washerwomen hang out their linen to the sun), passing over a shapeless confusion of modern edifices, piled rudely up with ancient brick and stone, and over the domes of Christian churches, built on the old pavements of heathen temples, and supported by the very pillars that once upheld them. At a distance beyond—yet but a little way, considering how much history is heaped into the intervening space—rises the great sweep of the Coliseum, with the blue sky brightening through its upper tier of arches. Far off, the view is shut in by the Alban Mountains, looking just the same, amid all this decay and change, as when Romulus gazed thitherward over his half finished wall.

We glance hastily at these things,—at this bright sky, and those blue distant mountains, and at the ruins, Etruscan, Roman, Christian, venerable with a threefold antiquity, and at the company of world-famous statues in the saloon,—in the hope of putting the reader into that state of feeling which is experienced oftenest at Rome. It is a vague sense of ponderous remembrances; a perception of such weight and density in a bygone life, of which this spot was the centre, that the present moment is pressed down or crowded out, and our individual affairs and interests are but half as real here as elsewhere. Viewed through this medium, our narrative—into which are woven some airy and unsubstantial threads, intermixed with others, twisted out of the commonest stuff of human existence—may seem not widely different from the texture of all our lives.

Side by side with the massiveness of the Roman Past, all matters that we handle or dream of nowadays look evanescent and visionary alike.

It might be that the four persons whom we are seeking to introduce were conscious of this dreamy character of the present, as compared with the square blocks of granite wherewith the Romans built their lives. Perhaps it even contributed to the fanciful merriment which was just now their mood. When we find ourselves fading into shadows and unrealities, it seems hardly worth while to be sad, but rather to laugh as gayly as we may, and ask little reason wherefore.

Of these four friends of ours, three were artists, or connected with art; and, at this moment, they had been simultaneously struck by a resemblance between one of the antique statues, a well-known masterpiece of Grecian sculpture, and a young Italian, the fourth member of their party.

"You must needs confess, Kenyon," said a dark-eyed young woman, whom her friends called Miriam, "that you never chiselled out of marble, nor wrought in clay, a more vivid likeness than this, cunning a bust-maker as you think yourself. The portraiture is perfect in character, sentiment, and feature. If it were a picture, the resemblance might be half illusive and imaginary; but here, in this Pentelic marble, it is a substantial fact, and may be tested by absolute touch and measurement. Our friend Donatello is the very Faun of Praxiteles. Is it not true, Hilda?"

"Not quite—almost—yes, I really think so," replied Hilda, a slender, brown-haired, New England girl, whose perceptions of form and expression were wonderfully clear and delicate. "If there is any difference between the two faces, the reason may be, I suppose, that the Faun dwelt in woods and fields, and consorted with his like; whereas Donatello has known cities a little, and such people as ourselves. But the resemblance is very close, and very strange."

"Not so strange," whispered Miriam mischievously; "for no Faun in Arcadia was ever a greater simpleton than Donatello. He has hardly a man's share of wit, small as that may be. It is a pity there are no longer any of this congenial race of rustic creatures for our friend to consort with!"

"Hush, naughty one!" returned Hilda. "You are very ungrateful, for you well know he has wit enough to worship you, at all events."

"Then the greater fool he!" said Miriam so bitterly that Hilda's quiet eyes were somewhat startled.

"Donatello, my dear friend," said Kenyon, in Italian, "pray gratify us all by taking the exact attitude of this statue."

The young man laughed, and threw himself into the position in which the statue has been standing for two or three thousand years. In truth, allowing for the difference of costume, and if a lion's skin could have been substituted for his modern talma, and a rustic pipe for his stick, Donatello might have figured perfectly as the marble Faun, miraculously softened into flesh and blood.

"Yes; the resemblance is wonderful," observed Kenyon, after examining the marble and the man with the accuracy of a sculptor's eye. "There is one point, however, or, rather, two points, in respect to which our friend Donatello's abundant curls will not permit us to say whether the likeness is carried into minute detail."

And the sculptor directed the attention of the party to the ears of the beautiful statue which they were contemplating.

But we must do more than merely refer to this exquisite work of art; it must be described, however inadequate may be the effort to express its magic peculiarity in words.

The Faun is the marble image of a young man, leaning his right arm on the trunk or stump of a tree; one hand hangs carelessly by his side; in the other he holds the fragment of a pipe, or some such sylvan instrument of music. His only garment—a lion's skin, with the claws upon his shoulder—falls halfway down his back, leaving the limbs and entire front of the figure nude. The form, thus displayed, is marvellously graceful, but has a fuller and more rounded outline, more flesh, and less of heroic muscle, than the old sculptors were wont to assign to their types of masculine beauty. The character of the face corresponds with the figure; it is most agreeable in outline and feature, but rounded and somewhat voluptuously developed, especially about the throat and chin; the nose is almost straight, but very slightly curves inward, thereby acquiring an indescribable charm of geniality and humor. The mouth, with its full yet delicate lips, seems so nearly to smile outright, that it calls forth a responsive smile. The whole statue—unlike anything else that ever was wrought in that severe material of marble—conveys the idea of an amiable and sensual creature, easy, mirthful, apt for jollity, yet not incapable of being touched by pathos. It is impossible to gaze long at this stone image without conceiving a kindly sentiment towards it, as if its substance were warm to the touch, and imbued with actual life. It comes very close to some of our pleasantest sympathies.

Perhaps it is the very lack of moral severity, of any high and heroic ingredient in the character of the Faun, that makes it so delightful an object to the human eye and to the frailty of the human heart. The being here represented is endowed with no principle of virtue, and would be incapable of comprehending such; but he would be true and honest by dint of his simplicity. We should expect from him no sacrifice or effort for an abstract cause; there is not an atom of martyr's stuff in all that softened marble; but he has a capacity for strong and warm attachment, and might act devotedly through its impulse, and even die for it at need. It is possible, too, that the Faun might be educated through the medium of his emotions, so that the coarser animal portion of his nature might eventually be thrown into the background, though never utterly expelled.

The animal nature, indeed, is a most essential part of the Faun's composition; for the characteristics of the brute creation meet and combine with those of humanity in this strange yet true and natural conception of antique poetry and art. Praxiteles has subtly diffused throughout his work that mute mystery, which so hopelessly perplexes us whenever we attempt to gain an intellectual or sympathetic knowledge of the lower orders of creation. The riddle is indicated, however, only by two definite signs: these are the two ears of the Faun, which are leaf shaped, terminating in little peaks, like those of some species of animals. Though not so seen in the marble, they are probably to be considered as clothed in fine, downy fur. In the coarser representations of this class of mythological creatures, there is another token of brute kindred,—a certain caudal appendage; which, if the Faun of Praxiteles must be supposed to possess it

The Marble Faun

at all, is hidden by the lion's skin that forms his garment. The pointed and furry ears, therefore, are the sole indications of his wild, forest nature.

Only a sculptor of the finest imagination, the most delicate taste, the sweetest feeling, and the rarest artistic skill—in a word, a sculptor and a poet too—could have first dreamed of a Faun in this guise, and then have succeeded in imprisoning the sportive and frisky thing in marble. Neither man nor animal, and yet no monster, but a being in whom both races meet on friendly ground. The idea grows coarse as we handle it, and hardens in our grasp. But, if the spectator broods long over the statue, he will be conscious of its spell; all the pleasantness of sylvan life, all the genial and happy characteristics of creatures that dwell in woods and fields, will seem to be mingled and kneaded into one substance, along with the kindred qualities in the human soul. Trees, grass, flowers, woodland streamlets, cattle, deer, and unsophisticated man. The essence of all these was compressed long ago, and still exists, within that discolored marble surface of the Faun of Praxiteles.

And, after all, the idea may have been no dream, but rather a poet's reminiscence of a period when man's affinity with nature was more strict, and his fellowship with every living thing more intimate and dear.

CHAPTER II
THE FAUN

"Donatello," playfully cried Miriam, "do not leave us in this perplexity! Shake aside those brown curls, my friend, and let us see whether this marvellous resemblance extends to the very tips of the ears. If so, we shall like you all the better!"

"No, no, dearest signorina," answered Donatello, laughing, but with a certain earnestness. "I entreat you to take the tips of my ears for granted." As he spoke, the young Italian made a skip and jump, light enough for a veritable faun; so as to place himself quite beyond the reach of the fair hand that was outstretched, as if to settle the matter by actual examination. "I shall be like a wolf of the Apennines," he continued, taking his stand on the other side of the Dying Gladiator, "if you touch my ears ever so softly. None of my race could endure it. It has always been a tender point with my forefathers and me."

He spoke in Italian, with the Tuscan rusticity of accent, and an unshaped sort of utterance, betokening that he must heretofore have been chiefly conversant with rural people.

"Well, well," said Miriam, "your tender point—your two tender points, if you have them—shall be safe, so far as I am concerned. But how strange this likeness is, after all! and how delightful, if it really includes the pointed ears! O, it is impossible, of course," she continued, in English, "with a real and commonplace young man like Donatello; but you see how this peculiarity defines the position of the Faun; and, while putting him where he cannot exactly assert his brotherhood, still disposes us kindly towards the kindred creature. He is not supernatural, but just on the verge of nature, and yet within it. What is the nameless charm of this idea, Hilda? You can feel it more delicately than I."

"It perplexes me," said Hilda thoughtfully, and shrinking a little; "neither do I quite like to think about it."

"But, surely," said Kenyon, "you agree with Miriam and me that there is something very touching and impressive in this statue of the Faun. In some long-past age, he must really have existed. Nature needed, and still needs, this beautiful creature; standing betwixt man and animal, sympathizing with each, comprehending the speech of either race, and interpreting the whole existence of one to the other. What a pity that he has forever vanished from the hard and dusty paths of life,— unless," added the sculptor, in a sportive whisper, "Donatello

The Marble Faun

be actually he!"

"You cannot conceive how this fantasy takes hold of me," responded Miriam, between jest and earnest. "Imagine, now, a real being, similar to this mythic Faun; how happy, how genial, how satisfactory would be his life, enjoying the warm, sensuous, earthy side of nature; revelling in the merriment of woods and streams; living as our four-footed kindred do,—as mankind did in its innocent childhood; before sin, sorrow or morality itself had ever been thought of! Ah! Kenyon, if Hilda and you and I—if I, at least—had pointed ears! For I suppose the Faun had no conscience, no remorse, no burden on the heart, no troublesome recollections of any sort; no dark future either."

"What a tragic tone was that last, Miriam!" said the sculptor; and, looking into her face, he was startled to behold it pale and tear-stained. "How suddenly this mood has come over you!"

"Let it go as it came," said Miriam, "like a thunder-shower in this Roman sky. All is sunshine again, you see!"

Donatello's refractoriness as regarded his ears had evidently cost him something, and he now came close to Miriam's side, gazing at her with an appealing air, as if to solicit forgiveness. His mute, helpless gesture of entreaty had something pathetic in it, and yet might well enough excite a laugh, so like it was to what you may see in the aspect of a hound when he thinks himself in fault or disgrace. It was difficult to make out the character of this young man. So full of animal life as he was, so joyous in his deportment, so handsome, so physically well-developed, he made no impression of incompleteness, of maimed or stinted nature. And yet, in social intercourse, these familiar friends of his habitually and instinctively allowed for him, as for a child or some other lawless thing, exacting no strict obedience to conventional rules, and hardly noticing his eccentricities enough to pardon them. There was an indefinable characteristic about Donatello that set him outside of rules.

He caught Miriam's hand, kissed it, and gazed into her eyes without saying a word. She smiled, and bestowed on him a little careless caress, singularly like what one would give to a pet dog when he puts himself in the way to receive it. Not that it was so decided a caress either, but only the merest touch, somewhere between a pat and a tap of the finger; it might be a mark of fondness, or perhaps a playful pretence of punishment. At all events, it appeared to afford Donatello exquisite pleasure; insomuch that he danced quite round the wooden railing that fences in the Dying Gladiator.

"It is the very step of the Dancing Faun," said Miriam, apart, to Hilda. "What a child, or what a simpleton, he is! I continually find myself treating Donatello as if he were the merest unfledged chicken; and yet he can claim no such privileges in the right of his tender age, for he is at least—how old should you think him, Hilda?"

"Twenty years, perhaps," replied Hilda, glancing at Donatello; "but, indeed, I cannot tell; hardly so old, on second thoughts, or possibly older. He has nothing to do with time, but has a look of eternal youth in his face."

"All underwitted people have that look," said Miriam scornfully.

"Donatello has certainly the gift of eternal youth, as Hilda suggests," observed Kenyon, laughing; "for, judging by the date of this statue, which, I am more and more convinced, Praxiteles carved on purpose for him, he must be at least twenty-five centuries old, and he still looks as young as ever."

"What age have you, Donatello?" asked Miriam.

"Signorina, I do not know," he answered; "no great age, however; for I have only lived since I met you."

"Now, what old man of society could have turned a silly compliment more smartly than that!" exclaimed Miriam. "Nature and art are just at one sometimes. But what a happy ignorance is this of our friend Donatello! Not to know his own age! It is equivalent to being immortal on earth. If I could only forget mine!"

"It is too soon to wish that," observed the sculptor; "you are scarcely older than Donatello looks."

"I shall be content, then," rejoined Miriam, "if I could only forget one day of all my life." Then she seemed to repent of this allusion, and hastily added, "A woman's days are so tedious that it is a boon to leave even one of them out of the account."

The foregoing conversation had been carried on in a mood in which all imaginative people, whether artists or poets, love to indulge. In this frame of mind, they sometimes find their profoundest truths side by side with the idlest jest, and utter one or the other, apparently without distinguishing which is the most valuable, or assigning any considerable value to either. The resemblance between the marble Faun and their living companion had made a deep, half-serious, half-mirthful

The Marble Faun

impression on these three friends, and had taken them into a certain airy region, lifting up, as it is so pleasant to feel them lifted, their heavy earthly feet from the actual soil of life. The world had been set afloat, as it were, for a moment, and relieved them, for just so long, of all customary responsibility for what they thought and said.

It might be under this influence—or, perhaps, because sculptors always abuse one another's works—that Kenyon threw in a criticism upon the Dying Gladiator.

"I used to admire this statue exceedingly," he remarked, "but, latterly, I find myself getting weary and annoyed that the man should be such a length of time leaning on his arm in the very act of death. If he is so terribly hurt, why does he not sink down and die without further ado? Flitting moments, imminent emergencies, imperceptible intervals between two breaths, ought not to be incrusted with the eternal repose of marble; in any sculptural subject, there should be a moral standstill, since there must of necessity be a physical one. Otherwise, it is like flinging a block of marble up into the air, and, by some trick of enchantment, causing it to stick there. You feel that it ought to come down, and are dissatisfied that it does not obey the natural law."

"I see," said Miriam mischievously, "you think that sculpture should be a sort of fossilizing process. But, in truth, your frozen art has nothing like the scope and freedom of Hilda's and mine. In painting there is no similar objection to the representation of brief snatches of time,—perhaps because a story can be so much more fully told in picture, and buttressed about with circumstances that give it an epoch. For instance, a painter never would have sent down yonder Faun out of his far antiquity, lonely and desolate, with no companion to keep his simple heart warm."

"Ah, the Faun!" cried Hilda, with a little gesture of impatience; "I have been looking at him too long; and now, instead of a beautiful statue, immortally young, I see only a corroded and discolored stone. This change is very apt to occur in statues."

"And a similar one in pictures, surely," retorted the sculptor. "It is the spectator's mood that transfigures the Transfiguration itself. I defy any painter to move and elevate me without my own consent and assistance."

"Then you are deficient of a sense," said Miriam.

The party now strayed onward from hall to hall of that rich

gallery, pausing here and there, to look at the multitude of noble and lovely shapes, which have been dug up out of the deep grave in which old Rome lies buried. And still, the realization of the antique Faun, in the person of Donatello, gave a more vivid character to all these marble ghosts. Why should not each statue grow warm with life! Antinous might lift his brow, and tell us why he is forever sad. The Lycian Apollo might strike his lyre; and, at the first vibration, that other Faun in red marble, who keeps up a motionless dance, should frisk gayly forth, leading yonder Satyrs, with shaggy goat-shanks, to clatter their little hoofs upon the floor, and all join hands with Donatello! Bacchus, too, a rosy flush diffusing itself over his time-stained surface, could come down from his pedestal, and offer a cluster of purple grapes to Donatello's lips; because the god recognizes him as the woodland elf who so often shared his revels. And here, in this sarcophagus, the exquisitely carved figures might assume life, and chase one another round its verge with that wild merriment which is so strangely represented on those old burial coffers: though still with some subtle allusion to death, carefully veiled, but forever peeping forth amid emblems of mirth and riot.

As the four friends descended the stairs, however, their play of fancy subsided into a much more sombre mood; a result apt to follow upon such exhilaration as that which had so recently taken possession of them.

"Do you know," said Miriam confidentially to Hilda, "I doubt the reality of this likeness of Donatello to the Faun, which we have been talking so much about? To say the truth, it never struck me so forcibly as it did Kenyon and yourself, though I gave in to whatever you were pleased to fancy, for the sake of a moment's mirth and wonder." "I was certainly in earnest, and you seemed equally so," replied Hilda, glancing back at Donatello, as if to reassure herself of the resemblance. "But faces change so much, from hour to hour, that the same set of features has often no keeping with itself; to an eye, at least, which looks at expression more than outline. How sad and sombre he has grown all of a sudden!" "Angry too, methinks! nay, it is anger much more than sadness," said Miriam. "I have seen Donatello in this mood once or twice before. If you consider him well, you will observe an odd mixture of the bulldog, or some other equally fierce brute, in our friend's composition; a trait of savageness hardly to be expected in such a gentle creature as he usually is. Donatello is a very strange young man. I wish he would not haunt my footsteps so continually."

"You have bewitched the poor lad," said the sculptor, laughing. "You have a faculty of bewitching people, and it is providing you with a singular train of followers. I see another of

The Marble Faun

them behind yonder pillar; and it is his presence that has aroused Donatello's wrath."

They had now emerged from the gateway of the palace; and partly concealed by one of the pillars of the portico stood a figure such as may often be encountered in the streets and piazzas of Rome, and nowhere else. He looked as if he might just have stepped out of a picture, and, in truth, was likely enough to find his way into a dozen pictures; being no other than one of those living models, dark, bushy bearded, wild of aspect and attire, whom artists convert into saints or assassins, according as their pictorial purposes demand.

"Miriam," whispered Hilda, a little startled, "it is your model!"

CHAPTER III
SUBTERRANEAN REMINISCENCES

Miriam's model has so important a connection with our story, that it is essential to describe the singular mode of his first appearance, and how he subsequently became a self-appointed follower of the young female artist. In the first place, however, we must devote a page or two to certain peculiarities in the position of Miriam herself.

There was an ambiguity about this young lady, which, though it did not necessarily imply anything wrong, would have operated unfavorably as regarded her reception in society, anywhere but in Rome. The truth was, that nobody knew anything about Miriam, either for good or evil. She had made her appearance without introduction, had taken a studio, put her card upon the door, and showed very considerable talent as a painter in oils. Her fellow professors of the brush, it is true, showered abundant criticisms upon her pictures, allowing them to be well enough for the idle half-efforts of an amateur, but lacking both the trained skill and the practice that distinguish the works of a true artist.

Nevertheless, be their faults what they might, Miriam's pictures met with good acceptance among the patrons of modern art. Whatever technical merit they lacked, its absence was more than supplied by a warmth and passionateness, which she had the faculty of putting into her productions, and which all the world could feel. Her nature had a great deal of color, and, in accordance with it, so likewise had her pictures.

Miriam had great apparent freedom of intercourse; her manners were so far from evincing shyness, that it seemed easy to become acquainted with her, and not difficult to develop a casual acquaintance into intimacy. Such, at least, was the impression which she made, upon brief contact, but not such the ultimate conclusion of those who really sought to know her. So airy, free, and affable was Miriam's deportment towards all who came within her sphere, that possibly they might never be conscious of the fact, but so it was, that they did not get on, and were seldom any further advanced into her good graces to-day than yesterday. By some subtle quality, she kept people at a distance, without so much as letting them know that they were excluded from her inner circle. She resembled one of those images of light, which conjurers evoke and cause to shine before us, in apparent tangibility, only an arm's length beyond our grasp: we make a step in advance, expecting to seize the illusion, but find it still precisely so far out of our reach. Finally, society began to recognize the impossibility of getting nearer to Miriam, and gruffly acquiesced.

There were two persons, however, whom she appeared to acknowledge as friends in the closer and truer sense of the word; and both of these more favored individuals did credit to Miriam's selection. One was a young American sculptor, of high promise and rapidly increasing celebrity; the other, a girl of the same country, a painter like Miriam herself, but in a widely different sphere of art. Her heart flowed out towards these two; she requited herself by their society and friendship (and especially by Hilda's) for all the loneliness with which, as regarded the rest of the world, she chose to be surrounded. Her two friends were conscious of the strong, yearning grasp which Miriam laid upon them, and gave her their affection in full measure; Hilda, indeed, responding with the fervency of a girl's first friendship, and Kenyon with a manly regard, in which there was nothing akin to what is distinctively called love.

A sort of intimacy subsequently grew up between these three friends and a fourth individual; it was a young Italian, who, casually visiting Rome, had been attracted by the beauty which Miriam possessed in a remarkable degree. He had sought her, followed her, and insisted, with simple perseverance, upon being admitted at least to her acquaintance; a boon which had been granted, when a more artful character, seeking it by a more subtle mode of pursuit, would probably have failed to obtain it. This young man, though anything but intellectually brilliant, had many agreeable characteristics which won him the kindly and half-contemptuous regard of Miriam and her two friends. It was he whom they called Donatello, and whose wonderful resemblance to the Faun of Praxiteles forms the keynote of our narrative.

Such was the position in which we find Miriam some few months after her establishment at Rome. It must be added, however, that the world did not permit her to hide her antecedents without making her the subject of a good deal of conjecture; as was natural enough, considering the abundance of her personal charms, and the degree of notice that she attracted as an artist. There were many stories about Miriam's origin and previous life, some of which had a very probable air, while others were evidently wild and romantic fables. We cite a few, leaving the reader to designate them either under the probable or the romantic head.

It was said, for example, that Miriam was the daughter and heiress of a great Jewish banker (an idea perhaps suggested by a certain rich Oriental character in her face), and had fled from her paternal home to escape a union with a cousin, the heir of another of that golden brotherhood; the object being to retain their vast accumulation of wealth within the family. Another story hinted that she was a German princess, whom, for reasons of state, it was proposed to give in marriage either to a decrepit sovereign, or a prince still in his cradle. According to a third statement, she was the off-spring of a Southern American planter, who had given her an elaborate education and endowed her with his wealth; but the one burning drop of African blood in her veins so affected her with a sense of ignominy, that she relinquished all and fled her country. By still another account she was the lady of an English nobleman; and, out of mere love and honor of art, had thrown aside the splendor of her rank, and come to seek a subsistence by her pencil in a Roman studio.

In all the above cases, the fable seemed to be instigated by the large and bounteous impression which Miriam invariably made, as if necessity and she could have nothing to do with one another. Whatever deprivations she underwent must needs be voluntary. But there were other surmises, taking such a commonplace view as that Miriam was the daughter of a merchant or financier, who had been ruined in a great commercial crisis; and, possessing a taste for art, she had attempted to support herself by the pencil, in preference to the alternative of going out as governess.

Be these things how they might, Miriam, fair as she looked, was plucked up out of a mystery, and had its roots still clinging to her. She was a beautiful and attractive woman, but based, as it were, upon a cloud, and all surrounded with misty substance; so that the result was to render her sprite-like in her most ordinary manifestations. This was the case even in respect to Kenyon and Hilda, her especial friends. But such was the effect of Miriam's natural language, her generosity, kindliness, and native truth of character, that these two received her as a dear friend into their hearts, taking her good qualities as evident and genuine, and never imagining that what was hidden must be therefore evil.

We now proceed with our narrative.

The same party of friends, whom we have seen at the sculpture-gallery of the Capitol, chanced to have gone together, some months before, to the catacomb of St. Calixtus. They went joyously down into that vast tomb, and wandered by torchlight through a sort of dream, in which reminiscences of church aisles and grimy cellars—and chiefly the latter—seemed to be broken into fragments, and hopelessly intermingled. The intricate passages along which they followed their guide had been hewn, in some forgotten age, out of a dark-red, crumbly stone. On either side were horizontal niches, where, if they held their torches closely, the shape of a human body was discernible in white ashes, into which the entire mortality of a man or woman had resolved itself. Among all this extinct dust, there might perchance be a thigh-bone, which crumbled at a touch; or possibly a skull, grinning at its own wretched plight, as is the ugly and empty habit of the thing.

Sometimes their gloomy pathway tended upward, so that, through a crevice, a little daylight glimmered down upon them, or even a streak of sunshine peeped into a burial niche; then again, they went downward by gradual descent, or by abrupt, rudely hewn steps, into deeper and deeper recesses of the earth. Here and there the narrow and tortuous passages widened somewhat, developing themselves into small chapels;—which once, no doubt, had been adorned with marble-work and lighted with ever-burning lamps and tapers. All such illumination and ornament, however, had long since been extinguished and stript away; except, indeed, that the low roofs of a few of these ancient sites of worship were covered with dingy stucco, and frescoed with scriptural scenes and subjects, in the dreariest stage of ruin.

In one such chapel, the guide showed them a low arch, beneath which the body of St. Cecilia had been buried after her martyrdom, and where it lay till a sculptor saw it, and rendered it forever beautiful in marble.

In a similar spot they found two sarcophagi, one containing a skeleton, and the other a shrivelled body, which still wore the garments of its former lifetime.

"How dismal all this is!" said Hilda, shuddering. "I do not know why we came here, nor why we should stay a moment longer."

"I hate it all!" cried Donatello with peculiar energy. "Dear friends, let us hasten back into the blessed daylight!"

From the first, Donatello had shown little fancy for the expedition; for, like most Italians, and in especial accordance with the law of his own simple and physically happy nature, this young man had an infinite repugnance to graves and skulls, and to all that ghastliness which the Gothic mind loves to associate with the idea of death. He shuddered, and looked fearfully round, drawing nearer to Miriam, whose attractive influence alone had enticed him into that gloomy region.

"What a child you are, poor Donatello!" she observed, with the freedom which she always used towards him. "You are afraid of ghosts!"

"Yes, signorina; terribly afraid!" said the truthful Donatello.

"I also believe in ghosts," answered Miriam, "and could tremble at them, in a suitable place. But these sepulchres are so old, and these skulls and white ashes so very dry, that methinks they have ceased to be haunted. The most awful idea connected with the catacombs is their interminable extent, and the possibility of going astray into this labyrinth of darkness, which broods around the little glimmer of our tapers."

"Has any one ever been lost here?" asked Kenyon of the guide.

"Surely, signor; one, no longer ago than my father's time," said the guide; and he added, with the air of a man who believed what he was telling, "but the first that went astray here was a pagan of old Rome, who hid himself in order to spy out and betray the blessed saints, who then dwelt and worshipped in these dismal places. You have heard the story, signor? A miracle was wrought upon the accursed one; and, ever since (for fifteen centuries at least), he has been groping in the darkness, seeking his way out of the catacomb."

"Has he ever been seen?" asked Hilda, who had great and tremulous faith in marvels of this kind.

"These eyes of mine never beheld him, signorina; the saints forbid!" answered the guide. "But it is well known that he watches near parties that come into the catacomb, especially if they be heretics, hoping to lead some straggler astray. What this lost wretch pines for, almost as much as for the blessed sunshine, is a companion to be miserable with him."

"Such an intense desire for sympathy indicates something amiable in the poor fellow, at all events," observed Kenyon.

They had now reached a larger chapel than those heretofore seen; it was of a circular shape, and, though hewn out of the solid mass of red sandstone, had pillars, and a carved roof, and other tokens of a regular architectural design. Nevertheless, considered as a church, it was exceedingly minute, being scarcely twice a man's stature in height, and only two or three paces from wall to wall; and while their collected torches illuminated this one small, consecrated spot, the great darkness spread all round it, like that immenser mystery which envelops our little life, and into which friends vanish from us, one by one. "Why, where is Miriam?" cried Hilda. The party gazed

The Marble Faun

hurriedly from face to face, and became aware that one of their party had vanished into the great darkness, even while they were shuddering at the remote possibility of such a misfortune.

CHAPTER IV
THE SPECTRE OF THE CATACOMB

"Surely, she cannot be lost!" exclaimed Kenyon. "It is but a moment since she was speaking."

"No, no!" said Hilda, in great alarm. "She was behind us all; and it is a long while since we have heard her voice!"

"Torches! torches!" cried Donatello desperately. "I will seek her, be the darkness ever so dismal!"

But the guide held him back, and assured them all that there was no possibility of assisting their lost companion, unless by shouting at the very top of their voices. As the sound would go very far along these close and narrow passages, there was a fair probability that Miriam might hear the call, and be able to retrace her steps.

Accordingly, they all—Kenyon with his bass voice; Donatello with his tenor; the guide with that high and hard Italian cry, which makes the streets of Rome so resonant; and Hilda with her slender scream, piercing farther than the united uproar of the rest—began to shriek, halloo, and bellow, with the utmost force of their lungs. And, not to prolong the reader's suspense (for we do not particularly seek to interest him in this scene, telling it only on account of the trouble and strange entanglement which followed), they soon heard a responsive call, in a female voice.

"It was the signorina!" cried Donatello joyfully.

"Yes; it was certainly dear Miriam's voice," said Hilda. "And here she comes! Thank Heaven! Thank Heaven!"

The figure of their friend was now discernible by her own torchlight, approaching out of one of the cavernous passages. Miriam came forward, but not with the eagerness and tremulous joy of a fearful girl, just rescued from a labyrinth of gloomy mystery. She made no immediate response to their inquiries and tumultuous congratulations; and, as they afterwards remembered, there was something absorbed, thoughtful, and self-concentrated in her deportment. She looked pale, as well she might, and held her torch with a nervous grasp, the tremor of which was seen in the irregular twinkling of the flame. This last was the chief perceptible sign of any recent agitation or alarm.

The Marble Faun

"Dearest, dearest Miriam," exclaimed Hilda, throwing her arms about her friend, "where have you been straying from us? Blessed be Providence, which has rescued you out of that miserable darkness!"

"Hush, dear Hilda!" whispered Miriam, with a strange little laugh. "Are you quite sure that it was Heaven's guidance which brought me back? If so, it was by an odd messenger, as you will confess. See; there he stands."

Startled at Miriam's words and manner, Hilda gazed into the duskiness whither she pointed, and there beheld a figure standing just on the doubtful limit of obscurity, at the threshold of the small, illuminated chapel. Kenyon discerned him at the same instant, and drew nearer with his torch; although the guide attempted to dissuade him, averring that, once beyond the consecrated precincts of the chapel, the apparition would have power to tear him limb from limb. It struck the sculptor, however, when he afterwards recurred to these circumstances, that the guide manifested no such apprehension on his own account as he professed on behalf of others; for he kept pace with Kenyon as the latter approached the figure, though still endeavoring to restrain 'him.

In fine, they both drew near enough to get as good a view of the spectre as the smoky light of their torches, struggling with the massive gloom, could supply.

The stranger was of exceedingly picturesque, and even melodramatic aspect. He was clad in a voluminous cloak, that seemed to be made of a buffalo's hide, and a pair of those goat-skin breeches, with the hair outward, which are still commonly worn by the peasants of the Roman Campagna. In this garb, they look like antique Satyrs; and, in truth, the Spectre of the Catacomb might have represented the last survivor of that vanished race, hiding himself in sepulchral gloom, and mourning over his lost life of woods and streams.

Furthermore, he had on a broad-brimmed, conical hat, beneath the shadow of which a wild visage was indistinctly seen, floating away, as it were, into a dusky wilderness of mustache and beard. His eyes winked, and turned uneasily from the torches, like a creature to whom midnight would be more congenial than noonday.

On the whole, the spectre might have made a considerable impression on the sculptor's nerves, only that he was in the habit of observing similar figures, almost every day, reclining on the Spanish steps, and waiting for some artist to invite them within the magic realm of picture. Nor, even thus familiarized with the stranger's peculiarities of appearance, could Kenyon help wondering to see such a personage, shaping himself so suddenly out of the void darkness of the catacomb.

"What are you?" said the sculptor, advancing his torch nearer. "And how long have you been wandering here?"

"A thousand and five hundred years!" muttered the guide, loud enough to be heard by all the party. "It is the old pagan phantom that I told you of, who sought to betray the blessed saints!"

"Yes; it is a phantom!" cried Donatello, with a shudder. "Ah, dearest signorina, what a fearful thing has beset you in those dark corridors!"

"Nonsense, Donatello," said the sculptor. "The man is no more a phantom than yourself. The only marvel is, how he comes to be hiding himself in the catacomb. Possibly our guide might solve the riddle."

The spectre himself here settled the point of his tangibility, at all events, and physical substance, by approaching a step nearer, and laying his hand on Kenyon's arm.

"Inquire not what I am, nor wherefore I abide in the darkness," said he, in a hoarse, harsh voice, as if a great deal of damp were clustering in his throat. "Henceforth, I am nothing but a shadow behind her footsteps. She came to me when I sought her not. She has called me forth, and must abide the consequences of my reappearance in the world."

"Holy Virgin! I wish the signorina joy of her prize," said the guide, half to himself. "And in any case, the catacomb is well rid of him."

We need follow the scene no further. So much is essential to the subsequent narrative, that, during the short period while astray in those tortuous passages, Miriam had encountered an unknown man, and led him forth with her, or was guided back by him, first into the torchlight, thence into the sunshine.

It was the further singularity of this affair, that the connection, thus briefly and casually formed, did not terminate with the incident that gave it birth. As if her service to him, or his service to her, whichever it might be, had given him an indefeasible claim on Miriam's regard and protection, the Spectre of the Catacomb never long allowed her to lose sight of him, from that day forward. He haunted her footsteps with more than the customary persistency of Italian mendicants, when once they have recognized a benefactor. For days together, it is true, he occasionally vanished, but always reappeared, gliding after her through the narrow streets, or climbing the hundred steps of her staircase and sitting at her threshold.

Being often admitted to her studio, he left his features, or some shadow or reminiscence of them, in many of her sketches and pictures. The moral atmosphere of these productions was thereby so influenced, that rival painters pronounced it a case of hopeless mannerism, which would destroy all Miriam's prospects of true excellence in art.

The story of this adventure spread abroad, and made its way beyond the usual gossip of the Forestieri, even into Italian circles, where, enhanced by a still potent spirit of superstition, it grew far more wonderful than as above recounted. Thence, it came back among the Anglo-Saxons, and was communicated to the German artists, who so richly supplied it with romantic ornaments and excrescences, after their fashion, that it became a fantasy worthy of Tieck or Hoffmann. For nobody has any conscience about adding to the improbabilities of a marvellous tale.

The most reasonable version of the incident, that could anywise be rendered acceptable to the auditors, was substantially the one suggested by the guide of the catacomb, in his allusion to the legend of Memmius. This man, or demon, or man-demon, was a spy during the persecutions of the early Christians, probably under the Emperor Diocletian, and penetrated into the catacomb of St. Calixtus, with the malignant purpose of tracing out the hiding-places of the refugees. But, while he stole craftily through those dark corridors, he chanced to come upon a little chapel, where tapers were burning before an altar and a crucifix, and a priest was in the performance of his sacred office. By divine indulgence, there was a single moment's grace allowed to Memmius, during which, had he been capable of Christian faith and love, he might have knelt before the cross, and received the holy light into his soul, and so have been blest forever. But he resisted the sacred impulse. As soon, therefore, as that one moment had glided by, the light of the consecrated tapers, which represent all truth, bewildered the wretched man with everlasting error, and the blessed cross itself was stamped as a seal upon his heart, so that it should never open to receive conviction.

Thenceforth, this heathen Memmius has haunted the wide and dreary precincts of the catacomb, seeking, as some say, to beguile new victims into his own misery; but, according to other statements, endeavoring to prevail on any unwary visitor to take him by the hand, and guide him out into the daylight. Should his wiles and entreaties take effect, however, the man-demon would remain only a little while above ground. He would gratify his fiendish malignity by perpetrating signal mischief on his benefactor, and perhaps bringing some old pestilence or other forgotten and long-buried evil on society; or, possibly, teaching the modern world some decayed and dusty kind of crime, which the antique Romans knew,—and then would hasten back to the catacomb, which, after so long haunting it, has grown his most congenial home.

Miriam herself, with her chosen friends, the sculptor and the gentle Hilda, often laughed at the monstrous fictions that had gone abroad in reference to her adventure. Her two confidants (for such they were, on all ordinary subjects) had not failed to ask an explanation of the mystery, since undeniably a mystery there was, and one sufficiently perplexing in itself, without any help from the imaginative faculty. And, sometimes responding to their inquiries with a melancholy sort of playfulness, Miriam let her fancy run off into wilder fables than any which German ingenuity or Italian superstition had contrived.

For example, with a strange air of seriousness over all her face, only belied by a laughing gleam in her dark eyes, she would aver that the spectre (who had been an artist in his mortal lifetime) had promised to teach her a long-lost, but invaluable secret of old Roman fresco painting. The knowledge of this process would place Miriam at the head of modern art; the sole condition being agreed upon, that she should return with him into his sightless gloom, after enriching a certain extent of stuccoed wall with the most brilliant and lovely designs. And what true votary of art would not purchase unrivalled excellence, even at so vast a sacrifice!

Or, if her friends still solicited a soberer account, Miriam replied, that, meeting the old infidel in one of the dismal passages of the catacomb, she had entered into controversy with him, hoping to achieve the glory and satisfaction of converting him to the Christian faith. For the sake of so excellent a result; she had even staked her own salvation against his, binding herself to accompany him back into his penal gloom, if, within a twelvemonth's space, she should not have convinced him of the errors through which he had so long groped and stumbled. But, alas! up to the present time, the controversy had gone direfully in favor of the man-demon; and Miriam (as she whispered in Hilda's ear) had awful forebodings, that, in a few more months, she must take an eternal farewell of the sun!

It was somewhat remarkable that all her romantic fantasies

arrived at this self-same dreary termination, — it appeared impossible for her even to imagine any other than a disastrous result from her connection with her ill-omened attendant.

This singularity might have meant nothing, however, had it not suggested a despondent state of mind, which was likewise indicated by many other tokens. Miriam's friends had no difficulty in perceiving that, in one way or another, her happiness was very seriously compromised. Her spirits were often depressed into deep melancholy. If ever she was gay, it was seldom with a healthy cheerfulness. She grew moody, moreover, and subject to fits of passionate ill temper; which usually wreaked itself on the heads of those who loved her best. Not that Miriam's indifferent acquaintances were safe from similar outbreaks of her displeasure, especially if they ventured upon any allusion to the model. In such cases, they were left with little disposition to renew the subject, but inclined, on the other hand, to interpret the whole matter as much to her discredit as the least favorable coloring of the facts would allow.

It may occur to the reader, that there was really no demand for so much rumor and speculation in regard to an incident, Which might well enough have been explained without going many steps beyond the limits of probability. The spectre might have been merely a Roman beggar, whose fraternity often harbor in stranger shelters than the catacombs; or one of those pilgrims, who still journey from remote countries to kneel and worship at the holy sites, among which these haunts of the early Christians are esteemed especially sacred. Or, as was perhaps a more plausible theory, he might be a thief of the city, a robber of the Campagna, a political offender, or an assassin, with blood upon his hand; whom the negligence or connivance of the police allowed to take refuge in those subterranean fastnesses, where such outlaws have been accustomed to hide themselves from a far antiquity downward. Or he might have been a lunatic, fleeing instinctively from man, and making it his dark pleasure to dwell among the tombs, like him whose awful cry echoes afar to us from Scripture times.

And, as for the stranger's attaching himself so devotedly to Miriam, her personal magnetism might be allowed a certain weight in the explanation. For what remains, his pertinacity need not seem so very singular to those who consider how slight a link serves to connect these vagabonds of idle Italy with any person that may have the ill-hap to bestow charity, or be otherwise serviceable to them, or betray the slightest interest in their fortunes.

Thus little would remain to be accounted for, except the deportment of Miriam herself; her reserve, her brooding melancholy, her petulance, and moody passion. If generously interpreted, even these morbid symptoms might have sufficient cause in the stimulating and exhaustive influences of imaginative art, exercised by a delicate young woman, in the nervous and unwholesome atmosphere of Rome. Such, at least, was the view of the case which Hilda and Kenyon endeavored to impress on their own minds, and impart to those whom their opinions might influence.

One of Miriam's friends took the matter sadly to heart. This was the young Italian. Donatello, as we have seen, had been an eyewitness of the stranger's first appearance, and had ever since nourished a singular prejudice against the mysterious, dusky, death-scented apparition. It resembled not so much a human dislike or hatred, as one of those instinctive, unreasoning antipathies which the lower animals sometimes display, and which generally prove more trustworthy than the acutest insight into character. The shadow of the model, always flung into the light which Miriam diffused around her, caused no slight trouble to Donatello. Yet he was of a nature so remarkably genial and joyous, so simply happy, that he might well afford to have something subtracted from his comfort, and make tolerable shift to live upon what remained.

CHAPTER V
MIRIAM'S STUDIO

The courtyard and staircase of a palace built three hundred years ago are a peculiar feature of modern Rome, and interest the stranger more than many things of which he has heard loftier descriptions. You pass through the grand breadth and height of a squalid entrance-way, and perhaps see a range of dusky pillars, forming a sort of cloister round the court, and in the intervals, from pillar to pillar, are strewn fragments of antique statues, headless and legless torsos, and busts that have invariably lost what it might be well if living men could lay aside in that unfragrant atmosphere—the nose. Bas-reliefs, the spoil of some far older palace, are set in the surrounding walls, every stone of which has been ravished from the Coliseum, or any other imperial ruin which earlier barbarism had not already levelled with the earth. Between two of the pillars, moreover, stands an old sarcophagus without its lid, and with all its more prominently projecting sculptures broken off; perhaps it once held famous dust, and the bony framework of some historic man, although now only a receptacle for the rubbish of the courtyard, and a half-worn broom.

In the centre of the court, under the blue Italian sky, and with the hundred windows of the vast palace gazing down upon it from four sides, appears a fountain. It brims over from one stone basin to another, or gushes from a Naiad's urn, or spurts its many little jets from the mouths of nameless monsters, which were merely grotesque and artificial when Bernini, or whoever was their unnatural father, first produced them; but now the patches of moss, the tufts of grass, the trailing maidenhair, and all sorts of verdant weeds that thrive in the cracks and crevices of moist marble, tell us that Nature takes the fountain back into her great heart, and cherishes it as kindly as if it were a woodland spring. And hark, the pleasant murmur, the gurgle, the plash! You might hear just those tinkling sounds from any tiny waterfall in the forest, though here they gain a delicious pathos from the stately echoes that reverberate their natural language. So the fountain is not altogether glad, after all its three centuries at play!

In one of the angles of the courtyard, a pillared doorway gives access to the staircase, with its spacious breadth of low marble steps, up which, in former times, have gone the princes and cardinals of the great Roman family who built this palace. Or they have come down, with still grander and loftier mien, on their way to the Vatican or the Quirinal, there to put off their scarlet hats in exchange for the triple crown. But, in fine, all these illustrious personages have gone down their hereditary staircase for the last time, leaving it to be the thoroughfare of ambassadors, English noblemen, American millionnaires, artists, tradesmen, washerwomen, and people of every degree, — all of whom find such gilded and marble-panelled saloons as their pomp and luxury demand, or such homely garrets as their necessity can pay for, within this one multifarious abode. Only, in not a single nook of the palace (built for splendor, and the accommodation of a vast retinue, but with no vision of a happy fireside or any mode of domestic enjoyment) does the humblest or the haughtiest occupant find comfort.

Up such a staircase, on the morning after the scene at the sculpture gallery, sprang the light foot of Donatello. He ascended from story to story, passing lofty doorways, set within rich frames of sculptured marble, and climbing unweariedly upward, until the glories of the first piano and the elegance of the middle height were exchanged for a sort of Alpine region, cold and naked in its aspect. Steps of rough stone, rude wooden balustrades, a brick pavement in the passages, a dingy whitewash on the walls; these were here the palatial features. Finally, he paused before an oaken door, on which was pinned a card, bearing the name of Miriam Schaefer, artist in oils. Here Donatello knocked, and the door immediately fell somewhat ajar; its latch having been pulled up by means of a string on the inside. Passing through a little anteroom, he found himself in Miriam's presence.

"Come in, wild Faun," she said, "and tell me the latest news from Arcady!"

The artist was not just then at her easel, but was busied with the feminine task of mending a pair of gloves.

There is something extremely pleasant, and even touching, — at least, of very sweet, soft, and winning effect, — in this peculiarity of needlework, distinguishing women from men. Our own sex is incapable of any such by-play aside from the main business of life; but women — be they of what earthly rank they may, however gifted with intellect or genius, or endowed with awful beauty — have always some little handiwork ready to fill the tiny gap of every vacant moment. A needle is familiar to the fingers of them all. A queen, no doubt, plies it on occasion; the woman poet can use it as adroitly as her pen; the woman's eye, that has discovered a new star, turns from its glory to send the polished little instrument gleaming along the hem of her kerchief, or to darn a casual fray in her dress. And they have greatly the advantage of us in this respect. The slender thread of silk or cotton keeps them united with the small, familiar, gentle interests of life, the continually operating influences of which do so much for the health of the character, and carry off what would otherwise be a dangerous accumulation of morbid sensibility. A vast deal of human sympathy runs along this electric line, stretching from the throne to the wicker chair of the humblest seamstress, and keeping high and low in a species of communion with their kindred beings. Methinks it is a token of healthy and gentle characteristics, when women of high thoughts and accomplishments love to sew; especially as they are never more at home with their own hearts than while so occupied.

And when the work falls in a woman's lap, of its own accord, and the needle involuntarily ceases to fly, it is a sign of trouble, quite as trustworthy as the throb of the heart itself. This was what happened to Miriam. Even while Donatello stood gazing at her, she seemed to have forgotten his presence, allowing him to drop out of her thoughts, and the torn glove to fall from her idle fingers. Simple as he was, the young man knew by his sympathies that something was amiss.

"Dear lady, you are sad," said he, drawing close to her.

"It is nothing, Donatello," she replied, resuming her work; "yes; a little sad, perhaps; but that is not strange for us people of the ordinary world, especially for women. You are of a cheerfuller race, my friend, and know nothing of this disease of sadness. But why do you come into this shadowy room of mine?"

"Why do you make it so shadowy?" asked he.

"We artists purposely exclude sunshine, and all but a partial light," said Miriam, "because we think it necessary to put ourselves at odds with Nature before trying to imitate her. That strikes you very strangely, does it not? But we make very pretty pictures sometimes with our artfully arranged lights and shadows. Amuse yourself with some of mine, Donatello, and by and by I shall be in the mood to begin the portrait we were talking about."

The room had the customary aspect of a painter's studio; one of those delightful spots that hardly seem to belong to the actual world, but rather to be the outward type of a poet's haunted imagination, where there are glimpses, sketches, and half-developed hints of beings and objects grander and more beautiful than we can anywhere find in reality. The windows were closed with shutters, or deeply curtained, except one, which was partly open to a sunless portion of the sky, admitting only from high upward that partial light which, with its strongly marked contrast of shadow, is the first requisite towards seeing objects pictorially. Pencil-drawings were pinned against the wall or scattered on the tables. Unframed canvases turned their backs on the spectator, presenting only a blank to the eye, and churlishly concealing whatever riches of scenery or human beauty Miriam's skill had depicted on the other side.

In the obscurest part of the room Donatello was half startled at perceiving duskily a woman with long dark hair, who threw up her arms with a wild gesture of tragic despair, and appeared to beckon him into the darkness along with her.

"Do not be afraid, Donatello," said Miriam, smiling to see him peering doubtfully into the mysterious dusk. "She means you no mischief, nor could perpetrate any if she wished it ever so much. It is a lady of exceedingly pliable disposition; now a heroine of romance, and now a rustic maid; yet all for show; being created, indeed, on purpose to wear rich shawls and other garments in a becoming fashion. This is the true end of her being, although she pretends to assume the most varied duties and perform many parts in life, while really the poor puppet has nothing on earth to do. Upon my word, I am satirical unawares, and seem to be describing nine women out of ten in the person of my lay-figure. For most purposes she has the advantage of the sisterhood. Would I were like her!"

"How it changes her aspect," exclaimed Donatello, "to know that she is but a jointed figure! When my eyes first fell upon her, I thought her arms moved, as if beckoning me to help her in some direful peril."

"Are you often troubled with such sinister freaks of fancy?" asked Miriam. "I should not have supposed it."

"To tell you the truth, dearest signorina," answered the young Italian, "I am apt to be fearful in old, gloomy houses, and in the dark. I love no dark or dusky corners, except it be in a grotto, or among the thick green leaves of an arbor, or in some nook of the woods, such as I know many in the neighborhood of my home. Even there, if a stray sunbeam steal in, the shadow is all the better for its cheerful glimmer."

"Yes; you are a Faun, you know," said the fair artist, laughing at the remembrance of the scene of the day before. "But the world is sadly changed nowadays; grievously changed, poor Donatello, since those happy times when your race used to dwell in the Arcadian woods, playing hide and seek with the nymphs in grottoes and nooks of shrubbery. You have reappeared on earth some centuries too late."

"I do not understand you now," answered Donatello,

The Marble Faun

looking perplexed; "only, signorina, I am glad to have my lifetime while you live; and where you are, be it in cities or fields, I would fain be there too."

"I wonder whether I ought to allow you to speak in this way," said Miriam, looking thoughtfully at him. "Many young women would think it behooved them to be offended. Hilda would never let you speak so, I dare say. But he is a mere boy," she added, aside, "a simple boy, putting his boyish heart to the proof on the first woman whom he chances to meet. If yonder lay-figure had had the luck to meet him first, she would have smitten him as deeply as I."

"Are you angry with me?" asked Donatello dolorously.

"Not in the least," answered Miriam, frankly giving him her hand. "Pray look over some of these sketches till I have leisure to chat with you a little. I hardly think I am in spirits enough to begin your portrait to-day."

Donatello was as gentle and docile as a pet spaniel; as playful, too, in his general disposition, or saddening with his mistress's variable mood like that or any other kindly animal which has the faculty of bestowing its sympathies more completely than men or women can ever do. Accordingly, as Miriam bade him, he tried to turn his attention to a great pile and confusion of pen and ink sketches and pencil drawings which lay tossed together on a table. As it chanced, however, they gave the poor youth little delight.

The first that he took up was a very impressive sketch, in which the artist had jotted down her rough ideas for a picture of Jael driving the nail through the temples of Sisera. It was dashed off with remarkable power, and showed a touch or two that were actually lifelike and deathlike, as if Miriam had been standing by when Jael gave the first stroke of her murderous hammer, or as if she herself were Jael, and felt irresistibly impelled to make her bloody confession in this guise.

Her first conception of the stern Jewess had evidently been that of perfect womanhood, a lovely form, and a high, heroic face of lofty beauty; but, dissatisfied either with her own work or the terrible story itself, Miriam had added a certain wayward quirk of her pencil, which at once converted the heroine into a vulgar murderess. It was evident that a Jael like this would be sure to search Sisera's pockets as soon as the breath was out of his body.

In another sketch she had attempted the story of Judith, which we see represented by the old masters so often, and in such various styles. Here, too, beginning with a passionate and fiery conception of the subject in all earnestness, she had given the last touches in utter scorn, as it were, of the feelings which at first took such powerful possession of her hand. The head of Holofernes (which, by the bye, had a pair of twisted mustaches, like those of a certain potentate of the day) being fairly cut off, was screwing its eyes upward and twirling its features into a diabolical grin of triumphant malice, which it flung right in Judith's face. On her part, she had the startled aspect that might be conceived of a cook if a calf's head should sneer at her when about to be popped into the dinner-pot.

Over and over again, there was the idea of woman, acting the part of a revengeful mischief towards man. It was, indeed, very singular to see how the artist's imagination seemed to run on these stories of bloodshed, in which woman's hand was crimsoned by the stain; and how, too, — in one form or another, grotesque or sternly sad, — she failed not to bring out the moral, that woman must strike through her own heart to reach a human life, whatever were the motive that impelled her.

One of the sketches represented the daughter of Herodias receiving the head of John the Baptist in a charger. The general conception appeared to be taken from Bernardo Luini's picture, in the Uffizzi Gallery at Florence; but Miriam had imparted to the saint's face a look of gentle and heavenly reproach, with sad and blessed eyes fixed upward at the maiden; by the force of which miraculous glance, her whole womanhood was at once awakened to love and endless remorse.

These sketches had a most disagreeable effect on Donatello's peculiar temperament. He gave a shudder; his face assumed a look of trouble, fear, and disgust; he snatched up one sketch after another, as if about to tear it in pieces. Finally, shoving away the pile of drawings, he shrank back from the table and clasped his hands over his eyes.

"What is the matter, Donatello?" asked Miriam, looking up from a letter which she was now writing. "Ah! I did not mean you to see those drawings. They are ugly phantoms that stole out of my mind; not things that I created, but things that haunt me. See! here are some trifles that perhaps will please you better."

She gave him a portfolio, the sketches in which indicated a happier mood of mind, and one, it is to be hoped, more truly characteristic of the artist. Supposing neither of these classes of subject to show anything of her own individuality, Miriam had evidently a great scope of fancy, and a singular faculty of putting what looked like heart into her productions. The latter sketches were domestic and common scenes, so finely and subtilely idealized that they seemed such as we may see at any moment, and eye, where; while still there was the indefinable something added, or taken away, which makes all the difference between sordid life and an earthly paradise. The feeling and sympathy in all of them were deep and true. There was the scene, that comes once in every life, of the lover winning the soft and pure avowal of bashful affection from the maiden whose slender form half leans towards his arm, half shrinks from it, we know not which. There was wedded affection in its successive stages, represented in a series of delicately conceived designs, touched with a holy fire, that burned from youth to age in those two hearts, and gave one identical beauty to the faces throughout all the changes of feature.

There was a drawing of an infant's shoe, half worn out, with the airy print of the blessed foot within; a thing that would make a mother smile or weep out of the very depths of her heart; and yet an actual mother would not have been likely to appreciate the poetry of the little shoe, until Miriam revealed it to her. It was wonderful, the depth and force with which the above, and other kindred subjects, were depicted, and the profound significance which they often acquired. The artist, still in her fresh youth, could not probably have drawn any of these dear and rich experiences from her own life; unless, perchance, that first sketch of all, the avowal of maiden affection, were a remembered incident, and not a prophecy. But it is more delightful to believe that, from first to last, they were the productions of a beautiful imagination, dealing with the warm and pure suggestions of a woman's heart, and thus idealizing a truer and lovelier picture of the life that belongs to woman, than an actual acquaintance with some of its hard and dusty facts could have inspired. So considered, the sketches intimated such a force and variety of imaginative sympathies as would enable Miriam to fill her life richly with the bliss and suffering of womanhood, however barren it might individually be.

There was one observable point, indeed, betokening that the artist relinquished, for her personal self, the happiness which she could so profoundly appreciate for others. In all those sketches of common life, and the affections that spiritualize it, a figure was portrayed apart, now it peeped between the branches of a shrubbery, amid which two lovers sat; now it was looking through a frosted window, from the outside, while a young wedded pair sat at their new fireside within; and once it leaned from a chariot, which six horses were whirling onward in pomp and pride, and gazed at a scene of humble enjoyment by a cottage door. Always it was the same figure, and always depicted with an expression of deep sadness; and in every instance, slightly as they were brought out, the face and form had the traits of Miriam's own.

"Do you like these sketches better, Donatello?" asked Miriam. "Yes," said Donatello rather doubtfully. "Not much, I fear," responded she, laughing. "And what should a boy like you — a Faun too, — know about the joys and sorrows, the intertwining light and shadow, of human life? I forgot that you were a Faun. You cannot suffer deeply; therefore you can but half enjoy. Here, now, is a subject which you can better appreciate."

The sketch represented merely a rustic dance, but with such extravagance of fun as was delightful to behold; and here there was no drawback, except that strange sigh and sadness which always come when we are merriest.

"I am going to paint the picture in oils," said the artist; "and I want you, Donatello, for the wildest dancer of them all. Will you sit for me, some day? — or, rather, dance for me?"

"O, most gladly, signorina!" exclaimed Donatello. "See; it shall be like this."

And forthwith he began to dance, and flit about the studio, like an incarnate sprite of jollity, pausing at last on the extremity of one toe, as if that were the only portion of himself whereby his frisky nature could come in contact with the earth. The effect in that shadowy chamber, whence the artist had so carefully excluded the sunshine, was as enlivening as if one bright ray had contrived to shimmer in and frolic around the walls, and finally rest just in the centre of the floor.

"That was admirable!" said Miriam, with an approving smile. "If I can catch you on my canvas, it will be a glorious picture; only I am afraid you will dance out of it, by the very truth of the representation, just when I shall have given it the last touch. We will try it one of these days. And now, to reward you for that jolly exhibition, you shall see what has been shown to no one else."

She went to her easel, on which was placed a picture with its back turned towards the spectator. Reversing the position, there appeared the portrait of a beautiful woman, such as one sees only two or three, if even so many times, in all a lifetime; so beautiful, that she seemed to get into your consciousness and memory, and could never afterwards be shut out, but haunted your dreams, for pleasure or for pain; holding your inner realm as a conquered territory, though without deigning to make herself at home there.

The Marble Faun

She was very youthful, and had what was usually thought to be a Jewish aspect; a complexion in which there was no roseate bloom, yet neither was it pale; dark eyes, into which you might look as deeply as your glance would go, and still be conscious of a depth that you had not sounded, though it lay open to the day. She had black, abundant hair, with none of the vulgar glossiness of other women's sable locks; if she were really of Jewish blood, then this was Jewish hair, and a dark glory such as crowns no Christian maiden's head. Gazing at this portrait, you saw what Rachel might have been, when Jacob deemed her worth the wooing seven years, and seven more; or perchance she might ripen to be what Judith was, when she vanquished Holofernes with her beauty, and slew him for too much adoring it.

Miriam watched Donatello's contemplation of the picture, and seeing his simple rapture, a smile of pleasure brightened on her face, mixed with a little scorn; at least, her lips curled, and her eyes gleamed, as if she disdained either his admiration or her own enjoyment of it.

"Then you like the picture, Donatello?" she asked.

"O, beyond what I can tell!" he answered. "So beautiful! — so beautiful!"

"And do you recognize the likeness?"

"Signorina," exclaimed Donatello, turning from the picture to the artist, in astonishment that she should ask the question, "the resemblance is as little to be mistaken as if you had bent over the smooth surface of a fountain, and possessed the witchcraft to call forth the image that you made there! It is yourself!"

Donatello said the truth; and we forebore to speak descriptively of Miriam's beauty earlier in our narrative, because we foresaw this occasion to bring it perhaps more forcibly before the reader.

We know not whether the portrait were a flattered likeness; probably not, regarding it merely as the delineation of a lovely face; although Miriam, like all self-painters, may have endowed herself with certain graces which Other eyes might not discern. Artists are fond of painting their own portraits; and, in Florence, there is a gallery of hundreds of them, including the most illustrious, in all of which there are autobiographical characteristics, so to speak, — traits, expressions, loftinesses, and amenities, which would have been invisible, had they not been painted from within. Yet their reality and truth are none the less. Miriam, in like manner, had doubtless conveyed some of the intimate results of her heart knowledge into her own portrait, and perhaps wished to try whether they would be perceptible to so simple and natural an observer as Donatello.

"Does the expression please you?" she asked.

"Yes," said Donatello hesitatingly; "if it would only smile so like the sunshine as you sometimes do. No, it is sadder than I thought at first. Cannot you make yourself smile a little, signorina?"

"A forced smile is uglier than a frown," said Miriam, a bright, natural smile breaking out over her face even as she spoke.

"O, catch it now!" cried Donatello, clapping his hands. "Let it shine upon the picture! There! it has vanished already! And you are sad again, very sad; and the picture gazes sadly forth at me, as if some evil had befallen it in the little time since I looked last."

"How perplexed you seem, my friend!" answered Miriam. "I really half believe you are a Faun, there is such a mystery and terror for you in these dark moods, which are just as natural as daylight to us people of ordinary mould. I advise you, at all events, to look at other faces with those innocent and happy eyes, and never more to gaze at mine!"

"You speak in vain," replied the young man, with a deeper emphasis than she had ever before heard in his voice; "shroud yourself in what gloom you will, I must needs follow you."

"Well, well, well," said Miriam impatiently; "but leave me now; for to speak plainly, my good friend, you grow a little wearisome. I walk this afternoon in the Borghese grounds. Meet me there, if it suits your pleasure."

CHAPTER VI

THE VIRGIN'S SHRINE

After Donatello had left the studio, Miriam herself came forth, and taking her way through some of the intricacies of the city, entered what might be called either a widening of a street, or a small piazza. The neighborhood comprised a baker's oven, emitting the usual fragrance of sour bread; a shoe shop; a linen-draper's shop; a pipe and cigar shop; a lottery office; a station for French soldiers, with a sentinel pacing in front; and a fruit-stand, at which a Roman matron was selling the dried kernels of chestnuts, wretched little figs, and some bouquets of yesterday. A church, of course, was near at hand, the facade of which ascended into lofty pinnacles, whereon were perched two or three winged figures of stone, either angelic or allegorical, blowing stone trumpets in close vicinity to the upper windows of an old and shabby palace. This palace was distinguished by a feature not very common in the architecture of Roman edifices; that is to say, a mediaeval tower, square, massive, lofty, and battlemented and machicolated at the summit.

At one of the angles of the battlements stood a shrine of the Virgin, such as we see everywhere at the street corners of Rome, but seldom or never, except in this solitary, instance, at a height above the ordinary level of men's views and aspirations. Connected with this old tower and its lofty shrine, there is a legend which we cannot here pause to tell; but for centuries a lamp has been burning before the Virgin's image, at noon, at midnight, and at all hours of the twenty-four, and must be kept burning forever, as long as the tower shall stand; or else the tower itself, the palace, and whatever estate belongs to it, shall pass from its hereditary possessor, in accordance with an ancient vow, and become the property of the Church.

As Miriam approached, she looked upward, and saw, — not, indeed, the flame of the never-dying lamp, which was swallowed up in the broad sunlight that brightened the shrine, but a flock of white doves, skimming, fluttering, and wheeling about the topmost height of the tower, their silver wings flashing in the pure transparency of the air. Several of them sat on the ledge of the upper window, pushing one another off by their eager struggle for this favorite station, and all tapping their beaks and flapping their wings tumultuously against the panes; some had alighted in the street, far below, but flew hastily upward, at the sound of the window being thrust ajar, and opening in the middle, on rusty hinges, as Roman windows do.

A fair young girl, dressed in white, showed herself at the

aperture for a single instant, and threw forth as much as her two small hands could hold of some kind of food, for the flock of eleemosynary doves. It seemed greatly to the taste of the feathered people; for they tried to snatch beakfuls of it from her grasp, caught it in the air, and rushed downward after it upon the pavement.

"What a pretty scene this is," thought Miriam, with a kindly smile, "and how like a dove she is herself, the fair, pure creature! The other doves know her for a sister, I am sure."

Miriam passed beneath the deep portal of the palace, and turning to the left, began to mount flight after flight of a staircase, which, for the loftiness of its aspiration, was worthy to be Jacob's ladder, or, at all events, the staircase of the Tower of Babel. The city bustle, which is heard even in Rome, the rumble of wheels over the uncomfortable paving-stones, the hard harsh cries reechoing in the high and narrow streets, grew faint and died away; as the turmoil of the world will always die, if we set our faces to climb heavenward. Higher, and higher still; and now, glancing through the successive windows that threw in their narrow light upon the stairs, her view stretched across the roofs of the city, unimpeded even by the stateliest palaces. Only the domes of churches ascend into this airy region, and hold up their golden crosses on a level with her eye; except that, out of the very heart of Rome, the column of Antoninus thrusts itself upward, with St. Paul upon its summit, the sole human form that seems to have kept her company.

Finally, the staircase came to an end; save that, on one side of the little entry where it terminated, a flight of a dozen steps gave access to the roof of the tower and the legendary shrine. On the other side was a door, at which Miriam knocked, but rather as a friendly announcement of her presence than with any doubt of hospitable welcome; for, awaiting no response, she lifted the latch and entered.

"What a hermitage you have found for yourself, dear Hilda!" she, exclaimed. "You breathe sweet air, above all the evil scents of Rome; and even so, in your maiden elevation, you dwell above our vanities and passions, our moral dust and mud, with the doves and the angels for your nearest neighbors. I should not wonder if the Catholics were to make a saint of you, like your namesake of old; especially as you have almost avowed yourself of their religion, by undertaking to keep the lamp alight before the Virgin's shrine."

"No, no, Miriam!" said Hilda, who had come joyfully forward to greet her friend. "You must not call me a Catholic. A Christian girl—even a daughter of the Puritans—may surely pay honor to the idea of divine Womanhood, without giving up the faith of her forefathers. But how kind you are to climb into my dove-cote!"

"It is no trifling proof of friendship, indeed," answered Miriam; "I should think there were three hundred stairs at least."

"But it will do you good," continued Hilda. "A height of some fifty feet above the roofs of Rome gives me all the advantages that I could get from fifty miles of distance. The air so exhilarates my spirits, that sometimes I feel half inclined to attempt a flight from the top of my tower, in the faith that I should float upward."

"O, pray don't try it!" said Miriam, laughing; "If it should turn out that you are less than an angel, you would find the stones of the Roman pavement very hard; and if an angel, indeed, I am afraid you would never come down among us again."

This young American girl was an example of the freedom of life which it is possible for a female artist to enjoy at Rome. She dwelt in her tower, as free to descend into the corrupted atmosphere of the city beneath, as one of her companion doves to fly downward into the street;—all alone, perfectly independent, under her own sole guardianship, unless watched over by the Virgin, whose shrine she tended; doing what she liked without a suspicion or a shadow upon the snowy whiteness of her fame. The customs of artist life bestow such liberty upon the sex, which is elsewhere restricted within so much narrower limits; and it is perhaps an indication that, whenever we admit women to a wider scope of pursuits and professions, we must also remove the shackles of our present conventional rules, which would then become an insufferable restraint on either maid or wife. The system seems to work unexceptionably in Rome; and in many other cases, as in Hilda's, purity of heart and life are allowed to assert themselves, and to be their own proof and security, to a degree unknown in the society of other cities.

Hilda, in her native land, had early shown what was pronounced by connoisseurs a decided genius for the pictorial art. Even in her schooldays—still not so very distant—she had produced sketches that were seized upon by men of taste, and hoarded as among the choicest treasures of their portfolios; scenes delicately imagined, lacking, perhaps, the reality which comes only from a close acquaintance with life, but so softly touched with feeling and fancy that you seemed to be looking at humanity with angels' eyes. With years and experience she might be expected to attain a darker and more forcible touch, which would impart to her designs the relief they needed. Had Hilda remained in her own country, it is not improbable that she might have produced original works worthy to hang in that gallery of native art which, we hope, is destined to extend its rich length through many future centuries. An orphan, however, without near relatives, and possessed of a little property, she had found it within her possibilities to come to Italy; that central clime, whither the eyes and the heart of every artist turn, as if pictures could not be made to glow in any other atmosphere, as if statues could not assume grace and expression, save in that land of whitest marble.

Hilda's gentle courage had brought her safely over land and sea; her mild, unflagging perseverance had made a place for her in the famous city, even like a flower that finds a chink for itself, and a little earth to grow in, on whatever ancient wall its slender roots may fasten. Here she dwelt, in her tower, possessing a friend or two in Rome, but no home companion except the flock of doves, whose cote was in a ruinous chamber contiguous to her own. They soon became as familiar with the fair-haired Saxon girl as if she were a born sister of their brood; and her customary white robe bore such an analogy to their snowy plumage that the confraternity of artists called Hilda the Dove, and recognized her aerial apartment as the Dovecote. And while the other doves flew far and wide in quest of what was good for them, Hilda likewise spread her wings, and sought such ethereal and imaginative sustenance as God ordains for creatures of her kind.

We know not whether the result of her Italian studies, so far as it could yet be seen, will be accepted as a good or desirable one. Certain it is, that since her arrival in the pictorial land, Hilda seemed to have entirely lost the impulse of original design, which brought her thither. No doubt the girl's early dreams had been of sending forms and hues of beauty into the visible world out of her own mind; of compelling scenes of poetry and history to live before men's eyes, through conceptions and by methods individual to herself. But more and more, as she grew familiar with the miracles of art that enrich so many galleries in Rome, Hilda had ceased to consider herself as an original artist. No, wonder that this change should have befallen her. She was endowed with a deep and sensitive faculty of appreciation; she had the gift of discerning and worshipping excellence in a most unusual measure. No other person, it is probable, recognized so adequately, and enjoyed with such deep delight, the pictorial wonders that were here displayed. She saw no, not saw, but felt through and through a picture; she bestowed upon it all the warmth and richness of a woman's sympathy; not by any intellectual effort, but by this strength of heart, and this guiding light of sympathy, she went straight to the central point, in which the master had conceived his work. Thus she viewed it, as it were, with his own eyes, and hence her comprehension of any picture that interested her was perfect.

This power and depth of appreciation depended partly upon Hilda's physical organization, which was at once healthful and exquisitely delicate; and, connected with this advantage, she had a command of hand, a nicety and force of touch, which is an endowment separate from pictorial genius, though indispensable to its exercise.

It has probably happened in many other instances, as it did in Hilda's case, that she ceased to aim at original achievement in consequence of the very gifts which so exquisitely fitted her to profit by familiarity with the works of the mighty old masters. Reverencing these wonderful men so deeply, she was too grateful for all they bestowed upon her, too loyal, too humble, in their awful presence, to think of enrolling herself in their society. Beholding the miracles of beauty which they had achieved, the world seemed already rich enough in original designs, and nothing more was so desirable as to diffuse those self-same beauties more widely among mankind. All the youthful hopes and ambitions, the fanciful ideas which she had brought from home, of great pictures to be conceived in her feminine mind, were flung aside, and, so far as those most intimate with her could discern, relinquished without a sigh. All that she would henceforth attempt and that most reverently, not to say religiously was to catch and reflect some of the glory which had been shed upon canvas from the immortal pencils of old.

So Hilda became a copyist: in the Pinacotheca of the Vatican, in the galleries of the Pam-fili-Doria palace, the Borghese, the Corsini, the Sciarra, her easel was set up before many a famous picture by Guido, Domenichino, Raphael, and the devout painters of earlier schools than these. Other artists and visitors from foreign lands beheld the slender, girlish figure in front of some world-known work, absorbed, unconscious of everything around her, seeming to live only in what she sought to do. They smiled, no doubt, at the audacity which led her to dream of copying those mighty achievements. But, if they paused to look over her shoulder, and had sensibility enough to understand what was before their eyes, they soon felt inclined to believe that the spirits of the old masters were hovering over Hilda, and guiding her delicate white hand. In truth, from whatever realm of bliss and many colored beauty those spirits might descend, it would have been no unworthy errand to help so gentle and pure a worshipper of their genius in giving the last divine touch to her repetitions of their works.

Her copies were indeed marvellous. Accuracy was not the phrase for them; a Chinese copy is accurate. Hilda's had that evanescent and ethereal life — that flitting fragrance, as it were, of the originals — which it is as difficult to catch and retain as it would be for a sculptor to get the very movement and varying color of a living man into his marble bust. Only by watching the efforts of the most skilful copyists — men who spend a lifetime, as some of them do, in multiplying copies of a single picture — and observing how invariably they leave out just the indefinable charm that involves the last, inestimable value, can we understand the difficulties of the task which they undertake.

It was not Hilda's general practice to attempt reproducing the whole of a great picture, but to select some high, noble, and delicate portion of it, in which the spirit and essence of the picture culminated: the Virgin's celestial sorrow, for example, or a hovering angel, imbued with immortal light, or a saint with the glow of heaven in his dying face, — and these would be rendered with her whole soul. If a picture had darkened into an indistinct shadow through time and neglect, or had been injured by cleaning, or retouched by some profane hand, she seemed to possess the faculty of seeing it in its pristine glory. The copy would come from her hands with what the beholder felt must be the light which the old master had left upon the original in bestowing his final and most ethereal touch. In some instances even (at least, so those believed who best appreciated Hilda's power and sensibility) she had been enabled to execute what the great master had conceived in his imagination, but had not so perfectly succeeded in putting upon canvas; a result surely not impossible when such depth of sympathy as she possessed was assisted by the delicate skill and accuracy of her slender hand. In such cases the girl was but a finer instrument, a more exquisitely effective piece of mechanism, by the help of which the spirit of some great departed painter now first achieved his ideal, centuries after his own earthly hand, that other tool, had turned to dust.

Not to describe her as too much a wonder, however, Hilda, or the Dove, as her well-wishers half laughingly delighted to call her, had been pronounced by good judges incomparably the best copyist in Rome. After minute examination of her works, the most skilful artists declared that she had been led to her results by following precisely the same process step by step through which the original painter had trodden to the development of his idea. Other copyists — if such they are worthy to be called — attempt only a superficial imitation. Copies of the old masters in this sense are produced by thousands; there are artists, as we have said, who spend their lives in painting the works, or perhaps one single work, of one illustrious painter over and over again: thus they convert themselves into Guido machines, or Raphaelic machines. Their performances, it is true, are often wonderfully deceptive to a careless eye; but working entirely from the outside, and seeking only to reproduce the surface, these men are sure to leave out that indefinable nothing, that inestimable something, that constitutes the life and soul through which the picture gets its immortality. Hilda was no such machine as this; she wrought religiously, and therefore wrought a miracle.

It strikes us that there is something far higher and nobler in all this, in her thus sacrificing herself to the devout recognition of the highest excellence in art, than there would have been in cultivating her not inconsiderable share of talent for the production of works from her own ideas. She might have set up for herself, and won no ignoble name; she might have helped to fill the already crowded and cumbered world with pictures, not destitute of merit, but falling short, if by ever so little, of the best that has been done; she might thus have gratified some tastes that were incapable of appreciating Raphael. But this could be done only by lowering the standard of art to the comprehension of the spectator. She chose the better and loftier and more unselfish part, laying her individual hopes, her fame, her prospects of enduring remembrance, at the feet of those great departed ones whom she so loved and venerated; and therefore the world was the richer for this feeble girl.

Since the beauty and glory of a great picture are confined within itself, she won out that glory by patient faith and self-devotion, and multiplied it for mankind. From the dark, chill corner of a gallery, — from some curtained chapel in a church, where the light came seldom and aslant, — from the prince's carefully guarded cabinet, where not one eye in thousands was permitted to behold it, she brought the wondrous picture into daylight, and gave all its magic splendor for the enjoyment of the world. Hilda's faculty of genuine admiration is one of the rarest to be found in human nature; and let us try to recompense her in kind by admiring her generous self-surrender, and her brave, humble magnanimity in choosing to be the handmaid of those old magicians, instead of a minor enchantress within a circle of her own.

The handmaid of Raphael, whom she loved with a virgin's love! Would it have been worth Hilda's while to relinquish this office for the sake of giving the world a picture or two which it would call original; pretty fancies of snow and moonlight; the counterpart in picture of so many feminine achievements in literature!

CHAPTER VII
BEATRICE

Miriam was glad to find the Dove in her turret-home; for being endowed with an infinite activity, and taking exquisite delight in the sweet labor of which her life was full, it was Hilda's practice to flee abroad betimes, and haunt the galleries till dusk. Happy were those (but they were very few) whom she ever chose to be the companions of her day; they saw the art treasures of Rome, under her guidance, as they had never seen them before. Not that Hilda could dissertate, or talk learnedly about pictures; she would probably have been puzzled by the technical terms of her own art. Not that she had much to say about what she most profoundly admired; but even her silent sympathy was so powerful that it drew your own along with it, endowing you with a second-sight that enabled you to see excellences with almost the depth and delicacy of her own perceptions.

All the Anglo-Saxon denizens of Rome, by this time, knew Hilda by sight. Unconsciously, the poor child had become one of the spectacles of the Eternal City, and was often pointed out to strangers, sitting at her easel among the wild-bearded young men, the white-haired old ones, and the shabbily dressed, painfully plain women, who make up the throng of copyists. The old custodes knew her well, and watched over her as their own child. Sometimes a young artist, instead of going on with a copy of the picture before which he had placed his easel, would enrich his canvas with an original portrait of Hilda at her work. A lovelier subject could not have been selected, nor one which required nicer skill and insight in doing it anything like justice. She was pretty at all times, in our native New England style, with her light-brown ringlets, her delicately tinged, but healthful cheek, her sensitive, intelligent, yet most feminine and kindly face. But, every few moments, this pretty and girlish face grew beautiful and striking, as some inward thought and feeling brightened, rose to the surface, and then, as it were, passed out of sight again; so that, taking into view this constantly recurring change, it really seemed as if Hilda were only visible by the sunshine of her soul.

In other respects, she was a good subject for a portrait, being distinguished by a gentle picturesqueness, which was perhaps unconsciously bestowed by some minute peculiarity of dress, such as artists seldom fail to assume. The effect was to make her appear like an inhabitant of pictureland, a partly ideal creature, not to be handled, nor even approached too closely. In her feminine self, Hilda was natural, and of pleasant deportment, endowed with a mild cheerfulness of temper, not overflowing with animal spirits, but never long despondent. There was a certain simplicity that made every one her friend, but it was combined with a subtle attribute of reserve, that insensibly kept those at a distance who were not suited to her sphere.

Miriam was the dearest friend whom she had ever known. Being a year or two the elder, of longer acquaintance with Italy, and better fitted to deal with its crafty and selfish inhabitants, she had helped Hilda to arrange her way of life, and had encouraged her through those first weeks, when Rome is so dreary to every newcomer.

"But how lucky that you are at home today," said Miriam, continuing the conversation which was begun, many pages back. "I hardly hoped to find you, though I had a favor to ask,—a commission to put into your charge. But what picture is this?"

"See!" said Hilda, taking her friend's hand, and leading her in front of the easel. "I wanted your opinion of it."

"If you have really succeeded," observed Miriam, recognizing the picture at the first glance, "it will be the greatest miracle you have yet achieved."

The picture represented simply a female head; a very youthful, girlish, perfectly beautiful face, enveloped in white drapery, from beneath which strayed a lock or two of what seemed a rich, though hidden luxuriance of auburn hair. The eyes were large and brown, and met those of the spectator, but evidently with a strange, ineffectual effort to escape. There was a little redness about the eyes, very slightly indicated, so that you would question whether or no the girl had been weeping. The whole face was quiet; there was no distortion or disturbance of any single feature; nor was it easy to see why the expression was not cheerful, or why a single touch of the artist's pencil should not brighten it into joyousness. But, in fact, it was the very saddest picture ever painted or conceived; it involved an unfathomable depth of sorrow, the sense of which came to the observer by a sort of intuition. It was a sorrow that removed this beautiful girl out of the sphere of humanity, and set her in a far-off region, the remoteness of which—while yet her face is so close before us—makes us shiver as at a spectre.

"Yes, Hilda," said her friend, after closely examining the picture, "you have done nothing else so wonderful as this. But by what unheard-of solicitations or secret interest have you obtained leave to copy Guido's Beatrice Cenci? It is an unexampled favor; and the impossibility of getting a genuine copy has filled the Roman picture shops with Beatrices, gay, grievous, or coquettish, but never a true one among them."

"There has been one exquisite copy, I have heard," said Hilda, "by an artist capable of appreciating the spirit of the picture. It was Thompson, who brought it away piecemeal, being forbidden (like the rest of us) to set up his easel before it. As for me, I knew the Prince Barberini would be deaf to all entreaties; so I had no resource but to sit down before the picture, day after day, and let it sink into my heart. I do believe it is now photographed there. It is a sad face to keep so close to one's heart; only what is so very beautiful can never be quite a pain. Well; after studying it in this way, I know not how many times, I came home, and have done my best to transfer the image to canvas."

"Here it is, then," said Miriam, contemplating Hilda's work with great interest and delight, mixed with the painful sympathy that the picture excited. "Everywhere we see oil-paintings, crayon sketches, cameos, engravings, lithographs, pretending to be Beatrice, and representing the poor girl with blubbered eyes, a leer of coquetry, a merry look as if she were dancing, a piteous look as if she were beaten, and twenty other modes of fantastic mistake. But here is Guido's very Beatrice; she that slept in the dungeon, and awoke, betimes, to ascend the scaffold, And now that you have done it, Hilda, can you interpret what the feeling is, that gives this picture such a mysterious force? For my part, though deeply sensible of its influence, I cannot seize it."

"Nor can I, in words," replied her friend. "But while I was painting her, I felt all the time as if she were trying to escape from my gaze. She knows that her sorrow is so strange and so immense, that she ought to be solitary forever, both for the world's sake and her own; and this is the reason we feel such a distance between Beatrice and ourselves, even when our eyes meet hers. It is infinitely heart-breaking to meet her glance, and to feel that nothing can be done to help or comfort her; neither does she ask help or comfort, knowing the hopelessness of her case better than we do. She is a fallen angel,—fallen, and yet sinless; and it is only this depth of sorrow, with its weight and darkness, that keeps her down upon earth, and brings her within our view even while it sets her beyond our reach."

"You deem her sinless?" asked Miriam; "that is not so plain to me. If I can pretend to see at all into that dim region, whence she gazes so strangely and sadly at us, Beatrice's own conscience does not acquit her of something evil, and never to be forgiven!"

"Sorrow so black as hers oppresses her very nearly as sin

would," said Hilda.

"Then," inquired Miriam, "do you think that there was no sin in the deed for which she suffered?"

"Ah!" replied Hilda, shuddering, "I really had quite forgotten Beatrice's history, and was thinking of her only as the picture seems to reveal her character. Yes, yes; it was terrible guilt, an inexpiable crime, and she feels it to be so. Therefore it is that the forlorn creature so longs to elude our eyes, and forever vanish away into nothingness! Her doom is just!"

"O Hilda, your innocence is like a sharp steel sword!" exclaimed her friend. "Your judgments are often terribly severe, though you seem all made up of gentleness and mercy. Beatrice's sin may not have been so great: perhaps it was no sin at all, but the best virtue possible in the circumstances. If she viewed it as a sin, it may have been because her nature was too feeble for the fate imposed upon her. Ah!" continued Miriam passionately, "if I could only get within her consciousness! — if I could but clasp Beatrice Cenci's ghost, and draw it into myself! I would give my life to know whether she thought herself innocent, or the one great criminal since time began."

As Miriam gave utterance to these words, Hilda looked from the picture into her face, and was startled to observe that her friend's expression had become almost exactly that of the portrait; as if her passionate wish and struggle to penetrate poor Beatrice's mystery had been successful.

"O, for Heaven's sake, Miriam, do not look so!" she cried. "What an actress you are! And I never guessed it before. Ah! now you are yourself again!" she added, kissing her. "Leave Beatrice to me in future."

"Cover up your magical picture, then," replied her friend, "else I never can look away from it. It is strange, dear Hilda, how an innocent, delicate, white soul like yours has been able to seize the subtle mystery of this portrait; as you surely must, in order to reproduce it so perfectly. Well; we will not talk of it any more. Do you know, I have come to you this morning on a small matter of business. Will you undertake it for me?"

"O, certainly," said Hilda, laughing; "if you choose to trust me with business."

"Nay, it is not a matter of any difficulty," answered Miriam; "merely to take charge of this packet, and keep it for me awhile."

"But why not keep it yourself?" asked Hilda.

"Partly because it will be safer in your charge," said her friend. "I am a careless sort of person in ordinary things; while you, for all you dwell so high above the world, have certain little housewifely ways of accuracy and order. The packet is of some slight importance; and yet, it may be, I shall not ask you for it again. In a week or two, you know, I am leaving Rome. You, setting at defiance the malarial fever, mean to stay here and haunt your beloved galleries through the summer. Now, four months hence, unless you hear more from me, I would have you deliver the packet according to its address."

Hilda read the direction; it was to Signore Luca Barboni, at the Plazzo Cenci, third piano.

"I will deliver it with my own hand," said she, "precisely four months from to-day, unless you bid me to the contrary. Perhaps I shall meet the ghost of Beatrice in that grim old palace of her forefathers."

"In that case," rejoined Miriam, "do not fail to speak to her, and try to win her confidence. Poor thing! she would be all the better for pouring her heart out freely, and would be glad to do it, if she were sure of sympathy. It irks my brain and heart to think of her, all shut up within herself." She withdrew the cloth that Hilda had drawn over the picture, and took another long look at it. "Poor sister Beatrice! for she was still a woman, Hilda, still a sister, be her sin or sorrow what they might. How well you have done it, Hilda! I knot not whether Guido will thank you, or be jealous of your rivalship."

"Jealous, indeed!" exclaimed Hilda. "If Guido had not wrought through me, my pains would have been thrown away."

"After all," resumed Miriam, "if a woman had painted the original picture, there might have been something in it which we miss now. I have a great mind to undertake a copy myself; and try to give it what it lacks. Well; goodby. But, stay! I am going for a little airing to the grounds of the Villa Borghese this afternoon. You will think it very foolish, but I always feel the safer in your company, Hilda, slender little maiden as you are. Will you come?"

"Ah, not to-day, dearest Miriam," she replied; "I have set my heart on giving another touch or two to this picture, and shall not stir abroad till nearly sunset."

"Farewell, then," said her visitor. "I leave you in your dovecote. What a sweet, strange life you lead here; conversing with the souls of the old masters, feeding and fondling your sister doves, and trimming the Virgin's lamp! Hilda, do you ever pray to the Virgin while you tend her shrine?"

"Sometimes I have been moved to do so," replied the Dove, blushing, and lowering her eyes; "she was a woman once. Do you think it would be wrong?"

"Nay, that is for you to judge," said Miriam; "but when you pray next, dear friend, remember me!"

She went down the long descent of the lower staircase, and just as she reached the street the flock of doves again took their hurried flight from the pavement to the topmost window. She threw her eyes upward and beheld them hovering about Hilda's head; for, after her friend's departure, the girl had been more impressed than before by something very sad and troubled in her manner. She was, therefore, leaning forth from her airy abode, and flinging down a kind, maidenly kiss, and a gesture of farewell, in the hope that these might alight upon Miriam's heart, and comfort its unknown sorrow a little. Kenyon the sculptor, who chanced to be passing the head of the street, took note of that ethereal kiss, and wished that he could have caught it in the air and got Hilda's leave to keep it.

CHAPTER VIII
THE SUBURBAN VILLA

Donatello, while it was still a doubtful question betwixt afternoon and morning, set forth to keep the appointment which Miriam had carelessly tendered him in the grounds of the Villa Borghese. The entrance to these grounds (as all my readers know, for everybody nowadays has been in Rome) is just outside of the Porta del Popolo. Passing beneath that not very impressive specimen of Michael Angelo's architecture, a minute's walk will transport the visitor from the small, uneasy, lava stones of the Roman pavement into broad, gravelled carriage-drives, whence a little farther stroll brings him to the soft turf of a beautiful seclusion. A seclusion, but seldom a solitude; for priest, noble, and populace, stranger and native, all who breathe Roman air, find free admission, and come hither to taste the languid enjoyment of the day-dream that they call life.

But Donatello's enjoyment was of a livelier kind. He soon began to draw long and delightful breaths among those shadowy walks. Judging by the pleasure which the sylvan character of the scene excited in him, it might be no merely fanciful theory to set him down as the kinsman, not far remote, of that wild, sweet, playful, rustic creature, to whose marble image he bore so striking a resemblance. How mirthful a discovery would it be (and yet with a touch of pathos in it), if the breeze which sported fondly with his clustering locks were to waft them suddenly aside, and show a pair of leaf-shaped, furry ears! What an honest strain of wildness would it indicate! and into what regions of rich mystery would it extend Donatello's sympathies, to be thus linked (and by no monstrous chain) with what we call the inferior trioes of being, whose simplicity, mingled with his human intelligence, might partly restore what man has lost of the divine!

The scenery amid which the youth now strayed was such as arrays itself in the imagination when we read the beautiful old myths, and fancy a brighter sky, a softer turf, a more picturesque arrangement of venerable trees, than we find in the rude and untrained landscapes of the Western world. The ilex-trees, so ancient and time-honored were they, seemed to have lived for ages undisturbed, and to feel no dread of profanation by the axe any more than overthrow by the thunder-stroke. It had already passed out of their dreamy old memories that only a few years ago they were grievously imperilled by the Gaul's last assault upon the walls of Rome. As if confident in the long peace of their lifetime, they assumed attitudes of indolent repose. They leaned over the green turf in ponderous grace, throwing abroad their great branches without danger of interfering with other trees, though other majestic trees grew near enough for dignified society, but too distant for constraint. Never was there a more venerable quietude than that which slept among their sheltering boughs; never a sweeter sunshine than that now gladdening the gentle gloom which these leafy patriarchs strove to diffuse over the swelling and subsiding lawns.

In other portions of the grounds the stone-pines lifted their dense clump of branches upon a slender length of stem, so high that they looked like green islands in the air, flinging down a shadow upon the turf so far off that you hardly knew which tree had made it. Again, there were avenues of cypress, resembling dark flames of huge funeral candles, which spread dusk and twilight round about them instead of cheerful radiance. The more open spots were all abloom, even so early in the season, with anemones of wondrous size, both white and rose-colored, and violets that betrayed themselves by their rich fragrance, even if their blue eyes failed to meet your own. Daisies, too, were abundant, but larger than the modest little English flower, and therefore of small account.

These wooded and flowery lawns are more beautiful than the finest of English park scenery, more touching, more impressive, through the neglect that leaves Nature so much to her own ways and methods. Since man seldom interferes with her, she sets to work in her quiet way and makes herself at home. There is enough of human care, it is true, bestowed, long ago and still bestowed, to prevent wildness from growing into deformity; and the result is an ideal landscape, a woodland scene that seems to have been projected out of the poet's mind. If the ancient Faun were other than a mere creation of old poetry, and could have reappeared anywhere, it must have been in such a scene as this.

In the openings of the wood there are fountains plashing into marble basins, the depths of which are shaggy with water-weeds; or they tumble like natural cascades from rock to rock, sending their murmur afar, to make the quiet and silence more appreciable. Scattered here and there with careless artifice, stand old altars bearing Roman inscriptions. Statues, gray with the long corrosion of even that soft atmosphere, half hide and half reveal themselves, high on pedestals, or perhaps fallen and broken on the turf. Terminal figures, columns of marble or granite porticos, arches, are seen in the vistas of the wood-paths, either veritable relics of antiquity, or with so exquisite a touch of artful ruin on them that they are better than if really antique. At all events, grass grows on the tops of the shattered pillars, and weeds and flowers root themselves in the chinks of the massive arches and fronts of temples, and clamber at large over their pediments, as if this were the thousandth summer since their winged seeds alighted there.

What a strange idea — what a needless labor — to construct artificial ruins in Rome, the native soil of ruin! But even these sportive imitations, wrought by man in emulation of what time has done to temples and palaces, are perhaps centuries old, and, beginning as illusions, have grown to be venerable in sober earnest. The result of all is a scene, pensive, lovely, dreamlike, enjoyable and sad, such as is to be found nowhere save in these princely villa-residences in the neighborhood of Rome; a scene that must have required generations and ages, during which growth, decay, and man's intelligence wrought kindly together, to render it so gently wild as we behold it now.

The final charm is bestowed by the malaria. There is a piercing, thrilling, delicious kind of regret in the idea of so much beauty thrown away, or only enjoyable at its half-development, in winter and early spring, and never to be dwelt amongst, as the home scenery of any human being. For if you come hither in summer, and stray through these glades in the golden sunset, fever walks arm in arm with you, and death awaits you at the end of the dim vista. Thus the scene is like Eden in its loveliness; like Eden, too, in the fatal spell that removes it beyond the scope of man's actual possessions. But Donatello felt nothing of this dream-like melancholy that haunts the spot. As he passed among the sunny shadows, his spirit seemed to acquire new elasticity. The flicker of the sunshine, the sparkle of the fountain's gush, the dance of the leaf upon the bough, the woodland fragrance, the green freshness, the old sylvan peace and freedom, were all intermingled in those long breaths which he drew.

The ancient dust, the mouldiness of Rome, the dead atmosphere in which he had wasted so many months, the hard pavements, the smell of ruin and decaying generations, the chill palaces, the convent bells, the heavy incense of altars, the life that he had led in those dark, narrow streets, among priests, soldiers, nobles, artists, and women, — all the sense of these things rose from the young man's consciousness like a cloud which had darkened over him without his knowing how densely.

He drank in the natural influences of the scene, and was intoxicated as by an exhilarating wine. He ran races with himself along the gleam and shadow of the wood-paths. He leapt up to catch the overhanging bough of an ilex, and swinging himself by it alighted far onward, as if he had flown thither through the air. In a sudden rapture he embraced the trunk of a sturdy tree, and seemed to imagine it a creature worthy of affection and capable of a tender response; he clasped it closely in his arms, as a Faun might have clasped the warm feminine grace of the nymph, whom antiquity supposed to dwell within that rough, encircling rind. Then, in order to bring himself closer to the genial earth, with which his kindred instincts linked him so strongly, he threw himself at full length on the turf, and pressed down his lips, kissing the violets and daisies, which kissed him back again, though shyly, in their maiden fashion.

While he lay there, it was pleasant to see how the green and blue lizards, who had beta basking on some rock or on a fallen pillar that absorbed the warmth of the sun, scrupled not to scramble over him with their small feet; and how the birds alighted on the nearest twigs and sang their little roundelays unbroken by any chirrup of alarm; they recognized him, it may be, as something akin to themselves, or else they fancied that he was rooted and grew there; for these wild pets of nature dreaded him no more in his buoyant life than if a mound of soil and grass and flowers had long since covered his dead body, converting it back to the sympathies from which human existence had estranged it.

All of us, after a long abode in cities, have felt the blood gush more joyously through our veins with the first breath of rural air; few could feel it so much as Donatello, a creature of simple elements, bred in the sweet sylvan life of Tuscany, and for months back dwelling amid the mouldy gloom and dim splendor of old Rome. Nature has been shut out for numberless centuries from those stony-hearted streets, to which he had latterly grown accustomed; there is no trace of her, except for what blades of grass spring out of the pavements of the less trodden piazzas, or what weeds cluster and tuft themselves on the cornices of ruins. Therefore his joy was like that of a child that had gone astray from home, and finds him suddenly in his mother's arms again.

At last, deeming it full time for Miriam to keep her tryst, he climbed to the tiptop of the tallest tree, and thence looked about him, swaying to and fro in the gentle breeze, which was like the respiration of that great leafy, living thing. Donatello saw beneath him the whole circuit of the enchanted ground; the statues and columns pointing upward from among the shrubbery, the fountains flashing in the sunlight, the paths winding hither and thither, and continually finding out some nook of new and ancient pleasantness. He saw the villa, too, with its marble front incrusted all over with basreliefs, and statues in its many niches. It was as beautiful as a fairy palace, and seemed an abode in which the lord and lady of this fair domain might fitly dwell, and come forth each morning to enjoy as sweet a life as their happiest dreams of the past night could have depicted. All this he saw, but his first glance had taken in too wide a sweep, and it was not till his eyes fell almost directly beneath him, that Donatello beheld Miriam just turning into the path that led across the roots of his very tree.

He descended among the foliage, waiting for her to come close to the trunk, and then suddenly dropped from an impending bough, and alighted at her side. It was as if the swaying of the branches had let a ray of sunlight through. The same ray likewise glimmered among the gloomy meditations that encompassed Miriam, and lit up the pale, dark beauty of her face, while it responded pleasantly to Donatello's glance.

"I hardly know," said she, smiling, "whether you have sprouted out of the earth, or fallen from the clouds. In either case you are welcome."

And they walked onward together.

CHAPTER IX
THE FAUN AND NYMPH

Miriam's sadder mood, it might be, had at first an effect on Donatello's spirits. It checked the joyous ebullition into which they would otherwise have effervesced when he found himself in her society, not, as heretofore, in the old gloom of Rome, but under that bright soft sky and in those Arcadian woods. He was silent for a while; it being, indeed, seldom Donatello's impulse to express himself copiously in words. His usual modes of demonstration were by the natural language of gesture, the instinctive movement of his agile frame, and the unconscious play of his features, which, within a limited range of thought and emotion, would speak volumes in a moment.

By and by, his own mood seemed to brighten Miriam's, and was reflected back upon himself. He began inevitably, as it were, to dance along the wood-path; flinging himself into attitudes of strange comic grace. Often, too, he ran a little way in advance of his companion, and then stood to watch her as she approached along the shadowy and sun-fleckered path. With every step she took, he expressed his joy at her nearer and nearer presence by what might be thought an extravagance of gesticulation, but which doubtless was the language of the natural man, though laid aside and forgotten by other men, now that words have been feebly substituted in the place of signs and symbols. He gave Miriam the idea of a being not precisely man, nor yet a child, but, in a high and beautiful sense, an animal, a creature in a state of development less than what mankind has attained, yet the more perfect within itself for that very deficiency. This idea filled her mobile imagination with agreeable fantasies, which, after smiling at them herself, she tried to convey to the young man.

"What are you, my friend?" she exclaimed, always keeping in mind his singular resemblance to the Faun of the Capitol. "If you are, in good truth, that wild and pleasant creature whose face you wear, pray make me known to your kindred. They will be found hereabouts, if anywhere. Knock at the rough rind of this ilex-tree, and summon forth the Dryad! Ask the water-nymph to rise dripping from yonder fountain, and exchange a moist pressure of the hand with me! Do not fear that I shall shrink; even if one of your rough cousins, a hairy Satyr, should come capering on his goat-legs out of the haunts of far antiquity, and propose to dance with me among these lawns! And will not Bacchus,—with whom you consorted so familiarly of old, and who loved you so well,—will he not meet us here, and squeeze rich grapes into his cup for you and me?"

Donatello smiled; he laughed heartily, indeed, in sympathy with the mirth that gleamed out of Miriam's deep, dark eyes. But he did not seem quite to understand her mirthful talk, nor to be disposed to explain what kind of creature he was, or to inquire with what divine or poetic kindred his companion feigned to link him. He appeared only to know that Miriam was beautiful, and that she smiled graciously upon him; that the present moment was very sweet, and himself most happy, with the sunshine, the sylvan scenery, and woman's kindly charm, which it enclosed within its small circumference. It was delightful to see the trust which he reposed in Miriam, and his pure joy in her propinquity; he asked nothing, sought nothing, save to be near the beloved object, and brimmed over with ecstasy at that simple boon. A creature of the happy tribes below us sometimes shows the capacity of this enjoyment; a man, seldom or never.

"Donatello," said Miriam, looking at him thoughtfully, but amused, yet not without a shade of sorrow, "you seem very happy; what makes you so?"

"Because I love you!" answered Donatello.

He made this momentous confession as if it were the most natural thing in the world; and on her part,—such was the contagion of his simplicity,—Miriam heard it without anger or disturbance, though with no responding emotion. It was as if they had strayed across the limits of Arcadia; and come under a civil polity where young men might avow their passion with as little restraint as a bird pipes its note to a similar purpose.

"Why should you love me, foolish boy?" said she. "We have no points of sympathy at all. There are not two creatures more unlike, in this wide world, than you and I!"

"You are yourself, and I am Donatello," replied he. "Therefore I love you! There needs no other reason."

Certainly, there was no better or more explicable reason. It might have been imagined that Donatello's unsophisticated heart would be more readily attracted to a feminine nature of clear simplicity like his own, than to one already turbid with grief or wrong, as Miriam's seemed to be. Perhaps, On the other hand, his character needed the dark element, which it found in her. The force and energy of will, that sometimes flashed through her eyes, may have taken him captive; or, not improbably, the varying lights and shadows of her temper, now so mirthful, and anon so sad with mysterious gloom, had bewitched the youth. Analyze the matter as we may, the reason assigned by Donatello himself was as satisfactory as we are likely to attain.

Miriam could not think seriously of the avowal that had passed. He held out his love so freely, in his open palm, that she felt it could be nothing but a toy, which she might play with for an instant, and give back again. And yet Donatello's heart was so fresh a fountain, that, had Miriam been more world-worn than she was, she might have found it exquisite to slake her thirst with the feelings that welled up and brimmed over from it. She was far, very far, from the dusty mediaeval epoch, when some women have a taste for such refreshment. Even for her, however, there was an inexpressible charm in the simplicity that prompted Donatello's words and deeds; though, unless she caught them in precisely the true light, they seemed but folly, the offspring of a maimed or imperfectly developed intellect. Alternately, she almost admired, or wholly scorned him, and knew not which estimate resulted from the deeper appreciation. But it could not, she decided for herself, be other than an innocent pastime, if they two — sure to be separated by their different paths in life, to-morrow — were to gather up some of the little pleasures that chanced to grow about their feet, like the violets and wood-anemones, to-day.

Yet an impulse of rectitude impelled Miriam to give him what she still held to be a needless warning against an imaginary peril.

"If you were wiser, Donatello, you would think me a dangerous person," said she, "If you follow my footsteps, they will lead you to no good. You ought to be afraid of me."

"I would as soon think of fearing the air we breathe," he replied.

"And well you may, for it is full of malaria," said Miriam; she went on, hinting at an intangible confession, such as persons with overburdened hearts often make to children or dumb animals, or to holes in the earth, where they think their secrets may be at once revealed and buried. "Those who come too near me are in danger of great mischiefs, I do assure you. Take warning, therefore! It is a sad fatality that has brought you from your home among the Apennines, — some rusty old castle, I suppose, with a village at its foot, and an Arcadian environment of vineyards, fig-trees, and olive orchards, — a sad mischance, I say, that has transported you to my side. You have had a happy life hitherto, have you not, Donatello?"

"O, yes," answered the young man; and, though not of a retrospective turn, he made the best effort he could to send his mind back into the past. "I remember thinking it happiness to dance with the contadinas at a village feast; to taste the new, sweet wine at vintage-time, and the old, ripened wine, which our podere is famous for, in the cold winter evenings; and to devour great, luscious figs, and apricots, peaches, cherries, and melons. I was often happy in the woods, too, with hounds and horses, and very happy in watching all sorts, of creatures and birds that haunt the leafy solitudes. But never half so happy as now!"

"In these delightful groves?" she asked.

"Here, and with you," answered Donatello. "Just as we are now."

"What a fulness of content in him! How silly, and how delightful!" said Miriam to herself. Then addressing him again: "But, Donatello, how long will this happiness last?"

"How long!" he exclaimed; for it perplexed him even more to think of the future than to remember the past. "Why should it have any end? How long! Forever! forever! forever!"

"The child! the simpleton!" said Miriam, with sudden laughter, and checking it as suddenly. "But is he a simpleton indeed? Here, in those few natural words, he has expressed that deep sense, that profound conviction of its own immortality, which genuine love never fails to bring. He perplexes me, — yes, and bewitches me, — wild, gentle, beautiful creature that he is! It is like playing with a young greyhound!"

Her eyes filled with tears, at the same time that a smile shone out of them. Then first she became sensible of a delight and grief at once, in feeling this zephyr of a new affection, with its untainted freshness, blow over her weary, stifled heart, which had no right to be revived by it. The very exquisiteness of the enjoyment made her know that it ought to be a forbidden one.

"Donatello," she hastily exclaimed, "for your own sake, leave me! It is not such a happy thing as you imagine it, to wander in these woods with me, a girl from another land, burdened with a doom that she tells to none. I might make you dread me, — perhaps hate me, — if I chose; and I must choose, if I find you loving me too well!"

"I fear nothing!" said Donatello, looking into her unfathomable eyes with perfect trust. "I love always!"

"I speak in vain," thought Miriam within herself.

"Well, then, for this one hour, let me be such as he imagines me. To-morrow will be time enough to come back to my reality. My reality! what is it? Is the past so indestructible? the future so immitigable? Is the dark dream, in which I walk, of such solid, stony substance, that there can be no escape out of its dungeon? Be it so! There is, at least, that ethereal quality in my spirit, that it can make me as gay as Donatello himself, — for this one hour!"

And immediately she brightened up, as if an inward flame, heretofore stifled, were now permitted to fill her with its happy lustre, glowing through her cheeks and dancing in her eye-beams.

Donatello, brisk and cheerful as he seemed before, showed a sensibility to Miriam's gladdened mood by breaking into still wilder and ever-varying activity. He frisked around her, bubbling over with joy, which clothed itself in words that had little individual meaning, and in snatches of song that seemed as natural as bird notes. Then they both laughed together, and heard their own laughter returning in the echoes, and laughed again at the response, so that the ancient and solemn grove became full of merriment for these two blithe spirits. A bird happening to sing cheerily, Donatello gave a peculiar call, and the little feathered creature came fluttering about his head, as if it had known him through many summers.

"How close he stands to nature!" said Miriam, observing this pleasant familiarity between her companion and the bird. "He shall make me as natural as himself for this one hour."

As they strayed through that sweet wilderness, she felt more and more the influence of his elastic temperament. Miriam was an impressible and impulsive creature, as unlike herself, in different moods, as if a melancholy maiden and a glad one were both bound within the girdle about her waist, and kept in magic thraldom by the brooch that clasped it. Naturally, it is true, she was the more inclined to melancholy, yet fully capable of that high frolic of the spirits which richly compensates for many gloomy hours; if her soul was apt to lurk in the darkness of a cavern, she could sport madly in the sunshine before the cavern's mouth. Except the freshest mirth of animal spirits, like Donatello's, there is no merriment, no wild exhilaration, comparable to that of melancholy people escaping from the dark region in which it is their custom to keep themselves imprisoned.

So the shadowy Miriam almost outdid Donatello on his own ground. They ran races with each other, side by side, with shouts and laughter; they pelted one another with early flowers, and gathering them up twined them with green leaves into garlands for both their heads. They played together like children, or creatures of immortal youth. So much had they flung aside the sombre habitudes of daily life, that they seemed born to be sportive forever, and endowed with eternal mirthfulness instead of any deeper joy. It was a glimpse far backward into Arcadian life, or, further still, into the Golden Age, before mankind was burdened with sin and sorrow, and before pleasure had been darkened with those shadows that bring it into high relief, and make it happiness.

"Hark!" cried Donatello, stopping short, as he was about to bind Miriam's fair hands with flowers, and lead her along in triumph, "there is music somewhere in the grove!"

"It is your kinsman, Pan, most likely," said Miriam, "playing on his pipe. Let us go seek him, and make him puff out his rough cheeks and pipe his merriest air! Come; the strain of music will guide us onward like a gayly colored thread of silk."

"Or like a chain of flowers," responded Donatello, drawing her along by that which he had twined. "This way!—Come!"

CHAPTER X
THE SYLVAN DANCE

As the music came fresher on their ears, they danced to its cadence, extemporizing new steps and attitudes. Each varying movement had a grace which might have been worth putting into marble, for the long delight of days to come, but vanished with the movement that gave it birth, and was effaced from memory by another. In Miriam's motion, freely as she flung herself into the frolic of the hour, there was still an artful beauty; in Donatello's, there was a charm of indescribable grotesqueness hand in hand with grace; sweet, bewitching, most provocative of laughter, and yet akin to pathos, so deeply did it touch the heart. This was the ultimate peculiarity, the final touch, distinguishing between the sylvan creature and the beautiful companion at his side. Setting apart only this, Miriam resembled a Nymph, as much as Donatello did a Faun.

There were flitting moments, indeed, when she played the sylvan character as perfectly as he. Catching glimpses of her, then, you would have fancied that an oak had sundered its rough bark to let her dance freely forth, endowed with the same spirit in her human form as that which rustles in the leaves; or that she had emerged through the pebbly bottom of a fountain, a water-nymph, to play and sparkle in the sunshine, flinging a quivering light around her, and suddenly disappearing in a shower of rainbow drops.

As the fountain sometimes subsides into its basin, so in Miriam there were symptoms that the frolic of her spirits would at last tire itself out.

"Ah! Donatello," cried she, laughing, as she stopped to take a breath; "you have an unfair advantage over me! I am no true creature of the woods; while you are a real Faun, I do believe. When your curls shook just now, methought I had a peep at the pointed ears."

Donatello snapped his fingers above his head, as fauns and satyrs taught us first to do, and seemed to radiate jollity out of his whole nimble person. Nevertheless, there was a kind of dim apprehension in his face, as if he dreaded that a moment's pause might break the spell, and snatch away the sportive companion whom he had waited for through so many dreary months.

"Dance! dance!" cried he joyously. "If we take breath, we shall be as we were yesterday. There, now, is the music, just beyond this clump of trees. Dance, Miriam, dance!"

They had now reached an open, grassy glade (of which there are many in that artfully constructed wilderness), set round with stone seats, on which the aged moss had kindly essayed to spread itself instead of cushions. On one of the stone benches sat the musicians, whose strains had enticed our wild couple thitherward. They proved to be a vagrant band, such as Rome, and all Italy, abounds with; comprising a harp, a flute, and a violin, which, though greatly the worse for wear, the performers had skill enough to provoke and modulate into tolerable harmony. It chanced to be a feast-day; and, instead of playing in the sun-scorched piazzas of the city, or beneath the windows of some unresponsive palace, they had bethought themselves to try the echoes of these woods; for, on the festas of the Church, Rome scatters its merrymakers all abroad, ripe for the dance or any other pastime.

As Miriam and Donatello emerged from among the trees, the musicians scraped, tinkled, or blew, each according to his various kind of instrument, more inspiringly than ever. A darkchecked little girl, with bright black eyes, stood by, shaking a tambourine set round with tinkling bells, and thumping it on its parchment head. Without interrupting his brisk, though measured movement, Donatello snatched away this unmelodious contrivance, and, flourishing it above his head, produced music of indescribable potency, still dancing with frisky step, and striking the tambourine, and ringing its little bells, all in one jovial act.

It might be that there was magic in the sound, or contagion, at least, in the spirit which had got possession of Miriam and himself, for very soon a number of festal people were drawn to the spot, and struck into the dance, singly or in pairs, as if they were all gone mad with jollity. Among them were some of the plebeian damsels whom we meet bareheaded in the Roman streets, with silver stilettos thrust through their glossy hair; the contadinas, too, from the Campagna and the villages, with their rich and picturesque costumes of scarlet and all bright hues, such as fairer maidens might not venture to put on. Then came the modern Roman from Trastevere, perchance, with his old cloak drawn about him like a toga, which anon, as his active motion heated him, he flung aside. Three French soldiers capered freely into the throng, in wide scarlet trousers, their short swords dangling at their sides; and three German artists in gray flaccid hats and flaunting beards; and one of the Pope's Swiss guardsmen in the strange motley garb which Michael Angelo contrived for them. Two young English tourists (one of them a lord) took contadine partners and dashed in, as did also a shaggy man in goat-skin breeches, who looked like rustic Pan in person, and footed it as merrily as he. Besides the above there was a herdsman or two from the Campagna, and a few peasants in sky-blue jackets, and small-clothes tied with ribbons at the knees; haggard and sallow were these last, poor serfs, having little to eat and nothing but the malaria to breathe; but still they plucked up a momentary spirit and joined hands in Donatello's dance.

Here, as it seemed, had the Golden Age come back again within the Precincts of this sunny glade, thawing mankind out of their cold formalities, releasing them from irksome restraint, mingling them together in such childlike gayety that new flowers (of which the old bosom of the earth is full) sprang up beneath their footsteps. The sole exception to the geniality of the moment, as we have understood, was seen in a countryman of our own, who sneered at the spectacle, and declined to compromise his dignity by making part of it.

The harper thrummed with rapid fingers; the violin player flashed his bow back and forth across the strings; the flautist poured his breath in quick puffs of jollity, while Donatello shook the tambourine above his head, and led the merry throng with unweariable steps. As they followed one another in a wild ring of mirth, it seemed the realization of one of those bas-reliefs where a dance of nymphs, satyrs, or bacchanals is twined around the circle of an antique vase; or it was like the sculptured scene on the front and sides of a sarcophagus, where, as often as any other device, a festive procession mocks the ashes and white bones that are treasured up within. You might take it for a marriage pageant; but after a while, if you look at these merry-makers, following them from end to end of the marble coffin, you doubt whether their gay movement is leading them to a happy close. A youth has suddenly fallen in the dance; a chariot is overturned and broken, flinging the charioteer headlong to the ground; a maiden seems to have grown faint or weary, and is drooping on the bosom of a friend. Always some tragic incident is shadowed forth or thrust sidelong into the spectacle; and when once it has caught your eye you can look no more at the festal portions of the scene, except with reference to this one slightly suggested doom and sorrow.

As in its mirth, so in the darker characteristic here alluded to, there was an analogy between the sculptured scene on the sarcophagus and the wild dance which we have been describing. In the midst of its madness and riot Miriam found herself suddenly confronted by a strange figure that shook its fantastic garments in the air, and pranced before her on its tiptoes, almost vying with the agility of Donatello himself. It was the model.

A moment afterwards Donatello was aware that she had retired from the dance. He hastened towards her, and flung himself on the grass beside the stone bench on which Miriam was sitting. But a strange distance and unapproachableness had all at once enveloped her; and though he saw her within reach of his arm, yet the light of her eyes seemed as far off as that of a star, nor was there any warmth in the melancholy smile with which she regarded him.

"Come back!" cried he. "Why should this happy hour end so soon?"

"It must end here, Donatello," said she, in answer to his words and outstretched hand; "and such hours, I believe, do not often repeat themselves in a lifetime. Let me go, my friend; let me vanish from you quietly among the shadows of these trees. See, the companions of our pastime are vanishing already!"

Whether it was that the harp-strings were broken, the violin out of tune, or the flautist out of breath, so it chanced that the music had ceased, and the dancers come abruptly to a pause. All that motley throng of rioters was dissolved as suddenly as it had been drawn together. In Miriam's remembrance the scene had a character of fantasy. It was as if a company of satyrs, fauns, and nymphs, with Pan in the midst of them, had been disporting themselves in these venerable woods only a moment ago; and now in another moment, because some profane eye had looked at them too closely, or some intruder had cast a shadow on their mirth, the sylvan pageant had utterly disappeared. If a few of the merry-makers lingered among the trees, they had hidden their racy peculiarities under the garb and aspect of ordinary people, and sheltered themselves in the weary commonplace of daily life. Just an instant before it was Arcadia and the Golden Age. The spell being broken, it was now only that old tract of pleasure ground, close by the people's gate of Rome,—a tract where the crimes and calamities of ages, the many battles, blood recklessly poured out, and deaths of myriads, have corrupted all the soil, creating an influence that makes the air deadly to human lungs.

"You must leave me," said Miriam to Donatello more imperatively than before; "have I not said it? Go; and look not behind you."

"Miriam," whispered Donatello, grasping her hand forcibly, "who is it that stands in the shadow yonder, beckoning you to follow him?"

"Hush; leave me!" repeated Miriam. "Your hour is past; his hour has come."

Donatello still gazed in the direction which he had indicated, and the expression of his face was fearfully changed, being so disordered, perhaps with terror, — at all events with anger and invincible repugnance, — that Miriam hardly knew him. His lips were drawn apart so as to disclose his set teeth, thus giving him a look of animal rage, which we seldom see except in persons of the simplest and rudest natures. A shudder seemed to pass through his very bones.

"I hate him!" muttered he.

"Be satisfied; I hate him too!" said Miriam.

She had no thought of making this avowal, but was irresistibly drawn to it by the sympathy of the dark emotion in her own breast with that so strongly expressed by Donatello. Two drops of water or of blood do not more naturally flow into each other than did her hatred into his.

"Shall I clutch him by the throat?" whispered Donatello, with a savage scowl. "Bid me do so, and we are rid of him forever."

"In Heaven's name, no violence!" exclaimed Miriam, affrighted out of the scornful control which she had hitherto held over her companion, by the fierceness that he so suddenly developed. "O, have pity on me, Donatello, if for nothing else, yet because in the midst of my wretchedness I let myself be your playmate for this one wild hour! Follow me no farther. Henceforth leave me to my doom. Dear friend, — kind, simple, loving friend, — make me not more wretched by the remembrance of having thrown fierce hates or loves into the wellspring of your happy life!"

"Not follow you!" repeated Donatello, soothed from anger into sorrow, less by the purport of what she said, than by the melancholy sweetness of her voice, — "not follow you! What other path have I?"

"We will talk of it once again," said Miriam still soothingly; "soon — to-morrow when you will; only leave me now."

CHAPTER XI
FRAGMENTARY SENTENCES

In the Borghese Grove, so recently uproarious with merriment and music, there remained only Miriam and her strange follower.

A solitude had suddenly spread itself around them. It perhaps symbolized a peculiar character in the relation of these two, insulating them, and building up an insuperable barrier between their life-streams and other currents, which might seem to flow in close vicinity. For it is one of the chief earthly incommodities of some species of misfortune, or of a great crime, that it makes the actor in the one, or the sufferer of the other, an alien in the world, by interposing a wholly unsympathetic medium betwixt himself and those whom he yearns to meet.

Owing, it may be, to this moral estrangement, — this chill remoteness of their position, — there have come to us but a few vague whisperings of what passed in Miriam's interview that afternoon with the sinister personage who had dogged her footsteps ever since the visit to the catacomb. In weaving these mystic utterances into a continuous scene, we undertake a task resembling in its perplexity that of gathering up and piecing together the fragments ora letter which has been torn and scattered to the winds. Many words of deep significance, many entire sentences, and those possibly the most important ones, have flown too far on the winged breeze to be recovered. If we insert our own conjectural amendments, we perhaps give a purport utterly at variance with the true one. Yet unless we attempt something in this way, there must remain an unsightly gap, and a lack of continuousness and dependence in our narrative; so that it would arrive at certain inevitable catastrophes without due warning of their imminence.

Of so much we are sure, that there seemed to be a sadly mysterious fascination in the influence of this ill-omened person over Miriam; it was such as beasts and reptiles of subtle and evil nature sometimes exercise upon their victims. Marvellous it was to see the hopelessness with which being naturally of so courageous a spirit she resigned herself to the thraldom in which he held her. That iron chain, of which some of the massive links were round her feminine waist, and the others in his ruthless hand, — or which, perhaps, bound the pair together by a bond equally torturing to each, — must have been forged in some such unhallowed furnace as is only kindled by evil passions, and fed by evil deeds.

The Marble Faun

Yet, let us trust, there may have been no crime in Miriam, but only one of those fatalities which are among the most insoluble riddles propounded to mortal comprehension; the fatal decree by which every crime is made to be the agony of many innocent persons, as well as of the single guilty one.

It was, at any rate, but a feeble and despairing kind of remonstrance which she had now the energy to oppose against his persecution.

"You follow me too closely," she said, in low, faltering accents; "you allow me too scanty room to draw my breath. Do you know what will be the end of this?" "I know well what must be the end," he replied.

"Tell me, then," said Miriam, "that I may compare your foreboding with my own. Mine is a very dark one."

"There can be but one result, and that soon," answered the model. "You must throw off your present mask and assume another. You must vanish out of the scene: quit Rome with me, and leave no trace whereby to follow you. It is in my power, as you well know, to compel your acquiescence in my bidding. You are aware of the penalty of a refusal."

"Not that penalty with which you would terrify me," said Miriam; "another there may be, but not so grievous." "What is that other?" he inquired. "Death! simply death!" she answered. "Death," said her persecutor, "is not so simple and opportune a thing as you imagine. You are strong and warm with life. Sensitive and irritable as your spirit is, these many months of trouble, this latter thraldom in which I hold you, have scarcely made your cheek paler than I saw it in your girlhood. Miriam,— for I forbear to speak another name, at which these leaves would shiver above our heads,—Miriam, you cannot die!"

"Might not a dagger find my heart?" said she, for the first time meeting his eyes. "Would not poison make an end of me? Will not the Tiber drown me?"

"It might," he answered; "for I allow that you are mortal. But, Miriam, believe me, it is not your fate to die while there remains so much to be sinned and suffered in the world. We have a destiny which we must needs fulfil together. I, too, have struggled to escape it. I was as anxious as yourself to break the tie between us,—to bury the past in a fathomless grave,—to make it impossible that we should ever meet, until you confront me at the bar of Judgment! You little can imagine what steps I took to render all this secure; and what was the result? Our strange interview in the bowels of the earth convinced me of the futility of my design."

"Ah, fatal chance!" cried Miriam, covering her face with her hands.

"Yes, your heart trembled with horror when you recognized me," rejoined he; "but you did not guess that there was an equal horror in my own!"

"Why would not the weight of earth above our heads have crumbled down upon us both, forcing us apart, but burying us equally?" cried Miriam, in a burst of vehement passion. "O, that we could have wandered in those dismal passages till we both perished, taking opposite paths in the darkness, so that when we lay down to die, our last breaths might not mingle!"

"It were vain to wish it," said the model. "In all that labyrinth of midnight paths, we should have found one another out to live or die together. Our fates cross and are entangled. The threads are twisted into a strong cord, which is dragging us to an evil doom. Could the knots be severed, we might escape. But neither can your slender fingers untie these knots, nor my masculine force break them. We must submit!"

"Pray for rescue, as I have," exclaimed Miriam. "Pray for deliverance from me, since I am your evil genius, as you mine. Dark as your life has been, I have known you to pray in times past!"

At these words of Miriam, a tremor and horror appeared to seize upon her persecutor, insomuch that he shook and grew ashy pale before her eyes. In this man's memory there was something that made it awful for him to think of prayer; nor would any torture be more intolerable than to be reminded of such divine comfort and succor as await pious souls merely for the asking; This torment was perhaps the token of a native temperament deeply susceptible of religious impressions, but which had been wronged, violated, and debased, until, at length, it was capable only of terror from the sources that were intended for our purest and loftiest consolation. He looked so fearfully at her, and with such intense pain struggling in his eyes, that Miriam felt pity.

And now, all at once, it struck her that he might be mad. It was an idea that had never before seriously occurred to her mind, although, as soon as suggested, it fitted marvellously into many circumstances that lay within her knowledge. But, alas! such was her evil fortune, that, whether mad or no, his power over her remained the same, and was likely to be used only the more tyrannously, if exercised by a lunatic.

The Marble Faun

"I would not give you pain," she said, soothingly; "your faith allows you the consolations of penance and absolution. Try what help there may be in these, and leave me to myself."

"Do not think it, Miriam," said he; "we are bound together, and can never part again." "Why should it seem so impossible?" she rejoined. "Think how I had escaped from all the past! I had made for myself a new sphere, and found new friends, new occupations, new hopes and enjoyments. My heart, methinks, was almost as unburdened as if there had been no miserable life behind me. The human spirit does not perish of a single wound, nor exhaust itself in a single trial of life. Let us but keep asunder, and all may go well for both." "We fancied ourselves forever sundered," he replied. "Yet we met once, in the bowels of the earth; and, were we to part now, our fates would fling us together again in a desert, on a mountain-top, or in whatever spot seemed safest. You speak in vain, therefore."

"You mistake your own will for an iron necessity," said Miriam; "otherwise, you might have suffered me to glide past you like a ghost, when we met among those ghosts of ancient days. Even now you might bid me pass as freely."

"Never!" said he, with unmitigable will; "your reappearance has destroyed the work of years. You know the power that I have over you. Obey my bidding; or, within a short time, it shall be exercised: nor will I cease to haunt you till the moment comes."

"Then," said Miriam more calmly, "I foresee the end, and have already warned you of it. It will be death!"

"Your own death, Miriam,—or mine?" he asked, looking fixedly at her.

"Do you imagine me a murderess?" said she, shuddering; "you, at least, have no right to think me so!"

"Yet," rejoined he, with a glance of dark meaning, "men have said that this white hand had once a crimson stain." He took her hand as he spoke, and held it in his own, in spite of the repugnance, amounting to nothing short of agony, with which she struggled to regain it. Holding it up to the fading light (for there was already dimness among the trees), he appeared to examine it closely, as if to discover the imaginary blood-stain with which he taunted her. He smiled as he let it go. "It looks very white," said he; "but I have known hands as white, which all the water in the ocean would not have washed clean."

"It had no stain," retorted Miriam bitterly, "until you grasped it in your own."

The wind has blown away whatever else they may have spoken.

They went together towards the town, and, on their way, continued to make reference, no doubt, to some strange and dreadful history of their former life, belonging equally to this dark man and to the fair and youthful woman whom he persecuted. In their words, or in the breath that uttered them, there seemed to be an odor of guilt, and a scent of blood. Yet, how can we imagine that a stain of ensanguined crime should attach to Miriam! Or how, on the other hand, should spotless innocence be subjected to a thraldom like that which she endured from the spectre, whom she herself had evoked out of the darkness! Be this as it might, Miriam, we have reason to believe, still continued to beseech him, humbly, passionately, wildly, only to go his way, and leave her free to follow her own sad path.

Thus they strayed onward through the green wilderness of the Borghese grounds, and soon came near the city wall, where, had Miriam raised her eyes, she might have seen Hilda and the sculptor leaning on the parapet. But she walked in a mist of trouble, and could distinguish little beyond its limits. As they came within public observation, her persecutor fell behind, throwing off the imperious manner which he had assumed during their solitary interview. The Porta del Popolo swarmed with life. The merry-makers, who had spent the feast-day outside the walls, were now thronging in; a party of horsemen were entering beneath the arch; a travelling carriage had been drawn up just within the verge, and was passing through the villainous ordeal of the papal custom-house. In the broad piazza, too, there was a motley crowd.

But the stream of Miriam's trouble kept its way through this flood of human life, and neither mingled with it nor was turned aside. With a sad kind of feminine ingenuity, she found a way to kneel before her tyrant undetected, though in full sight of all the people, still beseeching him for freedom, and in vain.

CHAPTER XII

A STROLL ON THE PINCIAN

Hilda, after giving the last touches to the picture of Beatrice Cenci, had flown down from her dove-cote, late in the afternoon, and gone to the Pincian Hill, in the hope of hearing a strain or two of exhilarating music. There, as it happened, she met the sculptor, for, to say the truth, Kenyon had well noted the fair artist's ordinary way of life, and was accustomed to shape his own movements so as to bring him often within her sphere.

The Pincian Hill is the favorite promenade of the Roman aristocracy. At the present day, however, like most other Roman possessions, it belongs less to the native inhabitants than to the barbarians from Gaul, Great Britain, anti beyond the sea, who have established a peaceful usurpation over whatever is enjoyable or memorable in the Eternal City. These foreign guests are indeed ungrateful, if they do not breathe a prayer for Pope Clement, or whatever Holy Father it may have been, who levelled the summit of the mount so skilfully, and bounded it with the parapet of the city wall; who laid out those broad walks and drives, and overhung them with the deepening shade of many kinds of tree; who scattered the flowers, of all seasons and of every clime, abundantly over those green, central lawns; who scooped out hollows in fit places, and, setting great basins of marble in them, caused ever-gushing fountains to fill them to the brim; who reared up the immemorial obelisk out of the soil that had long hidden it; who placed pedestals along the borders of the avenues, and crowned them with busts of that multitude of worthies — statesmen, heroes, artists, men of letters and of song — whom the whole world claims as its chief ornaments, though Italy produced them all. In a word, the Pincian garden is one of the things that reconcile the stranger (since he fully appreciates the enjoyment, and feels nothing of the cost) to the rule of an irresponsible dynasty of Holy Fathers, who seem to have aimed at making life as agreeable an affair as it can well be.

In this pleasant spot, the red-trousered French soldiers are always to be seen; bearded and grizzled veterans, perhaps with medals of Algiers or the Crimea on their breasts. To them is assigned the peaceful duty of seeing that children do not trample on the flower beds, nor any youthful lover rifle them of their fragrant blossoms to stick in the beloved one's hair. Here sits (drooping upon some marble bench, in the treacherous sunshine) the consumptive girl, whose friends have brought her, for cure, to a climate that instils poison into its very purest breath. Here, all day, come nursery-maids, burdened with rosy English babies, or guiding the footsteps of little travellers from the far Western world. Here, in the sunny afternoons, roll and rumble all kinds of equipages, from the cardinal's old-fashioned and gorgeous purple carriage to the gay barouche of modern date. Here horsemen gallop on thoroughbred steeds. Here, in short, all the transitory population of Rome, the world's great watering-place, rides, drives, or promenades! Here are beautiful sunsets; and here, whichever way you turn your eyes, are scenes as well worth gazing at, both in themselves and for their historic interest, as any that the sun ever rose and set upon. Here, too, on certain afternoons of the week, a French military band flings out rich music over the poor old city, floating her with strains as loud as those of her own echoless triumphs.

Hilda and the sculptor (by the contrivance of the latter, who loved best to be alone with his young countrywoman) had wandered beyond the throng of promenaders, whom they left in a dense cluster around the music. They strayed, indeed, to the farthest point of the Pincian Hill, and leaned over the parapet, looking down upon the Muro Torto, a massive fragment of the oldest Roman wall, which juts over, as if ready to tumble down by its own weight, yet seems still the most indestructible piece of work that men's hands ever piled together. In the blue distance rose Soracte, and other heights, which have gleamed afar, to our imaginations, but look scarcely real to our bodily eyes, because, being dreamed about so much, they have taken the aerial tints which belong only to a dream. These, nevertheless, are the solid framework of hills that shut in Rome, and its wide surrounding Campagna,—no land of dreams, but the broadest page of history, crowded so full with memorable events that one obliterates another; as if Time had crossed and recrossed his own records till they grew illegible.

But, not to meddle with history,—with which our narrative is no otherwise concerned, than that the very dust of Rome is historic, and inevitably settles on our page and mingles with our ink,—we will return to our two friends, who were still leaning over the wall. Beneath them lay the broad sweep of the Borghese grounds, covered with trees, amid which appeared the white gleam of pillars and statues, and the flash of an upspringing fountain, all to be overshadowed at a later period of the year by the thicker growth of foliage.

The advance of vegetation, in this softer climate, is less abrupt than the inhabitant of the cold North is accustomed to observe. Beginning earlier,—even in February,—Spring is not compelled to burst into Summer with such headlong haste; there is time to dwell upon each opening beauty, and to enjoy the budding leaf, the tender green, the sweet youth and freshness of the year; it gives us its maiden charm, before, settling into the married Summer, which, again, does not so soon sober itself into matronly Autumn. In our own country, the virgin Spring hastens to its bridal too abruptly. But here, after a month or two of kindly growth, the leaves of the young trees, which cover that portion of the Borghese grounds nearest the city wall, were still in their tender half-development.

In the remoter depths, among the old groves of ilex-trees, Hilda and Kenyon heard the faint sound of music, laughter, and mingling voices. It was probably the uproar—spreading even so far as the walls of Rome, and growing faded and melancholy in its passage—of that wild sylvan merriment, which we have already attempted to describe. By and by it ceased—although the two listeners still tried to distinguish it between the bursts of nearer music from the military band. But there was no renewal of that distant mirth. Soon afterwards they saw a solitary figure advancing along one of the paths that lead from the obscurer part of the ground towards the gateway.

"Look! is it not Donatello?" said Hilda.

"He it is, beyond a doubt," replied the sculptor. "But how gravely he walks, and with what long looks behind him! He seems either very weary, or very sad. I should not hesitate to call it sadness, if Donatello were a creature capable of the sin and folly of low spirits. In all these hundred paces, while we have been watching him, he has not made one of those little caprioles in the air which are characteristic of his natural gait. I begin to doubt whether he is a veritable Faun."

"Then," said Hilda, with perfect simplicity, "you have thought him—and do think him—one of that strange, wild, happy race of creatures, that used to laugh and sport in the woods, in the old, old times? So do I, indeed! But I never quite believed, till now, that fauns existed anywhere but in poetry."

The sculptor at first merely smiled. Then, as the idea took further possession of his mind, he laughed outright, and wished from the bottom of his heart (being in love with Hilda, though he had never told her so) that he could have rewarded or punished her for its pretty absurdity with a kiss.

"O Hilda, what a treasure of sweet faith and pure imagination you hide under that little straw hat!" cried he, at length. "A Faun! a Faun! Great Pan is not dead, then, after all! The whole tribe of mythical creatures yet live in the moonlit seclusion of a young girl's fancy, and find it a lovelier abode and play-place, I doubt not, than their Arcadian haunts of yore. What bliss, if a man of marble, like myself, could stray thither, too!"

"Why do you laugh so?" asked Hilda, reddening; for she was a little disturbed at Kenyon's ridicule, however kindly expressed. "What can I have said, that you think so very foolish?"

"Well, not foolish, then," rejoined the sculptor, "but wiser, it may be, than I can fathom. Really, however, the idea does strike one as delightfully fresh, when we consider Donatello's position and external environment. Why, my dear Hilda, he is a Tuscan born, of an old noble race in that part of Italy; and he has a moss-grown tower among the Apennines, where he and his forefathers have dwelt, under their own vines and fig-trees, from an unknown antiquity. His boyish passion for Miriam has introduced him familiarly to our little circle; and our republican and artistic simplicity of intercourse has included this young Italian, on the same terms as one of ourselves. But, if we paid due respect to rank and title, we should bend reverentially to Donatello, and salute him as his Excellency the Count di Monte Beni."

"That is a droll idea, much droller than his being a Faun!" said Hilda, laughing in her turn. "This does not quite satisfy me, however, especially as you yourself recognized and acknowledged his wonderful resemblance to the statue."

"Except as regards the pointed ears," said Kenyon; adding, aside, "and one other little peculiarity, generally observable in the statues of fauns."

"As for his Excellency the Count di Monte Beni's ears," replied Hilda, smiling again at the dignity with which this title invested their playful friend, "you know we could never see their shape, on account of his clustering curls. Nay, I remember, he once started back, as shyly as a wild deer, when Miriam made a pretence of examining them. How do you explain that?"

"O, I certainly shall not contend against such a weight of evidence, the fact of his faunship being otherwise so probable," answered the sculptor, still hardly retaining his gravity. "Faun or not, Donatello or the Count di Monte Beni—is a singularly wild creature, and, as I have remarked on other occasions, though very gentle, does not love to be touched. Speaking in no harsh sense, there is a great deal of animal nature in him, as if he had been born in the woods, and had run wild all his childhood, and were as yet but imperfectly domesticated. Life, even in our day, is very simple and unsophisticated in some of the shaggy nooks of the Apennines."

The Marble Faun

"It annoys me very much," said Hilda, "this inclination, which most people have, to explain away the wonder and the mystery out of everything. Why could not you allow me—and yourself, too—the satisfaction of thinking him a Faun?"

"Pray keep your belief, dear Hilda, if it makes you any happier," said the sculptor; "and I shall do my best to become a convert. Donatello has asked me to spend the summer with him, in his ancestral tower, where I purpose investigating the pedigree of these sylvan counts, his forefathers; and if their shadows beckon me into dreamland, I shall willingly follow. By the bye, speaking of Donatello, there is a point on which I should like to be enlightened."

"Can I help you, then?" said Hilda, in answer to his look.

"Is there the slightest chance of his winning Miriam's affections?" suggested Kenyon.

"Miriam! she, so accomplished and gifted!" exclaimed Hilda; "and he, a rude, uncultivated boy! No, no, no!"

"It would seem impossible," said the sculptor. "But, on the other hand, a gifted woman flings away her affections so unaccountably, sometimes! Miriam of late has been very morbid and miserable, as we both know. Young as she is, the morning light seems already to have faded out of her life; and now comes Donatello, with natural sunshine enough for himself and her, and offers her the opportunity of making her heart and life all new and cheery again. People of high intellectual endowments do not require similar ones in those they love. They are just the persons to appreciate the wholesome gush of natural feeling, the honest affection, the simple joy, the fulness of contentment with what he loves, which Miriam sees in Donatello. True; she may call him a simpleton. It is a necessity of the case; for a man loses the capacity for this kind of affection, in proportion as he cultivates and refines himself."

"Dear me!" said Hilda, drawing imperceptibly away from her companion. "Is this the penalty of refinement? Pardon me; I do not believe it. It is because you are a sculptor, that you think nothing can be finely wrought except it be cold and hard, like the marble in which your ideas take shape. I am a painter, and know that the most delicate beauty may be softened and warmed throughout."

"I said a foolish thing, indeed," answered the sculptor. "It surprises me, for I might have drawn a wiser knowledge out of my own experience. It is the surest test of genuine love, that it brings back our early simplicity to the worldliest of us."

Thus talking, they loitered slowly along beside the parapet which borders the level summit of the Pincian with its irregular sweep. At intervals they looked through the lattice-work of their thoughts at the varied prospects that lay before and beneath them.

From the terrace where they now stood there is an abrupt descent towards the Piazza del Popolo; and looking down into its broad space they beheld the tall palatial edifices, the church domes, and the ornamented gateway, which grew and were consolidated out of the thought of Michael Angelo. They saw, too, the red granite obelisk, oldest of things, even in Rome, which rises in the centre of the piazza, with a fourfold fountain at its base. All Roman works and ruins (whether of the empire, the far-off republic, or the still more distant kings) assume a transient, visionary, and impalpable character when we think that this indestructible monument supplied one of the recollections which Moses and the Israelites bore from Egypt into the desert. Perchance, on beholding the cloudy pillar and the fiery column, they whispered awestricken to one another, "In its shape it is like that old obelisk which we and our fathers have so often seen on the borders of the Nile." And now that very obelisk, with hardly a trace of decay upon it, is the first thing that the modern traveller sees after entering the Flaminian Gate!

Lifting their eyes, Hilda and her companion gazed westward, and saw beyond the invisible Tiber the Castle of St. Angelo; that immense tomb of a pagan emperor, with the archangel at its summit.

Still farther off appeared a mighty pile of buildings, surmounted by the vast dome, which all of us have shaped and swelled outward, like a huge bubble, to the utmost Scope of our imaginations, long before we see it floating over the worship of the city. It may be most worthily seen from precisely the point where our two friends were now standing. At any nearer view the grandeur of St. Peter's hides itself behind the immensity of its separate parts, — so that we see only the front, only the sides, only the pillared length and loftiness of the portico, and not the mighty whole. But at this distance the entire outline of the world's cathedral, as well as that of the palace of the world's chief priest, is taken in at once. In such remoteness, moreover, the imagination is not debarred from lending its assistance, even while we have the reality before our eyes, and helping the weakness of human sense to do justice to so grand an object. It requires both faith and fancy to enable us to feel, what is nevertheless so true, that yonder, in front of the purple outline of hills, is the grandest edifice ever built by man, painted against God's loveliest sky.

The Marble Faun

After contemplating a little while a scene which their long residence in Rome had made familiar to them, Kenyon and Hilda again let their glances fall into the piazza at their feet. They there beheld Miriam, who had just entered the Porta del Popolo, and was standing by the obelisk and fountain. With a gesture that impressed Kenyon as at once suppliant and imperious, she seemed to intimate to a figure which had attended her thus far, that it was now her desire to be left alone. The pertinacious model, however, remained immovable.

And the sculptor here noted a circumstance, which, according to the interpretation he might put upon it, was either too trivial to be mentioned, or else so mysteriously significant that he found it difficult to believe his eyes. Miriam knelt down on the steps of the fountain; so far there could be no question of the fact. To other observers, if any there were, she probably appeared to take this attitude merely for the convenience of dipping her fingers into the gush of water from the mouth of one of the stone lions. But as she clasped her hands together after thus bathing them, and glanced upward at the model, an idea took strong possession of Kenyon's mind that Miriam was kneeling to this dark follower there in the world's face!

"Do you see it?" he said to Hilda.

"See what?" asked she, surprised at the emotion of his tone. "I see Miriam, who has just bathed her hands in that delightfully cool water. I often dip my fingers into a Roman fountain, and think of the brook that used to be one of my playmates in my New England village."

"I fancied I saw something else," said Kenyon; "but it was doubtless a mistake."

But, allowing that he had caught a true glimpse into the hidden significance of Miriam's gesture, what a terrible thraldom did it suggest! Free as she seemed to be,—beggar as he looked,—the nameless vagrant must then be dragging the beautiful Miriam through the streets of Rome, fettered and shackled more cruelly than any captive queen of yore following in an emperor's triumph. And was it conceivable that she would have been thus enthralled unless some great error—how great Kenyon dared not think—or some fatal weakness had given this dark adversary a vantage ground?

"Hilda," said he abruptly, "who and what is Miriam? Pardon me; but are you sure of her?"

"Sure of her!" repeated Hilda, with an angry blush, for her friend's sake. "I am sure that she is kind, good, and generous; a true and faithful friend, whom I love dearly, and who loves me as well! What more than this need I be sure of?"

"And your delicate instincts say all this in her favor? — nothing against her?" continued the sculptor, without heeding the irritation of Hilda's tone. "These are my own impressions, too. But she is such a mystery! We do not even know whether she is a countrywoman of ours, or an Englishwoman, or a German. There is Anglo-Saxon blood in her veins, one would say, and a right English accent on her tongue, but much that is not English breeding, nor American. Nowhere else but in Rome, and as an artist, could she hold a place in society without giving some clew to her past life."

"I love her dearly," said Hilda, still with displeasure in her tone, "and trust her most entirely."

"My heart trusts her at least, whatever my head may do," replied Kenyon; "and Rome is not like one of our New England villages, where we need the permission of each individual neighbor for every act that we do, every word that we utter, and every friend that we make or keep. In these particulars the papal despotism allows us freer breath than our native air; and if we like to take generous views of our associates, we can do so, to a reasonable extent, without ruining ourselves."

"The music has ceased," said Hilda; "I am going now."

There are three streets that, beginning close beside each other, diverge from the Piazza del Popolo towards the heart of Rome: on the left, the Via del Babuino; on the right, the Via della Ripetta; and between these two that world-famous avenue, the Corso. It appeared that Miriam and her strange companion were passing up the first mentioned of these three, and were soon hidden from Hilda and the sculptor.

The two latter left the Pincian by the broad and stately walk that skirts along its brow. Beneath them, from the base of the abrupt descent, the city spread wide away in a close contiguity of red-earthen roofs, above which rose eminent the domes of a hundred churches, beside here and there a tower, and the upper windows of some taller or higher situated palace, looking down on a multitude of palatial abodes. At a distance, ascending out of the central mass of edifices, they could see the top of the Antonine column, and near it the circular roof of the Pantheon looking heavenward with its ever-open eye.

Except these two objects, almost everything that they beheld was mediaeval, though built, indeed, of the massive old stones and indestructible bricks of imperial Rome; for the ruins of the

Coliseum, the Golden House, and innumerable temples of Roman gods, and mansions of Caesars and senators, had supplied the material for all those gigantic hovels, and their walls were cemented with mortar of inestimable cost, being made of precious antique statues, burnt long ago for this petty purpose.

Rome, as it now exists, has grown up under the Popes, and seems like nothing but a heap of broken rubbish, thrown into the great chasm between our own days and the Empire, merely to fill it up; and, for the better part of two thousand years, its annals of obscure policies, and wars, and continually recurring misfortunes, seem also but broken rubbish, as compared with its classic history.

If we consider the present city as at all connected with the famous one of old, it is only because we find it built over its grave. A depth of thirty feet of soil has covered up the Rome of ancient days, so that it lies like the dead corpse of a giant, decaying for centuries, with no survivor mighty enough even to bury it, until the dust of all those years has gathered slowly over its recumbent form and made a casual sepulchre.

We know not how to characterize, in any accordant and compatible terms, the Rome that lies before us; its sunless alleys, and streets of palaces; its churches, lined with the gorgeous marbles that were originally polished for the adornment of pagan temples; its thousands of evil smells, mixed up with fragrance of rich incense, diffused from as many censers; its little life, deriving feeble nutriment from what has long been dead. Everywhere, some fragment of ruin suggesting the magnificence of a former epoch; everywhere, moreover, a Cross, — and nastiness at the foot of it. As the sum of all, there are recollections that kindle the soul, and a gloom and languor that depress it beyond any depth of melancholic sentiment that can be elsewhere known.

Yet how is it possible to say an unkind or irreverential word of Rome? The city of all time, and of all the world! The spot for which man's great life and deeds have done so much, and for which decay has done whatever glory and dominion could not do! At this moment, the evening sunshine is flinging its golden mantle over it, making all that we thought mean magnificent; the bells of all the churches suddenly ring out, as if it were a peal of triumph because Rome is still imperial.

"I sometimes fancy," said Hilda, on whose susceptibility the scene always made a strong impression, "that Rome — mere Rome — will crowd everything else out of my heart."

"Heaven forbid!" ejaculated the sculptor. They had now reached the grand stairs that ascend from the Piazza di Spagna to the hither brow of the Pincian Hill. Old Beppo, the millionnaire of his ragged fraternity, it is a wonder that no artist paints him as the cripple whom St. Peter heals at the Beautiful Gate of the Temple,—was just mounting his donkey to depart, laden with the rich spoil of the day's beggary.

Up the stairs, drawing his tattered cloak about his face, came the model, at whom Beppo looked askance, jealous of an encroacher on his rightful domain. The figure passed away, however, up the Via Sistina. In the piazza below, near the foot of the magnificent steps, stood Miriam, with her eyes bent on the ground, as if she were counting those little, square, uncomfortable paving-stones, that make it a penitential pilgrimage to walk in Rome. She kept this attitude for several minutes, and when, at last, the importunities of a beggar disturbed her from it, she seemed bewildered and pressed her hand upon her brow.

"She has been in some sad dream or other, poor thing!" said Kenyon sympathizingly; "and even now she is imprisoned there in a kind of cage, the iron bars of which are made of her own thoughts."

"I fear she is not well," said Hilda. "I am going down the stairs, and will join Miriam."

"Farewell, then," said the sculptor. "Dear Hilda, this is a perplexed and troubled world! It soothes me inexpressibly to think of you in your tower, with white doves and white thoughts for your companions, so high above us all, and With the Virgin for your household friend. You know not how far it throws its light, that lamp which you keep burning at her shrine! I passed beneath the tower last night, and the ray cheered me, because you lighted it."

"It has for me a religious significance," replied Hilda quietly, "and yet I am no Catholic."

They parted, and Kenyon made haste along the Via Sistina, in the hope of overtaking the model, whose haunts and character he was anxious to investigate, for Miriam's sake. He fancied that he saw him a long way in advance, but before he reached the Fountain of the Triton the dusky figure had vanished.

CHAPTER XIII
A SCULPTOR'S STUDIO

About this period, Miriam seems to have been goaded by a weary restlessness that drove her abroad on any errand or none. She went one morning to visit Kenyon in his studio, whither he had invited her to see a new statue, on which he had staked many hopes, and which was now almost completed in the clay. Next to Hilda, the person for whom Miriam felt most affection and confidence was Kenyon; and in all the difficulties that beset her life, it was her impulse to draw near Hilda for feminine sympathy, and the sculptor for brotherly counsel.

Yet it was to little purpose that she approached the edge of the voiceless gulf between herself and them. Standing on the utmost verge of that dark chasm, she might stretch out her hand, and never clasp a hand of theirs; she might strive to call out, "Help, friends! help!" but, as with dreamers when they shout, her voice would perish inaudibly in the remoteness that seemed such a little way. This perception of an infinite, shivering solitude, amid which we cannot come close enough to human beings to be warmed by them, and where they turn to cold, chilly shapes of mist, is one of the most forlorn results of any accident, misfortune, crime, or peculiarity of character, that puts an individual ajar with the world. Very often, as in Miriam's case, there is an insatiable instinct that demands friendship, love, and intimate communion, but is forced to pine in empty forms; a hunger of the heart, which finds only shadows to feed upon.

Kenyon's studio was in a cross-street, or, rather, an ugly and dirty little lane, between the Corso and the Via della Ripetta; and though chill, narrow, gloomy, and bordered with tall and shabby structures, the lane was not a whit more disagreeable than nine tenths of the Roman streets. Over the door of one of the houses was a marble tablet, bearing an inscription, to the purport that the sculpture-rooms within had formerly been occupied by the illustrious artist Canova. In these precincts (which Canova's genius was not quite of a character to render sacred, though it certainly made them interesting) the young American sculptor had now established himself.

The studio of a sculptor is generally but a rough and dreary-looking place, with a good deal the aspect, indeed, of a stone-mason's workshop. Bare floors of brick or plank, and plastered walls,—an old chair or two, or perhaps only a block of marble (containing, however, the possibility of ideal grace within it) to sit down upon; some hastily scrawled sketches of nude figures on the whitewash of the wall. These last are probably the sculptor's earliest glimpses of ideas that may hereafter be solidified into imperishable stone, or perhaps may remain as impalpable as a dream. Next there are a few very roughly modelled little figures in clay or plaster, exhibiting the second stage of the idea as it advances towards a marble immortality; and then is seen the exquisitely designed shape of clay, more interesting than even the final marble, as being the intimate production of the sculptor himself, moulded throughout with his loving hands, and nearest to his imagination and heart. In the plaster-cast, from this clay model, the beauty of the statue strangely disappears, to shine forth again with pure white radiance, in the precious marble of Carrara. Works in all these stages of advancement, and some with the final touch upon them, might be found in Kenyon's studio.

Here might be witnessed the process of actually chiselling the marble, with which (as it is not quite satisfactory to think) a sculptor in these days has very little to do. In Italy, there is a class of men whose merely mechanical skill is perhaps more exquisite than was possessed by the ancient artificers, who wrought out the designs of Praxiteles; or, very possibly, by Praxiteles himself. Whatever of illusive representation can be effected in marble, they are capable of achieving, if the object be before their eyes. The sculptor has but to present these men with a plaster-cast of his design, and a sufficient block of marble, and tell them that the figure is imbedded in the stone, and must be freed from its encumbering superfluities; and, in due time, without the necessity of his touching the work with his own finger, he will see before him the statue that is to make him renowned. His creative power has wrought it with a word.

In no other art, surely, does genius find such effective instruments, and so happily relieve itself of the drudgery, of actual performance; doing wonderfully nice things by the hands of other people, when it may be suspected they could not always be done by the sculptor's own. And how much of the admiration which our artists get for their buttons and buttonholes, their shoe-ties, their neckcloths,—and these, at our present epoch of taste, make a large share of the renown,— would be abated, if we were generally aware that the sculptor can claim no credit for such pretty performances, as immortalized in marble! They are not his work, but that of some nameless machine in human shape.

Miriam stopped an instant in an antechamber, to look at a half-finished bust, the features of which seemed to be struggling out of the stone; and, as it were, scattering and dissolving its hard substance by the glow of feeling and intelligence. As the skilful workman gave stroke after stroke of the chisel with

The Marble Faun

apparent carelessness, but sure effect, it was impossible not to think that the outer marble was merely an extraneous environment; the human countenance within its embrace must have existed there since the limestone ledges of Carrara were first made. Another bust was nearly completed, though still one of Kenyon's most trustworthy assistants was at work, giving delicate touches, shaving off an impalpable something, and leaving little heaps of marble dust to attest it.

"As these busts in the block of marble," thought Miriam, "so does our individual fate exist in the limestone of time. We fancy that we carve it out; but its ultimate shape is prior to all our action."

Kenyon was in the inner room, but, hearing a step in the antechamber, he threw a veil over what he was at work upon, and came out to receive his visitor. He was dressed in a gray blouse, with a little cap on the top of his head; a costume which became him better than the formal garments which he wore whenever he passed out of his own domains. The sculptor had a face which, when time had done a little more for it, would offer a worthy subject for as good an artist as himself: features finely cut, as if already marble; an ideal forehead, deeply set eyes, and a mouth much hidden in a light-brown beard, but apparently sensitive and delicate.

"I will not offer you my hand," said he; "it is grimy with Cleopatra's clay."

"No; I will not touch clay; it is earthy and human," answered Miriam. "I have come to try whether there is any calm and coolness among your marbles. My own art is too nervous, too passionate, too full of agitation, for me to work at it whole days together, without intervals of repose. So, what have you to show me?"

"Pray look at everything here," said Kenyon. "I love to have painters see my work. Their judgment is unprejudiced, and more valuable than that of the world generally, from the light which their own art throws on mine. More valuable, too, than that of my brother sculptors, who never judge me fairly,—nor I them, perhaps."

To gratify him, Miriam looked round at the specimens in marble or plaster, of which there were several in the room, comprising originals or casts of most of the designs that Kenyon had thus far produced. He was still too young to have accumulated a large gallery of such things. What he had to show were chiefly the attempts and experiments, in various directions, of a beginner in art, acting as a stern tutor to himself, and profiting more by his failures than by any successes of which he was yet capable. Some of them, however, had great merit; and in the pure, fine glow of the new marble, it may be, they dazzled the judgment into awarding them higher praise than they deserved. Miriam admired the statue of a beautiful youth, a pearlfisher; who had got entangled in the weeds at the bottom of the sea, and lay dead among the pearl-oysters, the rich shells, and the seaweeds, all of like value to him now.

"The poor young man has perished among the prizes that he sought," remarked she. "But what a strange efficacy there is in death! If we cannot all win pearls, it causes an empty shell to satisfy us just as well. I like this statue, though it is too cold and stern in its moral lesson; and, physically, the form has not settled itself into sufficient repose."

In another style, there was a grand, calm head of Milton, not copied from any one bust or picture, yet more authentic than any of them, because all known representations of the poet had been profoundly studied, and solved in the artist's mind. The bust over the tomb in Grey Friars Church, the original miniatures and pictures, wherever to be found, had mingled each its special truth in this one work; wherein, likewise, by long perusal and deep love of the Paradise Lost, the Comus, the Lycidas, and L'Allegro, the sculptor had succeeded, even better than he knew, in spiritualizing his marble with the poet's mighty genius. And this was a great thing to have achieved, such a length of time after the dry bones and dust of Milton were like those of any other dead man.

There were also several portrait-busts, comprising those of two or three of the illustrious men of our own country, whom Kenyon, before he left America, had asked permission to model. He had done so, because he sincerely believed that, whether he wrought the busts in marble or bronze, the one would corrode and the other crumble in the long lapse of time, beneath these great men's immortality. Possibly, however, the young artist may have underestimated the durability of his material. Other faces there were, too, of men who (if the brevity of their remembrance, after death, can be augured from their little value in life) should have been represented in snow rather than marble. Posterity will be puzzled what to do with busts like these, the concretions and petrifactions of a vain self-estimate; but will find, no doubt, that they serve to build into stone walls, or burn into quicklime, as well as if the marble had never been blocked into the guise of human heads.

But it is an awful thing, indeed, this endless endurance, this almost indestructibility, of a marble bust! Whether in our own case, or that of other men, it bids us sadly measure the little,

The Marble Faun

little time during which our lineaments are likely to be of interest to any human being. It is especially singular that Americans should care about perpetuating themselves in this mode. The brief duration of our families, as a hereditary household, renders it next to a certainty that the great-grandchildren will not know their father's grandfather, and that half a century hence at furthest, the hammer of the auctioneer will thump its knock-down blow against his blockhead, sold at so much for the pound of stone! And it ought to make us shiver, the idea of leaving our features to be a dusty-white ghost among strangers of another generation, who will take our nose between their thumb and fingers (as we have seen men do by Caesar's), and infallibly break it off if they can do so without detection!

"Yes," said Miriam, who had been revolving some such thoughts as the above, "it is a good state of mind for mortal man, when he is content to leave no more definite memorial than the grass, which will sprout kindly and speedily over his grave, if we do not make the spot barren with marble. Methinks, too, it will be a fresher and better world, when it flings off this great burden of stony memories, which the ages have deemed it a piety to heap upon its back."

"What you say," remarked Kenyon, "goes against my whole art. Sculpture, and the delight which men naturally take in it, appear to me a proof that it is good to work with all time before our view."

"Well, well," answered Miriam, "I must not quarrel with you for flinging your heavy stones at poor Posterity; and, to say the truth, I think you are as likely to hit the mark as anybody. These busts, now, much as I seem to scorn them, make me feel as if you were a magician.. You turn feverish men into cool, quiet marble. What a blessed change for them! Would you could do as much for me!"

"O, gladly!" cried Kenyon, who had long wished to model that beautiful and most expressive face. "When will you begin to sit?"

"Poh! that was not what I meant," said Miriam. "Come, show me something else."

"Do you recognize this?" asked the sculptor.

He took out of his desk a little old-fashioned ivory coffer, yellow with age; it was richly carved with antique figures and foliage; and had Kenyon thought fit to say that Benvenuto Cellini wrought this precious box, the skill and elaborate fancy of the work would by no means have discredited his word, nor the old artist's fame. At least, it was evidently a production of Benvenuto's school and century, and might once have been the jewel-case of some grand lady at the court of the De' Medici.

Lifting the lid, however, no blaze of diamonds was disclosed, but only, lapped in fleecy cotton, a small, beautifully shaped hand, most delicately sculptured in marble. Such loving care and nicest art had been lavished here, that the palm really seemed to have a tenderness in its very substance. Touching those lovely fingers,—had the jealous sculptor allowed you to touch,—you could hardly believe that a virgin warmth would not steal from them into your heart.

"Ah, this is very beautiful!" exclaimed Miriam, with a genial smile. "It is as good in its way as Loulie's hand with its baby-dimples, which Powers showed me at Florence, evidently valuing it as much as if he had wrought it out of a piece of his great heart. As good as Harriet Hosmer's clasped hands of Browning and his wife, symbolizing the individuality and heroic union of two high, poetic lives! Nay, I do not question that it is better than either of those, because you must have wrought it passionately, in spite of its maiden palm and dainty fingertips."

"Then you do recognize it?" asked Kenyon.

"There is but one right hand on earth that could have supplied the model," answered Miriam; "so small and slender, so perfectly symmetrical, and yet with a character of delicate energy. I have watched it a hundred times at its work; but I did not dream that you had won Hilda so far! How have you persuaded that shy maiden to let you take her hand in marble?"

"Never! She never knew it!" hastily replied Kenyon, anxious to vindicate his mistress's maidenly reserve. "I stole it from her. The hand is a reminiscence. After gazing at it so often, and even holding it once for an instant, when Hilda was not thinking of me, I should be a bungler indeed, if I could not now reproduce it to something like the life."

"May you win the original one day!" said Miriam kindly.

"I have little ground to hope it," answered the sculptor despondingly; "Hilda does not dwell in our mortal atmosphere; and gentle and soft as she appears, it will be as difficult to win her heart as to entice down a white bird from its sunny freedom in the sky. It is strange, with all her delicacy and fragility, the impression she makes of being utterly sufficient to herself. No; I shall never win her. She is abundantly capable of sympathy, and delights to receive it, but she has no need of love."

"I partly agree with you," said Miriam. "It is a mistaken idea, which men generally entertain, that nature has made women especially prone to throw their whole being into what is technically called love. We have, to say the least, no more necessity for it than yourselves; only we have nothing else to do with our hearts. When women have other objects in life, they are not apt to fall in love. I can think of many women distinguished in art, literature, and science, — and multitudes whose hearts and minds find good employment in less ostentatious ways, — who lead high, lonely lives, and are conscious of no sacrifice so far as your sex is concerned."

"And Hilda will be one of these!" said Kenyon sadly; "the thought makes me shiver for myself, and and for her, too."

"Well," said Miriam, smiling, "perhaps she may sprain the delicate wrist which you have sculptured to such perfection. In that case you may hope. These old masters to whom she has vowed herself, and whom her slender hand and woman's heart serve so faithfully, are your only rivals."

The sculptor sighed as he put away the treasure of Hilda's marble hand into the ivory coffer, and thought how slight was the possibility that he should ever feel responsive to his own the tender clasp of the original. He dared not even kiss the image that he himself had made: it had assumed its share of Hilda's remote and shy divinity.

"And now," said Miriam, "show me the new statue which you asked me hither to see."

CHAPTER XIV
CLEOPATRA

"My new statue!" said Kenyon, who had positively forgotten it in the thought of Hilda; "here it is, under this veil." "Not a nude figure, I hope," observed Miriam. "Every young sculptor seems to think that he must give the world some specimen of indecorous womanhood, and call it Eve, Venus, a Nymph, or any name that may apologize for a lack of decent clothing. I am weary, even more than I am ashamed, of seeing such things. Nowadays people are as good as born in their clothes, and there is practically not a nude human being in existence. An artist, therefore, as you must candidly confess, cannot sculpture nudity with a pure heart, if only because he is compelled to steal guilty glimpses at hired models. The marble inevitably loses its chastity under such circumstances. An old Greek sculptor, no doubt, found his models in the open sunshine, and among pure and princely maidens, and thus the nude statues of antiquity are as modest as violets, and sufficiently draped in their own beauty. But as for Mr. Gibson's colored Venuses (stained, I believe, with tobacco juice), and all other nudities of to-day, I really do not understand what they have to say to this generation, and would be glad to see as many heaps of quicklime in their stead."

"You are severe upon the professors of my art," said Kenyon, half smiling, half seriously; "not that you are wholly wrong, either. We are bound to accept drapery of some kind, and make the best of it. But what are we to do? Must we adopt the costume of to-day, and carve, for example, a Venus in a hoop-petticoat?"

"That would be a boulder, indeed!" rejoined Miriam, laughing. "But the difficulty goes to confirm me in my belief that, except for portrait-busts, sculpture has no longer a right to claim any place among living arts. It has wrought itself out, and come fairly to an end. There is never a new group nowadays; never even so much as a new attitude. Greenough (I take my examples among men of merit) imagined nothing new; nor Crawford either, except in the tailoring line. There are not, as you will own, more than half a dozen positively original statues or groups in the world, and these few are of immemorial antiquity. A person familiar with the Vatican, the Uffizzi Gallery, the Naples Gallery, and the Louvre, will at once refer any modern production to its antique prototype; which, moreover, had begun to get out of fashion, even in old Roman days."

The Marble Faun

"Pray stop, Miriam," cried Kenyon, "or I shall fling away the chisel forever!"

"Fairly own to me, then, my friend," rejoined Miriam, whose disturbed mind found a certain relief in this declamation, "that you sculptors are, of necessity, the greatest plagiarists in the world."

"I do not own it," said Kenyon, "yet cannot utterly contradict you, as regards the actual state of the art. But as long as the Carrara quarries still yield pure blocks, and while my own country has marble mountains, probably as fine in quality, I shall steadfastly believe that future sculptors will revive this noblest of the beautiful arts, and people the world with new shapes of delicate grace and massive grandeur. Perhaps," he added, smiling, "mankind will consent to wear a more manageable costume; or, at worst, we sculptors shall get the skill to make broadcloth transparent, and render a majestic human character visible through the coats and trousers of the present day."

"Be it so!" said Miriam; "you are past my counsel. Show me the veiled figure, which, I am afraid, I have criticised beforehand. To make amends, I am in the mood to praise it now."

But, as Kenyon was about to take the cloth off the clay model, she laid her hand on his arm.

"Tell me first what is the subject," said she, "for I have sometimes incurred great displeasure from members of your brotherhood by being too obtuse to puzzle out the purport of their productions. It is so difficult, you know, to compress and define a character or story, and make it patent at a glance, within the narrow scope attainable by sculpture! Indeed, I fancy it is still the ordinary habit with sculptors, first to finish their group of statuary, — in such development as the particular block of marble will allow, — and then to choose the subject; as John of Bologna did with his Rape of the Sabines. Have you followed that good example?"

"No; my statue is intended for Cleopatra," replied Kenyon, a little disturbed by Miriam's raillery. "The special epoch of her history you must make out for yourself."

He drew away the cloth that had served to keep the moisture of the clay model from being exhaled. The sitting figure of a woman was seen. She was draped from head to foot in a costume minutely and scrupulously studied from that of ancient Egypt, as revealed by the strange sculpture of that country, its coins, drawings, painted mummy-cases, and whatever other tokens have been dug out of its pyramids, graves, and catacombs. Even the stiff Egyptian head-dress was adhered to, but had been softened into a rich feminine adornment, without losing a particle of its truth. Difficulties that might well have seemed insurmountable had been courageously encountered and made flexible to purposes of grace and dignity; so that Cleopatra sat attired in a garb proper to her historic and queenly state, as a daughter of the Ptolemies, and yet such as the beautiful woman would have put on as best adapted to heighten the magnificence of her charms, and kindle a tropic fire in the cold eyes of Octavius.

A marvellous repose—that rare merit in statuary, except it be the lumpish repose native to the block of stone—was diffused throughout the figure. The spectator felt that Cleopatra had sunk down out of the fever and turmoil of her life, and for one instant—as it were, between two pulse throbs—had relinquished all activity, and was resting throughout every vein and muscle. It was the repose of despair, indeed; for Octavius had seen her, and remained insensible to her enchantments. But still there was a great smouldering furnace deep down in the woman's heart. The repose, no doubt, was as complete as if she were never to stir hand or foot again; and yet, such was the creature's latent energy and fierceness, she might spring upon you like a tigress, and stop the very breath that you were now drawing midway in your throat.

The face was a miraculous success. The sculptor had not shunned to give the full Nubian lips, and other characteristics of the Egyptian physiognomy. His courage and integrity had been abundantly rewarded; for Cleopatra's beauty shone out richer, warmer, more triumphantly beyond comparison, than if, shrinking timidly from the truth, he had chosen the tame Grecian type. The expression was of profound, gloomy, heavily revolving thought; a glance into her past life and present emergencies, while her spirit gathered itself up for some new struggle, or was getting sternly reconciled to impending doom. In one view, there was a certain softness and tenderness,—how breathed into the statue, among so many strong and passionate elements, it is impossible to say. Catching another glimpse, you beheld her as implacable as a stone and cruel as fire.

In a word, all Cleopatra—fierce, voluptuous, passionate, tender, wicked, terrible, and full of poisonous and rapturous enchantment—was kneaded into what, only a week or two before, had been a lump of wet clay from the Tiber. Soon, apotheosized in an indestructible material, she would be one of the images that men keep forever, finding a heat in them which does not cool down, throughout the centuries?

"What a woman is this!" exclaimed Miriam, after a long pause. "Tell me, did she ever try, even while you were creating her, to overcome you with her fury or her love? Were you not afraid to touch her, as she grew more and more towards hot life beneath your hand? My dear friend, it is a great work! How have you learned to do it?"

"It is the concretion of a good deal of thought, emotion, and toil of brain and hand," said Kenyon, not without a perception that his work was good; "but I know not how it came about at last. I kindled a great fire within my mind, and threw in the material,—as Aaron threw the gold of the Israelites into the furnace,—and in the midmost heat uprose Cleopatra, as you see her."

"What I most marvel at," said Miriam, "is the womanhood that you have so thoroughly mixed up with all those seemingly discordant elements. Where did you get that secret? You never found it in your gentle Hilda, yet I recognize its truth."

"No, surely, it was not in Hilda," said Kenyon. "Her womanhood is of the ethereal type, and incompatible with any shadow of darkness or evil."

"You are right," rejoined Miriam; "there are women of that ethereal type, as you term it, and Hilda is one of them. She would die of her first wrong-doing,—supposing for a moment that she could be capable of doing wrong. Of sorrow, slender as she seems, Hilda might bear a great burden; of sin, not a feather's weight. Methinks now, were it my doom, I could bear either, or both at once; but my conscience is still as white as Hilda's. Do you question it?"

"Heaven forbid, Miriam!" exclaimed the sculptor.

He was startled at the strange turn which she had so suddenly given to the conversation. Her voice, too,—so much emotion was stifled rather than expressed in it, sounded unnatural.

"O, my friend," cried she, with sudden passion, "will you be my friend indeed? I am lonely, lonely, lonely! There is a secret in my heart that burns me,—that tortures me! Sometimes I fear to go mad of it; sometimes I hope to die of it; but neither of the two happens. Ah, if I could but whisper it to only one human soul! And you—you see far into womanhood; you receive it widely into your large view. Perhaps—perhaps, but Heaven only knows, you might understand me! O, let me speak!"

"Miriam, dear friend," replied the sculptor, "if I can help you, speak freely, as to a brother."

"Help me? No!" said Miriam.

Kenyon's response had been perfectly frank and kind; and yet the subtlety of Miriam's emotion detected a certain reserve and alarm in his warmly expressed readiness to hear her story. In his secret soul, to say the truth, the sculptor doubted whether it were well for this poor, suffering girl to speak what she so yearned to say, or for him to listen. If there were any active duty of friendship to be performed, then, indeed, he would joyfully have come forward to do his best. But if it were only a pent-up heart that sought an outlet? in that case it was by no means so certain that a confession would do good. The more her secret struggled and fought to be told, the more certain would it be to change all former relations that had subsisted between herself and the friend to whom she might reveal it. Unless he could give her all the sympathy, and just the kind of sympathy that the occasion required, Miriam would hate him by and by, and herself still more, if he let her speak.

This was what Kenyon said to himself; but his reluctance, after all, and whether he were conscious of it or no, resulted from a suspicion that had crept into his heart and lay there in a dark corner. Obscure as it was, when Miriam looked into his eyes, she detected it at once.

"Ah, I shall hate you!" cried she, echoing the thought which he had not spoken; she was half choked with the gush of passion that was thus turned back upon her. "You are as cold and pitiless as your own marble."

"No; but full of sympathy, God knows!" replied he.

In truth, his suspicions, however warranted by the mystery in which Miriam was enveloped, had vanished in the earnestness of his kindly and sorrowful emotion. He was now ready to receive her trust.

"Keep your sympathy, then, for sorrows that admit of such solace," said she, making a strong effort to compose herself. "As for my griefs, I know how to manage them. It was all a mistake: you can do nothing for me, unless you petrify me into a marble companion for your Cleopatra there; and I am not of her sisterhood, I do assure you. Forget this foolish scene, my friend, and never let me see a reference to it in your eyes when they meet mine hereafter."

The Marble Faun

"Since you desire it, all shall be forgotten," answered the sculptor, pressing her hand as she departed; "or, if ever I can serve you, let my readiness to do so be remembered. Meanwhile, dear Miriam, let us meet in the same clear, friendly light as heretofore."

"You are less sincere than I thought you," said Miriam, "if you try to make me think that there will be no change."

As he attended her through the antechamber, she pointed to the statue of the pearl-diver.

"My secret is not a pearl," said she; "yet a man might drown himself in plunging after it."

After Kenyon had closed the door, she went wearily down the staircase, but paused midway, as if debating with herself whether to return.

"The mischief was done," thought she; "and I might as well have had the solace that ought to come with it. I have lost, — by staggering a little way beyond the mark, in the blindness of my distress, I have lost, as we shall hereafter find, the genuine friendship of this clear-minded, honorable, true-hearted young man, and all for nothing. What if I should go back this moment and compel him to listen?"

She ascended two or three of the stairs, but again paused, murmured to herself, and shook her head.

"No, no, no," she thought; "and I wonder how I ever came to dream of it. Unless I had his heart for my own, — and that is Hilda's, nor would I steal it from her, — it should never be the treasure Place of my secret. It is no precious pearl, as I just now told him; but my dark-red carbuncle — red as blood — is too rich a gem to put into a stranger's casket."

She went down the stairs, and found her shadow waiting for her in the street.

CHAPTER XV
AN AESTHETIC COMPANY

On the evening after Miriam's visit to Kenyon's studio, there was an assemblage composed almost entirely of Anglo-Saxons, and chiefly of American artists, with a sprinkling of their English brethren; and some few of the tourists who still lingered in Rome, now that Holy Week was past. Miriam, Hilda, and the sculptor were all three present, and with them Donatello, whose life was so far turned from fits natural bent that, like a pet spaniel, he followed his beloved mistress wherever he could gain admittance.

The place of meeting was in the palatial, but somewhat faded and gloomy apartment of an eminent member of the aesthetic body. It was no more formal an occasion than one of those weekly receptions, common among the foreign residents of Rome, at which pleasant people—or disagreeable ones, as the case may be—encounter one another with little ceremony.

If anywise interested in art, a man must be difficult to please who cannot find fit companionship among a crowd of persons, whose ideas and pursuits all tend towards the general purpose of enlarging the world's stock of beautiful productions.

One of the chief causes that make Rome the favorite residence of artists—their ideal home which they sigh for in advance, and are so loath to migrate from, after once breathing its enchanted air—is, doubtless, that they there find themselves in force, and are numerous enough to create a congenial atmosphere. In every other clime they are isolated strangers; in this land of art, they are free citizens.

Not that, individually, or in the mass, there appears to be any large stock of mutual affection among the brethren of the chisel and the pencil. On the contrary, it will impress the shrewd observer that the jealousies and petty animosities, which the poets of our day have flung aside, still irritate and gnaw into the hearts of this kindred class of imaginative men. It is not difficult to suggest reasons why this should be the fact. The public, in whose good graces lie the sculptor's or the painter's prospects of success, is infinitely smaller than the public to which literary men make their appeal. It is composed of a very limited body of wealthy patrons; and these, as the artist well knows, are but blind judges in matters that require the utmost delicacy of perception. Thus, success in art is apt to become partly an affair of intrigue; and it is almost inevitable that even a gifted artist should look askance at his gifted brother's fame, and be chary of the good word that might help him to sell still another statue or picture. You seldom hear a painter heap generous praise on anything in his special line of art; a sculptor never has a favorable eye for any marble but his own.

Nevertheless, in spite of all these professional grudges, artists are conscious of a social warmth from each other's presence and contiguity. They shiver at the remembrance of their lonely studios in the unsympathizing cities of their native land. For the sake of such brotherhood as they can find, more than for any good that they get from galleries, they linger year after year in Italy, while their originality dies out of them, or is polished away as a barbarism.

The company this evening included several men and women whom the world has heard of, and many others, beyond all question, whom it ought to know. It would be a pleasure to introduce them upon our humble pages, name by name, and had we confidence enough in our own taste—to crown each well-deserving brow according to its deserts. The opportunity is tempting, but not easily manageable, and far too perilous, both in respect to those individuals whom we might bring forward, and the far greater number that must needs be left in the shade. Ink, moreover, is apt to have a corrosive quality, and might chance to raise a blister, instead of any more agreeable titillation, on skins so sensitive as those of artists. We must therefore forego the delight of illuminating this chapter with personal allusions to men whose renown glows richly on canvas, or gleams in the white moonlight of marble.

Otherwise we might point to an artist who has studied Nature with such tender love that she takes him to her intimacy, enabling him to reproduce her in landscapes that seem the reality of a better earth, and yet are but the truth of the very scenes around us, observed by the painter's insight and interpreted for us by his skill. By his magic, the moon throws her light far out of the picture, and the crimson of the summer night absolutely glimmers on the beholder's face. Or we might indicate a poet-painter, whose song has the vividness of picture, and whose canvas is peopled with angels, fairies, and water sprites, done to the ethereal life, because he saw them face to face in his poetic mood. Or we might bow before an artist, who has wrought too sincerely, too religiously, with too earnest a feeling, and too delicate a touch, for the world at once to recognize how much toil and thought are compressed into the stately brow of Prospero, and Miranda's maiden loveliness; or from what a depth within this painter's heart the Angel is leading forth St. Peter.

Thus it would be easy to go on, perpetrating a score of little epigrammatical allusions, like the above, all kindly meant, but none of them quite hitting the mark, and often striking where they were not aimed. It may be allowable to say, however, that American art is much better represented at Rome in the pictorial than in the sculpturesque department. Yet the men of marble appear to have more weight with the public than the men of canvas; perhaps on account of the greater density and solid substance of the material in which they work, and the sort of physical advantage which their labors thus acquire over the illusive unreality of color. To be a sculptor seems a distinction in itself; whereas a painter is nothing, unless individually eminent.

One sculptor there was, an Englishman, endowed with a beautiful fancy, and possessing at his fingers' ends the capability of doing beautiful things. He was a quiet, simple, elderly personage, with eyes brown and bright, under a slightly impending brow, and a Grecian profile, such as he might have cut with his own chisel. He had spent his life, for forty years, in making Venuses, Cupids, Bacchuses, and a vast deal of other marble progeny of dreamwork, or rather frostwork: it was all a vapory exhalation out of the Grecian mythology, crystallizing on the dull window-panes of to-day. Gifted with a more delicate power than any other man alive, he had foregone to be a Christian reality, and perverted himself into a Pagan idealist, whose business or efficacy, in our present world, it would be exceedingly difficult to define. And, loving and reverencing the pure material in which he wrought, as surely this admirable sculptor did, he had nevertheless robbed the marble of its chastity, by giving it an artificial warmth of hue. Thus it became a sin and shame to look at his nude goddesses. They had revealed themselves to his imagination, no doubt, with all their deity about them; but, bedaubed with buff color, they stood forth to the eyes of the profane in the guise of naked women. But, whatever criticism may be ventured on his style, it was good to meet a man so modest and yet imbued with such thorough and simple conviction of his own right principles and practice, and so quietly satisfied that his kind of antique achievement was all that sculpture could effect for modern life.

This eminent person's weight and authority among his artistic brethren were very evident; for beginning unobtrusively to utter himself on a topic of art, he was soon the centre of a little crowd of younger sculptors. They drank in his wisdom, as if it would serve all the purposes of original inspiration; he, meanwhile, discoursing with gentle calmness, as if there could possibly be no other side, and often ratifying, as it were, his own conclusions by a mildly emphatic "Yes."

The veteran Sculptor's unsought audience was composed

mostly of our own countrymen. It is fair to say, that they were a body of very dexterous and capable artists, each of whom had probably given the delighted public a nude statue, or had won credit for even higher skill by the nice carving of buttonholes, shoe-ties, coat-seams, shirt-bosoms, and other such graceful peculiarities of modern costume. Smart, practical men they doubtless were, and some of them far more than this, but still not precisely what an uninitiated person looks for in a sculptor. A sculptor, indeed, to meet the demands which our preconceptions make upon him, should be even more indispensably a poet than those who deal in measured verse and rhyme. His material, or instrument, which serves him in the stead of shifting and transitory language, is a pure, white, undecaying substance. It insures immortality to whatever is wrought in it, and therefore makes it a religious obligation to commit no idea to its mighty guardianship, save such as may repay the marble for its faithful care, its incorruptible fidelity, by warming it with an ethereal life. Under this aspect, marble assumes a sacred character; and no man should dare to touch it unless he feels within himself a certain consecration and a priesthood, the only evidence of which, for the public eye, will be the high treatment of heroic subjects, or the delicate evolution of spiritual, through material beauty.

No ideas such as the foregoing—no misgivings suggested by them probably, troubled the self-complacency of most of these clever sculptors. Marble, in their view, had no such sanctity as we impute to it. It was merely a sort of white limestone from Carrara, cut into convenient blocks, and worth, in that state, about two or three dollars per pound; and it was susceptible of being wrought into certain shapes (by their own mechanical ingenuity, or that of artisans in their employment) which would enable them to sell it again at a much higher figure. Such men, on the strength of some small knack in handling clay, which might have been fitly employed in making wax-work, are bold to call themselves sculptors. How terrible should be the thought that the nude woman whom the modern artist patches together, bit by bit, from a dozen heterogeneous models, meaning nothing by her, shall last as long as the Venus of the Capitol!—that his group of—no matter what, since it has no moral or intellectual existence will not physically crumble any sooner than the immortal agony of the Laocoon!

Yet we love the artists, in every kind; even these, whose merits we are not quite able to appreciate. Sculptors, painters, crayon sketchers, or whatever branch of aesthetics they adopted, were certainly pleasanter people, as we saw them that evening, than the average whom we meet in ordinary society. They were not wholly confined within the sordid compass of practical life; they had a pursuit which, if followed faithfully out, would lead them to the beautiful, and always had a tendency thitherward, even if they lingered to gather up golden dross by the wayside. Their actual business (though they talked about it very much as other men talk of cotton, politics, flour barrels, and sugar) necessarily illuminated their conversation with something akin to the ideal. So, when the guests collected themselves in little groups, here and there, in the wide saloon, a cheerful and airy gossip began to be heard. The atmosphere ceased to be precisely that of common life; a hint, mellow tinge, such as we see in pictures, mingled itself with the lamplight.

This good effect was assisted by many curious little treasures of art, which the host had taken care to strew upon his tables. They were principally such bits of antiquity as the soil of Rome and its neighborhood are still rich in; seals, gems, small figures of bronze, mediaeval carvings in ivory; things which had been obtained at little cost, yet might have borne no inconsiderable value in the museum of a virtuoso.

As interesting as any of these relics was a large portfolio of old drawings, some of which, in the opinion of their possessor, bore evidence on their faces of the touch of master-hands. Very ragged and ill conditioned they mostly were, yellow with time, and tattered with rough usage; and, in their best estate, the designs had been scratched rudely with pen and ink, on coarse paper, or, if drawn with charcoal or a pencil, were now half rubbed out. You would not anywhere see rougher and homelier things than these. But this hasty rudeness made the sketches only the more valuable; because the artist seemed to have bestirred himself at the pinch of the moment, snatching up whatever material was nearest, so as to seize the first glimpse of an idea that might vanish in the twinkling of an eye. Thus, by the spell of a creased, soiled, and discolored scrap of paper, you were enabled to steal close to an old master, and watch him in the very effervescence of his genius.

According to the judgment of several connoisseurs, Raphael's own hand had communicated its magnetism to one of these sketches; and, if genuine, it was evidently his first conception of a favorite Madonna, now hanging in the private apartment of the Grand Duke, at Florence. Another drawing was attributed to Leonardo da Vinci, and appeared to be a somewhat varied design for his picture of Modesty and Vanity, in the Sciarra Palace. There were at least half a dozen others, to which the owner assigned as high an origin. It was delightful to believe in their authenticity, at all events; for these things make the spectator more vividly sensible of a great painter's power, than the final glow and perfected art of the most consummate picture that may have been elaborated from them. There is an effluence of divinity in the first sketch; and there, if anywhere,

The Marble Faun

you find the pure light of inspiration, which the subsequent toil of the artist serves to bring out in stronger lustre, indeed, but likewise adulterates it with what belongs to an inferior mood. The aroma and fragrance of new thoughts were perceptible in these designs, after three centuries of wear and tear. The charm lay partly in their very imperfection; for this is suggestive, and sets the imagination at work; whereas, the finished picture, if a good one, leaves the spectator nothing to do, and, if bad, confuses, stupefies, disenchants, and disheartens him.

Hilda was greatly interested in this rich portfolio. She lingered so long over one particular sketch, that Miriam asked her what discovery she had made.

"Look at it carefully," replied Hilda, putting the sketch into her hands. "If you take pains to disentangle the design from those pencil-marks that seem to have been scrawled over it, I think you will see something very curious."

"It is a hopeless affair, I am afraid," said Miriam. "I have neither your faith, dear Hilda, nor your perceptive faculty. Fie! what a blurred scrawl it is indeed!"

The drawing had originally been very slight, and had suffered more from time and hard usage than almost any other in the collection; it appeared, too, that there had been an attempt (perhaps by the very hand that drew it) to obliterate the design. By Hilda's help, however, Miriam pretty distinctly made out a winged figure with a drawn sword, and a dragon, or a demon, prostrate at his feet.

"I am convinced," said Hilda in a low, reverential tone, "that Guido's own touches are on that ancient scrap of paper! If so, it must be his original sketch for the picture of the Archangel Michael setting his foot upon the demon, in the Church of the Cappuccini. The composition and general arrangement of the sketch are the same with those of the picture; the only difference being, that the demon has a more upturned face, and scowls vindictively at the Archangel, who turns away his eyes in painful disgust."

"No wonder!" responded Miriam. "The expression suits the daintiness of Michael's character, as Guido represents him. He never could have looked the demon in the face!"

"Miriam!" exclaimed her friend reproachfully, "you grieve me, and you know it, by pretending to speak contemptuously of the most beautiful and the divinest figure that mortal painter ever drew."

"Forgive me, Hilda!" said Miriam. "You take these matters more religiously than I can, for my life. Guido's Archangel is a fine picture, of course, but it never impressed me as it does you."

"Well; we will not talk of that," answered Hilda. "What I wanted you to notice, in this sketch, is the face of the demon. It is entirely unlike the demon of the finished picture. Guido, you know, always affirmed that the resemblance to Cardinal Pamfili was either casual or imaginary. Now, here is the face as he first conceived it."

"And a more energetic demon, altogether, than that of the finished picture," said Kenyon, taking the sketch into his hand. "What a spirit is conveyed into the ugliness of this strong, writhing, squirming dragon, under the Archangel's foot! Neither is the face an impossible one. Upon my word, I have seen it somewhere, and on the shoulders of a living man!"

"And so have I," said Hilda. "It was what struck me from the first."

"Donatello, look at this face!" cried Kenyon.

The young Italian, as may be supposed, took little interest in matters of art, and seldom or never ventured an opinion respecting them. After holding the sketch a single instant in his hand, he flung it from him with a shudder of disgust and repugnance, and a frown that had all the bitterness of hatred.

"I know the face well!" whispered he. "It is Miriam's model!"

It was acknowledged both by Kenyon and Hilda that they had detected, or fancied, the resemblance which Donatello so strongly affirmed; and it added not a little to the grotesque and weird character which, half playfully, half seriously, they assigned to Miriam's attendant, to think of him as personating the demon's part in a picture of more than two centuries ago. Had Guido, in his effort to imagine the utmost of sin and misery, which his pencil could represent, hit ideally upon just this face? Or was it an actual portrait of somebody, that haunted the old master, as Miriam was haunted now? Did the ominous shadow follow him through all the sunshine of his earlier career, and into the gloom that gathered about its close? And when Guido died, did the spectre betake himself to those ancient sepulchres, there awaiting a new victim, till it was Miriam's ill-hap to encounter him?

The Marble Faun

"I do not acknowledge the resemblance at all," said Miriam, looking narrowly at the sketch; "and, as I have drawn the face twenty times, I think you will own that I am the best judge."

A discussion here arose, in reference to Guido's Archangel, and it was agreed that these four friends should visit the Church of the Cappuccini the next morning, and critically examine the picture in question; the similarity between it and the sketch being, at all events, a very curious circumstance.

It was now a little past ten o'clock, when some of the company, who had been standing in a balcony, declared the moonlight to be resplendent. They proposed a ramble through the streets, taking in their way some of those scenes of ruin which produced their best effects under the splendor of the Italian moon.

CHAPTER XVI
A MOONLIGHT RAMBLE

The proposal for a moonlight ramble was received with acclamation by all the younger portion of the company. They immediately set forth and descended from story to story, dimly lighting their way by waxen tapers, which are a necessary equipment to those whose thoroughfare, in the night-time, lies up and down a Roman staircase. Emerging from the courtyard of the edifice, they looked upward and saw the sky full of light, which seemed to have a delicate purple or crimson lustre, or, at least some richer tinge than the cold, white moonshine of other skies. It gleamed over the front of the opposite palace, showing the architectural ornaments of its cornice and pillared portal, as well as the iron-barred basement windows, that gave such a prison-like aspect to the structure, and the shabbiness and squalor that lay along its base. A cobbler was just shutting up his little shop, in the basement of the palace; a cigar vender's lantern flared in the blast that came through the archway; a French sentinel paced to and fro before the portal; a homeless dog, that haunted thereabouts, barked as obstreperously at the party as if he were the domestic guardian of the precincts.

The air was quietly full of the noise of falling water, the cause of which was nowhere visible, though apparently near at hand. This pleasant, natural sound, not unlike that of a distant cascade in the forest, may be heard in many of the Roman streets and piazzas, when the tumult of the city is hushed; for consuls, emperors, and popes, the great men of every age, have found no better way of immortalizing their memories than by the shifting, indestructible, ever new, yet unchanging, upgush and downfall of water. They have written their names in that unstable element, and proved it a more durable record than brass or marble.

"Donatello, you had better take one of those gay, boyish artists for your companion," said Miriam, when she found the Italian youth at her side. "I am not now in a merry mood, as when we set all the world a-dancing the other afternoon, in the Borghese grounds."

"I never wish to dance any more," answered Donatello.

"What a melancholy was in that tone!" exclaimed Miriam. "You are getting spoilt in this dreary Rome, and will be as wise and as wretched as all the rest of mankind, unless you go back soon to your Tuscan vineyards. Well; give me your arm, then! But take care that no friskiness comes over you. We must walk evenly and heavily to-night!"

The party arranged itself according to its natural affinities or casual likings; a sculptor generally choosing a painter, and a painter a sculp—tor, for his companion, in preference to brethren of their own art. Kenyon would gladly have taken Hilda to himself, and have drawn her a little aside from the throng of merry wayfarers. But she kept near Miriam, and seemed, in her gentle and quiet way, to decline a separate alliance either with him or any other of her acquaintances.

So they set forth, and had gone but a little way, when the narrow street emerged into a piazza, on one side of which, glistening and dimpling in the moonlight, was the most famous fountain in Rome. Its murmur—not to say its uproar—had been in the ears of the company, ever since they came into the open air. It was the Fountain of Trevi, which draws its precious water from a source far beyond the walls, whence it flows hitherward through old subterranean aqueducts, and sparkles forth as pure as the virgin who first led Agrippa to its well-spring, by her father's door.

"I shall sip as much of this water as the hollow of my hand will hold," said Miriam.

"I am leaving Rome in a few days; and the tradition goes, that a parting draught at the Fountain of Trevi insures the traveller's return, whatever obstacles and improbabilities may seem to beset him. Will you drink, Donatello?"

"Signorina, what you drink, I drink," said the youth.

They and the rest of the party descended some steps to the water's brim, and, after a sip or two, stood gazing at the absurd design of the fountain, where some sculptor of Bernini's school had gone absolutely mad in marble. It was a great palace front, with niches and many bas-reliefs, out of which looked Agrippa's legendary virgin, and several of the allegoric sisterhood; while, at the base, appeared Neptune, with his floundering steeds, and Tritons blowing their horns about him, and twenty other artificial fantasies, which the calm moonlight soothed into better taste than was native to them.

And, after all, it was as magnificent a piece of work as ever human skill contrived. At the foot of the palatial facade was strewn, with careful art and ordered irregularity, a broad and broken heap of massive rock, looking is if it might have lain there since the deluge. Over a central precipice fell the water, in a semicircular cascade; and from a hundred crevices, on all sides, snowy jets gushed up, and streams spouted out of the mouths and nostrils of stone monsters, and fell in glistening drops; while other rivulets, that had run wild, came leaping from one rude step to another, over stones that were mossy, slimy, and green with sedge, because, in a Century of their wild play, Nature had adopted the Fountain of Trevi, with all its elaborate devices, for her own. Finally, the water, tumbling, sparkling, and dashing, with joyous haste and never-ceasing murmur, poured itself into a great marble-brimmed reservoir, and filled it with a quivering tide; on which was seen, continually, a snowy semicircle of momentary foam from the principal cascade, as well as a multitude of snow points from smaller jets. The basin occupied the whole breadth of the piazza, whence flights of steps descended to its border. A boat might float, and make voyages from one shore to another in this mimic lake.

In the daytime, there is hardly a livelier scene in Rome than the neighborhood of the Fountain of Trevi; for the piazza is then filled with the stalls of vegetable and fruit dealers, chestnut roasters, cigar venders, and other people, whose petty and wandering traffic is transacted in the open air. It is likewise thronged with idlers, lounging over the iron railing, and with Forestieri, who came hither to see the famous fountain. Here, also, are seen men with buckets, urchins with cans, and maidens (a picture as old as the patriarchal times) bearing their pitchers upon their heads. For the water of Trevi is in request, far and wide, as the most refreshing draught for feverish lips, the pleasantest to mingle with wine, and the wholesomest to drink, in its native purity, that can anywhere be found. But now, at early midnight, the piazza was a solitude; and it was a delight to behold this untamable water, sporting by itself in the moonshine, and compelling all the elaborate trivialities of art to assume a natural aspect, in accordance with its own powerful simplicity.

"What would be done with this water power," suggested an artist, "if we had it in one of our American cities? Would they employ it to turn the machinery of a cotton mill, I wonder?"

"The good people would pull down those rampant marble deities," said Kenyon, "and, possibly, they would give me a commission to carve the one-and-thirty (is that the number?) sister States, each pouring a silver stream from a separate can into one vast basin, which should represent the grand reservoir of national prosperity."

"Or, if they wanted a bit of satire," remarked an English artist, "you could set those same one-and-thirty States to cleansing the national flag of any stains that it may have incurred. The Roman washerwomen at the lavatory yonder,

The Marble Faun

plying their labor in the open air, would serve admirably as models."

"I have often intended to visit this fountain by moonlight,", said Miriam, "because it was here that the interview took place between Corinne and Lord Neville, after their separation and temporary estrangement. Pray come behind me, one of you, and let me try whether the face can be recognized in the water."

Leaning over the stone brim of the basin, she heard footsteps stealing behind her, and knew that somebody was looking over her shoulder. The moonshine fell directly behind Miriam, illuminating the palace front and the whole scene of statues and rocks, and filling the basin, as it were, with tremulous and palpable light. Corinne, it will be remembered, knew Lord Neville by the reflection of his face in the water. In Miriam's case, however (owing to the agitation of the water, its transparency, and the angle at which she was compelled to lean over), no reflected image appeared; nor, from the same causes, would it have been possible for the recognition between Corinne and her lover to take place. The moon, indeed, flung Miriam's shadow at the bottom of the basin, as well as two more shadows of persons who had followed her, on either side.

"Three shadows!" exclaimed Miriam—"three separate shadows, all so black and heavy that they sink in the water! There they lie on the bottom, as if all three were drowned together. This shadow on my right is Donatello; I know him by his curls, and the turn of his head. My left-hand companion puzzles me; a shapeless mass, as indistinct as the premonition of calamity! Which of you can it be? Ah!"

She had turned round, while speaking, and saw beside her the strange creature whose attendance on her was already familiar, as a marvel and a jest; to the whole company of artists. A general burst of laughter followed the recognition; while the model leaned towards Miriam, as she shrank from him, and muttered something that was inaudible to those who witnessed the scene. By his gestures, however, they concluded that he was inviting her to bathe her hands.

"He cannot be an Italian; at least not a Roman," observed an artist. "I never knew one of them to care about ablution. See him now! It is as if he were trying to wash off' the time-stains and earthly soil of a thousand years!"

Dipping his hands into the capacious washbowl before him, the model rubbed them together with the utmost vehemence. Ever and anon, too, he peeped into the water, as if expecting to see the whole Fountain of Trevi turbid with the results of his ablution. Miriam looked at him, some little time, with an aspect of real terror, and even imitated him by leaning over to peep into the basin. Recovering herself, she took up some of the water in the hollow of her hand, and practised an old form of exorcism by flinging it in her persecutor's face.

"In the name of all the Saints," cried she, "vanish, Demon, and let me be free of you now and forever!"

"It will not suffice," said some of the mirthful party, "unless the Fountain of Trevi gushes with holy water."

In fact, the exorcism was quite ineffectual upon the pertinacious demon, or whatever the apparition might be. Still he washed his brown, bony talons; still he peered into the vast basin, as if all the water of that great drinking-cup of Rome must needs be stained black or sanguine; and still he gesticulated to Miriam to follow his example. The spectators laughed loudly, but yet with a kind of constraint; for the creature's aspect was strangely repulsive and hideous.

Miriam felt her arm seized violently by Donatello. She looked at him, and beheld a tigerlike fury gleaming from his wild eyes.

"Bid me drown him!" whispered he, shuddering between rage and horrible disgust. "You shall hear his death gurgle in another instant!"

"Peace, peace, Donatello!" said Miriam soothingly, for this naturally gentle and sportive being seemed all aflame with animal rage. "Do him no mischief! He is mad; and we are as mad as he, if we suffer ourselves to be disquieted by his antics. Let us leave him to bathe his hands till the fountain run dry, if he find solace and pastime in it. What is it to you or me, Donatello? There, there! Be quiet, foolish boy!"

Her tone and gesture were such as she might have used in taming down the wrath of a faithful hound, that had taken upon himself to avenge some supposed affront to his mistress. She smoothed the young man's curls (for his fierce and sudden fury seemed to bristle among his hair), and touched his cheek with her soft palm, till his angry mood was a little assuaged.

"Signorina, do I look as when you first knew me?" asked he, with a heavy, tremulous sigh, as they went onward, somewhat apart from their companions. "Methinks there has been a change upon me, these many months; and more and more, these last few days. The joy is gone out of my life; all gone! all gone! Feel my hand! Is it not very hot? Ah; and my heart burns hotter still!"

"My poor Donatello, you are ill!" said Miriam, with deep sympathy and pity. "This melancholy and sickly Rome is stealing away the rich, joyous life that belongs to you. Go back, my dear friend, to your home among the hills, where (as I gather from what you have told me) your days were filled with simple and blameless delights. Have you found aught in the world that is worth' what you there enjoyed? Tell me truly, Donatello!"

"Yes!" replied the young man.

"And what, in Heaven's name?" asked she.

"This burning pain in my heart," said Donatello; "for you are in the midst of it."

By this time, they had left the Fountain of Trevi considerably behind them. Little further allusion was made to the scene at its margin; for the party regarded Miriam's persecutor as diseased in his wits, and were hardly to be surprised by any eccentricity in his deportment.

Threading several narrow streets, they passed through the Piazza of the Holy Apostles, and soon came to Trajan's Forum. All over the surface of what once was Rome, it seems to be the effort of Time to bury up the ancient city, as if it were a corpse, and he the sexton; so that, in eighteen centuries, the soil over its grave has grown very deep, by the slow scattering of dust, and the accumulation of more modern decay upon older ruin.

This was the fate, also, of Trajan's Forum, until some papal antiquary, a few hundred years ago, began to hollow it out again, and disclosed the full height of the gigantic column wreathed round with bas-reliefs of the old emperor's warlike deeds. In the area before it stands a grove of stone, consisting of the broken and unequal shafts of a vanished temple, still keeping a majestic order, and apparently incapable of further demolition. The modern edifices of the piazza (wholly built, no doubt, out of the spoil of its old magnificence) look down into the hollow space whence these pillars rise.

One of the immense gray granite shafts lay in the piazza, on the verge of the area. It was a great, solid fact of the Past, making old Rome actually sensible to the touch and eye; and no study of history, nor force of thought, nor magic of song, could so vitally assure us that Rome once existed, as this sturdy specimen of what its rulers and people wrought.

"And see!" said Kenyon, laying his hand upon it, "there is still a polish remaining on the hard substance of the pillar; and even now, late as it is, I can feel very sensibly the warmth of the noonday sun, which did its best to heat it through. This shaft will endure forever. The polish of eighteen centuries ago, as yet but half rubbed off, and the heat of to-day's sunshine, lingering into the night, seem almost equally ephemeral in relation to it."

"There is comfort to be found in the pillar," remarked Miriam, "hard and heavy as it is. Lying here forever, as it will, it makes all human trouble appear but a momentary annoyance."

"And human happiness as evanescent too," observed Hilda, sighing; "and beautiful art hardly less so! I do not love to think that this dull stone, merely by its massiveness, will last infinitely longer than any picture, in spite of the spiritual life that ought to give it immortality!"

"My poor little Hilda," said Miriam, kissing her compassionately, "would you sacrifice this greatest mortal consolation, which we derive from the transitoriness of all things, from the right of saying, in every conjecture, 'This, too, will pass away,' would you give up this unspeakable boon, for the sake of making a picture eternal?"

Their moralizing strain was interrupted by a demonstration from the rest of the party, who, after talking and laughing together, suddenly joined their voices, and shouted at full pitch,

"Trajan! Trajan!"

"Why do you deafen us with such an uproar?" inquired Miriam.

In truth, the whole piazza had been filled with their idle vociferation; the echoes from the surrounding houses reverberating the cry of "Trajan," on all sides; as if there was a great search for that imperial personage, and not so much as a handful of his ashes to be found.

"Why, it was a good opportunity to air our voices in this resounding piazza," replied one of the artists. "Besides, we had really some hopes of summoning Trajan to look at his column, which, you know, he never saw in his lifetime. Here is your model (who, they say, lived and sinned before Trajan's death) still wandering about Rome; and why not the Emperor Trajan?"

The Marble Faun

"Dead emperors have very little delight in their columns, I am afraid," observed Kenyon. "All that rich sculpture of Trajan's bloody warfare, twining from the base of the pillar to its capital, may be but an ugly spectacle for his ghostly eyes, if he considers that this huge, storied shaft must be laid before the judgment-seat, as a piece of the evidence of what he did in the flesh. If ever I am employed to sculpture a hero's monument, I shall think of this, as I put in the bas-reliefs of the pedestal!"

"There are sermons in stones," said Hilda thoughtfully, smiling at Kenyon's morality; "and especially in the stones of Rome."

The party moved on, but deviated a little from the straight way, in order to glance at the ponderous remains of the temple of Mars Ultot, within which a convent of nuns is now established, — a dove-cote, in the war-god's mansion. At only a little distance, they passed the portico of a Temple of Minerva, most rich and beautiful in architecture, but woefully gnawed by time and shattered by violence, besides being buried midway in the accumulation of soil, that rises over dead Rome like a flood tide. Within this edifice of antique sanctity, a baker's shop was now established, with an entrance on one side; for, everywhere, the remnants of old grandeur and divinity have been made available for the meanest necessities of today.

"The baker is just drawing his loaves out of the oven," remarked Kenyon. "Do you smell how sour they are? I should fancy that Minerva (in revenge for the desecration of her temple) had slyly poured vinegar into the batch, if I did not know that the modern Romans prefer their bread in the acetous fermentation."

They turned into the Via Alessandria, and thus gained the rear of the Temple of Peace, and, passing beneath its great arches, pursued their way along a hedge-bordered lane. In all probability, a stately Roman street lay buried beneath that rustic-looking pathway; for they had now emerged from the close and narrow avenues of the modern city, and were treading on a soil where the seeds of antique grandeur had not yet produced the squalid crop that elsewhere sprouts from them. Grassy as the lane was, it skirted along heaps of shapeless ruin, and the bare site of the vast temple that Hadrian planned and built. It terminated on the edge of a somewhat abrupt descent, at the foot of which, with a muddy ditch between, rose, in the bright moonlight, the great curving wall and multitudinous arches of the Coliseum.

CHAPTER XVII
MIRIAM'S TROUBLE

As usual of a moonlight evening, several carriages stood at the entrance of this famous ruin, and the precincts and interior were anything but a solitude. The French sentinel on duty beneath the principal archway eyed our party curiously, but offered no obstacle to their admission. Within, the moonlight filled and flooded the great empty space; it glowed upon tier above tier of ruined, grass-grown arches, and made them even too distinctly visible. The splendor of the revelation took away that inestimable effect of dimness and mystery by which the imagination might be assisted to build a grander structure than the Coliseum, and to shatter it with a more picturesque decay. Byron's celebrated description is better than the reality. He beheld the scene in his mind's eye, through the witchery of many intervening years, and faintly illuminated it as if with starlight instead of this broad glow of moonshine.

The party of our friends sat down, three or four of them on a prostrate column, another on a shapeless lump of marble, once a Roman altar; others on the steps of one of the Christian shrines. Goths and barbarians though they were, they chatted as gayly together as if they belonged to the gentle and pleasant race of people who now inhabit Italy. There was much pastime and gayety just then in the area of the Coliseum, where so many gladiators and Wild beasts had fought and died, and where so much blood of Christian martyrs had been lapped up by that fiercest of wild beasts, the Roman populace of yore. Some youths and maidens were running merry races across the open space, and playing at hide and seek a little way within the duskiness of the ground tier of arches, whence now and then you could hear the half-shriek, halflaugh of a frolicsome girl, whom the shadow had betrayed into a young man's arms. Elder groups were seated on the fragments of pillars and blocks of marble that lay round the verge of the arena, talking in the quick, short ripple of the Italian tongue. On the steps of the great black cross in the centre of the Coliseum sat a party singing scraps of songs, with much laughter and merriment between the stanzas.

It was a strange place for song and mirth. That black cross marks one of the special blood-spots of the earth where, thousands of times over, the dying gladiator fell, and more of human agony has been endured for the mere pastime of the multitude than on the breadth of many battlefields. From all this crime and suffering, however, the spot has derived a more than common sanctity. An inscription promises seven years' indulgence, seven years of remission from the pains of purgatory, and earlier enjoyment of heavenly bliss, for each separate kiss imprinted on the black cross. What better use could be made of life, after middle age, when the accumulated sins are many and the remaining temptations few, than to spend it all in kissing the black cross of the Coliseum!

Besides its central consecration, the whole area has been made sacred by a range of shrines, which are erected round the circle, each commemorating some scene or circumstance of the Saviour's passion and suffering. In accordance with an ordinary custom, a pilgrim was making his progress from shrine to shrine upon his knees, and saying a penitential prayer at each. Light-footed girls ran across the path along which he crept, or sported with their friends close by the shrines where he was kneeling. The pilgrim took no heed, and the girls meant no irreverence; for in Italy religion jostles along side by side with business and sport, after a fashion of its own, and people are accustomed to kneel down and pray, or see others praying, between two fits of merriment, or between two sins.

To make an end of our description, a red twinkle of light was visible amid the breadth of shadow that fell across the upper part of the Coliseum. Now it glimmered through a line of arches, or threw a broader gleam as it rose out of some profound abyss of ruin; now it was muffled by a heap of shrubbery which had adventurously clambered to that dizzy height; and so the red light kept ascending to loftier and loftier ranges of the structure, until it stood like a star where the blue sky rested against the Coliseum's topmost wall. It indicated a party of English or Americans paying the inevitable visit by moonlight, and exalting themselves with raptures that were Byron's, not their own.

Our company of artists sat on the fallen column, the pagan altar, and the steps of the Christian shrine, enjoying the moonlight and shadow, the present gayety and the gloomy reminiscences of the scene, in almost equal share. Artists, indeed, are lifted by the ideality of their pursuits a little way off the earth, and are therefore able to catch the evanescent fragrance that floats in the atmosphere of life above the heads of the ordinary crowd. Even if they seem endowed with little imagination individually, yet there is a property, a gift, a talisman, common to their class, entitling them to partake somewhat more bountifully than other people in the thin delights of moonshine and romance.

"How delightful this is!" said Hilda; and she sighed for very pleasure.

"Yes," said Kenyon, who sat on the column, at her side. "The Coliseum is far more delightful, as we enjoy it now, than when eighty thousand persons sat squeezed together, row above row, to see their fellow creatures torn by lions and tigers limb from limb. What a strange thought that the Coliseum was really built for us, and has not come to its best uses till almost two thousand years after it was finished!"

"The Emperor Vespasian scarcely had us in his mind," said Hilda, smiling; "but I thank him none the less for building it."

"He gets small thanks, I fear, from the people whose bloody instincts he pampered," rejoined Kenyon. "Fancy a nightly assemblage of eighty thousand melancholy and remorseful ghosts, looking down from those tiers of broken arches, striving to repent of the savage pleasures which they once enjoyed, but still longing to enjoy them over again."

"You bring a Gothic horror into this peaceful moonlight scene," said Hilda.

"Nay, I have good authority for peopling the Coliseum with phantoms," replied the sculptor. "Do you remember that veritable scene in Benvenuto Cellini's autobiography, in which a necromancer of his acquaintance draws a magic circle—just where the black cross stands now, I suppose—and raises myriads of demons? Benvenuto saw them with his own eyes,— giants, pygmies, and other creatures of frightful aspect, capering and dancing on yonder walls. Those spectres must have been Romans, in their lifetime, and frequenters of this bloody amphitheatre."

"I see a spectre, now!" said Hilda, with a little thrill of uneasiness. "Have you watched that pilgrim, who is going round the whole circle of shrines, on his knees, and praying with such fervency at every one? Now that he has revolved so far in his orbit, and has the moonshine on his face as he turns towards us, methinks I recognize him!"

"And so do I," said Kenyon. "Poor Miriam! Do you think she sees him?"

They looked round, and perceived that Miriam had risen from the steps of the shrine and disappeared. She had shrunk back, in fact, into the deep obscurity of an arch that opened just behind them.

Donatello, whose faithful watch was no more to be eluded than that of a hound, had stolen after her, and became the innocent witness of a spectacle that had its own kind of horror. Unaware of his presence, and fancying herself wholly unseen, the beautiful Miriam began to gesticulate extravagantly, gnashing her teeth, flinging her arms wildly abroad, stamping with her foot.

It was as if she had stepped aside for an instant, solely to snatch the relief of a brief fit of madness. Persons in acute trouble, or laboring under strong excitement, with a necessity for concealing it, are prone to relieve their nerves in this wild way; although, when practicable, they find a more effectual solace in shrieking aloud.

Thus, as soon as she threw off her self-control, under the dusky arches of the Coliseum, we may consider Miriam as a mad woman, concentrating the elements of a long insanity into that instant.

"Signorina! signorina! have pity on me!" cried Donatello, approaching her; "this is too terrible!"

"How dare you look, at me!" exclaimed Miriam, with a start; then, whispering below her breath, "men have been struck dead for a less offence!"

"If you desire it, or need it," said Donatello humbly, "I shall not be loath to die."

"Donatello," said Miriam, coming close to the young man, and speaking low, but still the almost insanity of the moment vibrating in her voice, "if you love yourself; if you desire those earthly blessings, such as you, of all men, were made for; if you would come to a good old age among your olive orchards and your Tuscan vines, as your forefathers did; if you would leave children to enjoy the same peaceful, happy, innocent life, then flee from me. Look not behind you! Get you gone without another word." He gazed sadly at her, but did not stir. "I tell you," Miriam went on, "there is a great evil hanging over me! I know it; I see it in the sky; I feel it in the air! It will overwhelm me as utterly as if this arch should crumble down upon our heads! It will crush you, too, if you stand at my side! Depart, then; and make the sign of the cross, as your faith bids you, when an evil spirit is nigh. Cast me off, or you are lost forever."

A higher sentiment brightened upon Donatello's face than had hitherto seemed to belong to its simple expression and sensuous beauty.

"I will never quit you," he said; "you cannot drive me from

you."

"Poor Donatello!" said Miriam in a changed tone, and rather to herself than him. "Is there no other that seeks me out, follows me,—is obstinate to share my affliction and my doom,—but only you! They call me beautiful; and I used to fancy that, at my need, I could bring the whole world to my feet. And lo! here is my utmost need; and my beauty and my gifts have brought me only this poor, simple boy. Half-witted, they call him; and surely fit for nothing but to be happy. And I accept his aid! To-morrow, to-morrow, I will tell him all! Ah! what a sin to stain his joyous nature with the blackness of a woe like mine!"

She held out her hand to him, and smiled sadly as Donatello pressed it to his lips. They were now about to emerge from the depth of the arch; but just then the kneeling pilgrim, in his revolution round the orbit of the shrines, had reached the one on the steps of which Miriam had been sitting. There, as at the other shrines, he prayed, or seemed to pray. It struck Kenyon, however,—who sat close by, and saw his face distinctly, that the suppliant was merely performing an enjoined penance, and without the penitence that ought to have given it effectual life. Even as he knelt, his eyes wandered, and Miriam soon felt that he had detected her, half hidden as she was within the obscurity of the arch.

"He is evidently a good Catholic, however," whispered one of the party. "After all, I fear we cannot identify him with the ancient pagan who haunts the catacombs."

"The doctors of the Propaganda may have converted him," said another; "they have had fifteen hundred years to perform the task."

The company now deemed it time to continue their ramble. Emerging from a side entrance of the Coliseum, they had on their left the Arch of Constantine, and above it the shapeless ruins of the Palace of the Caesars; portions of which have taken shape anew, in mediaeval convents and modern villas. They turned their faces cityward, and, treading over the broad flagstones of the old Roman pavement, passed through the Arch of Titus. The moon shone brightly enough within it to show the seven-branched Jewish candlestick, cut in the marble of the interior. The original of that awful trophy lies buried, at this moment, in the yellow mud of the Tiber; and, could its gold of Ophir again be brought to light, it would be the most precious relic of past ages, in the estimation of both Jew and Gentile.

Standing amid so much ancient dust, it is difficult to spare the reader the commonplaces of enthusiasm, on which

The Marble Faun

hundreds of tourists have already insisted. Over this half-worn pavement, and beneath this Arch of Titus, the Roman armies had trodden in their outward march, to fight battles a world's width away. Returning victorious, with royal captives and inestimable spoil, a Roman triumph, that most gorgeous pageant of earthly pride, had streamed and flaunted in hundred-fold succession over these same flagstones, and through this yet stalwart archway. It is politic, however, to make few allusions to such a past; nor, if we would create an interest in the characters of our story, is it wise to suggest how Cicero's foot may have stepped on yonder stone, or how Horace was wont to stroll near by, making his footsteps chime with the measure of the ode that was ringing in his mind. The very ghosts of that massive and stately epoch have so much density that the actual people of to-day seem the thinner of the two, and stand more ghost-like by the arches and columns, letting the rich sculpture be discerned through their ill-compacted substance.

The party kept onward, often meeting pairs and groups of midnight strollers like themselves. On such a moonlight night as this, Rome keeps itself awake and stirring, and is full of song and pastime, the noise of which mingles with your dreams, if you have gone betimes to bed. But it is better to be abroad, and take our own share of the enjoyable time; for the languor that weighs so heavily in the Roman atmosphere by day is lightened beneath the moon and stars.

They had now reached the precincts of the Forum.

CHAPTER XVIII
ON THE EDGE OF A PRECIPICE

"Let us settle it," said Kenyon, stamping his foot firmly down, "that this is precisely the spot where the chasm opened, into which Curtius precipitated his good steed and himself. Imagine the great, dusky gap, impenetrably deep, and with half-shaped monsters and hideous faces looming upward out of it, to the vast affright of the good citizens who peeped over the brim! There, now, is a subject, hitherto unthought of, for a grim and ghastly story, and, methinks, with a moral as deep as the gulf itself. Within it, beyond a question, there were prophetic visions,—intimations of all the future calamities of Rome,—shades of Goths, and Gauls, and even of the French soldiers of to-day. It was a pity to close it up so soon! I would give much for a peep into such a chasm."

"I fancy," remarked Miriam, "that every person takes a peep into it in moments of gloom and despondency; that is to say, in his moments of deepest insight."

"Where is it, then?" asked Hilda. "I never peeped into it."

"Wait, and it will open for you," replied her friend. "The chasm was merely one of the orifices of that pit of blackness that lies beneath us, everywhere. The firmest substance of human happiness is but a thin crust spread over it, with just reality enough to bear up the illusive stage scenery amid which we tread. It needs no earthquake to open the chasm. A footstep, a little heavier than ordinary, will serve; and we must step very daintily, not to break through the crust at any moment. By and by, we inevitably sink! It was a foolish piece of heroism in Curtius to precipitate himself there, in advance; for all Rome, you see, has been swallowed up in that gulf, in spite of him. The Palace of the Caesars has gone down thither, with a hollow, rumbling sound of its fragments! All the temples have tumbled into it; and thousands of statues have been thrown after! All the armies and the triumphs have marched into the great chasm, with their martial music playing, as they stepped over the brink. All the heroes, the statesmen, and the poets! All piled upon poor Curtius, who thought to have saved them all! I am loath to smile at the self-conceit of that gallant horseman, but cannot well avoid it."

"It grieves me to hear you speak thus, Miriam," said Hilda, whose natural and cheerful piety was shocked by her friend's gloomy view of human destinies. "It seems to me that there is no chasm, nor any hideous emptiness under our feet, except

The Marble Faun

what the evil within us digs. If there be such a chasm, let us bridge it over with good thoughts and deeds, and we shall tread safely to the other side. It was the guilt of Rome, no doubt, that caused this gulf to open; and Curtius filled it up with his heroic self-sacrifice and patriotism, which was the best virtue that the old Romans knew. Every wrong thing makes the gulf deeper; every right one helps to fill it up. As the evil of Rome was far more than its good, the whole commonwealth finally sank into it, indeed, but of no original necessity."

"Well, Hilda, it came to the same thing at last," answered Miriam despondingly.

"Doubtless, too," resumed the sculptor (for his imagination was greatly excited by the idea of this wondrous chasm), "all the blood that the Romans shed, whether on battlefields, or in the Coliseum, or on the cross,—in whatever public or private murder,—ran into this fatal gulf, and formed a mighty subterranean lake of gore, right beneath our feet. The blood from the thirty wounds in Caesar's breast flowed hitherward, and that pure little rivulet from Virginia's bosom, too! Virginia, beyond all question, was stabbed by her father, precisely where we are standing."

"Then the spot is hallowed forever!" said Hilda.

"Is there such blessed potency in bloodshed?" asked Miriam. "Nay, Hilda, do not protest! I take your meaning rightly."

They again moved forward. And still, from the Forum and the Via Sacra, from beneath the arches of the Temple of Peace on one side, and the acclivity of the Palace of the Caesars on the other, there arose singing voices of parties that were strolling through the moonlight. Thus, the air was full of kindred melodies that encountered one another, and twined themselves into a broad, vague music, out of which no single strain could be disentangled. These good examples, as well as the harmonious influences of the hour, incited our artist friends to make proof of their own vocal powers. With what skill and breath they had, they set up a choral strain,—"Hail, Columbia!" we believe, which those old Roman echoes must have found it exceeding difficult to repeat aright. Even Hilda poured the slender sweetness of her note into her country's song. Miriam was at first silent, being perhaps unfamiliar with the air and burden. But suddenly she threw out such a swell and gush of sound, that it seemed to pervade the whole choir of other voices, and then to rise above them all, and become audible in what would else have been thee silence of an upper region. That volume of melodious voice was one of the tokens of a great trouble. There had long been an impulse upon her—amounting, at last, to a necessity to shriek aloud; but she had struggled against it, till the thunderous anthem gave her an opportunity to relieve her heart by a great cry.

They passed the solitary Column of Phocas, and looked down into the excavated space, where a confusion of pillars, arches, pavements, and shattered blocks and shafts—the crumbs of various ruin dropped from the devouring maw of Time stand, or lie, at the base of the Capitoline Hill. That renowned hillock (for it is little more) now arose abruptly above them. The ponderous masonry, with which the hillside is built up, is as old as Rome itself, and looks likely to endure while the world retains any substance or permanence. It once sustained the Capitol, and now bears up the great pile which the mediaeval builders raised on the antique foundation, and that still loftier tower, which looks abroad upon a larger page of deeper historic interest than any other scene can show. On the same pedestal of Roman masonry, other structures will doubtless rise, and vanish like ephemeral things.

To a spectator on the spot, it is remarkable that the events of Roman history, and Roman life itself, appear not so distant as the Gothic ages which succeeded them. We stand in the Forum, or on the height of the Capitol, and seem to see the Roman epoch close at hand. We forget that a chasm extends between it and ourselves, in which lie all those dark, rude, unlettered centuries, around the birth-time of Christianity, as well as the age of chivalry and romance, the feudal system, and the infancy of a better civilization than that of Rome. Or, if we remember these mediaeval times, they look further off than the Augustan age. The reason may be, that the old Roman literature survives, and creates for us an intimacy with the classic ages, which we have no means of forming with the subsequent ones.

The Italian climate, moreover, robs age of its reverence and makes it look newer than it is. Not the Coliseum, nor the tombs of the Appian Way, nor the oldest pillar in the Forum, nor any other Roman ruin, be it as dilapidated as it may, ever give the impression of venerable antiquity which we gather, along with the ivy, from the gray walls of an English abbey or castle. And yet every brick or stone, which we pick up among the former, had fallen ages before the foundation of the latter was begun. This is owing to the kindliness with which Natures takes an English ruin to her heart, covering it with ivy, as tenderly as Robin Redbreast covered the dead babes with forest leaves. She strives to make it a part of herself, gradually obliterating the handiwork of man, and supplanting it with her own mosses and trailing verdure, till she has won the whole structure back. But, in Italy, whenever man has once hewn a stone, Nature forthwith relinquishes her right to it, and never lays her finger on it again.

The Marble Faun

Age after age finds it bare and naked, in the barren sunshine, and leaves it so. Besides this natural disadvantage, too, each succeeding century, in Rome, has done its best to ruin the very ruins, so far as their picturesque effect is concerned, by stealing away the marble and hewn stone, and leaving only yellow bricks, which never can look venerable.

The party ascended the winding way that leads from the Forum to the Piazza of the Campidoglio on the summit of the Capitoline Hill. They stood awhile to contemplate the bronze equestrian statue of Marcus Aurelius. The moonlight glistened upon traces of the gilding which had once covered both rider and steed; these were almost gone, but the aspect of dignity was still perfect, clothing the figure as it were with an imperial robe of light. It is the most majestic representation of the kingly character that ever the world has seen. A sight of the old heathen emperor is enough to create an evanescent sentiment of loyalty even in a democratic bosom, so august does he look, so fit to rule, so worthy of man's profoundest homage and obedience, so inevitably attractive of his love. He stretches forth his hand with an air of grand beneficence and unlimited authority, as if uttering a decree from which no appeal was permissible, but in which the obedient subject would find his highest interests consulted; a command that was in itself a benediction.

"The sculptor of this statue knew what a king should be," observed Kenyon, "and knew, likewise, the heart of mankind, and how it craves a true ruler, under whatever title, as a child its father."

"O, if there were but one such man as this?" exclaimed Miriam. "One such man in an age, and one in all the world; then how speedily would the strife, wickedness, and sorrow of us poor creatures be relieved. We would come to him with our griefs, whatever they might be,—even a poor, frail woman burdened with her heavy heart,—and lay them at his feet, and never need to take them up again. The rightful king would see to all."

"What an idea of the regal office and duty!" said Kenyon, with a smile. "It is a woman's idea of the whole matter to perfection. It is Hilda's, too, no doubt?"

"No," answered the quiet Hilda; "I should never look for such assistance from an earthly king."

"Hilda, my religious Hilda," whispered Miriam, suddenly drawing the girl close to her, "do you know how it is with me? I would give all I have or hope—my life, O how freely—for one instant of your trust in God! You little guess my need of it. You really think, then, that He sees and cares for us?"

"Miriam, you frighten me."

"Hush, hush? do not let them hear yet!" whispered Miriam. "I frighten you, you say; for Heaven's sake, how? Am I strange? Is there anything wild in my behavior?"

"Only for that moment," replied Hilda, "because you seemed to doubt God's providence."

"We will talk of that another time," said her friend. "Just now it is very dark to me."

On the left of the Piazza of the Campidoglio, as you face cityward, and at the head of the long and stately flight of steps descending from the Capitoline Hill to the level of lower Rome, there is a narrow lane or passage. Into this the party of our friends now turned. The path ascended a little, and ran along under the walls of a palace, but soon passed through a gateway, and terminated in a small paved courtyard. It was bordered by a low parapet.

The spot, for some reason or other, impressed them as exceedingly lonely. On one side was the great height of the palace, with the moonshine falling over it, and showing all the windows barred and shuttered. Not a human eye could look down into the little courtyard, even if the seemingly deserted palace had a tenant. On all other sides of its narrow compass there was nothing but the parapet, which as it now appeared was built right on the edge of a steep precipice. Gazing from its imminent brow, the party beheld a crowded confusion of roofs spreading over the whole space between them and the line of hills that lay beyond the Tiber. A long, misty wreath, just dense enough to catch a little of the moonshine, floated above the houses, midway towards the hilly line, and showed the course of the unseen river. Far away on the right, the moon gleamed on the dome of St. Peter's as well as on many lesser and nearer domes.

"What a beautiful view of the city!" exclaimed Hilda; "and I never saw Rome from this point before."

"It ought to afford a good prospect," said the sculptor; "for it was from this point—at least we are at liberty to think so, if we choose—that many a famous Roman caught his last glimpse of his native city, and of all other earthly things. This is one of the sides of the Tarpeian Rock. Look over the parapet, and see what a sheer tumble there might still be for a traitor, in spite of the thirty feet of soil that have accumulated at the foot of the precipice."

They all bent over, and saw that the cliff fell perpendicularly downward to about the depth, or rather more, at which the tall palace rose in height above their heads. Not that it was still the natural, shaggy front of the original precipice; for it appeared to be cased in ancient stonework, through which the primeval rock showed its face here and there grimly and doubtfully. Mosses grew on the slight projections, and little shrubs sprouted out of the crevices, but could not much soften the stern aspect of the cliff. Brightly as the Italian moonlight fell adown the height, it scarcely showed what portion of it was man's work and what was nature's, but left it all in very much the same kind of ambiguity and half-knowledge in which antiquarians generally leave the identity of Roman remains.

The roofs of some poor-looking houses, which had been built against the base and sides of the cliff, rose nearly midway to the top; but from an angle of the parapet there was a precipitous plunge straight downward into a stonepaved court.

"I prefer this to any other site as having been veritably the Traitor's Leap," said Kenyon, "because it was so convenient to the Capitol. It was an admirable idea of those stern old fellows to fling their political criminals down from the very summit on which stood the Senate House and Jove's Temple, emblems of the institutions which they sought to violate. It symbolizes how sudden was the fall in those days from the utmost height of ambition to its profoundest ruin."

"Come, come; it is midnight," cried another artist, "too late to be moralizing here. We are literally dreaming on the edge of a precipice. Let us go home."

"It is time, indeed," said Hilda.

The sculptor was not without hopes that he might be favored with the sweet charge of escorting Hilda to the foot of her tower. Accordingly, when the party prepared to turn back, he offered her his arm. Hilda at first accepted it; but when they had partly threaded the passage between the little courtyard and the Piazza del Campidoglio, she discovered that Miriam had remained behind.

"I must go back," said she, withdrawing her arm from Kenyon's; "but pray do not come with me. Several times this evening I have had a fancy that Miriam had something on her mind, some sorrow or perplexity, which, perhaps, it would relieve her to tell me about. No, no; do not turn back! Donatello will be a sufficient guardian for Miriam and me."

The sculptor was a good deal mortified, and perhaps a little angry: but he knew Hilda's mood of gentle decision and independence too well not to obey her. He therefore suffered the fearless maiden to return alone.

Meanwhile Miriam had not noticed the departure of the rest of the company; she remained on the edge of the precipice and Donatello along with her.

"It would be a fatal fall, still," she said to herself, looking over the parapet, and shuddering as her eye measured the depth. "Yes; surely yes! Even without the weight of an overburdened heart, a human body would fall heavily enough upon those stones to shake all its joints asunder. How soon it would be over!"

Donatello, of whose presence she was possibly not aware, now pressed closer to her side; and he, too, like Miriam, bent over the low parapet and trembled violently. Yet he seemed to feel that perilous fascination which haunts the brow of precipices, tempting the unwary one to fling himself over for the very horror of the thing; for, after drawing hastily back, he again looked down, thrusting himself out farther than before. He then stood silent a brief space, struggling, perhaps, to make himself conscious of the historic associations of the scene.

"What are you thinking of, Donatello?" asked Miriam.

"Who are they," said he, looking earnestly in her face, "who have been flung over here in days gone by?"

"Men that cumbered the world," she replied. "Men whose lives were the bane of their fellow creatures. Men who poisoned the air, which is the common breath of all, for their own selfish purposes. There was short work with such men in old Roman times. Just in the moment of their triumph, a hand, as of an avenging giant, clutched them, and dashed the wretches down this precipice."

"Was it well done?" asked the young man.

"It was well done," answered Miriam; "innocent persons were saved by the destruction of a guilty one, who deserved his doom."

While this brief conversation passed, Donatello had once or

The Marble Faun

twice glanced aside with a watchful air, just as a hound may often be seen to take sidelong note of some suspicious object, while he gives his more direct attention to something nearer at hand. Miriam seemed now first to become aware of the silence that had followed upon the cheerful talk and laughter of a few moments before.

Looking round, she perceived that all her company of merry friends had retired, and Hilda, too, in whose soft and quiet presence she had always an indescribable feeling of security. All gone; and only herself and Donatello left hanging over the brow of the ominous precipice.

Not so, however; not entirely alone! In the basement wall of the palace, shaded from the moon, there was a deep, empty niche, that had probably once contained a statue; not empty, either; for a figure now came forth from it and approached Miriam. She must have had cause to dread some unspeakable evil from this strange persecutor, and to know that this was the very crisis of her calamity; for as he drew near, such a cold, sick despair crept over her that it impeded her breath, and benumbed her natural promptitude of thought. Miriam seemed dreamily to remember falling on her knees; but, in her whole recollection of that wild moment, she beheld herself as in a dim show, and could not well distinguish what was done and suffered; no, not even whether she were really an actor and sufferer in the scene.

Hilda, meanwhile, had separated herself from the sculptor, and turned back to rejoin her friend. At a distance, she still heard the mirth of her late companions, who were going down the cityward descent of the Capitoline Hill; they had set up a new stave of melody, in which her own soft voice, as well as the powerful sweetness of Miriam's, was sadly missed.

The door of the little courtyard had swung upon its hinges, and partly closed itself. Hilda (whose native gentleness pervaded all her movements) was quietly opening it, when she was startled, midway, by the noise of a struggle within, beginning and ending all in one breathless instant. Along with it, or closely succeeding it, was a loud, fearful cry, which quivered upward through the air, and sank quivering downward to the earth. Then, a silence! Poor Hilda had looked into the court-yard, and saw the whole quick passage of a deed, which took but that little time to grave itself in the eternal adamant.

CHAPTER XIX
THE FAUN'S TRANSFORMATION

The door of the courtyard swung slowly, and closed itself of its own accord. Miriam and Donatello were now alone there. She clasped her hands, and looked wildly at the young man, whose form seemed to have dilated, and whose eyes blazed with the fierce energy that had suddenly inspired him. It had kindled him into a man; it had developed within him an intelligence which was no native characteristic of the Donatello whom we have heretofore known. But that simple and joyous creature was gone forever.

"What have you done?" said Miriam, in a horror-stricken whisper.

The glow of rage was still lurid on Donatello's face, and now flashed out again from his eyes.

"I did what ought to be done to a traitor!" he replied. "I did what your eyes bade me do, when I asked them with mine, as I held the wretch over the precipice!"

These last words struck Miriam like a bullet. Could it be so? Had her eyes provoked or assented to this deed? She had not known it. But, alas! looking back into the frenzy and turmoil of the scene just acted, she could not deny—she was not sure whether it might be so, or no—that a wild joy had flamed up in her heart, when she beheld her persecutor in his mortal peril. Was it horror?—or ecstasy? or both in one? Be the emotion what it might, it had blazed up more madly, when Donatello flung his victim off the cliff, and more and more, while his shriek went quivering downward. With the dead thump upon the stones below had come an unutterable horror.

"And my eyes bade you do it!" repeated she.

They both leaned over the parapet, and gazed downward as earnestly as if some inestimable treasure had fallen over, and were yet recoverable. On the pavement below was a dark mass, lying in a heap, with little or nothing human in its appearance, except that the hands were stretched out, as if they might have clutched for a moment at the small square stones. But there was no motion in them now. Miriam watched the heap of mortality while she could count a hundred, which she took pains to do. No stir; not a finger moved!

"You have killed him, Donatello! He is quite dead!" said she.

"Stone dead! Would I were so, too!"

"Did you not mean that he should die?" sternly asked Donatello, still in the glow of that intelligence which passion had developed in him. "There was short time to weigh the matter; but he had his trial in that breath or two while I held him over the cliff, and his sentence in that one glance, when your eyes responded to mine! Say that I have slain him against your will,—say that he died without your whole consent,—and, in another breath, you shall see me lying beside him."

"O, never!" cried Miriam. "My one, own friend! Never, never, never!"

She turned to him,—the guilty, bloodstained, lonely woman,—she turned to her fellow criminal, the youth, so lately innocent, whom she had drawn into her doom. She pressed him close, close to her bosom, with a clinging embrace that brought their two hearts together, till the horror and agony of each was combined into one emotion, and that a kind of rapture.

"Yes, Donatello, you speak the truth!" said she; "my heart consented to what you did. We two slew yonder wretch. The deed knots us together, for time and eternity, like the coil of a serpent!"

They threw one other glance at the heap of death below, to assure themselves that it was there; so like a dream was the whole thing. Then they turned from that fatal precipice, and came out of the courtyard, arm in arm, heart in heart. Instinctively, they were heedful not to sever themselves so much as a pace or two from one another, for fear of the terror and deadly chill that would thenceforth wait for them in solitude. Their deed—the crime which Donatello wrought, and Miriam accepted on the instant—had wreathed itself, as she said, like a serpent, in inextricable links about both their souls, and drew them into one, by its terrible contractile power. It was closer than a marriage bond. So intimate, in those first moments, was the union, that it seemed as if their new sympathy annihilated all other ties, and that they were released from the chain of humanity; a new sphere, a special law, had been created for them alone. The world could not come near them; they were safe!

When they reached the flight of steps leading downward from the Capitol, there was a faroff noise of singing and laughter. Swift, indeed, had been the rush of the crisis that was come and gone! This was still the merriment of the party that had so recently been their companions. They recognized the voices which, a little while ago, had accorded and sung in cadence with their own. But they were familiar voices no more; they sounded strangely, and, as it were, out of the depths of space; so remote was all that pertained to the past life of these guilty ones, in the moral seclusion that had suddenly extended itself around them. But how close, and ever closer, did the breath of the immeasurable waste, that lay between them and all brotherhood or sisterhood, now press them one within the other!

"O friend!" cried Miriam, so putting her soul into the word that it took a heavy richness of meaning, and seemed never to have been spoken before, "O friend, are you conscious, as I am, of this companionship that knits our heart-strings together?"

"I feel it, Miriam," said Donatello. "We draw one breath; we live one life!"

"Only yesterday," continued Miriam; "nay, only a short half-hour ago, I shivered in an icy solitude. No friendship, no sisterhood, could come near enough to keep the warmth within my heart. In an instant all is changed! There can be no more loneliness!"

"None, Miriam!" said Donatello.

"None, my beautiful one!" responded Miriam, gazing in his face, which had taken a higher, almost an heroic aspect, from the strength of passion. "None, my innocent one! Surely, it is no crime that we have committed. One wretched and worthless life has been sacrificed to cement two other lives for evermore."

"For evermore, Miriam!" said Donatello; "cemented with his blood!"

The young man started at the word which he had himself spoken; it may be that it brought home, to the simplicity of his imagination, what he had not before dreamed of, — the ever-increasing loathsomeness of a union that consists in guilt. Cemented with blood, which would corrupt and grow more noisome forever and forever, but bind them none the less strictly for that.

"Forget it! Cast it all behind you!" said Miriam, detecting, by her sympathy, the pang that was in his heart. "The deed has done its office, and has no existence any more."

They flung the past behind them, as she counselled, or else distilled from it a fiery, intoxication, which sufficed to carry them triumphantly through those first moments of their doom.

The Marble Faun

For guilt has its moment of rapture too. The foremost result of a broken law is ever an ecstatic sense of freedom. And thus there exhaled upward (out of their dark sympathy, at the base of which lay a human corpse) a bliss, or an insanity, which the unhappy pair imagined to be well worth the sleepy innocence that was forever lost to them.

As their spirits rose to the solemn madness of the occasion, they went onward, not stealthily, not fearfully, but with a stately gait and aspect. Passion lent them (as it does to meaner shapes) its brief nobility of carriage. They trod through the streets of Rome, as if they, too, were among the majestic and guilty shadows, that, from ages long gone by, have haunted the blood-stained city. And, at Miriam's suggestion, they turned aside, for the sake of treading loftily past the old site of Pompey's Forum.

"For there was a great deed done here!" she said,—"a deed of blood like ours! Who knows but we may meet the high and ever-sad fraternity of Caesar's murderers, and exchange a salutation?"

"Are they our brethren, now?" asked Donatello.

"Yes; all of them," said Miriam,—"and many another, whom the world little dreams of, has been made our brother or our sister, by what we have done within this hour!"

And at the thought she shivered. Where then was the seclusion, the remoteness, the strange, lonesome Paradise, into which she and her one companion had been transported by their crime? Was there, indeed, no such refuge, but only a crowded thoroughfare and jostling throng of criminals? And was it true, that whatever hand had a blood-stain on it,—or had poured out poison,—or strangled a babe at its birth,—or clutched a grandsire's throat, he sleeping, and robbed him of his few last breaths,—had now the right to offer itself in fellowship with their two hands? Too certainly, that right existed. It is a terrible thought, that an individual wrong-doing melts into the great mass of human crime, and makes us, who dreamed only of our own little separate sin,—makes us guilty of the whole. And thus Miriam and her lover were not an insulated pair, but members of an innumerable confraternity of guilty ones, all shuddering at each other.

"But not now; not yet," she murmured to herself. "To-night, at least, there shall be no remorse!"

Wandering without a purpose, it so chanced that they turned into a street, at one extremity of which stood Hilda's tower. There was a light in her high chamber; a light, too, at the Virgin's shrine; and the glimmer of these two was the loftiest light beneath the stars. Miriam drew Donatello's arm, to make him stop, and while they stood at some distance looking at Hilda's window, they beheld her approach and throw it open. She leaned far forth, and extended her clasped hands towards the sky.

"The good, pure child! She is praying, Donatello," said Miriam, with a kind of simple joy at witnessing the devoutness of her friend. Then her own sin rushed upon her, and she shouted, with the rich strength of her voice, "Pray for us, Hilda; we need it!"

Whether Hilda heard and recognized the voice we cannot tell. The window was immediately closed, and her form disappeared from behind the snowy curtain. Miriam felt this to be a token that the cry of her condemned spirit was shut out of heaven.

CHAPTER XX
THE BURIAL CHANT

The Church of the Capuchins (where, as the reader may remember, some of our acquaintances had made an engagement to meet) stands a little aside from the Piazza Barberini. Thither, at the hour agreed upon, on the morning after the scenes last described, Miriam and Donatello directed their steps. At no time are people so sedulously careful to keep their trifling appointments, attend to their ordinary occupations, and thus put a commonplace aspect on life, as when conscious of some secret that if suspected would make them look monstrous in the general eye.

Yet how tame and wearisome is the impression of all ordinary things in the contrast with such a fact! How sick and tremulous, the next morning, is the spirit that has dared so much only the night before! How icy cold is the heart, when the fervor, the wild ecstasy of passion has faded away, and sunk down among the dead ashes of the fire that blazed so fiercely, and was fed by the very substance of its life! How faintly does the criminal stagger onward, lacking the impulse of that strong madness that hurried him into guilt, and treacherously deserts him in the midst of it!

When Miriam and Donatello drew near the church, they found only Kenyon awaiting them on the steps. Hilda had likewise promised to be of the party, but had not yet appeared. Meeting the sculptor, Miriam put a force upon herself and succeeded in creating an artificial flow of spirits, which, to any but the nicest observation, was quite as effective as a natural one. She spoke sympathizingly to the sculptor on the subject of Hilda's absence, and somewhat annoyed him by alluding in Donatello's hearing to an attachment which had never been openly avowed, though perhaps plainly enough betrayed. He fancied that Miriam did not quite recognize the limits of the strictest delicacy; he even went so far as to generalize, and conclude within himself, that this deficiency is a more general failing in woman than in man, the highest refinement being a masculine attribute.

But the idea was unjust to the sex at large, and especially so to this poor Miriam, who was hardly responsible for her frantic efforts to be gay. Possibly, moreover, the nice action of the mind is set ajar by any violent shock, as of great misfortune or great crime, so that the finer perceptions may be blurred thenceforth, and the effect be traceable in all the minutest conduct of life.

"Did you see anything of the dear child after you left us?" asked Miriam, still keeping Hilda as her topic of conversation. "I missed her sadly on my way homeward; for nothing insures me such delightful and innocent dreams (I have experienced it twenty times) as a talk late in the evening with Hilda."

"So I should imagine," said the sculptor gravely; "but it is an advantage that I have little or no opportunity of enjoying. I know not what became of Hilda after my parting from you. She was not especially my companion in any part of our walk. The last I saw of her she was hastening back to rejoin you in the courtyard of the Palazzo Caffarelli."

"Impossible!" cried Miriam, starting.

"Then did you not see her again?" inquired Kenyon, in some alarm.

"Not there," answered Miriam quietly; "indeed, I followed pretty closely on the heels of the rest of the party. But do not be alarmed on Hilda's account; the Virgin is bound to watch over the good child, for the sake of the piety with which she keeps the lamp alight at her shrine. And besides, I have always felt that Hilda is just as safe in these evil streets of Rome as her white doves when they fly downwards from the tower top, and run to and fro among the horses' feet. There is certainly a providence on purpose for Hilda, if for no other human creature."

"I religiously believe it," rejoined the sculptor; "and yet my mind would be the easier, if I knew that she had returned safely to her tower."

"Then make yourself quite easy," answered Miriam. "I saw her (and it is the last sweet sight that I remember) leaning from her window midway between earth and sky!"

Kenyon now looked at Donatello.

"You seem out of spirits, my dear friend," he observed. "This languid Roman atmosphere is not the airy wine that you were accustomed to breathe at home. I have not forgotten your hospitable invitation to meet you this summer at your castle among the Apennines. It is my fixed purpose to come, I assure you. We shall both be the better for some deep draughts of the mountain breezes."

"It may be," said Donatello, with unwonted sombreness; "the old house seemed joyous when I was a child. But as I remember it now it was a grim place, too."

The sculptor looked more attentively at the young man, and was surprised and alarmed to observe how entirely the fine, fresh glow of animal spirits had departed out of his face. Hitherto, moreover, even while he was standing perfectly still, there had been a kind of possible gambol indicated in his aspect. It was quite gone now. All his youthful gayety, and with it his simplicity of manner, was eclipsed, if not utterly extinct.

"You are surely ill, my dear fellow," exclaimed Kenyon.

"Am I? Perhaps so," said Donatello indifferently; "I never have been ill, and know not what it may be."

"Do not make the poor lad fancy-sink," whispered Miriam, pulling the sculptor's sleeve. "He is of a nature to lie down and die at once, if he finds himself drawing such melancholy breaths as we ordinary people are enforced to burden our lungs withal. But we must get him away from this old, dreamy and dreary Rome, where nobody but himself ever thought of being gay. Its influences are too heavy to sustain the life of such a creature."

The above conversation had passed chiefly on the steps of the Cappuccini; and, having said so much, Miriam lifted the leathern curtain that hangs before all church-doors in italy. "Hilda has forgotten her appointment," she observed, "or else her maiden slumbers are very sound this morning. We will wait for her no longer."

They entered the nave. The interior of the church was of moderate compass, but of good architecture, with a vaulted roof over the nave, and a row of dusky chapels on either side of it instead of the customary side-aisles. Each chapel had its saintly shrine, hung round with offerings; its picture above the altar, although closely veiled, if by any painter of renown; and its hallowed tapers, burning continually, to set alight the devotion of the worshippers. The pavement of the nave was chiefly of marble, and looked old and broken, and was shabbily patched here and there with tiles of brick; it was inlaid, moreover, with tombstones of the mediaeval taste, on which were quaintly sculptured borders, figures, and portraits in bas-relief, and Latin epitaphs, now grown illegible by the tread of footsteps over them. The church appertains to a convent of Capuchin monks; and, as usually happens when a reverend brotherhood have such an edifice in charge, the floor seemed never to have been scrubbed or swept, and had as little the aspect of sanctity as a kennel; whereas, in all churches of nunneries, the maiden sisterhood invariably show the purity of their own hearts by the virgin cleanliness and visible consecration of the walls and pavement.

As our friends entered the church, their eyes rested at once on a remarkable object in the centre of the nave. It was either the actual body, or, as might rather have been supposed at first glance, the cunningly wrought waxen face and suitably draped figure of a dead monk. This image of wax or clay-cold reality, whichever it might be, lay on a slightly elevated bier, with three tall candles burning on each side, another tall candle at the head, and another at the foot. There was music, too; in harmony with so funereal a spectacle. From beneath the pavement of the church came the deep, lugubrious strain of a De Profundis, which sounded like an utterance of the tomb itself; so dismally did it rumble through the burial vaults, and ooze up among the flat gravestones and sad epitaphs, filling the church as with a gloomy mist.

"I must look more closely at that dead monk before we leave the church," remarked the sculptor. "In the study of my art, I have gained many a hint from the dead which the living could never have given me."

"I can well imagine it," answered Miriam. "One clay image is readily copied from another. But let us first see Guido's picture. The light is favorable now."

Accordingly, they turned into the first chapel on the right hand, as you enter the nave; and there they beheld,—not the picture, indeed,—but a closely drawn curtain. The churchmen of Italy make no scruple of sacrificing the very purpose for which a work of sacred art has been created; that of opening the way; for religious sentiment through the quick medium of sight, by bringing angels, saints, and martyrs down visibly upon earth; of sacrificing this high purpose, and, for aught they know, the welfare of many souls along with it, to the hope of a paltry fee. Every work by an artist of celebrity is hidden behind a veil, and seldom revealed, except to Protestants, who scorn it as an object of devotion, and value it only for its artistic merit.

The sacristan was quickly found, however, and lost no time in disclosing the youthful Archangel, setting his divine foot on the head of his fallen adversary. It was an image of that greatest of future events, which we hope for so ardently, at least, while we are young,—but find so very long in coming, the triumph of goodness over the evil principle.

"Where can Hilda be?" exclaimed Kenyon. "It is not her custom ever to fail in an engagement; and the present one was made entirely on her account. Except herself, you know, we were all agreed in our recollection of the picture."

The Marble Faun

"But we were wrong, and Hilda right, as you perceive," said Miriam, directing his attention to the point on which their dispute of the night before had arisen. "It is not easy to detect her astray as regards any picture on which those clear, soft eyes of hers have ever rested."

"And she has studied and admired few pictures so much as this," observed the sculptor. "No wonder; for there is hardly another so beautiful in the world. What an expression of heavenly severity in the Archangel's face! There is a degree of pain, trouble, and disgust at being brought in contact with sin, even for the purpose of quelling and punishing it; and yet a celestial tranquillity pervades his whole being."

"I have never been able," said Miriam, "to admire this picture nearly so much as Hilda does, in its moral and intellectual aspect. If it cost her more trouble to be good, if her soul were less white and pure, she would be a more competent critic of this picture, and would estimate it not half so high. I see its defects today more clearly than ever before."

"What are some of them?" asked Kenyon.

"That Archangel, now," Miriam continued; "how fair he looks, with his unruffled wings, with his unhacked sword, and clad in his bright armor, and that exquisitely fitting sky-blue tunic, cut in the latest Paradisiacal mode! What a dainty air of the first celestial society! With what half-scornful delicacy he sets his prettily sandalled foot on the head of his prostrate foe! But, is it thus that virtue looks the moment after its death struggle with evil? No, no; I could have told Guido better. A full third of the Archangel's feathers should have been torn from his wings; the rest all ruffled, till they looked like Satan's own! His sword should be streaming with blood, and perhaps broken halfway to the hilt; his armor crushed, his robes rent, his breast gory; a bleeding gash on his brow, cutting right across the stern scowl of battle! He should press his foot hard down upon the old serpent, as if his very soul depended upon it, feeling him squirm mightily, and doubting whether the fight were half over yet, and how the victory might turn! And, with all this fierceness, this grimness, this unutterable horror, there should still be something high, tender, and holy in Michael's eyes, and around his mouth. But the battle never was such a child's play as Guido's dapper Archangel seems to have found it."

"For Heaven's sake, Miriam," cried Kenyon, astonished at the wild energy of her talk; "paint the picture of man's struggle against sin according to your own idea! I think it will be a masterpiece."

The Marble Faun

"The picture would have its share of truth, I assure you," she answered; "but I am sadly afraid the victory would fail on the wrong side. Just fancy a smoke-blackened, fiery-eyed demon bestriding that nice young angel, clutching his white throat with one of his hinder claws; and giving a triumphant whisk of his scaly tail, with a poisonous dart at the end of it! That is what they risk, poor souls, who do battle with Michael's enemy."

It now, perhaps, struck Miriam that her mental disquietude was impelling her to an undue vivacity; for she paused, and turned away from the picture, without saying a word more about it. All this while, moreover, Donatello had been very ill at ease, casting awe-stricken and inquiring glances at the dead monk; as if he could look nowhere but at that ghastly object, merely because it shocked him. Death has probably a peculiar horror and ugliness, when forced upon the contemplation of a person so naturally joyous as Donatello, who lived with completeness in the present moment, and was able to form but vague images of the future.

"What is the matter, Donatello?" whispered Miriam soothingly. "You are quite in a tremble, my poor friend! What is it?"

"This awful chant from beneath the church," answered Donatello; "it oppresses me; the air is so heavy with it that I can scarcely draw my breath. And yonder dead monk! I feel as if he were lying right across my heart."

"Take courage!" whispered she again "come, we will approach close to the dead monk. The only way, in such cases, is to stare the ugly horror right in the face; never a sidelong glance, nor half-look, for those are what show a frightfull thing in its frightfullest aspect. Lean on me, dearest friend! My heart is very strong for both of us. Be brave; and all is well."

Donatello hung back for a moment, but then pressed close to Miriam's side, and suffered her to lead him up to the bier. The sculptor followed. A number of persons, chiefly women, with several children among them, were standing about the corpse; and as our three friends drew nigh, a mother knelt down, and caused her little boy to kneel, both kissing the beads and crucifix that hung from the monk's girdle. Possibly he had died in the odor of sanctity; or, at all events, death and his brown frock and cowl made a sacred image of this reverend father.

CHAPTER XXI
THE DEAD CAPUCHIN

The dead monk was clad, as when alive, in the brown woollen frock of the Capuchins, with the hood drawn over his head, but so as to leave the features and a portion of the beard uncovered. His rosary and cross hung at his side; his hands were folded over his breast; his feet (he was of a barefooted order in his lifetime, and continued so in death) protruded from beneath his habit, stiff and stark, with a more waxen look than even his face. They were tied together at the ankles with a black ribbon.

The countenance, as we have already said, was fully displayed. It had a purplish hue upon it, unlike the paleness of an ordinary corpse, but as little resembling the flush of natural life. The eyelids were but partially drawn down, and showed the eyeballs beneath; as if the deceased friar were stealing a glimpse at the bystanders, to watch whether they were duly impressed with the solemnity of his obsequies. The shaggy eyebrows gave sternness to the look. Miriam passed between two of the lighted candles, and stood close beside the bier.

"My God!" murmured she. "What is this?"

She grasped Donatello's hand, and, at the same instant, felt him give a convulsive shudder, which she knew to have been caused by a sudden and terrible throb of the heart. His hand, by an instantaneous change, became like ice within hers, which likewise grew so icy that their insensible fingers might have rattled, one against the other. No wonder that their blood curdled; no wonder that their hearts leaped and paused! The dead face of the monk, gazing at them beneath its half-closed eyelids, was the same visage that had glared upon their naked souls, the past midnight, as Donatello flung him over the precipice.

The sculptor was standing at the foot of the bier, and had not yet seen the monk's features.

"Those naked feet!" said he. "I know not why, but they affect me strangely. They have walked to and fro over the hard pavements of Rome, and through a hundred other rough ways of this life, where the monk went begging for his brotherhood; along the cloisters and dreary corridors of his convent, too, from his youth upward! It is a suggestive idea, to track those worn feet backward through all the paths they have trodden, ever since they were the tender and rosy little feet of a baby, and (cold as they now are) were kept warm in his mother's hand."

As his companions, whom the sculptor supposed to be close by him, made no response to his fanciful musing, he looked up, and saw them at the head of the bier. He advanced thither himself.

"Ha!" exclaimed he.

He cast a horror-stricken and bewildered glance at Miriam, but withdrew it immediately. Not that he had any definite suspicion, or, it may be, even a remote idea, that she could be held responsible in the least degree for this man's sudden death. In truth, it seemed too wild a thought to connect, in reality, Miriam's persecutor of many past months and the vagabond of the preceding night, with the dead Capuchin of to-day. It resembled one of those unaccountable changes and interminglings of identity, which so often occur among the personages of a dream. But Kenyon, as befitted the professor of an imaginative art, was endowed with an exceedingly quick sensibility, which was apt to give him intimations of the true state of matters that lay beyond his actual vision. There was a whisper in his ear; it said, "Hush!" Without asking himself wherefore, he resolved to be silent as regarded the mysterious discovery which he had made, and to leave any remark or exclamation to be voluntarily offered by Miriam. If she never spoke, then let the riddle be unsolved.

And now occurred a circumstance that would seem too fantastic to be told, if it had not actually happened, precisely as we set it down. As the three friends stood by the bier, they saw that a little stream of blood had begun to ooze from the dead monk's nostrils; it crept slowly towards the thicket of his beard, where, in the course of a moment or two, it hid itself.

"How strange!" ejaculated Kenyon. "The monk died of apoplexy, I suppose, or by some sudden accident, and the blood has not yet congealed."

"Do you consider that a sufficient explanation?" asked Miriam, with a smile from which the sculptor involuntarily turned away his eyes. "Does it satisfy you?"

"And why not?" he inquired.

"Of course, you know the old superstition about this phenomenon of blood flowing from a dead body," she rejoined. "How can we tell but that the murderer of this monk (or, possibly, it may be only that privileged murderer, his physician) may have just entered the church?"

"I cannot jest about it," said Kenyon. "It is an ugly sight!"

"True, true; horrible to see, or dream of!" she replied, with one of those long, tremulous sighs, which so often betray a sick heart by escaping unexpectedly. "We will not look at it any more. Come away, Donatello. Let us escape from this dismal church. The sunshine will do you good."

When had ever a woman such a trial to sustain as this! By no possible supposition could Miriam explain the identity of the dead Capuchin, quietly and decorously laid out in the nave of his convent church, with that of her murdered persecutor, flung heedlessly at the foot of the precipice. The effect upon her imagination was as if a strange and unknown corpse had miraculously, while she was gazing at it, assumed the likeness of that face, so terrible henceforth in her remembrance. It was a symbol, perhaps, of the deadly iteration with which she was doomed to behold the image of her crime reflected back upon her in a thousand ways, and converting the great, calm face of Nature, in the whole, and in its innumerable details, into a manifold reminiscence of that one dead visage.

No sooner had Miriam turned away from the bier, and gone a few steps, than she fancied the likeness altogether an illusion, which would vanish at a closer and colder view. She must look at it again, therefore, and at once; or else the grave would close over the face, and leave the awful fantasy that had connected itself therewith fixed ineffaceably in her brain.

"Wait for me, one moment!" she said to her companions. "Only a moment!"

So she went back, and gazed once more at the corpse. Yes; these were the features that Miriam had known so well; this was the visage that she remembered from a far longer date than the most intimate of her friends suspected; this form of clay had held the evil spirit which blasted her sweet youth, and compelled her, as it were, to stain her womanhood with crime. But, whether it were the majesty of death, or something originally noble and lofty in the character of the dead, which the soul had stamped upon the features, as it left them; so it was that Miriam now quailed and shook, not for the vulgar horror of the spectacle, but for the severe, reproachful glance that seemed to come from between those half-closed lids. True, there had been nothing, in his lifetime, viler than this man. She knew it; there was no other fact within her consciousness that she felt to be so certain; and yet, because her persecutor found himself safe and irrefutable in death, he frowned upon his victim, and threw back the blame on her!

"Is it thou, indeed?" she murmured, under her breath. "Then thou hast no right to scowl upon me so! But art thou real, or a vision?" She bent down over the dead monk, till one of her rich curls brushed against his forehead. She touched one of his folded hands with her finger.

"It is he," said Miriam. "There is the scar, that I know so well, on his brow. And it is no vision; he is palpable to my touch! I will question the fact no longer, but deal with it as I best can."

It was wonderful to see how the crisis developed in Miriam its own proper strength, and the faculty of sustaining the demands which it made upon her fortitude. She ceased to tremble; the beautiful woman gazed sternly at her dead enemy, endeavoring to meet and quell the look of accusation that he threw from between his half-closed eyelids.

"No; thou shalt not scowl me down!" said she. "Neither now, nor when we stand together at the judgment-seat. I fear not to meet thee there. Farewell, till that next encounter!"

Haughtily waving her hand, Miriam rejoined her friends, who were awaiting her at the door of the church. As they went out, the sacristan stopped them, and proposed to show the cemetery of the convent, where the deceased members of the fraternity are laid to rest in sacred earth, brought long ago from Jerusalem.

"And will yonder monk be buried there?" she asked.

"Brother Antonio?" exclaimed the sacristan.

"Surely, our good brother will be put to bed there! His grave is already dug, and the last occupant has made room for him. Will you look at it, signorina?"

"I will!" said Miriam.

"Then excuse me," observed Kenyon; "for I shall leave you. One dead monk has more than sufficed me; and I am not bold enough to face the whole mortality of the convent."

It was easy to see, by Donatello's looks, that he, as well as the sculptor, would gladly have escaped a visit to the famous cemetery of the Cappuccini. But Miriam's nerves were strained to such a pitch, that she anticipated a certain solace and absolute

The Marble Faun

relief in passing from one ghastly spectacle to another of long-accumulated ugliness; and there was, besides, a singular sense of duty which impelled her to look at the final resting-place of the being whose fate had been so disastrously involved with her own. She therefore followed the sacristan's guidance, and drew her companion along with her, whispering encouragement as they went.

The cemetery is beneath the church, but entirely above ground, and lighted by a row of iron-grated windows without glass. A corridor runs along beside these windows, and gives access to three or four vaulted recesses, or chapels, of considerable breadth and height, the floor of which consists of the consecrated earth of Jerusalem. It is smoothed decorously over the deceased brethren of the convent, and is kept quite free from grass or weeds, such as would grow even in these gloomy recesses, if pains were not bestowed to root them up. But, as the cemetery is small, and it is a precious privilege to sleep in holy ground, the brotherhood are immemorially accustomed, when one of their number dies, to take the longest buried skeleton out of the oldest grave, and lay the new slumberer there instead. Thus, each of the good friars, in his turn, enjoys the luxury of a consecrated bed, attended with the slight drawback of being forced to get up long before daybreak, as it were, and make room for another lodger.

The arrangement of the unearthed skeletons is what makes the special interest of the cemetery. The arched and vaulted walls of the burial recesses are supported by massive pillars and pilasters made of thigh-bones and skulls; the whole material of the structure appears to be of a similar kind; and the knobs and embossed ornaments of this strange architecture are represented by the joints of the spine, and the more delicate tracery by the Smaller bones of the human frame. The summits of the arches are adorned with entire skeletons, looking as if they were wrought most skilfully in bas-relief. There is no possibility of describing how ugly and grotesque is the effect, combined with a certain artistic merit, nor how much perverted ingenuity has been shown in this queer way, nor what a multitude of dead monks, through how many hundred years, must have contributed their bony framework to build up these great arches of mortality. On some of the skulls there are inscriptions, purporting that such a monk, who formerly made use of that particular headpiece, died on such a day and year; but vastly the greater number are piled up indistinguishably into the architectural design, like the many deaths that make up the one glory of a victory.

In the side walls of the vaults are niches where skeleton monks sit or stand, clad in the brown habits that they wore in life, and labelled with their names and the dates of their decease. Their skulls (some quite bare, and others still covered with yellow skin, and hair that has known the earth-damps) look out from beneath their hoods, grinning hideously repulsive. One reverend father has his mouth wide open, as if he had died in the midst of a howl of terror and remorse, which perhaps is even now screeching through eternity. As a general thing, however, these frocked and hooded skeletons seem to take a more cheerful view of their position, and try with ghastly smiles to turn it into a jest. But the cemetery of the Capuchins is no place to nourish celestial hopes: the soul sinks forlorn and wretched under all this burden of dusty death; the holy earth from Jerusalem, so imbued is it with mortality, has grown as barren of the flowers of Paradise as it is of earthly weeds and grass. Thank Heaven for its blue sky; it needs a long, upward gaze to give us back our faith. Not here can we feel ourselves immortal, where the very altars in these chapels of horrible consecration are heaps of human bones.

Yet let us give the cemetery the praise that it deserves. There is no disagreeable scent, such as might have been expected from the decay of so many holy persons, in whatever odor of sanctity they may have taken their departure. The same number of living monks would not smell half so unexceptionably.

Miriam went gloomily along the corridor, from one vaulted Golgotha to another, until in the farthest recess she beheld an open grave.

"Is that for him who lies yonder in the nave?" she asked.

"Yes, signorina, this is to be the resting-place of Brother Antonio, who came to his death last night," answered the sacristan; "and in yonder niche, you see, sits a brother who was buried thirty years ago, and has risen to give him place."

"It is not a satisfactory idea," observed Miriam, "that you poor friars cannot call even your graves permanently your own. You must lie down in them, methinks, with a nervous anticipation of being disturbed, like weary men who know that they shall be summoned out of bed at midnight. Is it not possible (if money were to be paid for the privilege) to leave Brother Antonio — if that be his name — in the occupancy of that narrow grave till the last trumpet sounds?"

"By no means, signorina; neither is it needful or desirable," answered the sacristan. "A quarter of a century's sleep in the sweet earth of Jerusalem is better than a thousand years in any other soil. Our brethren find good rest there. No ghost was ever known to steal out of this blessed cemetery."

"That is well," responded Miriam; "may he whom you now lay to sleep prove no exception to the rule!"

As they left the cemetery she put money into the sacristan's hand to an amount that made his eyes open wide and glisten, and requested that it might be expended in masses for the repose of Father Antonio's soul.

CHAPTER XXII
THE MEDICI GARDENS

"Donatello," said Miriam anxiously, as they came through the Piazza Barberini, "what can I do for you, my beloved friend? You are shaking as with the cold fit of the Roman fever." "Yes," said Donatello; "my heart shivers." As soon as she could collect her thoughts, Miriam led the young man to the gardens of the Villa Medici, hoping that the quiet shade and sunshine of that delightful retreat would a little revive his spirits. The grounds are there laid out in the old fashion of straight paths, with borders of box, which form hedges of great height and density, and are shorn and trimmed to the evenness of a wall of stone, at the top and sides. There are green alleys, with long vistas overshadowed by ilex-trees; and at each intersection of the paths, the visitor finds seats of lichen-covered stone to repose upon, and marble statues that look forlornly at him, regretful of their lost noses. In the more open portions of the garden, before the sculptured front of the villa, you see fountains and flower-beds, and in their season a profusion of roses, from which the genial sun of Italy distils a fragrance, to be scattered abroad by the no less genial breeze.

But Donatello drew no delight from these things. He walked onward in silent apathy, and looked at Miriam with strangely half-awakened and bewildered eyes, when she sought to bring his mind into sympathy with hers, and so relieve his heart of the burden that lay lumpishly upon it.

She made him sit down on a stone bench, where two embowered alleys crossed each other; so that they could discern the approach of any casual intruder a long way down the path.

"My sweet friend," she said, taking one of his passive hands in both of hers, "what can I say to comfort you?"

"Nothing!" replied Donatello, with sombre reserve. "Nothing will ever comfort me."

"I accept my own misery," continued Miriam, "my own guilt, if guilt it be; and, whether guilt or misery, I shall know how to deal with it. But you, dearest friend, that were the rarest creature in all this world, and seemed a being to whom sorrow could not cling,—you, whom I half fancied to belong to a race that had vanished forever, you only surviving, to show mankind how genial and how joyous life used to be, in some long-gone age,—what had you to do with grief or crime?"

"They came to me as to other men," said Donatello broodingly. "Doubtless I was born to them."

"No, no; they came with me," replied Miriam. "Mine is the responsibility! Alas! wherefore was I born? Why did we ever meet? Why did I not drive you from me, knowing for my heart foreboded it—that the cloud in which I walked would likewise envelop you!"

Donatello stirred uneasily, with the irritable impatience that is often combined With a mood of leaden despondency. A brown lizard with two tails—a monster often engendered by the Roman sunshine—ran across his foot, and made him start. Then he sat silent awhile, and so did Miriam, trying to dissolve her whole heart into sympathy, and lavish it all upon him, were it only for a moment's cordial.

The young man lifted his hand to his breast, and, unintentionally, as Miriam's hand was within his, he lifted that along with it. "I have a great weight here!" said he. The fancy struck Miriam (but she drove it resolutely down) that Donatello almost imperceptibly shuddered, while, in pressing his own hand against his heart, he pressed hers there too.

"Rest your heart on me, dearest one!" she resumed. "Let me bear all its weight; I am well able to bear it; for I am a woman, and I love you! I love you, Donatello! Is there no comfort for you in this avowal? Look at me! Heretofore you have found me pleasant to your sight. Gaze into my eyes! Gaze into my soul! Search as deeply as you may, you can never see half the tenderness and devotion that I henceforth cherish for you. All that I ask is your acceptance of the utter self-sacrifice (but it shall be no sacrifice, to my great love) with which I seek to remedy the evil you have incurred for my sake!"

All this fervor on Miriam's part; on Donatello's, a heavy silence.

"O, speak to me!" she exclaimed. "Only promise me to be, by and by, a little happy!"

"Happy?" murmured Donatello. "Ah, never again! never again!"

"Never? Ah, that is a terrible word to say to me!" answered Miriam. "A terrible word to let fall upon a woman's heart, when she loves you, and is conscious of having caused your misery! If you love me, Donatello, speak it not again. And surely you did love me?"

"I did," replied Donatello gloomily and absently.

Miriam released the young man's hand, but suffered one of her own to lie close to his, and waited a moment to see whether he would make any effort to retain it. There was much depending upon that simple experiment.

With a deep sigh — as when, sometimes, a slumberer turns over in a troubled dream Donatello changed his position, and clasped both his hands over his forehead. The genial warmth of a Roman April kindling into May was in the atmosphere around them; but when Miriam saw that involuntary movement and heard that sigh of relief (for so she interpreted it), a shiver ran through her frame, as if the iciest wind of the Apennines were blowing over her.

"He has done himself a greater wrong than I dreamed of," thought she, with unutterable compassion. "Alas! it was a sad mistake! He might have had a kind of bliss in the consequences of this deed, had he been impelled to it by a love vital enough to survive the frenzy of that terrible moment, mighty enough to make its own law, and justify itself against the natural remorse. But to have perpetrated a dreadful murder (and such was his crime, unless love, annihilating moral distinctions, made it otherwise) on no better warrant than a boy's idle fantasy! I pity him from the very depths of my soul! As for myself, I am past my own or other's pity."

She arose from the young man's side, and stood before him with a sad, commiserating aspect; it was the look of a ruined soul, bewailing, in him, a grief less than what her profounder sympathies imposed upon herself.

"Donatello, we must part," she said, with melancholy firmness. "Yes; leave me! Go back to your old tower, which overlooks the green valley you have told me of among the Apennines. Then, all that has passed will be recognized as but an ugly dream. For in dreams the conscience sleeps, and we often stain ourselves with guilt of which we should be incapable in our waking moments. The deed you seemed to do, last night, was no more than such a dream; there was as little substance in what you fancied yourself doing. Go; and forget it all!"

"Ah, that terrible face!" said Donatello, pressing his hands over his eyes. "Do you call that unreal?"

"Yes; for you beheld it with dreaming eyes," replied Miriam. "It was unreal; and, that you may feel it so, it is requisite that you see this face of mine no more. Once, you may have thought it beautiful; now, it has lost its charm. Yet it would still retain a miserable potency' to bring back the past illusion, and, in its train, the remorse and anguish that would darken all your life. Leave me, therefore, and forget me."

"Forget you, Miriam!" said Donatello, roused somewhat from his apathy of despair.

"If I could remember you, and behold you, apart from that frightful visage which stares at me over your shoulder, that were a consolation, at least, if not a joy."

"But since that visage haunts you along with mine," rejoined Miriam, glancing behind her, "we needs must part. Farewell, then! But if ever—in distress, peril, shame, poverty, or whatever anguish is most poignant, whatever burden heaviest—you should require a life to be given wholly, only to make your own a little easier, then summon me! As the case now stands between us, you have bought me dear, and find me of little worth. Fling me away, therefore! May you never need me more! But, if otherwise, a wish—almost an unuttered wish will bring me to you!"

She stood a moment, expecting a reply. But Donatello's eyes had again fallen on the ground, and he had not, in his bewildered mind and overburdened heart, a word to respond.

"That hour I speak of may never come," said Miriam. "So farewell—farewell forever."

"Farewell," said Donatello.

His voice hardly made its way through the environment of unaccustomed thoughts and emotions which had settled over him like a dense and dark cloud. Not improbably, he beheld Miriam through so dim a medium that she looked visionary; heard her speak only in a thin, faint echo.

She turned from the young man, and, much as her heart yearned towards him, she would not profane that heavy parting by an embrace, or even a pressure of the hand. So soon after the semblance of such mighty love, and after it had been the impulse to so terrible a deed, they parted, in all outward show, as coldly as people part whose whole mutual intercourse has been encircled within a single hour.

And Donatello, when Miriam had departed, stretched himself at full length on the stone bench, and drew his hat over his eyes, as the idle and light-hearted youths of dreamy Italy are accustomed to do, when they lie down in the first convenient shade, and snatch a noonday slumber. A stupor was upon him, which he mistook for such drowsiness as he had known in his innocent past life. But, by and by, he raised himself slowly and left the garden. Sometimes poor Donatello started, as if he heard a shriek; sometimes he shrank back, as if a face, fearful to behold, were thrust close to his own. In this dismal mood, bewildered with the novelty of sin and grief, he had little left of that singular resemblance, on account of which, and for their sport, his three friends had fantastically recognized him as the veritable Faun of Praxiteles.

CHAPTER XXIII
MIRIAM AND HILDA

On leaving the Medici Gardens Miriam felt herself astray in the world; and having no special reason to seek one place more than another, she suffered chance to direct her steps as it would. Thus it happened, that, involving herself in the crookedness of Rome, she saw Hilda's tower rising before her, and was put in mind to climb to the young girl's eyry, and ask why she had broken her engagement at the church of the Capuchins. People often do the idlest acts of their lifetime in their heaviest and most anxious moments; so that it would have been no wonder had Miriam been impelled only by so slight a motive of curiosity as we have indicated. But she remembered, too, and with a quaking heart, what the sculptor had mentioned of Hilda's retracing her steps towards the courtyard of the Palazzo Caffarelli in quest of Miriam herself. Had she been compelled to choose between infamy in the eyes of the whole world, or in Hilda's eyes alone, she would unhesitatingly have accepted the former, on condition of remaining spotless in the estimation of her white-souled friend. This possibility, therefore, that Hilda had witnessed the scene of the past night, was unquestionably the cause that drew Miriam to the tower, and made her linger and falter as she approached it.

As she drew near, there were tokens to which her disturbed mind gave a sinister interpretation. Some of her friend's airy family, the doves, with their heads imbedded disconsolately in their bosoms, were huddled in a corner of the piazza; others had alighted on the heads, wings, shoulders, and trumpets of the marble angels which adorned the facade of the neighboring church; two or three had betaken themselves to the Virgin's shrine; and as many as could find room were sitting on Hilda's window-sill. But all of them, so Miriam fancied, had a look of weary expectation and disappointment, no flights, no flutterings, no cooing murmur; something that ought to have made their day glad and bright was evidently left out of this day's history. And, furthermore, Hilda's white window-curtain was closely drawn, with only that one little aperture at the side, which Miriam remembered noticing the night before.

"Be quiet," said Miriam to her own heart, pressing her hand hard upon it. "Why shouldst thou throb now? Hast thou not endured more terrible things than this?"

Whatever were her apprehensions, she would not turn back. It might be — and the solace would be worth a world — that Hilda, knowing nothing of the past night's calamity, would greet her friend with a sunny smile, and so restore a portion of the vital warmth, for lack of which her soul was frozen. But could Miriam, guilty as she was, permit Hilda to kiss her cheek, to clasp her hand, and thus be no longer so unspotted from the world as heretofore.

"I will never permit her sweet touch again," said Miriam, toiling up the staircase, "if I can find strength of heart to forbid it. But, O! it would be so soothing in this wintry fever-fit of my heart. There can be no harm to my white Hilda in one parting kiss. That shall be all!"

But, on reaching the upper landing-place, Miriam paused, and stirred not again till she had brought herself to an immovable resolve.

"My lips, my hand, shall never meet Hilda's more," said she.

Meanwhile, Hilda sat listlessly in her painting-room. Had you looked into the little adjoining chamber, you might have seen the slight imprint of her figure on the bed, but would also have detected at once that the white counterpane had not been turned down. The pillow was more disturbed; she had turned her face upon it, the poor child, and bedewed it with some of those tears (among the most chill and forlorn that gush from human sorrow) which the innocent heart pours forth at its first actual discovery that sin is in the world. The young and pure are not apt to find out that miserable truth until it is brought home to them by the guiltiness of some trusted friend. They may have heard much of the evil of the world, and seem to know it, but only as an impalpable theory. In due time, some mortal, whom they reverence too highly, is commissioned by Providence to teach them this direful lesson; he perpetrates a sin; and Adam falls anew, and Paradise, heretofore in unfaded bloom, is lost again, and closed forever, with the fiery swords gleaming at its gates.

The chair in which Hilda sat was near the portrait of Beatrice Cenci, which had not yet been taken from the easel. It is a peculiarity of this picture, that its profoundest expression eludes a straightforward glance, and can only be caught by side glimpses, or when the eye falls casually upon it; even as if the painted face had a life and consciousness of its own, and, resolving not to betray its secret of grief or guilt, permitted the true tokens to come forth only when it imagined itself unseen. No other such magical effect has ever been wrought by pencil.

Now, opposite the easel hung a looking-glass, in which Beatrice's face and Hilda's were both reflected. In one of her weary, nerveless changes of position, Hilda happened to throw

The Marble Faun

her eyes on the glass, and took in both these images at one unpremeditated glance. She fancied — nor was it without horror — that Beatrice's expression, seen aside and vanishing in a moment, had been depicted in her own face likewise, and flitted from it as timorously.

"Am I, too, stained with guilt?" thought the poor girl, hiding her face in her hands.

Not so, thank Heaven! But, as regards Beatrice's picture, the incident suggests a theory which may account for its unutterable grief and mysterious shadow of guilt, without detracting from the purity which we love to attribute to that ill-fated girl. Who, indeed, can look at that mouth, — with its lips half apart, as innocent as a babe's that has been crying, and not pronounce Beatrice sinless? It was the intimate consciousness of her father's sin that threw its shadow over her, and frightened her into a remote and inaccessible region, where no sympathy could come. It was the knowledge of Miriam's guilt that lent the same expression to Hilda's face.

But Hilda nervously moved her chair, so that the images in the glass should be no longer Visible. She now watched a speck of sunshine that came through a shuttered window, and crept from object to object, indicating each with a touch of its bright finger, and then letting them all vanish successively. In like manner her mind, so like sunlight in its natural cheerfulness, went from thought to thought, but found nothing that it could dwell upon for comfort. Never before had this young, energetic, active spirit known what it is to be despondent. It was the unreality of the world that made her so. Her dearest friend, whose heart seemed the most solid and richest of Hilda's possessions, had no existence for her any more; and in that dreary void, out of which Miriam had disappeared, the substance, the truth, the integrity of life, the motives of effort, the joy of success, had departed along with her.

It was long past noon, when a step came up the staircase. It had passed beyond the limits where there was communication with the lower regions of the palace, and was mounting the successive flights which led only to Hilda's precincts. Faint as the tread was, she heard and recognized it. It startled her into sudden life. Her first impulse was to spring to the door of the studio, and fasten it with lock and bolt. But a second thought made her feel that this would be an unworthy cowardice, on her own part, and also that Miriam — only yesterday her closest friend had a right to be told, face to face, that thenceforth they must be forever strangers.

She heard Miriam pause, outside of the door. We have

already seen what was the latter's resolve with respect to any kiss or pressure of the hand between Hilda and herself. We know not what became of the resolution. As Miriam was of a highly impulsive character, it may have vanished at the first sight of Hilda; but, at all events, she appeared to have dressed herself up in a garb of sunshine, and was disclosed, as the door swung open, in all the glow of her remarkable beauty. The truth was, her heart leaped conclusively towards the only refuge that it had, or hoped. She forgot, just one instant, all cause for holding herself aloof. Ordinarily there was a certain reserve in Miriam's demonstrations of affection, in consonance with the delicacy of her friend. To-day, she opened her arms to take Hilda in.

"Dearest, darling Hilda!" she exclaimed. "It gives me new life to see you!"

Hilda was standing in the middle of the room. When her friend made a step or two from the door, she put forth her hands with an involuntary repellent gesture, so expressive that Miriam at once felt a great chasm opening itself between them two. They might gaze at one another from the opposite side, but without the possibility of ever meeting more; or, at least, since the chasm could never be bridged over, they must tread the whole round of Eternity to meet on the other side. There was even a terror in the thought of their meeting again. It was as if Hilda or Miriam were dead, and could no longer hold intercourse without violating a spiritual law.

Yet, in the wantonness of her despair, Miriam made one more step towards the friend whom she had lost. "Do not come nearer, Miriam!" said Hilda. Her look and tone were those of sorrowful entreaty, and yet they expressed a kind of confidence, as if the girl were conscious of a safeguard that could not be violated.

"What has happened between us, Hilda?" asked Miriam. "Are we not friends?"

"No, no!" said Hilda, shuddering.

"At least we have been friends," continued Miriam. "I loved you dearly! I love you still! You were to me as a younger sister; yes, dearer than sisters of the same blood; for you and I were so lonely, Hilda, that the whole world pressed us together by its solitude and strangeness. Then, will you not touch my hand? Am I not the same as yesterday?"

"Alas! no, Miriam!" said Hilda.

The Marble Faun

"Yes, the same, the same for you, Hilda," rejoined her lost friend. "Were you to touch my hand, you would find it as warm to your grasp as ever. If you were sick or suffering, I would watch night and day for you. It is in such simple offices that true affection shows itself; and so I speak of them. Yet now, Hilda, your very look seems to put me beyond the limits of human kind!"

"It is not I, Miriam," said Hilda; "not I that have done this."

"You, and you only, Hilda," replied Miriam, stirred up to make her own cause good by the repellent force which her friend opposed to her. "I am a woman, as I was yesterday; endowed with the same truth of nature, the same warmth of heart, the same genuine and earnest love, which you have always known in me. In any regard that concerns yourself, I am not changed. And believe me, Hilda, when a human being has chosen a friend out of all the world, it is only some faithlessness between themselves, rendering true intercourse impossible, that can justify either friend in severing the bond. Have I deceived you? Then cast me off! Have I wronged you personally? Then forgive me, if you can. But, have I sinned against God and man, and deeply sinned? Then be more my friend than ever, for I need you more."

"Do not bewilder me thus, Miriam!" exclaimed Hilda, who had not forborne to express, by look and gesture, the anguish which this interview inflicted on her. "If I were one of God's angels, with a nature incapable of stain, and garments that never could be spotted, I would keep ever at your side, and try to lead you upward. But I am a poor, lonely girl, whom God has set here in an evil world, and given her only a white robe, and bid her wear it back to Him, as white as when she put it on. Your powerful magnetism would be too much for me. The pure, white atmosphere, in which I try to discern what things are good and true, would be discolored. And therefore, Miriam, before it is too late, I mean to put faith in this awful heartquake which warns me henceforth to avoid you."

"Ah, this is hard! Ah, this is terrible!" murmured Miriam, dropping her forehead in her hands. In a moment or two she looked up again, as pale as death, but with a composed countenance: "I always said, Hilda, that you were merciless; for I had a perception of it, even while you loved me best. You have no sin, nor any conception of what it is; and therefore you are so terribly severe! As an angel, you are not amiss; but, as a human creature, and a woman among earthly men and women, you need a sin to soften you."

"God forgive me," said Hilda, "if I have said a needlessly

cruel word!"

"Let it pass," answered Miriam; "I, whose heart it has smitten upon, forgive you. And tell me, before we part forever, what have you seen or known of me, since we last met?"

"A terrible thing, Miriam," said Hilda, growing paler than before.

"Do you see it written in my face, or painted in my eyes?" inquired Miriam, her trouble seeking relief in a half-frenzied raillery. "I would fain know how it is that Providence, or fate, brings eye-witnesses to watch us, when we fancy ourselves acting in the remotest privacy. Did all Rome see it, then? Or, at least, our merry company of artists? Or is it some blood-stain on me, or death-scent in my garments? They say that monstrous deformities sprout out of fiends, who once were lovely angels. Do you perceive such in me already? Tell me, by our past friendship, Hilda, all you know."

Thus adjured, and frightened by the wild emotion which Miriam could not suppress, Hilda strove to tell what she had witnessed.

"After the rest of the party had passed on, I went back to speak to you," she said; "for there seemed to be a trouble on your mind, and I wished to share it with you, if you could permit me. The door of the little courtyard was partly shut; but I pushed it open, and saw you within, and Donatello, and a third person, whom I had before noticed in the shadow of a niche. He approached you, Miriam. You knelt to him! I saw Donatello spring upon him! I would have shrieked, but my throat was dry. I would have rushed forward, but my limbs seemed rooted to the earth. It was like a flash of lightning. A look passed from your eyes to Donatello's — a look." — "Yes, Hilda, yes!" exclaimed Miriam, with intense eagerness. "Do not pause now! That look?"

"It revealed all your heart, Miriam," continued Hilda, covering her eyes as if to shut out the recollection; "a look of hatred, triumph, vengeance, and, as it were, joy at some unhoped-for relief."

"Ah! Donatello was right, then," murmured Miriam, who shook throughout all her frame. "My eyes bade him do it! Go on, Hilda."

"It all passed so quickly, all like a glare of lightning," said Hilda, "and yet it seemed to me that Donatello had paused, while one might draw a breath. But that look! Ah, Miriam, spare me. Need I tell more?"

"No more; there needs no more, Hilda," replied Miriam, bowing her head, as if listening to a sentence of condemnation from a supreme tribunal. "It is enough! You have satisfied my mind on a point where it was greatly disturbed. Henceforward I shall be quiet. Thank you, Hilda."

She was on the point of departing, but turned back again from the threshold.

"This is a terrible secret to be kept in a young girl's bosom," she observed; "what will you do with it, my poor child?"

"Heaven help and guide me," answered Hilda, bursting into tears; "for the burden of it crushes me to the earth! It seems a crime to know of such a thing, and to keep it to myself. It knocks within my heart continually, threatening, imploring, insisting to be let out! O my mother!—my mother! Were she yet living, I would travel over land and sea to tell her this dark secret, as I told all the little troubles of my infancy. But I am alone—alone! Miriam, you were my dearest, only friend. Advise me what to do."

This was a singular appeal, no doubt, from the stainless maiden to the guilty woman, whom she had just banished from her heart forever. But it bore striking testimony to the impression which Miriam's natural uprightness and impulsive generosity had made on the friend who knew her best; and it deeply comforted the poor criminal, by proving to her that the bond between Hilda and herself was vital yet.

As far as she was able, Miriam at once responded to the girl's cry for help.

"If I deemed it good for your peace of mind," she said, "to bear testimony against me for this deed in the face of all the world, no consideration of myself should weigh with me an instant. But I believe that you would find no relief in such a course. What men call justice lies chiefly in outward formalities, and has never the close application and fitness that would be satisfactory to a soul like yours. I cannot be fairly tried and judged before an earthly tribunal; and of this, Hilda, you would perhaps become fatally conscious when it was too late. Roman justice, above all things, is a byword. What have you to do with it? Leave all such thoughts aside! Yet, Hilda, I would not have you keep my secret imprisoned in your heart if it tries to leap out, and stings you, like a wild, venomous thing, when you thrust it back again. Have you no other friend, now that you have been forced to give me up?"

"No other," answered Hilda sadly.

"Yes; Kenyon!" rejoined Miriam.

"He cannot be my friend," said Hilda, "because—because—I have fancied that he sought to be something more."

"Fear nothing!" replied Miriam, shaking her head, with a strange smile. "This story will frighten his new-born love out of its little life, if that be what you wish. Tell him the secret, then, and take his wise and honorable counsel as to what should next be done. I know not what else to say."

"I never dreamed," said Hilda,—"how could you think it?— of betraying you to justice. But I see how it is, Miriam. I must keep your secret, and die of it, unless God sends me some relief by methods which are now beyond my power to imagine. It is very dreadful. Ah! now I understand how the sins of generations past have created an atmosphere of sin for those that follow. While there is a single guilty person in the universe, each innocent one must feel his innocence tortured by that guilt. Your deed, Miriam, has darkened the whole sky!"

Poor Hilda turned from her unhappy friend, and, sinking on her knees in a corner of the chamber, could not be prevailed upon to utter another word. And Miriam, with a long regard from the threshold, bade farewell to this doves' nest, this one little nook of pure thoughts and innocent enthusiasms, into which she had brought such trouble. Every crime destroys more Edens than our own!

Milton Keynes UK
Ingram Content Group UK Ltd.
UKHW021939081024
449407UK00008B/159